MEETING ON THE HIGHWAY

A convertible, robin-egg blue, came at a fast clip, giving me just a glimpse of blonde, long hair blowing in the wind. The car passed me and slowed, swerved, and pulled over to the side and stopped.

She had a flat tire.

She got out of the car and walked around it. She wore shorts and she had long legs, flashing legs that were deeply tanned, beautifully proportioned, long and lovely.

"I'm glad to see you," she said.

"This is the second time you've seen me," I said. "You saw me the first time when you passed me."

Her laughter gurgled. "You're right," she said. "Well, run along. Someone will stop."

"I'll fix your tire."

She stood back and watched as I got the key out of the car, opened the trunk, pulled out the tools. I didn't talk and she didn't talk the whole time it took me to change the tire.

"How much do I owe you?" she asked.

"Nothing. I didn't fix your tire for money."

She smiled, shrugged. "Well, thank you," she said. "Thank you very much."

Without another word, without another glance, she got into her car and drove away.

I'd see her again…

—from *SO CURSE THE DAY*
by Jada M. Davis

The Stark House
ANTHOLOGY

**Edited by Rick Ollerman
& Gregory Shepard**

Stark House Press • Eureka California

THE STARK HOUSE ANTHOLOGY

Published by Stark House Press
1315 H Street
Eureka, CA 95501
griffinskye3@sbcglobal.net
www.starkhousepress.com

ISBN: 979-8-88601-043-5

Cover design by Jeff Vorzimmer, ¡caliente!design, Austin, Texas
Book design by Mark Shepard, shepgraphics.com

First Stark House Edition: June 2024

CONTENTS

Stark House Press: The First 25 Years

by Gregory Shepard

When my dad and I first talked about starting up a publishing venture, neither of us had an idea where this might go. It was just a wild idea. I think my dad, Bill Shepard, was the one who brought it up. He had recently retired from the newspaper and magazine business, his last gig editing a horse magazine in Texas. He was the one with the experience. I owned a book distribution company called Firebird Distributing. Brother Mark was a graphic designer, and my wife at the time, Cammy Shepard, was an artist. With my mom Joanne on board as proofreader, we figured we had all the personnel we needed.

And thus, Stark House Press was born.

That was 1998. Our first book came out a year later.

I thought it would be a great idea to start off with a collection of fantasy stories by Storm Constantine. I contacted her and she agreed. And since I had been distributing a lot of small presses, I figured the best place to start would be a signed/numbered/limited edition hardback edition. We printed 1,000 copies of *The Oracle Lips* and Storm graciously signed all 1,000 signature pages.

It sold fairly well for a first book. But a thousand copies? Let's just say that our initial capital outlay could have been better spent on half that amount. Simply put, it didn't pay for itself. And the family was not encouraged to jump into book number two.

So I used the Stark House set-up and my own capital and contracted with Storm to reprint two of her earlier novels—this time in affordable trade paperback—plus a second original collection called *The Thorn Boy*. I followed this up with a reprint of Algernon Blackwood's *Incredible Adventures*.

With very little arm twisting, the rest of the family let me buy them out. Which led to another Blackwood collection, *Pan's Garden*. But you can only reprint so many vintage supernatural collections. So I turned to my rather large paperback collection and asked myself, what next? Where do I go from here? Mysteries! Of course! No one is reprinting Elisabeth Sanxay Holding. What a great place to start. I had loved her old Ace Double mysteries. I wonder who holds the rights?…

I think it was Ed Gorman who put me in touch with the Holding heir, which eventually led to our first Stark House two-fer of *Lady Killer/Miasma*. Why two books instead of one? It wasn't a nod to the Ace Doubles, though that would be natural assumption. No, it was cost that got me thinking of double trade paperback volumes. It simply cost too much to publish a single book and sell it at a reasonable price. The books were going to have to be priced at $19.95 anyway, why not include two books and make it an affordable deal. And with new introductions and handy bibliographies....

The idea took off in my head. So I went back to Ed and asked him if he knew how to get in touch with the Peter Rabe copyright holder. I loved the old Gold Medal thrillers and Rabe was one of my favorites. After that Ed must have figured I was serious about this reprint thing so he started making suggestions of his own: Day Keene, Stephen Marlowe, Benjamin Appel. And off we went. With Ed Gorman's generous and invaluable help, Stark House stood up and walked.

And now, 25 years later, we're publishing 4-5 books per month. We've added a mass market line with Black Gat Books, Jazz-Age classics under the Staccato Crime imprint, Film Noir Classics, more vintage supernatural tales and mysteries from the early 1900s, and even the occasional science fiction and western book.

I have my dad to thank for the idea of Stark House. Mark still handles most of the text design, and Cammy (now C. B. Williams) still does a few covers. Rick Ollerman (who came up with the idea behind Black Gat) joined as associate editor back in 2010. And when he got too busy, Jeff Vorzimmer was right there with his aid and advice (and those cool retro covers), not to mention all the *Manhunt* and Beacon collections he's edited for Stark House (he and David Rachels also edit the Staccato line). Bill Kelly became our proofreader, also contributing a lot of ideas, introductions and encouragement (and film noir links). And my wife Cindy manages the website, when she isn't doing a little of everything else (honestly, it wouldn't happen without her).

But, really, Stark House Press wouldn't exist without lots of help, so it's imperative that I give credit where credit is due. So thank you to everyone else who helped Stark House along the way: Kevin Fox, Joanne Applen (Barstow), Roger Schwed, Anne Devlin, Day James, Maxim Jakubowski, Ann Marlowe, Lucas Crown, Frank Loose, Ted & Dorrie Lee, Gary Phillips, David Wilson, JT Lindroos, Nicholas Litchfield, James Heimer, Jay Herzog, Suzy Roderbach, Terrie Wolf, Charlie Stella, David Rachels, Casey & Cathleen Coburn, Mike Ashley, Timothy J. Lockhart, the Yates Family, Gary Lovisi, Tom Simon, Eric Compton, Don Blyly, J.B., Otto Filip, Jeff Battis, Brian Greene, S. T. Joshi, Cullen Gallagher, James Reasoner, Mark & Cindy Ziesing, Curtis Evans, Ben Boulden, Scott Montgomery, George Kelley, Kevin Burton Smith, Steve Lewis, Daniel Morrison, Ted Hertel, John Norris, Michael Dirda, Richard Krauss, Lou Boxer, Donna Seaman, Matthew Sorrento, Cari Ballinger, Deb Potts, Carol Lee Hamilton, James A. Cox, Bill Pronzini, Robert Silverberg, Barry Malzberg, Robert Friedman, Corey Field, Ben LeRoy, Chris Duffy, Scott Brown, Michael Hitchens, Sue

Tarvin, Rod Lott, Paul Burke, Martin Edwards, Mike Ripley, Woody Haut, Kate Jackson, Sergio Angelini, Jon Breen, Kate Stine, Peter Rozovsky, Bruce Grossman, Craig Tenney, Anne Fleischman Miller, Alan Cranis, Noelle Mays, Julia Rhodes, Sherry Lee Wert, Marvin Lee III, Belle Marko, Jonathan E. Lewis, Joyce Gordon, the Appel sisters, John Douglas Sanderson, James Burnett, Marijane Meaker, Patrick Millikin, Joe Bratcher and John Goddard (just because).

Twenty-five years of Stark House Books. It's still a labor of love, and it's still fun!

—March 2024
Eureka, CA

Introduction

by Rick Ollerman

The origins of Stark House Press stretch back to 1998 when members of the Shepard family decided to get into the publishing business. Their first offering was a signed, limited edition of dark fantasy stories called *Oracle Lips* by British author Storm Constantine. It wasn't very long before Greg Shepard became the sole publisher and his general intention was to bring back "the good stuff." I use the word "general" because as the years have passed Stark House has published old stuff and new stuff across most genres but the bread and butter became, and continues to be, crime fiction.

In 2003 Greg made the decision to start releasing books in two-in-one omnibus editions. Sometimes three-in-one, sometimes single books, but it's all a nod to Stark House's ability to be flexible with its list.

I became aware of Stark House around 2011. I'd gone to the wonderful St. Petersburg Antiquarian Book Fair and saw some pristine Fawcett Gold Medal paperbacks that looked as if they'd never even touched a spinner rack. There was no yellowing, fading, foxing, dog-ears— probably not even fingerprints based on the way they were bagged and being displayed. The seller said some guy in North Carolina had bought all the Gold Medals he could find as they were published and stored them away in his attic, without even reading them. He had the idea they'd be worth something some day. Smart guy.

And maybe that was the day, but not for me. Thirty-five bucks apiece was a bit steep for me at the time (although I did spend a couple hundred bucks on a beautiful two-book first edition set of *Three Years of Arctic Service, An Account of the Lady Franklin Bay Expedition of 1881-84 and the Attainment of the Farthest North* by Adolphus W. Greely. Written by the expedition leader, it is the tale of a General Sir John Franklin rescue expedition, one that ended in various forms of disaster, including cannibalism and a last minute rescue.). The weekend drove me to search online for Peter Rabe books to see what I could find. And lo and behold I found a two-in-one omnibus volume of Rabe's first-rate *The Box* paired with his *Journey Into Terror.*

This was exciting stuff, especially after reading Donald E. Westlake's appreciation of Rabe's work in his introduction to the Gregg Press edition of the Richard Stark novel, *The Hunter.* At that point I was unfamiliar with Rabe, not even having read any of the Black Lizard reprints. I ordered a copy and read it with relish, discovering one of the all-time greats, or as Harlan Ellison said, "In the most golden of the Golden Days of exquisite hardboiled suspense writing, not one of us considered the Best could wait for the next new Rabe. Peter Rabe was an entire genre unto himself. Paying attention to him was, and is, a banquet."

The Box was a revelation. As Westlake had intimated, Rabe painted pictures with words in ways that no one else ever has: "His use of language, his handling of emotion, and his eye for the dramatic detail inside the normal were an inspiration for me." My opinion aside, *The Box* isn't even widely considered his best book, though he has so many titles that could qualify it doesn't really matter. Especially since Stark House has reprinted nearly all of Rabe's work, with the sole exception being his work-for-hire novelization of the TV show *Mannix*.

In other words, there was excitement here, new discoveries to be made, and Stark House kicked open that door wide and hard, and continues to do so today. For a book lover, a crime fiction devourer, Stark House provides an endless smorgasbord of discoveries and has given the world a chance to discover or rediscover the lost talents of both giants and should-have-been giants from the past. These are the building blocks today's crime fiction was built on. Often they are done subjectively better than what we see today. For instance, read Bill S. Ballinger's *Portrait in Smoke* before you read (after works, too) Gillian Flynn's *Gone Girl* and see what you think.

That sense of discovery is key to the Stark House appeal. You don't have to be familiar with Peter Rabe or Elisabeth Sanxay Holding or Bill S. Ballinger or Lionel White or dozens of others to trust that Stark House is producing, or reproducing, the goods.

There is plenty to unearth in this collection. The majority of stories here haven't been reprinted since their original publication, and some have never before been published anywhere.

The crown jewel here is Jada M. Davis's terrific *So Curse the Day*. Davis published only two books in his lifetime, *One for Hell*, which for my money belongs on every shelf right next to every copy of Thompson's *The Killer Inside Me;* and *The Outraged Sect*, sort of a mirror-image to *One for Hell*. Instead of a bad guy (to be sure a *really* bad guy) coming to a good town, we have a good guy going to a bad one, as corrupt as can be. Stark House reprinted *One for Hell* as well as *Midnight Road*, a very fine coming-of-age crime story. Now we bring you what should have been a bestselling Gold Medal title. It has all of the noir elements you find in the best of James M. Cain and the book should have seen print long before now.

Peter Rabe wrote only two short stories and one of them, "A Matter of Balance," has never seen print—until now. (His other story, "Hard Case Redhead," was reprinted by Stark House along with two previously unpublished novels: *The Silent Wall* and *The Return of Marvin Palaver*). Here also is a Bruno Fischer story that has only been published once, in a small press collection. Orrie Hitt is represented with the only short story he ever published, "Nothing in My Way."

There's a lot more here to discover, from Jean Potts to Helen Nielsen to the private detectives of Henry Kane, Frank Kane and Stephen Marlowe; there's a trio of stories representing St. Petersburg, Florida's own Harry Whittington, Gil Brewer and Day Keene; we have a fascinating look at a different kind of crime story from the legendary Robert Silverberg; and many more.

Whether you're familiar with all the authors between these covers or if they're new to you, if any of them can tickle that innate but sometimes buried sense of discovery, of *I want more of that,* then you've found the right place.

January, 2024
Compass Lake, FL

A Trio of Gold Medals is one my favorite Stark House books. It's a three-in-one volume that gives you novels by no less than Dan J. Marlowe, Fletcher Flora, and Charles Runyon. Runyon's entry is the gritty The Prettiest Girl I Ever Killed. *As prolific as they come, Runyon wrote both crime and science fiction and you would have been hard-pressed to pick up a digest magazine in the sixties without finding one of his stories. He is always very readable and skillful in his writing and I've never read a book or story of his I didn't like. He is a vastly underrated and forgotten author but then, so many are…*

HANGOVER

Charles Runyon

I couldn't feel the hammers in my head when I woke up. But I knew they were poised to thud into the base of my skull the moment I lifted my head from the pillow. My nose felt stuffed and swollen, as though someone were pinching the bridge tightly between thumb and forefinger.

I heard a noise in the kitchen. Something made of tin tipped over, rolled for what seemed like an hour, then hit the floor with a sound like the cymbals in a Wagner overture. My head began to throb. I tried to deal with the noise passively, without moving: "Marian! Are you in the kitchen?"

The only answer was a metallic echo, the kind you get from an empty house. I forced an eye open and saw that the opposite bed was empty. The spread lay neatly folded at the foot. The sheet was turned back as crisp and smooth as glass, ready to receive her body. But Marian hadn't slept there; she'd been gone for nearly two weeks.

I closed my eyes, and fragments of despair dropped like lead weights into my mind. I'd been thinking she came back last night. She smiled down at me the way she always did before coming to bed; with her eyes, hardly moving her lips. She was wearing the pale blue nightdress I'd given her two months ago on our tenth anniversary….

Hell, I must have dreamed it. I wanted her home, and that's the kind of impossible wish that keeps distilleries in business.

I felt a warm weight pressing against my back. I turned quickly, but it wasn't Marian. This girl's hair was the same dark auburn color; but Marian had never let her hair get into such a tangled mess, *with* matted rat's nests above the ears.

I drew away from her. She frowned in her sleep and moved toward me. I slid out of bed, pulled on my robe and looked down at her. She was somewhere between twenty and twenty-five. If she was pretty, I couldn't see it; not with her face lumpy and sagging in sleep. Her upper lip arched outward to reveal two slightly protruding teeth. A line of saliva trailed from her mouth to the pillow, where it mixed with lipstick and formed a stain the color of diluted blood.

I hated to deal with her now; even the intimacy of conversation made my stomach queasy. But I wanted her out of my house, so I shook her shoulder.

"Baby…." Without opening her eyes, she rolled her tongue around her mouth. "Let's sleep a little longer, baby."

I could feel my patience slipping away. I hated that sticky, stupid, shopworn endearment; in thirty-five years I'd come to tolerate everything but being called "Baby." I shook her until her eyes popped open. "What's your name?"

"God, did you wake me up for *that*?" She jerked the sheet over her head. "Marian… you been calling me Marian."

I jerked the sheet off her head. "Dammit! That's my wife's name."

"I know, Baby, I know." She kicked off the sheet and stretched, her legs forming a straight line from toe to torso. "I'm Sandra. You can call me Sandy."

She gave me a heavy-lidded smile she probably meant to be sweet and seductive. To me it was like having syrup smeared on my face. Her nakedness aroused me somewhat less than a tree with the bark stripped off, though she had the fleshy, over-blown kind of figure that's supposed to be the American dream. She wasn't my dream and that's why her presence threw me. I couldn't remember where I'd picked her up or why. My last sharp memory was coming home from the office Wednesday and feeling the emptiness of this house hit me like a fist in the stomach. I knew I couldn't spend another night talking to the furniture, so I'd gone out and started throwing down vodka martinis.

"Okay, Sandy," I said. "Where'd I meet you?"

She raised her eyebrows. "Hey, you really had a blackout. I'm a hostess at the Dolly Bar. That's a strip joint on Fourth Street. Don't you remember *that?*"

"Would I ask if I did?"

"Aw… Baby's got a hangover, hasn't he?" She slid off the bed and started toward the door. "I'll get you something for that."

"Never mind. Just tell me when and why you came to my house."

She stopped in the door and turned. A hip stuck out and she cupped her palm over it. "Okay. You came into the Dolly Wednesday night. You bought me a few drinks, then a… former friend of mine tried to move in and you hit him. You hit him several times before they threw you out, and I liked the way you handled yourself. I took you with me to my hotel and next morning we came out here."

"What time was that?"

"About eleven."

"*Eleven?* Oh, Jesus." I saw myself staggering into my new tri-level house with a B-girl on my arm. That sort of thing wasn't done in Elysia. It was really PTA and cub scout country—even though its name conveyed a vision of satyrs and fat-hipped Greek women dressed in bunches of grapes. Elysia meant home and family to the men who worked in the city, and I'd broken one of the club by-laws. "Did anyone see you?"

"Well, I guess." Sandy shrugged. "You didn't tell me to sneak in." She paused. "Look, if there's any more questions, I'll be in the john."

She walked away and slammed the bathroom door. A second later I heard a glass shatter in the kitchen.

I padded barefoot down the half-flight of stairs, walking with a bent-knee shuffle to stabilize my aching head. In the kitchen, I found that Marian's gray cat had overturned a flour canister and was anointing the room with white paw prints.

I cornered her and imprisoned her under my arm. I rubbed her behind the ears and surveyed the kitchen.

It was a mess. Odors of stale food and liquor rose from a sink piled high with dirty dishes and glasses. The stove held a stew pan filled with black pebbles which once were beans. I wondered what Marian would have said; she was the kind of woman who jumped up from the table and started washing dishes before they even cooled.

I saw two plates on the table. One held a puddle of gray grease with a slab of bacon in the center, garnished by a long, auburn hair. My stomach did a half gainer; eating with Sandy was even less appetizing than sleeping with her.

The cat mewed. "All right, kid," I said. "You first, then the other one."

I shuffled through the long living room and found the front door open. The carpet around it was damp; the door had stood open all night and it had rained. I set the cat on the lawn and nudged her away with my toe.

Around the front steps lay proof that life in Elysia had flowed on without me. Several milk bottles warmed in the sun; I tried to count them but they kept moving. Two newspapers formed a wet, gluey mass on the sidewalk. A third lay near the door, crisp and dry and smelling of ink as I picked it up. I read the date beneath the flag: *Tuesday, July 19.*

Five days, I thought. A drop of sweat traced a cold path down my spine. *Oh, Jesus. Five days gone like bootleg liquor down the drain.*

I dropped the paper and stood there trying to remember. Nothing came but sweat, cool and clammy under my robe. The sun was a whit-hot rivet tacked on a sheet of blue steel. It couldn't have been much past eight in the morning; I still had time to get to the office. But I remembered the winter sales program I was supposed to have presented to the board last Friday, and I knew that one more day would add little to the devastation.

I raised my eyes and saw my car crosswise in the drive. The back wheels rested on my neighbor's lawn. Now the whole damn town would know. Two women walked past, pushing empty grocery carts. They stared at me, then walked on with the studied concentration of students coming late to class. I was suddenly aware of my bare legs sticking out beneath my robe.

I went inside and slammed the door on the painful sunlight. I needed a drink. My nerves were rubbing together, rasping like the hind legs of a cricket.

The bar was a half-flight down in a basement room with sand-colored tile on the floor. The walls were lined with desert murals, and I reached the bar feeling like I'd just trekked across the Quattara depression on my hands and knees.

But the bar held no bourbon; no scotch. I searched beneath it for the exotic liqueurs Marian had stocked against the day I reached the level of a party-giving executive. I wondered if she was sitting in her hotel room now, regretting that she'd ripped apart all those detailed blueprints for the future.

All the bottles were empty; we'd even drained the tall, slim containers of fiery Metaxa. Apparently we'd finished up on crème de cacao; I found two glasses containing a brown, concave residue, dry on the edge and damp in the center, like a pond in a drought.

I prowled the room and found a beer mug containing an inch of bourbon and a shredded cigaret butt. I fished out the butt, gulped down the bourbon, and shuddered like a volcano about to erupt. I swallowed three times before the bourbon gave up and decided to stay down.

After a minute I felt well enough to climb the stairs and call a cab. I felt even better when I'd done that; it would be a relief to get Sandy out of my house.

When I hung up, I found myself looking at the words I'd scrawled on the pad a week before: *Regent Hotel, CA-72700.* The number had cost me an eighty-dollar detective fee, but I'd never used it. I kept reminding myself that it was Marian who got caught cheating; not me. She had to come to me.

I got up and walked upstairs, away from the telephone. Outside the bedroom, I found my suit. It was crumpled, damp and muddy. I lifted it with a bare toe and saw that it had bleached the hardwood beneath it, as skin is bleached by a bandage. I couldn't imagine what fuzz-brained impulse had driven me out into the rain. Maybe Sandy would know....

I found her in the bathroom, standing under the shower with her back to me. Behind the portiere of needle-spray she looked like Marian—though a Marian drawn with thick pencil strokes that made my chest ache for the original. I felt a curious urge to shove the girl's head under water and hold it there.

Instead, I tried to make my voice pleasant but brisk. "About finished?"

She halted in the act of lathering her belly. She turned, suds squeezing out between her fingers. "I like it slow, Baby." She smiled with one side of her mouth. "Wanta wash my back?"

I stretched out my hand and jerked the shower curtain together. Once I'd washed Marian's back; but that honeymoon ritual had been shelved several years ago. "Hurry up," I said. "I called a cab."

I could feel my tiny supply of patience seeping away. "*You'll* use it, Sandy—the minute it gets here."

"Wearing nothing but soap bubbles?" She ripped off a laugh that tweaked my nerves like a fingernail drawn across a blackboard. "Anyway, I can't leave you, Baby."

"Dammit! My name is Greg. Greg Maxwell."

"I know, Baby...."

"Don't call me that!"

"You liked it yesterday."

I walked to the washbasin and started throwing cold water on my face. Talking to Sandy was a pointless ordeal; she'd leave when the cab arrived. I wondered ho much money she'd want....

I wiped off the mirror and looked at my dripping image with detached, alcoholic disdain. I looked like someone who sang hymns in a skid row mission; a red-haired joker whose big frame hung loose inside an expensive bathrobe, as though tacked together by a hurried carpenter. The pallid face was patched here and there with red-black stubble, interspersed with tiny razor nicks.

I looked down at my hands. The knobby knuckles were scraped raw; the nails were cracked and chipped and tipped with black, dirt-filled crescents. I remembered my wet, muddy suit in the hall, and tried to recall what happened yesterday.

But yesterday was gone. So was the day before, and the day before that. Five days were lost, buried deep among three billion brain cells. A strange, violent character had taken over my body; an idiot who enjoyed being called baby, and went for women who measured an axe-handle or more across the hips. Now he sat back in my mind and smirked from a perch atop a filing cabinet full of memories. "*Get out of here, Maxwell,*" he was saying. "*Those five days were mine, old buddy.*"

"What?"

I jumped at the sound of Sandy's voice. "I didn't say anything."

"You said something about getting out of here."

"Oh, Jesus." My mind was splitting apart; I couldn't remember saying anything. I put both hands to my forehead and squeezed. "Sandy.... What was I doing in the rain?"

"Don't you even remember *that*?"

I clamped my teeth together. "Sandy, all I know is that my suit's in a wet, muddy heap in the hall."

"Oh. Well...." She was silent a minute, then the shower curtain screeched. She came to stand behind me, enclosing me in her aura of scented bath soap. "You did that Friday night when the guy came to see why you hadn't come to work."

"What guy?"

"Gosh, I don't know his name…."

"Dammit! What did he look like?"

"Bug-eyed little fella. Kept eating candy."

"Candy…." My mouth went dry, and my skin felt hot and prickly. My boss was Harvey Reed, sales manager. His protruding eyes gave him a look of never quite believing what he saw. He chewed mints chain fashion to blunt a craving for cigarets. "Go on," I told her.

"Well, he didn't stay long. He acted kind of teed off… didn't even taste the drink I fixed for him."

I whirled to face her. "Why the hell didn't you stay out of sight?"

She froze in the act of wiping her left ear. "Gee…. I was trying to *help*. You said he was your boss and I wanted to treat him nice…."

"Oh, for God's sake!" I turned back and gripped the washbasin. Harvey was a nut on family integrity: *"A man who can't run his home has no business dealing with customers."* I remembered him saying that, looking like a surprised chipmunk with the mint tucked in his cheek. "Okay, Sandy. So he saw you. Now how'd the rain get into the picture?"

"I…. Are you sure you wanta hear?"

I spoke softly, watching my lips move in the mirror. "Sandy, for the last time, I wouldn't be asking if I didn't."

"Okay. Okay. Jesus, I wish you'd get drunk again. You're a lot more fun when you're drunk." She sighed. "Well… so when the guy left, you followed him outside telling him he couldn't fire you because you already quit. You had a lot better job with United Oil, you told him. When he drove off you was standing on the lawn yelling at him—"

"Yelling?"

"Yeah, you were giving him hell, only I couldn't hear you so clear in the house. Then it started raining and you got down on your hands and knees and dug your fingers into the lawn. I went out and asked what you lost. You said we were about to fall off the world and you wanted me to help you hold on…." She started to laugh, then cut it short. "I'm sorry, but you did act… kind of funny."

I shook my head, trying to clear it. Dark fragments of memory swirled like storm clouds; I remembered feeling that the earth was tipping away from the sun, pitching me into darkness. I'd been afraid of losing contact and flying off into cold, deep space without Marian there to anchor me….

"Was it a good job?" asked Sandy. "I mean… I guess it was, but you mentioned the deal with the other company…."

"I made it up, Sandy. Now let's drop it." The concern in her voice sickened me. I didn't want sympathy; that's why I couldn't go back to the office. I'd mail my resignation; let them believe the story about United Oil. I might even be able to get on there, with a good recommendation—

Oh, sure. Harvey would grab at a chance to recommend me: *"Good man, Maxwell; aside from a drinking problem. Can't blame the boy, of course, considering his domestic situation."* Damn, damn, damn. Nobody would touch me with a ten foot pole.

An electric shaver whirred, sawing at my nerves. I had a vision of Marian shaving her gently tapered legs. She didn't like me to watch her; shaving was a masculine act that made her feel coarse and indelicate.

I turned to see Sandy with her leg propped on the edge of the bathtub, running a tiny electric shaver along her thick calf. For a moment I watched it chew away the faint stubble, then it dawned on my that it was Marian's shaver. I jerked the cord from the wall plug and the whirring died.

Sandy looked up with her mouth open. "What the hell...?"

"Where'd you get that shaver?"

"Why... you gave it to me last night."

Last night. I'd been almost sure that Marian had taken it with her; apparently I was mistaken.

I held out my hand. "Let's have it."

She gave it to me, watching my face. I wrapped the cord around the shaver and put it in the medicine cabinet; I'd have to clean it later, when my stomach settled. The air in the bathroom was mushy with the scent of bath soap.

"Did you bring any luggage?" I asked her.

"A suitcase, like you told me."

"Good. I'll help you pack."

She blinked in surprise. "Baby, *wait* a minute...."

"Clean up in here first. Then get dressed." I walked to the door. "And stop calling me baby."

I walked into the hall and took a deep breath. It didn't help much; I was sick with the knowledge that I'd thrown away ten years of work Friday night.

I found Sandy's cheap pasteboard suitcase in the bedroom and prowled through the house, carrying it open under my arm. Sandy had treated the place like a burlesque runway. I found shoes in the living room, a negligee in my den, and underwear in the basement bar. They were black, sleazy garments that clung to my fingers.

I was nearly finished with the house when I heard a dog barking out back. It wasn't ours; Marian didn't like dogs. I went out and found our neighbor's Dalmatian spraddled on the naked black earth at the edge of the unfinished patio. He was growling at a beagle I'd never seen before.

I yelled, and they ran off. Then I wondered why the hell I bothered. The patio was Marian's idea; another page torn from her futures book. She'd had it started during my last two-month trip around our sales divisions. The night I came home, I'd found her with the contractor who had the job. He wasn't building a patio then....

I went back inside and slammed the door. The next owner could finish the patio. Let him worry about the house and its twenty-five year mortgage. I couldn't handle the payments without a job.

I'd have to move into a cheaper home in a different neighborhood. I had to start fresh in another job; maybe I'd even go back to pushing doorbells. *Damn*, I missed Marian. I needed her calm, realistic approach to problems; without her I was like a centipede with each leg trying to run in a different direction.

First I had to get rid of Sandy. I walked upstairs and found her wet footprints leading to the bedroom. She hadn't cleaned up the bathroom. In the bedroom, I found Marian's closet open, the clothes disarranged. I felt anger rise inside me.

I found Sandy in the kitchen drinking coffee. She wore the blue nightdress I'd given Marian on our last anniversary. I felt a stab of disappointment that Marian had left it behind, then the disappointment changed to anger. "Stand up," I told Sandy.

She rose slowly, her face blank.

"Now take off the robe."

Her face twisted in confusion. "But you *told* me to wear it yesterday."

I covered the distance between us in tow quick steps. I gripped her arm and said: "Slip it off gently. I don't want it damaged." Gradually I tightened my grip until she began to move. "That's it. Now the other arm… easy."

When it was off she dropped back in her chair, rubbing her arm. "Your hands are strong, you know that? You ought a see the other marks you gave me." Her lower lip trembled. "I didn't mind them, though. You know why? Because you made me feel like a wife and I went for that. All of a sudden you change…." Her eyes grew shiny and her face became pouchy and ugly.

I watched a tear roll down her cheek and felt my skin crawl. I didn't want her tears. "Isn't your cab here yet?"

"Sure." Her mouth twisted. "It's under the table."

"If it doesn't come you can walk. Now get dressed. I want you out of here when my wife comes back."

"Your *wife*? But you—" She closed her eyes for a minute, then opened them. "You sent her away because you caught her cheating on you."

"I didn't actually *catch* her…."

"She didn't deny it, you said."

I didn't want to argue, but the urge to justify myself pulled me in like quicksand. "Sandy, I'd been away for two months. During that time I wasn't exactly a… perfect husband myself. Anyway, I don't care what she did. She's coming back."

"What about your promise?"

"Promise?"

She stood up, and her weak mouth seemed suddenly firm. "You said we'd go to Mexico. You'd sell the house, draw your money out of the bank, sell your stocks...."

"Oh, hell. Don't you realize I have no job? The house is mortgaged, I still owe money on the car, I've borrowed against my stocks. Sandy, you're trying to con the wrong man. I'm damn near broke."

Her chin came up at that. "I'm not trying to con you!"

"Then why don't you leave?"

"Because... you said you hated your wife because she was a cold, efficient machine. You liked me because I was warm and passionate and... and sloppy."

Suddenly I was tired of the conversation. "Listen, whatever happened during those five days, it's ended. I'm a different man. I've turned inside out. What I hated before, I like now. What I liked before, I now hate. You understand?"

"You hate me?"

"It isn't your fault, Sandy. It's just the way it works out."

"Thanks a lot." She walked to the door, then turned to face me. "You should've stayed drunk, Baby."

She walked out and up the stairs, grabbing her suitcase on the way. I watched her disappear into the bedroom, feeling as though I'd just detached a terrier from my leg.

While I waited for her to come down again, the cab arrived. I went out and told him to wait, then went back inside. I paced the long living room, impatient now that I'd decided to get Marian back. She'd be grateful, I thought, though she wouldn't show it. She'd be anxious to please, and I'd accept that. I'd have her make chocolate brownies and bring me coffee in bed. I'd loaf for a day or so, warm and musty under the covers with the soft feel of flannel. We'd make small talk and lazy daytime love. Though she thought there was something perverted about love in the daytime, she wouldn't deny me. Later I'd tell her about the job and we'd decide what to do....

Sandy came down then, clad in a black sequined gown that must have been her working dress. It covered her just a little better than nothing, but I didn't care. I felt almost grateful to her, the way you feel toward a bore when he goes out the door after a long, trying evening. I pressed a twenty into her hand and said, "That's for the cab, Sandy."

She looked down at it sullenly, then stuffed it into her purse and walked out, the gown tight across her haunches. I hurried to the phone and dialed the Regent Hotel. "Give me Mrs. Maxwell's room," I told the operator.

"Just a moment, sir."

I drummed my fingers on the telephone stand while I waited. In my mind I saw Marian sitting in her room. Her small white hands reposed in her lap, palms up. Her nose had a faint blush of red on the end, just where it began to turn up. She'd been crying or was about to cry. After a moment she rose, picked up her purse, and walked to the door. She paused before the mirror; a small woman fashioned without waste of bone and flesh. Her dark auburn hair was pulled back from her temples, the comb-marks straight as plow-furrows on bottomland. On top the hair lay in careful, frozen curls, like a stylized Chinese drawing of the sea. She lifted her hand to touch an imperfection visible only to herself. Suddenly the phone rang…

.

The operator's voice pierced my ear. "Sorry, sir. Mrs. Maxwell checked out yesterday."

My stomach flipped over and a drop of sweat rolled slowly down my back. "Did she… leave an address?"

"No sir. Sorry."

I replaced the receiver, tasting a bitterness in my throat. I couldn't think; my mind was like an electrical appliance which had been struck by lightning. It seemed to give off smoke and a faint buzzing sound, but no power.

I heard a noise behind me. I turned to see Sandy standing there.

"I knew she wouldn't be there," she said. "She came here last night."

I could only look at her.

"You… sent her away again," said Sandy.

My mouth went dry. I thought of Marian coming home, hoping to be forgiven, finding me in that insane, drunken state and the house ravaged by a four-day orgy. "What… what did I say to her?"

"Gee, I don't know. You shoved me into the bathroom when she came. A long time later you came in and said she wouldn't get in our way again."

My face felt tight, as though someone had grabbed the skin at the back of my head and pulled, slitting my eyes and pulling my lips tight across my teeth so that my words came out blurred an fuzzy:

"Was that when I gave you the shaver and the nightdress?"

"Yes." Slowly her eyes grew round. "Baby, you look like you need a drink."

"Oh, Jesus. Jesus Christ." I squeezed my eyes shut and pressed my forehead against the cool, firm wood of the telephone stand. The memory came back all at once, like light returning to a city when the current is restored. It was bright, vivid and unbearable….

The argument had lasted a long time, and we'd moved from room to room. Now we faced each other on the patio, and my voice was hoarse and my breath was ragged. Marian was stiff, sober, and firm as a tree; she'd seen the house, she'd sensed the other woman's presence, and now she was leaving. "This time, Greg, I'll never come back." I screamed curses at her. She regarded me with a cool, quizzical expression that drove my fury higher until there was only hate swirling in my mind. I knocked her down and pried a stone from the patio, lifted it above my head, and smashed it down with all my strength. Afterward, as I pried up more stones, I laughed at the way my hands were shaking.

Sandy's voice came to me from a distant, peaceful land, speaking with a sweetness that curdled my soul. "Let's get drunk, Baby. Don't worry about her. I'll stick with you. Always."

I heard dogs on the patio, fighting again. This time I knew what they were fighting over.

No one ever wrote like Peter Rabe. The best of his writing is like reading through some sort of literary lens, where his prose bears one direction while other writers go in the other; he'll give you a zig when everyone else would zag. Not just in terms of plot twists but in his choice of words and his sentence structure. He simply makes choices other people do not and it makes the best of his novels special. *Read* The Box *or* Kill the Boss Goodby *or* Murder Me for Nickels *or… well, the list goes on. Rabe wrote only two short stories in his career and only one—*Hard Case Redhead*—was published. Here is his second, a nuanced story that hints at the subtlety that Rabe was often capable of, finally making its long overdue appearance.*

A MATTER OF BALANCE

Peter Rabe

The Captain reached back until his hand touched the table and he kept talking without any rise or fall in his voice.

"The point is readiness. A fine matter of balance, because you must make your rage come to a point—"

He watched his man all the time while his hand felt over the table behind him. He felt the stick, the Italian foil, the brass knuckles, the knife. He took the knife.

"Corporal," he said. "You're not watching it right. Your eyes are stiff."

"I'm watching…."

"I know what you're watching. But you must try and see everything."

The soldier opposite thought he saw everything. He saw the bars on the collar, the thin face with the lines, the name card on the breast pocket, and even the print, "Captain Tyll." He saw the arm held back to the table, the starched suntans stretched over the Captain's flat chest. The arm moved quite slowly.

"You're watching exactly what I want you to watch," said Captain Tyll and the Corporal kept his eyes on the knife.

When it struck, it wasn't the knife. The knife was still out there in Tyll's hand, weaving slowly, when Tyll's other arm shot out from below with the fingers stiff like darts and straight into the soft nook where the ribs come together.

The Corporal felt like two things instead of one, with the fear splitting all of him into parts, one of him useless to do anything further, the other will in him doubling the body into a small knot with everything weak deep inside, safe. Or that's how it felt.

Then the knife hit.

The Corporal heard Captain Tyll's grunt, like a raw cough, and after that his deep breath showing that he was done.

"You can relax now, Corporal Bush."

Captain Tyll put the knife back on the table, putting it in the same place where it had been before.

"You would be dead now," he said, "if this were not a demonstration. Or at least bleeding to death, from here," and the Captain touched the side of his neck with the same movement he had used when taking the knife. The movement had the even pitch he kept in his voice, and the sense of no real completion.

Captain Tyll walked to the edge of the stage and looked over the hall. It was dim and empty except for the few rows in front. Two squads of men. They sat very still.

"He loves it," said one of the men. "Lookit him there," and he and his neighbor looked up at the stage, at Captain Tyll and the Corporal. Tyll showed nothing, but there were nervous blotches of sweat on the Corporal's shirt. His dark face seemed indistinct, except for the open-mouthed look, as if waiting to breathe. He stood with arms hanging and the hands like weights.

"So would you," said another. They both felt sure they knew how Tyll felt.

"You have a question?" asked Tyll from the stage.

They had no question. They had seen how Corporal Bush had been theoretically killed, how it was done, and they also thought they knew how Tyll felt in all this. They felt this almost as strongly as Bush did.

"The son of a bitch loves it. For twenty years straight he's been doing what he loves best and it doesn't even raise a sweat on the son of a bitch anymore he's so used to doing what he loves best. He'd die from the lack of it, if he didn't have his twenty year constant love of giving one enemy after another this sharp, sudden dose of fright—"

This was not all true. Captain Tyll did not very much care how the trainee felt. His interest had little to do with the man he attacked—

He turned his head towards Bush and said,

"You all right, Corporal?"

"Yes, sir."

"Fine. Corporal?"

"Yes, sir."

"Don't leave yet."

Captain Tyll folded his arms and waited until Bush had come back. When Bush stood as before, Tyll said, "Thank you, Corporal," and turned away.

Corporal Bush said nothing, just touched his neck. He felt like a slaughter animal. He looked down at his shoes and started to hate.

Captain Tyll folded his hands behind him and looked past the men in the hall, to the end of the hall, but not seeing it. He talked as he always did.

"You have seen, gentlemen, what you might call a ruse. That is not important, though. It is important to know how it was possible." He turned toward Bush and said, "Corporal?"

"Yes, sir."

"Take something from the table."

"Yes, sir," and Bush walked to the table without looking at Tyll.

He stopped before the table and looked at everything there. His eyes wouldn't focus. He coughed, and then he licked his lips.

"Take something," said Captain Tyll. "Go ahead, Corporal."

It was important to remember that this wasn't for real. This was a class— a class— Corporal Bush moved his lips.

"Well?" said Tyll.

(The sweatless bastard—if this were real—if this were someplace else— not done by the numbers—)

"Pick it up, Corporal."

"Yes, sir.— What should I take, sir?"

"Anything, Corporal. This isn't done by the numbers, you know."

Bush moved his big shoulders. His mouth was open again and he licked his lips.

He picked up the brass knuckles.

Tyll turned back to the men in front and said,

"He picked up the brass knuckles." It was obvious that Tyll didn't care what Bush had picked up. "He took one of the four things on the table, and if this were the real thing, gentlemen, he could have picked one of a hundred weapons. A chair is a weapon, a cup is, or a newspaper rolled into a tight stick. Or the hands, gentlemen. You will learn this. The fist for one, the fingers for another, the edge of the hand. But for the moment, gentlemen, the details don't matter."

Captain Tyll stepped back and nodded at Bush. "Go ahead."

Bush swallowed and his weapon hand worked as if kneeding dough. Tyll stepped terribly close.

"The way I'm going to handle this," said Captain Tyll, "is to assume nothing," and he turned his head slightly so that the men in front of the stage could hear him well.

As if I didn't matter, thought Bush. As if I wasn't here— Or maybe he thinks he knows everything, even my insides—and he held himself so that nothing would show. But he sweated. The hate leaked out in a sweat, crawling all over him.

"And so, remember," said Tyll, loud now. "I know nothing about my enemy. Nothing!" He nodded at Bush. "Any time, Corporal. Any ..." He ducked.

The brass teeth whistled with air. They bit through a whistling arch but they meant nothing else. The obvious ruse of flaunting the obvious weapon. But the leg! That was good of Bush. It shot out like a piston and aimed for the weakest low spot, the knee, which could be buckled the wrong way with a very small effort. Bush, as a matter of fact, was kicking too hard, much too seriously—

Tyll made a funny, small trip, then swung one leg to the side, a Charleston kick almost, and Corporal Bush fell lengthwise making a board-like clatter.

"You have seen," said Captain Tyll to the hall, "what I meant.—Please stay, Corporal. Thank you.—My defense, gentlemen, was to know nothing ahead of time. It is like holding your breath, not committing yourself to exhale. But you are ready!"

I'm melting with it, said Bush to his own hands. It's dripping off my face and my hands are shaking because I'm not done. I'm stopped half-way done. I stink like rutting buck from the pressure— And him, dry like something dead in the sun for two seasons— He loves it, stopping me this way. He lives on this thing—

But the Captain was talking.

"The way you will stay alive, gentlemen, the only way, is this matter of staying suspended. Your enemy is one man with one weapon. You see this. But you know better! Because you don't know what he will do, how he will strike. All you know is a danger. And now the fear almost splits you in two. There are two kinds of fear, gentlemen. One, the stiff kind, which makes you lame and you die on your feet. The enemy is saved the trouble, except for the *coup de grace*. The other fear is more painful, a fluid fear, an unbearable urge to act. 'Strike!' it says. 'Attack, act, spill over!'"

Captain Tyll took a small breath. It was clear he felt the thing he was talking about. His monotone became very delicate.

"But you wait. And then when this pressure is worse than fear and ready to make you fly apart—" Captain Tyll talked very softly. "The condition is delicate, wants to turn into something sudden—"

He exhaled. For a moment he seemed almost off-hand.

"Now you are ready for the kill. But that's not a problem anymore."

He looked down at the creases in his pants and kept talking with no special emphasis.

"That's why a mock kill—here—is as important as what you might do in close combat. Learn this. The kill is nothing—" and then he looked up again. "But this tension, gentlemen! This state of a breaking balance—and holding it!"

He was through. It hung there, unfinished, but that was the point with Captain Tyll.

He was through and stepped away from the edge of the stage. He nodded at Bush that he could leave, but Bush stood a moment longer. He hadn't seen this happen before: the two large blotches of sweat on Captain Tyll's shirt.

Corporal Bush left the empty barrack and walked down the company street. It was almost dark and a warm pine odor hung in the air. At home the woods smelled of leaf and water. Bush rubbed his face and felt annoyed.

He had smelled the difference before but it had never rankled him. His annoyance was dull, without direction, and held in like a stiff-chested breath. Like the thing Tyll talked about.

Bush kept walking and once he touched the side of his neck where the collar covered it. He did not really touch, left it a gesture, and then stuck his hands in his pockets. It did not make him look casual but humped and bunched up.

The PX was big with counters the whole length of the building and the tables in a short L at the end. Bush walked all the way through to the back, as if it were any night between paydays. Somebody called him and Bush took his hands out of the pockets and went to the table. He sat down and nodded at the two men.

"Hi," he said and sighed.

"You ain't drinking?" said Ralph.

Bush shook his head.

"Somebody else here isn't drinking," said the other man at the table. He grinned when he said it and kept watching Bush.

"Who?" said Bush.

"Him there," and when Bush turned to look where Matty was nodding he saw Captain Tyll at another table.

The Captain sat there smoking a cigarette and he had packages lying in front of him.

"Must have been shopping," said Ralph. "That reminds me, Matty, I gotta get…."

"You know," said Matty, and he kept smiling as if he had forgotten that he was doing it, "I think of Captain Tyll, I don't think at all of a man who comes to the PX and buys groceries."

"He's gotta eat," said Ralph.

"I don't think of him that way either."

"So maybe he's bought something else. Maybe a present for the wife or something."

"He isn't married. Can you think of Tyll married?" and Matty looked over to Bush.

Bush shrugged, doing it carefully so his collar would not scrape on his neck. Then he looked down at his hands, trying to see nothing else.

"Bush," said Matty. "You know him good, Bush. What about him?" and it sounded to Bush like the voice was smiling.

This Matt was needling him. This guy whom he didn't know except for a man in his squad, except for talk over beer, had started to strike at him like Tyll did.

"I don't know Tyll," he said. "No better than you."

"Then how come," Matty said right away, "you don't like him?"

"Hell, man," said Ralph. "It's like envy."

But that had nothing to do with it. Matty knew this, because he was clever, and Bush knew this, because he felt it. He disliked Tyll in the same way he disliked freezing rain in the summer. It did no good and it didn't fit anywhere.

"Here he comes," said Ralph and he hunched himself behind his bottle, with his eyes up, undecided and shiny.

"Gentlemen," said Captain Tyll and bowed to the three men.

"How are you, Captain— Geez, you got an armful, huh, Captain?" and Ralph giggled.

"Yes." Captain Tyll looked at his packages and then he laughed too. It went 'he-he,' like laugh printed.

He had nowhere in particular to go and stood by the table.

"Uh— You like beer, Captain?" said Ralph. "I mean, if you...."

"Thank you. No, I don't drink beer," said Captain Tyll. He said "thank you" again and sat down at the table with the three men.

Ralph helped get the packages stowed, Matty moved beer bottles around, and Bush sat still. He wanted to leave, but didn't know how. A familiar feeling by now—whenever Tyll was involved—this being stopped—

"Very nice of you men to ask me," said Captain Tyll. "Very nice."

They all felt awkward with Captain Tyll. They felt it in one way or another that Captain Tyll was truly grateful and that this did not fit.

"Are you—uh—have you been on this post very long?" Matty asked the Captain.

"Oh no. Just before you men came for your course. Japan and Korea before that."

"Gee—" said Ralph.

"Mostly Korea."

"Gee— And the Second World War, you been in that too?"

"Why, yes. My career, you know," and Captain Tyll laughed to make his career sound like any other.

"I was thinking of signing up for another hitch," said Ralph. "When this one is over."

"Oh? That's very nice. Not many good men signing up anymore." Captain Tyll turned his head so he saw Bush, as if now it was Bush's turn. "And you, Corporal? What'll you do when you get out?"

"Go home. I guess," said Bush.

"Don't you know?"

It was just conversational, as far as Tyll was concerned, just said because the air was so dead and he wished that there were some more conversation.

"It's a word I use," said Bush. "I'm going home for sure."

"No offense meant, Corporal. Really, no offense meant." Tyll smiled it, hoping to be understood.

He's pushing himself my way, Bush felt. He's like a stone in a shoe—

"And what do you do, Corporal Bush? Got a job waiting?"

"Job? No. I got no job."

"How do you make your living?" said Matty. "The question was asked *that* way. Wasn't it, Captain Sir?"

"I got a place," said Bush. "And I hunt."

"Ah!" Captain Tyll hitched around in his chair and showed interest. A topic, now. Something to talk about—

"Then our course must come naturally to you," he said. "You must enjoy it."

Bush started to prickle all over his skin, and to sweat.

"No," he said.

They all looked at each other at the table, leaving Bush out, each wishing to show that they would excuse the remark. But Tyll did not want to lose a conversational topic. He wanted to sit awhile talking to somebody.

"But you will, Corporal," he said. "When it feels more familiar. It's the same thing, really, like your hunting."

"No," said Bush. He looked sullen now. "Mine's different."

"Oh? Well, but look at it, Corporal. The stalk, what you do, and what I'm teaching you—"

"I kill 'em," said Bush. He looked up at Tyll, straight and vicious. "The stalk don't pleasure me."

It was now sort of a conversation, like Tyll had wanted. It was just that to Matty and Ralph. It wasn't to Bush—never had been—and now, it wasn't to Tyll. The two men looked at each other and knew this.

"No feeling of sport," said Matty, but the air didn't change.

"I don't hold with 'sport'," said Bush.

They waited for Captain Tyll, because it was his turn. He sat looking down at his hands, at the nails which were small and pink, and next he looked up as if he felt very casual.

"Pleasure?" he said. "Sport and pleasure?" This time he did not bother to smile. He looked at Bush and said, "Are you imputing something, Corporal? What are you imputing?"

For a moment Bush got confused because Tyll looked so sure and the bars on his collar were blinking with the man's very slow breathing. But then the dislike gave Bush his direction again and he said, "I don't know what impute means."

He pushed back his chair and wanted to leave.

"Corporal," said Captain Tyll. "One moment, please, Corporal Bush."

Bush, of course, had to stop and listen.

"You have an objection, perhaps? You know what objection means. There is something you don't like. Is it killing? After all, I prepare you to kill."

"I kill," said Bush. "I kill 'em to eat."

"Aha." And now Captain Tyll smiled again, but wasn't pleasant. "I thought for a moment that killing was somehow your objection." He leaned back. "It is mine, you know," and he looked at Bush with a slow satisfaction.

Bush said nothing, nor did the other two men.

"You are surprised," said Tyll.

"No."

All along the two men had understood each other and so Captain Tyll's sudden rage now had nothing to do with surprise or with taking affront.

He would shout this down. He held his breath so that first of all everything would be interrupted and then he would measure it out, thin and civilized, an officer's edge to the voice—no more—and so pull down his fear to something acceptable.

"What I teach is clean, like a science, Corporal. Nothing thoughtless, but a discipline, which is safety. I teach safety! For years, Corporal."

"And in the Second World War and Korea both!" Ralph said fast.

"I'm thinking about that," said Matty, and his face, looking up, showed pleasure.

"Well," said Captain Tyll, "that is hardly the point," but he left it hang there, left each of them with his own impressions. "What does matter," he said, "is that you, Corporal Bush, needn't worry. You don't have to be afraid in the least."

He smiled at Bush very briefly, then at the other man, longer. It meant they were together, understanding each other, and that Corporal Bush could leave.

Nobody looked at him anymore and Bush went away without saying another word. Talking did nothing for him—

He walked fast. The further he got away from the PX the darker it got and the noise fell off to nothing. Just the thunk of his shoes on the pavement and his clothes rasping slightly. He stopped once and then there was nothing except his breathing. It was very loud.

Afraid of Tyll? Of his fastness and his way with a knife? That was one kind of fear, but it did not make Bush crawl. Tyll made him crawl. Bush had sometimes seen a buck stop in his tracks while there had been no sound and no tell-tale wind anywhere and the animal's feet twitching and testing and the nose making very small trembles. The buck would look straight at Bush in his cover *knowing* he was there but would just stand still, because he did not trust his signs.

Bush felt that way. He had none of the natural signs of fear coming to him, and that was the worst.

Bush coughed and looked around to get his bearings. He saw the warehouse by the side of the rail spur, the road curving around there, and the short, dark stretch between two squares of light from the marker spots at the ends of the building. Bush went on and started to curse very slowly with each step he took, listening to himself as if to a lesson. He cursed so the meaning of it would massage his feelings into a full heat.

He stopped by the black wall of the building with light right and left but none where he stood. Just a deep blackness where he was with the same feel he knew on a hunt. Small and still, waiting, and then came the game. He would wait for it, finish it. That's how: *finish it!* Not like Tyll and his ways. Bush took a deep breath and the picture was at last clear and simple. He hated Tyll and no reason why not. Finish it.

Tyll came the way Bush knew he would because Captain Tyll lived in the officer's quarters. He was carrying the packages in his arms and was humming. He looked black and white when he passed under the light, thin and with many lines showing. Then he came into the dark and was a silhouette.

"Now," said Bush. "Now we do it my way."

Tyll stopped and the packages crackled. But there was nothing dramatic about this. Tyll craned his neck to see in the dark and Bush walked over to him.

"Well! Corporal Bush— Isn't it?" and Tyll's voice went up at the end.

"Put down the junk, Captain Tyll."

"What?"

"I'm gonna beat you."

Captain Tyll did not put the packages down but held on to them with a sudden tight squeeze. To do anything else now would be insane. A million things he could do now, all insane. If this were a demonstration—

"Skaaa!" said Bush, exploding his voice the way he would do it to flush a bird.

Captain Tyll held on to the packages which, right then, made all the difference. He pressed air into his throat and said, "Soldier. I suppose you know what this means."

Bush didn't answer. He was measuring.

"You know who I am. You are wearing your uniform. I'm wearing my uniform. I remind you...."

"Put down the junk."

Captain Tyll did not know he was going to smile but he was smiling and hoping that Bush would be able to see it.

"Very well," he said, "I'll do what you say. I'll put my packages here on the ramp and then you and I talk this over. Now, I'm not the kind of man... " but at this point the packages were out of the way and Bush made his pass.

He feigned for the head and came through with the heel of his other hand aiming for the chin, but never get there.

Tyll reflexed. It needed no thought. With old practice he dropped back and jabbed out his foot which connected. It cracked on Bush's shin, not too hard, but it hurt like hell.

He's going to fight, Bush said to himself. He's going to come through and open up, my way—

But right then, Tyll did not do anything else. He stayed where he was, holding himself where he was, and kept very still. His own kick had surprised him. He had acted without any thought, and now—in this moment—the fact was unnerving.

"Bush," he said. "Listen to me, Corporal Bush!"

"Stop talking—" and Bush made a slow half-circle.

"You *know* I can break you. You know that—"

"Go ahead," and Bush stopped moving, loose and ready the way he had learned it.

"Now, please," said Captain Tyll. He cleared his throat, as if nothing was very important, and with a wave of his hand, "Listen to me, Corporal Bush. Fine—you're listening, Corporal Bush, fine—stay there. I want you to know, Corporal Bush, that you are quite safe. Believe me. Don't be afraid. I want you to know I have never hurt anyone. You are safe—"

Nuts. He was nuts with his talk. The rage came up inside Bush, shaking his voice.

"Lookit!" and he ripped at his collar, tearing it open. "Can you see what you did? Lookit, you son of a bitch!"

Bush stepped close, twisting his neck. There was a thin line of black dried blood on the base of the neck. There was a cut like a slice in the trunk of a pine tapped for sap.

Nothing from Tyll.

"Your sweet talk don't count for nothing. You didn't hold back good enough!"

Then Bush had meant to hit out again but he heard Tyll say something and the voice was a shock.

"Oh my God—"

It was mostly a breath fearing to draw very deeply. Under the dim light two black patches of sweat could be seen growing on Captain Tyll's shirt.

"Shut up," said Bush. "Shut up, shut up," very low, so his trembling would not break out all over him.

"My God, man, you've seen how I work! You've seen me!" Tyll had his bearings again, in a desperate way. "This is an accident! I have never...."

"You're a killer," said Bush. He crouched and the trembling left him.

"You're safe. Bush! In all my years...."

"Twenty years and two wars. And a killer all of that time. Don't stand there and tell me...."

"*No!* I mean this!" He was pleading now, with great force and pain in his voice. "I have never in all that time, Bush, *never* touched anyone!"

Bush let his hands sink down very slowly, without knowing it. He was staring at Tyll and had to believe him.

"Jeesis—" he said.

Bush stared at the man and his skin started to crawl. His neck burned from the cut. The first cut in a lifetime, the first time that it had leaked out of the Captain and past his dead-handed control. The thought of that murder held back gave Bush his hate again.

"Finish it!" he said and that time he connected.

It was a fast play with a jab which meant nothing, but a jab that left Bush's head close and wide open so that it drew Tyll's reaction the same way a magnet draws. Tyll's hand, with unconscious intent, shot out but it was this momentum Bush had been waiting for. He did everything he had learned from Tyll except not for Tyll's reasons.

Tyll yelled with the pain in his wrist and spun with the leverage, crashing hard into the wall.

"Wait— WAIT!"

Bush kicked him hard, dropped back for the next pass.

"My God, man!" Tyll's voice strained terribly. "I can kill you!"

Bush said nothing, made no move, so there was nothing else but Tyll's voice, Tyll's own voice made him talk more, made him break out with his fear. "I can! In a hundred ways! I can cripple the life out of you so you know every minute of it! You hear what I'm saying? I can do it— It takes only a second— Listen, man I can make you choke on your own flesh, I can show you your bones, I can."

"Finish!" said Bush and horror of the talking man was fever all over his skin.

It was very fast after that, fast like fright. Bush came to attack but before he had really connected the Captain's neck bloated up with the coarse screams that broke out, the face wasn't thin anymore but glutted with blood, and the whole man came apart in wild flailing and twisting and lashing. His motions were thick and solid with force, unpointed, so that they sprayed out the same way a buckshot charge loses itself. That's how Tyll lost himself—

Bush didn't come near him. This wasn't aimed at him and he stood back, watching: Tyll going to pieces with the violence in each swing, each thrash like another crack in his careful clean science, and nothing there that came to a point but everything coming out like splash—

When Tyll ran down and stopped it was finished for Bush. He stood aside, his hands hanging down, and he let Tyll be. The Captain's breath made a bad sound on the inhale but was deep and tired when it came out. In a while he pushed himself away from the wall, walked away.

There was nothing else, as far as Bush was concerned. He could walk his way, and Tyll the other. Tyll forgot to pick up his packages and Bush took them after the Captain and said, "You forgot these." Then Tyll walked one way and Bush the other. It was finished.

"Wade Miller" was merely one of many pseudonyms used by the team of childhood friends, Robert Wade and Bill Miller. Like Peter Rabe, they didn't tend to write a lot of short stories, instead favoring novels. Together they wrote one of the best private investigator series ever about a character named Max Thursday. Over the course of six books they do a truly remarkable job of showing Thursday's character on an arc, where he begins the first book with a very certain kind of reputation. Every succeeding entry in the series shows Thursday continue on his evolutionary course, changing into something else while struggling with the problems of each story. Fascinating stuff and done as well as anyone has ever done it. Highly entertaining as well as highly recommended.

INVITATION TO AN ACCIDENT

Wade Miller

Perhaps Albert Magnum was still unmarried because he had never rescued a damsel in distress. Certainly everyone who mattered liked him, whenever they noticed him. They admired his slim grace, his courtly manners, even his precise mustache, but no one ever seemed to see the cavalier gleam in his eyes. It was a reflection of the burning gallantry in his heart. He was one of those rare men who could see nothing especially funny about Don Quixote. Womanhood he worshiped, and he was a perennial escort, but he preferred a woman to be on his arm rather than in his arms.

A hot wind was blowing out to sea the night Albert Magnum came to dine with the Ponds. It parched and rustled everything in its path, respecting nothing, although Bedsole Drive is the oldest and most staid neighborhood in Orchestra Beach, possibly in all San Diego. The wind made Magnum himself feel uncommonly like a dry leaf, lost and purposeless. Being a bachelor past 40 has its moody moments.

Yet he smiled bravely as he rang the bell of what was still known as "the old Skillet house." Virgilia, whose surname had been changed to Pond for two years, answered the door in person. "Albert!" she welcomed her old friend. And he did feel old tonight, despite her twinkling and beaming at him in the entry hall. The slender hands to which he relinquished his hat looked so much younger than his own, although Virgilia and he had grown up together on Bedsole Drive.

"As lovely as ever," he complimented her. "I don't believe you've changed since our first dancing class. Tell me your secret." His bow lacked much of its usual flourish. Tonight he wasn't too eager to expose the bald spot on top of his head.

"My secret?" said Virgilia with a squeak of anxiety. Then she laughed quickly in relief and understanding. "Oh, your same old chivalry." She led him along the hall. He was disappointed: not a word from her to halt time in its flight.

Well, perhaps marriage kept a woman young, and this was Virgilia's second. She was willowy and pallid and her chestnut hair was extremely fine in texture. With her fragile features, the total effect was that of centuries of choice inbreeding, but it was actually the result of strict dieting and sedulously keeping out of the sun. She was one of the hardware Skillets and her grandfather had come to California with his wares in a wagon. Remembering this was some comfort to Albert Magnum since his *great*-grandfather had arrived by ship and, furthermore, had owned the ship; its figurehead could be seen on display any afternoon in the very museum where Albert sat on the board of directors.

"It's been ages!" Virgilia was saying, with more excitement than seemed necessary. "Since we've even spoken, Albert—more than to say hello, I mean. You've met my husband, haven't you? Joseph thought he and I were keeping to ourselves much too much. He insisted I shouldn't forget life-long friends simply because of marriage and—well, here you are!"

Here he was, in the living room. The grand old carved furniture looked the same, he was glad to see, polished and permanent. Just think, last week he had almost forgotten that he had ever taken the sweet Virgilia Skillet dancing or boating or picnicking; tonight he was dining with Virgilia Pond. And between these two eras, she had been Mrs. Campbell Bedsole. A pity that Virgilia had seen fit to give up the Bedsole name. After all, great-great-grandfather Bedsole had come to Orchestra Beach even before the Magnums, and it had been a Bedsole who built the pier and bandstand for Sunday afternoon concerts over the ocean. Of course, the bandstand had been an abandoned sinking derelict for a full generation now, and certainly the present Campbell Bedsole was not one to confine his charm to a wife, but nevertheless Virgilia shouldn't have….

When Joseph Pond shook hands he hurt Albert Magnum's fingers. Pond managed to be hearty without smiling. He said, "you've got a choice, Al. Manhattan or whiskey?"

"Would you have any port?" Luckily, the Ponds did, so Magnum drank port as his father had, and Virgilia subsisted on several manhattans, and Pond drank his whiskey unadulterated by anything except a single ice cube.

Pond was quite cubical, a heavy ruddy man with a grainy complexion like red sandstone. He had hair along the outer edges of his hands. Magnum recognized him from the Yacht Club where some referred to him as "young Pond" only because he had made all his own money, and because he hadn't even been born in Southern California, much less on Bedsole Drive in Orchestra Beach. He was in real estate. Magnum, while keeping up his third of the small talk, decided that pretty, vivacious Virgilia was wasted. She would have been better off with the profligate Cam Bedsole who at least pretended to add water to his whiskey.

Pond crushed the small talk with, "What's this I read about the mural at your museum, Al? A bunch of naked women or something."

"Oh, you know the newspapers." Magnum smiled like a martyr. "The mural was simply unsuitable, that's all." The mural, as contracted for, had been intended to show the activities of the original San Diego Indians, but not as the artist had depicted them.

"Absolutely undressed?" inquired Virgilia with unsuitable interest. It was probably the manhattans that brought the eager glow to her pale eyes. "Really now, why haven't I read about that?"

"Well," said Magnum uncomfortably, "the men wore codpieces, I suppose you'd call them." As for what the women wore, he was at a loss. He wasn't a very physical person. When driven to mention any of the usually clothed parts of the body, he would seek refuge in a euphemism, such as "tummy" instead of "stomach" or "abdomen" or, Heaven forbid, "belly." But, recalling those Indian girls, he was stuck for a decent term.

"Mixed company, yet," commented Pond. "I guess you were the one who blackballed it."

"There were two of us forthright enough to cast vetoes." The other was old Mrs. Bedsole, bless her. She was 85.

Virgilia sighed. "A shame," she said. "I mean, a shame that Joseph hasn't time to serve on any civic committees. But he works so hard now that he's scarcely ever home. I can't make him slow down."

"I believe in getting things done, dear." Pond gestured impatiently with one stubby hand. "In your shoes, Al, I'd either hang the mural or hang the artist."

The wind raised its voice then and some massive object struck the rear of the house a resounding blow. Magnum started but he was grateful for the interruption. "What was that—a tree?" it had sounded more like The Fall of the House of Usher: enter Lady Madeline, fresh from her tomb.

"No. I've had painters refinishing the back end of this place. They left their scaffolding up on the second floor, like fools. Guess they didn't expect the wind to come up."

During dinner, Pond discussed sewage. This was in connection with the property values of an adjacent district where the voters stubbornly preferred their septic tanks to progress in the form of a bond issue. Pond was for progress, property values, and sewers, no matter what the cost was—to others. Virgilia tried to divert the conversation to the improvements her husband had made about the house and grounds. "Oh, the garden furniture!" she exclaimed. "I'm really fond of that, myself. Joseph made it all with his own hands. Perhaps you'd like to see it, Albert."

Pond said, "If you're going outside, dear, you'll need a coat in this wind."

He pushed back his coffee cup and strode from the room.

After a moment of listening to her husband plod up the stairs, Virgilia rose. "We might as well go ahead, Albert. He'll be along before I catch my death of anything."

They went into the rear garden through the French doors of the billiard room. The warm east wind still moaned, making the pepper trees tremble and causing the banana trees to flap in anguish. Virgilia groped for an outside electric-light switch and clicked it. When nothing happened, she philosophized. "Bulbs will burn out."

Over their heads the rope-hung scaffold swung and hammered twice against the frame wall of the house. Magnum chuckled to excuse his little jump of fright. "Your husband should lower that thing. It's likely to keep you awake tonight."

"No, I'm the world's best sleeper."

They crossed the tiles of the terrace an Magnum admired the iron garden furniture Joseph Pond had himself constructed, what little he could see of it in the dark.

"He likes to bend things," explained Virgilia. "He's converted the old carriage house into a workshop and shares it with the gardener. He and the gardener are like friends." There was a hibiscus bush near the door she opened. She picked the single pale pink blossom and fastened it on top of her brown hair. She grinned, her breath still sweet with manhattans. "I feel paganish. Were those Indian girls really naked?"

"Your father would have disapproved too," said Magnum defensively. She turned on the lights in the former carriage house and he glanced around at objects unfamiliar to him. Work benches, machines he supposed were lathes, rows of hacksaws and bristly files. A great many gardening tools were ranged along the wall next to the door, beneath a shelf of insecticides. The boxes and bottles each displayed its printed skull and crossbones and list of ingredients. The nearest was arsenate of something-or-other.

He never found out exactly what because Virgilia flipped the light off suddenly. She muttered, "I wish *I'd* been born naked. I mean, I suppose I was, of course, but I wish I could live nakedly, not have to hide anything."

"Now really, old girl."

"You've just never lived with an adage, that's all." She hiccupped defiantly. Then she twisted her head hastily toward the house. The upstairs windows were black. "All work and no play. He's been laboriously constructing my happiness for two years. I've got to tell someone!"

"Tell me what?" They were standing together in the doorway of the carriage house, and Magnum abruptly felt romantic, in a benevolent and protective way. He patted her shoulder as he would have petted an animal, provided it was clean and friendly. This particular animal seemed feverish, even through the dusky material of her dress.

She withdrew slightly, musing. Suddenly she told him her secret. "I've seen Cam once or twice lately."

What was the proper reply to that? Good luck? Carry on, dear childhood friend? Magnum never condoned these extramarital doings despite the distinguished line of precedents—Queen Guenevere, for example—but on the other hand he had a lot more respect for Cam Bedsole than for Joseph Pond. And after all she *had* been Mrs. Campbell Bedsole for a while, which should make some sort of difference. Magnum felt excited, in on something. He cleared his throat, preparatory to saying nothing.

With a delicious stroke of logic, Virgilia said next, "Well, let's go back to the house and play some high-fidelity recordings. I don't know what can be taking Joseph so long."

They crossed the garden silently. The wind had stopped. Magnum paused beneath a jacaranda tree while Virgilia went ahead. Ostensibly he was searching his pockets for his cigarette holder; actually, he wanted to be alone for a moment to deplore the primitive complications of the Pond household. To think such thoughts while walking beside Virgilia would not have been gallant.

She was on the tiled terrace, swaying toward the open French doors when Magnum heard the scaffolding thud against the house again. Automatically, he peered up through the still branches of the jacaranda.

In that disastrous moment, he couldn't move. He wanted to run to Virgilia, seize her, shelter her body with his own—but all he could do was stand with his mouth open and his hands rigid in his pockets. "Virgilia!" The voice sounded something like his own except that it was too high and cracked unbecomingly with panic.

Her face turned back toward him, whitely. Her eyes were huge and fearful as they rolled upward. From the night above, one end of the painting scaffold plunged to earth. The timbers struck the porch with a ringing sound, then the half-suspended platform danced about like a monster marionette. It banged against the wall of the house and smashed at the French doors. In a moment the dance was over and the scaffold curtsied lazily, its sudden wild energy spent.

Albert Magnum ran awkwardly across the terrace. He heard his voice shouting again. Virgilia lay like a bundle of clothes just inside the billiard room, splinters of glass sparkling on her dress.

Pond came into the room from the other direction, his wife's coat draped over his arm. "Virgilia! For God's sake!"

The two men kneeled beside her at the same time. She was uninjured, but her hands fluttered out of control against the carpet. "I fell," she whispered. "I fell. It missed me."

After the doctor had come and gone, the two men stood again in the big living room. With the excitement past, with Virgilia put to sleep upstairs, Magnum shivered. The truth settling in his bones was piercing cold. Virgilia had nearly been killed. Only his shout had saved her, so rudely close had death come. He puckered his forehead in impotence. "But how could it have happened?"

"Fool painters," growled Pond. His fingers angrily shredded the pale flesh of the hibiscus blossom that had fallen from his wife's hair. "They never should have left their gear up there in this wind. I should've had sense enough to lower it myself."

"But the rope was new, brand new and an inch thick. A break was—"

"It didn't just break," Pond interrupted sharply. "You saw the rope, Al. It frayed through. Must have been a splinter of iron on the pulley that's been wearing against it. It frayed through until the wind and the weight of those planks snapped the last few strands."

It sounded perfectly plausible as told by Pond's matter-of-fact voice in a fully lighted room. But it was in the dark that Albert Magnum lay awake through the rest of the night, listening to the wind rattle the windows of his bachelor apartment.

He twisted and turned, reliving the evening's adventure many times. Nothing so violent had ever happened to him before. This comes, he thought, of going only where one is invited; tonight he had been invited to an accident. Such a queer notion… more likely thought by the wind than by his usually ordered mind…. And then suddenly he sat bolt upright in his bed, trembling with excitement. *There had been no wind when the scaffold fell!*

In his first frenzy of imagination he nearly telephoned the police. Luckily, he foresaw the ultimate reaches of that conversation. "Officer, I want to report an attempted murder. Mr. Joseph Pond of Bedsole Drive tried to kill his wife this evening."

Attempted murder on *Bedsole Drive*? Have you any proof, sir?

He had none. Trying to recollect something damning, he rubbed at his mustache with a knuckle but all he produced was an irritated lip. He *knew* it had been intended that he be the corroborative witness to an accidental death, yet what good was his sensitive intuition without facts? At a time like this, he nearly hated facts.

All he could remember were those intangibles which Virgilia's husband might easily explain away. Pond had taken a long time upstairs. He had not turned on any lights visible from the garden. Even the garden light itself had not been working. No—because it might have reflected the knife blade in the second-story window where Pond had waited by the scaffold rope, waiting for his wife to pass below on her return to the house.

But the rope had been frayed, not cut.

That detail baffled Magnum for a while. Then he recalled the files and rasps in Pond's workshop. Of course! Joseph Pond would construct the murder of his wife with tools. Magnum could easily picture those square thick hands moving back and forth over the rope, practicing their craft.

Exhilarated, Magnum slid to the floor and commenced his setting-up exercises although it was not dawn yet, much less his usual hour for rising. But he was faithful to his bedroom calisthenics, and he was now rising to the emergency. Protect Virgilia—that was the watchword. He must get dressed despite the unholy hour, drive to Bedsole Drive, and guard the house where a drugged wife lay at the mercy of her brute husband. He exercised faster than usual, feeling young and intense. He had a Cause. The ringing in his ears as he bent and stretched was like massed trumpets.

A ghastly possibility occurred to him just as he finished his counting and grunting. Bedsole Drive, being a wealthy neighborhood, was well patrolled by police cars. He might be asked why he was parked there at this time of night. And how did one answer a suspicious policeman? "If you must know, I am protecting a lady."

"Why?"

"Because she is having an affair with her ex-husband."

"Hey, Ed, listen to this one."

Albert Magnum sank back in his bed with a shudder. Protect Virgilia, certainly, but protect her good name too. He presumed that Virgilia, like any woman, would rather be strangled in her sleep than have her reputation dirtied on the city streets. So he didn't race to her side, after all. He didn't even get dressed until a decent time. He made himself wait, for Virgilia's sake.

After breakfast, about 10 o'clock, he telephoned. To his amazement, Virgilia answered, alive and unslain.

"Are you all right?"

"Certainly, Albert. A bit dopey, perhaps. I'm sorry about the silly way I folded up last night."

"I mean—really all right?"

She actually giggled. "But I just told you! It's very sweet of you to call. I'm always such a bother to people."

His ears began to burn with an asinine feeling. Through the window he could see the clean safe sunlight, and the melodramatic wind had blown itself away and his dark forebodings seemed ridiculous in the bright of day. Despite this treachery, he pressed on. "Virgilia, have any other accidents happened to you recently?"

"Of course not. What do you mean?"

He didn't dare tell her for fear she would laugh at him. He thanked her for last night's dinner, said cautiously to say hello to Cam Bedsole for him, and hung up. His bald spot was damp with the perspiration of embarrassment. He sat in sulky contemplation of the fool he had almost made of himself. The shining armor vanished from his imagination to be replaced by cap and bells....

For the next week Albert Magnum plunged resolutely into a series of committee meetings. He managed to keep the Ponds out of his mind except for an occasional twinge of self-resentment.

So it was with a faint vexation on Saturday that he raised his eyes from his luncheon table at the Yacht Club to see Virgilia beaming down at him. "Don't get up," she insisted. "I'm late for an engagement and I can only stop a moment. How are you?"

He rose anyway. "Disappointed, of course." His gallantry was purely automatic although Virgilia did appear as radiant as the bay waters outside. "I see you've recovered completely from your escape."

"Escape? Oh, that scaffold business. You know, Albert, we've had a perfect rush of bad luck at our house."

It was good luck that she didn't see the suspicion spring to life in his eyes. She didn't see his appetite disappear. She didn't see his shoulders straighten martially.

"Well," she inquired gaily, "aren't you going to ask me what sort of bad luck?"

"I can imagine."

"Joseph is ill."

"Oh." After a breath of relief, he added hastily, "That's a shame. What's the trouble?"

"We don't know exactly. The doctor says a touch of ptomaine. He'll be up and about in a day or so, but it certainly has tied me down taking care of him. Why don't you drop by tonight and see him? You know Joseph— confinement makes him restless as a bear."

Virgilia peeked at her wrist watch and said that she really must run. Puzzled, Magnum watched her thread her way among the tables. She slid into a car that had pulled up at the front steps of the Yacht Club. It appeared to be Cam Bedsole at the wheel.

When he called dutifully at the Pond home that evening the maid informed him that Virgilia had not yet returned. Joseph Pond was napping. Albert Magnum waited, finally wandering out into the rear garden. It was seven o'clock and he reflected that Virgilia was being rather flagrant about her private life.

Nevertheless, she didn't deserve to be executed merely for the pursuit of happiness.

The thought was back again, nagging. Magnum found himself standing beneath the jacaranda tree, looking up as he had that night a week before. The upper floor of the old house was dark, as it had been then. But the painting was completed and the scaffold gone. The French doors had been repaired.

He scuffled along the paths irritably, doing battle with his imagination. Why should he attribute evil motives to Joseph Pond? The fall of the scaffold was an unusual accident, but still credible. And this second bit of bad luck had harmed the husband, not the wife. It was melodramatic nonsense.

He hesitated beside the hibiscus bush where Virgilia had plucked the blossom for her hair just before the—yes, the accident. Furtively, Magnum tried the door to the converted carriage house. It swung open invitingly. He stepped inside.

The overhead light shone on the skeletal shapes of Pond's tools and machinery. Nothing was different and Magnum didn't know why he had expected any change. The neat rack of files drew him like a magnet. Blushing with shame, he peered at their corrugated blades. There was no trace of hempen strands caught in any of the tiny spikes. He had the final proof that he was a fool. He hurried back to the door and turned off the light. Then, slowly, he reached for the switch again.

Something *was* different.

It was a very small thing, concerning the shelf of insecticides above the garden tools beside the door. He remembered that a week ago he had scanned the table of ingredients of the first box on that shelf. The table had began with "arsenate of" something-or-other.

Tonight that box was not there. A spray gun sat in its place. Quickly, Magnum went through the array of boxes and bottles. The label of which he remembered such a scanty fragment was no longer there.

With more delight than apprehension, Albert Magnum now understood everything. Virgilia needed a protector, after all! For it was obvious that Joseph Pond was proceeding with his plans. His first attempt on Virgilia had failed; he was constructing the second more carefully. He was ill because he was experimenting on himself.

Another accident was going to happen. By some skillfully clumsy error, both Virgilia and Joseph would be poisoned by an arsenic substance. Joseph Pond, being the stronger, would recover after a few days of illness. But Virgilia would die from in identical amount of arsenic, an amount which her husband's acquired tolerance could withstand.

Magnum almost ran back to the house.

Virgilia Pond had just come in. She was stripping off her gloves and spreading a sweet air of manhattans throughout the entry hall. She looked mischievous, glowing, and remote from disaster. "Sorry I'm late, Albert. Have you seen poor Joseph yet?"

"I understand he's sleeping."

"We'll wake him."

As they went upstairs Magnum wondered if it would do any good to warn her. No, he decided. All he could tell her were those conjectures to which a wife might listen soberly and then repeat, giggling, to her husband. Charming as she was, Virgilia was not deep. Magnum doubted that she could perceive the barbarity of her husband's nature, the bleak jealousy there that could ever forgive, only punish.

Joseph Pond was awake and sitting up. In his woolen robe, his legs under the blankets, he looked more self-conscious than barbaric. Virgilia kissed his drawn cheek lightly. Magnum condemned Pond's bad luck in a convincing manner while in the back of his head he mulled over the problem of how best to rescue Pond's wife. It seemed a pity that the duel had gone out of fashion, as well as the hired assassin.

Pond was saying, "Doc says day after tomorrow. He wants me to take some time off, go camping or something. Don't see how I can, though, with so much to do."

Virgilia patted his hand affectionately. "Really, you should, you know. It may be your working so hard that helped to upset your stomach."

Tummy, Magnum corrected her mentally. Then it came to him, a strategy suggested by Pond himself. Magnum smiled casually. "Perhaps we could take a run down into Mexico for some surf fishing, Joseph. The weather's balmy enough and open air is the best medicine in the world."

"Fishing, Al?" Pond squinted in disbelief. "I would never have picked you for a sportsman."

"I know a spot below the border, although I haven't been there for twenty years. I'm certain we can borrow some equipment at the club. Lying around on the beach should do you good. And me too, of course."

The scheme appeared perfect to Magnum. It would separate Pond from his wife just when the intended murderer was first recovered and ready to try the second helping of poison. And though Virgilia might not take a warning seriously, Magnum was certain Pond would. He would frame it carefully so that there would be no uncivilized break between Pond and himself. Simply an unmistakable reference to the so-called accident and a clear indication that Albert Magnum was watching and aware should another attempt be made. The man would not dare go ahead if his plans were uncovered beforehand, for Joseph Pond would be in danger if anything befell his wife.

Pond shot a questioning look toward the woman. She said, "Well, if the wide open spaces are the only thing that will keep you from your real estate, I'm for it. I'll miss you, though."

Her husband shrugged after a moment. "I had planned to do a few things around the house, but surf fishing sounds good to me."

It was settled. Magnum collected the largest items of equipment from various club acquaintances and purchased such pieces as were liable to become lost or used up. He had an opportunity to borrow at least one heavy rod from Cam Bedsole but desisted. This was no time for irony. After several telephone consultations with Pond, who was becoming more and more enthusiastic about the outing, he laid in the few provisions required. Pond happened to have two sleeping bags and said he could supply what cooking gear they would need.

They left at dawn on Monday and Magnum was disappointed that Virgilia did not get up to see them off. He had pictured her waving a handkerchief from an upstairs window but, of course, she didn't realize the importance of this adventure.

Fifty miles below the Mexican border, he located the stretch of beach he remembered from his youth. White and clean, the broad belt of sand melted undisturbed into opposite horizons. The pound of surf seemed muffled by the utter loneliness. The dirt road bore no traffic for days at a time and even this faint evidence of man was hidden from the beach itself by soft dunes festooned with creeping plants. The primeval beauty reminded Magnum of the scenery in the mural rejected by his museum.

Pond too was exhilarated. He appeared to expand physically as he crunched across the dunes, scarcely bowed beneath three-quarters of the camping paraphernalia. His last traces of pallor vanished under the hot blue sky. He wore no hat but Magnum did, to protect his easily burned bald spot.

Though they talked little while making camp, Magnum discovered a camaraderie rising between himself and his companion. The very stolidity of Virgilia's husband attracted and refreshed him. Yet the same quiet directness of Pond's every move served to stabilize Magnum's determination to set him right. In warning Pond away from murder Albert Magnum was sure he was making the manful, the civilized gesture. He would be saving, not only Virgilia, but Joseph Pond too.

All through the afternoon they cast and recast their lines until the breakers were growling and frothing dimly against velvet darkness. During the long descent of the sun, neither man relaxed by planting the butt of his rod in the sand. Both Magnum and Pond kept the leather hilts braced against their bodies, playing the drag of the water and the false strikes of kelp with a sort of mutual exaltation. Magnum suspected he would be stiff in the morning but he couldn't resist the fervor of the battle.

At last, Pond said, "Guess we better leave some for tomorrow," and they trudged back to their camp. Pond had caught three perch and a croaker. Magnum's catch was one fish, a corbina weighing about six pounds, but it was more of a prize than his companion's four. He felt bold and successful. He stored the spare fish in the trunk cooler in the car while Pond began preparing the evening meal.

When Magnum returned to the cooking-hole where the fire blazed, Pond was boiling coffee in a battered can and cursing his own forgetfulness in leaving the coffee pot behind. They dined in silent grandeur on the flaky crispness of corbina and draughts of the bitter coffee. They squatted like Indians on opposite sides of the fire-pit while the flames sank lower and the circle of night closed in.

When he began thinking longingly of the sleeping bags, Magnum recalled with a start his reason for this expedition. A Crusader letting the Saracens slip from his mind could not have been more shocked. Magnum opened the subject with more abruptness than he intended. "It's hard to believe that we give up all this peace simply to crowd ourselves into cities. I often wonder, do we gain anything worthwhile? Only jealousy and disease and so on."

For a despairing instant he feared that Joseph Pond had fallen asleep. Then the stony bulk across the way stirred and scratched itself. "Well, Al, property came first. The first towns were single families. The main reason for family is still to protect property." With a lazy grunt, Pond stopped speaking and left Magnum without a single idea for another foray.

Luckily, after a long pause, Pond added dreamily, "I'd like to live on a ranch, myself. But Virgilia can't be talked into selling that old barn on Bedsole Drive. She's strong on memories, on living in the past. You know."

Magnum knew. He also deplored Pond's disrespect for the old Skillet house, but it did give him an opening.

"Then you'll admit that what are annoyances in town fade away out her in the open. It's the constant, grating proximity that gives rise to jealousy and the unnatural deaths that go with it."

"What kinds of death aren't natural?"

"Oh, war, for example." Magnum drained his coffee cup with trembling hands before delivering his *coup de grace*. "And murder, if you want to include the petty things."

"I never saw a man who called his own death a petty thing."

"I meant that most motives for murder are pretty slight, compared to the value the murderer places on his own life." Breathlessly, Magnum watched the flickering face across the fire.

After some consideration Pond snorted. "What right-thinking murderer is going to imagine his own life ending? No one ever applies that notion to himself."

"I know a man who did." Again Magnum waited for Pond to show an avid interest and was disappointed. "I know a man who intended to kill."

"Oh?" Pond was engrossed in gingerly plucking the coffee can off the coals and dividing the remainder of its contents between their two cups. Magnum, once more dismayed by doubt, gulped at it for strength. Surely, he couldn't have made a mistake! But never had he seen a face as magnificently unconcerned as Pond's. At his last pronouncement, Magnum had expected to observe the twitching mouth, the sliding eye of a cornered criminal. Yet Pond merely inquired, "Do I know him?"

"I don't think you'd recognize him."

"You say he didn't go through with it?"

"No."

"Then he couldn't have had his mind much set on it."

"Oh, yes, he did! He had a frank, straightforward mind, and murder was its obsessing idea for a time. But because he had that type of mind, he was reasoned out of it. A simple use of civilized logic. You see, a third person came to the rescue—a disinterested unselfish person who was a friend of both the intended murderer and the intended victim."

"But how did this third person catch on, Al?"

"Well, the murderer was such a practical fellow that he rehearsed his crime beforehand. Our third person, thank Heaven, was astute and alert. He saw through the murderer's plan."

Pond sat very still, thinking. At last, he shook his head bullishly. "Much as I've come to like you, Al, sometimes you don't make good sense. This business of talking a murderer out of his murder—what possible argument could be used?"

Magnum smiled with relief. Pond not only understood him, he was also trying hard to comprehend his viewpoint. So far disarmed, Pond would succumb, Magnum knew. It was just a pity that Virgilia could never be told about his triumph in her behalf. However, his own accolade would have to suffice. He said, "As I mentioned, Joseph, it's a matter of simple logic. The murderer was invited to weigh his own life against the small satisfaction he'd gain from killing his wife."

Magnum smiled but Joseph Pond laughed. It was a jolly roar that broke over the beach in waves of merriment. Magnum would have joined in if Pond hadn't held up his hand for silence. "Al, excuse me! That was a sweet lesson in logic but what if you had made a mistake? What if nothing you said applied to the case at hand?"

"But how could that be?"

"Excuse me," gasped Pond, still choking with amusement, "and listen.

"I also know a man who decided to kill. But he wasn't anything like your nitwit friend. No, when he heard his wife was playing around, he very logically set out to protect his property. Protect it, Al—not destroy it. He told his wife to bring her friends around to the house. He knew darn well who she'd invite right off. Women are pretty obvious."

He smiled.

"This man specialized in accidents, Al, but the first time he tried the darkness fooled him. The darkness made him mistake a flower in his wife's hair for his victim's bald spot. But he got her lover the second time around. It seems they went camping in a lonely place and the coffee was boiled in a can which formerly contained a very potent insecticide. Only the husband recovered from...."

Albert Magnum was no longer listening. He had rolled face downward on the sand with the first clawing agony in his belly.

Known for writing strong characters and often from the victims' point of view, James McKimmey was able to create a strong sense of suspense and tension in his books. Here's a story that invokes two well-known adages: the best revenge is living well, and don't count your chickens prematurely. McKimmey takes the same kind of stress he puts on the characters in his novels and uses it here to great effect. A prolific short story writer, one of them, "Last Reunion," was adapted into an episode of GE Theater *starring Lee Marvin, no stranger himself to crime stories on the screen. Read McKimmey to really get into the minds of the characters. Is there a better place to be?*

THE TORMENTED

James McKimmey

A chilling evening wind blew across the small crossroads town on the spine of the Coast Range Mountains. Inside the Copper Lantern Bar and Restaurant the air was fragrant and warm from logs blazing in the huge stone fireplace. The aroma of charcoal-broiled steaks and garlic bread came from the restaurant section, whose broad windows overlooked the vast spread of the San Francisco Peninsula below.

David Farrel sat at the L-shaped bar and ordered another beer. It was a Thursday and customers were sparse. Only two parties were dining. Farrel and three other locals sat at the bar; one was Vince Ecker, a regular.

"Eggskull!" Ecker boomed to Farrel from down the bar. Loudly, Farrel thought. Always loudly.

He turned his head to look at the large, sinewy man whose eyes were the color of gun metal—which was appropriate, Farrel thought. "I'm thinking, Ecker."

Ecker wheezed—there was no other description for his laughter. "That's what you do, all right, Eggskull. Think. But it don't make you any money."

The man wore a black nylon jacket, tan Levis and hunting boots. A white Stetson was pushed back from his pulpy, cruel face. His ski-styled sun glasses rested on the dark wood beside his beer bottle. He grasped the bottle with a broad, stub-fingered hand and drank.

He was a primitive, Farrel thought bitterly, born into an advanced civilization that had done little to bring him up beyond his animal status. Yet he had been able to secure himself a good living as a construction foreman. He also owned a shrewd child-like ability to make the savage cut, as he had just done again.

He knew that Farrel had received a lengthy college education, but Ecker also knew that Farrel was presently living near pauper-hood, trying to support a wife and child on the meager pay he received as a book clerk in Palo Alto, ten miles below. But that particular situation was going to be corrected, Farrel thought.

"Is that the extent of your contribution?" he asked acidly. He was as large as Ecker, but there was a difference in their physiques. Beneath Farrel's bulk was fat, not muscle. His face was pale, against the weathered brownness of Ecker's. He would have liked to have suddenly transformed into a tough and muscular specimen in order to take care of Ecker physically. But there were more realistic ways.

"I was wondering if you want to go night-cooning again," Ecker said.

Farrel turned away as Ecker began wheezing again. He remembered vividly that night two weeks ago when he'd gone hunting with Ecker. Out of some foolish belief that he should test his courage in Ecker's presence, he'd agreed to it despite the fact that unlike Ecker, he had never wanted to see any animal killed.

He'd got into the man's pickup truck with four lean hounds inside the special compartment built on the flatbed behind. They'd drive on to a narrow road at the rear of the large rental ranch owned by Martin Brindmart, a retired investor who lived in seclusion in sizeable house built on that land.

He'd got out of the cab as the carbine-carrying Ecker had walked behind the truck to open the dog's compartment. The hounds sprang out in smooth, stretching leans and immediately began ranging, noses to the ground and yipping.

Ecker switched on his powerful flashlight as the dogs found a scent and gathered to bound into the darkness.

Farrel was a lover of nature. He particularly liked animals. He loved to hike through the hills to observe deer grazing on the highest slopes. He liked to see rabbits springing away from his step. He liked cats and dogs—even the hounds owned by Ecker, who had been bred and trained to lead the butcher to his quarry. All animals, he thought, could be categorized into just what they were.

The devious breed was human. He cared little for anyone of those, including his son Jolly, and certainly his wife Milly, who refused to allow him to own a pet of any kind.

Yet here he was, walking across a field with a killer of deer, raccoons, anything on which he could sight his gun. Because he was growing increasingly more nervous, he tried to make conversation: "Doesn't Brindmart mind our being out here at night?"

"Minds any time, Eggskull. To hell with him. I've took more deer meat off this land of his than you could figure. What's he going to do about it?"

"He's peculiar, isn't he?"

"Hermit, that's what he is. Even his own foreman don't get beyond his fence. Only me, when I deliver his supplies every Saturday."

"How come you, Ecker?"

"I trained his dogs. You ever see them?"

"I hiked in one day to where Rawl's' house is by the gate. I saw them."

He pictured those two dogs running back and forth behind the steel barbed-wire topped fence that Martin Brindmart had ordered built around his house: German shepherds, trained to attack on command. Trained, he now learned, by Vince Ecker.

"Them dogs would listen to two people only. Brindmart and me. No more, though. They're dead and buried."

"What happened?"

"Someone threw them a hunk of poisoned meat. Now I got to train me two more for him."

Farrel stepped gingerly over the tufted grass. "I hear Brindmart's rich."

"Yeah," Ecker said shortly.

"Why does he hide away like that?"

"Who knows? He's a nut."

But Farrel was not so sure about that. Having seen Brindmart's sanctuary, he'd become increasingly envious of the man. Brindmart's life, he'd decided, was one of perfection. Free of all worries and all responsibilities, he could live exactly as he chose.

As Farrel moved apprehensively through the night, with the dogs running ahead of them, he was regretting everything. Because of a small inheritance, he'd been able to remain in college for graduate study in English literature. He'd been content there. But then he'd met Milly and made the unfortunate mistake of marrying her on a slightly drunken weekend in Reno. Now they had Jolly, a bit under two years old. Farrel, who'd failed at a brief stint of teaching, had been required to become a clerk in a book store to support them. He would gladly, he thought, trade places with Martin Brindmart.

The sound of the dogs turned into a wild chorus of barks and yelps.

Ecker hurried his pace. "They got one."

Farrel followed him reluctantly over the rise of a hill, then down where the dogs were gathered around the trunk of an oak. Ecker pointed his flashlight upward to find the treed raccoon. The animal's eyes glowed against the light. Ecker handed Farrel the flash.

Listening to the bedlam of the dogs, feeling his throat dry, Farrel held the beam on the raccoon as Ecker carefully lifted his carbine. There was the crack of the rifle, and Farrel closed his eyes. As Ecker reclaimed the flashlight, Farrel looked again and saw that the raccoon had dropped to the ground, where it was slashing, biting and growling viciously, as the dogs darted at it.

"You didn't kill him," he managed.

"Hell, no!" Ecker said happily. "The dogs do that. I just winged him."

Farrel watched in horror as a small hound's belly was slashed by the raccoon's claws. "You're letting your own dogs get killed!"

"I get some more!" Ecker said in delight.

Farrel looked again at the bloody, raging battle. Then he trotted away. He stumbled over another small rise and sat down weakly beside the trunk of a small, wind-warped tree. He thought he would be sick for a time, listening to that wild sound of battle behind him. Then he came to himself.

He finally realized that he was sitting in a small cleft of a hill which rose directly above Martin Brindmart's house, no more than five hundred yards below. Outside the fencing, there were the lights of the smaller house used by the foreman, Cass Rawl. Then the long run of dark space to the larger house where light shown from a wide window.

Farrel used his excellent eyes to see that Brindmart was reading a book in a leather chair beside a desk and fireplace. He was lean, white-haired, and wore dark-rimmed glasses. He put the book down and walked to a wall.

He reached under a corner of the desk, and a panel of the knotty pine wall slid back. He reached inside the recess and drew out what was obviously a packet of currency. He put his hand beneath the corner of the desk again; the panel closed. He placed the packet in a drawer of the desk, then returned to his chair and began reading again.

Farrel rubbed his mouth. Finally he returned to the truck, where he waited in the cab until he was startled to find Ecker's flash suddenly lighting the hood. A ripped carcass of a raccoon was slapped down on the metal. Ecker wheezed with laughter. "What's the matter, Eggskull? You don't like a little fun?"

Farrel poured beer from his new bottle and listened to Ecker wheezing again.

"He just don't like that night-cooning no way!"

The bartender diplomatically refused comment. Instead he said, "How's that new Winchester working out, Vince?"

"Best you can buy," Ecker said with enthusiasm. "I got that thing zeroed in so I could shoot the eye out of a gnat at a thousand yards."

Farrel sat holding his glass, staring straight ahead, reviewing everything he'd learned since he'd seen Martin Brindmart remove that currency from the recess hidden behind the paneling. By discreet questioning, he'd found out that Brindmart never left the privacy of his fenced acreage. One of the single personal contacts he made was with Cass Rawl, his foreman. Most of that was accomplished by phone. Fees for renting his ranch land were collected in cash by Rawl, who then turned them over to Brindmart. Farrel was reasonably certain that the man used no bank.

The only other person who dealt with Brindmart was Ecker, who was paid to bring in Brindmart's supplies every Saturday morning, a habit begun when Brindmart had added the attack dogs to his protection; no one but Ecker could have gone past them.

But Brindmart was now temporarily without dogs, and that, Farrel thought, was going to make the difference. Give credit to Ecker for it.

Farrel had heard the general community opinion that it had been Ecker himself who'd poisoned the animals—they would have accepted meat from no one but Ecker or Brindmart—in order to sell Brindmart two new ones. Ecker was disliked by most everyone who knew him. And that too, Farrel told himself, was going to count.

The door opened; the cutting wind blew through the interior. The logs in the great fireplace snapped as blue-yellow flames wavered. Cass Rawl stepped in, wearing a cowhide jacket with butter-colored Sherpa pile, a full black Stetson, overall pants and worn cowboy boots.

He was a thin man in his early thirties; but his face was already deeply lined from exposure to weather. He nodded briefly to Farrel, who had talked to him casually last week, when Rawl had stated his dislike for Ecker in his North Texas drawl: "A damned sadistic butcher. If Mr. Brindmart hadn't got hooked up with him on account of the dogs, I'd never let him set foot on the ranch. The way it is, he delivers supplies every Saturday, nine in the morning. I press the switch and open the gate and wave him through. That's all I'll have to do with him. I ever catch him hunting on Mr. Brindmart's property, I'll see he's prosecuted."

Rawl walked to Ecker, who smiled and looked at his beer bottle. Rawl handed him a folded sheet of paper. "List of stuff he wants Saturday."

"Okay."

"Somebody was coon-hunting two weeks ago. Heard it, at night. If I catch a man doing that on Mr. Brindmart's property, I go for him personally."

"You told me that already. Think it was me?"

"I know it was."

"Maybe it was Farrel over there. Give him the lecture."

"Somebody's been night-hunting deer, too. Freezing them with a flashlight and shooting them that way. Next time he does it, he'll get the book thrown at him."

"Wonder who it was?" Ecker said, still smiling.

"Somebody using a Winchester Seventy."

"How do you know?"

"Know the sound."

Ecker shrugged. "Doubt it. But even if you do, lots of people use a Winchester Seventy."

"Deliver the supplies, Ecker," Rawl said tightly. "Train the dogs. Otherwise, stay off the land and away from Mr. Brindmart." He wheeled and left.

Ecker delivered his laugh and pushed his empty beer bottle away.

"I got to get home and feed them dogs. Seven I got now, counting the new shepherds."

Farrel tapped the bar and placed a bill on the wood. "Buy him a beer."

Ecker looked at him in surprise. "What's got into you?"

"I'm trying to make friends. Complaining?"

"Hell, no," he said contemptuously. "Let's have the beer."

Farrel observed the few cars parked in the near darkness outside. There were no street lamps; the only lighting came from an orange neon sign on top of the building and another in the window of the general store down the street. Ecker's pickup was parked beside Farrel's old Plymouth sedan.

He stepped between the two vehicles and looked into the interior of the pickup. The keys were in the ignition. Ecker's Winchester, with its mounted scope, was held by specially installed clamps along the front edge of the seat just above the flooring. The habits of a man, Farrel thought, were in direct ratio to his personality. Ecker was an egotistical bully, he believed that no one would dare take something he owned. As a result he carelessly left his car in this condition.

Looking toward the bar, hoping the extra beer would hold Ecker in there, Farrel opened the left-hand door. He leaned inside and carefully removed the rifle from the clamps.

He moved quickly to the rear of his own car, lifted the door of the trunk and placed Ecker's rifle there. Then he picked up a second rifle—same model with an identical scope—and closed the trunk. He stepped back to the pickup, pushed the second Winchester into the clamps, then softly closed the truck's door.

As he got into his Plymouth, he realized that he was breathing quickly. He drove away, regretting only the money he'd paid for that rifle at a large and busy sporting goods store in San Francisco where, he was certain, he would never be remembered. It had taken most of what meager savings he'd had in the bank. But it was an investment that would pay returns— if it worked.

He stopped his car beside the small cabin he'd rented to house his family, then walked through the wet wind into a steamy kitchen which smelled familiarly of ham and lima beans. Milly looked at him reproachfully.

Her hair was in curlers—her permanent do, he thought dismally. The lines of her plump face— she was fifteen pounds heavier now than when he'd married her—were set in that vacant expression worn ever since Jolly had been delivered. Her voice came forth in a thin, high whine: "I have to hold dinner every night!"

"So you do," he said wearily, and looked into the living room, where Jolly was trying to work his portable crib into a wall by yanking back and forth on a top slat.

"Night after night!" Milly shrilled.

He walked into the living room and sat down in an ancient easy chair. Jolly saw him and started babbling loudly, shifting the direction of his manipulation. Moments later the crib jarred into one of Farrel's shins. Grunting with pain, he stared back in fury at the wet, wicked smile Jolly was showing him.

Vince Ecker's redwood house, its shingles catching the last light of the following day, was in a secluded hollow at the north edge of the sparsely housed community. Farrel stood in the protection of a thick grove of trees above, watching the man working one of the shepherds in the fenced area of his dog run. He wore the protective gear of an attack-dog trainer and held a small leather whip with frayed ends, which he repeatedly snapped into the dog's nose. The dog, its eyes growing brighter, snarled and attacked with greater vengeance.

Farrel jogged a hundred yards back to where he'd parked his car. He dove to the crossroads and got out to enter a public telephone booth. As he dialed, he felt his blood warming. He let the rings repeat until he heard the breathless, angry voice of Ecker: "Yeah?"

He assumed a nasal drawl which he'd practiced repeatedly through the week. "Rawl, Ecker."

"So?"

"Forget bringing in those supplies tomorrow morning."

"Why the hell not?"

"He doesn't want to be disturbed."

"All right! Let him starve."

"Hurry it up on those dogs."

"That's what I'm doing!" Ecker said.

He returned to his car as darkness began enveloping the community. The macadam leading in the direction of Martin Brindmart's land ran south in dipping curves. Farrel drove in that direction, passing the ranch, then turning right on another highway. When he reached the small road at the rear of the property where Vince Ecker had brought him the night of the hunt, he got out and opened the trunk to remove the rifle.

A cow was sounding in the distance, but he could not see it because of the increasing darkness. He moved swiftly over the tufted field, over a rise and into the small valley where the raccoon had been killed by the dogs. He walked over another rise and stopped beside the small, wind-shaped tree.

The windows of the house used by Cass Rawl were dark; he truly hoped that Rawl was gone. The wide window of the large main house was lighted. Feeling his nerves tingling, he saw that Martin Brindmart was reading in the chair near the desk and fireplace.

Farrel lifted the rifle and sighted through the scope. His heart was bumping. But he forced himself to hold the rifle steady. His finger squeezed. The report sounded cannon-like in his ears. The kick of the rifle spun him half-around. Then he looked again. Brindmart was slumped in the chair.

He hurried to his car and placed the rifle in the back seat. As he drove away, he was thinking that he might not have been able to shoot a deer, or a raccoon, or even a rabbit. But Brindmart was just another human being.

When he reached the edge of the community, he stopped the car off the highway. He put on leather gloves and quickly cleaned, then oiled the rifle. He returned it to the trunk, and minutes later parked in front of the Copper Lantern. He was seated at the bar sipping a beer when Ecker arrived. Ecker ignored him and sat down angrily. "Damn, stupid dog!"

Farrel half-smiled. "How's the hunting, Ecker?"

"Might be all right if they knew how to make rifles!"

"Thought you said that Winchester was the best."

"Tried it this morning. I'd have done better with the carbine! It was off a mile! Had to fix it all over again!"

"Maybe now you can hit a raccoon clean enough to kill it," Farrel said drily.

"Raccoon! I'm going for the big stuff from now on."

"Like what?"

"Maybe go up to the Sierra and get a bear. Cat maybe. Maybe go down south and find a pig—I told you about them wild boars, didn't I?"

"Yes," Farrel said, and finished his beer. He walked outside and stood beside his car until another pulled away from the general store down the street. Then he put on the gloves again and exchanged the Winchester from the trunk with the one held by the clamps in Ecker's pickup. He placed that in the back section of the Plymouth, on the floor, then drove down a winding road to Palo Alto. He crossed through town to the Dumbarton Bridge, where traffic was light. Halfway across, he stopped and leaned from a window to throw the rifle over a guardrail into the Bay.

At twenty minutes to nine the next morning, he again stood inside the public telephone booth dialing Vince Ecker's number.

"Who?" Ecker demanded.

"Farrel."

"So?"

"You were talking about cats last night. I saw one down the highway."

Ecker's voice assumed immediate interest. "Where?"

"You know that little road that cuts off the highway just north of the road to Brindmart's place?"

"What kind of cat?"

"Big."

"Wildcat?"

"Looked bigger."

"*How* big?"

"Five feet long, maybe six."

He could hear Ecker's breath drawing in.

"Mean-looking," Farrel said. "Mountain lion, I figure. Maybe came down from the north. I ought to phone the sheriff. Animal like that—"

"You leave it to me, you hear? *I'll* take care of it! Small Creek Road, is that the place?"

"That's it."

Farrel drove south, meeting a single car. He turned onto the narrow length of blacktop marked Small Creek Road and stopped out of sight from the highway. Minutes later Ecker's truck skidded to a halt behind the Plymouth. Ecker got out with his rifle held tightly in one large hand. He released three dogs from their compartment.

"Which way?" The sun glinted against his sun glasses.

"Down," Farrel said. "Through those trees, along the creek, toward the valley."

"Five, six feet?"

"Swear it was."

Ecker motioned his dogs ahead and followed, running. Farrel waited until he hard them deep in the trees. Then, from a pocket, he drew a bottle of tan make-up purchased at a variety store; he smoothed it over his face. He fitted on a pair of ski-type sun glasses. Finally he removed from a foil-lined carton a black parka and a white medium-brimmed Stetson. He put them on and placed the carton on the right-hand side of the seat of Ecker's truck. He turned the key of the pickup and backed to the highway. Then he drove to the road leading to Martin Brindmart's fenced acreage.

When he neared the small house used by Cass Rawl, his palms had become so wet he could no longer hold on to the steering wheel. He stopped and put on his gloves. Then he forced himself to drive the truck to the gate. Through the dark glasses, he saw Rawl appear at the doorway of his house. Rawl glared at him; but the gate opened. Farrel drove through, breathing hard.

He stopped at a side door of the large house and carried the empty carton out of the truck. His worst moment arrived when he became certain that the door would be locked. It wasn't. He stepped inside and began looking for the room where Brindmart would be in that leather chair. After several tries, he found it.

He looked at the man—at what was left of him after the tearing slug from the high-powered rifle had created its destruction. Then he strode to the desk and located the lever beneath the corner. Paneling slid back. Farrel stared at the packets of currency stacked there. Finally, with shaking, gloved hands, he was able to transfer the packets into the carton. He looked around the room, feeling an increasing greed, and noticed a sheet of paper on the surface of the desk. He stepped closer and read the beginning of the note.

> *To Whom It May Concern, I, Martin Brindmart, hereby*
> *reveal the following events....*

He read no further, feeling a fresh panic. Had Brindmart somehow known that he'd been observed? Had Farrel been seen that night of the raccoon hunt? And had Brindmart written something…?

Farrel grabbed the paper, folded it swiftly and slid it into an inner compartment of his wallet. He picked up the carton and returned to the truck. He did not look at Rawl's house as he drove through the gate. Through a rear-view mirror, he saw it closing behind him.

He reparked the truck where he'd met Ecker and carried the carton to the trunk of his car, where he placed it beside a small spade. He removed the sun glasses, parka and hat, put them in the carton and closed the trunk. He wiped his face with a handkerchief, then got behind the wheel of the Plymouth and drove back to the highway.

Following the undulating road, he drove fifteen miles south. He stopped on a turn-out in a heavily wooded area. When no other cars were in sight, he got out and retrieved the carton. He carried it with the spade into the woods. In a small clearing, he dug a deep hole, fitted the carton down, then scooped earth back and smoothed pine needles over the surface.

On the way home, he threw the spade and make-up stained handkerchief from the window. When he walked into his small cabin and sat down in his chair. He was exhausted. His mind went entirely blank. Milly kept complaining to him. But her voice seemed very far away, and the words she spoke were unintelligible.

One year, two months and five days later, David Farrel sat near a window of a large stone house. Encircled by a corrugated steel fence, the structure had a fortress-like quality and blended smoothly with the flat Nevada sagebrush land.

Located well off the highway, outside Reno, Farrel could see nothing immediate but sage and brown earth and rock. In the distance, the bluish rise of mountains was fading in the wavering light of late afternoon.

He stood up feeling edgy; there were smudges of darkness beneath his eyes. He paced slowly through the silent house, from room to room, trying to find satisfaction in this haven and finding none.

He thought of going out to the front patio to sit for a while before the cold night sharpened the air. But he decided against it, as he had for weeks. A bit later he would have to walk out to the gate any way, to see if there was mail. That would be enough exposure. You could never be certain. He knew what a good rifle could do at five hundred yards.

He sat down in his baroque living room and stared at a cold fireplace. He thought back, as he did every day, to how well it had gone, once Cass Rawl had decided to go into Martin Brindmart's house and found him dead in the library. They arrested Vince Ecker two hours later. The next day a sheriff's detective had come to question Farrel at length. When Ecker's case had come to trial, Farrel had been required to go on the witness stand.

Ecker kept shouting his accusations; several times he had to be physically restrained. But Farrel had answered the questions in a polite, shy manner which, he knew, had suited the jury; his performance had been in complete contrast to Ecker's screaming and shouting.

"The defendant has made the claim, Mr. Farrel, that he was, in his words, framed—that you, in fact, fired the rifle that ballistic tests have proven to be the murder weapon."

"I'm aware of that."

"Is there any truth to it?"

"Certainly not."

Ecker, swearing, was in high fury, his face mottled with rage.

"It is the defendant's contention that you switched rifles in his truck, shot the deceased yourself from a hill, then tricked the defendant into trailing a non-existent cat of some description while you entered the fenced retreat of the deceased in the disguise of the defendant to steal valuables which might have been hidden behind paneling in the library. Did you?"

Farrel displayed a certain amount of incredulity at the proposition. "I've heard the contention, sir. I continue to be surprised by it. No, sir—nothing like that happened."

The cords of Ecker's neck bulged like taut ropes.

"You did not exchange rifles with the defendant?"

"I did not."

"You did not shoot the deceased?"

"I wouldn't kill a rabbit, sir, let alone Mr. Brindmart. I did not."

"You did not phone the defendant to explain that you'd seen a wild animal, which caused him to meet you at a location called Small Creek Road?"

"No, sir."

"You did not send the defendant on a chase after that animal, then disguise yourself in apparel similar to his and drive his truck onto the property of the deceased?"

"Certainly not."

"You did not see the defendant at all, that day?"

"Yes sir. As I was driving south on the highway near nine o'clock as I often do on a Saturday, I saw him drive his truck onto the road leading to the house of the deceased."

When his testimony had been completed, he'd smiled at the jury, then left the stand. He'd known fairly certainly that it was going to work when he'd heard the testimony of Cass Rawl.

"Please tell me, Mr. Rawl, are you absolutely certain that the driver of the truck who went through the gate the day following the established murder time of the deceased was Vincent Albert Ecker?"

Farrel watched Cass Rawl's eyes shine with the hatred of the devoted servant who has lost his master at the hands of the enemy. Cass Rawl said, "Vince Ecker, all right."

He knew positively that it was going to work when the prosecuting attorney summarized his case by characterizing Ecker as a sadistic killer who would go to any means to accomplish his selfish mission—in this case, the theft of an undetermined amount of money, still unfound, because it had been hidden away by the defendant.

Ecker had put the finishing touch on the performance by shouting, accusing and raging in such a fashion that not a juror felt him to be anything but what he had been portrayed to be by the prosecution.

Farrel had hoped that he would be given the gas chamber. But Ecker had gotten a life sentence instead. That had been good enough anyway. Farrel had since learned that Ecker's performance in prison as a surly, hating, bullying, provocative inmate continually precluded any possibility for eventual parole.

Farrel stalked into his library lined with every book he had ever wanted to read. But he had not been able to concentrate on anything these past weeks. He was nervous, feeling a growing fear of some unknown quantity which could destroy him. Yet he knew that was absurd. He had perfect protection here. He had not made the mistakes Brindmart had. He had refused to bring in dogs, because that would have required dependance upon a trainer. He allowed his supplies to be brought only to the gate and left outside until he picked them up—nobody came through that gate but himself.

Yet, he had to walk through the open to reach that gate and collect supplies and mail. Each time that he was required to do it, his apprehension became greater.

He sat down and rubbed his palms over his knees. He'd also been thinking about women. Not Milly, certainly. He'd taken care of her easily, after Ecker had been sent to prison. He had picked up an easy brunette in the Copper Lantern, then began an obvious affair that had reached Milly's ears quickly, in that small community. She'd divorced him.

But, based on his book clerk's income, she had gotten very little from him. She'd remarried in a short time, and even that small alimony was no longer necessary. No, he did not want Milly. But any other woman. Yet how could he risk leaving this place to find one?

He tried not to think about that by repeating his most familiar thoughts: reviewing the possibility of having made a mistake somewhere. The largest, he was certain, had been taking that sheet of paper from Martin Brindmart's desk.

He stood up again and resumed pacing, feeling his blood pumping. At first he had worried most about the condition of that money in the foil-lined carton. But when he had finally dug it up, he'd discovered that it had been preserved perfectly. Then he'd worried about demonstrating any sort of affluence by spending some of it. But he'd gotten the idea of moving to Reno, where he had claimed heavy winnings on small stakes, in the casinos.

He had even declared the winnings on his income-tax report, and paid taxes on them. No one had questioned anything.

It all came back to having taken that note Brindmart had written. Because of the state of shock that had hit him that evening, he could not remember removing from his pocket the wallet which contained the note. But he must have, because it disappeared.

He recalled that he had demanded of Milly that she find it. But she could not. Finally he had looked at the moist, wicked face of Jolly, and realized that the baby had picked it up and hidden it somewhere. But up to the time of his divorce, he had not found where that was.

What, he asked himself, had been contained in the rest of that note? Where was it now? Who had read it? Would it be enough to implicate him? And did Milly have it, waiting to use it on him?

He turned on a transistor radio on a shelf, wanting to remove that thought. Then he switched the radio off immediately. Voices coming into this house and telling him of the outside world had ceased to interest him and only made him more nervous. He'd also canceled his newspaper subscription weeks ago.

He paced again, thinking of all he had planned to do if he should ever gain the seclusion and independence owned by Martin Brindmart. Now that he had achieved them, he could concentrate on nothing. He had even begun to hate his once-loved animals, which had become hated sounds in the night. Rabbits. Coyotes. Wildcats. Mountain lions. Prowling and searching, padding, climbing, causing him to lie in his bed with sweat beading on his forehead and his nerves trembling.

All he could honestly think of was having made a mistake somewhere, leaving a small gate open, something that would bring destruction down on him....

At the near gloom of twilight, he stood beside a window and peered toward the highway as the red mail truck stopped beside his box on the other side of the gate. He watched the carrier, who was a slope-shouldered man with a reddish mustache, deposit something. The man had, in the beginning, tried to stall till Farrel came out to inspect that box. But Farrel would have none of it. Even now the man looked curiously and hopefully toward the house, as though Farrel might come out. Oh, yes? Farrel thought.

The truck finally rolled on. Farrel tried to get up his nerve for his daily forage outside. Then he walked to the heavy front door, which he kept locked and bolted—he well remembered that Martin Brindmart had failed to do that. He stood there, feeling a familiar weakness going through him. His palms became moist. Finally he slid the bolt, then turned the handle. He pushed the door open and stepped out.

He looked across the expanse of white-graveled drive that he would have to traverse in order to reach the gate. Then he would have to unlock that gate and hurry out to check the contents of the mailbox, all of which had become a nearly unbearable task these past days. But his curiosity was too strong. The mailman had placed something in there. It might be a bill. Or it might only be junk mail. But he had to know.

He ran along the gravel to the gate and inserted a key into the lock. He turned it, then jumped out to yank the lid of the box down. He grabbed a small package wrapped in brown paper, seeing that it had been addressed to him in Milly's familiar hand.

He returned through the gate, kicked it shut and locked it, then trotted back toward the house. When he had nearly reached the door, he was certain that he saw something moving beyond the fence to the east. He stopped, heart speeding. There was a clumping of sage there. Whatever it had been he was certain, had moved behind that protection. But the light, now, was deceiving. He broke into a run and leaped into the house to close the door behind him and bolt it.

He threw the package on a sofa, then hurried to an east window. He looked out, his face by the sill. But he could see nothing.

Imagination, he thought. Or something harmless, like a jackrabbit. He returned to the sofa and sat down, not assured.

He picked up the package and looked at it more carefully to see that it was correctly addressed. Well, he had made no effort to go into absolute hiding—he'd given a forwarding address to the small post office in that crossroads community. If he had tried to disappear entirely, it would definitely have been suspicious. She'd probably inquired of the postmistress, and gotten the address that way.

He tore the brown paper away from a flat pasteboard box. He opened it to see his wallet. He removed it, as a small white card fell away. He read the message:

David,

I found this when I was cleaning the house, as George and I are moving to much larger quarters. It was inside the register of the heater in the living room, where I guess Jolly put it, sliding it down a vent. As you will notice, there are only two dollars inside, which I did not touch. I am sending it not out of any respect for you, as you hurt me, all right. But because it has your various cards you were so upset about losing. I am only trying to be honorable, no matter how much anguish you have caused me.

Yours truly,

Milly.

He opened the compartment which contained his various cards. Then he looked inside the second compartment where he'd placed the note from Brindmart's desk. He pulled out the folded paper. Had she opened that compartment too, to find this?

He threw the wallet aside and got up with the paper. He walked in a fast circle around the room. Then he hurried to his library where he switched on a desk light and sat down to read:

To Whom It May Concern,

I, Martin Brindmart, hereby reveal the following events, beginning with the decline of my partner, Albert Henshaw. It was true that Albert engaged in dishonest measures which profited him greatly, at the expense of many innocent people—as was stated in his suicide note found beside his body in his car where he died of carbon-monoxide poisoning.

What is not true is that he later filtered away those profits, as was stated in his note. What is not true is that I knew nothing of his dealings. What is not true is that he willingly committed suicide.

I discovered his manipulations, after which time I confronted Albert with my knowledge. By threatening exposure of him, to his wife, to his daughter, to his son, to his friends, I was able to extract the whereabouts of that money. By working on his shame and guilt, I was also able to get him drunk, after which I carried him to his garage and placed him in the car. It will be remembered that a large percentage of alcohol was found in Albert's blood as well as a half-consumed bottle beside him in the death car. But Albert was intoxicated before the car's engine was started—by me.

I have since experienced an increasing torment for that deed. The money, first gained by Albert, is tainted money. It has made me a prisoner in this hated stockade I have created in these wretched hills. I have received nothing but hell in exchange. Secluding myself in this fashion—afraid, afraid, nerves nearly shot—I damn the money and all it has caused. All that I desire now, as Albert did before me, is some release from my torment. I invite, welcome any release....

The handwriting became nearly illegible near the end; the letter had not been completed.

Farrel continued to stare at the words. Then he stood up suddenly, eyes shining with fear. Milly had read it, he thought.

Yet—why had she sent it to him? Giving the evidence away that he had been in Brindmart's house? Then he nodded quickly, a muscle flickering along a cheek. She was playing with him. Like Ecker, playing with a wounded raccoon. Sadistic. Devilish....

He whirled, hearing something moving outside. He ran to the window and yanked the cord to snap the drapes shut.

His mouth had turned dry. He tried to swallow and could not. Ecker he thought, reaching that absolute and inevitable conclusion he should have reached months ago. *You couldn't cage a man like that; somehow, some way....*

He switched off the desk lamp and stood in the darkness, shaking with a strong chill.

His hearing for any alien sound had become acute. Now he heard something very alien: someone running out there. He fell to the floor and pressed his cheek tightly against the rug. He listened, shaking badly, licking his dry lips. But now there was only silence.

Slowly he crawled toward the shelf where the transistor radio rested. He reached up and turned on the switch. Soft music played through the room. He lay shaking very badly now. The music stopped abruptly and a man's voice said, "There have been no further developments on the escape of a convicted killer believed to have fled to this area...."

As his hand jerked up to turn up the volume, the radio was jarred from the shelf. It crashed to the floor and the voice was gone.

He pressed his cheek against the rug again, breathing hard, listening.

He should have known that he could never have defeated an animal like that. It was like trying to defeat a wild boar, as Ecker had so often described: you shot to kill, and if it didn't work, it came looking for you, tracking you, mean and vicious.

Farrel began to whimper, eyes hot with tears. He thought of Martin Brindmart's written words: "I damn the money and all it has caused...."

Cheek to rug, lying flat beside the desk, he envisioned the special womb he had created for it with his own hands: a trap-doored recess right there beneath the desk.

He heard that sound of running again, closer now. He whimpered once more, shaking violently.

Finally he rolled to his stomach, then began inching closer to the desk. He slid his trembling fingers along the grain of the rug, searching. He found the clasps that held the fabric flat, loosened them, then peeled the rug back. He managed to find a key in his pocket and inserted it into a heavy lock built into the oak planking of the floor. He turned the key and lifted the trap door. He began removing packets of currency.

At last he pushed himself up to his knees, then to his feet. He stood swaying drunkenly, holding one of the packets. He staggered to the drape cord and yanked it. The drapes were drawn open with a thin, whistling sound. With his free hand, he reached out and switched on the ceiling lights, bathing himself in hard, white brightness.

Gasping for breath, eyes wild, he unlatched the window and threw it open, staring into the darkness. "Ecker?" He listened and heard nothing. He held up the packet of money and shook it, wanting only to be free of his torment. *"Vince Ecker!"*

He saw the muzzle flash. He did not hear the explosion.

Dusty, thick-soled shoes stopped beside the bloodied body. A stub-fingered hand gathered up the packets of currency. A pulpy, ultimately cruel face creased with a smile.

Minutes later David Farrel was alone in his house.

Women writers are sometimes overlooked when considering hardboiled and noir fiction of the paperback original era (and even before). The term "domestic suspense" was often coined but I'm not sure how much of a pejorative that term may be. Elisabeth Sanxay Holding was one of these writers, another was Margaret Millar, both of whom have been published by Stark House. But the woman writer who may have come closest of all to writing books with the same kind of noirish sense of tone we look for when we think of authors like Thompson or Woolrich may be Jean Potts. Stark House paired her 1954 Edgar winner Go, Lovely Rose *along with her 1963 Edgar runner-up* The Evil Wish, *completing the entirety of her crime fiction oeuvre. Read her story below then check them out....*

MURDERER #2

Jean Potts

It would never have occurred to Rolfe Jackson to kill his mother if it had not been absolutely necessary.

He was not a criminal. He was an artist. (True, there were those who held that the pictures Rolfe painted were crimes of a particularly brutal sort. They were fools, of course; he had not yet found himself, that was all.)

Besides, he was really quite fond of the old girl. He had her to thank for his name, for instance. She might so easily have called him Henry or Albert, both of which were traditional family names. Henry Jackson. Albert Jackson. Why, with such a name he might never have had the heart to embark on his artistic career at all! Certainly the identity he had created for himseslf as Rolfe J.—which was the way he chose to sign his pictures— would have been inconceivable.

He was quite a character, this Rolfe J. who had been built up with such care and who would someday come into his own. Hard-boiled. Dedicated. A Hemingway among painters. There was his stubby beard to prove it, and his lumberjack taste in clothes. Without them, he would have looked what he was—short and pudgy. With them he was impressively burly. Rolfe J. talked tough. He had choice unprintable phrases for the critics and for the work of other artists. He sneered at creature comforts. Publicly, that is. Very few people ever saw the inside of his apartment, and so very few people knew how much he loved luxury.

None of it—his whole beloved, outwardly rough-hewn, secretly luxurious life—had set up the trust fund, and the trust fund saved Rolfe J. from having to make a living.

Yet it was also the trust fund that made it absolutely necessary for him to kill Mother. The realization hit him, like a blow from a fist, while he and

Mr. Webb were having their little talk. Mr. Webb was Mother's attorney, and a friend of many years' standing; he lived in an apartment just across the hall from hers. Rolfe was instantly wary when one night Mr. Webb asked him to come in. His own relations with the man had always been notable for their lack of cordiality. No open quarrels. Just a mutual case of low estimation. Mr. Webb looked like a Yankee farmer—stringy, lantern-jawed, granite-eyed. His study was just what you would expect. Rolfe had never in his life sat on a more uncomfortable chair.

"I've been meaning to have a little talk with you for some time," Mr. Webb began. "Ever since your mother had this stroke. How are things going with the nurse?"

Mr. Webb had found the nurse for Mother. An ugly, devoted woman named Stella, who came in every day. By now Mother could manage alone, at night. But she was never going to get beyond the wheelchair stage. Poor old girl. What a change after all the bustle and pressure of the job she had had for years with one of the ladies' magazines.

"Stella? She's a paragon," said Rolfe. He felt, as usual, an impulse to shock Mr. Webb, jolt him out of his flinty composure. "If she wasn't god-awful ugly I'd marry her, to save her salary."

Mr. Webb just looked at him. He had a talent for the unsettling silence. Finally he said, "That's what your mother's worried about. Money. She shouldn't be. But she is. So I thought we ought to get the whole thing straightened out."

"What's to straighten out? She's got the pension from her office—"

"Peanuts," said Mr. Webb curtly. "Hardly pays the rent. That's why she's worried. She knows she's going to have to dip into your trust fund to pay the nurse and the doctors' bills." He opened his brief case and spread some papers out on the desk in front of him. "I don't know how familiar you are with the terms of your grandfather's will. It might be well to review them. He left his money in trust for you, with the proviso that your mother may draw on it, in case of emergency. Now I don't believe anyone would question the fact that your mother's illness constitutes an emergency."

"Who's questioning it?" said Rolfe irritably.."Not me."

"I'm glad of that. It's only fair to warn you that the drain on your trust fund will be considerable Very likely you will find it necessary to curtail your present and future expenses." Mr. Webb said this with relish. "Your living arrangements, for example, aren't exactly economical. My own suggestion would be that you move in with your mother. Why not? You're already in the same apartment house. It would simply mean paying rent on one apartment, instead of two. As far as Stella's salary, and her appearance, are concerned"—he produced a wintry smile—"it's not necessary for you to marry her. Since you don't go out to work anyway, I don't see why you shouldn't take over some of the care of your mother. Combine art and nursing, say, two or three days a week. It would mean quite a saving."

It was Rolfe's turn to just look at Mr. Webb. For once in his life he had nothing whatever to say. Mr. Webb did not seem to notice. Having curtailed living expenses to his Yankee heart's content, he was now proceeding to "go over the figures."

They appalled Rolfe. He had not realized their true nature until now; it was like the moment when the dentist's drill touches a live nerve, sending out shoots of excruciating pain. He sat bolt upright (there was no other way to sit in that contemptible chair of Mr. Webb's), his eyes riveted on Mr. Webb's bony face, while he watched his beautiful trust fund trickle away day after day, year after year. The doctor had said Mother might live for years. Fifteen, even twenty. And every day of every one of those years meant ten dollars for Stella, at least another ten for food and medicine and miscellaneous expenses.

And Rolfe was supposed to stand for this without a murmur of protest; he was—yes, Mr. Webb was making it quite clear—he was supposed to stand for it *gladly*, just because Mother had gone out of her way to keep the trust fund intact, until now. As if that were Rolfe's fault! He hadn't asked her to pay for his education, the summers in France, all the rest of it, out of her own earnings. It was her business, how she chose to spend her salary. And yet, now that there was no more salary, he was to be penalized, his very life was to go down the drain!

Well, he *wouldn't* stand for it. They were dealing with a man, not a mouse. And no ordinary man, either; he would show them, once and for all, the caliber of Rolfe J. The dream, the vision of himself as a man among men, touched with genius, ruthlessly molding his own destiny, had never been more vivid. He would—

"As I say," Mr Webb was concluding, as he shuffled his papers back into their folder, "I'm glad you're taking a sensible attitude about this. Even if you weren't, it wouldn't make any difference. There's not a thing you can do about it."

That was what Mr. Webb thought. Rolfe knew better. It had hit him in the second before Mr. Webb stopped speaking: the flash of crystal understanding, and the resolution.

Nothing he could do about it? Ah, but there was, there was. Something so obvious, so necessary and right (or why should Mother, simply by living, cheat him of what was rightfully his?) that even a fool like Mr. Webb ought to see it. He didn't though. There was a gleam of satisfaction in his granite eyes as he said good-night. He thought he had scored, in this little talk of theirs. He thought he had taken Rolfe down a notch or two.

Out in the hall, Rolfe paused a moment, waiting for his heart to stop pounding. Then he let himself into Mother's apartment and called cheerily, "Anybody home? How about a glass of sherry?"

Mother was in bed—Stella always got her settled for the night before she left—but bright-eyed obviously brimming over with news. She was a fat little woman, with a halo of white curly hair. "You'll never guess what happened to me today," she began, while Rolfe poured the sherry. "I was approached by an ex-narcotics addict!"

"What? Now really, Mother—"

"Really. Oh, a strictly business approach. He wants me to help him write a book. 'I Was a Narcotics Addict'—that sort of thing. I must say, he doesn't look like a man with a lurid past. Quite presentable. I don't know why I— Maybe it was his missionary zeal that put me off. This project seems to be kind of a crusade to him."

"That's normal, isn't it?" said Rolfe. "Look at the reformed drunks that go around spreading the good word. I suppose it works the same with dope addicts."

"I suppose. Or maybe it was his name. It's Borden, and all I could think of was that little verse about Lizzie Borden taking an axe…. It's awful to have a free-wheeling mind like mine."

They both laughed. Rolfe became aware of a prickle at the back of his neck, a tremor of obscure excitement. But he kept his voice casual.

"You turned him down, then?"

"No, I told him I'd think it over and let him know tomorrow. It *would* be fun, you know." Just the thought made her look, for a moment, quite like her old busy, enthusiastic self. "And then supposing it turned out to be a best seller and we all got rich."

"I wasn't thinking of the money," said Rolfe truthfully. "Nice as it would be. I was just thinking how much you'd enjoy having something to do again."

"You think I'm being silly?" she asked wistfully. "You think I ought to do it?" She waited for his answer, and at once the illusion of vigor vanished. For in the old days she would not have needed Rolfe's advice, she would have known her own mind. Now uncertainty clouded her eyes. Her whole face sagged into lines of doubt, almost of fear. But it was the delicacy of her temple that fascinated Rolfe. Above her plump cheek it was slightly sunken and threaded with blue. It looked fragile as an egg shell.

"Good Lord, Mother, I've never seen the man, so how can I tell! And I've been wondering, how'd he happen to get in touch with you?"

"Well, he works in a bindery, a book bindery. Someone there suggested an editor, who in turn suggested me. So he looked me up in the phone book—"

"If you want me to look him over when he turns up again tomorrow," said Rolfe, "I'll be glad to…."

The deal was clinched next day, on the spot. Mother, now that Rolfe had disposed of her original vague doubts, was frankly delighted at the prospect. So was Borden.

Only Stella held out. She cornered Rolfe as he left; she had been lurking in the kitchen, waiting to speak her piece. Which she did, in an ominous whisper. "I don't like it, Mr. Jackson. I just think you and your mother are taking an awful chance, letting that dope fiend in here three evenings a week. Oh, I know. He claims he's cured. I've heard that one before. They're none of them ever cured. Not for sure. I don't like it. Not one little bit."

Good old Stella. Under her white nylon uniform she wore what appeared to be a suit of armor; it jutted out in ridges across her meaty shoulders and back. Lumpy wriggles of varicose veins showed through her white stockings. And she dyed her hair shoe-polish black. As ugly as ever, and yet Rolfe regarded her with something very like affection. Good old doubting Stella.

"*Sh*," he whispered back. "The only reason I'm going along with it is she needs something to keep her occupied. It's brightened her up already. Don't worry, I'll make sure she's never left alone with him. That's why I insisted on meeting the fellow, to make sure he seemed all right."

"All right!" Stella snorted. "With those gooseberry eyes of his, and those long twitchy hands? Gives me the shivers just to think of him."

But even Stella seemed to forget her doubts as two weeks, three weeks, went by, with no danger signals from Borden. Rolfe found it necessary to remind her now and then in an unobtrusive way.

He himself was busy exploring. He had been quick to sense Borden's potentialities. But they would remain only potentialities until he had found the way to use them. To use them he must know his man, through and through.

He found the whole project almost alarmingly easy. No one could have been more cooperative than Borden, either in striking up a friendship or in promoting the exploration of his own character. The circumstances were favorable too. In his capacity as watchdog, Rolfe was always present on Borden evenings, for Stella—having first given Mother her early dinner and settled her in be—left at seven thirty. Rolfe did not intrude on the book sessions, which were held in the bedroom; he lounged in the living room, pretending to read, waiting for Borden to emerge, ready with his suggestion—so natural—that they drop into the bar and grill next door for a sociable drink. Borden snapped at the invitation like a hungry dog at a bone. The drink or two often stretched out to dinner and beyond: a whole solid evening of analyzing Borden.

It was a subject that fascinated them both. Borden's experiences as a psychiatric patient had left him with an insatiable interest in his own mental processes. Sometimes he would work himself up into a transport of confession, like a religious convert glorying in the spectacle of his remembered sins. His prominent green eyes dilated even more than usual, and he would sway on his bar stool, making jerky gestures or running his hand through his lank blond hair.

At other times he was coldly objective. "It's a classic type," he would say. "The rejected child." And he would tick off the "classic" elements—the family-deserting father, the indifferent mother, the succession of even more indifferent substitute parents. The few friends he had managed to make always ended by sloughing him off—frightened away, probably, by the violence of his attachment to them. For he was violent. He was so famished for affection that he could not help it.

"You'll never know what it's meant to me, meeting you and your mother. You've always had friends, so you can't possibly understand—" He broke off with an embarrassed laugh, and went on more calmly. "You see, it's not just a question of getting cured of the dope habit. You've go to get cured of whatever it was that made you turn into a dope addict in the first place. That's where you can't ever be sure. I'm 'cured' now, and I can stay 'cured' as long as I've got my job at the bindery, and the book to work on, and most of all you and your mother. But let something go wrong maybe the least little thing—"

It was the truth. When Rolfe tested it out a few nights later by breaking a dinner date they had made, Borden's face turned quite white and into his eyes flashed a look of desperate presentiment: here it was again, the pattern as before. Rolfe and his mother, like all the others, were going to cast him off. He wrote Rolfe a cringing, overwrought letter: What had he done to offend Rolfe? How could he make amends? It took Rolfe several days to quiet the fears he had set off with trivial slight.

He was excited, even a little bit scared, at how easy it was going to be.

The crucial slight, he decided, must come from Mother, because the full force of Borden's devotion was focused on her rather than on Rolfe. It would have to be faked. Though Borden sometime made Mother nervous ("He's so intense, poor fellow!") still she sympathized with him; she would stick with him as long as he behaved himself. Of course if she thought for one minute that he had gone back to drugs....

A little manipulation by Rolfe, and that was exactly what she thought. She couldn't understand it when Borden failed to turn up for three sessions in a row. (The doctor, Rolfe had explained to him, felt that Mother might be overdoing; she was showing signs of strain.) Why didn't Borden call? Why didn't he explain? ("Whatever you do, please don't call her," Rolfe had cautioned. "It would only upset her, and we're trying to keep her as quiet as possible.") She fretted. She hoped against hope—until Rolfe, commissioned to investigate, brought back a report that confirmed her worst fears.

Of course there was nothing to do but call the whole project off. They couldn't risk letting Borden come back now, under any circumstance. But Mother didn't know when she had been so disappointed in anyone. And just when she had thought he was doing so well! She had a good cry over it. Then—with Rolfe's help—she wrote the letter that had to be written to Borden.

It was all that was needed to push Borden over the edge. A prey, as always, to his own insecurity, he had been suspicious from the first. "You're not telling me the truth," he had raged to Rolfe. "It isn't doctor's orders. She hadn't been overdoing. I've offended her somehow, the way I always do, with everybody I've ever cared about. She wants to get rid of me. Doesn't she? Doesn't she? Why won't you admit it?" And Rolfe had been just kind enough, just evasive enough, to keep him simmering.

He had expected an immediate explosion after the letter. But it was several days before he heard from Borden. No letter this time. None of the frantic telephone calls he had grown used to. His doorbell rang very late one night, and there was Borden—an ominously different, glassy-eyed Borden who at first seemed to have nothing to say and then suddenly burst into a flood of abject pleading. He couldn't stand it, that was all. They had to give him another chance. It was true that he had lost his job and hocked most of his clothes (he was not even wearing a jacket, though the night was raw and windy) but only because he couldn't stand it, they couldn't do this to him, another chance and he would be all right again.

"But that's why I've been trying to get hold of you!" Rolfe broke in—all sincerity, the distressed friend eager to help. "I've told Mother all along she was being unfair. Only I didn't know where to find you, and here she is, all but convinced that she ought to give you another chance—"

"Let me see her! Now! Right away!" Trembling with excitement, Borden jerked himself out of his chair. "I'll do anything, anything. Let me see her. You come with me, Rolfe, she'll listen to you—"

"Are you crazy?" said Rolfe coldly. "At this hour of the night? And you in the shape you're in? We wouldn't have a prayer. I'll tell you right now, I'm not doing one thing for you unless you pull yourself together. Is that understood? You've got until tomorrow night. Let's say tomorrow night at nine thirty. We can meet next door at the bar and if you're okay I'll take you to see Mother and I'll do all I can for you. But remember, it's up to you."

"Anything, I told you I'll do anything—" Borden drew a long shaky breath. "Can't we make it earlier?" he whispered. "It's so long to wait. Nine thirty. I don't know if I can wait."

"You'd damn well better," Rolfe told him. "I can't make it till then."

He thought he never was going to get rid of the fellow. Borden promised, over and over again. Agonized hope flared in his eyes; he knew that if he could just see Mother, speak to her for only a minute, he could convince her. He apologized, he explained, he all but licked Rolfe's hand in a transport of gratitude.

When he was leaving, as an afterthought, Rolfe lent him his own sports jacket. It seemed like the least he could do.

He may have slept some, during what was left of the night, but very little.

Mostly, he paced the floor and planned. And as the hours of the next day slid by into afternoon, into evening, a mystical calm spread through him. Here was what he had waited for all his life—the moment (and of his own choosing, brought about by his own contrivance) that would change Rolfe J. in one incandescent flash from vision to reality. Soon, very soon. A bare half hour from now. He had only to slip down the fire escape and into Mother's bedroom through the window he had surreptitiously unlatched when he said goodnight to her, and then— and then—

It would take a very few minutes. He knew so well the exact location of the paperweight, in the desk beside her bed. He knew so well the way she would be lying, with the blanket pulled up to her chin and above it that egg-shell temple exposed, waiting for the blow. Asleep. She would be fast asleep. She would never know what hit her. Or who. Or why.

Back up the fire escape, because he could not afford the risk of being seen in the elevator a few minutes later he would emerge from his own apartment quite openly, take the elevator to the street floor, and go into the bar next door. Most likely Borden would already be there, wild with anticipation. "Come on," Rolfe would say, "Mother's expecting us." And into the apartment house they would go, up in the elevator to Mother's door, where Rolfe would suddenly pause in the act of turning his key in the lock. "Oh, damn! (slapping his pockets) "I forgot my pipe. I'll just run up to my place and get it. Go on in, I'll be right back." Opening the door, he would call in to Mother the business about the pipe, just as though she could hear. Up to his own place again. Five, ten minutes.

When he came back, Borden would have discovered what had happened in the bedroom. He might be standing there, stunned; he might—even better—have fled in panic. Rolfe's story to the police would fit, in any case. "I never trusted the guy," he would say. "Stella can tell you. I made a point of always being here, when he came for his sessions with Mother. But it never occurred to me— It couldn't have been ten minutes. Just while I went upstairs for my pipe. I shouldn't have left him there. God, if only I hadn't!" as for what Borden would try to tell the police— Well, who was going to take the word of a hophead? He didn't have a prayer. Like as not, before it was allover, Borden, along with everybody else, would become convinced of his guilt.

It had been snowing lightly, Rolfe found when he stepped noiselessly through his window. The fire escape steps looked ghostly under the thin white coat. The windows of the two floors between him and Mother's apartment were dark. So was the church next door. No one to see or hear him. Everything was just as he had planned: the swift, silent descent, Mother's window opening smoothly under his hands, his leg thrusting inside, feeling for the floor, avoiding the little chintz chair...

He was inside. And suddenly nothing was as he had planned: the paperweight was not there on the desk. He stumbled into the medicine table, setting off a nervous clash of silver against glass, and still there was no stir or sound from the hump in the bed. His own rapid breathing unnerved him; he could not make it slow down. He became aware of a smell in the room, and that too was wrong because it was unfamiliar—pervasive, yet not like Mother's medicine; sweetish, yet not like her dusting powder. The smell of fear? Might Mother, having heard the intruder, be lying there frozen with terror? It could not be that Rolfe himself was afraid.

It was just that he could not see to find the paperweight. But to turn on the lamp would be to meet Mother's eyes…. Again he groped over the desk; for a moment he thought he had it, his fingers closed convulsively, and at once a snatch of wistful music tinkled out. Horrified, he clapped the lid back on the damned-fool contraption: one of those musical cigarette boxes. Mother loved such trinkets. He braced himself for what must surely come now—some movement, some sound from the bed. It did not come. He held his own breath, listening for hers. It was not there.

He turned on the lamp.

The shock came not so much from what had been done to Mother—after all, he himself had planned it—as from the fact that it had been done without his realizing it. For his first nightmarish conviction was that his memory had betrayed him, tricked him by blanking out. How could I have done it, he thought, and I have absolutely no recollection of if? Why, there I was, fumbling around for the paperweight, when all the time I had already….

The paperweight was on the bed, where it had been dropped once it had served its purpose. Mother's smashed-in head lay sideways on the pillow. She had put up quite a struggle for her poor life; one fat dimpled hand reached vainly toward the telephone, and her eyes, glazed and terrible with knowledge, stared up at him. She had know who hit her, and why.

It could not have been Rolfe. At last his mind grasped the truth. Memory was not playing tricks on him. Someone else had beaten him to it, had carried out his plan for him. A glance around the room, and he had the answer. The someone else was Borden. There across the chintz chair was Rolfe's jacket, the one Borden had borrowed last night. Maybe he had left it here on impulse—simply shucking off anything connected with Rolfe or his mother—or maybe on purpose in the hope (the dirty little rat) of implicating Rolfe. Well, Rolfe wasn't having any of that. He had come down in his shirt sleeves. With a feeling of triumph he slipped into the jacket. The comfortable set of it on his shoulders seemed to steady him.

Not that he was really shaken, of course. Not Rolfe J. Naturally it was a jolt, to find that Borden had come barging in ahead of time. But only a minor jolt, only momentary.

How had the fellow gotten in? The open fire-escape window? No, Rolfe remembered. There had been a key to Mother's apartment, an extra one, in his jacket pocket. Finding it must have been the spark that set Borden off. There right in his hands was the means of cutting short the agony of waiting; he could not resist using it. And Mother—taken by surprise, unaware that she was supposed to be on the verge of giving Borden another chance—would not have minced words. A flat, harsh turndown. What followed was inevitable.

Yes, there was the key on the desk, where Borden must have tossed it when he came in. Rolfe reached for it. And hesitated.

Supposing the police didn't believe him? He had never doubted that he could convince them of a lie. But now, in a chilling flash, he saw the situation as it would look, for example, to someone walking in on him at that moment. Standing there with the weapon in his hand (hastily, he slipped it into his pocket), the open fire-escape window behind him….

But of course nothing like that was going to happen. It wouldn't take them long to catch up with Borden, and he would crack. He had none of Rolfe's stamina, he was sure to crack. Guilty as he was, he might already be turning himself in. He would spill everything—the jacket borrowed from Rolfe, the extra key accidentally left in the pocket.

So it was a mistake to wear the jacket away. He must leave everything just as it was. And it would be a mistake to call the police quite yet. Because the other key to Mother's apartment was upstairs, on his chest of drawers, and it would be hard to explain why, with it lying there, Rolfe had chosen to come down the fire escape. Thank God he had thought of it in time! He drew a breath of relief at the simplicity of what he had to do—another trip up the fire escape for his key, down again in the elevator, back here to the bedroom (he must remember to lock the fire-escape window) and then the distraught call to the police. He had it made.

All the same, he had one leg through the window when he realized he was still wearing the jacket. The near-blunder shook him; it gave him a grim glimpse of how treacherous his mind could be. But must not be. Would not be.

The trouble was that everything happened at once; he discovered in his hurry to shed the jacket why Borden had left it behind. There was blood on the sleeve; it was already beginning to stiffen. And he heard the voice and the footsteps. His whole body locked in a paralysis of listening. Someone was in the apartment. Someone who was moving through the living room, on toward the bedroom. That fool Borden must have left the door ajar, simply walked out and….

Move. Get out of here. But get out of the jacket too, the damning jacket because the footsteps were appallingly close now! At the last moment his arms and legs unlocked, but only to a flurry of witless jerks that neither got him through the window nor out of the jacket. And it was all too late. He was lost. Ignominiously straddling the window sill, with one arm still trying to fumble its way out of the jacket, he looked into the granite eyes of Mr. Webb and knew that disaster was upon him.

Complete disaster. He felt Rolfe J.—the masterful man of destiny—disintegrate, once and for all, into the reality of what Mr. Webb saw—a pudgy, guilty wretch, caught red-handed and babbling (somehow that was the worst of all, that he could not stop babbling) an incoherent story that no one was going to believe.

"Tell it to the police," said Mr. Webb, and reached for the telephone.

So Rolfe went on babbling to the police that they must find Borden, all they had to do was find Borden. He babbled on and on.

They found Borden. What was left of him. He had either fallen or jumped from the window of his room to the alley below. Nobody knew exactly when. Or why. As the police said, who knew what made hopheads do any of the screwball things they did?

Luck had been with Borden—until he went out the window, of course. Nobody had seen him entering or leaving Mother's apartment. Nobody had seen him wearing Rolfe's jacket; there was only Rolfe's word that he had ever borrowed it. Only Rolfe's word, which nobody believed.

Yet there was nothing else for Rolfe to do but to go on hopelessly telling the truth. At the very end, while he was waiting in the death cell, he said, "I am guilty. I did not do it, but I am guilty."

A garbled sort of confession? Or just some more crazy babbling? No one recognized it for what it was. The deepest truth of all.

Lionel White was justly known as the master of the heist novel though his work crossed many boundaries. His complex plots were so well laid out that his book Clean Break *became Stanley Kubrick's first major movie,* The Killing, *precisely because the scenes were so clear cut; Kubrick didn't have to spend a lot of time reworking the story into a flimable script. The scenes were already there. He often wrote from the criminal's point of view so when things began to unravel, the tension levels went to work on the minds of his characters. The best of his work stands with anyone's of the time.*

TO KILL A WIFE

Lionel White

This boy was sitting on a tall stool at the bar, facing the cash register.

He had a fleshy, muscled face; there was a reddish tinge to his hair and it curled a little. He looked Irish. But his looks were deceiving, for he was a Dutchman.

He was around five foot ten, stocky, and wore a white shirt under a badly cut suit. Somebody, somewhere along the line, had probably told him that a white shirt was a sign of culture. Perhaps twenty-two or twenty-three, his face was unlined, his skin healthy, his nose upturned over incongruously narrow lips. He seemed a nice enough kid. Only people like myself might take him for what he really was.

I edged around the corner of the table and brushed against a slender, peroxide girl who looked as though she were drinking to yesterday, moved a bar stool close to where the boy was sitting, beckoned to the bartender. I knew the barkeep's name and had talked to him frequently, but I didn't call him by name; just held up one finger and he nodded and a minute later I had a bourbon and soda in front of me.

I casually turned on my stool, and looking at this boy, I said to the bartender, "Maybe he wants one, too."

The kid looked up and stared at me coldly, without expression. He didn't say a word and turned back to facing the cash register.

Well, Joey, who has known me a long time, figured that I must have some approximate idea of what I was doing so when he brought my drink, he also brought over a bottle of Bud and put it in front of the kid. Bud was what he had been drinking.

The kid didn't make a move until Joey walked away. Then he stared at the bottle for a minute, picked it up and poured the amber liquid into his glass. I pointedly looked into the mirror over the bar, ignoring him.

He drained the glass, sat it back on the mahogany, and out of the corner of his mouth muttered, "Thanks."

It was a beginning, anyway.

The kid sat there with the beer for about a half hour. I went back to my table after awhile and the thin blonde was still drinking to yesterday, only she was drinking a little faster to yesterday than was probably good for her.

I ordered a drink at the table and kept watching the kid, and I noticed he was catching me in the mirror over the bar now and then. So when the place cleared out a little, I walked back to the bar.

This time I didn't fool around at all. I walked right up to him, and said, "My name is Dacey. D A C E Y, Dacey. I've got a last name and when you're ready to tell me yours, I'll probably tell you mine. I keep a room upstairs in the hotel and I've been around here a long time. Joey knows me; a lot people around here know me. You're a stranger, I can see that. I'd like you to come over to my table and have a drink with me."

He gave me that peculiarly cold stare again and then, suddenly, he smiled. But the smile didn't mean anything because I noticed that everything smiled except his eyes.

We went back to the booth and Joey didn't have to be told. He just brought the drinks over and the kid sat there saying nothing. I waited a few minutes and then we had a second drink. Again he gave me that peculiar expressionless stare and then, once more using the side of his mouth, said, "So what?"

I gave him my smile and said, "So I gather you're hanging around here for some reason or other. Are you looking for something in particular?"

"What are you looking for?" he asked.

"I'm looking for a kid," I said, "who probably thinks like you think. I want someone to do a little job for me."

He laughed, but there was nothing funny about his laugh. "Look fella," he said, "I don't know what your racket is. I don't know you and I don't particularly care to know you. So if you've something to say to me, I think you'd better say it and get it off your chest."

I didn't answer the kid for a minute. Instead, I took out my wallet. I leafed through it until I found a century note and I took it out and laid it on the table.

"That's yours," I said, "for being nice enough to listen to me for a few minutes. Now just a second."

I reached back into the wallet and took out four more single hundred dollar bills, and then I went on, "Now if you want to behave yourself for the next few minutes, these are all yours. If you don't like what I have to say, when I get finished you can pick up those five bills and get your god damned little self out of here!"

He sat there, bland, expressionless and with an odd attitude of tense expectancy and let me talk.

I told him the story. It took almost a half hour to tell it.

When I was through, he gave me the strangest look, and instead of picking up the money and leaving, he folded it very neatly and handed it back to me.

"You see," he said, "I'm paying you now to listen to me."

I took the money he handed back and pocketed it. "Go ahead and talk," I said.

It didn't take him any half hour. He said what he had to say in about two minutes flat.

"I've got no record," he started out. "I've never done anything that you can go to jail for, and I'm never going to—I mean, I'm never going to jail. You're hanging around this crumb joint, where you seem to be known. You're probably some sort of petty racketeer. So you got five hundred dollars. Well, you still got five hundred dollars. If you've got anything to say that really makes sense, not just that you know ways in which young fellas like me can make a fast buck or so, but if you got something that really makes sense, why I'm down at the Mills Hotel. The Bleeker Street Mills Hotel. I'm going to be down there for two or three days. They don't have no telephone service there, you know, but you can drop me a card. My name is Smith. Pat Smith. When I get to know you a little better, I may give you another name. But Pat Smith will reach me. Goodbye."

He stood up, turned and walked out of the place.

I smiled. I knew I had my kid then!

You see, what I'd asked him to do was to commit a murder. I wanted my wife murdered.

I had told him the first five hundred was actually just for listening to me. That there was another forty-five hundred dollars. That there would be no really serious risk and that I had all the arrangements made. I told him that the only thing missing was the person to commit the actual crime itself. That I thought he looked like a likely candidate.

Well, he sure was a likely candidate. And, in a sense, he more or less ended up committing murder. But not for any lousy five thousand dollars. No, he was much too smart for that. He really made it pay off. But I had better start from the beginning.

When I started out I was a bell hop in a hotel. Later on, because I saved my money and stole a dollar here and there, I was able to buy a couple of juke boxes. I parlayed those juke boxes into a half interest in a rather disreputable dance hall and then I bought a hotel. The hotel was really something else, but we called it a hotel and it had a café and a lot of girls around the place all the time. It made money.

There was a bookie at the hotel, who paid me a few dollars now and then, and I had several taxi cabs and a few other little things going. All thoroughly legitimate, but all not quite respectable. You can't make too much money if you stay too respectable—or at least I couldn't.

So I was doing pretty good around the time I became thirty years old. I'd learned to talk right and I dressed pretty well. I got along with a fairly decent type of people. I couldn't go certain places, but then I really didn't want to go to a lot of places. I just wanted to be around the places I had an interest in.

It never occurred to me that I might get married, but I did. I met one of the girls who worked in one of my dance hall joints and I went all the way. I've made a lot of money out of girls, but I'd never played around with them myself. Not until I met Judy.

The day we got married she told me she wasn't in love with me, that she doubted very much if she ever would be, but that I wasn't a bad guy and a hell of a lot easier to take than a lot of other things she'd had to take.

As it turned out, Judy was a very good wife. She did everything a wife is supposed to do. We didn't have any children, but that wasn't Judy's fault, particularly. That was just the way things turned out. We lived in a nice little house out in Hastings and I came home nights. I didn't fool around with anything, except my businesses, of course. And I'd say Judy was fairly contented.

I provided what I thought I should, including a Caddie convertible, the usual mink coat, and trips to Miami. But I didn't give Judy the one thing you can't buy for your wife, and that's give her a husband in whom she was in love.

So after four years, I knew I was missing something in Judy I'd tried very desperately to find. And this was about the time things began going bad with my rackets.

And, of course, that's when Judy ran into this guy. He was a pretty nice guy. He had a job as a salesman and he used to stop by the house. He couldn't get any other kind of job, I guess, and so he was selling some gadget or other.

He'd stop and talk with Judy and of course she'd buy anything from anybody who'd talk with her. But he came back too many times just to be selling that gadget of his.

It never occurred to me what was really going on until Judy, who is pretty honest, told me she wanted a divorce so she could marry this guy with whom she'd fallen in love.

Well, I was still pretty crazy about Judy and I knew that for me there was only one possible solution. I couldn't give her up and I couldn't stand living with her while she was in love with this guy, so I decided that Judy would have to go.

As I've said I'd always had a tough time making a dollar, so once I'd made that decision about Judy, I figured the only way to become completely cold about it and not have too many regrets, would be to take out a combination hundred thousand dollar insurance policy on each of our lives.

And that is how, after making preliminary arrangements, I happened to be looking for the kind of kid that this Pat Smith seemed to be.

That was the story, right off the cuff, which I told Pat Smith in the bar, after offering him the five hundred dollars just to listen to it.

So, he had given me the five hundred back and walked out, after letting me know how to get in touch with him. That was how I knew I had him.

If he'd have taken the five C's and blown, I would never have seen him again. If he'd got sore or hot-headed, or asked a lot of questions, I wouldn't have wanted him for the job. But he'd merely told me off and walked out after making a second contact possible. So I figured he didn't want five hundred or even five thousand. He wanted twenty or twenty-five thousand.

I couldn't blame him. He'd go to the chair if anything went wrong. And the biggest chance of anything going wrong, of course, would be during the time he was actually committing the murder.

So he knew what the job was really worth and I knew that was why he was playing hard-to-get. It was after he left the table that I decided I'd let him make his twenty-five thousand or whatever it was he wanted, but at the same time I also decided I would have to kill him too. Killing him would accomplish two things: it would save me the twenty-five grand, but more important, it would eliminate the one person who would know I was implicated in Judy's death.

I gave him three days to cool off and worry a little bit and regret the fact that he hadn't snapped up my five hundred bucks. I then mailed him a short letter that suggested he call me as soon as convenient. I included the telephone number of the hotel bar where he had first met me and where I usually hung out in the afternoons.

His call came the very next day. I arranged to pick him up downtown at six that evening.

After meeting him on Bleeker Street, I drove west to the Elevated Highway which was as jammed as usual. We drove on north, past the Hendrick Hudson Bridge and on up into Westchester. I turned the radio on and let him stew. After we had passed through Riverdale, I muted the radio. Traffic had thinned out and I started talking.

I didn't let him get a word in edgewise. I told him I realized he must be interested and that he probably wanted more money than the suggested five thousand and that I guessed it was a job which called for a slightly heavier expenditure. I said the only thing was, if he wanted more money, I would have to change my plans about the way I wanted the job done. I said that instead of one of those mysterious deals, where a stranger kills another stranger and nobody knows why or anything else, that I thought it would be a good idea to bring him home with me for a while. I could justify his hanging around on the grounds that he was doing some very private "research" for me on one of my new ventures. I could also explain that he was a friend of a friend of mine, a kid who didn't exactly have a place of his own and therefore ought to move in and make use of our spare room.

It was easy to see as I talked that he wasn't quite following me. He was too busy trying to figure the angle.

I went on to explain that I had evolved a new and rather subtle plan for the way the whole thing was to operate.

I knew he would go for the idea, because I knew he was anxious to be close to me for a while in order to find out how much dough I really did have and exactly what my motives in this thing really were.

Even at this stage of the game, I could see him beginning to figure out the angles in his own mind. Well, that's what I wanted. Because if he was shooting an angle at me, his defenses would be down a little, and they had to be down if I was to pull this caper the way I *really* planned it.

We drove back to the city, after stopping at a roadhouse and having dinner and a couple of drinks.

The next night I brought him home with me.

"This is Pat Smith," I said to Judy. "He's a friend of Harry's."

Of course she didn't know who Harry was, and, as a matter of fact, I didn't either.

Judy said, "Hello."

He said, "How do you do, Madam."

That "Madam" almost got her for a second, but she saved herself a blush and walked over to the sideboard. "What'll it be?" she asked.

He said beer. I didn't have to tell her what I wanted because she'd been mixing drinks for me every evening for almost four years.

He dropped his bag, put his hat on the floor, and sat on the couch. We lifted our drinks.

"Pat here," I told Judy, "is going to help me out with some work I gotta do here at the house. Sort of bookkeeping stuff. He won't be any trouble or get in the way. We'll give him the guest room and he can get his grub outside. I'll be working with him in the evenings, for the next week or so. He'll have his own key and you won't even know he's around. Pat don't do much but read comics and go to the movies, anyway."

So all the arrangements were made and we had another drink and then went in and had dinner. Later we went upstairs and I showed Pat his room. He took the room in his stride, although it was a very comfortable room with its own fireplace and bath. Late that evening, after Judy had gone to bed with a confession magazine, I went to talk with Pat. I found him sitting on the edge of the bed, stripped to the waist, staring at the floor.

I told Pat that he was to completely ignore Judy, to be polite to her if he saw her around the place, but to stay away from her as much as possible.

If he should run across Heming—Robert Heming, the fellow with whom Judy was having her love affair—he should ignore him completely. I told him, "Be polite to him if you have to say anything. But don't let on you know anything is going on. After all the guy's a salesman, and he'll probably want to do all the talking anyway. Let him think you think everything is okay and above board. I don't want the guy getting suspicious."

Pat nodded.

And I thought that now I could begin working on the second stage of my plan.

I had never been one for mixing much with the neighbors or passing the time of day with the village tradesmen, but now I made it a point to see people around the local stores. I would stop at the corner stationery store in the evenings, for my newspapers, and I made it a point to talk to the clerk who worked there. Later, I found out he was the owner and probably had more money than I had.

I first started by just discussing the weather. And then gradually I began talking more and more about myself. I told him I was in business in New York and spent a lot of time in the city. And then I casually brought out the fact that I had this young fellow staying at our house. I explained that he was a boy I'd picked up hiking along the Post Road. Said I didn't know too much about him, but that I understood he had some sort of criminal record and that I was trying to help get him straightened out and thought he would turn out to be a pretty good citizen after a while.

Then, later, I'd bring Pat into the store with me. Of course, I'd already asked the man not to let on he knew anything about the boy. I'd buy a handful of cigars and Pat would order a pack of cigarettes.

Pat was always polite enough, but I noticed the storekeeper looked at him with a rather peculiar expression. I knew I had planted the seed which was going to be very important to me if my plan were to work out.

At the same time, I followed a similar procedure at the gas station which serviced my car and at two or three other spots in the neighborhood. I wanted Pat to be seen with me and I wanted everyone around to know as much about him as I could let them know, so that later on when things developed and they were questioned they would back up certain ideas I had planted in their minds.

At the same time, I began working on Judy. I made a point of asking her to meet me in town for lunch.

One day we went to a midtown restaurant where I obtained a quiet, secluded table. Judy looked very lovely in the dimly lighted room with her dark blue eyes like smudges and her red, red mouth. She wore a large picture hat which partly concealed her face. I knew I was still in love with her and that I probably always would be. It made me feel sad.

We had lunch and then we talked.

"Judy," I said, "I've been thinking a lot about your being in love with this guy Heming and his being in love with you. I've thought the whole thing over. One thing I don't want, baby, is for you to be unhappy."

I went on along this line for some time. Then I told her it was all right for her to go ahead and get her divorce. I did have a couple of requests to make, however. I wanted her to wait a couple of weeks so I'd have a chance to get some business straightened out and loosen up some cash. I wanted time to get some extra money so I could get her a good lawyer and give her a stake to go out to Reno on, where she could plan to get her decree.

"One thing I want you to do, baby," I said. "For the next two or three weeks, until I get things straightened out, I want you not to see much of this Heming guy. We don't want no scandal and we can do this thing right, like friends, which I hope we still are."

Judy told me she thought I was being very fair about everything. At one point, she got very sentimental and almost cried. It was a funny thing, I damn near felt like crying myself. Because, I still loved her. But with Judy it was strictly sentimentality. She just didn't want to hurt me.

She had a sidecar—that made her third—and got a little weepy. I had a double brandy and thought it was a damned shame I was going to have to do what I was going to do. Judy promised she wouldn't see Heming again until after she got her divorce. And then she went shopping and I went down to the hotel to see Joey and get a bet down on the third race at Washington Park.

I've always made it a practice not to carry large sums of money with me; I do most of my business by check. But now I began violating a lifelong rule. I began making it a practice to stop by my bank every day or so to draw out large amounts of cash, anywhere from a thousand to five or six thousand dollars in fairly large bills.

After the third or fourth time, my banker took me into his private office and warned me that it was a bad idea having large transactions when there were no check records kept. He also said it was unsafe to carry large sums.

I told him a long story about being involved in a new venture and that I was conducting most of the business from my home. I said I was buying services from various men who met me at the house and whom I paid off in cash. He nodded, but I knew he didn't have the faintest idea of what I was saying. I didn't even know myself. But the point was, I had it firmly implanted in his mind that I was carrying large sums, and that I had substantial amounts of money around my house.

Pat had been with us about ten days when I figured the time had come to make the next move. He was getting a little jittery, just sitting around doing nothing all day but reading comic books.

One night I told Judy that Pat would be going into town with me the following day. She nodded, hardly listening.

"When do I go to Reno, Dacey?" she asked.

"Soon, baby," I told her. "Maybe next week. I'll let you know in a couple of days. I'm just getting the money together now."

She kissed my cheek in a careless gesture of affection. In a way, it was worse than if she hated me and had struck me.

The next morning Pat got into the car beside me. We drove into New York without speaking. Pat had the car radio turned on full blast. He liked cowboy music. I explained when I let Pat off that I was going to the hotel. I gave him the room number and told him to give me a few minutes and then come on up. He arrived some ten minutes after I'd opened the windows to air the place out. I don't use the room much and it gets stuffy.

Joey sent up a bottle of bourbon and after I had a drink all mixed and was ready to sit down and talk, Pat reminded me he drank beer.

I sent down a second time, this time for beer. The beer was warm and that gave me a certain amount of satisfaction. By now I was getting just a little tired of Pat.

The windows closed again, and seated at last, I told Pat my plans. These were the arrangements, as I explained them to him.

When we went back to the house that night, we'd let a couple of days slide by. That would bring it up to Wednesday. Wednesday was the day the servants, a man and his wife, had off. Wednesday morning Pat was to pack his bag and get ready to leave.

I went on to explain to Pat that I had already arranged for Judy to meet me in town Wednesday night to take in a Broadway opening. She would be home alone during the afternoon and would be ready to leave the house for town to meet me at eight thirty.

I would leave the house for town around noon.

At ten minutes to seven, while Judy was sitting at her dressing table getting her face made up, Pat was to go to her room. Knowing Judy as I did, it was a fifty-to-one bet that she would follow her usual routine. She always waited until the last minute. And it took her a good hour to get ready to go anywhere.

From my inside breast pocket, I took a snub nosed thirty-two caliber revolver with a short silencer on its barrel.

"This is the gun," I said. "You walk into her bedroom, the door is always unlocked. She may hear you and she may not. It doesn't make much difference. The minute you open that door, shoot her. Let her have three or four slugs. I don't want any mistakes."

As I talked, Pat sat there staring at me without expression.

"My watch will be timed with yours," I said. "Five minutes before you shoot Judy, I'm going to be talking on the phone with Robert Heming. I'm going to tell him Judy has been in a serious accident and is calling for him, that he is to come at once to the house. He lives about two miles away, down in Yonkers."

"How do you know he'll be in?"

"Listen, kid," I said. "It's my business to know things like that. You just let me plan this job and be sure to handle your end of it."

Pat nodded.

"Heming should reach the house at no later than seven o'clock. By this time Judy should certainly be taken care of. When the doorbell rings, answer it at once. He won't know who you are, but that doesn't matter.

He'll be all up in the air at the time. The thing is, you're to take him to Judy's bedroom immediately. Explain it any way you want. Let him get in the room before you enter. The thing he'll do first is rush over to Judy and lean down to see what has happened. That's when you let him have it. From as short a distance as possible, and in the left side over the heart."

Pat nodded, still noncommittal.

I took twenty-five hundred dollars from a long fat wallet I carried in my jacket pocket. I counted out the bills and handed them to him.

He looked up without touching them.

"Take 'em," I said. "A down payment. I'll explain the rest in a minute."

I next told Pat he was to carefully wipe the murder weapon and then place it in or as near as possible to Heming's hand. In any case, he was to get the man's print on the grip. I again told Pat to try and hit Heming in the left side, over the heart if possible. I explained how necessary it was to have it look like murder and suicide. Necessary for both our sakes.

I handed Pat a note. It was a pretty good forgery of Judy's handwriting. It was a suicide note, signed with her name. The idea was that Heming and Judy had had a suicide pact. Pat was to leave the note on Judy's dressing table.

That done he was to take his bag and leave the house from his own entrance.

It would be dark and he was to walk directly north on the street on which we live. Three blocks from the house, I would pick him up. I'd drive him into New York and drop him at the airport. I would then return to the house and find the bodies. I would be the one to call the police.

"How do I know the cops will figure a suicide pact?" Pat asked.

"It will be the only conclusion possible," I explained to him. "My lawyer will testify that I had arranged to let Judy get a divorce. Today I told the mouthpiece that I'd changed my mind and had told Judy so. My lawyer knows that the two of them were in love; Judy herself told him so. The fact that I refused to give her a divorce will establish a motive for the suicide pact. If they don't go for that, the evidence will have to lead to a conclusion of murder and suicide. In any case, you'll be out of it. And should you ever be questioned, I'll have your alibi all set. The same as I'll have my own."

Pat nodded. "You've got twenty-five hundred now," I went on. "When I meet you to take you to the airport after we're all through, I'm giving you another fifteen thousand. That's all I can raise in cash. Later on, after I collect the hundred thousand on Judy from the insurance people, I'm giving you an additional ten thousand."

Pat looked up quickly and I knew I'd made a good plan. I wanted him to squawk about the money end of it. It would divert any suspicions he might have of my real plan.

"You said I'd get twenty-five thousand cash," he said.

"Right. But damn it, this way you get even more. So what if you do have to wait a while?"

"Look here," Pat said. "That's not the idea at all. Get up the twenty-five."

"All right," I said. "Suppose we do it this way. Fifteen more when you finish the job and then another fifteen when I get the insurance. That's thirty-two fifty in all. Thirty-two thousand five hundred dollars."

Well, we batted it around for a half hour and finally he gave in and we shook hands on it. He was surly about it though.

We returned to the house separately that night. On Tuesday, after breakfast, I had a long talk with Judy. I told her I had made the final arrangements with the attorneys and that within four days she would be able to leave for Reno. I also asked that she say nothing to Robert Heming until the day before she left and at that time I would turn over a sufficient amount of money to her to see her through.

"One thing, though, baby," I added. "Tomorrow is Wednesday. I have tickets for a new show, and in view of our four years together, I'd like to take you to a nice dinner and the theater. Make a sort of farewell party out of it. It will be our last evening together. Tomorrow I'm checking into a suite at the hotel. After you've gone, I'm going to sell this house. I'll split whatever I get for it, with you."

Judy looked a little unhappy, the way a child looks unhappy at any unexpected request. But she also looked sort of relieved. She readily agreed with my plans.

Wednesday turned out to be a bleak, wintery day. The skies were leaden and the bare trees appeared naked and cold in the chill wind.

I drove into town late in the morning and went at once to the hotel. Joey mixed me a couple of sours as I looked over the scratch sheet. Nothing looked very good, but I laid a fifty on a long shot in the sixth anyway. I followed my usual routine.

Pat, of course, was at the house. I'd got him a new batch of comic books, and he already had the fake suicide note, the gun with the silencer and the advance dough. His bag was packed.

I had told Pat that once we hit the airport, I'd give him the other fifteen thousand. I let him believe I didn't quite trust him to go ahead with the murder once he had that much cash on him. I was still working on the basic psychological principle that the more Pat thought I distrusted him, the less he was likely to distrust me.

I hung around the hotel bar long enough to get the results on the sixth race and, contrary to my expectations, my horse came in and paid off sixteen-fifty. It made me a profit of three-hundred and sixty-two dollars and fifty cents.

There was snow in the air as I left the city. I was timing myself carefully. Everything from this point on out depended on people being at certain exact places at certain exact times. As I drove up the Parkway, a thin ice was forming on the roads. I passed two accidents.

My nerves, however, were in excellent shape. I was glad about the weather. Few persons would be out on a night like this.

At twenty minutes to seven I was parked in front of a vacant lot, some hundred and fifty yards down the street from my home. I noticed a Ford sedan across the street, a block away, and it looked vaguely familiar. But I paid no attention to it. My eyes were on my own place and nowhere else.

At this exact moment, as I glanced at my wrist watch in the dim light of the shaded dashboard, I knew Judy would be sitting in front of her dressing table in our bedroom. She would be leaning forward slightly, tracing her lips with carmine. I could visualize the scene. She would be in her bra and panties and nothing else. I'd watched her a thousand times as she made up. It was always the same.

And then, as I realized that now, this very second, the door would be opening and Pat would be there with the silenced revolver, I think I had a moment of regret. In a sense, it was a shame to destroy anything as beautiful as Judy. She would be looking up now, half turning in her chair. And then she would be dead.

I checked my wrist watch with the dashboard clock. The hands of both pointed to six forty-five.

Perhaps I shuddered, I don't really know. But the sense of regret was deeper than ever, and I am a man who has never regretted easily.

There were five minutes to kill, so I turned on the radio. It's odd how I remember it now, but there was a violinist playing "Caprice Venoir," and I hunched back in the heavy leather upholstery of the seat and felt a sense of infinite sadness as the soft, deep, sentimental strains of the music came to me. I have always been a sucker for classical music and particularly for violin solos.

It lasted a little more than five minutes, but I waited it out anyway. Then I snapped off the radio and stepped from the car, slamming the door behind me.

Strangely enough I felt the urgent need for hurrying, but I controlled myself and was almost casual as I walked toward my home. Dimly I was conscious of the fact that there were no lights visible from the street. The windows in Pat's room, however, were lighted and the shades were down.

Pat's work was over, that I knew full well. And Pat was waiting for the bell to ring. A cold, ruthless murderer, with one body still not cold, waiting for Robert Heming, his second victim.

I reached inside my coat for the shoulder holster under my left armpit.

The gun I took out was a .22 caliber on a .32 frame. That morning I had loaded it with soft nosed dum-dums. I carried a permit for the gun so I knew there would be no trouble later on. There were three bullets in the revolver and I would use them all.

It was dark on the porch, but I had no trouble finding the bell. Again it struck me as odd that there were no lights in the front of the house. But I had no time for thinking now. I heard the steps as they approached. That would be Pat. My left hand rested lightly on the door knob. I felt the knob begin to turn.

I waited no longer. Quickly leaning my weight against the door, I shoved it inward. There was some slight resistance and I believe there was a sort of muttered sound of surprise. I could just barely make out his outline, but I am sure that I got him with the first slug. The other two followed rapidly and went into him as he sank to the floor.

Even as the body struck with a dull thud, I dropped my gun into my side coat pocket.

Time now was of the essence. Those shots were bound to have been heard in the neighborhood. I had to get into that bedroom and get the suicide note from the dresser where Pat had left it. I didn't bother with the lights, for I knew my way through the house blindfolded.

I hurriedly crossed the room and ran down the long hall. I could see the crack of light coming from the door as I approached. A second later and I had pushed into the bedroom. My eyes were drawn as by a magnet to Judy's dressing table.

That was when I really knew that this kid, Pat Smith, was just as tough as they come.

That was when I realized that Judy, whom I had loved for the past four years, but who had never really loved me, must have, somewhere along the line, learned to hate me.

That's my story, Father. That's my confession. Of course, you remember the trial. You remember when I was fighting for my life against a charge of being the murderer of Robert Heming, a man whom the State's Attorney said was my wife's lover.

You remember the testimony of my own attorney. He stood there and told the jury that I had made arrangements to give my wife, Judy, a divorce. And then, just two days before the shooting, how I had gone to him and changed my plans and said I would never give her up.

You remember the testimony of Pat Smith, himself. Pat who perjured himself when he told the judge and the jury that I had hired him as a spy to watch my wife and to report on her affair with this man Heming, whom I was accused of killing. You remember how he told the jury that I was desperately jealous and had threatened to kill Heming.

Of course you remember Judy's own story, which she gave to the newspapers after she realized she wouldn't be able to appear in court as a witness against me. How she told of going to a moving picture show with Pat on that Wednesday afternoon. And then having dinner with Pat, from six-thirty to seven-thirty, on the night of the murder. And about the witnesses who saw them at dinner. That was a diabolically clever touch.

And then, most damning of all, was the testimony of Heming's landlady.

About the letter I was supposed to have sent him asking him to come to the house and wait for me. That the door would be open. That letter, written on my own typewriter, but which I never wrote, telling Heming that I was going to give Judy her freedom and to come and talk with me about it.

And so tonight, Father, I'm going to the electric chair for the murder of this man Robert Heming. And probably, within a week of the time the state buries my burned and shriveled body, Judy will collect the hundred thousand dollars insurance on my life. And she and this boy Pat Smith will be married and they will spend the money. In a way, it's a sort of wedding present from me to them.

I don't know if they'll ever be really happy.

For you can see what they have done to me. For although I planned to commit a double murder, I didn't actually commit any murder. I shot a man by accident and I shall pay for that with my life.

And that's why, Father, before I pass through that door in less than a half hour from now, I wanted to make this last confession.

I don't say that I didn't kill Robert Heming. I don't say that I didn't plan Judy's death and the death of Pat Smith or that I didn't plan to frame Pat for Judy's murder after I had killed him. But I do say that I never deliberately planned to kill Robert Heming, and that if I had not run into Pat Smith I might not be going through that little gray door tonight, alone.

So you may leave now, Father, and I guess that's everything I have to say, except that I hope Judy has finally found someone she is able to love.

If you pick up this book for only one reason, Jada M. Davis's previously unpublished novel should be it. Had Davis chosen to see it published in his lifetime, So Curse the Day *surely would have topped many "best of" lists. It reads as a prototypical Gold Medal paperback: it's a classic noir in the sense that the main character and his malleable morals are subject to facile molding by an irresistible femme fatale. If you like truly hardboiled fiction one can do no better than reading his* One for Hell. *Davis was a writer who knew how to punch his readers in the gut in so many different ways. Talk about an undiscovered jewel….*

SO CURSE THE DAY

Jada M. Davis

It was an adobe house.

There was an old nanny goat baa-ing her head off in the front yard, advancing on me, long skinny neck out-thrust.

Bright colored clothing flapped on a rusty wire line stretched between two cracked cedar posts.

The little house was in a hollow, flat roofed, dirty brown, a part of the country, grown out of the earth, quiet and sun-soaked and peaceful. Three or four brown hens scratched earth in the yard and a long-eared pup rolled in the dust.

I wanted to lie down, close my eyes, forget, lie down forever.

Long ago and dim distant there'd been a place like this, a quiet sun-warmed place like this, where insects hummed gently in the trees, hummed gently and not too loudly, where chickens scratched in the dust and a dog slept in the sun.

Long ago and dim distant there'd been a place like this, when I'd been small, when I'd stood in a front yard under a chinaberry tree, still and small and happy, with only the humming sounds of insects and the subdued chuckle of the chickens to break the stillness.

That was before they took my mother away and before my father locked me in the house and went away forever. That was before the man in black found me in the house, before the orphanage, before a lot of things.

And now I wanted to lie down and close my eyes.

"Hello, the house!" I called.

Stillness, dead stillness, no answer but the answering hum of insects.

Nobody home.

The door was open, and I went in, blinking in the cool shadow of the room.

A rough pine table, rough pine chairs, a kerosene stove, pots and pans on the wall, a pine bench in the middle of the floor, a sewing machine.

An odor.

The smell of chili, the smell of peppers, the warm smell of people not there.

A Mexican sombrero on the floor, in the corner.

An open doorway, another room, a room with three beds, rudely fashioned from cedar. Clothing hung from the rafters.

A pair of khaki pants, a khaki shirt.

So I changed clothes.

The khakis were clean, freshly washed, a little snug but all right.

It was a fair trade.

Back in the front room, hungry now, I found a can of tomatoes, some cold tamales, some leather-stiff tortillas, some tepid water in a bucket. And I ate my fill, ate until I was tired of chewing, full stomached to the point of sickness.

When I left the house I felt better.

My step was almost springy as I followed a dim rutted trail to somewhere.

CHAPTER I

The sun was just going down when I hit the highway. I was tired, a little hungry again, a little thirsty, a little scared.

It was the middle of nowhere, the exact middle, but it didn't matter. The highway spelled civilization. Cars whizzed past, trucks lumbered past, and I stood by that strip of asphalt and waved my thumb. Once a car slowed down, almost stopped, and I started running. But the driver looked back over his shoulder and stepped on the gas.

That made me mad.

The sun was going down, almost red, spreading a pinkish tinge to the low-flying clouds, edging them with pink gold and fringing the round swelling hills with soft touches of orange.

You have to remember scenes like that, because artists can't paint them. So I drank it in, stood there with my mouth open, my face hanging out, and drank it in, etched it on my mind, swallowed it and rubbed it into me so I'd remember it so long as I lived.

Three or four cars hummed by, zoomed by while I was looking. But I didn't care.

An army jeep rolled up, soft and easy, out of the hazy mist of sundown, pulled over to the side of the road and stopped.

The soldier was a beefy guy, red of face and thick of lip, the kind that leans over to speak in a low voice, as if someone could overhear.

"Want a ride, bud?"

"Sure," I said, the laughter bubbling inside, boiling inside, almost spilling over.

"Hop in," he said. "We're not suppose to pick up anybody, but I can't leave you out here."

"I appreciate it," I said.

"The coyotes might get you," he said, nudging me with his elbow.

"Don't scare me." I said. "I'm terrified of coyotes."

"Hell," he said. "I've never even seen a coyote. Or rattlesnake either. They tell me rattlesnakes are thick out here but I've never seen one of the damned things."

"They're not pretty."

"I'm from Chicago, myself," he said.

"What are you doing out here?"

"We've been looking for a joker."

"A soldier?" I asked.

"Yeah."

"What'd he do? Refuse to salute a looey?"

The guy just grunted, so I let it drop.

"Where you headed?" he asked. "To see your girl friend?"

"Yeah."

"What's she like?"

"Black eyes. Olive skin. A figure that'll knock your eyes out."

"A señorita."

"Right."

"Tell me" he said. "I've always wondered."

"It's true."

"That I don't understand. Everybody says Mex girls are hotter, but I don't know why."

"The pepper," I said.

"That wouldn't do it. I knew a girl in Chicago who ate pepper all the time and she was coldern'n an Eskimo's ice box."

Dusk came suddenly, floated in like fog, settled softly.

"How come you're not in the army?" the soldier asked.

Just the way he said it irked me.

"I've been in," I said. "Got shot up a little."

"You look okay to me," he said.

"Have you been shot at?"

"No. but I've...."

"You've been sitting on your fat behind," I said. "What Uncle Sam needs is a few less chiefs and more Indians."

"Can I help it if they haven't sent me overseas?"

"Have you asked for overseas?"

"Twice."

I laughed.

"That's what they all say! Every time you meet a soldier, every damned time, he begins talking about how he begged to be sent overseas!"

"Look, buster," the soldier said, "how do I know you've been overseas? How do I even know you've been in the army? You may have been out on some sheep ranch since the war started for all I know."

"I told you I'd been in the army," I said. "I told you I'd been overseas. You calling me a liar?"

"Now, wait a minute!" he said, slowing the jeep a little. "Just hold up a little! Don't get tough with me!"

"Aw, shut up," I said, the anger fading.

"That does it!" He slammed on the brakes. "Get the hell out! From here in you can walk!"

So I got out, feeling foolish, wishing I had better control of my temper, dreading the walk.

"How far to town?" I asked.

"Five miles. And I hope you walk every step!"

It made me laugh, it was so silly.

The soldier started off, zoomed the jeep a hundred yards down the road, stopped and began to back up. Like I knew he would.

"Get in," he said, his voice sullen. "I wouldn't leave a dog out here."

"Thanks, soldier. Sorry I got mad."

"Maybe I got out of line," he said.

"No, I'm a crazy coot. Sometimes I blow up for no reason at all. Most times I'm mad at the world in general, but sometimes I take it out on anybody near me."

The cool gray dusk was a soft and shimmery veil and we drove the rest of the way in silence. At the edge of a small town, visible from a swelling hill, the soldier pulled over to the side of the road and stopped.

"I can't let anybody see you in the vehicle," he said. "It's not far to town."

"Thanks a lot. Good luck."

"Same here."

He drove away, his tail light blinking, and I hoofed on past the service stations, the honky-tonks, on into the center of the town, the one-streeted town, through the town and out the other side.

It's no fun to stand beside a road and wait for a ride, wish for a ride, watch the cars whizz past, listen to the humming sound of tires on pavement. It's no fun. Especially when you don't know where you're going. It's no fun by day and worse by night, because at night you get sleepy and can't lie down for fear a car will come along.

Here, in this hot-by-day country, it was cold at night. Not really cold, but more cold than cool, too cool for comfort. My eyes felt gritty, raw and gritty, the lids heavy. I wanted to sleep, close my eyes and sleep my way back to another time, another place, another life.

In the night, deep in the night, I hoofed back to the center of town. One café was open. I went in.

The waitress must have been all of six feet tall, bony and mop-haired, lanky and buck-toothed, flat of chest and thin of face.

She was the only person in the place, the only one I could see.

"What'll it be?" she asked.

"Well," I said, "if you don't mind... I'd just like to sit here and get warm."

She glanced at the back of the room. There was an oval-shaped opening there, with a shelf, an opening into the kitchen.

"You broke?" She leaned across the counter

"Flat."

"Hungry?"

"Starved."

She glanced at the back again, turned and loped toward the coffee urn, filled a cup and returned.

"Drink this," she said.

"Thanks," I said. "I can use that."

"I think the cook is asleep," she said. "Or maybe he stepped out."

She loped toward the back, disappeared through a swinging door.

I heard dishes clattering.

The old girl brought meat and potatoes, green beans and turnips, a roll and a slice of corn bread.

"Eat that," she said.

"Lady," I said, "I'd like to marry you."

"I just happen to have a license in my purse," she said, giggling a little. "No kidding. I know how it is to be broke."

"Well, there are worse things."

"Yeah. What?"

I wolfed the food, sipped the coffee, fumbled in my pocket.

"Here," the tall girl said, handing me a cigarette.

That made me laugh.

"What's so funny?" she wanted to know, sullen.

"Not you," I said. "Me."

"You don't look very funny. You look like you need a bath and a shave and some sleep... and some money."

"Sure I do. That's what makes it so funny. Here I am, tough and strong, and there you are."

"Yeah," she said. "Here I am. My feet hurt and I get thirty lousy bucks a week."

"You're working," I said. "Take me, now. I'm a bum and you're feeding me."

She swabbed the counter with a dirty rag, watching me from the corners of her eyes.

"You got a place to sleep tonight?" she asked.

"The ground."

She swabbed, glancing at me now and then, nervous, breathing fast, lips parted.

Something inside me turned over.

She had a mustache, almost a mustache, and her lips were thin and colorless, her ears too big and her neck skinny and long. Her hair was straggly, mouse colored and straggly.

"I can fix you up on the couch at my place," she said. "It won't be the best bed in the world, but it'll beat sleeping on the ground."

No thank you.

Not for me.

Some other time, when I'm blind and old and crippled and desperate.

But what could I do?

I didn't want to hurt her feelings.

She must have been a lonely creature, looking like that, lonely and lost and unloved, plodding through life, hoping and wishing and dreaming.

"That'd be swell," I said. "How do you know I won't cut your throat?"

"You won't."

She was radiant with some inner light from somewhere deep down, deep buried, and for a minute, a moment, half a moment, she was almost pretty.

"We'll be closing in a few minutes," she said.

"Good. I could use some sleep."

"I'll get you some more coffee."

She brought some more coffee, went up front, came back with a package of cigarettes.

"These are on the house," she said.

"I wouldn't want to get you in trouble."

"You won't."

After about ten minutes she started turning off the lights. I heard a door bang in back, so the cook must have returned. The girl waved her hand at me and I followed her to the door, went out first, waited while she flicked the night latch.

"It's not far," she said.

She was tall, toothpick tall, awkward, long legged and awkward and tall, striding like a man beside me, in a hurry to be home.

For a minute, as we walked in silence, I considered bolting. It would have been easy. We'd left the main street, left the lights, and it would have been easy to dart away into the darkness.

Something, maybe pity, kept me walking beside her, uneasy and uncomfortable.

She lived in a tiny frame house, unpainted, old and rickety, down an alley. We walked through a yard darkened by some giant tree, some wide-branched, thick-leaved tree, onto a roofed porch, walked in darkness until I walked by feel rather than sight.

The girl's breathing was labored, raspy, and the odor of desire hung around her like a perfume, tickled some part of my senses until I, too, breathed hard, prickled, tingled, breathed hard and sweated icy sweat.

Sex is a funny thing, blind as a bat.

A door squeaked. The girl fumbled around, found a light switch, stood there inside the doorway, staring at me, her eyes dilated, her chest rising and falling.

I told my feet to move and they went the wrong way.

It wasn't much of a place, little more than a dump, but she'd done her best to make it livable. She had a bunch of Mexican blankets, gaily colored, some Mexican pottery and some brightly painted chairs and a table, a bed with fluffy pillows, and at least a hundred dolls. At least a hundred dolls.

The pitiful gimcrackery, the cheap throw rugs and blankets, the pottery and pictures and pillows and dolls couldn't hide the peeling wall paper, the worn linoleum on the floor, the shabby couch and rickety chairs and table.

Still, it was better than the road.

"How about a beer?" she asked, flirty, eyebrows arched.

"Fine."

She had one of those old wooden ice boxes that opened at the top. I could see a pan underneath, half full of ice drippings. But the beer was cold.

I sat on the couch, belly full of food and lungs full of smoke, drinking my beer and watching the girl. She was perched on a chair, stiff and straight, drinking beer, closing her eyes when she raised the bottle to her lips.

She twisted and turned, cleared her throat.

"Where you heading?" she asked.

I shrugged my shoulders.

"Don't you know?"

Well, I didn't even care. To hell with it. Now was now and yesterday was gone. Tomorrow would be another day.

I shrugged my shoulders, drained my bottle.

"Let's get some rest," I said.

CHAPTER II

The sun was just coming up when I hit the road, and the night past was a sour taste in my mind. I was anxious to be gone from there, anxious to escape the memory of the night.

It was big out there, lonely and big out there. I could see a million miles, drank in the sharp air, the bitingly sharp air fresh from the night just gone. I felt good, strong and alive, free, but I would have felt better over a cup of coffee.

For some reason I felt confident. I even felt like planning ahead. I found myself wanting to find a small town and settle down, burrow down and stay down, become a part of the town, get to know everybody, get everybody to know me.

A car whooshed by, going fast. A couple of kids waved, peered at me through the rear window, made faces. It didn't even make me mad, I just laughed.

The sun climbed higher and it got warmer. A road-runner darted across the road, long tail bobbing, and I chunked a rock at it.

A convertible, robin-egg blue, came at a fast clip, giving me just a glimpse of blonde, long hair blowing in the wind. The car passed me and slowed, swerved, and pulled over to the side and stopped.

She had a flat tire.

That tickled me.

Maybe she'd get her pinkies dirty.

No, she wouldn't. Some jerk would stop and fix her tire for her, some married jerk with five kids at home, some timid jerk hoping he'd get somewhere with the babe in the robin-egg blue convertible.

She got out of the car and walked around it, stooping to look at the tires, kicking them. She wore shorts and she had long legs, flashing legs that looked white in the distance but turned tan as I approached, until finally I could see they were deeply tanned, golden brown tanned, beautifully proportioned, long and lovely.

I walked to the car and stood watching.

The rest of her was lovely, all lovely. Her blouse was high-necked, buttoned to the top, long-sleeved and prim except for its tight fit that proved all of her was lovely. Her face was tanned, too, the lips full and scarlet, wide, bow-shaped naturally and not shaped with the scarlet lip stick she wore. Her eyes were blue and slanted, the eyebrows dark and carefully shaped to emphasize the slant of her eyes.

She smiled a dazzling smile, white teeth showing, and even her eyes smiled.

"I'm glad to see you," she said.

"This is the second time you've seen me," I said. She frowned, wrinkling her brow, looked puzzled, and still smiled.

"Beg pardon?"

"You saw me the first time when you passed me."

"Oh."

"I'm afoot," I said. "My feet hurt. Your car has plenty of room."

"I'm sorry," she said.

"You're sorry now. You wouldn't be sorry if you hadn't had a flat tire."

Her laughter gurgled. "You're right," she said. "Well, run along. Someone will stop."

"I'll fix your tire."

"Never mind," she said. Her eyes turned frosty and the smile went away.

"I'll fix it," I said.

She stood back and watched as I got the key out of the car, opened the trunk, pulled out the tools. I didn't talk and she didn't talk the whole time it took me to change the tire.

When I'd finished putting the tools away the girl had her purse open.

"How much do I owe you?" she asked.

"Nothing."

She had a bill in her hand. "I insist," she said.

"I didn't fix your tire for money."

She smiled, shrugged. "Well, thank you," she said. "Thank you very much."

Without another word, without another glance, she got into her car and drove away.

Sometimes the anger boils up black inside me, like a suffocating cloud, slow and easy, until everything is black and angry, and sometimes the anger bursts in a shower of red gold green.

Like now.

And just as suddenly the anger was gone.

I'd see her again.

Someday I'd see her again. I knew it, because it had to be.

She was lovely.

A big truck, a semi, came barreling down the road, and I didn't even bother to lift my thumb. But the truck stopped. Of all the fool luck, the truck stopped. I climbed in the cab and screwed myself into the corner of the seat and the driver let her roll. He was hauling pipe and it was heavy, but he sent that rig across country and the miles fell behind.

We rode until mid-afternoon and by that time I was groggy. My belly rumbled. My mind was a little fuzzy, too. You know how it is when you're so hungry your belly aches and grumbles and tightens up into a knot as if some big sore was eating away and drawing away and pulling away at your insides. I was that way.

The skinny waitress had been asleep when I left her house, mouth wide open asleep, face wrinkled and sallow and drawn asleep, neck thin and scrawny and corded asleep, ugly as hell asleep.

So I'd left without my breakfast.

The trucker pulled in at one of those stucco places beside the road, all signs and neon, fly specked and dirty, gravel-yarded and beer can littered. We went inside and right away I knew it wasn't the home cooking that caused the driver to stop. A swishy hipped waitress with curly blonde hair, short curly blonde hair, was the attraction. She came over to the booth and leaned down to clean the table. Her type always does. Her two top buttons were unbuttoned. I knew they would be. She leaned over more than was necessary.

I knew she would.

First she leaned toward the trucker, the big greasy trucker with the yellowed teeth, and began wiping the table top. Then she turned my way, giving me an eye full. The trucker didn't like that.

I didn't mind, just pulled my eyes away from where they wanted to look and pretended not to notice when the big boy patted the girl's fanny.

It was food I wanted.

More than anything else.

The dump was the same as a thousand others. Half a dozen booths along one wall, a counter along the other, a juke box and a cigarette machine and the usual number of punch boards, the usual amount of gimcrackery on shelves. Clocks that look like cats, with pendulums for tails. Dolls and knives and key chains. There were signs you'd expect to see. Stuff like WE DON'T TRUST OURSELVES SO WHY SHOULD WE TRUST YOU, and THE BANK WON'T SERVE FOOD IF WE DON'T CASH CHECKS.

"What'll it be?" the waitress asked.

"Apple pie and coffee," the trucker said.

"Coffee and doughnut," I said, wondering what the traffic would bear.

The waitress hovered around, talking to the trucker and eyeing me, but I was enjoying the doughnut and coffee too much to worry about her. I sipped the coffee slowly, took small bites of the doughnut and chewed every ounce of flavor from each bite, made it last. When the coffee was half gone I filled the cup with water, dipped in four heaping spoons of sugar and sipped it slowly. The waitress noticed.

"How about another doughnut?" she asked.

"Thanks, no."

The trucker finished his pie in about three bites and drank his coffee. He pulled a cigarette out of his shirt pocket and lighted up. It smelled good.

"Give me a cigarette, Charlie," the girl said.

He fished out the pack and handed it over. She took one and tossed it to me, took another for herself, dug matches out of the silly little pocket on her apron and gave me a light.

The trucker didn't like that, either.

"I gotta roll," he said. "See you next trip."

"Hurry back," the girl said.

Charlie turned to me. "Guess I'll be dropping you here," he said.

"How come? I'm going your way."

He shrugged. "Too close to home. We're not suppose to pick up hikers."

"Give the guy a break," the blonde said. "I've seen you haul plenty of hikers past here."

"Sorry," the big fellow said. "I got called on the carpet. Can't take a chance."

"Forget it," I said. "Wouldn't want to get you in trouble."

He started walking toward the door.

I was suppose to pay for the snack.

"Hey, Charlie," the blonde called.

"Yeah?"

He was sucking a toothpick.

"That'll be fifty cents. I love you and all that, but we can't dish out free grub."

I drew a dirty look from Charlie.

"How come fifty cents?" he asked. "I only had pie and coffee."

"Fifty cents," the babe said.

Charlie shrugged again, threw me another dirty look and paid up.

I drank my coffee and smoked my cigarette. The blonde sat on a stool, legs crossed and skirt high, leaning back against the counter to get the last fraction of an inch of out-thrust to her breasts, and gave me the eye.

"Thanks for the coffee and doughnut," I said, just to have something to say.

"Charlie paid," she said.

"You made him."

She sighed, a heavy sigh, eyelids fluttery. "Why is it all the nice looking ones are broke?" she asked.

I grinned, careful to show my teeth. "Women take us for all our money," I said.

"You're conceited," she said. She simpered.

They all do. I could have gone through the whole line, what I'd say and what she'd say.

"My husband owns the joint."

"Oh."

She laughed.

"He's in Colorado," she said. "On vacation."

"Oh?"

She laughed again. "Don't be getting ideas," she said. "I do what I feel like doing when I want to do it."

I wished I had another doughnut but I wasn't going to ask.

"It's time I hit the road," I said.

"What's your hurry?" Her voice was tight, strained. "You in a hurry to get somewhere?"

"Not in a hurry to get somewhere," I said. "I just always seem to be in a hurry to get away from where I am."

"That's why you're broke."

"Guess so. Well, it was nice talking to you. Thanks again for the feed."

She didn't answer. Just slid off the stool and walked to the back of the room, jiggling her rear end.

Nice.

I was still hungry.

CHAPTER III

It was hot. The wind was blowing and it was full of sand that stung like buckshot. The road, black asphalt, was bubbling, actually bubbling, shiny slick, stretching off like a black ribbon, straight as a string for what looked like a hundred empty miles.

There was a beer sign beside the road and I leaned against it, squinting my eyes against the sun.

Time dragged.

My face was scratchy, I needed a shave and a bath, didn't even own a razor.

The door of the café squeaked and I turned to look. Blondie was standing in the doorway of the café, not looking at me, posed as all hell.

I heard the sound of a motor.

The car was coming from a side road, one of those dirt roads that take off from the highway and seemingly go nowhere. It was a pickup truck, shabby and battered, but it was moving fast toward the highway. I watched, wondering which way it would turn, and it turned my way. Then I watched to see if it would head for the café, but it didn't.

A big guy with one of those cowboy hats was driving. He slid to a stop and yelled at me. I moved, opened the door and slid in beside him.

He looked like a cowboy, brown as leather, dressed in blue jeans and khaki shirt, even boots.

"It's too hot to stand out there without a hat," he said. "That sun's murder."

"You said it."

"Where you headed?"

"Where you going?"

"Onarka."

"Then I'm going to Onarka."

He raised his eyebrows. "Good town," he said. "Did you go inside the café?"

"Yeah."

"Was Chesty all alone?"

"The blonde?"

"Yeah."

"She said she was."

He laughed, a deep laugh. "You get fixed up?"

"No."

"You should have. She's always ready."

The big fellow let me out in Onarka, but Onarka wasn't the town I was looking for. It was the kind of dump I wouldn't be caught dead in after dark, one of those little built-around-the-square deals with farmers and ranchers sitting on their heels in the shade. Some sat in the shade of the moth-eaten stores. Others sat under stunted hackberry trees in front of the courthouse.

The pickings looked pretty slim.

All the loafers watched me. One grizzled old boy squirted tobacco juice near my feet, but I didn't look his way. He wasn't worth getting excited about.

A little knot of men burst around the corner at the end of the block, huddled together.

I could hear laughter, shouts, squeals, but couldn't see what was going on.

And then I saw.

A fat boy ran out of the ring of men, his mouth open, a shrill cry trailing him, running as if the hounds of hell had hold of the seat of his pants. He was scared, bad scared.

He wasn't all there, either.

His face was square, vacant, and the expression was almost the expression of the idiot, almost but not quite.

A big boy was chasing him, a big boy in blue denims and T-shirt, wearing boots and a wide belt with lots of silver, lots of buckle.

There was something in the big boy's hand, but not until he neared me could I see what it was.

A snake.

A tiny little snake, not much longer than your finger, and the big boy was scaring the simpleton with it.

Without thinking, without having time to think, I stuck out my foot and tripped the goon, watched him sprawl, watched the little snake wriggle out of his hand and slide off the walk.

The simpleton stopped and turned around, grinned at me, mouthed something, winked.

He should worry.

The big kid got up. He was young, maybe twenty, but big and quick and mad. Plenty mad. His face was red. He didn't say a word, just dusted off his pants and began hitching up his belt.

There was no way to avoid a fight. I'd walked through his yard, lifted my leg in his yard, and he'd do more than bark.

It started without a word. A crowd collected, silently, and the big boy waded in. He came in a crouch, not fast and not slow, on his toes, jabbing with his left and keeping his right cocked. All I could do was dance and feel him out and I didn't feel strong enough to do that for long.

It didn't last long.

He must have tagged me with his right, but I never saw it coming. Something just exploded in my face and the sidewalk bounced up and hit me in the back. I wasn't out, but I might as well have been. By the time they picked me up the sheriff was tapping me on the shoulder.

"Come along, punk."

"When I'm able."

"You can walk. Come along." He jerked my arm and I tried to pull away, so he clouted me across the face with the back of his hand.

It hurt.

My head cleared and pulsing singing throbbing rage came up from nowhere, made me strong, made me want to kill, made me want to get the sheriff's throat between my hands so I could squeeze and squeeze and keep on squeezing.

They pulled me off, but I left the sheriff in pretty bad shape. His face was clawed and scratched, his shirt was torn to shreds, and the mark of my hands stayed on his throat for a while.

So I landed in the clink.

They fed me at sundown. Beans and cornbread and buttermilk. It wasn't bad.

I slept like a baby.

Onarka didn't look any better the next morning. The sheriff came in bright and early, icy mac, polite as the devil, and I figured he'd pistol whip me out of town.

He asked me questions instead.

What's your name.... Where you from.... Where you headed....

He badgered me for thirty minutes, and then he let me go.

"Just don't come back," he said.

"I won't."

It wasn't a long walk out of town. No traffic. A road sign made a good leaning post, so I leaned a while and then backed off and chunked pebbles at the A in P A L E Y. According to the sign, it was fifteen miles to Paley.

A few cars came by but I was still standing there at two o'clock. A hayseed in a jalopy finally picked me up, but he was going two miles down the road. Where he let me out was the northwest corner of hell, dusty dry and hot.

There wasn't even grass in the ditches. As far as I could see the land rolled and heaved in gentle dunes.

Walking was better than standing, so I walked. My feet got hot and began to hurt, but standing still didn't help any. After a while I saw some cow skulls over in the pasture, and then I began seeing the rotting carcasses of coyotes hanging across the fence.

I was thirsty. All I could think about was how thirsty I was. The bright sunlight hurt my eyes and I got a headache and my feet were screaming.

I walked in the ditch, but the sand got in my shoes, so I headed back for the highway. It was then I heard a dry, scratchy, rattling noise and looked down and saw a big rattler all coiled up and vibrating his tail. The fool thing scared me. I jumped.

After that I lost all track of time, just heel-and-toed-it down the line, staggering a little bit, coming to now and then to see things clearly and to think clearly, only to fall back into a sort of half daze. One time I came out of it long enough to notice the sun going down, realized it would get cooler, noticed I was biting my tongue and that my lips were swollen and cracked, and then I went back into another stupor.

The rain brought me out of it for good.

It was cold, that rain, and it fell in sheets. I just stood there with my face up and my mouth open, made a scoop out of my hands, stuck out my tongue, held my eyes open and let tree water rinse my eyeballs.

I was inside the city limits of Paley before I realized it. The rain came again, and it was dark as your mother's womb. The town was in a hollow, so I didn't see any lights until I hit the edge of town. It startled me. One minute I was out in the middle of nowhere, in the dark, and the next minute I was at the edge of town, with acres of lights stretching out before me. Dark blobs of houses loomed beside the road. A dog barked. Somewhere a foolish rooster crowed.

Maybe this was it, the town.

I passed a service station with a row of lights across its front. I could see batteries and tires and cans of oil inside, but the attendant was nowhere in sight. I went across and looked inside for a water cooler. There was a pop box, but no cooler.

The attendant wasn't around and there was the cash register. I drank from a hose.

The rain stopped and I walked the streets, through the residential section, and the streets were lighted. The houses were neat, with grassy yards and trees. It was a good town.

I wondered what would happen if I knocked at a door and asked for food. Somebody would call the police, probably.

Main street was like all small town main streets, starting at the railroad at one end and snaking straight as a string, with the better business section starting two or three blocks from the tracks, stretching four or five blocks, then petering out and becoming shabbier and shabbier until, finally, way out at the edge there were nothing but honky-tonks and service stations and tin garages.

I clopped along, my mind in my stomach. I would have vomited if there'd been anything to vomit.

There was a café in every block, but I walked along until I found one with dirty windows. It was crowded. I wandered in, took a seat, ordered a dinner. Some hashed meat, browned potatoes, string beans, plenty of bread and butter. When I'd finished, I ordered coffee.

The man next to me got up to leave. He left a quarter by his plate, I grabbed the quarter and followed him to the front, dropped the quarter in the cigarette machine, grabbed the cigarettes and stood by the door until the man had paid his check. Then I followed him out the door, moved fast away from there, turned off the main drag and walked in darkness, walked in darkness down a side street, walked in darkness, period.

The night wind came up, cold, and I started looking for a place to sleep. I was tired, dead tired, cold and tired and sleepy and low down blue.

There was a light in the next block and I heard a rumbling sound. Newspaper office. Maybe I could sweep the joint out for the price of a flop.

It was a frame building with big glass windows in front. I went inside. There were a couple of desks and a table with a typewriter on it, a big map on the wall. A door, bearing a sign, COMPOSING ROOM, was closed.

The thrump, thrump, thrump of the press was deafening.

I pushed open the composing-room door. A young man, dark and good looking, was feeding an old beat-up press, hand feeding it, and a girl was feeding a folder. She wore slacks and a man's shirt and she was stacked. Her hair was jet black and hung to her shoulders. Even in the poor light I could see she had tiny freckles on her nose. Freckles get me. What I liked most about her, though, were her lips. The lower lip was thicker than the upper, pouty. She looked up, saw me, smiled.

She was a looker.

An old man, wearing a green eyeshade, was stooped over the stone. Five or six kids were on the floor folding papers. The old man looked up, smiled, nodded.

"I've no place to sleep," I yelled. "Mind if I stay here?"

He couldn't hear me, just nodded and shrugged his shoulders.

I stepped closer. "I'd like to sleep here!" I yelled. "I've no place to stay!"

"Suits me!"

I watched him for a while, glancing now and then at the girl. Every time I looked I'd find her looking at me. She smiled every time. She was zipping the papers through the folder, big sheets of printed papers. She'd grab a sheet by the corner, flip it, and it would start through the folder, stopping and folding and starting again, zipping along on tapes. She was good at her job. The papers were piling up at the bottom of the folder. I moved over there, picked up a load and carried them over to the kids.

She smiled, said something, I couldn't hear what she said, so I went over and stood behind her.

"Thanks!" she said, looking back over her shoulder.

"You're welcome!"

I watched her for a while. Once I looked up at the man on the press. He was looking at me and he smiled.

"Would you like to try?" the girl asked.

"Yes."

She stepped back and I took her place. I tried to pick up a sheet of the paper, but it stuck. Static electricity. I gave it a shake. Some rollers caught the other end of the paper and pulled it out of my hand. It went through the folder crooked, jammed up, and the girl flipped a switch to stop the machinery.

"I'm sorry," I said.

"No harm done," she said, leaning close so I could hear.

She pulled the paper from the folder and walked over to the press, reached up and pulled at the pressman's trousers leg. He looked down, leaned down, listened to her. I could see her lips move but couldn't hear what she was saying.

The pressman turned off the press.

Sudden quiet.

It hurt my ear drums, that quiet.

The pressman stepped down and came across to me. He held out his hand.

"I'm Jerry Norton," he said. "This is my sister, Melissa."

"Glad to know you," I said, taking his hand. "I'm Dun Lattner."

"Let's have some coffee," the girl said.

She pulled a little hot plate from a shelf beneath the stone and plugged it in. I was careful not to stare, careful not to let her brother or the old man see me stare, but I tingled, felt my heart speed, noticed my breathing was faster, felt a stirring stirring stirring in my belly, in my groin.

"Hope you don't mind my barging in," I said to her brother. "I'll be truthful. I just hit town and I'm broke and wet. I'm nothing. Thought I might find a place to sleep."

He pointed at all the paper on the floor.

"We'll be working all night," he said. "You can curl up in the paper and sleep."

He couldn't have been more than thirty, dark like his sister, thin-faced, good-looking, long straight nose, full lips, dark brown eyes and black hair, heavy black eyebrows, high cheek bones. He was well built. Weighed, maybe, a hundred and sixty or seventy.

The girl was something else.

Maybe she was five feet. Like I said, her hair was black and it hung to her shoulders, her skin creamy, her eyes dark and dreamy. I can't describe her face, but you've seen heart-shaped faces. Little pointed chin.

I've seen a lot of beautiful women.

This one took the cake, first prize, hands down.

The old printer knocked off work, wiped his hands on his apron, and came over. He stuck out his hand. I took it. His name, he said, was Herb. Just Herb.

Friendly crowd.

The girl had the pot on the hot plate and it was beginning to perk.

Coffee smelled good.

Jerry Norton offered me a cigarette and the girl poured coffee into battered cups. We chatted. The kid owned the paper and he had big plans.

While he talked I sized up what he had. Not much. Battered equipment, worn out, so all he had was a dream and a lot of guts. The girl, Melissa, helped him out on press nights. Her name was Melissa Marlin, not Norton, and I felt better when she told me her husband had been killed in Germany. In fact, I was glad and I felt selfish that this girl was so unattached.

They were nice people, but I was sorry for Norton. He was bucking a daily, a chain deal, and having tough sledding.

We finished our coffee and they went back to work. I watched for a while and then I couldn't take it any longer. I went to the back and raked up pile of paper and turned in. Even the noise of the press didn't bother me.

It was broad daylight when I awakened and I had the building to myself. The coffee pot and cups were on the stone, along with a couple of doughnuts. They were nice people.

The front door was locked.

I found a washroom in the back. There was a can of coffee on a shelf, so I started brewing coffee and moseyed up to the front while I waited. There was a metal money box in one of the desks, unlocked. I opened it.

Four ones and some change.

I took four-bits. They wouldn't miss it.

The doughnuts were stale but I ate them. I drank almost the whole pot of coffee. There were papers on the floor and I read one. It was a tri-weekly, THE GLOBE. I noticed the dateline. It was Sunday. So Jerry and Melissa wouldn't be down today.

I started out the front door, but there was the money box. Fifty cents wouldn't help me much, so I took a dollar. I closed the box, started to close the drawer, then saw the razor.

Why not shave?

There was a cracked mirror in the washroom and I looked like the devil. Tough, I looked, with a heavy black beard and matted hair. I rubbed gritty soap on my face and shaved, nicked myself a couple of times. My face smarted when I'd finished but it felt good to have the whiskers off. Next, I washed my hair, rinsed it good, took off my undershirt and used it for a cloth to bathe my body. Then, when I'd combed my hair and rolled my sleeves, I didn't look bad at all.

The key to the front door was in the money box. For some fool reason I decided not to keep the money I'd taken, but I took the key. The way I figured it, the Norton kid wouldn't care if I slept there again.

The town was pretty dead.

Church bells were ringing. Cars rolled quietly along the streets, filled with people headed for church. Downtown, on main street, a few men lounged around, leaning against parking meters or against walls, talking, eyeing the high school girls in their blue jeans and tails-out white shirts. The men were eyeing the young chicks and I got a kick out of the way the girls let on they didn't know they were being watched, but stuck out their tight little breasts and wiggled their firm and jouncy little tails just the same.

I moseyed down the street all the way to the railroad station and stood looking at the wrong side of the tracks.

Maybe I should catch a freight.

But I decided against it.

This town had something. A man might do all right in such a town. Besides, the girl, Melissa, interested me. I wanted to see her again.

So I decided to stay.

Maybe I could get a job.

Hell is paved with good intentions. I hadn't taken money from the newspaper cash box because Norton had been nice to me. But beggars can't be choosers and there's no use worrying about the fit of your britches when your tail is hanging out.

I went back to the newspaper office and took two bucks from the cash drawer.

They didn't serve beer on Sunday mornings. The pool rooms were open but beer wasn't served until one o'clock.

So I had a real breakfast and tipped the waitress a quarter.

I walked out on main street, north from the depot, until the business district was far behind. There were honky-tonks open, with girls in shorts out front, but they weren't serving beer. There were oil field supply houses at the edge of town, big places with fleets of trailer-trucks parked in the yards, pipe stacked all over the place. Two or three of the places had help wanted signs out, but it looked too much like work.

My feet hurt, so I went back to town. I went into a pool hall and watched high school kids play. They weren't so hot, so I let them talk me into playing. I won six bucks, all they had, and gave them a buck so they could see a show.

There were two movies on the main drag, both showing Westerns. I killed a couple of hours watching Gary Cooper and then I had a steak. That made two meals for the day. I was getting fat. The pool halls were serving beer and I treated myself to one bottle. By that time, it was five o'clock.

I jiggled the key in my pocket, wondering whether to stay or go. I thought of the girl, Melissa, and for the first time in a long time I thought of a girl as more than just a bed companion. Sure, I thought of her that way, too. With the face and body she had, how could I help it? But there was more to it than desire, more to it than physical attraction.

That kind of thinking can be dangerous. Maybe more dangerous than taking it on the lam.

All of a sudden I had my mind made up. I'd blow the town. First, though, I decided to return the key to its place in the metal box, maybe leave a note thanking Norton for his kindness. Then, maybe, I'd head for California or Old Mexico.

The only trouble was that Melissa was waiting in the GLOBE office.

She was wearing a print dress, a little girl dress, and a ribbon in her hair. She took my breath. Part of her appeal came from that little-girl look, that helpless little-girl look, and the other part from the full beauty of her body. Contrast.

"Why, hello," she said, "I was afraid you'd left town."

I pulled the key from my pocket and held it up. "I took the key so I could get back in," I said. "But I hope you don't think...."

"That you were going to rob the joint?" She had dimples.

"Yeah."

"If we'd thought that," she said, "we wouldn't have left you here. You have an honest face."

"First time I've heard that," I said. "But I've already robbed the place. I took two dollars, but I can pay it back now."

She stepped back from the door, hands locked behind her back, turned around, arching her back, strutting a little on tip-toe, and went over to the desk and sat down on it.

"Tell me about you," she said.

"Not much to tell. I'm just a bum."

She laughed. "No," she said. "You're not old enough to be a confirmed bum. I thought about you today and I decided you probably got out of the army not too long ago and that you're looking around the country before deciding to settle down."

I lifted my eyebrows. "Something like that," I said.

"Your parents had a job all picked out for you the day you got your discharge," she said, narrowing her eyes a little, dreaming it up as she went along. "But you rebelled. Your nerves were shot and you weren't ready to settle down."

"Go on," I said.

"Maybe they had a girl picked out for you, too."

It wasn't a question, but almost a question.

I just grinned.

"Why don't you settle down here?" she asked. "You'd like it here."

"Maybe I would."

"Maybe my brother can help you find a job."

"Fine."

"Now," she said, hopping off the desk. "I've told you all about you, so now you tell me all about you."

"I don't know all about me," I said.

"What are you looking for? What do you want?"

"That's the trouble. I haven't decided yet." I kept my voice low, light.

"Everybody wants something."

"Oh, I want lots of things. But nothing very badly."

She frowned. By now she was standing right in front of me, almost touching me, her head back, looking up.

"That's bad," she said.

"Yeah."

"You really don't know what you want?"

"Really. My trouble is that I want everything I want *now*. Right now. I don't want to wait, I don't want to start because then I'll know it'll take all my life to get what I want."

"I've felt like that," she said.

This had to stop.

"Maybe I'd better go."

"Go where?"

"Away from here."

"Why?"

The little devil was breathing hard.

She felt it, too.

"The other side of the fence, I guess."

She stepped back, cocked that little head, put her hands on her hips and looked me over from head to foot.

"You're a big boy now," she said. "Why don't you make yourself settle down and act grown up?"

"Maybe I'm afraid of what I'll find out about myself," I said, half teasing now, baiting her.

Give a woman a problem child and she's happy.

"Find out what?" she wanted to know.

"That I don't have it, maybe. I was a pretty good fighter once," I said. "But I quit before I found out whether or not I was any good."

"Maybe you just haven't found out what you're good at," she argued. "Maybe you're better than you think."

"Maybe," I said, losing interest. "Anyway, think I'd better go."

"Go on, then," she said.

I wanted to kiss her.

So I did.

She kissed back.

It was like, well, I don't know what. Like kissing a blow torch, so flaming was that kiss. It was like drinking a pint of corn liquor on an empty stomach, like being drunk on wine, pleasantly drunk.

She had to stand on tip-toe to put her arms around my neck, and I crushed her, lifted her, pressed her body to mine, strained against her, felt her soft flesh melt into mine, strain against me.

And then I ended it.

"You'll stay?"

Her voice shook.

"Yeah."

"You'll get a job?"

I nodded.

She smiled.

Women are in there pitching every minute. They never let down. They're strongest when men are weakest.

"You'll spend the night here," she said. "I'll be down early in the morning."

"Wait," I said, stepping forward.

She laughed and stepped around me.

"I don't trust you," she said. "For that matter, I don't trust myself. We'll talk more tomorrow."

She was out the door and gone and I stood there feeling like a fool.

Somewhere, not far off, a train whistled.

My feet had the itch but the rest of me didn't feel like moving.

I went to the back and lay down on a pile of paper.

CHAPTER IV

I thought of the girl, dreamed of the girl, came wide awake at break of day with my mind made up, I'd stay away from her, let her be, forget her completely.

Breakfast put me in business, almost made me ambitious, and I walked the town looking for work. The oil-supply houses still had help-wanted signs out, but it still looked too much like work. I wasn't that ambitious.

There was a big stucco night club at the edge of town. Beyond that, off the road, stood a row of straggling honky-tonks, box-like and paint-peeled. One last service station hid behind its signs beside the road and, beyond that, there was nothing but the framework of a church with a tiny steeple. Men were working there and the sounds of their hammers and saws sounded better than the jukebox music from the honky-tonks.

It was a funny place for a church, but it looked like a job.

I circled the church and stood around watching the carpenters. A tall man, dressed in a worn black suit, was sitting on a keg, looking my way. He nodded and I nodded back. He had a good face, long and thin, eyes that were blacker than brown, shaggy eyebrows. A poor man's Abe Lincoln.

"Are you the boss?" I asked.

"Well," he said, thinking it over. "Well, I guess you could say I'm the boss."

"I'm looking for work."

"Are you a carpenter?"

I had to laugh. "Always mash my thumb when I use a hammer," I said. "But I'm strong and willing to work, so there ought to be something I could do."

He stood up and offered me his hand. "I'm Brother Brock," he said.

"Dun Lattner."

"Would you be willing to haul lumber and nails and clean away debris and make yourself useful?"

"When do I start?"

"The pay is eighty cents an hour. That's all we can afford. Most of our work is done by our members."

"I'll take it."

It didn't sound like much of a job, but the carpenters kept me hopping. I carried bundles of shingles on my back, up a ladder in the hot sun. Twice I took a battered old truck to town for lumber, loaded and unloaded it myself. My hands were blistered before noon and my back was a solid ache by mid-afternoon. The more it hurt the harder I worked, and I grinned when I thought of the way I'd ducked those oil-field jobs because they seemed too much like work.

Once, just before five, I took a load of scrap across the highway to burn. Just as I reached it a car came along, a blue convertible.

It was the blonde babe, the blonde with the flat tire, the blonde who left me standing beside a desert road. She wasn't driving fast and I got a good look at her. There was no doubt about it at all. It was the same babe.

Maybe she lived here. Maybe I'd see her. Maybe some day I could claw my way up, make some money, get even. I got a kick just thinking about it.

Brother Brock paid me for six hours of work, four dollars and eighty cents. It was a good thing because I had two-bits in my pocket.

"Come on back tomorrow, son," he said. "You're a good worker."

"Thanks."

"I'm pretty good at sizing men up," he said. "I knew you were a good boy the minute I laid eyes on you."

"Thanks again," I said.

Brother Brock let me off a couple of hours and I headed for the other side of the tracks, figuring room rent would be cheaper there. I looked all over and was about to give up when I saw Nora Simmons. She looked to be around fifty years old, maybe sixty.

She was standing at an upstairs window when first I saw her, idly staring out on the street, the wide dusty street, lost in a world of her own.

It was a big house, well kept, but it was a lonely looking house.

I had it taped right from the start.

The woman disappeared from the window, but in a moment she came out on the porch with a broom in her hands. She began to sweep, not looking up, but I could see her stealing peeks at me.

She had white hair but she looked spry enough. She wasn't fat, but plump and surprisingly enough her face was thin and wrinkled. She wore too much powder and lipstick and she was hideous.

I went through the gate and up the walk, paused at the foot of the steps.

"Excuse me." I said.

She looked up, startled, and I almost shuddered.

"My name is Dun Lattner," I said. "I'm looking for a place to board and room."

"Well, for goodness sakes" she said. "You slipped up on me!"

"I'm sorry. Hope I didn't startle you."

"Not a bit. No, it's just that when I'm busy I just don't hear or see what's going on about me. I'm Nora Simmons."

I gave her my best smile, the tender lost smile, and I could almost see her melt.

"I'm working on the new church out at the edge of town," I said. "Brother Brock said I'd probably find a good place to stay down here."

"Well, now," she said. "I don't make a practice of taking in boarders, but you seem like a nice young man."

"I'd be no bother, ma'am. If you have room to spare, that is."

"Room to spare?" She giggled. "There are rooms in this house I haven't seen in months!"

"You live here alone?"

"All alone. My husband passed on last year, you see."

"I'm very sorry to hear it."

"Sometimes I get so lonesome I could scream. Of course, there's the church. And I have many friends. But, somehow, I just feel that there's not a soul in the world that cares whether I live or die."

"I know what you mean."

"You do? And you so young?"

"I've been alone all my life."

She clucked with her tongue, like an old mother hen, and I knew she was hooked.

"Your life's ahead of you," she said. "At least you have that to cheer you. Take me, now. My life's behind me."

"Aw, ma'am, you've got a long row to hoe."

Nora Simmons laughed. "Come look at your room," she said.

"Maybe we'd better talk about money first," I said. "You see, I'm broke. I got a job working on a new church building, but I don't have any money."

"That's all right. Room and board won't be more than... well, let's say eight dollars a week."

"Sounds fair."

"Then it's settled. Come look at your room and then you can go get your things."

I laughed. "All I own is on my back."

"You do need looking after," she said.

"I'll tell you what. I'll look at the room this evening. Right now I'd better get back to the job."

She was sitting on the porch swing when I turned the corner.

I thought about Nora Simmons all afternoon, couldn't get her out of my mind.

She probably had money.

About three o'clock I stopped by the water can for a drink of water, stood there until Brother Brock walked up.

"Did you find a room, son?" he asked.

"Sure did. Across the tracks. A woman, Nora Simmons, is going to rent me a room and feed me for eight bucks a week."

"That's cheap enough," the preacher said. "But, then, Nora can afford it."

"Do you know her?"

"I knew her husband. He owned quite a bit of property around here. Left Nora pretty well off, they say."

"She seems like a nice old lady."

"I'm sure she is."

I wondered how much money she had.

Nora's house was really something. The furniture wasn't bad. Old and massive and ugly, sure, but good stuff. There were some pretty good pictures in some of the rooms and some pretty bad pictures in other rooms. The rugs were worn, but still good, and the wallpaper was good, the woodwork clean and white. There were twenty rooms, most of them dusty and unused, musty and dark. Nora could have a fortune just renting out rooms.

I learned the town pretty well, heard some of the gossip, read the papers and walked the streets and visited the stores. It was a good town, a prosperous town, just the right size.

Nora didn't mind when I spent all my first week's salary on clothing and wasn't able to pay my rent.

"Pay it later," she said, a smile on that prune face of hers. "A man can't get ahead in this old world unless he looks respectable."

Her false teeth clicked when she talked.

The way she dressed killed me. Her dresses were short, long waisted and short, and her hats were flapper hats, close fitting to the head, covering the ears, covering both sides of her face. She wore black silk stockings and pumps.

I flattered her.

"You look young enough to be my sister," I'd say. "I swear I don't know how you do it."

That gave her a bang, made her worse, and she'd deck herself out in brightly colored dresses, all cut alike, all too long in the waist and too tight, too short. Maybe she was a good soul, but she'd have looked more natural with a mug of beer in one hand and a cigarette in the other.

On Sunday she insisted I go to church with her, simpered when she introduced me to her friends as her boarder, stressing that word, underlining it, hoping somebody would make something of it, hoping for talk.

We went to church again the second Sunday. By that time I was a part of the community, that part of town on the wrong side of the tracks. Nora's part of town, the old part of town.

The church was coming along and there wasn't much left for me to do. Brother Brock hated to let me go, so I told him I'd find something else.

"Finish out the day, Dun," he said. "Take the truck and go to Onarka for me. Go to the Smith Lumber Company and tell them I sent you. They're donating some amber wood for the wainscoting."

I took off in the old truck, nursing it along, remembering how I'd walked that road.

The same loafers sat along the curbs, around the courthouse steps, and I hoped I wouldn't run into the sheriff. I found the lumber company and helped load the truck, and then I decided to get something to drink. For some reason, I walked the block to town, found a pool hall, drank a bottle of beer.

I started to leave and met the sheriff at the door.

He stared.

I stared.

He opened his mouth to say something and I let him have it in the stomach, let him have a right in the stomach, and then I ran.

Right through the middle of town I ran, ducked down an alley, heard a whistle blow.

I flew.

I hit a street, turned left, and had a straight shot at the street leading to the lumber yard. I didn't meet a soul. Not even a car passed. I got in the truck, backed out, circled side streets until I hit the highway, and drove back to Paley.

CHAPTER V

I applied for a police job.

They weren't hiring, but I walked into the police station and talked to the chief, talked to the captain of police, left my application.

"Try the water department, Lattner," the captain said. "They'll probably give you a job. It won't be much, but it'll be a start. Meanwhile, you can be looking around. There's a lot of work here, especially if you want to work in the fields."

"I don't know a thing about oil work," I said. "Maybe I can find something else."

"Come back and see us from time to time, then," the captain said. "We may have something later if you can qualify."

So I went to the water department.

"Ever dig ditches?" an old codger asked me.

"Not until now."

"We pay two bucks an hour."

"I'll give it a whirl."

"Catch the truck at the side of the building at eight o'clock in the morning."

I'd gone into a drug store for razor blades and I ran into Melissa at the door. I bumped her pretty hard with my shoulder, half knocked her off balance so she had to take a step back.

"I beg your pardon," I said.

"It's all right," she said, and smiled. "Gosh, I didn't know you were still in town. Why haven't I seen you? Where've you been? What've you been doing?"

She took my breath. This time she wore her hair in pigtails and she looked like six years old until you dropped your eyes.

"I've been getting established," I said. "Honest, I was going to call as soon as I got my feet on the ground."

She looked me over pretty good and grinned. "You seem to have your feet on the ground," she said. "You're clean and you're wearing good clothes and your hair is cut and you don't need a shave. I'd say you've done all right."

"Can't complain," I said. "How about a drink?"

"Sure."

We sat at the counter and sucked cokes through straws, ill at ease, both trying to talk at the same time or lapsing into dumb silence.

"Look," she said. "If you're not going to say it, I will. Come out and see me."

The way she said it put a lump in my throat, and it wasn't just the way she said it but it was the way she looked, too, the look in her eyes.

"You make me feel like a heel," I said. "You don't have to ask me to come see you."

"Don't I?"

"Tell me where you live."

"Forty-six-o-eight Oak," she said. "That's at the edge of town."

"Do you live alone?"

"All alone. My brother's married and our parents are dead. John and I bought the house just before he went overseas and...."

"I'll find it."

"Look," she said, "I have an idea. Let's go rabbit hunting."

"With dogs?"

"With guns. We'll take my car and drive across the desert. We can take turns shooting."

"Sounds good. You got guns?"

"Twenty-twos. Can you shoot?"

"Let's go."

Her car was a late model, an Oldsmobile, and she drove it pretty fast.

Her house was really at the edge of town, almost out of town, a neat white frame cottage. I went in with her to get the guns. The house looked lived-in and comfortable, books and magazines everywhere. The guns were in a closet in her bedroom and she gathered up panties and slips and stockings from the bed, scooped them up and stuffed them in a chest drawer, blushing a little.

I grinned at her.

"I'll put on some slacks," she said, "Wait for me in the car."

"Okay." I took the guns outside.

She drove out a country road, across a cattle guard, and then drove across the prairie. We saw jackrabbits jump from clumps of sage, but I didn't have a chance shooting out the car window.

"Sit on the fender," Melissa said.

I got out and sat on the fender, holding on with my left hand, cradling the gun in my right arm. A jack jumped and Melissa swerved the car, stepped on the gas. I tried to lift the gun, turned loose of my hand-hold with my left, snapped a shot and missed.

The car hit a dune and off I went, on my face in the sand, rolled over and over, narrowly missing a clump of cactus.

Melissa stopped the car and jumped out, took one look at me and began to laugh.

I flipped sand in her face.

It went into her eyes, blinded her, and she staggered in circles, rubbing her eyes with her hands. She cried. I went to her, took her in my arms, pulled her down, took my handkerchief and held her hands back, held the lids back, and dabbed the sand from her eyes.

I kissed her.

She turned her face, her lips twisting beneath mine.

"You didn't have to do that," she said.

"And you didn't have to laugh."

Her lips were soft and warm. Her lips drove me wild. I held her close and closer, drowned in her kiss, and let my hands slide over her body.

She pushed my hands away, pulled her head back, tried to speak.

She fought me, twisted and turned and fought me, tried to knee me in the crotch, slashed at my face with her nails, slapped me and pulled my hair.

We rolled in the sand.

She got up to run and I reached out and caught her foot, tripped her. She kicked, got to her hands and knees. My hand slipped, but my fingers caught the leg of her slacks. I pulled her to me, but at the last moment she got to her feet and tried to run. I made it to my knees, hooked my fingers in her belt, tried to pull her down.

The belt broke, buttons popped off, and the slacks slid down over her hips.

She pulled them up, wriggling and squirming, and began to cry.

"I'm sorry," I said. "Honey, I'm sorry."

"Leave me alone," she moaned.

I tried to put my arms around her, tried to hold her close, but she pushed me away.

"I'm sorry," I said. "I shouldn't have treated you that way."

"Why be sorry? That's the way you are, isn't it?"

"I guess it is," I said. "Let's go to town."

Nora thought it was a shame for me to dig ditches for the water department.

"You're too smart for that kind of work," she said. "There must be easier ways to make a living."

"There must be," I said. "Believe me, with a little time to think I'll find an easier way."

I wanted to call Melissa, wanted to apologize again, but decided she'd need time to cool off. I sat in the living room, reading the paper and listening to the radio. Nora went into the kitchen, washed the dishes, and then went upstairs.

There was soft music on the radio. I dropped the paper and closed my eyes.

A noise.

Nora had entered the room. She was wearing a dress that barely covered her knees. Her face was painted and powdered, plastered with paint and powder, and her lips were garish red. She was bare-legged.

Her hair was flowing loose.

The white hair, that gray white hair, stringy and long, was hanging loose, falling about her shoulders.

She was smiling.

Panic seized me, flowed through me, made me sick. I wanted to cry out, wanted to jump up and run from the house.

"How well you look, Nora," I said. "I'd swear you couldn't be more than thirty eight."

CHAPTER VI

Paley belonged to the oil men at seven in the morning, the oil stiffs with their crash helmets and drillers' boots, their khaki clothing bleached almost white from many washings, their tin lunch pails.

The cafés swarmed with the men of the fields. Men clustered at the curbs, waiting for their trucks to roll along. Gears meshed. Men laughed, cursed, grumbled and joked.

I walked through the town to city hall, stood on the sidewalk and waited for my work gang.

A truck turned off the street into the driveway and stopped. A big guy got out of the cab. He must have weighed two hundred and fifty pounds and he looked hard. He didn't wear a hat. His hair was blonde, almost white, making his red face look redder. His eyes were pale blue, almost white.

"You Lattner?" he asked.

"Yeah."

"You gonna work?"

"Yeah."

"Get your tail into the truck, then."

He should have slapped me. I was trembling with anger as I crawled into the truck.

The big boy was gone thirty minutes, finally came out of the fire house with five men. The word for them was motley. One guy was tall and skinny and freckled and one was short and fat. There's always a short, fat guy in a crowd like that. Right away I knew he'd be the butt of all the corny jokes. One of the five was old and shaky, a drunk, and one was just a fuzzy-faced kid. The last one was a tough character, dark and handsome. Even his clothes looked good. I couldn't figure him.

They nodded at me and crawled into the back of the truck, all except the handsome guy. He sat in the cab with the big boy.

"Who's the boss?" I asked.

"His name is Flynn," the old fellow said. "He's poison."

Flynn drove us right through the middle of town.

… once, long ago, the county sent a truck to the orphanage. We'd been loaded in like cattle, but hadn't been told where we were going. We were driven through the town and people stopped on the street to stare. I always remembered that ride, all of it, and remembered the baseball game they'd taken us to see....

The four guys in the back chatted, chaffed each other, with the fat boy getting ribbed the most. I leaned back against the side of the truck and thought of Melissa, wondered whether I should see her again or leave her alone.

We went east on the highway, past the drilling companies and the supply houses, past the last of the honky-tonks and frowzy night clubs, hit open country, flat country studded with derricks gaunt against the sky.

The truck left the highway and ground along a sandy road across the plain, up what would have to pass for a hill in such country, and stopped.

What a prospect.

Already the sun was beating down and I knew why the other men wore big hats. I was hatless.

"You'll get sun stroke," the fat boy said. "Won't last half a day."

"Thanks," I said.

"Tie a handkerchief around your head if you've got one," he said.

"Don't have one."

He pulled a big red bandanna from a hip pocket and handed it over. I thanked him and tied it around my head.

"You look like a pirate," he said.

There was a ditch about a hundred feet long, three feet deep, a narrow ditch stretching across the top of the rise. The Irish boss, Flynn, climbed up in the truck and began tossing out shovels and picks.

"Hit it, men," he said. "You're getting paid for digging dirt."

I grabbed a shovel and followed the others.

My muscles started screaming before I'd been digging an hour. Dirt flew in my face. The wind came up, carrying sand, stinging sand, and blowing my shovels full of dirt right back into my face. Flynn went back to town and brought out a can of water. It was tepid and tasted like mud. My hands got sore and raw. The handkerchief didn't keep the sun from burning my head. I got a headache.

Flynn must have been around some place.

The sun stood still.

It was two weeks to the minute from eight o'clock until noon. Everybody had lunches, but I hadn't brought one, couldn't have eaten. I threw myself to the ground in the shade of the truck and lay there until time to go to work.

Still, I needed the money. Two bucks an hour would set me up... if I could put in enough hours.

Somehow, I don't know how, I lasted until five.

Nora went to a prayer meeting. I stayed home and stared at the telephone, wanting to use it, wanting to call Melissa.

I couldn't figure it. No woman had ever made me think about her twice, until now.

Nora must have been gone an hour when I decided to look around a bit. I didn't have anything in mind, didn't have any idea what I was looking for, but nosed around from room to room, opening drawers and peeking in closets.

There was a cardboard box in a dresser drawer in one of the unused rooms. I opened it, found a pile of papers, old letters, bits of ribbon, a ball of yarn.

I picked up a paper, a folded paper.

It was a will.

My eyes scanned it, scanned the wherefores and herebys, caught the words "to my beloved wife," scanned on, saw the words "all my worldly possessions" and, further down, "all my monies, including insurance in the amount of...."

The front door opened.

I froze.

"Dun?"

"Here I am," I called. "I'm upstairs."

I dropped the paper in the box, shoved the box in the drawer, closed the drawer and went out into the hallway.

"Up here," I called. "I've been exploring."

Nora laughed. "Don't get lost," she said.

"Don't worry," I said. "One thing I can do well... I can find my way around."

Two bucks an hour for eight hours a day comes to sixteen dollars. I worked five days, so that gave me eighty bucks for the week. That would buy me a pretty good suit, a hat and tie, some new shoes.

The fifth day was a scorcher, but the exercise had been good for me. I was holding my own all right, doing as much work as any of the men, more than some.

Five o'clock came and Flynn paid us in cash, paid me first.

He counted sixty bucks into my hand.

"Wait a minute," I said. "Your arithmetic's not so hot."

"That's correct," he said. "Eighty less twenty comes to sixty."

"Eighty less twenty does come to sixty," I said. "But why are you subtracting twenty from eighty in the first place?"

"Don't you know?"

"What is it? Income tax? Social Security? You don't hold that out on these occasional jobs."

"You got a job," Flynn said, "so you know what the deal is. Nobody else is complaining."

I turned to the other men.

"Is that right?" I asked. "Do they hold twenty bucks out of our pay?"

The fat boy nodded.

"Who gets the kickback?" I asked Flynn. "You?"

"Don't start trouble," he said. "Take your sixty bucks and don't come back. Start walking."

"You didn't hire me," I said. "Maybe you can't fire me."

He was big. I sized him up, wondering if I could take him, noticing his big, hairy hands, the size of his wrists, the wide shoulders and narrow waist. He was in good shape, hard and tough.

I boiled over.

"I want my twenty bucks," I said. "Do you give it to me or do I take it?"

He grinned.

"Why don't you try to take it?" he asked. "That ought to be pretty interesting."

The other ditch diggers were licking their chops, hoping to see a fight.

"Get your behind off city property," Flynn said. "Get moving before I kick your twat all the way to town."

"Start kicking," I said.

The devil was wearing drillers' boots. He was wearing heavy oil-field boots, and he kicked out hard and fast. I took the first one on the thigh, but grabbed his heel and spilled him hard. He'd no more than hit the ground before I was on him. I grabbed him by the hair with my left hand, slammed his head back hard into the ground and drove my right into that big red face. I felt the nose give, felt the bones break, and I pounded him again and again, his face a blur but not enough of a blur to keep me from hitting where I wanted to hit.

He was strong and the blows didn't weaken him. They hurt, but didn't weaken. He exploded under me, threw me back hard, so hard I couldn't keep to my feet, but staggered back, reaching back and down so that my hands raked the ground, but still I went down and over.

My head hit the ground, hit a rock, hit something hard.

There was plenty of time.

Flynn moved in slow motion. I saw the ditch diggers scatter, saw them move slowly, so slowly, out of the way. A buzzard circled overhead, the only thing moving at normal speed, and I began to move in slow motion, began to gather myself, began to get to my feet.

A car passed on the highway, creeping along, taking forever to pass by.

Something seemed to click. The ditch diggers were scrambling out of the way and the buzzard circled faster. The car on the highway zoomed past.

Flynn was coming at me.

The big man thought he had me. He came charging in and he looked a mile high, a mile broad. Fear of those big fists helped my speed, and I got up, went in, went low in a dive and clipped him shin high, knocked him head over tail gate.

He landed on his head and he wasn't so chipper when he got up. He didn't look so tall and wide, either, and worry showed in his eyes, on his face.

I figured he'd been cut down to my size, so I went in.

He threw a few, grunting, powerful blows, roundhouse lefts and rights, knockout punches if they'd landed. I buried a right in his gut, heard the wind whoosh out of him, and then started cutting away at his face.

It was fun.

I made a mess of his face, gave him scars to carry to his grave. You can do that if you know how to flick your wrist just so. He was game and he could take a punch. I could knock him down but I couldn't keep him down. Even after he was too weak to fight, let his hands drop, stood there with blood covering his face, I couldn't keep him down.

No use breaking my hands.

Wiley pulled me off after they'd seen enough blood. They pulled me back and Flynn sat down.

"Give me the money now, Flynn," I said.

He mouthed something but I couldn't understand what he said. The fat boy went over to him and dug in his pocket, came up finally with some bills, peeled off two tens and handed them to me.

I don't know why, but I just had to hit that fat boy. Maybe it was because he let himself be the goat for all our jokes. Maybe I had one more punch left in me. Anyway, I hit him and knocked him flat. And I felt better.

The dark guy, the good-looking boy, didn't like it.

"You had no cause to hit Fatso," he said. "He was helping you out."

I kneed the pretty boy in the crotch, laughed when he doubled up, and walked away from there.

It was a long way to town, a long hot way, and I walked every step. I was still burning when I got to my room, growled a hello at Nora when she spoke, hurt her feelings, and lay down for a nap.

Melissa's face floated in my dreams.

CHAPTER VII

Melissa hung up on me.

I called her after supper, but she didn't give me time to apologize.

"This is Dun," I said. "I just want to say...."

Click.

So that was okay. I'd never run after a woman before, and now didn't seem like a good time to start. She was a little fluff. I only wanted her body, anyway.

But I couldn't fool myself.

I thought of the blonde girl I'd seen on the New Mexico road, and whom I'd seen again in Paley. She was a dish, and I wished I could find her.

Right then and there I decided I wouldn't see Melissa again, decided I wouldn't get involved.

Nora came into the room.

"Here's my girl," I said. "What say we go see a movie?"

She giggled.

"What would people say?" she asked.

"They see us together at church. So why shouldn't we be seen at a movie?"

She giggled again. "I'll get dressed," she said.

You can't get rich digging a ditch, and you can't get rich building a church. Manual labor is for the birds.

There were jobs in the fields, but I couldn't see myself driving a truck or dressing tools or climbing around on a derrick. Neither could I see myself handling nitro. That kind of work is dangerous.

City hall smelled good to me. Besides, I was still burning from the raw deal Flynn had given me.

The mayor's name was Harris. From what I heard, he made a fortune in the oil fields and invested it in ranches and stores and bonds, ran for mayor because he wanted to run the town.

He was a hard man to see.

Twice I went to city hall and twice his secretary let me cool my heels. I could hear him inside his office both times talking in a booming voice, but I had to sit there and watch other men go in and out ahead of me.

Twice was enough, so I called him.

"Harris," he said. "Speak up, it's your nickel."

He was a card.

"My name is Lattner," I said. "I want to talk to you about a little matter of kick-backs on city jobs."

He took his time answering.

"I'd like to see you at three o'clock," I said.

"Sure," he said. "Come around, I'll work you in."

It was three on the nose when I climbed the steps. I was half way up them when the blonde babe opened the door and came out, the blonde babe who let me fix her flat tire so long ago, how long ago, not long ago.

She hadn't changed a bit.

She'd worn shorts the first time I'd seen her, but this time she was dressed to kill. Her suit must have cost a small fortune.

I blocked her path. She walked down the steps, straight at me, stopped and waited for me to move.

We stared.

I stood aside and let her pass, turned to watch her. She knew I was watching.

She got into the blue convertible at the curb, glanced up at me, smiled just a little, backed out and drove away.

Now I knew she lived in Paley.

I could wait.

Some day, some not-so-distant day, she'd wish she hadn't left me beside that road.

She was beautiful, blonde and beautiful, lush beautiful, almost but not quite plump, just right.

I went inside. The secretary gave me the old cold eye.

"Lattner," I said. "The mayor's expecting me."

She double checked me just the same, buzzed the boss, and sent me in.

Harris was heavy. His beard was blue black, the kind that shows even after a close shave, blue black under the skin. His cheeks were fat, pendulous, forming creases at the corners of his mouth, creases that started beside his nose and fanned down and out to form creases at the corners of his mouth. His chin was small, almost lost in the fat face, a weak chin. He had thin blond hair, combed back, plastered to hide a bald spot. The rest of him wasn't so bad. His mouth was good and so were his eyes. He had a massive head, but his body was heavy, not fat.

"I'm Harris," he said, standing up, offering his hand.

"Dun Lattner."

"Have a seat."

"Thanks."

"Let's see now, Lattner, you said something about kickbacks on city jobs."

"I was fired Friday because I wouldn't kick back twenty out of eighty."

"You must be the man who whipped Flynn."

"Yes."

"Was that what the fight was about?"

"Yes."

"Flynn says you wouldn't work. Says he fired you and you got mad. The other men in the gang back him up."

"They're lying."

"That's what you say. Flynn's been with us six years, never been in any trouble. So why should I take your word for it?"

"Okay," I said. "I see how it is."

Harris scowled.

"And how is it?" he asked. "What do you mean?"

"Looks like I complained to the wrong men."

His laugh was ugly, short and ugly.

"Young man," he said, "I don't have to take twenty-dollar kickbacks for a living."

"That's what I hear."

"You come in here and prove Flynn asked you for a twenty-dollar kickback and I'll fire him."

"I can't prove it," I said. "But I can damned sure tell it where it'll hurt."

He rubbed his chin. The bristles made a dry, scratching sound.

"Yeah," he said. "You can do that. And election day is coming up."

He stared at me a moment, made up his mind.

"What do you want?" he asked. "Money?"

"I'm not trying to blackmail you," I said. "All I want is a chance to earn a living. I had a job and now I don't have a job, all because a dirty crook wanted part of my pay."

"You were digging ditches," he said. "You can get that kind of job all over town. Better jobs than that are going begging."

"I wanted to work for the city."

"I'll tell you what I'll do," he said. "I own a hardware store. An old man and his wife run it for me. They're good people but they don't push things, don't make money for me. I'll give you a job in the store, let you learn the business. I'll pay you eighty dollars a week. Do a good job, learn your business, and some day you can be my store manager."

"When do I start?"

"Tomorrow at eight o'clock. Now listen. Briggs is getting old. He and his wife feel like they own the store. They'll resent you a little and it'll be up to you to do the getting along."

"We won't have any trouble."

"What's your background? Ever work in a store before?"

"No."

He hesitated.... "Well, I'll tell Briggs to expect you in the morning."

We shook hands. He had a strong grip, strong enough to make me wince.

Not seeing Melissa became sort of a game, something like trying to stop smoking or drinking. I worked hard in the store, worked until I was tired to the bone when the sun went down. It was better than ditch digging, but Harris had been right about the old man, Briggs, and his wife. They welcomed me like the plague. The old man, frail and feeble, tried to be fair. He taught me all I was willing to learn. But the old woman was bitter as a pill, sharp faced and pinch-nosed, gimlet-eyed and mean. Her voice was shrill and she liked to nag me, liked to point out my mistakes.

The summer sun was a wicked thing. Sandstorms blew in with the wind. No rains fell. The earth became dry and parched, cracked. Nora worked for hours in her yard, watered and nursed her grass and flowers, but they turned yellow, withered.

Once I saw Melissa on the street. She didn't see me, but I was tempted to call to her, go to her, and the wanting of her was an ache in my heart. She was wearing white, swinging along the street in white, the prettiest thing I'd ever seen.

I was afraid of that woman, of her only, because I wanted her more than any woman I'd ever seen.

She never came into the store. Once I saw her pass, saw her look in, lifted my arm to wave. She didn't see me.

Business wasn't good. Sometimes we didn't take in a hundred dollars a day. Old Briggs and his sour wife had run the store too long and people were buying some place else.

Harris came in one afternoon and looked the place over. He didn't drop by often. He was too busy being the big man about town.

"How are things going?" he asked.

"Why don't you close it up or sell it?" I asked. "You're not making any money out of it. You're not even trying."

"It made money before the war."

"Other stores advertise," I said. "Other stores don't have a couple of corpses frowning on their customers."

Harris glanced across the room at Briggs and his wife.

"They're getting old," he said.

"Look," I said. "I could run this store and make it pay. I could run some ads and sell some of this stuff."

"Why don't you do it?"

"Briggs won't hear of it."

Harris sighed. "Just be patient," he said. "Learn what Briggs knows and then we'll see about pushing things a bit."

I called Melissa again and tried to apologize, but she hung up on me again. I think it was then I decided to marry Nora Simmons. It was a crazy idea and I knew it. The idea itself was enough to make me laugh, but at the time it looked like an easy way to take a long step the easy way.

The old girl couldn't live forever. She had money and I needed money.

There was a chance she wouldn't marry me, but she was always acting coy and girlish, always tittering like a young girl, always dressing up for me, always giving me motherly pecks on the cheek.

I didn't exactly waste time paying court to the old bat. There was a flower shop near the house, so I invested in a half dozen roses.

Her face gave the show away. She'd rather have had those roses than all the tea in China.

It was her big moment.

It was rough. She seemed to take me for granted, seemed to read deep meaning into my act of giving her flowers. She couldn't keep her hands off me, patted me and pinched me, tweaked my cheeks. I had to get myself in hand, had to force myself to be nice.

We went to the movies.

From then on in I spread it on pretty thick, soft soaped her, careful not to go too far too fast. I wanted marriage to be her idea, not mine. That way, whatever happened, she'd have herself to blame.

Once or twice I said something about our ages, the difference in our ages, and what a shame it was.

"I should have been born sooner," I said. "The wonderful women are the women of your generation."

We went to the movies, went to church, went out to eat. In the show I'd hold her bony hand, gently as a son. Later, not much later, I began kissing her cheek before I went up to my room at night.

She loved flattery.

"Nora," I'd say. "I don't know how you do it. You look like a woman half your age."

She began to talk of my future, began to make plans for me.

"There's something fine in you, Dun," she'd say. "I can see it. In a way, you remind me of my husband, bless him, when he was your age. You've got that same honest look in your eye, and you're ambitious like he was. You'll get somewhere, Dun. You'll be somebody."

"I hope I don't let you down," I said. "My father wasn't much. He went off and left me and I don't even know whether or not he's still living. I don't know anything about my mother's family and I don't know anything about my father's family. But whatever they were, I'm going to be better."

Briggs and his wife always went out for coffee at ten o'clock, rain or shine, without fail. They always stayed away fifteen minutes.

On Monday, a blazing hot Monday, a young woman came into the store just as the Briggs couple went out. She wanted a washing machine and I showed her our new automatics.

"How much is this one?" she wanted to know.

"Two hundred dollars."

Her eyebrows arched. "Are you sure? I thought they cost much more than that."

"Well, we got a break on our last shipment. This is the last one I can let go at that price, though, so you're lucky."

She wrote a check, filled in the amount and signed it. I took it.

"I have a stamp for the firm name," I said.

We talked for a while about the new automatics. The minutes were speeding by and I wished she'd leave.

"I read in a magazine that they're making combination washers and dryers," she said. "Some of the big city stores have a few now."

"It'll be a long while before we get them," I said. "Our distributor tells us they're working the bugs out of them now."

"When will you deliver the machine?"

"Tonight, if you'll be home."

"Oh. I'll be home. It's Six-thirty-three Parkland. That's on a corner, left hand side as you go south."

"I'll find it."

"Well, thank you ever so much. My old machine has been repaired once a week for months and the repairman says he can't fix it any more."

"Just don't tell any one you got the new one for two hundred," I said. "I don't want a swarm of housewives descending on me."

"I won't say a word."

Would she never leave?

Time was up, nearly up, but the woman just didn't seem to be in a hurry to leave and I kept watching the clock. I tried to break it up, wrote down her address and told her I'd deliver the machine before nine.

Still she talked, prattled, told me again how lucky she was to get the machine so cheaply.

She had me sweating.

"I can't wait until the combination machines come out," she was saying as Briggs opened the front door. "You can put me down for one as soon as they come in."

"Right," I said, just waiting for her to spill the beans.

"You won't forget the address?" she asked.

"I have it."

She went away.

We had little business all day. Once the old man suggested we straighten up the stock room, but I told him I didn't feel like it. He grumbled and let it drop.

"Tomorrow we'll straighten up all you want," I said. "We've got plenty of time."

Just before five I went to the back and slid back the bar to the door, turned out the lights and went up front.

"All locked up back there?" Briggs asked.

"All locked up."

He worked on the books for a bit, counted the cash and locked the register. I dusted the counter and made a job of sweeping the floor, taking my time. Whistling as I worked, doing my best to look industrious. It was ten after five when I'd finished, so the old man couldn't say I was a clock watcher.

There was a used-car lot a couple of blocks off main street and I went there. For ten bucks I rented a pickup truck, drove to a café at the edge of town, ate dinner and drank beer until it was dark.

After cruising the town a while I saw a burly young man standing on a street corner, offered him five bucks to help me with the machine.

It was a snap.

I parked in the alley, pushed the door open, switched on the lights and called my helper inside. He was a little nervous, not sure I really had any right in the store.

"It's all right," I said. "If you think I'm robbing the joint, just run up the alley and find a cop."

That calmed him down.

The washing machines were in crates, I went up front and got a hammer, carefully opened the crate, just as carefully nailed it back together. Shoved it back into a corner behind the other crates.

We loaded the machine and delivered it.

CHAPTER VIII

It was a hot Saturday. Few people were in town and business wasn't much better than weekday business. Ma Briggs had a headache, and at four o'clock I told the old man he should take her home.

"I'm afraid you might get rushed," he said.

"A kid could handle all the business we get."

"You've been talking to Harris," he said.

"What makes you think that?"

"Well, you're always complaining about business being slow, always wanting to run advertisements in the paper and on the radio. Harris called me last night and said I'd have to do a better business. He said I ought to start running some ads."

"Harris is not as dumb as I thought," I said. "Times are better than they've ever been before and this is the only store in town losing business. You're getting old, Briggs. You ought to quit or at least listen to somebody once in a while."

I couldn't have hurt him more if I'd slapped him. His lips tightened, his face whitened, and then his lips began to tremble. I thought he was going to cry.

"I'll take Ma home," he said.

They'd been gone about ten minutes when the blonde of the flat tire walked in.

I stared.

Again she wore shorts, only this time her blouse wasn't high necked, wasn't modest. Her hair, her honey hair, was loose, hanging loose about bare shoulders, golden bare shoulders. She was all round and soft curved, full bosomed, her breasts half covered. Her waist was bare and the shorts were too short, the long legs bare and deeply tanned. She wore sandals.

She stared at me, a little puzzled. I could tell she remembered me from the time I'd blocked her way on the city hall steps, but she didn't remember me from the time I'd fixed her flat tire on that lonely road in New Mexico.

"Hello," she said.

"Hello."

"You're new here."

"Yes."

"Where's Mister Briggs?"

"His wife was ill so he took her home."

"That's too bad. Will you tell him I was by?"

"Yeah," I said. "If you'll give me your name."

"Cyd Harris," she said. "Mayor Harris is my father."

"I'll tell him," I said.

She looked me over, almost smiled, and left. I stared after her, wondering how a guy like Harris could have a daughter like that.

Sooner or later, but maybe not sooner, the old man would discover the washing machine missing. He was jealous of that store, thought he owned it. Not once did he worry about sales dropping off. Sometimes I thought he'd have been happier if no customers came in at all. He got pleasure out of handling the merchandise, liked to take inventory, liked to walk around with his hands behind his back, feasting his eyes on pipes and nuts and bolts and saws and rakes and shovels.

He almost discovered the empty box a couple of days after I'd sold the machine.

We were working in the stockroom, only I was doing most of the work. Briggs stood around and told me what to do. It was hot and I got mad, I snapped at him a couple of times and he got nervous.

"That'll do for today," he said. "Unless you want to help me line these washing machines up against the wall. The way they're stacked takes up most of that end of the room."

"We don't need the space," I said.

"We will in time. I can get a hand truck and we can line them up against the wall."

"Do it yourself if you want," I said. "It's too hot back here and I'm not feeling well."

He went for the hand truck, came back and tried to push one of the big cartons up on it. I just stood and watched, knowing he thought I'd help.

"You'll have to give me a hand," he said.

"Leave them where they are," I said. "They're too heavy for the two of us."

"I could get somebody to help."

"Look!" I said. "We're losing money every day! If you don't care about saving money, I do! What we ought to do is do some advertising and start moving some of the merchandise through here! Every store in town is making a killing! This is the only place in town sitting on its dead can!"

"Maybe you could run things better!" he flared.

"Just give me a chance." I changed my tune. "Listen, Briggs! You're behind the times! Keep on like this another year and Harris will sell this place right out from under you! Then how would you live?"

He rubbed his chin.

"Well," he said. "I have been worrying about things."

"Will you take my advice just for two weeks? Will you let me try things my way? If I don't put it over... I'll quit."

"All right," he said. "We'll try it your way."

I didn't waste any time, didn't give the old man a chance to change his mind. An hour later I'd placed ads in the daily, on the radio station, and arranged for a thousand circulars.

Three days later we were doing business. A week later we hired a boy to juggle the heavy stock.

Harris was tickled pink.

He came in one day and made me manager of the store, jumped my salary to a hundred dollars a week.

He was a little rough on Briggs.

"Dun is the boss from now on in," he said. "You can advise him and keep the books, but Dun has a free hand."

Briggs didn't like it and his wife liked it even less. I couldn't blame them, even felt a little sorry for them, but I had my own row to hoe.

Two days later old Briggs lowered the boom. He'd found the empty washing-machine crate in the back. What he was doing back there I don't know. Maybe he'd heard something. Maybe he just suspected something. Anyway, he went straight to that crate, like a cat to a mousehole, and came right back up front and called Harris.

I didn't have a leg to stand on. Old Briggs had me. Harris came over and squirmed, but it was no use.

"Why accuse me?" I asked. "How do I even know there was ever a washing machine in that crate? For all you know, that machine could have been gone long before I came to work!"

Harris was no fool.

"Maybe," Harris said, his face white and pinched. "But something tells me different."

"How much was the machine worth?" I asked,

"Three hundred and fifty dollars," Briggs said.

"Take it out of the pay I've got coming," I told Harris. "When you decide I'm innocent, come around and pay me."

"You don't have half that much pay coming," he said.

"Whistle for the rest," I said.

I told Nora I'd quit my job and she didn't like it. It was on her face, just the shadow of doubt flitting across her face.

"It's all right, Nora," I said. "In fact, Harris wants me to open a used furniture store on this side of the tracks."

I moped around the house for a couple of days. Nora was a little sharp, kept asking questions, kept prodding me.

"The bank will call me this week," I said. "The man I want to see is out of town."

"You're going to borrow money?" Nora asked.

"If I can."

"But Harris has plenty of money," she said. "Why can't he finance you?"

"He thinks I have some money," I said. "You know how it is with rich guys like him. If he thought I was broke he wouldn't think about doing business with me. Maybe I was wrong, but I let him think I had enough money to swing this deal by myself."

"Oh," she said.

Another day passed, and the next day I pretended to get my telephone call from the bank. Nora was in the back yard and I went out on the back steps.

"The bank called," I said. "Wish me luck. If I make a good impression I'll be an honest-to-goodness business man by this time tomorrow."

I went to town and had a couple of beers, went to the drug store and bought a bottle of iodine. On the way home I stopped at a café and ordered a soft drink, poured a touch of iodine into the glass of water and downed it. I was sick as a dog by the time I got home.

Nora was on the front porch.

I vomited in the front yard and I wasn't faking. My insides were twisting and turning and I thought I was going to die. It scared Nora, scared her badly. She came running out, caught me by the arm, helped me inside, put me to bed.

Later, when I was feeling better, I sat up in bed and took her gnarled old hand in both of mine.

"I'm going to leave, Nora. You've been wonderful to me, but I don't seem to be getting anywhere."

"The bank wouldn't let you have the money," she said.

"No."

"Don't worry, Dun. There are other things."

"Not for me," I said. "Not here. I don't want to work for wages all my life and I don't have any friends here to help me. I think I'll go back to where I came from, back where I can walk into a bank and get the kind of backing I need."

"You have friends here, Dun."

"I need friends with some money, Nora," I smiled. "And it takes time to make friends like that."

"Don't worry," she said. "Take a nap. We'll talk about it later."

She left the room.

I almost laughed aloud.

It was going to work. I could feel it. Nora was going to let me have the money.

By supper time I was feeling pretty good, got up and dressed, went downstairs to eat. Nora was chipper, working overtime to cheer me up.

I didn't eat much, kept pecking at my food, stared into space and wore a long face.

"Dun?"

"Yes."

"How much money would it take to get you started in your used furniture business?"

How much?

Not too much. Mustn't make it too high. Better to start out easy.

"About two thousand dollars," I said. "All I need is an old building and a little working capital. I'd never stock much at one time. Turnover is the thing in the used furniture business."

"But what about Harris?"

"He'll put in another two thousand," I lied. "Used furniture will move in a hurry, see, so four thousand should be more than enough to get us going. After a couple of weeks I can have enough cash on hand to expand."

"I'll let you have the money, Dun."

Just like that.

I argued, protested, told her I didn't want to gamble with her money. She insisted. At bedtime I still hadn't agreed to take the money.

She talked me into it at the breakfast table next morning.

CHAPTER IX

Luck was a strong tide flowing my way. I couldn't miss. I'm luckiest when I feel lucky, and I felt lucky.

There was a building on the wrong side of the tracks that suited my needs. It was a ramshackle building, unpainted and drab, but it was on the main street and that's the kind of building you need for a used-furniture store. A man named Craig had it, but was leaving town. He sub-let it to me for fifty bucks a month.

Nora got the money for me, two thousand dollars, and I ran my first advertisement in the daily, placed some spots on the radio, took a display ad in Jerry Norton's tri-weekly.

Melissa took my ad.

It was an awkward meeting. I had hoped she'd be there, hoped she wouldn't, but told myself I needed that advertisement, talked myself into placing it.

She had everything Cyd Harris had, in miniature. Cyd Harris had jolted me, but Melissa jolted me more because she had as much as Cyd had, every bit as much, only there wasn't as much of it because she was smaller, but more of it because there wasn't as much of it, if that makes sense. Her breasts were smaller, but not smaller in the sense that they were smaller in proportion to the rest of her body. The rest of her was the same. Her legs were not as long as Cyd's legs, but as long in proportion to the rest of her.

A little girl with the body of a woman, and that's what got me.

"Hello, there," she said, her voice trembling.

"Hello," I said.

"You've been a stranger."

"I tried to talk to you, I called you. I wanted to apologize."

"Let's not talk about it," she said, walking toward me, an electric current walking toward me, making my body tremble, making my hands want to reach out and grab.

"Well, I am sorry," I said. "I was wrong, I shouldn't have treated you like that."

"I'm glad you're sorry."

I laughed.

"Look," I said. "We're going in circles, I could say I'm glad you're glad that I'm sorry."

"Well, anyway, I'm glad you're here. And you're looking awfully prosperous."

"It's the only suit I own."

"It's more than you had the first time I saw you. I hear you're working at the hardware store."

"Was working. I'm opening a used-furniture place."

She arched her brows, puckered her lips and whistled. "You'll get rich. Maybe I'd better grab you before it's too late."

"I wish you would," and I meant it.

It was getting too serious around there. She felt it, too.

"Let's go to my house," she said. "I have some beer and we can talk."

"Fine with me. But, first, I want to place an ad in your paper."

We laid out the ad together, laughing and arguing, our heads together. I had to fight myself. Sometimes she leaned against me, touched me, and her very touches burned.

Jerry Norton came in. We shook hands. Melissa told him the news.

"I'm real glad," he said. "I'm glad you're getting a break."

We finished the ad and drove to Melissa's house in her car.

I was almost afraid to go in, didn't trust myself, didn't want to get off base with her again, didn't want to anger her. As much as I wanted her, I wanted to be with her more. Somehow, with her, everything was fine.

We had a beer, sitting at the kitchen table, laughed and chatted. She listened to my plans, listened to me with wide eyes, encouraged me to talk.

I killed two beers and got up to go. It was getting dark and she hadn't turned on the lights. She saw me to the door and I put my hand on the knob, turned to say good-bye.

She was standing there, so small beside me, looking up.

I stooped and kissed her, a gentle kiss, and her arms went around me, locked hard around me, and I forgot about leaving.

Nora wasn't feeling well. She wasn't looking well either.

No man living could leave a woman as beautiful as Melissa and go home to an old crow like Nora without a feeling of revulsion.

It made me sick to look at Nora and it was hard to be nice to her. I had to pretend I was sorry she was ill, had to urge her to go to bed, had to take her a bowl of hot soup, had to sit beside her bed and talk, had to read a chapter from the Bible aloud.

I was glad when she went to sleep.

For all I cared....

Right away I had a stroke of luck.

The day after my ads started running a man and woman drove up in front of my store. They were in a good car, a new car, and well dressed. I'd seen the kind before. They were broke, but classy broke. They were leaving town and had five rooms of furniture for sale. I got it for three hundred bucks, cash, and it was worth a thousand if it was worth a dime. I moved most of it the first week, bought more furniture, and ran more ads.

Things looked good. By the end of the second week I could see I was losing business when I locked up and went out to look for furniture.

My double life almost killed me.

Every night I'd have supper with Nora, sit around with her for a while or take her driving in her car, forcing myself to butter her up. And every night I'd go to my room, and then slip out of the house.

Melissa would be waiting for me.

We drove in the country, took long walks and held hands like a couple of kids, stared at the stars and made love.

It was three o'clock in the morning.

Time to go home.

Time to go home and steal to my room, shoes off for fear Nora would hear.

"Dun?"

A small, sleepy voice.

"Yeah."

"Can't you sleep?"

"Time to go."

"No. Light me a cigarette."

I flipped on the light, grinned as Melissa scrambled for cover.

"Why do you have to go?" she asked.

"My landlady is a respectable woman. I like my room and don't want to give it up."

"I wish you could stay. I've never had breakfast with you."

"Some day I'll be with you all the time."

She sat up in bed, the sheet held around her shoulders. I leaned over and kissed her nose.

"Will we, Dun? Will we be together all the time... some day?" She giggled, wrinkled her nose. "Are your intentions honorable, Dun?"

It wasn't funny. I ran my fingers through her hair, pulled her to me and kissed her.

"I've had a lot of dishonorable intentions," I said, "but this time I mean what I say. We'll be married, honey, and we'll live right here in this house. I'll build my business up. Some day I'll have a store right spang in the middle of town. I'll make a lot of money and buy you a blue convertible to drive round."

She rubbed her cheek against mine.

"Dun."

"Yeah."

"You don't think... I mean, do you...."

Women.

All alike, all of them alike.

"I don't think anything," I said. "We're together because we love each other and can't wait to get married. Don't worry about it."

"I love you, Dun. I love you more than I've ever loved anyone."

I cupped her chin in my hands. "I'll tell you something," I said. "In all my life I've never loved but one person. Me. But now I love you more than I love myself. That's a lot."

It hurt like the devil, but I paid Nora five hundred of the two thousand I'd borrowed. It tickled her. Right then I could have borrowed five thousand.

Melissa worried me. It's a sign of weakness to want a women as much as I wanted Melissa, so that made her dangerous. Every night I told myself I'd see her once more, one last time, and then break it off, stay away, forget her.

How do you stop breathing?

Business got better. Oil towns are funny that way. Cadillacs sit beside shacks. People are in the chips one day, broke the next, in the chips one day and broke the next and willing to sell everything they have except their flashy automobiles. They go broke, sell their furniture, move on to other fields, greener pastures, always hoping to make the big strike.

I ran a help-wanted ad in the daily. Three women and one man answered the ad.

One of the women was a honey. She was a tall, willowy brunette, narrow waisted and swishy-hipped, and she knew how to wear clothes. Her eyes were brown, liquid brown, and she had full red lips and straight, white teeth.

I wondered if she could make me forget Melissa.

I was sitting at my desk adding up my day's take when she walked in. She looked around and added things up, but she wasn't looking for anything to buy.

"You'll do," I said.

"I'll do what?" she asked, smiling a lazy smile, daring me with those eyes.

"You'll do well whatever you do," I said. "But I was thinking you'd do for the job you came to see me about."

"I'm glad I came."

"You were looking for work."

"I'll take the job," she said.

"Don't you want to know about the pay?"

"I'll take the job," she said. And again she gave me that lazy smile. "What do I do?"

"Sell this stuff," I said. "It'll be price tagged. You can knock off twenty per cent if the customer shies away. The pay is fifty dollars a week. All right?"

"Fine," she said.

"Now tell me about yourself. What's your name?"

"Sandra," she said. "Sandra Wittling."

I left her with the store and went out to buy some furniture, didn't return until after five. She'd locked up the joint and that burned me. I wanted to talk to her.

Melissa was expecting me but I decided not to see her.

I went home, a roll of bills in my pocket big enough to choke a horse, and paid Nora another two hundred dollars. You'd have thought I'd given her all the gold from Fort Knox.

I knocked myself out to please her, took her to dinner at a place I knew at the edge of town, listened to her insane chatter, suggested a movie and didn't argue when she said no. A beer would have tasted good, but she didn't like me to drink beer. I had coffee.

We drove around a while and went home. She wanted me to listen while she read a chapter of the Bible, so I listened. I even nodded my head and looked impressed when she gave me a lecture on the evils of drink and the value of hard work and honesty.

"You know," I said, "I've been thinking."

"What, Dun?"

"If this furniture business goes over I might move up town some day. Maybe I'll open a hardware store up there. Sell furniture and radios and hardware and toys and variety-store stuff. Sell anything people buy, like the big drug stores."

"Maybe you can some day," she said.

It seemed best to let it ride.

She went up to bed and I sat down to read. It was slow going. I finished the paper and picked up a book, read the same page over twice and gave it up.

"Nora?" I called.

No answer.

I left the house and walked over to South Main, turned right one block to Ben's Tavern, went inside. A jukebox was blatting its brains out. They had a loudspeaker outside for the customers in the cars, but it was louder inside. Two girls in sleazy pink dresses danced around, posturing, their rumps swaying and swinging, giving the high sign to anything in pants. A man stood at the jukebox looking at the selections. He wore a big hat pulled low over his eyes, a red shirt and skin-tight pants, cowboy boots. Maybe he had a dollar in his pocket. A couple sat in a booth, drinking beer, and a fat woman sat at a table near the wall, glassy eyed, slack mouthed, stringy hair falling over her face, a cigarette hanging between her lips.

Calendars on the wall, garage calendars with nudes, long-legged nudes. A steer skull on a wall. Two tired waitresses, not bad, dressed alike in gingham and bows. I went to a booth and sat down, ordered a beer, lit a cigarette.

Sandra Wittling, my new employee, walked in.

She saw me almost as soon as I saw her.

It didn't surprise me. For some reason I half expected her, but it was sheer coincidence. I'd never been in the place before.

She didn't pause, but walked straight to my booth and sat down.

"Cigarette?" she asked.

I gave her one, gave her a light. The girl brought my beer and I ordered another.

We finished our beers, not talking.

"Let's go to the store and take inventory," I said.

I fired her the next day.

Greed is a funny thing.

For all the deep passions inside me, the unknown buried and unpredictable passions that made me want Cyd Harris for a time and Melissa forever, I wanted Nora's money most.

What made it funny, what scared me, was that I didn't know for sure that Nora had enough money to worry about.

Sometimes I got scared because I wanted Melissa, loved Melissa, and sometimes I got scared and wanted to run because I was afraid of Nora.

It was wrong, all wrong, not natural. I didn't want to think about Nora, about her money, didn't want to be nice to her.

Spring and winter, June and December, fire and ashes.

Nora almost drove me away, almost caused me to chuck everything. She began harping because I went out at night. She wasn't nagging, just harping in a motherly way, constantly harping. On Sunday she wanted me to go to church with her, wanted me to go every Sunday.

"Look," I said. "I've nothing against going to church. I enjoy going to church, but I don't like to be forced to go. Just let me go when I want to go. Don't act like my mother."

"Why, Dun," she said. "I didn't know I was acting like a mother."

"You know I don't think of you as a mother," I said. "You're too young to be my mother."

She liked that.

She was a real hag in the morning, a real hag all the time but a real old hag in the morning. I'd dress and go downstairs, find her in the kitchen dressed in a too-young kimono, a tight and thin thing, her wrinkled old prune face already smeared with rouge, scarlet lipstick on her horrible thin lips.

My entrance was the signal for her tongue to start flapping. She'd talk about my business, about my future, flirt a little, but always she got around to my going out at night.

The old crow was jealous.

"'Where were you last night?" she'd ask. "Out with some sweet young thing?"

"Visiting around. Doing a little business."

"Until three o'clock in the morning?" She wagged her finger at me. "You're a naughty boy."

"Well, I ran into a man I know. We got to drinking coffee and talking."

She never believed me, tried hard to believe me, flirted and gabbled until I'd finished my coffee and gone to work. I might as well have been married to her.

CHAPTER X

A slick customer barged into the store late in the afternoon. He was sickly pale, sported a tiny mustache, dressed like a rich rancher.

He looked around like he owned the place.

"You interested in some furniture?" I asked.

He ignored my question, just kept looking, and I went back to work on a cabinet with a broken leg.

"You're a little slow, aren't you?" he asked.

"Well, I'm new at this sort of thing."

"I wasn't talking about your work," he said.

"No?"

"No."

"Look," I said. "It's hot outside. Maybe you had a couple too many and the sun got to you. Now, run along and let me work."

"They told me you'd be cocky," he said. "Suppose you let me do the talking. You just save your breath and listen."

The guy interested me.

I stood up and took a deep breath so he could see my muscles.

"Go ahead and talk," I said.

"That's better," he said, fishing a cigar from a coat pocket. "Now, listen to me. You said you'd do the job for five hundred dollars. That was steep, but we heard about your results in El Paso and figured you could deliver here."

"Wait a minute," I said.

"You agreed to let me do the talking. So listen."

"Okay, Buster."

"The election's not far off," he said. "It's a close race and we figure the Negroes will spell the difference. Harris thinks you should do something and do it fast."

I didn't know what he was talking about, but he'd mentioned Harris. So I figured I'd let him talk, let him hang himself.

"It's going to be a real close race," he said. "Now, if you can deliver the Negro votes it might just make the difference. We figure five hundred votes will put us over the top."

"Any suggestions?" I asked.

He thrust his hands deep into his pockets and began to pace the floor, his head down, back and forth and back and forth.

The man was really worried.

"Well, we paid their poll taxes," he said. "That usually does the trick. But this time it's not enough. Now, I don't know your methods and I don't want to know. Maybe you've done your job and maybe you haven't. I don't even know what you told Harris, but I want your guarantee to leave town on election day. That way we can claim we never heard of you if anything comes up. And, that way, we don't have to keep any promises you make to the Negroes."

"I haven't made them any promises," I said.

That surprised him.

"What did you do?" he asked.

"Nothing."

"You mean you haven't even tried?"

I shook my head.

"Brother," I said, "I don't even know what you're talking about."

He turned a little white and looked around, beginning to get the idea.

"You're Craig," he said, pointing the cigar at me, almost jabbing me.

"I'm Lattner."

He began to laugh. He roared. I didn't think he was laughing because he thought it was funny.

After a while he walked to the door and looked up and down the street, turned back to me and looked me up and down.

"What happened to Craig?" he asked.

I spread my hands and shrugged my shoulders. "He had this building," I said, "but he didn't have anything in it except a desk and a chair and a telephone. There was a for-rent sign out front."

"So you rented it."

I nodded.

"You've been took," he said. "I own this building."

It was my turn to laugh. "I think you're the one who got took."

"Yeah," he said. "It looks like it."

"You paid this Craig in advance to deliver the Negro vote?"

"Harris did. I didn't have anything to do with it."

I had to laugh, couldn't help it. He turned red. He paced the floor again, hands in his pockets, mad and worried.

"You've got me at a disadvantage," he complained. "In all fairness you should have stopped me before I spilled the beans."

Again I laughed.

"I know," he said. "You didn't have much of a chance. That's one of my biggest faults, I guess, blurting out what's on my mind without giving the other fellow a chance to talk."

"Who are you, anyway?" I asked. "What are you in this town?"

He looked at me, giving me one of those sizing-up looks. I could almost hear wheels going around in his head.

"I'm city clerk," he said. "I'm the man behind the scenes, the errand boy when things go right and the whipping boy when things go wrong. My name's Crossland. Ross Crossland. Harris and two councilmen are my... benefactors."

"You should be in a pretty good spot," I said.

"What do you mean?"

"Well," I shrugged, "it seems to me a city clerk should be able to make some dough."

"I do all right," he said.

"What are you going to do about that Negro vote?" I asked. "Craig must not have done anything if he skipped town."

"I don't know," he said. "I just don't know."

"Well, maybe I could help you. I've had some experience with Negroes."

"Yeah," he said. "You probably read a book on race relations."

"I'll take on the job and deliver the votes. If I fail, Harris doesn't pay. If Harris wins, I get a thousand bucks."

Crossland whistled.

"You wouldn't have much time to work," he said. "Besides, I don't know whether Harris would want to take the risk."

"What's he got to lose? It costs him nothing if I don't deliver."

"Yeah," he said. "There's that. Maybe...."

"Why don't you talk to Harris?"

"I will."

"You'd have to let me know in a hurry. Tomorrow at the latest."

"I'll do that."

CHAPTER XI

I married Nora Simmons

It was funny how it happened. The old girl proposed to me.

The way she laid it on the line made sense. She had some money and the house and there wasn't anybody to leave it to when she died.

"You're a long way from dying," I said. "You shouldn't talk like that."

"I'm worth twenty thousand dollars in cash," she said. "I own some buildings in town and five rent houses. I've thought of leaving it to the church. But I got to thinking. Maybe it's not right, considering the difference in our ages, but I couldn't see the harm in it, either."

"What do you mean?"

"Well, we could be married. Mind you," she said, "I know there couldn't be any... well, any romantic attachment... but, well, we seem to like each other and...."

There was something nasty about the idea, something repulsive.

"You don't know a thing about me," I said.

"I know as much as I need to know, Dun, and I want your companionship."

"I'm honored," I said.

We drove over to Onarka on Monday to buy the license. I figured it wouldn't get into the Paley newspapers if we got married in another town. Nora wanted to get married the following Thursday but I put it off, hoping

I'd hear from Crossland or Harris, hoping something would happen, anything. But Crossland didn't call, so I figured Harris had refused to let me try for the Negro vote.

Thursday came and Nora got all dressed up for the wedding. Her hat had feathers and flowers and fruit and beads. With a veil. The veil helped some. Her dress swallowed her, dragged her ankles, a brightly flowered dress cut like a gunny sack.

We were married by a justice of the peace. A couple of loafers were our witnesses, and I wanted to spit in their faces. They snickered, and so did the old justice.

I slipped the justice a five-dollar bill and led Nora out of his office. We went to a drug store and had a coke. She was giggling like a girl, like a young bride.

"Wonder if we look like newlyweds?" she asked once, looking up coyly, her veil thrown back so she could sip her drink through a straw.

"They'll think I'm your son," I said.

She didn't like that.

I don't know why I wanted to hurt her, but I did.

On the way home she said I was driving too fast. Henry never drove faster than thirty miles an hour.

"Who in hell is Henry?" I asked.

"Don't swear, Dun," she said in a sad little voice. "You never used to swear. I honestly don't know what's got into you! You've been acting funny all day!"

"Well, I'm sorry! I'm sorry! But you didn't answer my question! Who is Henry?"

"Henry was my husband, Dun."

"Let's forget him, then! Let's not mention him again! He's dead and gone and that's all there is to it!"

She sighed. "He was a good man," she said. "A good man and a smart man. Never spoke a cross word to me. Never raised his voice."

"Any man who lives with a woman more than a week without speaking a cross word should have his head examined," I said. "Show me a man who never gets mad at his wife and I'll show you a man with something wrong with him. More than likely he hates his wife."

"What a thing to say! Why, Henry loved me!"

"There goes Henry," I said. "Don't tell me you married me so you could compare me to Henry!"

She sat up stiff and straight, so mad she was shaking.

"Young man," she said. "I've done you a favor! When I die you'll be better off than you ever dreamed of being! But if you think I'm just a silly old woman who intends to sit around and let you run over me you've got another thing coming! Now, I'm easy to get along with! Always have been! Even Henry said I had the soul of a saint! But it takes two to get along, and you're going to have to do your share! Let's have an understanding, Dun! Let's agree to get along or let's call the whole thing quits right now!"

Then I knew I'd gone too far.

She couldn't be bullied.

"Take it easy," I said. "Sure I'm grouchy today. First time I ever got married. Besides, all you want to talk about is your Henry."

It was hard to do, but my voice sounded sulky. She giggled.

I could have vomited.

"Don't be jealous," she said, throwing her veil back. "I'll remember not to talk about him in front of you."

By that time we were in the outskirts of Paley, so I pulled in and stopped at a honky-tonk. A girl in shorts, plump and blonde, flounced over to the car and leaned on the door.

"What'll it be?" she asked.

"Hi, Pauline," I said. "I'll have a beer." I turned to Nora and asked her what she'd have.

She was staring straight ahead, didn't answer.

"You want a drink, Nora?" I asked.

She didn't answer.

"One beer," I told the girl.

The floozy shook her tail away and I turned to Nora. She was plenty burned up about something.

"What's eating you, honey?" I asked, almost choking over the word honey.

"How did you know that girl's name?" she asked.

"You mean Pauline? Why shouldn't I know her name?"

"A common honky-tonk girl!" she said. "Is that the kind of person you associate with?"

"Listen," I said, and my voice was tough. "You don't know a thing about that girl in the first place! She's making a living and she's not hurting you doing it! Plenty of nice girls work in these places! And as for my knowing her name, dear, it was embroidered on her blouse! I never laid eyes on the girl in my life!"

"You ordered beer," she said.

"Hell," I said.

I started the motor and backed out of there, slammed down the street full blast, blind with rage, killing mad and blind red mad, mostly mad-at-myself mad.

You've seen those concrete roads with narrow asphalt strips across them every few feet. This street was like that. The tires bumped bumped bumped over them as a train clickity clicks over the rails, bumped bumped and mocked and talked to me and said what have you done have you done and as I stepped on the gas the bumpety bump speeded up and said what have you done have you done have you done done done and my brain felt like mush and my nerves were wriggling writhing twisting snakes in my body, inside my body, all coiled up and twisting and turning and knotting and wriggling wriggling tightly twisting and wriggling.

I wanted to scream, wanted to open my mouth and scream, wanted to hit my head on the steering wheel and make the blood and life and snaky wriggling nerves spill out.

Understand, I didn't want to hurt Nora.

It was myself I hated and despised.

Her voice was far away. I could hear the words, but she had to say them over and over before I could understand what it was she was saying.

"Slow down, Dun, slowdown! We'll be, killed, Dun! Slow down!"

"Shut up!" I said.

And then, just like that, I was myself again. Inside me, deep down inside me, the nerves untwisted and went limp. I could think again, could see again, and I took my foot off the pedal and braked the car down.

"I'm sorry, Nora," I said. "Believe me, I don't want to hurt you in any way, not even your feelings. It's just that I feel kind of trapped and scared and for a minute there things went a little bit crazy."

"It's all right, son," she said. "I think I understand. Just don't worry about it."

And I drove through town, feeling foolish, watching the people, afraid I'd see Melissa and afraid I wouldn't, feeling all panicky and lost because she was out of it now, out of my life, out of my dreams even, better off forgotten.

What I needed was a drink.

And then I remembered it was my wedding day, and for the first time I thought of the night.

Nora cooked a steak and we ate, and then she wanted to talk about my future.

"I know some of the richest men in town," she said. "You can sell your furniture store and go into insurance or real estate. There's a real future in insurance."

"No insurance," I said. "No real estate."

"I'm a good deal older than you, Dun," she said. "At least listen to me."

"I want a store in town," I said. "I've proved I can run a business. With a little backing, just a little, I could start a store in town."

She raised her eyebrows and I knew what she was thinking.

"Where will you get the backing?" she asked.

"I have half of all your money, Nora. There's a community property law in this state, so everything you have is half mine."

Again she raised those eyebrows, those scraggly gray eyebrows.

"Well," she said, "I guess you do own half this house and half the furniture and car. But you can't sell your half unless I agree, so I don't think you can raise much cash that way."

"You said you had some money," I said.

"So I did."

She screwed up her lips until they formed a small, tight O, and her eyes glinted. There was a look almost of triumph on her face.

"Were you lying?" I asked.

"I never tell lies," she said. "The money is in cash and it's where you can't touch it. You can't even prove I have it, because it's in a bank box and not even the bank knows how much I have."

She was gloating.

My anger didn't show on my face. I stood up and went over to the table, set the cup on the table and turned to face her.

"Why did you do this to me?" I asked. "You don't love me and you know damned well I'm not in love with you! I've no doubt you're a fine woman, but you don't have any sort of attraction for me."

"Dun," she said, rocking gently, hands folded in her lap. "I will do exactly what I said I'd do. When I die, everything I have will be yours. Until I die, what I have is mine. I may choose to help you along. Indeed, I want you to amount to something. I'll do everything in my power to help you amount to something."

"This has been a mistake," I said. "We've both made a mistake."

A man's wedding night should be a night to remember.

Mine was.

I sat around in the kitchen drinking coffee and smoking, nervous as a cat on a tin roof. Nora went into the living room and switched on the radio. Once, when I went into the hall, I saw her in her rocking chair, glasses perched on the end of her nose, rocking gently and sewing.

A motherly sight.

The way I figured it, Nora would go up to bed in her same old room and I could go to bed in my room. I even thought of going to my room and locking the door, and would have except that I wanted to talk.

Nora didn't have much to say.

I went back into the kitchen and drank a pot of coffee while I waited for her to go to bed. She always turned in at nine o'clock, but on this night, our wedding night, she was still up at ten.

What was she thinking about?

I hoped she didn't have any ideas.

And then I laughed at myself, laughed at the idea of Nora getting ideas about the fountain of youth.

It was ten-thirty when she came into the kitchen with a silly smile on her face.

"Time for bed," she said.

"You go on up," I said. "I'm not tired."

"Young people should get their sleep, Dun."

"I'm not sleepy."

"Good night, Dun," she said, and went upstairs.

I took Nora's car, didn't even try to slip it out of the drive, raced the rotor and backed out.

Melissa's house was dark.

I knocked on the door.

She flicked on the porch light, peered at me through the glass pane, opened the door and let me in. She was wearing pajamas, baggy pajamas.

She was grave, unsmiling.

"Where have you been?" she asked. "I thought maybe you'd left town."

"I've been around."

"Not around here."

"I've been thinking about you," I said.

"Sit down," she said. "Be comfortable. Make yourself at home."

"Thanks."

She began to cry, suddenly, began to cry like a child, standing there with her arms straight and stiff, with the tears streaming down her cheeks, making no sound.

I went to her, picked her up, kissed the tears away.

"Dun?"

"Yeah?"

"Do you really love me?"

I laughed, laughed softly in the darkness, fumbled for the light.

It was four o'clock.

"How many times do I have to tell you? Why do you doubt me?"

"You come around when... well, sometimes I wonder."

"Melissa, I love you. I've said that to other women when I didn't mean it, but I mean it when I say it to you."

She sat up in bed, lighted two cigarettes, gave me one.

"Why don't you marry me?" she asked.

"I will marry you. I want to marry you and I will marry you when I think I can support you."

"You said the store was doing well. What do you have to have, a million dollars?"

"No, baby. Just a little more time. Give me a little time and then I'll come around and beg you to marry me."

"Maybe I'll find another boy friend," she said. "Maybe I won't want to marry you in a month."

"Don't say that, baby. Don't ever say that. I can't live without you, so don't say that. Just don't go away. Always be here. Always be here when I need you."

"Just don't wait too long, Dun. Please. Don't wait too long."

The light was on in Nora's room. I parked the car at the curb and went upstairs, paused outside her door, thought I heard her moan.

She didn't wake me next morning. I dressed and went downstairs, expecting to find her sulking in the kitchen. She wasn't there.

I went upstairs.

She was ill, really ill, pale and drawn, in pain.

"What's the matter?" I asked. "Headache?"

"I don't know," she gasped. "My head hurts, but I ache all over. Feel feverish. Maybe you'd better call a doctor."

"Let me take your temperature," I said.

She had a fever. Not much. Couple of degrees.

"You have a touch of flu," I said. "Stay in bed all day. I'll bring your breakfast up and see about you at noon."

She couldn't eat breakfast, just sipped her coffee and moaned, felt sorry for herself and moaned.

"I'll see about you at noon," I said. "Promise you won't get out of bed."

"I promise," she said.

"You'll be all right."

I stooped over and kissed her cheek.

When I left the house, I locked the front door.

CHAPTER XII

Crossland came by the store at ten o'clock, tooted his horn and waited for me to come out.

"Harris wants you to drop by his house tonight," he said. "He wants to talk about the Negro votes."

"He's taken his own time about it. There's not enough time to do anything now."

"You could try. If you succeed you'll be in solid with Harris. He can do you a lot of good."

"Yeah."

"Give it a whirl."

"Well, I don't know. He doesn't exactly love me."

Crossland grinned. "That's what I gathered. I didn't know you two had met."

"We've met. All right. I'll go to his house."

"About eight."

"Will you be there?"

Crossland shook his head. "I don't socialize with Harris."

I went home at noon and found Nora in bed. She was running more temperature and this time she begged for a doctor.

"I'll call right away," I promised.

"Doctor Lever," she said. "He's in the book."

"I'll give him a ring."

I looked up the doctor's number and called his office.

He wasn't in.

"Any message?" his receptionist asked.

"No," I said. "I'll... call back later."

I took Nora up a bowl of soup, but she wouldn't eat it. Did she think I was poisoning her?

"Is the doctor coming?" she asked.

"He said he'd be a little late," I said. "There's a lot of summer flu around town and he's got some calls to make."

"Oh."

"You should eat that soup. You haven't eaten today."

"I'm not hungry," she said.

"You stay in bed," I said. "I'm going to the store, but I'll be back to see about you in an hour."

But I didn't go to the store.

Nora had said her money was in a bank box, in cash, and I wanted to see the bank's safe-deposit boxes.

Maybe I could work an angle.

I locked the front door of the house. It wouldn't keep Nora inside but it would keep any chance visitor outside. And I didn't want Nora seeing any visitors. She'd not seen anyone since the wedding and I wanted our marriage kept secret. For just a little while.

I walked to town, walked fast, and headed straight for the bank.

There were two banks in town, both small, but Nora's bank was a hick place, a cracker box, and I'd teased her about it, told her it was unsafe. But her husband had banked there and so would she.

It wasn't much of a bank.

Three men could have knocked it over without any trouble. There was an office with a frosted glass door at the front, an open space with three desks, a mahogany partition with barred windows for the cashiers, a couple of owl-faced men in the front, a fat man and two collared kids at the windows, three or four girls running clicking machines at the back.

There were half a dozen people inside, standing at the windows or at tables along the walls.

I didn't know any of them.

One of the owl-faced boys would suit me fine.

The one I picked wore horn-rimmed glasses. A desk tab was lettered with his name.

Mr. J. Tarbot.

"My name is Lattner," I said. "J. D. Lattner. I'd like to rent a safe-deposit box."

"Why, fine, Mr. Lattner. I'm Jess Tarbot."

His hand was like a wet fish.

"Do you have an account with us, Mister Lattner?" he asked, smiling with his lips, his eyes unsmiling, questioning.

"Not at present. I'll transfer my account from Phoenix in a few days."

He actually rubbed his hands.

"Well, let me welcome you to our city, Mister Lattner. You are new here, are you not?"

"I've been here a while."

"I hope you find us cooperative, Mister Lattner. We certainly try to be. We try to help our clients here, try to look out for their interests, so to speak. Are you in oil, Mister Lattner?"

"Let us say that I'm here to look around," I said. "If everything turns out as I plan I may settle here."

He became all business, tried to show me how efficiently his bank operated: filled out a form, had me sign it, gave me a key, stood up and rapped on his desk.

A girl came from the back of the room, a sallow-faced girl, a dull-eyed girl with drooping shoulders.

"Norma," Tarbot said, "this is Mister Lattner. Will you show him safe-deposit box number thirty-three, please?"

The girl moved her lips and bobbed her head.

"Just follow Norma, Mister Lattner. And drop in to see us any time we can be of help."

"Thanks, I will."

Again we shook.

I followed the girl the length of the room, through a doorway, down a wall-scarred hallway, through an open doorway into a small, windowless room.

It was a joke.

The safe-deposit boxes were light steel boxes with ten-cent locks, stacked on shelves. The numbers were taped on the fronts.

All at once I wanted to laugh, wanted to sit down and laugh.

This was going to be a snap. I could learn the number of Nora's box, get her key, slip in and open her box instead of mine. That would take some doing, all right, because the bank probably wouldn't let anyone go into that room alone. But there would be a way. I'd find a way.

The girl stood in the doorway and stared at me as I unlocked my box and transferred some envelopes from my coat pocket to the box, closed the lid, locked it.

Now was the test.

Maybe they'd ask for the key back.

I put the key in my pocket, half expecting the girl to say I'd have to turn it in.

She just stood there.

So all customers kept their own keys. That was a break. As I left the bank I thought of that house, that big bleak house, and wondered where in that house Nora kept the key to her box.

I'd have to find it, spot it without Nora knowing, and then take it when I was ready.

Nora was on the front porch when I got home. It scared me.

"What are you doing down here, Nora? Have you lost your mind?"

"I called the doctor."

"Oh?"

"You didn't call him, Dun."

"I called him."

"That isn't what his receptionist told me."

"I called him just the same."

"Never mind," she said, her lips tight.

"Are you feeling better?"

"Much better, thanks."

"Is the doctor coming?"

"I don't need him now."

"Come on inside and I'll fix something to eat."

"I can prepare supper," she said.

We ate scrambled eggs and toast, both of us forcing our food down, not talking, not even looking at each other. There was hate in the room.

"I have an appointment," I said. "I'll be back early. You get to bed and get some sleep."

She didn't reply. I dressed and took the car, went to a tavern and drank beer until it was dark.

Harris lived in a big house out in the country. He must have had money to burn. I've seen layouts like that in California, but this house seemed out of place. It was part stucco, part wood and part glass, with the glass winning out. The yard was beautifully landscaped and I wondered where Harris got the water for his grass and trees. He even had a swimming pool, so he must have had his own wells.

There were cars in the yard, sleek convertibles and station wagons. That bothered me. Crossland hadn't said anything about a party.

I was all dressed up in my new suit. My tie and socks matched, so I wasn't worried about my looks.

Harris had a butler and he asked me to wait in the foyer or whatever you call it, and that burned me up.

Harris came out with the butler, all smiles and slick words.

"Glad to see you, Lattner," he said. "Glad you could make it. My daughter's throwing a little party for some of her friends, so come in and have a drink."

We went into a living room copied from some magazine. It was too so-so, a big room with couches and tables and modernistic chairs. There was a baby grand piano over in the corner and about a dozen people standing around, men in sport coats and classy chicks in off-the-shoulder dresses. Way off-the-shoulder. Their breasts wanted to jump out over the tops of their dresses and they were bright and tinny false, brittle as hell.

All except Cyd Harris.

I wondered if she remembered me, wondered if she would remember me, hoped she wouldn't remember me as I'd looked the day I'd fixed her flat.

She was a real bitch, that woman, a bitch in a tight green dress. She didn't have to wear a low-cut dress. She could have worn a blanket and still she would have looked better than the other women. Her shoulders were magnificent and her breasts were outlined by tight fitted material, outlined, moulded. I was puzzled by her figure, couldn't decide whether she was on the plump side but not plump or just big and all woman.

Again I looked into that lovely face, that tanned face with the full, scarlet lips and the blue, slanted eyes.

"I'm Cyd Harris," she said, and her voice was low pitched as her voice should be.

"My name is Lattner," I said. "Dun Lattner."

She held out her hand and I ignored it.

It embarrassed her. She let the hand fall to her side.

"Your face is familiar," she said. "Have we met?"

I looked her over, looked her over boldly, top to bottom, lingeringly.

"We've met," I said.

"I saw you in town," she said, "but I've a feeling I met you before that."

Again I let my eyes slide up and down her body.

"We met before," I said. "Believe me, I didn't remember your face but I remembered the body."

She was mad, mad all the way through, shaking with rage, wanting to put the slug on me and biting her lip to keep herself under control. Her head went up and the chin went out, and she was beautiful.

Her voice shook.

"Mind telling me where?" she asked.

"You think about it," I said. "It'll come back to you."

Now it was her turn.

She turned her back on me and went back to the creeps at the piano.

"Where can we talk?" I asked Harris.

He was smiling.

"In the library," he said.

"I knew you'd say that," I said. "Shall we have our coffee there?"

He was puzzled, but smart enough to know he was being razzed.

I followed him into the library. Maybe there were ten books in there, some easy chairs and tables and lamps.

"Have a seat," he said.

I sat down.

He rubbed his hands and walked the floor. He made me nervous.

"What about our drinks?" I asked.

He pressed a buzzer and then paced back and forth with his hands clasped behind his back until the butler brought the drinks.

"Now, Lattner," he said. "Let's conclude our little business arrangement. But, first, I want to apologize for that, eh, little washing-machine incident."

"Aw, crap," I said. "You make my twat want to dip snuff. You're not apologizing about the washing-machine incident and you know it."

It got his goat and it made me feel good because I'd been able to get under his skin.

"You're mistaken," he said. "In the first place, I blame myself for not paying you more money. I should have sized you up better. To be perfectly frank, I should have known you'd steal if you couldn't get the money any other way. You're in a hurry. I know how it feels to be in a hurry."

He made me uncomfortable.

"Let's get down to brass tacks," I said.

"All right. Here it is. I need the Negro vote. I'll lose the election without it. There's not much time."

"You wasted valuable time," I said. "You should have contacted me right after Crossland came around."

"I know. But that's spilt milk. Right now I want to know if you can swing the Negro vote or part of the Negro vote."

"Well," I said, "I have one idea. It may work."

"What is it?"

"Send me a city truck and two men down in the Flats," I said. "Have them bring some surveying instruments."

"What's the idea?" he asked.

"I'm going to be subtle," I said. "I'm going to make the Negroes want to vote for you and they won't know we ever made an effort to influence them."

"Listen," he said. "Don't make any fool promises I can't keep."

"Don't worry," I said. "Leave it to me and forget about it."

He paced the floor some more, nipping at his drink, chewing at his cigar.

"All right," he said. "I don't think you can swing it in the time we've got left. But I don't have time to bring in a professional. I can run ads and make speeches and hand out cards, but that's not enough."

"Just one thing," I said.

"Yeah?"

"When do I get paid? Crossland said it would be a thousand."

"A thousand if you produce. Nothing if you fail."

"And you'll pay right after the election?"

"If I win."

"Let's say you win by a landslide," I said. "Let's say you don't even need the Negro votes to win. Do I still get paid?"

"You'll get paid if I win. You'll get paid if I win by one vote and you'll get paid if I win by a thousand votes."

He didn't see me out.

The crowd had gone, but the girl was in the living room, standing at the piano, picking out some mournful tune, waiting for me.

I pretended not to notice her. She couldn't take that.

"Just a moment," she called. "I'd like to talk to you."

"Oh," I said. "Hello."

"You're not very nice," she said, coming toward me, swaying toward me in a back-bowed, shoulders back, head back, swaying walk that was suggestive and inviting and calculated.

"Lady, I don't even like myself."

"I didn't say I don't like you," she said, standing close to me, almost touching me.

"I think you probably like to play with naughty little boys," I said.

The practiced look of the seductress left her face, left her eyes, but only for a moment.

"You're the naughtiest of the lot," she said. "Tell me where I met you the first time."

"Some day you'll remember, sweetheart. Some day I'll make you remember. And then I'll never let you forget."

She laughed, and her laugh was a little shaky.

"That could be a threat," she said. "But it sounds interesting."

"Lady, I may not be nice... but I'm interesting."

"Sit down and tell me about you," she said, nodding her head at a couch. "Or maybe you'd like to hear about me."

That made me laugh.

My laughter angered her.

She flounced, wanted to leave the room, wanted to stay with me, wanted to make a conquest.

"You don't have to tell me about you," I told her. "I can tell your life story as well as you can."

"Tell it." Her voice was flat.

"You were a poor little girl until you were ten years old. Your dad worked in the oil fields. First you lived in East Texas and then you went up into New Mexico and Oklahoma, and then you came out here. Your dad bought some leases cheap and got some backing so he could drill. He hit oil and you became a rich little girl. You had your own car when you were a high school freshman. Your mother was a social leader, but she died. At seventeen you were engaged, and then you got engaged five or six times. You went to three colleges and got kicked out of them all. Now you're playing the field."

"Pretty close," she said. "Only you don't tell it so nice."

"It's not a bad story. In fact, the only reason it's not a good story is because you never helped it any. You just drifted along."

"What's the matter with you?" she asked. "Don't you like people with money? Did a rich girl throw you over? Did your mother take in washing?"

"It's been fine talking to you, honey," I said. "Just dandy. Maybe we'll bump into each other again."

"Do you have to go?"

"No."

"Then sit down."

"I have to go now."

She smiled a mocking smile, arched her brows, shrugged. There was no promise in her smile, no promise in the eyes, but the hint of a promise, somewhere a promise.

I turned to leave.

She followed me to the door, stood there a moment and, when I paused, followed me outside.

"Let's walk," she said.

Nora's car looked cheap and out-of-place in the yard, in front of the big house, and I wondered what the girl was thinking. She took my arm and walked me toward the pool, her hand light and hot on my arm.

We paused at the pool edge, not talking, and faced each other.

She kissed me.

She swayed toward me, face uplifted, eyes closed, and her arms went around my neck, her body pressed tight and hard and hotly soft against my body, and her lips were velvety soft moist warm hot against my lips.

The bitch pushed me into the pool.

Without warning, snake fast, she pushed me, pushed me with her body, and I went backward into the pool.

She was laughing when I came up.

When I dragged myself out, sick at the belly with rage, she was gone.

CHAPTER XIII

Nora's light was burning.

I heard her thin screaming the moment I opened the door. She was calling Henry, her dead husband, begging him to save her from me.

I rushed upstairs, pushed her door open, drew back at the sight of her, the ugly sight of her, the screaming clawing wild-eyed sight of her.

She was sick crazy, in a delirium, burning with fever, deathly ill, so ill it scared me.

She couldn't die. Not like that. Not without a doctor.

It wouldn't be right.

I went downstairs to the telephone and Nora stopped screaming.

It was deathly quiet. I stood there in my wet clothes, shivering a little, cold.

There was a noise, a slight noise at the top of the stairs.

It was Nora.

She started down, fell, tumbled down the stairs like a limp doll, bouncing and thudding, fell all the way and landed in a loose heap.

Panic was a bitter thing, a bitter burning bile, not lessening but increasing, the panic turning my legs to pulpy useless things, making me tremble, making me gibber insane drivel, making me run from room to room, looking for something but not knowing what to look for.

She was dead.

I could tell by the way she ley there, limp, dishrag limp, her head twisted to one side, the neck stretched and twisted, the hair flowing out over the floor in a dirty gray mess, the mouth open, eyes dilated, the face a purplish color.

Stone cold dead.

They'll think I killed her, think I tripped her, think I married her and killed her for her money.

They'll find Melissa, learn of my love for Melissa, and they'll send me to the chair.

They'll go to Onarka and look up the records. Or some smart hick cop or some wet-behind-the-ears country reporter will dig it up, or some long-nosed county clerk will add two and two together. Or the justice of the peace will remember marrying me to Nora.

I was a dead duck, cold turkey.

Ninety-nine years.

Or death.

They'll have me where it hurts, by the short hairs, and I can squirm or beg or explain or swear and it won't make any difference.

A small town loves a juicy morsel, and the law loves an open-and-shut case. Give them a goat to hang something on and they won't look past the warts on their noses.

Ninety-nine years, long long years, ninety-nine years or death.

Which?

Well, life is life, even if it's ninety-nine years. Best to run, make a break, bolt and run, head for the border, any border, but do it in a hurry.

In Nora's car.

They'll be after me.

Fast.

They'll be after me fast and they'll get me sooner or later.

And all the time I was scurrying from room to room, touching nothing, holding my hands in the air, afraid to touch a thing.

Something clicked and I found myself, came to myself, found myself running from room to room, caught myself in mid-air, stopped dead still where I was and began to think.

Turn off some lights. No sense letting any passer-by see me scurrying around like a chicken with its head cut off.

Calm down and think.

I switched out all the lights except the kitchen light, and then I bolted the front and back doors. Slowly, calmly, I made myself go to the icebox, get a bottle of beer and open it.

It tasted good.

I was thinking now, thinking smoothly, counting the odds.

… all right; so she's dead, forever dead and gone, and she's got a safe-deposit box stuffed full of money…. Maybe nobody'll find out about the marriage, so let it ride, ride it out, play it straight and ride it out….

The key to Nora's box.

Where?

I'd have to get the key to the box and get that money, somehow get that money.

But first have to get into some dry clothes. I changed, dumping the wet clothing in my closet.

It was a big house and a key is a small thing, easily hidden.

Where would Nora hide it?

In her room, maybe.

It's hard to believe, but I was half afraid to go into Nora's room. I hated to go there, but go I did. It was a tomb, a real tomb, dark and sad, a thing of the past, smelling of the past, thick carpeted, furnished with massive pieces. There were pictures on the wall, pictures of Nora in her youth, pictures of her dead husband, pictures of relatives or friends, and one picture of a child.

Her child?

Dead, maybe?

I looked through bureau drawers, careful to replace the clothing.

No key.

A chest was filled with trinkets, small boxes of jewelry. A small box held keys, but not the key to the safe-deposit box. I opened a trunk. It was filled with purses, new purses, shiny new purses, unused. There must have been fifty. A funny thing, because the purse Nora had carried was shabby and worn.

I looked in every drawer, turned back the covers on her bed and looked.

No key.

From room to room I went, opening drawers, heedless of the time, but growing more and more impatient.

I had to find that key. Had to.

Time came rushing down the funnel, all at once, and I moved faster, faster from room to room. But I couldn't move fast enough because I had to leave everything tidy. How much time had passed?

I had to get out of that house, had to go somewhere, had to be seen somewhere, had to be gone all night.

Where to look?

If I could only put myself in Nora's place, think where I would hide a key... if I had a husband, a young unloving husband I didn't trust.

It had to be in her room.

I went back up the stairs, down the long hallway, and opened the door to her room, switched on the light.

Her dead husband's picture wasn't hanging straight, not quite straight.

He must have been a big man.

With a walrus mustache.

His picture was in a massive frame, a massive gilt frame, hanging right over the bureau.

The key was hanging from a nail behind it.

I grabbed it and ran out of the room, pausing only to turn out the light, ran back down the hallway to the living room.

There was a number on the key.

Thirty-six.

My box number was thirty-three.

I went to the bathroom and found tape, tore off a piece, went back to the living room and printed my box number on the tape.

Thirty-three.

I wrapped the tape in a piece of paper, lightly, and put it in my coat pocket.

Thirty minutes later I was drinking beer in a honky-tonk. I talked to people, bought drinks, flirted with the waitress, tipped her two bucks.

She'd remember that.

The place closed at one o'clock. I had to go somewhere, had to get somewhere in a hurry.

I called a cab and had him take me to Melissa. I felt a little tight, not much, and I wasn't worried about Nora. For tonight I could forget about Nora. She was dead and a weight gone from my shoulders.

Good-bye, Nora.

I tipped the cabbie five dollars and got out at the corner near Melissa's house, walked up the street feeling a little fuzzy, a little tight and fuzzy, but good. I felt free and it felt good.

A noise.

Door opening.

Dimly, dark dimly, a figure moved from Melissa's door way, across the darkness of the porch, and into the yard.

Melissa.

Melissa in a nightgown, a shiny sheening nightgown, walking wild and strange across the yard, barefoot in the moonlight, long hair streaming down her back, her face pale and featureless in the dim moonlight.

I stood still and stared.

She stood there, a lovely ghost in the moonlight, with head thrown back, staring at the stars, and I stood there with my blood racing and my heart pounding and my breath coming ragged and fast, remembering her kiss, the wildness of her kiss, remembered the odor of her, the tingling woman odor of her and the way she looked and the way she talked and the way her eyebrows lifted and eyes smiled, mocking and teasing and tender and somehow sweet sad.

Beyond her, across the street, was the desert, shimmering silver, lonely and wind washed, but she stood motionless, head thrown back.

And then she was gone, running, back into the house. I felt I'd been dreaming.

When I knocked at the door it must have scared her. I heard her move inside. Her voice, when she spoke, was little more than a whisper, trembly and thin.

"Who is it?" she quavered.

"Dun."

"Dun!"

"Let me in."

She opened the door and was in my arms, warm and soft and smooth in my arms, and her kiss was a living flame, consuming me, making me wild.

I slept with her in my arms, lying across the bed, and it was the first time in my life, the first time I could remember, that I'd felt safe and secure, at peace with myself, at peace with the world.

CHAPTER XIV

The bank opened at nine o'clock. I went to a café next door for a cup of coffee, dawdled over it for half an hour, chain smoked and eyed the clock.

There were a few people in the bank. I went directly to the girl at the front desk, behind the railing, and showed her my key.

"I'd like to get into my box," I said.

"Name, please."

"Lattner."

She flipped through a card file, studied it, and handed me a pen.

"Sign here, please."

I hadn't counted on that, but I signed.

She pressed a buzzer and the mousey girl, the one who had shown me to my box the first time, came up from the back.

"Mister Lattner wants to open his box," the girl at the desk said.

The mousey girl walked toward the back and I followed her. She unlocked the door to the little room, went inside and flicked on the light.

I looked among the boxes for thirty-six.

It was taking too long.

There was my box, thirty-three but thirty-six wasn't where it should be.

None of the boxes were where they should be, but scattered without order, or maybe scattered with some kind of order in mind.

Would the girl remember my box number? She hadn't picked up the card, hadn't asked me for my number, hadn't asked me for my key.

It wasn't working out as I had planned. The way I had figured it, thirty-six should be near thirty-three.

The girl cleared her throat.

"That's a mighty bright light," I said. "It blinded me for a minute."

And all the time my eyes were searching, searching and searching, frantically searching.

There it was.

It wasn't even on the side of the room where my box lay, but at the end of the room.

I'd have to chance it.

Walking toward it, taking my hand from my pocket, palming the adhesive, I tried to think of something bright to say.

"Maybe I should have a checking account," I said. "I thought I could stash away some money for a rainy day, but it rained sooner than I expected."

The girl gave a polite smile.

I took the box, pressed it against my belly front side out, stooped a bit and stuck the adhesive on top of the original number. Then, tucking the box under my arm, I walked toward a small table in the middle of the room. I dropped it on the table, letting it bang, wanting the girl to see my number on the tape.

Do it right.

Take your time.

I fumbled in my pockets, hunting my key, making a show of it.

"Never know where I put anything," I said.

She laughed a little, but her eyes flicked toward the box. I had the key, turned to the box, inserted it in the lock and twisted.

Nothing happened.

It was the key to my own box.

"Car key," I said. "I hope I didn't leave the box key in the car."

This time I didn't have to pretend, but searched my pockets with trembling fingers.

Nora's key was in my coat pocket, in the tiny pocket at the top of my coat pocket, the change pocket, the nuisance pocket.

I could feel sweat on my face.

This time I stood between the girl and the box, hiding the box from her, not wanting her to see.

Unlocked it.

Pulled back the lid.

Neat stacks of greenbacks, rubber banded, stacks and stacks of greenbacks.

Some rings, some necklaces, some brooches.

I scooped out the money, jamming it in my inside coat pocket. The rings and things I left.

Closed the lid. I'm not greedy.

I walked with the box back to the shelf, peeled the tape off, crumpled it into a ball in my hand.

"That should hold me for a while. Maybe you could help me spend some of it one night."

Again she smiled, but this time she blushed, dropped her eyes.

"I'd love to," she said.

"Fine. Where do you live?"

"Thirty-three-one-six South Oak," she said.

"I'll be around. What's your name, anyway?"

"Norma," she said. "Norma Amel."

"Well, then, Norma. I'll call you soon."

She smiled, half giggled, stood aside for me to leave the room.

It took twenty minutes to get home, to Nora's house, to the house that was never home.

Nora was still there.

Dead as a door-nail, cold as a fish, offal.

I ran upstairs to her room, hung the key on the nail behind her dead husband's picture, and ran back down the stairs.

Nora was still there.

Still dead, cold dead.

She'd changed color. She was bluish, blackish bluish, repulsive. Still she wore that smile, that horrible smile, and her eyes were wide, staring, filmed and cold blank.

I ran out of the door, yelling.

"Call an ambulance!" I screamed. "Call the police! Call a doctor!"

People came from everywhere. Funny, I hadn't paid any attention to neighbors. I'd seen them, sure. I even knew a few of them by name, recognized them on sight, but I'd just never paid any attention to them.

Women came, women in wrappers, fat women and tall women, frowzy and ugly and curious, morbidly curious, excited as all hell, hoping for the worse.

They got what they were looking for.

One woman fainted.

A couple of men came on the run, took one look and ran away again. They must have called all emergency numbers, though, because an ambulance came, a doctor came, and the police came.

It was quite a session. Even a newspaper reporter came.

This had to be good.

This game was for keeps.

The police were pretty nosey, suspicious and nosey, but my neighbors rallied round me. A fat woman, and I swear I'd never laid eyes on her before, became indignant.

"That woman was like a mother to this boy!" she said. "The very idea! You sound like you think he might have hurt that poor old soul! Why, if I've heard her say it once I've heard her say it a hundred times! She said this boy was like her own flesh and blood, like the son she never had!"

The policeman, red of face, told the woman to run along home.

"This is serious business, ma'am," he said. "A woman's dead here."

"That doesn't mean you have to treat this boy like a criminal!" she said. "Look at him! Look at how white he is! Can't you see he's stricken with grief?"

"Please go home, ma'am," the cop said, nudging his companion, urging him to act.

The fat woman walked away, muttering, and the others followed her.

"Now," the red-faced cop said. "Tell us what happened here."

"I came in a few minutes ago," I said. "There she was, just as you see her. I didn't touch a thing. I've warned her about those stairs before."

"Who are you anyway?"

"Lattner. Dun Lattner. I room here."

"What's your line? What do you do?"

"I'm in the used furniture business."

"Yeah. I've seen your place. Where were you all night?"

"At the home of a friend... after about one o'clock this morning. Before that I was at the mayor's house. I left there about nine and went to a tavern out on the highway."

"Can you prove where you were?"

"If necessary."

"Well, it looks like this woman fell down the stairs and broke her neck. The doc can tell us. Anyway, the sheriff should be along after a while. There'll be an inquest, more'n likely."

The doctor, a small, busy man, bustled into the room without a word. He examined the body briefly, nodded at the cops.

"I'll send you my report," he said. "Have you notified the county authorities?"

"Yeah."

"Don't move the body until the sheriff and the coroner have been here," the doctor said.

The ambulance arrived, two men in the cab.

I smoked, sat on the stair steps and smoked.

A car pulled in at the curb and two men got out. One was old, fat and old and lame, the coroner. The other was young, wet behind the ears, sporting a gun on his hip and a deputy sheriff's badge on his vest.

The coroner didn't even stoop over, didn't touch Nora, just stood over her and stared.

"Guess she fell," he said. "The doctor been here?"

"Just left," the red-faced cop said.

"We'll have the inquest in my office at two o'clock tomorrow afternoon."

The deputy pointed at me. "Who's he?"

"I'm Dun Lattner," I said, standing up. "I board here. I found the body a little while ago."

He stared at me, his eyes cool and questioning. He looked around, asked to see my room, pried, and peered, even poked the pile of clothing I'd dumped in the closet.

"How come these things are damp?" he asked.

"I fell in the mayor's swimming pool."

"Be at the courthouse at two o'clock tomorrow," he said. "Second floor, Room 210, north end."

They left. The two men got out of the ambulance, brought in a stretcher, rolled Nora on it.

"Say," I said. "What gives with the coroner in this state? He didn't even examine the body."

"He's not a doctor," one of them said. "He's the justice of the peace."

"Oh."

I went into the kitchen, found a beer in the ice box, sat down at the kitchen table and emptied my pockets of money.

Ten thousand dollars.

Where was the rest of it? Nora had said she had twenty thousand.

In the house?

Where in the house?

I searched room by room, under mattresses, in vases, behind pictures. It could have been in the house, but I couldn't find it.

One thing I did know. I wasn't going to stay in that house, wasn't going to sleep there.

It didn't take long to pack a bag.

Nora's old car was in the garage, but I didn't take it. From now on in there was no Nora, had been no Nora, would never be a Nora and never be the memory of a Nora... if I was lucky.

I'd take her money and leave her memory behind.

CHAPTER XV

I went down to the store and swept out. It wasn't much, that store, but it made me feel good to be in it, working in it, hoping to make a sale or hoping somebody would come along and sell me some furniture.

At nine o'clock, on the nose, a panel truck pulled up in front and a couple of guys got out. They wore shiny boots and boot pants.

"Mayor Harris sent us," one of the men said.

"Did you bring your instruments?"

He nodded.

"Let me lock up."

We all crowded in the front seat. Both men were young, pretty much impressed with themselves, curious but not wanting to ask questions.

"Drive to the middle of the Flats," I said.

They tried to make conversation and I only grunted in reply.

I wanted to think.

The breaks had been in my favor. The cops had been dumb. I had the world by the tail.

Every town has a Flats, if it's small enough, or a Belt or a District if it's large enough. This Flats was like all other small-town Flats, a ghetto of tin dwellings, boxboard stores, a hodge-podge of crude shacks with tarpaper roofs or rusty tin roofs, dingy honky-tonks and cluttered grocery stores, cafés and barbecue pits.

Kids were everywhere, barefoot and happy, their faces shining.

Men and women, fat and black women, slim brown women, zoot suit men and work clothed men, ambled across the street, down the street, popped from nowhere.

We stopped in the middle of the shack town, pulled over to the side of the road.

"Get your instruments out of the car," I said. "If anybody asks what you're doing, which they will, just say you're surveying for the new paved streets, the mayor's going to put in."

"The mayor's not going to build any streets," the blond boy, Hibbs, said.

"How do you know?" I asked. "Have you asked him?"

"No, but I know he's not fixing to pave any streets down here."

"Shut up, Henry," said Dillon, the dark boy. "Do as you're told. The mayor said do whatever this guy said do."

"Start surveying," I said. "Do it right. Drive stakes and everything. Some of these lads aren't as dumb as they pretend."

They started surveying. I sat on the steps of a honky-tonk and watched them sweat. They didn't like it, but they worked.

A black man, black as the ace of spades, waddled out of a barbecue joint. He was picking his teeth, watching the surveyors. He was fat and prosperous and he had an eye for business.

"What they doin' out there?" he asked, smiling, bowing a little, gesturing at the surveyors.

"The mayor's going to pave the streets through here," I said.

"Is he now?" The fat man's eyebrows shot up.

"Yeah," I said. "This street's first and then we'll get to the side streets."

"How come?" he asked. "They ain't paved no streets here before. How come they startin' to pave now?"

"Well, the mayor might not get elected for another term," I said. "He's always wanted to get money enough to pave down here and now he's got it. So he's rushing the paving while he's in office because he's afraid the next man might use the money for something else."

"Is... that... right! Interestin' to be sure! Yes... sir... ree!"

"Yeah," I said, getting up and stretching. "I sure hope we can get this paving done before the mayor goes out of office. It's slow work, though, so I don't know...."

"Maybe the mayor will get hisself elected again."

"Maybe."

"You think he'll get beat?"

"I think so. He's worried, too. Not that he cares for the office, but he's worked hard trying to raise money for this section of town and he'd sort of like to see it through."

"I'm John Sylvester Brown," the man said. "Maybe you've heard of me."

"Can't say that I have."

He strutted a little walking down the steps, puffing out his chest, throwing back his head.

"Well," he said, "I own just about everything worth owning down here. You might say I'm the mayor of the Flats."

"Glad to know you," I said.

"Maybe I could throw some votes to the mayor."

"Well, maybe."

"The people down here'll vote the way I say," he said.

"Maybe." I shrugged my shoulders.

"Honest," he said. "I run things down here."

"Maybe you can help the mayor a little, then. Say, where's the school?"

"Two blocks over." He pointed.

"Mind walking over there with me?"

"I'll walk you. What you want to go over there for?"

"There's talk of a new school," I said.

"The mayor can't build a new school, mister. The school board does that."

He wasn't dumb.

"The mayor's been talking to the board," I said. "He told those bastards that the school down here is a crime and disgrace. Said the board better get busy or he was going to raise hell."

We walked over and looked at the school. Actually, it was better than the school I went to when I was a kid. Even at that it wasn't much of a school.

"They crowd too many kids in there," John Sylvester said. "It's cold in winter and hot in summer. The windows're gone and it's dark in there."

"The mayor's going to fix all that," I said. "He told the school board he wants a modernistic school down here. Said the kids down here need a gymnasium and a swimming pool. What's more, all the councilmen on the ticket with him are going to back him up."

John Sylvester rubbed his hands. "Man!" he said. "That sure sounds good! I can swing plenty of votes down here!"

"Trouble is," I said, shaking my head and looking glum, "there's not much time. You can see a few people, sure, but you can't see enough to help much."

Laughter, gurgling deep laughter.

"Man," John Sylvester said, "I can see you ain't never heard of me. Why, man, I'll call a meeting every night until election! I'll go to the churches! I'll pack people in that old school house! Why, man, I'll just naturally pass the word all over these old Flats before you know what's goin' on! And, besides, darn near everybody down here owes me money!"

"How do you know they'll listen to you?"

John Sylvester smiled. "Because you come down here to make a deal," he said. "You think I walked out on the street and started askin' questions by accident? You think I wasn't up in my room when a boy come up and told me they was surveyin' the street? You think I didn't know you come down here to put on an act to suck up some votes?"

"You think I'm not on the level?"

He waved a hand at the school, at the tumbled shacks and dusty streets.

"It's the same as it was ten years ago," he said. "But it ain't the same as it'll be in ten more years. You know why? Because we can't be fooled any more. From now on we get! When a white man makes a promise, he delivers!"

"You'll get your paved streets," I said. "The school was a bluff."

"I'll settle for the streets. The mayor can't do anything about the school. Anyway, bigger people than me will take care of the schools."

"Will you deliver the votes?"

John Sylvester took a deep breath.

He looked me square in the eye.

"I can deliver the votes, but how do I know you can deliver the streets?"

"I'm pledging the mayor to pave the streets."

"White man, that don't mean nothing to me."

"You talk a big game, fat man."

The man was mad, so mad he forgot I was white and he was black and there was a whole world between us, a wide world bridged by a long bridge he could never cross.

He shook his finger at me.

"I'll take a chance on you," he said. "I'll deliver the votes and you deliver the streets. But you damned sure better deliver the streets!"

"All right," I said. "You've got my word for it. My word binds the mayor and I'll see to it he delivers."

"See that you do," he said. "Just see that you do."

I walked away, telling myself he had no right to talk to me like that. I tried my best to get mad, but I couldn't.

And I didn't feel good about the look in his eyes, either.

The inquest wasn't bad. They didn't give me a hard time. The mayor stated I'd visited in his home. The waitress from the honky-tonk told them

I'd been there until one in the morning. I'd given them Melissa's name and address privately, but they didn't bother to call her.

So I was in the clear... if I stayed lucky. Small towns are like that.

They kept me about an hour and dismissed me. I was starting out of the room when a seedy little man with a sad, droopy, tobacco-stained mustache caught me by the arm.

"Jaggers," he said. "Henry Jaggers."

"Lattner."

His eyes were watery.

"She was a fine woman," he said.

"She certainly was."

"Had you known her long?"

"Not very long. I've been boarding there. But the place was like home to me. Nora took me under her wing, in a manner of speaking, and I... well, I never had a mother."

His face was sorrowful. "You must have thought a great deal of her. She was a fine woman."

"Like a mother to me."

"My heart goes out to you," he said.

Was he kidding?

"I was her attorney," he said. "Handled her affairs for years."

A cold, shocking, almost electrical chill swept up my back, prickled the hairs on my neck.

He'd know about the bank box, about Nora's money.

"We'll read the will tomorrow," he said. "Right after the funeral."

"The will?"

"Oh," he said. "You wouldn't know about that."

"We didn't talk about her personal affairs."

"She was a fine woman."

There was a pause, an awkward pause, but I couldn't think of anything to say.

"In my office," he said. "Shall we say four o'clock? The funeral's at two, so that should be about right."

"In your office," I said.

"I won't detain you. Know you're busy. Must attend to the funeral arrangements myself."

"Can I help?"

"Thanks," he said. "I can manage."

He turned back into the room, his whole body dripping with sadness, and I went outside.

Nora must have had a will. She might have written a new one after our marriage. I'd be mentioned and I'd be cooked. The will would mention the money in the bank box, and the money wouldn't be in the box.

But they couldn't prove anything, couldn't prove I'd taken the money from the box.

The girl, the tall girl, the ugly girl, hadn't seen me take the money, hadn't seen me take the money from Nora's box. She'd have squealed if she'd seen, and she hadn't squealed.

They couldn't pin it on me. The bank couldn't admit they'd been careless. It was time to start living.

I went to a drug store for a drink and a paper, turned to the classified ads and started checking rooms for rent.

The room I took was a cheerless place, in a big house, old and ugly. An old man and woman lived alone. They gave me a room with a private entrance for fifteen dollars a week. The bed was hard and lumpy and I kept thinking about that will.

It's hard to think straight when you're tired and sleepy and can't fall asleep. Your thoughts start twisting around, start running off on tangents, and finally you build the problem up and up, out of proportion, until it gets you in a sweat.

That's what happened to me. I kept thinking about that will, thinking about all the possibilities. Nora could leave her money and house to me and they'd put me in the chair. Circumstantial evidence could do it. I'd be dead. They'd burn me. I wouldn't have a chance, not the ghost of a chance.

Motive?

Any jury in the world would convict me just on general suspicion. And... if Nora had written a new will I'd be dead. They'd say I had the motive, say I expected to benefit from the will, even if she didn't leave me a cent.

I got my bowels in an uproar just thinking about it. For a while there I was on the point of bolting.

It's funny how muddled was my thinking, how I twisted and turned and rolled and tossed and sweated. Then, all of a sudden, some little me inside me pointed a finger and laughed and said, look, kid, you're losing a screw, acting the fool, because Nora didn't have time to make a new will, didn't have time to mention you as her husband in a will, because she was sick the next morning after the wedding and then she fell down the stairs and broke her neck... remember?

She could have called her lawyer.

But she hadn't. She was feeling better that afternoon and wasn't planning to fall down a flight of stairs.

I had one chance and one only. To sit still. Besides, I had the world by the tail on a downhill pull. All I had to do was keep the grip I had.

All night long I rolled and tossed, thought and thought, and more than once I was ready to chuck the whole thing and pull out of there. Finally, toward morning, I got a to-hell-with-it feeling and dropped off to sleep. A cool fall wind blew in with the morning, brought me wide awake, and I got out of bed.

The bathroom was down the hall, cold and ugly. I shivered through a shave, skipped a bath, doused my head under the cold tap and went back to my room to dress. There was a gas stove there, which I lighted, stood before, warmed my legs. Then I dressed and walked to town.

A short stack with a couple of eggs over easy, three cups of coffee, and I felt like a new man.

I felt good enough to attend Nora's funeral.

Poor Nora.

It was a long morning. I must have had a dozen cups of coffee, must have smoked forty cigarettes, and the morning dragged, taunted and tortured, and my nerves were screaming before two o'clock.

Two o'clock came. I took a cab to the cemetery.

Poor old Nora.

I got out at the cemetery gate and walked a gravel road toward a cluster of cars. Stunted fir trees marched in orderly rows, but the graves were grassless mounds of red earth and the entire cemetery looked unkempt, uncared for.

A black cloud bank was blowing in from the Southwest, lowering, gold rimmed, threatening. A cool gust of wind hit me in the face, smelling of rain, and the first spattering drops fell before I reached the burial site. They plopped on the ground, splattered, rolled in the dust, formed little balls, and then the cloud burst and the rain fell in torrents.

I was soaked.

By the time I'd reached the grave the heavy rain was gone and it just drizzled.

The preacher, an elderly man with white hair and open, square face, was telling about Nora's life, about what a fine woman she had been. He repeated all the stock phrases, quoted all the appropriate Scriptures, and then said a prayer.

It didn't take long.

The preacher picked up a handful of earth and dropped it into the grave. I heard it strike the boarding, heard the sodden thump, and fought down an insane desire to give the preacher my handkerchief to wipe his muddy hand.

There couldn't have been more than fifty people there. I stayed until they had gone, watched three men fill the grave, and then I walked back to town.

It was just four when I walked past the courthouse, five past when I got to the little row of brick buildings two blocks beyond the courthouse square. There was a small black directory in the hallway of one of the buildings. Jaggers was in number two.

The minister was there, still soaked from the rain, still wearing his funeral expression. Another man was there, too, a small man, bald and pickle-faced, a quick and nervous man.

Jaggers, poring over papers at his desk, looked up. "Ah, there you are," he said. "Meet Reverend Peters and Doctor Buell."

We all murmured something, shook hands, sat down.

"Gentlemen," Jaggers said, "this won't take long. I've asked you all here because you are the beneficiaries or the representatives who benefit from the will."

He began to read. It took ten minutes.

Nora left half her insurance and money to the church, the other half to the hospital.

My name wasn't mentioned.

Forty thousand bucks in a savings account.

Twenty thousand in insurance.

… and all monies in my safe deposit box….

A lot of dough. Half to the hospital and half to the church.

What a chump I'd been.

I should have planned better. I should have found the body as a grieving husband instead of a mere boarder. I should have gambled, should have defied them to prove I'd pushed Nora down those stairs. As a husband I could have contested the will.

Jaggers cleared his throats.

"Mr. Lattner," he said, "Nora Simmons called me about you some two weeks before her death."

"Oh?"

"She wanted you to have her picture."

My laugh cackled out, more of a giggle than a laugh, and I staggered out of there, bent almost double, hands clasped over my belly, tears streaming from my eyes.

I'll never forget the way they looked.

CHAPTER XVI

Harris called me next day.

"How'd it go in the Flats?" he asked.

"Maybe we'd better meet somewhere for coffee," I suggested. "There are customers in the store."

"Tell you what, Lattner. I've got a business appointment. There's a party at the country club tonight. Why don't you drop by out there about eight?"

"I'll be there."

It was a good day. By five I was dreaming of a store in town.

Melissa called and wanted me to take her swimming. I told her I had to go look at some furniture, promised to see her the following night.

I bought a new suit, new shoes, a half dozen shirts, new underwear, socks and ties, got a haircut and a manicure.

I took a cab to the country club, paid the driver, walked slowly toward the music and lights.

The bar was in the back. To get there I had to circle the dance floor.

Cyd Harris was there, lovely and blonde and expensive, dancing like a dream, head thrown back, saying something, laughing a little.

She saw me.

I grinned and kept on walking, looked back once to see her glide away.

Harris was in the bar.

"Well, hello," he said. "Glad to see you could make it."

"What are we drinking?"

"You name it and we've got it."

"Bourbon and water."

"Bartender!"

The barkeeper almost jumped over the bar.

We took our drinks to a table and sat down. Women, attached and unattached, wandered into the bar for drinks. Their laughter was too loud, too forced, too gay. They were killing themselves having fun.

"Do you go for this?" I asked.

Harris shrugged. "It's good for business," he said. "And besides, I'm in politics."

We drank.

"How's it going in the Flats?" he asked finally.

"I ran into a fat black boy over there," I said. "He had a gold tooth with a white diamond cut in it."

"John Sylvester Brown," Harris said. "What happened?"

"We ran a survey over there. John Sylvester wanted to know what gives, so I told him you were going to pave the streets."

Harris turned red. He turned red like a thermometer, the red starting at his shirt collar and roving upward, slowly, evenly.

"You told Brown that?"

"Yes."

He almost choked. "Do you know what that means?"

"It means votes for you," I said. "So before you blow your gasket, just chew that for a while."

"Maybe it means votes!" he said. "But it means I'll have to pave those streets!"

"So pave them," I said. "It shouldn't cost so much. Those Negroes pay taxes."

"And what do you think my white neighbors will say about that? You think they're going to sit around and let me pave the Flats when there are streets uptown that need paving?"

"You can cross that bridge when you come to it," I said. "If you're smart you can get the newspaper to back you. Make it a crusade. Be the upright and forward-looking mayor. Have vision. Get the churches behind you."

Harris laughed.

"I can see the newspaper getting behind me," he said. But I could tell he was liking it. He had some hope now. Already he was seeing the headlines.

Suddenly he was all smiles, all laughter and light, ready to play, a load gone from his shoulders.

"Come on," he said. "A young man like you ought to be dancing."

"Just a minute," I said. "There's something else I want to talk about."

The old boy's eyes narrowed. He could smell it coming. The touch. Rich men see the touch played like a violin, from every angle, over and over and endlessly, until they begin to freeze up before the touch comes.

"What's on your mind?"

"You saw my little store. Today I cleared three hundred dollars on used furniture. Yesterday I cleared three and a quarter. I made a cool thousand last week."

His face cleared. He didn't figure I wanted money, not after what I'd just said.

"Is that right?" he asked. "I didn't know there was that much money in used furniture."

"There is," I said. "Take any oil town, any town where people come and go, and you've got a used furniture market. What makes it better is that the first guy usually corners the market. Well, I wasn't first, but I was the first to play it right. I advertise and keep on advertising. I turn the stuff over for a quick profit. People get bargains from me."

"So?"

"So I'm ambitious. I want to move up town."

"With used furniture?"

"With new furniture. Hardware and toys and new furniture and radios and washing machines and iceboxes and cosmetics."

"That would cost some money."

"I can raise ten thousand."

"That wouldn't be enough."

"I know it."

"What's your deal?"

"A partnership. You've got a dead store and I can bring it to life and pay you the rest out of my share of the profits."

Harris was all business now, his face cold and set with that cold and set ruthless blood-sucking look that men with money wear when they're talking to men without money who want money.

"I don't know you from Adam's off ox," he said. "For all I know you're not worth the powder to blow your head off. I do know you sold one of my washing machines. Stole it, to be blunt."

"You don't know that," I said. "The odds are fifty-fifty I'm honest."

"If the odds were that good I'd take chances on more people," he said. "But between me and you, I'd say the odds are about ninety to one."

"You didn't make your money without cutting some throats along the way."

"Maybe I didn't," he said. "But I didn't steal."

"You never stole a lease? Never cheated another man?"

"Business is business."

"Look," I said. "Given time, I can build my own store right in the middle of town. I can do it in a year, the way I'm going. But I'm in a hurry. The money's here now. It won't be here forever. Your store isn't earning you a dime and you know it. I can make it pay, and I've got ten thousand dollars to start with."

"We'll talk about it some more," he said. "Give me a chance to look you over a little. And let's see how the election comes out."

I tossed off my drink and stood up.

"Be seeing you," I said. "Good night."

Harris nodded. "I'll keep in touch with you."

I went to the ballroom, stood with my back to the wall. Cyd Harris danced by, sleek and tall and brown-smooth lovely, the dress molded to her body, shoulders round and brown bare, smooth round bare, the long blonde hair touching the shoulders, just touching the shoulders, the breasts taut and firm, the legs long and lovely and sharply etched beneath the skin-tight blue slick tight dress.

She saw me.

Smiled.

Wrinkled her nose and smiled and looked away again, looked into the face of her partner, danced away with him. I wanted her.

It was time to get out of there, but I wanted another drink.

I had another bourbon and water, sitting at a table in the corner, drank and felt my body relax, drank deeply and fought the girl from my mind.

A hand fell on my shoulder, lightly, so lightly, burning through the coat and through the shirt, burning a brand into my shoulder.

I looked into her face.

It was the first time I'd really looked at her face. The eyes were wide spaced, gray blue green, green and cool and blue and hot, brown flecked, under thin black upward outward curling eyebrows, a face high cheeked and full cheeked and square chinned and wide mouthed, red lipped and creamy tan white, blonde and sexy as sin and dangerous as hell.

"You're dry," she said.

"Dry all over. Sit down and have a drink."

She sat down, saying nothing, elbows on the table, chin in cupped hands, the eyes cool and appraising, studying me, figuring what made me tick, figuring my potential, figuring my maleness, primitive and wild and coolly calculating.

"I owe you an apology," she said.

"Skip it. Maybe I had it coming."

"Tell me why you disliked me so that night," she said.

"You still haven't placed me?"

"No."

"I was out on the highway one day. You had a flat and I fixed it. And you drove off and left me."

She was erect, biting her lips, and snapped her fingers.

"That's it!"

"That's it."

"No wonder you disliked me." She laughed, a full throaty laugh.

"If you'll pardon my saying so," I said, "you acted like a bitch."

She narrowed her eyes. "A she-bitch."

"I couldn't have worded it better myself."

"You don't have to be so damned agreeable. It's time you started saying it was your fault all the time."

"But it wasn't," I said. "First you insulted me by trying to give me money. Then you drove off and left me standing beside the road."

"I resented you. I resented the way you looked at me. And I resented that superior air of yours. There you were, dirty and long haired and broke and hungry and you acted like you were better than me."

"Maybe I am."

She didn't like that.

"Maybe you are, Buster." Her voice was brusque, rough around the edges.

"Take it easy," I said. "I'm baiting you."

She smiled then, making my backbone shiver, making my belly tickle, sending a stream of desire through my body.

The girl knew her business, unconsciously, knew her female business in an unconscious born-with-it sureness, knew how to use her femaleness as a weapon.

"Let's dance," she said.

So we danced.

It was more than dancing. It was almost a union of our bodies, almost but not quite, both of us straining to touch the other with all our bodies, with the secret parts of our bodies, both striving to touch the other without the other being aware of the striving, dipping and swaying and leaning into each other, touching and clinging and pressing.

"Let's get out of here," she said at last, her lips close to my ear, her hair brushing my cheek.

"What about your date?"

"To hell with my date."

We left in her car.

She drove fast, hair streaming, the radio playing, along the highway and off onto a country lane, a smooth oil field lane, across the flat prairie, the shimmery moon-touched flat white sand sage-studded prairie, the girl a golden dream with long blonde hair flying in the wind, flying to the pulse of music, floating across the flatland of the prairie.

The road must have made a wide circle, away from the town and half-moon circle back to the town, for the lights loomed ahead of us, close ahead of us, and within minutes we were driving through the town.

"We'll stop by my place for a drink," she said.

I grunted.

She drove on through town, slowly, into the country and we were on the road leading to her house, her monstrosity of a house.

Parked.

Radio still playing.

We sat there a long while, not speaking, and made a contract, an unspoken contract, until both of us moved at the same time, moved to get out, moved toward the fulfillment of the contract unspoken.

The butler let us in.

Cyd led the way to the living room and poured drinks.

Still we had not spoken.

We toasted one the other, silently, toasted silently and drank our drinks.

She smiled a lazy smile, an unspeakably lovely smile, and my hands itched to bury themselves in warm soft flesh.

I followed her up a flight of stairs, into a bedroom, a huge bedroom with soft carpeting and concealed lighting, studded leather doors, sliding doors that partitioned the room, a bedroom with a huge bed, an enormous bed, a satiny smooth bed with pink sheets, skin smooth sheets.

In that bedroom, in that house, in that bed, that warm satiny smooth bed, I lay with Cyd, drowned myself in Cyd, branded myself with the hot sweet fire of Cyd's kisses, the mad sad glad passion of Cyd.

And then I dressed to go, leaving her on the bed, lovely brown smooth long limbed lovely on the bed.

I took a bill from my pocket, a crumpled dollar bill, held it between my fingers, and let it fall gently like an autumn leaf, twisting and turning lazily to land silently, to lie silently on the bed beside her.

The political pot boiled over and things looked bad for Harris. Some of the young business men, the punks, the kind that played around in the businesses their fathers founded, threw their support to the reform group opposing the Harris ticket. There was a hot editorial in the Norton newspaper, aimed at the city administration, and circulars littered the streets. The daily paper came out for Harris, but it was a wishy-washy endorsement, too weak to do much good.

Harris was worried. He came into the store just before sundown. I was alone, drinking a beer, counting the day's take.

He sat down in an old rocker, leaned back and unbuttoned his collar.

"It's hot," he said.

"Yeah. I'd offer you a beer if I had another."

"How do you think that Brown fellow will do with the vote in the Flats?"

"He's smart."

"You think he fell for that paving trick?"

"He wasn't fooled, but he'll go along. I wouldn't think of that paving as being a trick. I'd figure on paving those streets down there."

Harris grunted.

"I'm not kidding," I said. "That Brown impressed me as a tough cookie."

"What can he do?"

"He can talk. And, after all, you may need those votes again."

"One more term in office is all I need... all I want."

"Well, Brown can talk. And he might find somebody willing to listen."

"What kind of talk?"

"He could tell it around that you bought the vote down there. I don't know much about things like that, but some people might consider that as unethical, to say the least. Maybe somebody would contest the election."

"Who'd listen to Brown?"

"You're forgetting who Brown is, Harris. He's not just a Negro. He's a rich Negro. What's more, he's got influence. After all, who do you go see when you want to buy a vote in the Flats?"

"I never talked with him," Harris grinned. "Just remember, I've never made that man a promise."

"I talked to him. And you sent two men in a city truck to survey down there."

That rocked him a little. He stood up, stretched, buttoned his collar.

"You're worrying too much," he said. "You just get me the votes. I'll worry about the paving."

Melissa called.

"Where have you been?" she asked.

"Honey, I'm making money so fast I have to sit up at night and count it."

"Come over tonight."

There was a pleading note in her voice.

"Gosh, I can't. A guy wants me look at a house full of furniture."

"You could come if you wanted to."

"I'm doing this for you, baby. For us."

"I wish I could believe you."

"Honey! You know I love you."

"You won't come?"

"Tell you what I'll do. I'll come by about nine if I can manage it."

"The lights will be on."

I hung up and called Cyd Harris.

"This is Dun," I said.

"Go to hell," she said, and hung up on me.

Well, she had a right to be mad.

I called her again in ten minutes.

"Look," I said. "We should be about even new. What say we declare a truce."

"An armed truce," she said. "You're way ahead of me."

"I'll give you another chance to get even. I'll come by about eight and we'll go somewhere."

"Just this once," she said.

CHAPTER XVII

The polls opened at eight and closed at six. The voting box for the Flats was across the street from my store and I watched it all day. A few people voted before noon, only a few, and I began to worry.

I called Harris.

"Send a city truck back to the Flats," I said. "Have a couple of men drive a few more stakes. In about an hour I want you to send a truckload of gravel and a truckload of sand. Have them dump it right in the middle of Flat Town."

"Does it look bad down there?"

"Brown hasn't delivered you a dozen votes yet."

"All right. We'll give him a signal."

"Don't slip up. Get that stuff moving."

The votes began to trickle in about three. I saw Brown bring some old people in a truck, saw others brought in cars, saw the line begin to form, saw the people of the Flats voting for paved streets.

The returns were in by nine. Harris and his councilmen won, barely won, and I was in solid.

Harris picked me up and took me to the country club for a celebration. Cyd was there.

Melissa was there, too. She was with an army officer. I danced with Cyd, steered her away from Melissa, felt Melissa's eyes on me and cried inside.

"Let's go somewhere," I told Cyd.

"We can go somewhere later. Let's dance."

"Tonight I don't feel like dancing. I'd rather go somewhere and hold you close."

That low, lazy, slow lazy sensuous smile.

"I'd rather we'd go somewhere and you hold me close, too," she said. "Let's go."

I got up early and took the bus to Onarka, bought a marriage license.

Cyd would be surprised.

Her father would be surprised. He'd have a stroke. He'd die laughing. He'd blow a fuse.

Wouldn't Melissa be surprised'?

That hurt. The thought of Melissa hurt. I closed my eyes and saw her face just as it would look when she heard the news, and it hurt.

I could have cried.

Poor Melissa.

Poor Melissa, poor me, because I loved Melissa and she loved me, and never the twain shall meet.

A couple of weeks passed, the days mellow and golden, the trace of a fall nip in the air.

I took Cyd out every night, fought myself in an effort to stay away from Melissa, fought myself every waking moment to stay away from her, dreamed of her at night. It wasn't so bad when I was with Cyd. I didn't think of Melissa when I was with Cyd, but I thought of her constantly when I was alone.

Harris paid me the thousand dollars and I made another effort to buy into his store.

"You're rushing me," he said. "Give me some recommendations. For all I know you've got a record somewhere. Understand, I like you. I think you'll amount to something some day because you've got the drive. But I've got my reputation to think about."

"I've never been in business before," I said. "The people who could recommend me wouldn't satisfy you because they're just plain people."

"Well, let's let it ride for a while. You're doing well in furniture. Show me what you can do. Stick to it for a year and then we'll talk."

John Sylvester Brown came to see me. He was mad, but he wasn't in the Flats and he held himself under control.

"It was a trick," he said. "The mayor didn't ever mean to pave the Flats."

"He promised."

"You promised," John Sylvester said. "I never talked to the mayor until today."

"Today? You've seen Harris?"

"I went to his office. They wouldn't let me in."

"But you saw him!"

"When he went to the john."

"What did he say?"

Brown laughed. "What you expect he said? I'll tell you what he said. That he never heard of me! That he never promised to pave the Flats! That he didn't know what I was talkin' about! That's what he said!"

"We'll go see Harris. We'll go right now."

"He won't see me. I'm good enough to get him votes. All us black people are good for votes, but he won't let us in his office!"

"We'll see. Come along."

He had a car, a shiny new car, and we drove to city hall.

The blonde secretary said the mayor wasn't in.

"I can hear him in there," I said.

"He's busy. I'm sorry."

"Come on, John," I said. "We're going in."

The girl stood, but I stepped between her and Brown, pushed him ahead of me.

Harris could have shot us.

"You told John you weren't going to pave the Flats," I said. "How come?"

"It would be political suicide."

"You promised."

"No. You did the promising, Dun, and I didn't authorize it."

"You got the votes. John delivered them."

"How do I know he delivered them?"

"You know it."

"This will get you nowhere," Harris said. "I won't pressure."

"All right. We're not making threats, but you'll wish you'd done the paving."

"I'm busy," Harris said. "You'll please excuse me now."

Melissa called. We chatted a bit, sparring with words.

"I saw you with Cyd Harris," she said, finally.

"Yeah. I've been seeing her."

A pause, an awkward pause.

There was nothing to say.

"Dun?"

"Yeah?"

"What's the matter?"

"Nothing. Why?"

"What's the matter between us, Dun?"

"Nothing. Darling, there's nothing the matter between us."

"Yes, there is. What is it, Dun? Something I've done? If so, I'm sorry."

"You've done nothing, baby. Nothing. It's just me. Don't let it bother you. I've been trying to make money, trying to make contacts, trying to get ahead. But everything I do is for you. For us. Remember that."

"When will I see you?"

"Tonight. At eight."

"I hope you'll come this time, Dun. Please come."

"Don't worry. I'll be there."

All day I worried, fretted and stewed. I didn't want to hurt Melissa and I didn't want to get hurt. I had a course charted and the sailing was clear. Melissa was a quiet harbor and I couldn't get rich settling for a berth in a quiet harbor.

I didn't see Melissa.

I took Cyd dancing, broke it up early and went to my room. For an hour I rolled and tossed, and then I dressed and left the house.

I went to Melissa, held her in my arms and slept, buried my face in the hollow of her neck, held her tight and buried myself in sleep.

Harris sent a kid with a note. He wanted to see me, wanted me to meet him on the corner of Elm and Main at six o'clock.

I went to his office, barged in, and he frowned when I opened the door.

"You shouldn't have come here," he said. "I told you I'd pick you up at six."

"I'm ready to talk now," I said. "Maybe you'd better say your piece first."

"You've been seeing Cyd. I think she's in love with you. And I've been seen with you. That connects you with me. That Negro, Brown, has been spouting off about the paving you promised in the Flats. If he decides to squawk I'm bound to be hurt. So what do you want, Dun? How much will it take to buy you a ticket out of town?"

"Let's talk about your store first," I said.

"What's the store got to do with it?"

"I still want an interest in it," I said.

He flicked ashes from his cigar, gazed out the window.

"A lot of men would like to buy an interest in the store," he said.

"Let's put it like this. I'll buy a quarter interest in your store. I'll pay you ten thousand in cash, run the place and make it pay, and the rest of my interest will be paid out of profits."

"Let's say you just get out of town and stay out."

"And leave Cyd at the altar?"

Harris jumped, blanched, started to speak and thought better of it.

"Cyd and I are going to be married. Didn't she tell you?"

"I'll kill you first!"

"Mayors don't run around shooting prospective sons-in-law."

Harris stood up, leaned across his desk, shook his finger in my face.

"I'll see you in hell before you marry Cyd! I'll kill you if I hang for it!"

"Calm down, Mayor. Calm down and let's think about this thing a bit."

He stared at me, and then he slumped back in his chair.

"I sewed up the vote in the Flats," I said. "You might say I put you in the mayor's office. I promised Brown paving in the Flats if he delivered the vote, and then you welched on that promise. That wouldn't be a pretty story for me to tell, would it?"

Harris just stared.

"I can prove I had nothing to do with what you promised Brown."

"Can you? How? I'll say you were in on it. People know I've been seeing Cyd. People have seen us together. I even worked in your store for a while. People will believe Brown... and me."

"You've got me by the short hair," Harris said.

"Looks like it. And don't forget this. I can marry Cyd."

"She wouldn't marry you, Dun. She's playing. Besides, I can tell her about this conversation and she won't even see you again."

"Tell her, Mayor. Tell her about the Negro vote. Tell her how you paid me a thousand dollars to get their votes for you."

"What do you want, Dun?"

"I told you. Sell me a quarter interest in your store. Have the papers drawn up and ready to sign by tomorrow afternoon."

"And what about Cyd?"

"I'll drop her like a hot potato. I'm in love with someone else, anyway."

He walked to the window and stood there, his back to me, his shoulders drooping.

"Call me at two o'clock tomorrow," he said. "I'll either have the papers ready to sign or I'll have a warrant for your arrest."

"You won't have me arrested, Harris."

"Get out," he said.

"Sure. I'll call you at two tomorrow."

Harris told me to go to hell.

I didn't call him at two, but waited until three, and he told me to go to hell.

"We'll call it a draw," he said. "You leave Cyd alone and get out of town and I'll not make trouble for you."

"You're nuts," I said.

"I'll get you, Dun. I'll get you if you stick around."

"Here I stay," I said.

"Stay away from Cyd."

I hung up.

It was still early. I called Cyd.

"Meet me in front of the courthouse," I said. "I feel like driving and drinking and things like that."

"I'm busy, Dun."

"Look, baby, I've got something to tell you. Dress up and meet me at that courthouse in thirty minutes."

I waited an hour, stood around for an hour with a bottle of whiskey in my coat pocket. I was burning, but only smiled when she pulled in at the curb.

"You take too much for granted," she said as I entered the car. "You think all you have to do is crook your finger and I'll come running."

"You came."

She stepped on the gas and headed out of town. I opened the bottle, took a swig, handed it to her.

"Let's get something straight," she said. "I like you a lot. We have good times together. But don't be possessive. Don't crowd me. Just remember that sex isn't everything."

"It is with us."

I took another drink, gave her another drink.

"Look," I said. "Don't be mad. I'm just acting smart."

She pulled in at a service station, ordered some soft drinks for chasers, and drove fast along the highway. I switched on the radio, found some music and sat watching her, watched the anger fade, saw her relax.

"Pull over," I said. "I'm in the mood for a drink."

I poured half a soft drink from a bottle, slugged it hard, gave it to her.

We sat there an hour. The drinks hit her, but I cheated, drank sparingly and slugged her drinks, pretended to be tight and loaded her drinks.

Cyd got mushy, lovey-dovey and mushy, became all arms and lips and body.

"You're beautiful," I murmured against her lips. "You're beautiful and I want you and can't live without you."

"You're beautiful, too," she said.

I caught her shoulders, held her away, looked into her eyes.

"You know something," I said. "I've got a beautiful idea."

"All your ideas are beautiful," she said.

"Not as beautiful as you."

"I know it, but beautiful."

Her eyes wouldn't focus right. She giggled. Her head fell forward and she slumped against me.

"Let's get married," I said.

"That might be fun."

"You want to get married?"

"Sure, I think that would be fun. Then we could sleep together in public."

"I'd rather sleep with you in private."

"Let's get married," she said. "I've got a perfectly beautiful idea. Let's get married."

"All right, baby. You talked me into it."

"We don't have a license," she said. "Where can we get a license? Cars and people and dogs have to have licenses."

"I just happen to have one."

"That's beautiful," she said. "Let's get married."

"I'd better drive."

She slid over and I climbed under the wheel, headed for Onarka.

It was dangerous and I knew it. I was taking a big chance going back to Onarka to be married. But I was afraid to marry in Paley. Harris was a big man in Paley. No preacher would perform a ceremony for a drunken girl, and a Paley justice of the peace would be afraid of Harris. The whiskey was gone and it was sixty miles to any other town, so it had to be Onarka.

I had to walk with my arm around Cyd, had to hold her up, had to walk slowly to the courthouse. I hoped I wouldn't meet the sheriff.

There was a directory in the hallway and I studied it, breathed easier when I saw there were four justices of the peace in Onarka.

Nora and I had been married on the second floor. I picked a justice with an office on the first floor. I had to slip him a twenty-dollar bill.

"You're drunk," he said. "I don't marry drunks."

So I slipped him another twenty and he overhauled his ethics.

We met Jerry Norton in the hallway. He stared after us. I looked over my shoulder as I went out the door, saw him go into the office of the justice of the peace.

I steered Cyd to a café across the street, made her drink some coffee. She felt better for it.

Jerry Norton was standing beside her car when we came out. He nodded. "Hello, Jerry," I said.

He didn't say a word, just stood aside to let us pass, but his face was white and his hands formed fists. I hadn't noticed before, but he looked like Melissa, looked like an angry Melissa, and suddenly there were tears burning my eyes, tears to be blinked away.

CHAPTER XVIII

The news would break in a hurry and Harris would be furious. He would be furious, but he'd be stymied. Still, I was glad I didn't have to face him.

I headed for the Big Bend country. Cyd had a headache. She was sullen, withdrawn into herself. Part of the time she slept. We ate on the run. I picked up sandwiches and drinks and drove until nightfall.

We stopped at a small town at the edge of the Big Bend.

It wasn't a honeymoon.

Cyd wouldn't talk to me, wouldn't let me touch her, insisted we take separate cabins. I took a long walk, climbed a ragged ugly peak. She was polite, but that was all.

"It won't work, Dun," she said. "I don't love you and never will. You tricked me and everything worked out just as you planned. All right. We'll see what happens next."

So I took her home.

I let her out and drove back to town.

Melissa was backing out of her driveway when I drove up, almost backed into me, slammed on the brakes and got out of the car, leaving the door open.

Her face was white, the tiny freckles etched sharply against the whiteness.

"Come inside," she said.

I followed her, dreading it, wondering what I could say, wondering what I could do, wondering if I could undo what I'd done, and tell her I loved her.

She slammed the door and leaned against it.

"Why did you come?" she asked.

"To explain," I said.

She slapped me, the sound of the slap splatting loudly in the silence of the room, seeming to echo.

It hurt and I wanted it to hurt, wanted her to slap me again, wished she'd shoot me.

"That was for the times I've given myself to you," she said. "The trouble is, I can't punish myself for being such a fool."

"Don't," I said. "Don't be sorry."

She slapped me again, stood there trembling, breathing hard.

"Don't hate me," I said.

"I'd like to kill you!" she gritted. "I hope your life will be a hell on earth!"

"I love you," I said.

She laughed, head thrown back, laughed without mirth.

"Get out!" she said. "Stay out of my sight! Go to your Cyd! She can give you everything I can give you and she's got money, too! That's what you wanted, wasn't it? You'd do anything for money, wouldn't you?"

I walked toward her, tried to take her in my arms, but she stepped back. I could feel the scorn she felt for me, could actually feel the hatred she felt for me.

"Please," I said.

"Get out, Dun," she said. "Get out, now."

I stumbled to the car, felt despair, drove aimlessly around the town.

I took a hotel room for the night, wished I had Cyd with me to keep my feet warm, wondered what would happen if I went to the Harris home and knocked on the door, wished I had the nerve to do it, wished I could see the look on the mayor's face.

I got up early and went down to the store, took an inventory of the stock and found a buyer. There wasn't much stock left and I sold it for a song, glad to be free of it.

It was time to see Harris.

Jerry Norton stopped me on the street, caught me by the arm and pulled me around.

"Let's drink some coffee, Dun. I'd like to have a little chat with you."

"Sure, Jerry."

The wind whistled around corners, forced us to walk with heads down, collars up, blew our pants legs tight against our legs, tugged at our jackets.

We went into a café, took a booth, ordered coffee.

"I don't want you fooling around Melissa," Jerry said. "She told me you came there last night."

"Yeah. I had to see her, Jerry."

"Leave her alone, Dun. You're no good. You're no good for her and you're married. You could have married her, Dun, but you took Cyd and her money. So leave Melissa alone."

"I love her, Jerry."

"I'm warning you, Dun."

"Give me some time, Jerry. Give me some time to straighten things out."

"Don't make me warn you again, Dun."

"Give me time, Jerry. Lay off and give me some time."

Jerry flipped a quarter on the table and walked out of the café.

Harris wasn't in his office.

"He's at his store, I think," his secretary said. "Anyway, he said he wouldn't be in all day."

"Thanks."

I wanted to see Harris, wanted to get it over, but I didn't want to see him before witnesses. It had to be in private, where I could apply the screws, screw the vise tight, grab him by the short hairs.

It was three o'clock when I decided to take Cyd's car to her.

She opened the door at my knock and slammed the door in my face.

So all right.

I drove back to town, killed some time, drank coffee and had a beer. I called Harris at the store a little before five.

"This is Dun," I said.

"Go to hell."

"This is Dun, Mayor. Your favorite son-in-law. When can we talk?"

"Get out of town, Dun. I'm warning you."

"Why should I do that, now?" I asked, laughing a little. "What are you so upset about?"

"I'll give you one last warning, Dun. Get out of town while you can."

"Listen," I said. "I want to talk to you and I want to talk now."

"All right, then. Come around to the store in about fifteen minutes. I'll be alone then."

That was better.

Harris opened the door for me. He was mad, all-the-way-through mad, trembling mad, about ready to blow up. Great purple veins stood out on his neck, on his forehead, pulsed and throbbed. His face was flushed and his lips trembled.

"Come back here," he said, pointing to the rear.

I followed him to the stock room. He closed the door behind him and leaned against it, breathing hard.

"Dun," he said, "you've gone too far."

"I don't know what you're talking about. Cyd and I are in love. So we got married. That's natural, isn't it?"

"You married Cyd so I couldn't get at you," he said. "You got her drunk and married her, thinking you'd have me all sewed up. You think you'll be in clover, don't you Dun? You think you've arrived, don't you?"

"I don't expect anything from you, mayor. All my life I've made my own way. I'll support myself and I'll support Cyd. Of course, if you insist on taking me into the family business...."

His laugh was harsh.

"You'd love that," he said. "Harris and Lattner. Partners. From rags to riches in ten easy lessons."

"You're not being fair, Mayor."

"You're in for a big surprise, Dun. You're in for a big surprise."

We stared at each other.

"I always thought it was pretty funny the way you got ahead so fast," Harris said. "You blew into town and dug ditches and worked on a church building. Next thing anybody knew, you had that used furniture place. Then, in no time, you said you had ten thousand dollars to invest in my store."

"What's so funny about that?"

"Where'd you get the money, Dun?"

"I had backing. Is that a crime?"

"Where did you get the backing?"

"I'd rather not say."

"Did Nora Simmons let you have the money?"

"No."

"The ten thousand dollars?"

"No. One thousand dollars to start the furniture store. And I paid it back, every cent of it."

"Where did you get the ten thousand?"

"I didn't have ten thousand," I said. "I just told you I had that much, figuring I could borrow it if you agreed to let me buy in."

He was baiting me, enjoying it, watching me squirm.

"What was Nora Simmons to you, Dun?"

"A friend."

"She didn't die a natural death. Did she, Dun?"

Baiting me.

"She fell down some stairs," I said.

"You wouldn't have pushed her, would you, Dun?"

There was a sly smile on his face, an evil smile.

"The poor thing fell down a flight of stairs, like I said. It broke her neck. She was like a... mother... to me."

"Yeah," Harris said. "I'll bet."

"What are you driving at, Harris? What are you trying to say?"

"I think you know."

"Somebody's crazy," I said. "You've been out in the sun too long. What are you trying to say?"

"You took that money from Nora Simmons. I think the sheriff would be interested."

I began to laugh, began to laugh real laughter, began to laugh at myself, at the big joke.

"I've arranged to annul your marriage to Cyd," he said. "I can prove you didn't sleep with her."

I laughed.

He moved across the room and sat on a nail keg. Part of his anger was spent and he had a smirk on his fat face. He was still breathing hard.

Danger smell was in the room, thick and heavy in the room.

I was trembling.

Scared.

I was scared, trembling and scared and mad, hating Harris, hating his guts.

"It looks like you win, Harris."

"Yeah," he said. "I've got it all figured out, Dun. The old woman fell down a flight of stairs and you showed up with ten thousand dollars. Very convenient."

"The used furniture business has been good."

"Not that good. Dun. You took the old woman's money and you pushed her down the stairs."

"She fell down those stairs."

"That's what you say."

"You're talking through your hat, Harris."

Harris laughed.

"What about your girl friend, Dun?"

"I don't have a girl friend."

"Look," he said. "Don't try that line on me. I know you've been sleeping with Norton's sister."

"Don't say anything nasty about Melissa. Just don't say it."

He raised his eyebrows, cocked his head.

"You're in love with the girl," he said.

"That wasn't what I said, but make of it what you want. It doesn't matter what you think now."

"It'll matter," he said. "It'll matter before I'm finished."

He meant to see it through, meant to pin Nora's death on me.

"Spill it, Dun. You might as well spill it."

"Spill what?"

"Spill it about the old woman."

I was trembling.

"Come on," he said, baiting me. "Tell me the truth, Dun. Tell me the truth and I may let you go. Tell me everything and promise to get out for good and I may let you go."

He laughed a crazy little laugh, a head back, belly rumbling little laugh.

"You're taking it too far, Harris. You're pushing too hard. I don't know what you're talking about."

He laughed again, laughed silently, doubled over, pointed his finger at me.

"You'll laugh on the other side of your face," I said. "When my kid climbs up on your knee you'll laugh on the other side of your face."

His laughter faded.

He was paralyzed.

"What do you mean?" he asked.

"Cyd's with child," I lied. "That's why we were married."

He lost his marbles, flipped his lid, mouthed curses and gibberish, threats and curses and gibberish.

I let him rave.

He didn't calm down. Sweat poured from his face.

The sap jumped me.

Not once did he swing a fist. I hit him at will, cut his face, slugged him in the belly, but he came on and on and all the time his big hands were reaching and clawing, tearing at my shirt and my flesh, raking my arms and shoulders and chest, drawing blood, trying to get at my face.

Once he gave me the knee.

It doubled me up and I went down.

He kicked me in the ribs. I rolled over, caught the toe of his shoe in the small of my back and cried out, fire stabbing my kidneys, my spine.

Somehow I made it to my knees, but his knee caught me on the shoulder and sent me over on my back.

He was a mess, streaming blood, his face already puffed.

But he wasn't even breathing hard.

On my back, flat on my back, I doubled my knees and lashed out, caught him in the stomach. He seemed to float back, seemed to float a long time, a long way, and he went over backward, his back arched, head down and face up, and it was his face that hit the wall, the full weight of his body behind it.

I lay there a long time, and then I rolled over, vomited, rolled away from the vomit and sat up.

Harris wasn't moving.

It hit me like a ton of bricks.

He looked dead.

Maybe I blacked out. I must have blacked out, because when I could see again, think again feel again, I was on my knees beside Harris, his hand in mine, and I was crying.

Suddenly I froze.

Tingling little icicles tickled my spine.

Footsteps?

There I stood, frozen, glued to the spot, and it wouldn't do. I had to move, had to hide.

The footsteps were real now, loud and firm, louder, getting nearer.

I jumped as high as I could jump, caught hold of a rafter, pulled myself up, huddled against the wall in the open attic.

Ice-cold sweat poured down my face. I was ready to scream, wanted to run, but I perched on the rafter and stared at the door.

It opened slowly, so slowly, so very slowly.

The black man, the Negro, John Sylvester Brown.

I was cooked.

He stared at the body of Harris, glanced around the room, and then he was gone. I could hear his footsteps as he made his way toward the front door.

I heard the front door slam.

He was gone.

But where had he gone

Would he call the police?

I headed for the back door, unbarred it, slipped through and out into the alley.

I walked to Melissa, walked all the way, and she wasn't home.

The door was open but the house was dark, empty and dark, and Melissa was gone when I needed her most.

It was quiet, dark and quiet, and I relaxed. There in the quiet room, the dark quiet of the room, with somewhere a clock tick-tick-ticking, I lay down on the couch, lay warm and still and alone and safe on the couch and went to sleep.

And then I was awake and the light was bright and harsh in the room. A radio was blaring, blaring, blaring, and there was harsh light that hurt my eyes and noise that shredded my nerves, frayed the bare nerves, and I sat up and yelled, screamed, yelled, my mouth wide open and my eyes tight shut and the yell bubbling out of my mouth.

"What is it?" Melissa was shaking me. "What's wrong? What are you doing here?"

"Let me stay," I said.

"Go to your wife," she said.

"Cyd's not my wife. The marriage is being annulled."

"You're a liar!" she said. "Go home to your wife!"

"Cyd and I are finished," I said. "It was a mistake and the marriage is being annulled."

"Why?" she asked flatly.

"You know why."

"No."

"There was no love there, baby. You know that."

"You married her."

"It was a mistake."

"What do you expect me to do, Dun?"

"I thought you'd be glad."

"Maybe I am glad. I don't know. Please go now."

CHAPTER XIX

The gray days of fall are days of despair, when all the bad things of life come back to haunt you. The gray days darken into blots of night, and the nights are rain filled, slow drizzly rain filled, cold wind whipped slow drizzly rain filled, dark and desolate and blue black, blue sad black.

I'd killed a man.

I stopped at a drug store, bought a couple of magazines, and picked up a beer at a tavern. My room was dark, cold dark, bare cold dark and depressing. The bed, without coverlet, sagged in the middle, and its gaunt paint-chipped headboard and footboard were reminders of the bed in which I'd slept as a child.

The naked bulb was too bright, blinding bright, revealing the torn wallpaper, the rickety chair with the frayed upholstery, the scarred dresser and cracked mirror.

Nothing is colder than a bare floor in a rickety frame building, an unpainted frame building with high ceilings, and this floor oozed cold, generated cold, bred cold and nursed cold.

I stooped, struck a match, turned on the gas and lit the heater. The flame was uneven, blue red, a hissing blue red that fought vainly against the embedded cold, the ever-present cold of the bleak room.

I was as low as you could get, almost as low as you could get without getting as low as it's possible to get, one step away from the road, one step away from bumming, with only the paid-up rent and the bed with covers and a chair to sit on and a bathroom at the end of the hall and the suits hanging in the closet between me and the road again.

Except for fifteen thousand dollars. Ten thousand of Nora's and five thousand of mine.

I would have given all the money to bring Harris back to life.

I stripped off my clothes, threw them across a chair, tossed cigarettes and matches on the bureau beside the bed, took my toothbrush and paste and towel from a drawer, pulled a quilt from the bed and draped it across my shoulders.

The hallway was empty and I made a dash.

There was linoleum on the bathroom floor, but it was even colder than the bare floor of my room. I brushed my teeth and doused my face, dried myself and made a dash back to the room, turned back the covers and crawled in.

Rain beat a rattle-te-tattle on the windows, on the roof, a drumbeat of sadness, a slow drumbeat of dark sadness and I lay shivering in a cold bed under a white light and stared at the ceiling.

An hour passed.

Another.

For another hour I sat propped up in bed, a pillow doubled under my back, heart heavy and sick inside, a bitter taste in my mouth, in my brain and throat, soul sick and hungry to start things over, turn the page back, begin again and do and be as Melissa had told me to do and be.

I even thought of Nora, and shivered.

Poor Nora.

Poor old Nora with the prune face and shriveled heart, the pickled heart, the unfeeling un-blood pumping heart.

Once I dozed off, came wide awake to hear the slow rolling drumbeat of the rain. Water was seeping in through cracks around the window frame, blotching the wallpaper, forming a puddle on the floor.

I should worry.

For a while I lay there and watched the water trickle, listened to the mournful howling sigh of the wind and the staccato rapping of the rain, and then I pushed myself out of bed, turned off the gas, flicked off the light and crawled back into bed.

The sound and smell and feel of things took me back, made me think of far ago and long away gone, to a time when I'd crawled into a culvert to escape the cold and rain. It had been a dark tunnel on a lonely road somewhere far away and I'd found it just as the rain started. At first it was dry and warm, but after a while the water from little gullies poured into the ditch beside the road so that water flowed through the culvert, a trickle at first and then a stream that lapped against my body, wet my body with icy fingers so that finally I had to get up again and walk the road through darkness, keeping on the road by the sound of my feet and the feel of my feet against the pavement, on and on for hours and days and weeks and months through the icy cold rain, the slowly pattering rain, until after a century or two or three the dawn came and the rain ceased and I was able to leave the road and gather wood for a fire.

Only to discover I had no matches.

That was the story of my life.

I shuddered, lost alone lost.

An odor, a penetrating odor of decay, filled the room. Even the sheets felt clammy.

Sleep came again, uneasy sleep, cat-nap snatches of sleep that didn't rest me but made me long for deep sleep.

I heard footsteps in the hall, half heard footsteps in the hall, and there was a knock at the door.

At this hour?

It had to be the police. They must have found Harris, must have found him dead, and now they had come for me. Well, let them come.

I stumbled against a chair, cursed softly, stood in the middle of the room rubbing my shin and listening to the pattering drizzle of the rain.

No other sound, not even in the hallway a sound. Had I imagined it?

I went to the door and opened it, saw a dark blob in the darkness, a small dark blob and knew it was Melissa.

She moved in on me. I felt her wet arms go around me, felt her wet body press against mine. She was shivering and then I shivered, but the shiver turned to icy fire and I held her close, buried my face in the soft wet hair, breathed the fragrance of soft wet hair.

After a moment I pulled her inside, closed the door, pushed her away and fumbled for matches, lit the fire and pulled her close, huddled before the fire, huddled in the dim glow of the fire and held her close.

"What is it?" I asked. "What's the matter?"

"They're going to arrest you," she said.

"I'll turn myself in first."

"You didn't do it, Dun."

"I did it," I said. "I didn't intend to kill him, but I did. Melissa, you've got to believe that."

She pulled away from me. "Killed who, Dun?"

"Harris."

She began to laugh and I couldn't stop her. I shook her, but I couldn't stop her. After a while she was quiet. I held her close and she whispered something.

"What?" I asked. "What did you say?"

"Jerry saw Harris at the sheriff's office less than an hour ago. He was bloody and battered, but he wasn't dead."

Happiness was a surging thing.

For a moment.

For a moment only.

"Then why are they going to arrest me?" I asked.

"Harris says you took money from an old woman and that you might have killed her."

So my goose was cooked.

They'd convict me of killing Nora for her money.

It was too late, too late.

In that darkened room, squatted beside a flickering gas flame, in that clammy cold room huddled with Melissa in my arms I said a prayer, a short prayer, a too-late prayer. I prayed for the beginning again, not the absolute beginning but only a little beginning, back to the time I'd met Melissa, back to the time I had a chance to dig dirt or carry boards or collect garbage or work in the oil fields or herd sheep, and, praying, knew it was too late.

I could run, break and run, and that's all I could do, all there was left to do.

Well, you only live once.

The money was under my pillow. That, at least, I had. That and Melissa. We could go somewhere, live a while, have fun and see the sights, laugh and love together, be happy until they caught me.

I dressed, taking my time, found a coat in the closet and put it on. I stuck the money under my shirt.

"Is your car outside?"

She looked up.

"Yes," she whispered.

"Are you going with me?"

"Yes."

"Do you know what you're letting yourself in for?"

"No."

"Do you know what I am?"

She didn't answer for a long moment, a long, long moment, and I thought she'd never answer.

"You don't know me," I said. "You don't know what I am or where I came from."

"What are you, Dun?"

"Can't you guess?"

"Did you kill that old woman, the one you boarded with?"

"No."

"Then why are you running?"

"Because I was married to her and I was there when she fell down the stairs. I wouldn't have a chance with a jury."

She gasped, as if I'd slapped her, whimpered something, moaned a little, and then all I could hear was the sound of raindrops outside.

"I didn't kill her, Melissa."

"Then why don't you stay and face them?"

"I wouldn't have a chance."

"Did... she leave you her... money?"

"No."

"Then why wouldn't you have a chance?"

"Because the motive was there! Because I couldn't have known she wouldn't leave me her money!"

"Oh."

"Are you still going with me?"

"Yes."

"Do you love me that much, Melissa?"

"Yes."

"Do you know what else I am? Do you know what I was before I came here?"

"No."

"I was nothing. I've never been anything but nothing."

Her voice was little more than a whisper, and there was a pleading note in it.

"You're something to me, Dun. You should be something."

"Do you still love me?"

Pause.

"Yes." the answer came, faintly.

"Still want to go with me?"

"Yes."

"Let's go."

We went together into the night, the dripping night, my arm around her to hold her close. I opened the door for her, went around and slid in under the wheel.

I drove out of town, hit the highway and made tracks, but my heart wasn't in the going. Melissa wasn't happy about it. I knew that. I knew, too, that the running away would stand as a wall between us.

Once or twice in a man's life he has to face the music.

I turned the car around and drove back into town, headed for the courthouse.

I parked at the curb, cut the motor and the lights and sat there gathering courage or moral strength or something.

"Think, Dun," Melissa said. "What I want and what you should do are two different things. I don't want to be the cause of your doing the wrong thing."

"You haven't said a word," I said. "You're not causing me to turn myself in."

"I am, though. You felt it. You're doing this for me."

"We can't run forever," I said, arguing with myself. "They'd get me sooner or later. Besides, I didn't kill Nora and I've nothing to fear but fear itself."

Rain splattered against the car, drummed on the top and on the hood, splashed against the glass and rolled.

A siren wailed, trailed off, and the sheriff's car swished past us, turned in at the courthouse drive. Three men got out and ran, stooped and huddled against the rain, toward the front door.

"I'm going in," I said.

"I'll go with you."

"No. Wait here for thirty minutes and then come inside. If they jug me I want them to know you know it. They're less likely to work me over if they know I'm not completely friendless."

"Kiss me," she breathed, leaning toward me, and her kiss was bittersweet and full of longing.

I ran across the lawn, the rain cold and wet on my face, went up the steps and into the building.

It was a big building, all hallway and tobacco spit, musty and foul and dark. The sheriff office was on the first floor, near the front door.

The office was like an oven, and I could hardly see for cigarette smoke. A half dozen chairs lined one wall. A high counter cut the room almost in half and the sheriff and his deputies were behind the counter. The sheriff was slim and hard, half bald, dressed in expensive gabardine and rancher's hat, thin-faced with a dot of mustache under his nose. Three deputies flanked him, young and fresh-faced, students of small-town politics, their eyes on the sheriff's job.

"I'm Dun Lattner," I said. "I think you want me."

The sheriff looked up. His eyes were blue and they almost made me shiver.

"Yeah," he said.

"Why am I wanted?"

"You'd better come into my private office." He nodded at a steel door.

His office was big enough for a desk and two chairs, and I had the feeling blood had been shed in there. It was too small for comfort and the door looked thick and solid.

"You gave Mister Harris a hard time," he said. "The man was mighty mad when he came in here."

"He wanted to fight."

"I figured."

He fiddled with some papers on his desk and I waited until my nerves twisted into knots.

"Look," I said. "Let's get this over."

He pursed his lips and squinted up at me, nodded at a chair and leaned back with hands clasped behind his head.

"Harris decided not to charge you with assault and battery, Lattner."

"That was nice of him."

"Oh, he wasn't being nice. He finally decided he didn't want everybody knowing you gave him a whipping."

"That's great," I said. "That was the charge that worried me."

The sheriff picked up a piece of paper and studied it, handed it to me. It was a statement by Harris, in which he swore I had stolen a washing machine from his store.

"That worries me, too," I said. "Now, listen. Stop playing cat and mouse and get down to brass tacks."

The sheriff grinned. "You're nervous, Lattner. Now, tell me. Are you willing to pay for that washing machine?"

"If it will make Harris happy."

"He says he held back some of your wages, so he's willing to settle for two hundred dollars."

"All right."

He lighted a cigarette and offered me one, inhaled, leaned back and stared at the ceiling.

"I guess," he said, "that brings us to Nora Simmons."

"I guess it does."

"Harris thinks you might have killed her."

I couldn't decide whether he was playing cat and mouse or whether he was fishing for information. At any rate, I felt the thrill of hope.

"Harris was mad enough to say anything," I said.

The sheriff nodded.

"Why would I have killed Nora Simmons?" I asked, afraid he'd have a motive to throw at me.

"I don't know," he said. "Why would you?"

"I wouldn't. She was a nice old lady and she was nice to me. I was down and out and she gave me room and board on credit until I got on my feet."

"Well, I can't hold you on what I've got to go on," he said. "Harris is willing to settle for the washing machine. That's provided, of course, that you get out of town."

"I'll get out of town."

"Harris says he'll fix you good if you fool around his daughter."

"I won't even see his daughter."

He clucked. "Well, you're not like me. If I had that girl's name on a marriage register I'd fight the devil to keep it there."

"The girl doesn't happen to want to stay married to me, Sheriff."

He sighed, pushed his chair back, stood up. "Let's see that two hundred, Lattner. That'll square you with Harris and you can go."

I reached for my bundle of money and drew my hand back fast. The sheriff would throw me in the pokey and throw away the key if he caught sight of that much dough in one stack.

"I don't have that much on me," I said. "I'll have to go to my room for it."

He blew a smoke ring and swiped it away with his hand.

"You will come back?"

"I'll be back, sheriff. After all, I came here of my own free will."

"Yeah," he said thoughtfully. "You know, Lattner, if you hadn't come in I would have thought there might have been something in what Harris said. About you and that old lady, I mean."

"I'll get the money," I said.

The deputies didn't even look up when I walked through the outer office.

I walked outside and moved away from the steps, away from the light, unbuttoned my shirt and brought out the money. I stooped over to keep the stuff dry, moved a few paces toward the building to get some light, peeled off two bills and stuck the rest of the money back under my shirt.

A car horn tooted and I turned to wave. The lights flashed on and I walked toward the car.

"Are you all right, Dun?" Melissa called.

"Everything's all right, honey. Wait for me. I won't be a minute."

I went back to the courthouse, ran up the steps, hurried down the dark hall to the sheriff's office. The sheriff was leaning against the counter and I slapped the two bills down beside his hand.

He picked them up, looked at them, took an envelope from a drawer and slid the bills inside.

"I'll give you a receipt," he said.

I waited while he scribbled on a piece of paper, took the paper from him and placed it in my billfold.

"Goodbye, Sheriff," I said. "I guess I won't be seeing you again."

"Don't change your mind," he said. "Something tells me I'm making a mistake. Still… I could be wrong. Just don't come back, Lattner."

"Look," I said. "Just say the word and I'll drop you a postcard so you'll know where to find me. Just in case you ever want me, that is."

He grinned and I almost liked him. "Don't bother, son. I've got enough trouble already."

I turned to go and he called me back.

"What is it?" I asked, turning, and fear was a cold chill.

"Tell me," he said, his voice pitched too low for the deputies to hear. "Tell me how it felt to smash a fist into Harris's face?"

I relaxed.

"Good," I said. "Real good."

"Yeah," he said. "I know you're right."

I ran all the way to the car, slid in beside Melissa and held her close.

"It's all right," I said. "I can go. We'll leave this town and start over somewhere else. Where do you want to go, baby?"

"To the Valley," she said. "Let's go to the Valley, Dun. Let's get us some land and build us a house and grow oranges and flowers."

She snuggled against me as we drove out of town.

"I'll have to go back for just a minute," I said. "I forgot something."

I turned in at a honky-tonk, circled around and headed back to town, pulled in at the curb in front of a drug store.

"I won't be a minute," I said, getting out.

Inside, I bought two packs of cigarettes and a Coke to go, went through a door into a storeroom, stepped out a back door into an alley and walked to a service station three blocks away. A semi, loaded with pipe, was ready to pull out.

"I need a ride to the next town," I told the driver.

"I'm not allowed."

"I'll pay you twenty."

"Get in the cab."

The rain was cold and the wind was cold. I was cold, my heart cold, my bones aching cold, all the life I'd lived dark bleak cold.

It was an adobe house.

There was an old nanny goat baa-ing her head off in the front yard, advancing on me, long skinny neck out-thrust. Bright colored clothing flapped on a rusty wire line stretched between two cracked cedar posts.

The little house was in a hollow, flat roofed, dirty brown, a part of the country, grown out of the earth, quiet and sun-soaked and peaceful. Three or four brown hens scratched earth in the yard and a long-eared pup rolled in the dust. I wanted to lie down, close my eyes, forget, lie down forever.

This time, though, a brown man and a brown woman sat in the shade of the front porch and two brown children played in the yard.

"Señor," the man said.

"I came into your house a few months ago," I said. "I ate some food and took some clothing."

"So you are the one."

I peeled a hundred dollar bill from my roll, placed it on a table near the man, weighted it with a clay pitcher.

"I'm not a thief," I said, and turned to go.

"Vaya con Dios," the man said, and the woman echoed his words softly.

Dan J. Marlowe wrote one of the all-time best noirs in his The Name of the Game Is Death. *Defining "noir" is a tricky subject with a lot of people listing "must-have" elements: you need a man who makes decisions not in his best interest, their must be a femme fatale, etc. I choose to simplify it by saying noir is where "your character starts out screwed and ends up screweder." This allows for a bit more flexibility. For instance, some say a noir novel* cannot *have a sequel, the implication being the protagonist is so close to the end after the first book that there cannot be another. Marlowe blows that requirement up with* One Endless Hour, *the follow-up to* Name of the Game. *Charles Kelly's biography tells of Marlowe's bizarre life and is well worth the read....*

ART FOR MONEY'S SAKE

Dan J. Marlowe

My name is Carl Widner. I have none of the characteristics people usually associate with men of daring. I'm balding, pink-cheeked, far too short, and on the wrong side of sixty. On the other hand, I'm a chain-smoker who is loaded with nervous energy, I drive a bright red sport scar, I'm a young sixty-four, and I know I'm considered something of an eccentric by my associates at the museum.

I have a background in daring too. All my life I've been reading mystery stories and planning perfect crimes. What began as an intellectual exercise prepared me for reality. Spurred to action by circumstances, I had just such a plan in operation.

It was really very shortsighted of the museum trustees. After a hundred years of laissez-faire operation in regard to employees' retirement ages, they suddenly decided to invoke a mandatory retirement-at-sixty-five clause. The word reached me eventually in the restoring and retouching section which I had headed for fifteen years. At the moment my total worldly assets approximated $900 plus my car. Since my combined museum pension and social security would barely keep me in the quantities of unfiltered cigarettes to which I was accustomed, the precipitous action of the museum board left me no alternative but to feather my nest against my fast approaching involuntary retirement.

I borrowed $2,000 that afternoon and wrote an airmail letter that night. I enclosed the $2,000 in the form of a bank draft. Three weeks later I received a notice from the air express office at the local airport that they were holding a package for me.

I drove to the airport, weaving in and out of traffic. Upon the occasion of one of his infrequent rides with me, my young assistant, Henry Sansom, remarked in an awed tone: "Mr. Widner, you really *use* a car!"

I skidded to a stop in the NO PARKING zone at the airport terminal building. There were several signs with arrows pointing toward the location of airport facilities. I climbed from the car and followed the set of arrows marked AIR EXPRESS.

Five minutes later I returned to the car carrying a large, flat crate. The policeman must have arrived a couple of minutes sooner. He gave me an impersonal glance as I placed the crate on the passenger's-side bucket seat and then got into the car. He continued to write in his summons book as he stood with one foot on my rear bumper. It irked me that this crass arbiter of automotive injustice seemed determined to ignore me personally.

When he bent to get the license number, I gunned the car forward. The bumper was yanked from under his foot as I pulled into the moving traffic stream. The discomfited minion of the law was still rolling on his back in the dust when the airport disappeared from my rear-view mirror.

Twenty minutes later I parked outside my studio apartment. I'm fond of the place. It has one large room with a skylight, and the walls of the room are covered with my paintings. I'd prefer to have the walls bare and the paintings sold, but I've become reconciled to the fact that we live in an imperfect world.

The apartment also has a small bedroom, a bath, and a kitchenette. A cleaning woman takes care of those three rooms for me, but I don't permit her to touch anything in the studio. The floor is littered with cigarette butts and the twisted remains of paint tubes. There is no order in the haphazard placement of cabinets, easels, drawing tables, and paint boxes. The entire atmosphere, in fact, is perfect for the creation of rare and original works of art.

The critics are all agreed, unfortunately, that I have never created anything that was rare, original, or a work of art. Their attitude and their aspersions are all the more dastardly when it's considered that never once have I asked for their opinions. Almost as much as the museum board, the critics were responsible for forcing me into my chosen course of action.

Have you ever heard of Hans van Meegeren? Quite simply, he was a genius, the world's greatest art forger. He created Vermeers so perfect that even Jan Vermeer would have thought they were his own. And van Meegeren's deceptions might never have been detected at all if he hadn't confessed due to a bizarre combination of circumstances.

At the end of World War II, van Meegeren was put on trial by the Dutch for selling national art treasures to the Nazis. The only way he could hope to avoid a prison sentence was to admit that he'd painted the "masterpieces" himself. He wasn't believed, of course. The critics and experts had all certified his paintings as genuine Vermeers. To prove his point, he created another Vermeer in his jail cell, and the experts all had to admit that they'd been wrong.

Van Meegeren's story always appealed to me because he showed up the critics from whom he'd suffered just as I had. His first forgery was begun for no other reason than to fool them. A profit motive was soon involved, however. In all, van Meegeren created six false Vermeers which he sold for a total of $3,200,000. One might be able to find fault with his ethics but never with his arithmetic.

If you're not an artist yourself, you can't possibly imagine the knowledge, skill, and patience the man needed to bring off his coup. Each new painting had to be the equal of a genuine Vermeer. It had to be consistent with the master's known works. It had to be a subject which Vermeer himself might have selected. The color, the perspective, and the style of execution all had to be as technically perfect as a genuine Vermeer.

But that's not the half of it. In addition to making the Vermeer the subject of years of intensive study, van Meegeren had other difficulties to overcome. A painting is made up of four layers: the support, usually canvas or wood; the painting ground, the prepared surface upon which the picture is painted; the paint itself, made from particles of colored pigment suspended in a medium such as linseed oil; and finally a film of varnish to give brilliance to the colors and to act as a protective covering.

A forger not only must be a fine artist, he must choose his materials with care. A modern canvas would never pass for a canvas 200 years old. The modern weave is too uniform, obviously the product of a superior technology. A forger must also know what pigments were used by the artist he's imitating, because many of the pigments in use today are comparatively recent discoveries.

A forger must know, for instance, that Renaissance painters used ultramarine for the blue in their canvases; the Prussian blue wasn't discovered until 1704; that cobalt blue first appeared in 1802; and that synthetic ultramarine, first used in 1824, is distinguishable from the natural product because it lacks impurities and its particles are all the same size.

A forger must have similar knowledge of all other color pigments. He must be careful to use nothing that will date his work earlier than he intends. A simple brush made from badger hair can destroy the illusion of authenticity. If brush error like using a modern brush made from hog bristles instead of a period-piece bristles are discovered in a painting, they had better be the right kind.

Although I didn't plan to forge a Vermeer, I did plan to employ many of van Meegeren's tested techniques. Before I was finished, I expected to have enough money to end my days on the French Riviera, surrounded by beautiful, bikini-clad mermaids. When I dream, you understand, I really dream.

In the studio I found a claw hammer and pulled the nails from one end of the crate I'd brought from the airport. Out came the most expensive piece of trash I'd ever owned. It was a painting by Albretti, a Renaissance artist so minor that few people have ever heard of him. I'd gone $2,000 in debt to purchase the painting from a private collection.

What I planned to do was produce a Delgardi, and my newly acquired canvas had been painted in Delgardi's own studio. Albretti had been one of Delgardi's least accomplished students, but the materials he used were identical with those employed by the master. As soon as I made up my mind to paint a Delgardi, I knew this was the type of support I had to have.

Van Meegeren again had pointed the way for me. Knowing that old wood or canvas can't be faked successfully, he bought old paintings of minor artists of the proper time period, removed their work, and substituted his own. He once paid $400 for a painting just for its support and later sold the "Vermeer" he created upon it for $700,000.

I began the tedious task of carefully removing the varnish and the paint of Albretti's work. The next day I stayed in the museum until long after closing. When I was sure I was alone, I took several color photos of the museum's most recent acquisition, a Delgardi madonna that had been in the private collection of a Spanish family for centuries. The museum had acquired it at auction in Sotheby's London showroom. I examined the painting in detail, and was delighted to find that the support for the Delgardi was in every way identical to the support I was salvaging from the Albretti. So far, so good.

I'm not stupid. I knew I couldn't hope to create a painting that would be accepted as a long-lost Delgardi. I didn't know enough about the master's style and technique to create something totally new as van Meegeren had done with his Vermeers. The years I'd spent restoring and retouching old masters, however, more than qualified me to copy any existing Delgardi.

By the time the photo lab delivered my color enlargements of the Delgardi madonna, I had removed all traces of the Albretti from my support and had collected pigments and brushes of the proper period. I got right to work then duplicating the Delgardi masterpiece.

My plan was simplicity itself. First I would duplicate the museum's painting, then I would remove the original from the museum and leave the copy in its place. Next I would announce that while trying to restore my Albretti I had discovered another painting underneath, identical to the one on display in the museum. After that it would be up to the experts to decide which was the genuine Delgardi and which was the work of a copyist.

Just to make sure there could be no mistake, I used a little cobalt blue on a couple of spots to give my copied Delgardi a date too late for the original. This would show the experts beyond a shadow of a doubt that the copy hanging in the museum was indeed a copy.

I couldn't afford to be in a hurry. I allowed the painting to age for a few months, then brushed on a coat of special varnish. The next-to-final step was to place the canvas in an oven and bake it delicately until a network of fine cracks spread over its entire surface. I sprayed it then with a thin coating of ancient grime I'd scraped from my original Albretti.

I had a key to the museum because I often worked weekends. That same night I let myself into the museum and turned off the alarms guarding the collections of old masters. I substituted my copy for the original Delgardi and made my departure after the closest inspection showing the paintings to be presumably identical. Back in my apartment I gloated for most of the balance of the night over my "copy."

In the morning I called on the curator and told him about my fantastic discovery. He telephoned the chairman of the museum board, and the excitement began. No one doubted for an instant that the Delgardi madonna in the museum display case was the same one that had always been there. The only question to be resolved was which painting was authentic. I was glad I'd had the foresight to put the two spots of cobalt blue on the forgery, because I didn't have much faith that the experts would come up with the right answer unless there was an obvious flaw.

They used X rays, alcohol tests, spectroscopic analyses, and a few tests unknown to me. It took several weeks, but no one hurries where a half-million-dollar painting is concerned. Then one Saturday afternoon, as I was lounging in the apartment, reading a travel brochure about the Riviera, I received a phone call from the curator. It was the unanimous opinion of the experts that the painting on display in the museum was the genuine one.

I was staggered. "Are you sure?" I asked.

"We're certain. There's no doubt at all. We even found traces of cobalt blue on the museum's Delgardi."

"But doesn't that prove it's a copy?" I argued. "Cobalt blue wasn't discovered until the early 1800's." It annoyed me that I had to do their thinking for them too.

"On the contrary. It proves the painting's age. You understand that if a copy was made from your painting, it would have had to be done hundreds of years ago, before Albretti covered it. Besides, anyone able to duplicate a Delgardi would know enough to use the proper pigments. Everyone knows how recent cobalt blue is. The cobalt blue that was used undoubtedly occurred when the painting required retouching, perhaps 150 years ago. An artist doing retouching, as you very well know, Carl, is concerned with color and effect, not in using pigments identical to those of the original painter."

I stared at the far wall. "Then what about *my* painting?" I asked finally.

"A copy. It wasn't uncommon for students to duplicate the works of their teacher, including the signature. Yours is most likely the work of Albretti. It's an uncommonly fine job, everyone agrees, but then, you see, he painted over it. We can't imagine any artist covering such fine work unless he knew it was a copy and placed more value upon the original work he planned to put over it."

The infuriating part of it was that their logic made a certain weird sense. Or could it be that I was the victim of the experts' commercialism rather than their stupidity? After all, the museum had half a million tied up in the painting on their wall.

I paced the room while I tried to think. I now owned a "copy" of a Delgardi by Albretti instead of a mediocre Albretti original. The "copy" was worth more than the original, but hardly enough to pay my debts and transport me to a lifetime of ease on the French Riviera.

The irony of it struck me afresh. That was *my* work hanging in the museum. I had fooled all the experts, or so they were prepared to swear. Hundreds of people would stop in front of the Delgardi in the museum every day and admire the skill of the artist, who was me. Art magazines would publish articles praising the painting. And it would all be for my work. It was exactly what I'd always dreamed of during those scarifying moments while reading the critics' cutting reviews of my work.

Wasn't that better than going to the Riviera?

Of course it was.

I might not be able to retire to a life of leisure, but after all, when a man passes sixty, bikini-clad mermaids present a problem not even van Meegeren could solve.

The next few stories showcase three authors most closely associated with their private investigator characters. Stephen Marlowe wrote twenty novels featuring his man Chester Drum, including one co-written with Richard S. Prather called Double In Trouble *that co-starred Prather's own character, Shell Scott. Chester Drum is a PI who travels the world and fit in with Marlowe's ability to write first-class spy and intrigue fiction. Like Charles Runyon, Marlowe also wrote science fiction but under his real name, Milton Lesser. Both men also ghosted titles for the Ellery Queen series (Marlowe did one, Runyon three) and Marlowe wrote several very good historical novels, including one about Edgar Allan Poe,* The Lighthouse at the End of the World.

CHESTER DRUM TAKES OVER

Stephen Marlowe

"Signor Drum? Signor Chester Drum?"

I looked at my watch. One in the morning and a small bit. I had drifted off in bed with a book face down on my chest. A stiff wind was lashing cold March rain against the windowpanes.

"Or a sleepy facsimile thereof," I said into the phone.

"Prego, signore?"

"Yeah, this is Drum."

"One moment, please," she said in English. "For Domodossola, Italy."

I lit a cigarette and jacked myself partially upright. The book slid off my chest and thumped on the floor. Well, I thought, at least they'd come back as far as Domodossola. It was better than I had expected, with Vinnie Hatcher running things, Domodossola was the first town of any size on the Italian side of the border, down over the Simplon Pass. It was four hours from the bedroom of my apartment if you drove like hell. I thought there was a pretty good chance I would be driving like hell.

"Mr. Drum?" Another girl's voice, not the operator. The connection was sharp. She could have been calling from a phone right here in Geneva.

I admitted my identity again.

"This is Miss Sabra. We're in Domodossola, on the way back."

"I know where you are," I said. "What's up?"

"Trouble. The worst kind of trouble." Her voice was twanging like a taut bowstring. She was all keyed up for a scream.

"You mean the deal's off?"

"No. We left Rome this morning and got this far. The Grand Hotel in Domodossola. We had an auto accident. Mr. Shalom couldn't go on. You knew about his heart."

I smiled a little at the corny noms de guerre. Miss Native-of-Israel and Mr. Peace.

"And of course you can't risk a doctor, is that it?"

"A doctor wouldn't help," Miss Sabra said flatly. "He's dead. He died a half hour ago. What are we going to do?"

I thought for a minute, wondering why Vinnie Hatcher couldn't tell her what to do. He was right there. "Do corpses give you the willies?" I asked.

"I am a lieutenant in the Israeli Army," Miss Sabra said. "I'm not squeamish."

"Okay. Get him in the car. You sit in back with him, like he's sleeping, and Hatcher drives you back over the Simplon into Switzerland. What's the problem? They don't make a big thing about the frontier between Italy and Switzerland. You'll be in Geneva before breakfast."

"Mr. Hatcher smashed the car. That's why we stopped here. You'd better speak to him."

"The next voice you hear…" a man's voice said after slight pause. "Hi, Chet old buddy."

He sounded pretty drunk.

"Hello, Vinnie," I said. "Can you rent a car?"

"In the middle of the night in Domowhat's-its-name? We need you, old buddy. With chariot."

"How'd it happen?"

"A guy passed me coming into town and I kind of wandered into a ditch. Busted the front axle."

"I should be there in four hours," I said. "Lay off the sauce, will you?"

"Who pays for the damages?" Vinnie whined. "I don't have that kind of insurance."

"We'll discuss it with Miss Sabra later. Just lay off the sauce."

"I am cold stone disgusting sober," Vinnie said.

He wasn't, but I told him, "Stay that way. Tell Miss Sabra four hours. I'll see you."

I hung up and dressed in a hurry. I needed a shave, but no one was going to stop me at the border, either coming or going, for that. I loaded five cartridges into the Smith & Wesson Magnum .44 and shoved it into my raincoat pocket. The car that forced Vinnie into the ditch could have been driven by an Arab.

Two packs of cigarettes, and no time for coffee. Forty minutes on the auto route to Lausanne and then three hours and some to reach and cross the Simplon Pass into Italy. I went downstairs and ran a couple of blocks through the rain to where I'd parked my VW in front of the big Gothic church. I always park there, and they never ticket the heap. Maybe they figure I'm clergy, which is a laugh in my line of work. I'm a private detective, same as Vinnie Hatcher. Only most of the time I don't drink on the job.

Hatcher came to the door of one of the rooms they'd taken in the hotel in

Domodossola with a half-empty bottle of Strega in his hand. "Four hours right on the nose," he said.

"I told you to lay off the sauce. Where are they?"

"Room 207. Right down the hall. It raining or snowing on the pass?"

"Raining, but that could change."

Hatcher raised the bottle toward his face. I slapped it out of his hand, caught it in mid-air, and took it past him into the bathroom and poured it out in the sink. He got a big hand on my shoulder while I was doing that, and I turned and slapped it away as I had slapped the bottle out of his hand.

We looked at each other, a full half minute of it. Then Hatcher shrugged and smiled. "Okay, boss," he said, mockingly. "Anything you say, boss."

"Be ready to roll in ten minutes."

"I'm ready right now."

Vinnie Hatcher was a big man, palely blond and freckled, with washed-out blue eyes and a face dames would find attractive, complete with broken nose and a mean prow of a jaw. He was maybe 35 or 40. He had been a captain in Uncle's Army, running the counterintelligence show at a base in Germany until they'd given him the boot for such as falling down dead drunk on the floor of the officers' open mess about five times too often. He'd drifted into private work in Switzerland, as more than one American had, including me, because American corporations with European headquarters in Geneva, Zug, and Lausanne pay pretty good rates for private snooping. Word was on the Rue de Rhone that his drinking problem was getting worse. He'd probably needed Miss Sabra's assignment for eating money. Or drinking money.

That wasn't enough for her to be sure of the voice. "Say something else."

"I just poured half a bottle of Strega down the sink in Hatcher's room."

She opened the door. Black raincoat, unbuttoned, and the butt of a cigarette clenched nervously between thumb and forefinger. A high-cheekboned face and the dark eyes enormous, but looking tired and defeated now. Short black hair, cut so she'd have no trouble with it under an Israeli Army helmet, if dames in the Israeli Army wear helmets. She was 25, give or take a year or two, pretty, and stacked in an intriguing lean and hungry way. I didn't know her real name.

She shut the door behind me. We were in a small sitting room dominated by one of those wild Venetian glass chandeliers in about fourteen colors.

"Where is he?"

"On the bed."

I went inside and pulled the sheet back. He was a small bald man in his sixties, wearing gaudy pajamas. Face gray now, grayer than a face ever gets unless it belongs to a dead man. I raised one arm by the wrist. Miss Sabra started to say something, then changed her mind. I let the arm drop.

Stiff, and it would get stiffer. Rigor mortis was just setting in.

"Where are his clothes?"

She pointed to the armoire. I went over and got his trousers and wrestled him into them. Shoes on the bare feet and an ancient, not-quite-threadbare trenchcoat finished the job. I threw the rest of his stuff into his canvas suitcase.

"What kind of passports are you carrying?"

"American," she said, looking at me defiantly.

"They any good?"

"They got us across the border once."

"Stamped?"

"No."

They rarely stamp passports at border crossings in Western Europe these days. All they want is a quick look at the date.

"Deal all set?" I asked.

"Yes and no."

"You'll burn your hand," I told her.

She looked down at the butt of the cigarette and crushed it out in an ashtray. Her fingers were stained yellow from the tar. She lit another cigarette.

"He was nervous," she told me. "It's against the law where he gets the parts, to sell arms to Israel. Of course the fact that everyone is selling arms to the Arabs so they can have another try at—"

"Skip the politics," I said.

"You don't like us, do you?"

"Miss Sabra," I said, "none of my best friends are Arabs."

"Why are you angry with me then?"

"Because you hired me and I set the deal up for you and then you fired me and got Hatcher."

"It was a mistake. I admit that."

"Okay, forget it. I'll get you back across the border. How'd it go with Mr. Milo?"

Milo was an expatriate Greek dealer in jet-plane parts, He had a police permit to stay in Italy. At the moment he could go nowhere else, which meant that he'd had to see Miss Sabra and Mr. Shalom in Italy, if they arranged a deal for the sale of military hardware the Israelis needed to keep their Air Force flying. Prove that Miss Sabra and Mr. Shalom had been in Italy, and Milo might find himself cut off at the source of supply, which would put him out of business. He sold for cash on the barrelhead and he didn't care who he sold to as long as his profits ran in the neighborhood of 200 percent. But the possibly senile, possibly paranoid president of the country of origin was mad at Israel. If it could be proved that Milo sold to Miss Sabra and Mr. Shalom he'd have to look around for another commodity, such as guano or eiderdown feathers.

"Mr. Milo was worried because he was our obvious contact," Miss Sabra said.

"You paid in advance?"

"We had to."

"Check?"

"Cash. A great deal of money. The hardware will be shipped from Naples to Haifa in a Greek freighter later this week, disguised as agricultural equipment."

"With the customs people paid to look the other way."

"Of course. But if it is learned that Mr. Shalom and I were in Italy, the deal is off. That's what Milo said."

"We'll cross over in a few hours. What are you worried about?"

"We have to cross the frontier with a dead man."

Miss Sabra's face crumpled suddenly, and she was crying. She looked very young and defenseless. I felt awkward.

"I'll get you across," I said. "He'll be in his own bed in Geneva in the morning. You'll have a death certificate saying he died in Switzerland. Take it easy."

"You don't understand."

"Pull yourself together," I said harshly. I wanted to get going.

She went on crying. Her voice keened against the damp lapel of my raincoat. "My parents died during the first war with the Arabs, when I was a baby. He—he was like my own father."

I patted her shoulder stiffly, not knowing what else to do. I wished we were in the car and driving up the Simplon Pass.

There was a knock at the door. "What're you guys waiting for?" Vinnie Hatcher called.

The first part of it was easy because the Grand Hotel in Domodossola was grand in name only and because it was still this side of six in the morning.

I went down the service stairs and found the back way out through the kitchen. It was dark and smelled of garlic and olive oil. I ducked outside and around the block through the heavy rain to drive the VW behind the hotel, then took a peek into the lobby before returning to Hatcher and Miss Sabra. An old night porter in a black uniform with the crossed keys of his calling on the left lapel was snoozing in his lodge. The reception desk was deserted. Satisfied, I returned to the service stairs and climbed them.

The door was open and Hatcher's head appeared in it.

"Miss Sabra pays your bill," I said. "You and me take him down the back way and put him in the car. Then you go back for the bags."

Hatcher looked at me. "Just like that?"

"There's nobody here but us chickens."

Miss Sabra went away before we tackled the body. Even in the few minutes that had passed, it had grown stiffer. We propped it between us like a drunk, an arm on my shoulder and an arm on Hatcher's shoulder. The legs trailed like logs. The shoes dug a furrow in the worn rug in the hall.

Hatcher began to pant right away. All that drinking had taken his wind. "He weighs a damn ton."

"It's just two flights down."

We got him down the stairs and through the kitchen and to the car. Hatcher kept him from falling while I opened the door and pulled the back of the seat forward. Then I went around to the other side and got in, and Hatcher pushed and I pulled, and pretty soon Mr. Shalom was sitting in one corner in back like a wooden Indian.

"Get the bags," I told Hatcher. "I'll drive around front."

"Will he fall?"

"I don't think so, but what if he does?"

"Sure, just us chickens."

Hatcher took off and I chauffeured Mr. Shalom to the front of the hotel, lit a cigarette, and waited. The body remained seated in an upright position. I kept the motor going and watched the windshield wipers thumping back and forth. It was still dark.

Miss Sabra ran out. "The porter," she said. "He insisted on getting our bags."

Hatcher and the porter came out together. The old man was burdened down with Mr. Shalom's canvas bag, an overnighter for Miss Sabra, and Hatcher's flight bag. I hoped they would all fit under the hood of the VW. Otherwise we'd have to move the body to get at the luggage space behind the rear seat.

I yanked the hood release and got out and opened the snout of the VW. Canvas bag first, and then the overnighter. I stuffed Hatcher's little grip in and slammed the hood down. It wouldn't lock. I got the flight bag out and tried again. The lock caught. Miss Sabra had climbed into the back of the car with the dead man. I dropped the flight bag at her feet and got behind the wheel alongside Hatcher.

"Buon viaggio," the man said. Hatcher gave him some change.

"Arrivederci," I said.

I started driving.

"A thousand francs," Hatcher said. "Or maybe fifteen hundred."

"For what?"

"To fix my car."

"Work it out with Miss Sabra after we get to Geneva."

"She has the dough on her. I want it now."

"I'll give you the money later," Miss Sabra said.

"No. I want it now."

I heard her sigh from the back seat and her hand appeared with money.

Hatcher took it and her hand went away.

The road starts climbing as soon as it leaves Domodossola. You turn left and there is a steep rise and then a switchback and you see the few early-morning lights of the town as you turn and start climbing again. Sempione, the sign says. Sempione is Simplon in Italian, and, unless you want to drive through the tunnel of the Grand St. Bernard, where the border guards are snug and dry and might give you more of a once-over, it is the way to go.

I took the Italian side of the pass in second gear. The road was potholed after the winter snows and the early spring thaw. We rumbled and bounced along, reasonably warm with the heater and defroster going. I was chainsmoking and wished I had a drink. That was nothing compared to what Vinnie Hatcher was wishing. He couldn't keep his hands still. The sweat stood out like droplets of oil on his face. He was staring straight ahead and seeing nothing and blinking rapidly.

I glanced at the rearview mirror every now and then. Miss Sabra sat very still, not quite in contact with the dead man but close enough to keep him from falling across the seat if a turn dislodged him. Her eyes were shut.

Ten kilometers this side of the frontier the night dark gave way to a dirty gray dawn. The rain had changed to snow, which seemed to fall from a point ahead of our headlights and move horizontally toward us and around us. There was snow on the high crags to our right and snow falling into the still-dark chasm to our left. We turned into a long narrow valley that followed a riverbed and then there were patches of snow on the road, and soon more snow than pot-holed frost-buckled blacktop, and finally all snow, fresh powder a couple of inches deep and ours the only tire tracks on it.

"You got chains?" Hatcher asked.

"Yeah, but we ought to be able to make it without them."

"You're the jock."

With the weight of its engine in back over the rear wheels, the VW surged forward. A low cloud hung over the road and enveloped us like thick white smoke. I took my foot off the gas pedal to slow down and stared through the windshield. I could see almost nothing. The road curved to the right gradually and then very sharply.

I turned the wheel hard and we fishtailed a few yards and found traction again. I heard movement in the back seat and took a quick glance at the rearview mirror. The wooden Indian had fallen across Miss Sabra's lap. She was trying to right him and biting down hard on her lip, her eyes tight shut.

"He's so cold," she said. "He's so cold."

They gave us no trouble on the Italian side of the frontier. A man poked his head out of the shack and said in bad French that I had to hand in my gasoline carnet. That was no problem, since they had given it to me on the down from Switzerland. It entitled me to a tourist rake-off at gas stations in Italy. I handed it over and we were waved ahead. Nobody even looked at our passports.

We drove for a while through the high timberline no-man's-land between countries. I threw away my empty pack of cigarettes and started a fresh one.

Ahead a big Swiss flag was flapping in the wind and snow. The road widened into four lanes and went under a big roof on stanchions and I followed a yellow arrow to the control point. A tall Swiss border guard in a loden cape and a big campaign hat came out as I rolled the window down.

"Grüss Gott."

"Grüss Gott."

He had taken a look at the license plate first. I didn't like that. If you have a foreign plate, they will glance at your passports, ask if you have anything to declare and expect a negative answer, look at your car papers, and send you on your way. If you have a Swiss plate they will examine your luggage. If you have, as I had, a Swiss "Z" plate—the "Z" standing for temporary resident—it could go either way.

"Passports."

I had already collected the passports. All four, including the two ersatz ones, were American. That was good. Four people in a car in the wee hours of the morning ought to be from the same country.

He held the passports under the brim of the big campaign hat and flipped through them. He handed them back.

"Green card," he said in French.

That was to establish the fact that I was carrying the right kind of international insurance for the car. I gave him the little green booklet and he flipped through that, too, and found the date and nodded and returned it to me.

"Have you anything to declare?" he said. He sounded bored. I was glad he was bored.

I was about to say no.

Vinnie Hatcher beat me to the punch. He said, "Oui, monsieur."

I had my hand in the pocket of my raincoat and the butt of the gun in it and the muzzle against Hatcher's thigh before anyone said anything else. What happened next would depend on how scared Hatcher was. If he was calm enough to realize that the gun would do me as much good here as an extra pack of cigarettes, we were all through.

"Yes?" the border guard said, in English this time and a little less bored.

Hatcher stared past me at the blur of a face under the campaign hat. He looked on the point of speaking. A muscle in his cheek twitched. I jabbed the gun against him hard, wondering what the hell I could declare now that Hatcher had opened his mouth-assuming he would say nothing else.

"Yes?" the border guard said again. There was a light in the window of the office behind him and a few other guards sitting around a table, probably waiting for their buddy to return to their card game.

"Wrist watch," I said, poking my left hand through the rolled down window and showing him the watch.

He looked at it. "But it is Swiss."

"Bought it in Italy."

He gave me the sort of look that said what he thought of anyone foolish enough to buy a Swiss watch in Italy and pay the duty both places.

"You have a receipt?"

"I lost it."

"How much did it cost?"

"Twenty-five thousand lire," I said. "They told me it was a bargain."

He looked at the watch. He hadn't asked me to take it off yet. If he did, I was all through because then I'd have to take my hand off the gun. Even if he didn't, I was all through if he kept us much longer because Hatcher, even if he was scared blue, as apparently he was, would begin to get the idea I was helpless.

"Twenty-five thousand lire," he said. "Then in that case there is no duty."

Twenty-five thousand lire is less than fifty bucks.

"Anything else?"

"No," I said, fast.

The campaign hat moved toward me and looked past me at Hatcher and then moved to the side back window for a look at Miss Sabra and Mr. Shalom. The face under the campaign hat grinned. "Sleeping," it said.

"We had a long drive."

"From where?"

"Rome," I said.

"Welcome back to Switzerland."

A big hand touched the brim of the campaign hat, and I put the car in gear and we were in Switzerland.

I drove maybe five kilometers through the snow, past earth-moving equipment and steamrollers and a sign that said to watch out for road work, though the workers hadn't arrived on the job and probably wouldn't today now that it was snowing. I found an overlook with a fine view of a dense cloud and pulled off the road.

Hatcher gave me a quick frightened look. "What are you going to do?"

"Talk," I said.

"So talk."

"You insisted on payment to repair your car in advance," I said. "But you didn't stay back there to get it done. That should have told me."

"Told you what?"

"Not to mention driving into a ditch in the first place. I ought to break your back."

Hatcher just licked his lips.

"You were going to declare a dead man, weren't you? That's why you came with us. That would have been one way of proving Mr. Shalom was in Italy."

"I didn't."

"Get out of the car," I said. "And don't try to make a run for it."

He got out and I got out with the gun in my hand. I frisked him and found his own hardware. It was a Luger. Something small and hard was in his raincoat pocket with it. I jammed the Luger into my own pocket.

"Who are you working for?"

"A guy," he said. "A guy in Geneva."

I hit him.

"I swear I don't know his name. He wanted the deal stopped, that's all. Like by accident, without any involvement on his part. You know?"

"No, tell me."

"An accident, so the cops would come. But then Shalom got sick so I figured that would be even better. He had a bad heart. He'd need a doctor."

"Only he died."

"And the girl called you."

By then he was over his fright and smirking. He still had us, short of my killing him. All he had to do was reach a phone and say a dead man had just been transported across the border. He could even wait until we reached Geneva to do that and someone would check with the frontier station where the guard would remember the old man sleeping in the back of the car, and it might not be enough to prove anything in a court of law but it would be enough to make Mr. Milo call the deal off. Not as good as the accident in Domodossola, not as good as a dead man at the border itself, but plenty good enough if Milo was as nervous as Miss Sabra thought he was.

I wasn't in this deep enough to kill Hatcher. I had just been hired to do a job. I felt sorry for Miss Sabra, but there was nothing I could do.

"Is it going to be all right?" Miss Sabra asked from the car.

I didn't know what to tell her. "Do we get to drive on now, boss?" Vinnie Hatcher smirked.

On one of those hunches that are all you have left I said, "Let's see what else is in your pocket, Vinnie."

"There's nothing," he said.

But he stood still while I reached into his pocket again and found the small hard something and withdrew it.

That left me holding a small unlabeled pill bottle in my hand—dark green glass, a plastic screw-on cap, and a single pill inside.

I unscrewed the cap one-handed and held the bottle out toward Vinnie. "Take it," I said.

"Are you nuts or something?"

"Take it, I said."

He shook his head.

"What is it?"

"Pep pill, for when I'm not drinking."

"You're not drinking now. Take it."

He stood there in the snow, looking at the bottle and the single pill. He shook his head.

"What kind of heart disease did Mr. Shalom have?" I asked the girl.

"Angina."

"He have pills for it?"

"A glycerin compound. You put them under the tongue. They always worked before."

"You have them?"

"Yes."

"Let's have a look."

She handed a pill bottle out the front window on the driver's side, a bottle the same size as Hatcher's but amber instead of green. There was a label from the Pharmacie Principale in Geneva.

Most of the time, if you can pop a pill in your mouth, angina is a painful but not a fatal disease.

The little white pills were the same size as Vinnie's.

"Could he have switched them on you?" I asked.

"I—yes!" Her dark eyes narrowed. "I was nervous. I dropped the bottle. He picked it up and opened it for me. He could have had his own pill ready."

"That's crazy," Vinnie Hatcher said.

He said nothing else for about ten seconds. Then he said, "What the hell, I'll take it, if it will convince you. I didn't kill the old man."

He took the green bottle. He swallowed the pill.

"See?" he laughed. "Quick-acting poison. I'm dead only don't know it."

"It probably is a pep pill," I said. "Not giving Mr. Shalom his own medicine was enough to kill him. If he couldn't be found in Italy alive, you decided he'd be found there dead."

Hatcher said nothing.

"Didn't you?"

Hatcher shrugged. "You'd have a rough time proving that in court. Can we get in out the hot sun now, boss?"

He still had us, and he still knew it.

Miss Sabra asked, in a very calm voice, "Are you quite sure that was the way it happened, Mr. Drum?"

"I'm sure, but I can't prove it."

In the same calm voice: "Would you stand aside, please, Mr. Drum?"

I looked at her. She had a small handgun. Later, before I disposed of it, I learned it was a Berretta.

Vinnie Hatcher looked where I was looking. He turned and started running, and the small handgun made a flat sound and spurted orange, just once. Hatcher kept running three more steps to the edge of the overlook, out of control now and either hit or not hit, and struck the guard rail with his legs and went on over headfirst, soaring for an instant, completely clear of the ground, and then down into the low cloud and gone in it. A few seconds later we heard him striking rock and bouncing and striking again out of sight far below.

I didn't say anything. I got back into the car and shut the door on the other side and on my side. I started driving. We went through a short tunnel and met our first traffic coming up the other way, a rattling little 2CV Citroën. It went past and there was a water runoff from the roof of the tunnel and we were through that and out the other side. It was snowing harder.

"Give me your gun," I said.

Finally Miss Sabra said, "Are you going to report this?"

She gave it to me, and I shoved it in my pocket. She didn't ask any more questions.

It was like the pep pill all over again. If she hadn't hit him, he'd have gone over the guardrail under his own steam. No matter what it said in the papers in a week or a month, after they found the body.

"You sure are a lousy shot," I said. "You missed him by a mile."

*Early in his career, Frank Kane wrote radio scripts for crime shows like
The Shadow and later he wrote teleplays for the Darren McGavin vehicle
Mickey Spillane's Mike Hammer. In between he wrote a lot of short stories
and novels, chiefly about his PI, Johnny Liddell. Unlike Marlowe's Chester
Drum character, Liddell usually stayed home in New York City. His prose
was tough and so was the action. Like Henry Kane (no relation), their PI
stories tended to be mostly novel or novella length. Here is one of his shorter
Liddell stories set in a milieu Kane was quite familiar with….*

SLEEP WITHOUT DREAMS

Frank Kane

The control room was close and hot.

Johnny Liddell sat near the control panel, his jacket over the back of his
chair. He shifted uncomfortably on the hard seat, wiped the tiny beads of
perspiration from his upper lip with the side of his hand. This was the
fourth run-through on Sunday's *Phantom* script and from the look on the
director's face, it wouldn't be the last.

Hal Lewis looked up from his marked script, checked the time notations
in the margin, shook his head. He glared through the plate glass window
at the small group of actors spaced around the two mikes in the studio
beyond.

"Pretty sad for a gang that's been doing the same show for over six years,"
he growled to no one in particular. He jabbed at a button on the panel in
front of him. "It's still no good, fellows."

The groans and growls in the studio came through the amplifier into the
control room.

Lewis waved for quiet. "Let's take it again from the top." He slipped his
script to page one, ran his eye down the penciled notations. "Manny, it's all
right to lisp playing the mobster. But when you're supposed to be fingering
the Phantom for the cops, you're supposed to say 'He's one of them,' not
'He's one of us!'" He barked a few other criticisms into the mike. "Let's take
it."

"He's one of us, not one of them."

It was Lewis's voice but Liddell, watching, felt like a runner caught off
first base by the old hidden-ball trick.

Lewis cut their laughter dead. He was sore. "All right, comedians. Want
to get home tonight? I said let's take it!"

He glanced sidewise at Liddell. "Lousy mimics I have on my hands as
well as lousy actors. Be glad you work mostly with corpses." He frowned.
"Though it's a live one I asked you to come see me about tonight."

The fifth rehearsal went according to the director's liking; he signaled an okay to the cast touching the tip of his forefinger and the tip of his thumb. He waited until the small knot of men around the mike broke up and headed for the exits for a fast smoke.

"Sorry to make you sit through all that, Liddell." He reached for a pack of cigarettes on the control panel, held it out to the private detective. "They're not usually that sloppy." He waited until Liddell had lit his cigarette. "Kurt Davis is beginning to get a little stale, I'm afraid. Playing the same part for six years can do that to the best of them."

"He the fellow that played the lead?"

Lewis grinned. "Let's say he has the lead. Confidentially, most of those guys in there with him could play rings around him." He turned to the engineer. "We won't be doing a dress before the show, Lou. They're as ready as they're ever going to be. Want to grab a cup of coffee?"

The engineer was a tall, thin man with unruly black hair and the dark stubble of a beard along the line of his jaw. He consulted his watch. "It's only four. We've got two hours to air time. The cast know we're skipping the dress?"

Lewis shrugged. "I'll tell them when they come back in." He waited until the engineer had turned off the panel, pulled himself to his feet. "Better get back by 5:30. Some of those levels need checking."

The thin man scowled at him, stamped through the iron, soundproof door.

The director sighed. "Everybody's a prima donna in this business, Liddell. You can't tell the cast they're reading a line wrong and tell the engineer he's got to check his levels without hurting their feelings. You know what that makes me? A fourteen-carat bastard."

Liddell grinned his sympathy.

"Everybody has troubles." He studied the rumpled hair, the tired droop to the man's lips, the reddened eyes. "You look like you could stand a rest, Hal."

Lewis nodded absently. "That's what the doc said. After tonight's show, I'm taking off for a three-week trip. Maybe by the time I get back my understudy will have figured out something to do with that ham Davis. He's taking years off my life."

"If he's that bad, why don't you replace him?"

The director screwed his face up grimace. "And have every brat in the country boycott the program? Haven't you ever heard the little so-and-sos imitating every place you go? You take that tag line 'Justice Must Prevail' off the show and you'd have no show. It would be just as if the Lone Ranger stopped saying 'Hi-Ho Silver.' Our headache is that Davis's voice is so damn distinctive, we'd never get away with a substitution. They'd spot it in a minute."

Liddell considered it, nodded. "I never thought about it, but I guess you're right. I'm certainly no fan of the Phantom's, but I'd know that bellow of his any place."

The director nodded sadly, chain-lit a cigarette from the half consumed one he held in his hand. "But I didn't get you down here to discuss my lead." He licked at his lips, seemed to be fumbling for words. "Libby won't be making the trip with me, Liddell."

Liddell raised his eyebrows, said nothing.

The other man raked at his hair with clenched fingers. "She can't get away. She does the lead in that soap on Columbia and she's written in every day for the next six weeks." He sucked at the cigarette with short, nervous puffs. "That's part of the racket, and…" He looked at Liddell, then dropped his eyes. "Who the hell am I kidding? She didn't want to go with me. She could have taped the next twenty sequences if she wanted to." He wiped the dampness along his jowls with the back of his hand. "I think we've had it, Johnny. I think I'm getting dealt out."

Liddell looked uncomfortable, muttered a few words of sympathy. "Another guy?"

The director nodded. "It figures. But I don't know who." He got up, paced the narrow confines of the booth. "I found out about it pretty much by accident." He stopped near Liddell's chair, crushed out his cigarette in a metal ashtray. "Like I said, she does the lead in an across-the-board soap. It's on from three-thirty to four every weekday. From force of habit, I tune it in. No reason—just to see how she's doing. You understand?"

Liddell nodded.

Lewis scratched at his head again. "Two weeks ago, I happened to catch a sequence and Libby fluffed twice in one of her long speeches. I figured I'd have a little fun with her, tease her about the fluffs. When the show went off the air, I called over to Columbia and asked for her studio. They seemed surprised that I didn't know the show had been on tape for the past few weeks."

He sat down, stared at Liddell. "She never mentioned it to me, Liddell. She never mentioned that for two weeks, every afternoon she was spending a couple of hours away from the house. Where? Who with?" He jabbed another cigarette into his mouth, lit it with a shaking hand. "It's been driving me crazy, Liddell. I've got to know."

"Where do I come in?"

The director leaned over, put his hand on the detective's arm. "You're going to find out for me. I'll be away for weeks. She won't have to hide."

Liddell shook his head. "That's not my field, Hal. You know that. That takes a special kind of talent, a kind I don't have."

Lewis licked at his lips. A pleading note came into his voice. "You're my friend, Liddell. I don't know where else to turn."

Liddell massaged his brow with the tips of his fingers. "Anything else I can do for you, I'd do in a minute. But I won't do you any good and I wouldn't do myself any good if I started peeking through keyholes or over transoms, Hal." He stared at the sweat-shiny face of the other man. "I know a good reliable man in that field, though. I'll have him drop by and see you."

"You won't change your mind, Liddell? Price is no object and—"

Liddell got up, clapped the other man on the shoulder. "Price doesn't come into it, chum. I'm just not the man for the job. But I'll see to it that you do get the man who is." He took his jacket off the back of the chair, shrugged into it. "Don't look so gloomy. Maybe it isn't what you think."

"How do you think she's been spending her afternoons? Learning to crochet?" Lewis pulled the half-smoked butt from between his lips, added it to the pile on the ashtray in front of him. "I've got to know who it is, Liddell. I've got to know!"

Johnny Liddell had almost forgotten Hal Lewis's problems two weeks later when he walked into his office. The pert little redhead behind the reception desk grinned as he pushed through the glass door.

"Anything new?" was his stock greeting.

She tossed her head in the direction of the private office. "Company." She rolled her eyes lasciviously. "Real lush."

"How come you put her in there?"

Pinky grinned at him. "She said she was a friend of yours. I wouldn't dare have a friend of yours sit on the dirty old customer's bench in the dingy old reception room."

Liddell growled at her under his breath, walked over to the door to the private office, pushed it open.

Libby Lewis was a natural ash blonde. She wore her hair clipped close until it looked almost like a halo around her face. Her eyes were slanted, green. Her mouth was a vivid slash of color in the cocoa brown of her face. She wore no hat, and a pale green sweater did an indifferent job of disguising outstanding assets in her profession. Her lips parted, showing a perfect set of gleaming teeth. She got up, walked toward him with outstretched hand.

"Johnny. I'm so glad to see you." Her hand was cool, soft. She brought off with her a clean, fresh smell. Standing, she was tall for a girl. Her waist was small, the fullness of her skirt hinted at rounded hips, long shapely legs. "I hope you didn't mind my coming here?"

"It's the nicest thing that's happened to me all week." He led her back to the customer's chair, walked around the desk, dropped into his armchair. "I'd like to think it was my fatal fascination that brought you, but something tells me it wasn't."

A momentary frown marred the placidity of her forehead. "I wish it were just a social visit. It isn't." She chewed on her full lower lip for a moment. "I'm in a jam, Johnny. I need advice."

"I wish you had talked to me before you got into the jam," Liddell told her. He reached down into his bottom drawer, brought up a half filled bottle of bourbon. "Better late than never, though."

"You knew Hal was away, of course?" The detective walked across the room to where a water cooler stood humming to itself against the wall. He drew two paper cups, spilled some water into them and returned to the desk. "He's been touring the country visiting old friends along the net, holding a few auditions, taking it easy." She laced her fingers in her lap, stared at them. "I'm dreading the day he comes back."

Liddell spilled some bourbon into the cups on top of the water. He handed one to the girl. "The bloom off the romance?"

Her eyes were wide, clear, made no attempt to evade his. "It has been for a long, long time, Johnny. I never did anything about it because I had my work to keep me occupied. Hal had his, and we just didn't get into each other's way." She sipped at the drink, coughed. "It's different now."

Liddell perched on the corner of the desk. "How?"

"I've found a man I really love, Johnny. The man I thought Hal was when I married him."

"You made a mistake once. How do you know you're not making another one?"

"I know. Kurt's not as good an actor as Hal was." She chuckled. "We don't fool ourselves. Kurt's strictly a one-part man. When the Phantom goes off the air, so does Kurt. And we don't mind, Johnny. Both of us have had it with radio. It doesn't leave you much time to live."

"Kurt?" Liddell set his drink down. "Kurt Davis?"

"The fellow who plays the name role in the Phantom every Sunday. Hal directs him."

Liddell nodded, picked up his drink, emptied the cup in one swallow. "I'll bet Hal will love that."

The blonde sipped at her drink. "They hate each other. Kurt has been wanting to go to Hal and tell him he's got to give me my freedom. I wanted to wait. I know Hal's pride." She shrugged helplessly. "Now I guess it's too late. He's been having me followed. Now that he knows, he'll never let me go."

Liddell crushed the paper cup into a ball, threw it at the waste basket. "When does Hal get back?"

"Sometime this week. He's scheduled to do the Phantom on Sunday."

Liddell walked around the desk, dropped into his chair. He picked a silver pencil from the desk, rolled it between his thumb and forefinger. "You've been pretty stupid about the whole mess," he told her bluntly. "You should have gone to Hal right at the beginning."

"I couldn't. He wouldn't understand."

"I suppose he'll understand better when he gets it in a report from a private detective agency?" He slammed the pencil on the top of the desk. "You should have known you couldn't get away with it."

The blonde's full lips drooped. "It never occurred to me he'd call the station. I knew he checked up on me every day by tuning into the show, but—"

The telephone jangled on the desk at Liddell's elbow. He scooped it from its cradle, held it to his ear. "Yeah?" His lower lip sagged. "When?" The instrument chattered at him again. "Call the police. I'll be right over." He dropped the instrument back on its hook, stared at the girl. "Hal's home."

"He is?" Some of the color had drained from her face. "You said something about the police. What's happened?"

"Kurt Davis is dead. He tried to kill Hal, but Hal killed him first. In self defense."

The blonde shrank back into the chair, tried to squeeze her little fist into her mouth.

Sergeant Eddie Neal of Homicide opened the door in response to Johnny Liddell's knock. He was a tired-looking, middle-aged man in a rumpled blue suit and a battered grey fedora stuck on the back of his head. He seemed surprised to see Liddell.

"What's the gimmick? You following the meat wagon these days?" Neal shifted his bulk from one foot to the other.

"Hal Lewis called me after it happened. He wanted me to come over."

Neal shrugged, stepped aside. "He's inside. The study."

The director sat on an oversized couch at the far end of the room. He seemed incapable of pulling his eyes away from a blanket-draped bulge in the center of the room. As he watched, two white-coated attendants from the coroner's office transferred the body to a stretcher and strapped it on. While they were obtaining an initialed release from one of the Homicide team, Liddell walked over to Lewis.

The director's face was damp and gleamed wetly in the half light. His eyes moved from the corpse to Liddell's face; he licked at his lips. "He's dead, Liddell," he muttered unnecessarily.

The homicide man turned back from the form he was initialing, grinned humorlessly. "It's a cinch he ain't wearing that hole in the head for a decoration." He eyed Liddell coldly. "You're the private eye, Liddell, eh?" He said it as though it left a bad taste in his mouth.

Liddell nodded.

The homicide man put his hand out. "You got the report?"

"What report?"

The homicide man nodded to Lewis. "Man here says he's had you watching his wife for the past couple weeks. Don't he get a report?"

"Not from me. I don't peep keyholes. He had another agency on that job." He watched while Neal ambled over.

"What's your job here, then?"

Liddell dug his cigarettes from his pocket, stuck one in his mouth. "Being a friend. It looks like he might need one."

"Lay off the guy, Mike," Neal told the other Homicide man. "He's okay. He works pretty close with the Inspector's office." He turned to Liddell. "This is Mike Herrnan, Johnny. He's just been transferred over to us from Central Office. He's teamed with me."

Liddell nodded. "Glad to know you. Mind filling me in?"

Herrnan looked to his partner, drew a nod. "Your friend here calls us. We pick up the squeal. Says he's killed his wife's lover. Guy pulled a gun on him first, he says, so it's self defense."

Hal Lewis swabbed at his face with a balled-up handkerchief. "That's right, Johnny. The guy called me, cussed me out for having a tail on Libby. He dared me to come over, said we'd settle it once and for all." He swabbed at his face again. "I picked up an old .38 I had around." He nodded in the direction of a table on which lay two guns. "As soon as I walk in Davis's door, he pulls a gun and aims it at me." Lewis shook his head, "I don't know what happened then. All I know is that I started shooting and when it was all over he was lying there."

Neal squinted at the man in the chair. "You weren't taking much of a chance, were you?" He looked up at Liddell. "The other guy's gun was loaded with blanks." The eyes rolled back to Lewis. "Two of them were fired. He had four holes in him—one in the head. That's the big one."

Lewis dry-washed his hands. "I didn't know his gun was loaded with blanks. All I know is he started aiming at me. So I—" He looked from face to face, didn't find what he was looking for. "I got a right to defend myself against a guy who was breaking up my home."

Herrnan pulled a dog-eared leather notebook from his pocket, wet the tip of his index finger, flipped through the pages. "You say you got a call from the dead man today, daring you to come over. Right?"

Hal Lewis nodded, watched the homicide man warily.

"This private eye you had watching your wife. What was his name?"

Lewis looked at Liddell, got no encouragement. "Ted Derbers. He has an agency at—"

Neal grunted. "We know all about Derbers." He looked sideways at Liddell. "The kind of guy that's giving the racket a bad name. Wire tapping and all the dirty tricks. Right, Liddell?"

Liddell shrugged. "He's not my kind of op."

Herrnan chewed on the cuticle of his thumb. "If Derbers was doing a good job, he probably had a tap on the phone here." He looked thoughtfully at Lewis. "In that case, he could verify what you just said."

Lewis nodded eagerly. "Call him and see."

"We'll do better than that, mister. We'll invite him to drop down to headquarters and play us all the stuff he's picked up. You wouldn't object to that, would you?"

"Does he have a choice?" Liddell said.

"No."

"In that case, what are we waiting for?"

Neal grinned. "You weren't figuring on joining the party, were you, Liddell? It's strictly by invitation—and you're not invited."

The blonde was still in his office when Liddell got back. Her eyes were puffy, showed signs of crying. She jumped out of the chair when he opened the door, her eyes searching his face.

"It's pretty bad, baby," he shook his head. "Hal went over to Kurt's place, killed him." He walked around the desk, dropped wearily into his chair. "He told the police Kurt had called him and threatened him, dared him to come over for a showdown."

"But if it was self defense—"

"Kurt never called him." He opened the desk drawer, brought out an opened pack of cigarettes, dumped one on the desk, held the pack out to the girl, drew a shake of the head. "Hal had a private eye watching you. You know that." He lit the cigarette, blew a feathery stream of smoke ceilingward. "The guy he hired is a wire tap artist. He put a bug on Kurt's wire. Kurt never called all day, and he didn't leave the house."

Libby sat down hard, her eyes wide, staring. "Then—then, it was murder?"

Liddell speared a flake of tobacco from the tip of his tongue. "It looks that way. You see, Derbers—that's the wire tap guy—told me he didn't have a single call from Kurt's place. But there was one to Kurt. From Hal."

The blonde chewed on her finger. "What about?"

"Hal told Kurt he was on his way over to kill him. That he had all the evidence he needed to claim the Unwritten Law and that's what he'd been waiting for all these years."

"He hated him. He always hated him. But I never knew—"

Liddell leaned back, raked his hair with clenched fingers. "As soon as Homicide gets those records, Hal will be charged, Libby. My guess is they'll try to make a Murder One charge stick."

"Can they?"

Liddell shrugged. "They can try. They have all the elements—premeditation, motive, opportunity. They can make a real college try at it."

The blonde got up from her chair. "I've got to go to him, Johnny."

Liddell looked at her.

She shook her head. "I'm his wife. And I guess I'm as much to blame as he is. Thanks for everything." Liddell sat at his desk for minutes after the girl had left, staring at the door. Finally, he crushed out his cigarette, picked up his hat from the corner of the desk and left.

Frank Cole, producer of the *Phantom* for Seasweet Tuna, looked like a stroke on its way to happen. Thick veins stood out on his neck, his cheeks had assumed a purple hue, his eyeballs threatened to pop from their sockets as he tried to speak into three phones at once.

Johnny Liddell stood by the window, listened sympathetically while the producer tried to assure the cast that the show would go on as scheduled, calm the sponsor with a promise of an adequate replacement and browbeat an assistant into stepping up auditions for a new Phantom.

When he finally got off the phone, he leaned back, wiped at his forehead. He jabbed at a button on the base of the phone. When his secretary's voice came through the intercom, he told her he'd take no more calls.

"What the hell is going on, Liddell?" he started. "All I know is the police called the agency told us Kurt was dead and Hal under arrest. What happened?"

Liddell shrugged. "Hal claims Kurt was playing house with Libby. He defended the honor of his household."

Cole looked thoughtful. "I suppose there's no accounting for tastes, but I wouldn't figure Kurt Davis to be Libby's dream boy." He picked up a pencil, doodled on a desk pad. "He wasn't in her league. Not that Hal was either, but he got her before she blossomed out." He looked up. "Picking Kurt to follow Hal would be like stepping out of the frying pan into the fire."

"How so?"

Cole shrugged, resumed shading his doodle. "Libby could write her own ticket in Hollywood. Neither Hal or Kurt could get into a movie studio on a pass. The only thing that's ever held her back was Hal."

"What was wrong with Kurt? I thought he was a good enough actor."

"Typed, I guess. He's been booming that 'Justice Must Prevail' tag for so long, the minute his name is announced everybody yells 'Justice Must Prevail' and it breaks up the show. Hell, we can't even use him on our other programs because he's so identified with that character."

"Could he do a job on another show? Like imitations may be?"

"How'd you know? The guy's a good mimic. Could keep the whole cast in stitches. Hal complained more than once about Kurt delaying rehearsals by doing take-offs of the other players."

"You think Hal disliked Kurt enough to kill him? Aside from his messing around with Libby, I mean."

Cole shrugged. "Who knows? Guys like Hal take this business pretty seriously. He always thought Kurt was smelling up the Phantom, that with another lead he could do real things with it." He smiled wryly. "Maybe it was half for the honor of his household and half for the good of the show."

The clock on the night table said four o'clock. Liddell got up on his elbow, glared at the telephone, but it continued to shrill at him. He reached over, yanked it from its cradle.

"Johnny? This is Libby. I'm downstairs. Can I come up?"

Liddell pushed back the covers, picked up the clock, held it to his ear. It was ticking. "You know what time it is?"

"I know." There was a pause. "I just left Police Headquarters. Johnny, Hal is dead."

"He's what?"

"He's dead. They notified me about an hour ago, and sent a car her for me. He must have had some pills with him. When the keeper went past his cell, he—"

"I'm in 4B."

He stuffed his legs into his pants, pulled a bathrobe over his pajama tops. In less than ten minutes the girl was knocking at his door. The cocoa color of her face was a yellowish tint in the half light, she wore no make-up but lipstick. She closed the door behind her, leaned against it. Her full breasts rose and fell spasmodically. "He's dead, Johnny. He killed himself."

Liddell caught her by the arm, led her to a chair. "I've got some coffee working." He disappeared in the direction of the kitchenette, reappeared with a steaming cup of coffee. A bottle of cognac was tucked under his arm. He laced the coffee with the cognac, pushed it into the girl's hand. "Drink that. But be careful. It's hot."

He dropped into a chair facing her, waited until she had taken a few long sips from the cup. Then he lit two cigarettes, passed one to her.

She took a deep drag, leaned her head against the back of the chair, blew a feathery stream of smoke ceilingward. Her round breasts strained against the flimsy blouse.

"I had a little talk with Frank Cole this evening after you left, Libby."

"Poor Frank. He must be nearly crazy. Losing his lead and director the same day."

Liddell smoked glumly. "He is. He had a lot of respect for Kurt's ability, apparently."

Libby shrugged. "As the Phantom, sure. But as anything else, Kurt was in left field."

"That's not what Cole thinks. He thought Kurt would have done well if he hadn't been typed. He was a good mimic, could make the cast laugh at his take-offs."

"That was one of the things that made Hal furious. Kurt would break up rehearsals with his silly imitations, and—"

"Was he any good doing a take-off of Hal?"

The slanted green eyes studied his face soberly. A puzzled frown wrinkled her forehead. "Why?"

"The telephone conversation Derbers picked up between Hal and Kurt. When Hal threatened to kill him."

"You're not getting to me, Johnny. What are you trying to say?"

Liddell grinned at her bleakly. "Hal never made that call to Kurt. He knew Kurt's phone was tapped. He'd have to be insane to put it on record that he was going to kill Kurt."

"But he did make the call. Derbers recorded it."

"That's what he was supposed to do." Liddell leaned back, sighed. "Here's the way I figure it. When Kurt found out that Hal had his phone tapped, he saw a chance to set up a self-defense plea if he were to kill Hal. He did a take-off of Hal threatening his life and put it on tape. Then, all he had to do was wait until Hal came home and play the record from some other phone and answer from his own. So, it wasn't Hal. It was Kurt playing both roles—one on tape and one live."

The girl chewed on her full lower lip. "Go on."

"Once the threat was on the record, Kurt went to another phone, probably one in the lobby of his building and called Hal, daring him to come over and settle the whole mess."

"Then his plan miscarried. Kurt's the one who got killed. Remember?"

Liddell stared at her for a moment. "Did it miscarry?" He chain-lit a fresh cigarette, took his time about crushing out the butt. "I just said the recording was played from one phone and Kurt answered from his." His eyes moved from the ashtray, met hers. "That means he had an accomplice."

Libby started to get up from her chair.

"You may as well hear the way I figure the rest of it." He waited until she had sunk back. "Kurt needled Hal into coming over to shoot it out with him because the accomplice had one other little job to do. She was supposed to fill Hal's gun with blanks. Then, after Hal was dead, Kurt would replace the blanks with shells."

The blonde stared at him, made no attempt to interrupt.

"But instead, his accomplice put the blanks into Kurt's gun so that he was a sitting duck for Hal. With Hal's threat on the record, she knew he wouldn't stand a chance. With all the evidence stacked against him the chance of acquittal was almost nothing, wasn't it, Libby?"

The blonde continued to stare at him for a moment, then her lips parted in a taunting smile. "You ought to be writing the *Phantom* script, Johnny. You're real good. But you'd never get anybody to swallow that wild yarn."

Liddell shook his head. "Never in a million years," he conceded. "But you couldn't let well enough alone, could you? You had to kick over the whole apple cart."

"How?"

"What did you slip Hal when you went to see him? What did you tell him it was, sleeping pills?"

Some of the taunting quality drained from the smile. "I didn't slip him anything. He had them with him."

Liddell shook his head. "Not a chance. Before they bedded him down, he was searched to the skin, his shoelaces and his tie were taken away along with his belt. It's routine." He exhaled twin streams of smoke from his nostrils. "You got rid of the two men who were complicating your life, all right, but where do you go from here, baby?"

The blonde studied his face from under lowered lids. "You couldn't prove a thing. But you don't have to try, do you?"

Liddell shook his head. "I don't intend to."

A self-satisfied smile wiped the worry from her face. "I'll make it up to you, Johnny."

Liddell consulted his watch. "You won't have the time, baby. I figure you have twelve hours at most. By now, the medical examiner knows what was in those pills you slipped in Hal and both Herrnan and Neal are out checking to find out where you got it." His eyes ran over the girl's lush figure. "No drug clerk's going to forget a customer like you, baby." He looked at her sympathetically. "Twelve hours at the outside and they'll be coming for you. Just twelve hours—how are you going to spend it, baby?"

Her glance met his levelly. "I guess I'll sleep. I have a few pills left. I guess I didn't realize how tired I was."

She got up, walked to the door. Standing in the doorway, she touched her fingers to her lips, blew him a kiss. Then she walked out.

Peter Chambers is the name of Henry Kane's private investigator and similarly to Frank Kane (again, no relation) the stories take place mostly in New York City. Kane was noted for the humor and sexual innuendo in his work and was every bit as prolific as Frank Kane, at times appearing in the same digest magazines. Kane also wrote another series featuring Inspector McGregor, a more restrained, more sophisticated sort of protagonist than Chambers. Kane also ghosted an Ellery Queen as well as published other pseudonymous works, including a book on how to write a song. All this and with a law degree too....

THE MEMORY GUY

Henry Kane

It was early morning, but I had a worried client. I pushed her door bell and waited until the peephole moved. I saw the bright blue eye, and the peephole closed. Then she opened the door and she said, "You're a doll to come so early."

"Nine-thirty," I said. "That was our appointment."

"You're usually asleep at nine-thirty."

"I don't usually have a client as frightened as you."

"Frightened to death. You can't imagine what a week it's been."

"I can, Rosie, but I tell you again—people who make threats over the phone rarely do much else." I walked through the living room to the phone on the desk and lifted the receiver. The phone was dead. "Good girl," I said.

"I did what you told me."

"When was it disconnected?"

"Yesterday. There's a man coming to switch it to a new number."

"Good girl."

"Hungry?"

"Starved."

"You'll have breakfast with me?"

"You bet."

I followed her to the kitchen and watched her as she puttered at the stove. She was nervous as a filly and jumpy as a hare but she was a gorgeous creature: Rosanne Hamilton, rising young actress, driven, obsessed, fighting the world—even her father—in pursuit of her career.

I thought about the father while the daughter performed at the skillets. Judge David Hamilton, recently retired from General Sessions. The old man, a widower and a millionaire many times over, had gone along with what he had considered temporary whims on the part of his only child. Upon her graduation from college, he had consented to her having her own apartment although he had insisted that he have a key. He was a conservative man, straitlaced as an old-fashioned corset. Her interest in dramatics had, to put it mildly, distressed him, but the old Judge had applied psychology: he had voiced objection but he had made no overt move; not at the beginning; he had hoped it was a disease that would run its course and end.

"Bacon with your eggs?" Rosanne called.

"Yes ma'am."

"How do you like your bacon?"

"Crisp."

"The eggs?"

"Over lightly."

She returned to her skillets and I returned to my contemplation of Papa. The disease had not ended, it had progressed; and then the Judge had made many overt moves, none subtle. The old man was past seventy, a craggy New Englander, a Victorian throwback, a relic. There are not many any more; in today's aura they are anomalies; but they exist; and in their own way they suffer. The Judge suffered, and would not suffer his daughter to be an actress. To him an actress was akin to a tart, a strumpet—not for his daughter!—and the old Judge had taken steps. He had ceased paying the rent for her apartment. He had cut off her substantial allowance. He had implored, then commanded, then threatened. He had even engineered—evoked—her marriage to a young lawyer, George Hudson. Nothing had helped: The daughter was as adamant as the father. The contest had progressed to conflict, and then to schism.

Now she brought eggs, bacon, toast, and coffee to a pine-paneled breakfast nook and we ate.

"It's been hell, a week of hell," she said.

"I'm sure."

"The calls at all hours. The obscenities. The threats."

"But not to you."

"Pardon?"

"The threats weren't directed to you, Rosie. 'Tell the Judge I'll murder him; tell the Judge I'll knife him.'"

"And then the stream of filth." She shuddered.

"But when you told the Judge—"

"He just shook it off. Maybe he's accustomed to cranks. I'm not."

I stirred sugar into my coffee.

"How're you two getting along?"

"We're not." Her eyes filled with tears. "He's impossible. He's over the hump. He's senile, I tell you. We had a terrible scene yesterday in Mr. Swanson's office. Probably the last—"

The bell rang.

She jumped, gasped.

"Easy," I said. "I'll get it."

I went to the door and opened it for a smiling young man carrying equipment.

"Telephone Company," he said.

I led him into the living room. "Right there on the desk."

"Thank you, sir."

He went to work and I went back to the breakfast nook.

"Phone man," I said.

"Yes, I heard."

"By the way, anyone else—aside from your father—have a key to this place?"

"No."

"The Memory Guy?"

She squinted. "Who?"

"George. Your husband, you know? George Hudson."

"No. George doesn't have a key. He returned his key… when… when we decided to live apart." She pushed away her coffee cup. "Now, Peter, please. I've been patient, I haven't badgered you, but you've been working, and you *must* have something to tell me, *something*!"

"I've got a hunch we're going to resolve it today."

"Oh, I hope to God!"

She stood up and took away the dishes. Obviously her nerves had bitten through: she needed something to do. Despite the strain—and the strain showed—she was very beautiful: thick red hair, enormous blue eyes, tall defiant carriage. She was Rosanne Hamilton, actress, and she wore it like an emblem. She was Rosanne Hamilton, now in rehearsal for an important role, female lead in a Broadway play, and that strain showed, and other strains: the strain of the marriage that had broken up, the strain of the long struggle with her father, and now the strain of the harassment by the anonymous caller.

She brought coffee in fresh cups and sat opposite me.

"Well, Peter?"

"I've done a check on all the recently released prisoners who were sentenced by your father." I lit a cigarette, inhaled, sipped coffee on top of it. "Every now and then a psycho stores up animus against the sentencing judge. Now there was only one such prisoner-release within the last month and it's my hunch—"

"Pardon me." It was the telephone man, smiling in the doorway. "I have disconnected the old instrument and put in a new one unlisted and if you have any further annoyance, ma'am, please let us know and we'll do it all over again."

"Thank you," Rosanne said.

"Would you sign here, Miss Hamilton?"

She signed and I let the guy out and locked the door and came back to the breakfast nook.

"Where was I?" I said.

"The released prisoner."

"Sentenced a year ago, just before your father retired. Jeff Anderson, lives with his parents at 2 West 18th. A kid of twenty-two, sneak thief, petty burglar. I've talked with his Parole Officer. He fits. A kook-type, a coward, a grudge bearer. A sick type kid who can let loose like that over a phone. We've an appointment with him at noon."

"We?"

"You may be able to identify the voice. The Parole Officer will be there too. If he's our boy, we'll put a stop to this once and for all."

"But I promised to be at the lawyer's office at eleven. And at one o'clock I've got rehearsal."

"So? Noon fits right in between."

"Will you go to the lawyer with me, please, Peter?"

"Sure."

"I… I'm afraid to go about alone these days."

"Sure," I said.

Adam Swanson had his office in the Empire State Building and there the receptionist talked to her mouthpiece and then said to us, "Mr. Swanson is busy but Mr. Hudson will be right out," and then George Hudson pushed through the leather swinging doors.

He was tall, dark, handsome, ruddy, with a wide white smile: the Memory Guy. He was quite famous for that quirk of his: what the eye saw the brain registered—a photographic memory. He was also a brilliant young lawyer. It was that combination—the photographic memory and the brilliant mind that had won him the job as legal secretary to Judge Hamilton. When the Judge had retired he had recommended his protégé to his closest friend and former law partner, Adam Swanson.

We did "Hi" all around and then George Hudson took us to his office. "Adam is finishing up with a client. He knows you're here and he'll be with us in a jiffy. How are you, Rosanne?"

"Fine, thank you," she said.

"I tried to call you a number of times yesterday, couldn't get through. Phone disconnected, they told me."

"I had a new phone put in today."

There was a knock and Adam Swanson came in, unsmiling. He was lean, frost-haired, young for fifty, usually genial. Today he was tight-lipped and abrupt to the point of discourtesy. He gave us no greeting, no hello, nothing. He said, "I'm glad you're here, Peter. Maybe you can help."

"So?" I said.

"You're a friend of both father and daughter. Perhaps your good influence may ameliorate matters. Sit, sit, won't you?" We sat, and then he sat, on the edge of a chair. "They had a horrible wrangle yesterday, right out in front of George and myself. Ugly things were said."

Rosanne lit a cigarette. "Why don't you tell him about the day before yesterday?"

"You tell Mr. Chambers, my dear."

"Sure." She blew a plume of cigarette smoke. "My father burst in on rehearsal, acting like crazy. He ranted, raved, demanded that the producer discharge me, threatened to sue for God knows what. They had to put him out. Correct. The Judge was ejected. You can imagine how bitterly embarrassed I was, and still am. Well, yesterday, here, in Mr. Swanson's office I finally told him off...."

Swanson folded his arms. "Do you remember how you told him off?"

"I said what I thought. That he had flipped, that he was overboard—senile, crazy, nutty, and a total embarrassment. I told him I'm no longer a child...."

"You said worse." Swanson was grim.

"I have a temper."

"So does your father. And I don't think he's crazy, senile—not at all."

"You've a right to your opinion."

"Tell Mr. Chambers what else you said."

She shrugged. "I don't know. I don't care. I don't remember."

"Well, I remember and so does George and so does your father. You ought to be ashamed of yourself."

"What did she say?" I said.

"That if he ever got in her way again, she'd kill him. Nice talk, from a daughter to a father. *'I swear, by God, I'll kill you.'*"

The Memory Guy raised both hands as though he were pushing back a falling fence. "Now hold it, Adam! People say wild things in moments of hysteria. Who takes it seriously?"

"The old man took it damned seriously."

"Hell, I'm a grown woman," Rosanne said. "I've got a right to live my own life in my own way. Nobody interferes."

"Your own way may prove very difficult, my dear."

"I'm willing to risk that."

Swanson sat back in his chair, talked directly at me.

"The old man has finally had his fill. You see, Peter, the Judge never wrote a will, no need. There's only Rosanne. No wife, parents, brothers, sisters, nephews, nieces, cousins—no one but Rosanne. Dying intestate, his estate would go to her—his only next of kin. But now"—Swanson moistened his lips—"he's determined to cut her off—completely."

I looked toward Rosanne. She sat stiff, stubborn, dry-eyed.

"This office has been instructed to draft a will," Swanson said. "In the circumstances it's no breach of ethics to inform you of its provisions. Young George here gets fifty thousand dollars. The rest of the estate is to be divided in half—half to me and the other half to certain specified charities.

The daughter gets nothing."

"Unconscionable and unfair," George Hudson said, "but a person does have that legal right. He can cut off his own flesh and blood without a penny."

Swanson sat forward. "I do believe, however, that the Judge, at this extreme of pique, has gone too far."

"Damn right," I said.

"On the other hand, no will exists as yet. Just remember that, Rosanne. Nothing, as yet, has been executed."

"What's the point?" I said.

"Just this. I've persuaded the Judge—before he acts—to have one final talk with his daughter. Now if you please, Rosanne."

"Yes sir?"

"He's promised to be at your apartment directly after your rehearsal today. That's over at five o'clock, isn't it?"

"Yes."

"And it takes you about fifteen minutes from the theater to your place?"

"Yes."

"You'll please go straight to your apartment. And you'll please try to be sensible."

She flared. "Just what do you mean by sensible?"

Swanson slapped his knees and stood up. "Please try to talk some sense into her, Peter. She's stubborn, headstrong, bad tempered…."

"Temperamental," I said.

"This is a matter of many millions," he said. "Hell, I've known this kid since she was born. In all good conscience, I couldn't accept this legacy if I didn't try to persuade her to think carefully about it. All the old man wants is that she quits the stage, no more. Right or wrong, that's all he wants. If she does that, there'll be no will, and we'll all be back in status quo. Just remember— there's no will yet. Now try to talk some sense into her, Peter…."

It was a warm and lovely day and for a while in the cab going to 18th street we just sat and breathed the air and did not talk. Then Rosanne said, "Simply this. Money, per se, just doesn't mean that much to me."

"But, Rosie, you heard the man. This isn't just money. It's millions. That's money!"

"You can only eat one steak at a time, wear one dress, one pair of shoes. Nobody's going to talk me out of my life, Peter. Not you, not anybody. I don't need his millions. I can get along on my own. Now let's drop the subject."

I dropped that subject and shifted to another. "What about the Memory Guy?"

"What about him?"

"Are you going back with him?"

She shook her head. "No. That was a mistake. Even my dear father knows that…."

"I don't get it."

"Daddy worked out that marriage. He threw us together constantly and kept us together as often as possible. He told me it would please him if I married George and he told the same to George. I admit there was a physical attraction between us but physical attraction isn't love."

"But you did get married."

"Daddy pressed. George comes from a poor family, he's never had any real money in his life. George believed he was marrying an heiress with all the perquisites that go with such. And Daddy believed that once I married I would give up the business of career and settle down to having babies. Well, as you know, it didn't work out."

"So?"

"When Daddy cut off all the money, George was hooked to a girl without a dime, and I was hooked to a device that my father had concocted, and I resented that and was nasty to George and George resented that and got nasty with me and so it went, on and on, until poor George was happy to move out."

"But I was under the impression the separation was temporary—"

"No. Neither of us has made a move for divorce simply out of sheer inertia, that's all. But it's obvious that my dear father realizes the selfish trick he played on George and hopes the bequest of fifty thousand dollars will balance the scale. Money talks with Daddy, only sometimes it just doesn't talk loud enough…."

The Anderson apartment was on the second floor of a walkup and the Parole Officer, Tom Murphy, opened the door for us and led us into a small cramped living room. There he introduced us to Jeff Anderson, and to the worn grey-haired woman who was his mother, and to the worn grey-haired man who was his father. All three were seated, looking scared. Tom said, "Stand up, Jeff."

The guy got up. He was thin, sallow, small-boned, and narrow-faced, with long-fingered trembling hands.

"Talk to Miss Hamilton," Tom Murphy said.

"Whadaya want me to say?"

I was holding Rosanne's arm. I felt the muscles constrict.

Instantly she said, "He's the one!"

Mildly Tom Murphy said, "Talk some more, Jeff."

"Whadaya want me to say, Mr. Murphy?"

"Well," Tom drawled. "Say something like 'Tell the Judge I'm going to murder him. Tell your father—'"

"No! Please! No!" The narrow face twisted in a grimace and the boy began to cry. "Please! I'm sorry! Sorry!"

"You admit making these calls, Jeff?"

"I only wanted like to get even…."

"We're going to have to revoke your parole, Jeff."

The worn grey-haired woman said, "I beg you, no."

Rosanne said, "I'd rather not press charges."

I said, "Maybe he's had his lesson, Tom."

Tom said, "Sit down, Jeff. We're going to have a long talk, you and me and your mother and father…."

I went with her to rehearsal and watched and admired. She had an enormous talent, there was no question she was on her way: whether it was worth the sacrifice of millions was not for me to decide. At least she was not fooling herself, she was not relinquishing an inheritance under some form of delusion: she was an accomplished actress.

Later, at five minutes to five, in her dressing room, as she creamed off make-up, I said, "I'm glad you invited me. I enjoyed it."

"How did it go? How was I?"

"Only great."

"Thank you. I wish I could sit here and listen to more. I devour praise, but let's save it for the cab. Dear old Daddy is waiting, you know."

I rode her by cab to her house, but I stayed in the cab.

"Good luck," I said.

I gave the driver my address and he pulled away but after a few blocks I told him to turn back. It was wrong to let her face up to the old man alone, a cold confrontation, each with a deep grievance and both with fierce tempers. The old man was fond of me: at least at the beginning I might be able to pave the way, use whatever small influence I had to try to effect some sort of reconciliation.

The cab stopped and I paid my fare and went up in the elevator and put my finger on the button. There was no answer. I tried the knob: the door was not locked. I went into the living room and saw Judge David Hamilton on the floor, rigid in death, bleeding from a bullet hole in his forehead. Above him stood Rosanne Hamilton with a gun in her hand.

Detective-lieutenant Louis Parker, Homicide, was the man in charge. While his men worked—fingerprint men, photographers, uniformed policemen, Medical Examiner—I acquainted him with all the details. Then he took the girl aside for quiet questioning and I buttonholed one of the uniformed policemen. "You'll pick up a Jeff Anderson at 2 West 18th and bring him here. And you'll get Tom Murphy at the Parole Office. It's okay with the Lieutenant."

The policeman verified with Parker and departed and I called Adam Swanson at his home. "Please come up to Rosanne's apartment, Mr. Swanson. It's urgent. Thank you." I hung up and called George Hudson. I got his answering-service:

"Sorry, Mr. Hudson isn't at home. Any message?"

"Yes. Tell him Peter Chambers called. Tell him to come over to Rosanne Hamilton's apartment as soon as he gets this message. Tell him it's very important, urgent."

And then I went to where Parker was talking to the girl.

He was pointing at a pearl-handled .22 calibre Smith & Wesson revolver. "…and it is your gun, isn't it?"

"Yes, my gun."

"And where'd you keep this gun, Miss Hamilton?"

"Right hand drawer of the desk."

"And now will you repeat exactly what happened here?"

"I came in. The door wasn't locked."

"That didn't surprise you?"

"No. I knew my father was going to be here. He has a key. He needn't have locked the door. I came in and… I saw him… lying like that… touched him. He was dead. The pistol was on the floor. I… I picked it up… just stood there, bewildered, shocked. I… I suppose I would have gone to the phone, called the police, but then Peter, Mr. Chambers, was here."

"What time, Pete?"

"I dropped her off downstairs at about five-fifteen. I came back within the next, oh-five-ten minutes."

The Medical Examiner came to us.

"Time of death?" Parker said.

"Very close. I'd say within a half hour of when we got here."

"How's five-fifteen?"

"It would fit."

"Suppose we give it the full stretch," Parker said. "Between ten to five and twenty after five."

"That would tie it," the Medical Examiner said and went away.

The bell rang. A policeman ushered in Jeff Anderson and Tom Murphy. "Who's that?" Parker said.

"The Anderson boy I told you about."

"Thanks, Pete." The Lieutenant went to the boy at once. "One question, quick. Where were you between ten to five and twenty after?"

"I can answer that, Lieutenant," Tom Murphy said.

"Hello, Tom."

"Hello, Lieutenant. He was at home with me and his parents."

"Okay, that's it. Get him out of here. Thank you, Tom."

In the bustle of their exit, Adam Swanson joined the party.

I was about to greet him when the phone rang. I grabbed it. It was George Hudson. I talked quickly. "Hustle your can over here, George. There's been, well, trouble, bad trouble. Yes. Right away, please. Good boy." When I hung up Parker was beside me with Rosanne. "That was George," I said to her. To Parker I said, "The husband. He lives only a few streets away. I think you ought to hold up until he gets here. Matter of minutes."

Parker nodded, then said to the girl, "Who knew you had this pistol? Anybody?"

"Everybody," she said. "Everybody who knows me. My father bought it for me. Mr. Swanson got the permit for me."

"And they knew where you kept it?"

"It wasn't a secret."

I went to Swanson and talked with him and then the bell rang and George Hudson was with us and then Parker began his summation. "We've got three ways on this—all of them, of course, involving Miss Hamilton."

"Three ways?" said Adam Swanson.

"First, *her* way. She came in and found him like that and was going to call the police. That has complications, of course."

"What complications?" George Hudson said.

"Well…." Parker jutted his jaw. "The fact that she didn't call the police."

"She didn't have time," I said.

"That's *her* story, and maybe it's true. Then the gun was in her hand. She was shocked, bewildered—but that's still *her* story. Then it gets further complicated by the business of the will, the bad feeling between the two of them, and the fact that she made an actual threat before witnesses."

"What's the second way?" Adam Swanson said.

"Heat of passion killing. They got caught up in an argument; maybe he took the gun out; maybe she did—and boom."

"And the third way?" George Hudson said.

"Deliberate premeditated murder."

"Are you crazy?" I said.

"Maybe. Maybe not. But that way she'd have her career and her millions."

"What way?" George Hudson said.

"She didn't expect Peter Chambers to pop in on her."

"So?" I said.

"Let's project it. She's an actress. She could carry it off."

"Carry *what* off, for Christ sake?" George Hudson said.

"She shoots him, wipes the gun, puts it in his hand, maybe explodes another bullet, and then runs out screaming. What would we have then, gentlemen? We would have, ostensibly, a suicide."

"No," George Hamilton said. "She couldn't."

"Why not, Mr. Hudson?"

"It's just not in her."

"Nonsense, it's in all of us, given sufficient provocation. Her provocation: two-pronged: career and money. If he's dead before he executes his will, she gets it all. Right? And could we disprove that suicide? Hardly—when we're dealing with one whose business it is to dissemble, an actress. She didn't know that Pete was going to walk in on her and she sure did know that the old man was here waiting for her."

"So did Mr. Hudson," I said. "And so did Mr. Swanson."

"But neither of these gentlemen could be involved because neither would have purpose. If the Judge was killed *after* he made his will…." Parker shrugged. "But before? Before—George Hudson would be out fifty thousand dollars. Before?—Adam Swanson would be out millions. No, sir. Where there's no motive, there's no sense. What's the matter, Pete? You look unhappy."

I must have continued to look unhappy because Parker grunted and picked up with routine interrogation. "Mr. Swanson."

"Yes, Lieutenant?"

"Could you tell us where you were between ten to five and twenty after?"

"At home. George and I left the office together at about four o'clock."

"Anyone at home to corroborate that you were at home, Mr. Swanson?"

"Actually, no. My kids are up at school, and my wife returned from the beauty parlor just as Peter called me."

"Were you here, at this apartment, at any time today?"

"Absolutely not."

"Mr. Hudson."

"Yes, Lieutenant?"

"You heard my questions to Mr. Swanson?"

"Yes, Lieutenant."

"Well, how about you?"

"Left the office with Adam. He took a taxi, I walked. It's beautiful day— I walked all the way home. There I called my Service and they gave me Peter's message. I called back immediately and Peter told me to come here at once, urgent, and I did exactly that."

"And were you here, at this apartment, at any time today?"

"Absolutely not."

"Now both you gentlemen did hear this girl threaten her father?"

Neither one answered.

"Mr. Swanson," Parker said.

"Yes, I heard."

"Heard what?"

"Heard her threaten."

"Just what did she say? Do you remember?"

Swanson cleared his throat. "She said that if he ever interfered with her again, she'd kill him. She said, *'I swear, by God, I'll kill you.'*"

"You heard that too, Mr. Hudson?"

"Now, please, Lieutenant! This makes no sense at all! I'm certain she didn't mean it. People say ridiculous things in moments of crisis, in the passion of argument. That was no threat."

"Very gallant," I said.

It came out sharp, like a shot.

Heads snapped up. Policemen moved near.

"Why the sarcasm?" George Hudson said.

"Because you and I—we both know Rosie didn't kill her father."

"I don't *think* she did but I *know* nothing. And I certainly don't know what you know."

"I know that you killed him."

He rushed at me. A clip on the chin rushed him right back. The cops held him.

"What in hell are you talking about?" Parker said.

"Murder, First degree. Deliberate and premeditated."

"Bastard!" The Memory Guy pulled forward for another clip on the chin but the cops restrained him.

Parker wrinkled his eyes. "What reason, what purpose? The best that could happen to him would be the loss of fifty thousand dollars."

"Not quite," I said. "He's a brilliant young man, with an exquisite legal mind, once chosen to be the legal secretary to Judge Hamilton himself. He knows the law and the convolutions of the law."

"Convolutions," Parker said, but encouragingly.

I blew a sigh. "If Judge Hamilton died before the execution of his will, true, George Hamilton would miss out on a bequest of fifty thousand dollars. But now let us inquire, somewhat more carefully, just what would happen in such circumstances."

"Okay," Parker said. "Inquire."

"The old guy would die intestate. No will."

"No will," Parker said.

"The Judge had no other heir—except his daughter. But there's a rule of law that a wrongdoer cannot profit by his own wrongdoing, isn't there, Mr. Swanson?"

"There is."

"Thus if there were a decision that she killed her father, she couldn't inherit, could she?"

"Correct," Swanson said.

"Then what would happen to the estate?"

"It would devolve to her next of kin."

"Which would be the husband, George Hudson. They're separated but still legally married. But even if his nice little scheme didn't work—even if it was decided that she *didn't* kill her father—then he would still be the legally wedded husband of a woman who had inherited millions, and it would cost her plenty—more than fifty thousand dollars—to buy her freedom when she wanted it. Motive, Lieutenant?"

"Liar!" George Hudson screamed. "He can't prove a word of this!"

"Oh yes I can, Memory Guy."

"Let's have it," Parker said.

"He says he wasn't in the apartment today."

"I swear to Christ I wasn't!"

"I can prove you were, Georgie."

"Not on your life!"

"You just prove that, Peter." And now Parker was very close to the policeman holding George Hudson.

"There's a new telephone in this apartment," I said.

"Telephone!" It was a groan. The gravel in Parker's voice was disappointment. "Now what in hell has a telephone to do with this?"

"It was installed this morning. I used that very telephone to call our Memory Guy. He wasn't at home. I left a message with his Service for him to come here at once. He didn't come right away. He called first."

"So, damn, *what?*" Parker said.

"Unless he was here in this apartment today—he could not have called."

Parker blinked. "Brother, somewhere along the way you've lost me."

"I was with Rosie Hamilton all day—since this new phone was installed. She didn't give the number to anyone...."

"But Information would have it," Adam Swanson said.

"Information would *not* have it. As the telephone man mentioned after he put in the new phone—*it's an unlisted number.*"

"You're beginning to find me again, Peter." And now Parker was smiling.

"George came here pretending it was a social call. The Judge opened the door for him, and they probably exchanged casual amenities. Then George went to the desk, opened the drawer, took out the gun, shot the Judge, wiped the gun, dropped it on the floor beside the body, and blew the joint."

"Knowing Miss Hamilton would arrive at about five-fifteen," Parker said.

"He knew the phone had been disconnected yesterday. Rosie told him. And she told him a new one was installed today. So when he was here, taking the gun out of the desk, he must have flicked a glance at the telephone plaque, and with his kind of mind the number automatically registered. He had to be here in this apartment today to know the number—to be able to call back."

George Hudson was a brilliant young man, with an exquisite legal mind, once chosen to be the legal secretary to a Judge of General Sessions. He could bluster and bellow at what he considered random accusations but he could not resist the indictment of unimpeachable logic. He sagged and the policemen held him up. The fight was out of him. He was docile as they led him away.

Orrie Hitt wrote more than 150 books, many of them the racy erotica we know as "sleaze." He also wrote crime novels, and sometimes racy crime novels, and over the length of his career he published but one short story. It appeared in a late-coming pulp called Smashing Detective Stories *which began publishing in 1951 and ending seven years later as a digest with a different name. Hitt was always entertaining and anyone overlooking his work because of his association with publishers like Beacon or Midwood are doing themselves a disservice. Hitt wrote fast, as his market demanded, in much the way studios couldn't pump out enough movies in the later video rental boom. Despite his rapid pace, Hitt consistently brings the goods….*

NOTHING IN MY WAY

Orrie Hitt

It was past midnight when the train pulled in at Bowling Green Station. A porter with a five dollar smile that earned him a quarter tip helped me off with my bags and then I went on through the station, carrying them. Outside, I found the taxi I was looking for and hung around while the driver opened up the trunk.

"Kind of cold," he said.

I nodded and walked around the car. He'd said the same thing to me on a thousand different nights, but now he didn't even know who I was. I got into the cab, feeling good. It was the one test I'd been waiting for; Mike Nickles would know me if anybody would, and he didn't. That made the whole thing right and with it being right it meant that the year's work was worth two hundred thousand bucks.

Mike got in and started the engine. "Where to, mister, hotel?"

"I guess. You got any suggestions?"

"Well, the Mayflower House is a nice place."

"All right."

The cab moved out easily into the street.

"Nothing fancy," Mike said. "Good food and good rooms. That's all. Nothing else."

"I'll get the rest by myself," I said.

We rode a couple of blocks in silence.

"First trip to town?" Mike wanted to know, turning left on Lake Avenue.

I told him it was.

"Salesman?"

"Well, not right now. I'm just knocking around sort of visiting." I lit a cigarette and watched the lights slide by the cab windows. "I've got a friend in town. Doc Martin—Harry Martin. Do you happen to know him?"

"I used to," Mike said. "Before he died."

"You mean, he's dead?"

"Yeah. Last year."

"Cripes," I said. "I didn't know that."

"Heart attack or something."

"God! And at his age."

"Out at the country club; at a dance. They found him in his car, cold as a rock."

We went through a dark section of street and I grinned at the back of Mike's head. The world, I decided, was jammed up with suckers and insurance companies. Suckers who would believe the obvious, and insurance companies that had plenty of cash to count out.

"The doc was a good guy," Mike was saying. "I used to take him down to the station every morning and out to his house every night. A real guy. That's the trouble with this stinking life; the good ones always get the whistle blowed on them early. Now, you take the guy I've got out at Westminster Park, some railroad lawyer, why he—"

I shut my ears to Mike's talk. I'd heard all I wanted to hear. I'd been sure that I'd done a good job on my face, but I'd needed this extra lift to make me positive. I leaned back, relaxing, feeling great.

"You ever met the doc's wife?" Mike wanted to know.

"No."

"Rita." He rolled the word around in his mouth as though he'd been after her, too. "A slut," Mike said; "I'll bet she hasn't had a lonely night since the doc's been dead."

I thought of her then, of her black hair and her wet red smile and how I hated her. I hated her because she wasn't any good, and she'd never been any good and I'd had to use her. I'd had five years of marriage to her, five years of despising her, and now it would soon be over and I'd be able to go back to Wilmington and the little girl with the sandy eyes and the white gold hair.

"Tough," I said. "The doc was a fine fellow."

I looked down at my hands. It seemed funny to be talking about myself that way, as though I were dead. Something twisted painfully at my insides and I could feel the cold sweat on my forehead. I was dead. There had been a body, and they had said it was mine, and they had buried the body. I was as dead as a guy could get and still know about it.

Mike pulled up in front of the hotel and a kid came out for my luggage. I gave Mike a five and told him that made us square.

"I got a hint for you," he said, grinning. "Maybe you was a friend of the doc's and all that, but I wouldn't leave town without seeing his widow." He winked. "If you know what I mean."

"Sure," I said. "I'll see her."

I would; and she'd be dead when I left her.

I followed the kid inside and signed the register. I used the name Frank McCay, the name of the man who occupied my grave. Then I rode upstairs in the elevator with the kid and entered a three dollar room that had cost me ten.

"Just ring if you want anything," the kid said.

"Okay."

There was only one thing I wanted. Two hundred thousand dollars, in cash—and before morning.

I left my bags packed and went over to the dresser mirror. What I saw reflected in the mirror rather pleased me. It was a lot better looking face than the one I'd had before. There wasn't the blunt nose, or the receding chin, or the lips that had been too puffy. I wondered what they'd have said if I'd had the same face when I'd been in college. My guess was that no one would have called me ugly, or any those names, and they wouldn't have joked so much about my ambition to be a plastic surgeon. Yes, the face was all right; it was fine, but it would even better when it had a pile of green bills to stare at.

I turned away from the dresser and I went over to the phone. I stood there for a moment before I picked it up, wondering just what I was going to say, how I'd finally do it. I began to feel a little sick. I'd been married to her for five years, slept with her almost every night, and she was still my wife. But pretty soon I laughed and picked up the phone. How could she be my wife when I was already dead?

The phone rang several times before she answered it. I could almost see her out there at our place in the country, not too far out of town but just far enough, walking around with her clothes off, maybe, the way she used to do, trying to find someplace to put her drink while she talked in the phone.

"Hello."

She had one of those flypaper voices, the kind of a voice that sticks to you and won't let go, the voice of a woman ready to live at a moment's notice.

"Rita."

I heard her breath slide down into her chest and end in a deep sigh. I closed my eyes and I could imagine how her breasts rose up, full and hard, the way they always did when she was thinking—or whenever she was the least bit excited.

"Harry!"

"Not Harry. This is Frank."

"Oh," she said quietly. "Yes. Frank. How are you, Frank?"

"Good."

"I didn't expect you until tomorrow."

"Well, I got in early. Just now."

There was another brief silence and then the air rushed out of her lungs at me.

"When do you want to see me?"

"It's been a year," I told her. "What do you think?"

She laughed and I could tell that she was sober. I was almost sorry about that. It would be easier if she had a load on and she couldn't know from nothing.

"I'll drive in for you," she said.

"Okay." I told her where I was and that I'd meet her on the corner. "One thing," I wanted to know. "Did you do like I said?"

"They thought I was nuts, wanting that much money."

"But did you get it?"

"Yes. Yes, I got all of it."

"That's good," I said.

"I'll pick you up in a few minutes—Frank."

"All right."

"On the corner."

"Sure."

I put the phone back on the cradle and went over to the bed. I opened up one of the suitcases and found the hypodermic needle. I tried it once on a rubber capped bottle, to see if it was okay and if it pumped air. Then I held the needle up to the light and stared at it. It had killed before and it would kill again. It didn't mean a thing; there was that two hundred thousand and the girl in Wilmington and they were all that mattered.

I had some time so I sat down on the bed and thought about it. I'd tried not to, but I'd thought of it before, how Frank McCay had appeared up out of Rita's past and how easy it had been. He'd said he'd gotten drunk and fallen down some steps and he'd wanted his face fixed. At first, Rita and I hadn't said very much about it, how Frank was lying upstairs with his face all wrapped up. I guess we'd been a little scared at first, realizing what a break this was for us, and we hadn't believed it right away.

"Just think," Rita had whispered one night after we'd gone to bed. "You've been looking all over for a man like that—and he just walks in on us."

"Yeah."

"Who says my friends aren't any good?"

I'd laughed and kissed her, telling myself that her friends were good for one thing—dying.

"It's a lot of money." She'd sighed and her body had been very warm. "A lot of money, Harry."

I suppose that was the night that I'd really started counting what I could get, the night we'd first talked about Frank. I'd lain there beside her for a long time, thinking about it, how long I'd waited and how good my plan was. I'd tried then, and later, to remember just when it was that I'd decided to kill. Maybe it had been in college when they'd laughed at my face, or maybe it had been during the weeks prior to the old man going broke, or perhaps it had been during those bitter months after he had gone broke. I had no way of knowing, because it was all mixed up and lost in a haze. For a while we'd had money and a good house and nice things and then, all of a sudden, there had been nothing. They'd thrown the old man in jail for trying to make a fast buck during the war and he'd grown old quickly and he'd died very soon.

It was about this time that I'd made my plans and applied for a life insurance policy on my life. At first, I'd had the idea of trying for a half a million dollar policy but I'd given that up because the premiums were too high, even on term, and the agent had said something about limits and re-insurance and all that stuff. It had been during my second year of practice and, while they'd held my application for a while, they'd finally issued the policy. After that it had only been a question of finding somebody I could fix up, with plastic surgery, to look like me. Somebody to die for me.

The phone rang again and I answered it. It was Rita.

"Look," she said. "I've got all this money here; what'll I do with it?"

"Shove it in the car."

"Do you think it'll be safe enough?"

"Don't worry. It'll be safe."

And it would be—after she was dead.

"Well, all right," she said. "I'll hurry."

I put the phone down and went back to the bed again. I found a leather case between a pair of socks. I slipped the needle into it and put that in my inside coat pocket. Then I found the pint of Wilson's and put that in there with it. After that I went out into the hall, locked the door and rang for the elevator.

She didn't come right away and I kept hanging around the street corner, waiting for her. It was getting cold and I could see my breath in the air, against the glow of the street light, and I didn't like it at all. She had the money and she might do a hideout on me and I'd be up the creek without a paddle if she did that. It was the only thing in my plan that I hadn't liked but I hadn't been able to change it. Somebody had to get the money as my beneficiary and, since I didn't have any living relatives, it had to be my wife. At the beginning, I'd wondered how I could keep it away from her but my agent had helped me with that one. He had suggested that I program my insurance, set it up in installments, and that's what I'd done—installments of seven hundred dollars a month for one year and then the balance all in one shot. The agent hadn't liked the last part of it but I'd said, what the hell, if she wanted to blow it away after I was gone let her blow it away, and the agent had said, sure, and we'd done it my way.

So it'd been set up like that and she'd had an income big enough to stay potted on while I'd taken a whole year in Wilmington, making my face over. I'd been a long year and I'd had to call her several times for money so I could see the blonde once in a while and buy food. Rita had been real big about it. Once she'd sent me a hundred bucks, but she must have been drunk when she did it because she'd written in the letter that she was sending ten.

A car came around the corner and stopped. It was a forty-nine Ford but right at the moment it was worth more than a whole train load of new cars. I flipped my cigarette into the street and opened the door. "Hello, baby," I said.

There wasn't much light inside the car, just enough so that I could see her. She had dark eyes and they looked wide awake and her hair was fixed different, sort of pulled back over her ears. She was wearing a coat but it was open down the middle and I could see the red dress underneath and how it swelled out toward the top.

"Kiss me," she said.

I did like she said and she came back at me hard, pushing her body in tight.

"Let's get out to the house," I said.

She straightened slowly and her mouth looked hurt. "You haven't missed me at all," she said.

I gave her a grin and lit a cigarette.

"Wait'll we get out to the house." I told her. "I'll show you."

She laughed and started the car and we rolled off down the street. The Ford had heavy duty shocks on it and it rode good and she let it pick up fast. We were out of town in a couple of minutes and we pulled into the driveway alongside the house in less than ten.

"The suitcase is in back," she said. "Bring it in."

She didn't have to tell me twice. I hauled the suitcase out and carried it up the steps. I'd never thought that money could weight so much. She looked up at me as I laughed. Hell, it could tip the scales at a ton and I'd carry it out of there on my back.

The house hadn't changed much. The living room was still sunken, there was newspapers in a couple of the chairs and some empty glasses nested on one of the end tables.

"Drink?" she wanted to know.

"I could use one."

She went across the room and I watched her go. She had a nice body, long and full and moving. It was almost a shame that she'd wasted it the way she had. She'd been born and brought up in Pennsylvania and the men had passed her around from one coal mine to the other before she was fifteen. At sixteen she'd been pregnant and she'd run away from home; the guy she'd bunked in with, in Philly, had tossed her down the stairs and she'd lost the kid. After that she'd danced with a carnival, and slept in some strange places; when I'd met her she'd been ready for almost anything, even me with my face.

"Straight?" she asked.

"Of course."

She glanced at me and smiled.

"That's one way you haven't changed," she said.

She was dead wrong. I'd changed in a lot of ways. The dusty eyes of the blonde and the long nights in Wilmington had done that. And my face, the work I'd done on that, that had changed me, too. There had been long hours before the mirror, staring at the picture beside me, using the deadening shots, making the cuts and the fills myself, swabbing my own blood and suffering the pain. And, then, that infection, the one I'd gotten near my right eye. For a week I hadn't wanted the money. All I had wanted was to live.

"Skoal!"

The glass was in my hand and she was there before me, looking up, her eyes bright and her lips curving.

"You always say that."

"It means luck."

I nodded and lifted my glass. The liquor was strong and smooth and it went down easy. She drank hers all the way and stepped back, watching me. "You look almost pretty," she said.

I remembered how she'd looked at me before, and then away, like she couldn't stand the sight of my face anymore. I wouldn't have much trouble killing her. "It's the way you wanted me," I said.

"I know. Thanks."

It was funny, but it was the only thing I'd ever done for her. And it was funny, too, how I'd gotten the pattern for my new face. It had been right after Frank McCay started living with us and we'd been lying there in bed talking about it, when she'd suddenly turned on the light and started talking real excited.

"Would you do something for me, Harry? Please!"

"Why, sure, I guess so."

She'd dug around in the drawer of the stand and she'd brought out this picture, the one of the guy with the good looking face. "Please, Harry. I'd like you to be this way. You've got to change yourself, anyway—you know, make your face over—so why can't you do it to look like him?"

I'd looked at the picture and I'd liked what I'd seen and I'd told her all right. One face was about as good as another, as long as it wasn't a duplicate of my own. And, now, there she was in front of me, looking up at my new face and liking it—and she wouldn't live long enough to see what I looked like with a beard.

"The money," I said. "You've got it all here?"

She nodded.

"And did I have a time getting it! Why, I had to drive all the way in to New York to get it at a bank there. I just got home a few minutes before you called."

I glanced away from her, going over it in my mind again. I'd timed it right, hit it on the day after she'd received the check and the same day she'd gotten the money. Two hundred thousand. In cash. Well, not quite two hundred thousand. Only two hundred thousand, less whatever they'd given her, plus the interest on the principal. Who the hell could tell? And who cared? It was still a wad big enough to stuff a pillow.

"How about another drink, Harry?"

"For Lord's sake, don't call me Harry!"

"Well, Frank."

"I don't know, why not?"

While she was filling the glasses again, I walked down into the middle of the living room, and it was then that I noticed the luggage piled on the landing above. I'd caught up with her just in time. She'd been set to pull a squeaker on me.

This time when she handed me the drink, I was the one who proposed the toast. "To a long and lovely night," I said.

We drank slowly, watching each other, and then she put her glass on a side table and walked straight into my arms. I was a man and her lips were hungry and I could feel the need in her body. I kissed her hard and I kept my right hand on her neck, pushing down on the nerve I knew was there. It wasn't long before the urgency in her lips slid away and her body got slack. I stopped kissing her and carried her over to the davenport. I put her down on that and got the needle case out of my pocket. I found the vein in her arm and slipped the needle into it. She moved a little as I jabbed the plunger home but that was all. I took out the needle, lifted her to her feet and let her fall face down on the floor. She moaned once and lay still. Before she had the urge to wake up she'd be chasing a harp across the sky. I wiped off the glasses, picked up the suitcase and got out of there.

It was getting colder and it was a long walk back to town but I didn't mind it. I drank some of the whiskey and thought about things and pretty soon I began to feel better. They hadn't discovered anything when I'd killed Frank McCay and they'd miss this one on Rita, too. That was one nice thing about a small town and a politician for a coroner; a guy who was ambitious didn't have much trouble getting ahead.

I finished the bottle before I got to the city limits and I threw it in a ditch. My insides were hot, my brain was getting numb, I had two hundred thousand bucks and everything was fine. The only thing I kept remembering was that guy Frank and how I'd gotten him out to the country club that night, building him up about a strange date for his new face, and how I'd done it, easy, by telling him that he needed a shot to steady his nerves before we switched on the inside light and he got a first look at himself. He'd been looking in the mirror, and then at me, he'd dropped over dead.

The liquor began to wear off by the time I got to the hotel. When I blinked my eyes I could see Rita's smile and the next time I blinked them I was seeing that girl down in Wilmington.

I went through the lobby and the kid took me upstairs in the elevator. He said something about how it was supposed to be warmer the next day but I didn't answer him. I just got off at my floor and walked down to my room and went inside.

"Hello," the guy sitting on the bed said.

I started to turn around but there was a guy standing by the door and he didn't look very friendly.

"Just a couple of questions." The man on the bed got up and the springs creaked. He came forward and held out his hand. "That your picture?"

I looked at the picture and my new face stared back at me.

"Sure," I said.

The man put the picture away and nodded to his companion.

"That Mrs. Martin was right," he said. "This guy is Frank McCay."

I put the suitcase down on the floor and laughed at them. "Sure, I'm Frank McKay," I said. "So what if I am?"

"Well, that's nice," the man said. "There's been a flier out on you for over a year. You know, one of those things you see hanging in post offices and police stations. Only it was rumored that your face had been banged up and that this picture might not be any good." He smiled and looked at the picture again. "That rumor sure must have been wrong; you look all right to me."

And, suddenly, I felt it closing in, felt everything falling down around me.

"Cripes," I said. "I don't even know what I did."

"Well, we do," the cop said. "You killed a man in a holdup in Sunnyside, Long Island, and you got away. Until now you got away, that is. And now you're done."

I didn't say anything. I couldn't say anything.

"They burn you for that," the cop said.

And I knew that they would.

Harry Whittington, justly known as the King of the Paperbacks, was at the center of a number of writers working out of St. Petersburg, Florida. These included Gil Brewer, Day Keene, Jonathan Craig, and Talmage Powell. Whittington would host and the men would talk writing while their wives worked up a meal. John D. MacDonald even made the trip down from Sarasota but that was in the days before interstates so he only did it once. A number of Harry's books should be required reading for paperback enthusiasts. Included here is a story that leaves a few things unsaid, forcing the audience to read between the lines. It works out very well....

PREVENTIVE MEDICINE

Harry Whittington

He came home tired from a night call. When he saw Herb Mason's Buick he grimaced, thinking Donna had planned another night out and neglected to tell him.

He parked behind Herb's car, cut off the engine, hefted his medical kit and crossed the lawn. Mixed with his weariness he felt pride in his white brick, ranch-type home set in rich lawn back from the pleasant street. Doctor Ben Taylor's place. He had come a long way.

Lights were subdued in the living room and the rest of the house was dark. Passing, he glanced in the lighted window, and stopped. He stopped breathing.

They were on the piano bench. At least Herb Mason was, and what Donna was doing hit Ben like a fist in the face.

He stumbled away from the window, hand loosening on the kit so he almost dropped it.

He didn't know how long he stood paralyzed, watching without wanting to watch, the way his hands moved in her short-clipped hair, the way he looked at her.

Ben turned, walked back across the lawn. Rich grass, white bricks. Doctor Ben Taylor's place. He really had come a long way.

He opened his car door and sat down, letting his kit topple to the curb between his legs.

He fumbled in his pocket, found a cigarette. It tasted dry, hot. It burned his throat, he thought he'd vomit. He couldn't, that was too easy. He stared at that lighted window.

It's different when you're a doctor in a small town. It's different when you were a poor kid, when you worked your way through pre-med, borrowed to make the last hitch and had been repaying ever since. It's different when it's your best friend, when it's Donna.

Donna. Everybody'd said she was too rich for him, too much for him. But he'd known what he wanted or he'd never have gotten through eight years of school. If she was an extravagance, he'd afford her somehow.

He was thirty-nine now, and that meant for nine years Donna had been his only love. He'd worked hard, maybe too hard, maybe he'd neglected her.

Herb was from Donna's country club set, puttered around with golf, puttered around with law. His law office was down the corridor from Ben's in the Bank building.

He picked up the kit, slid over, started the car and pulled into the drive, listening to the gravel cry under the tires.

He walked woodenly to the front door.

She opened it before he got there. Her hair had snapped into place—those clever Italian cuts—it looked blonde and rich with the lights in it. Her mouth looked swollen and bruised when she turned it up for Ben to kiss. He pressed his cheek against hers. He felt her stiffen, knowing something was wrong. In nine years wives get attuned.

Herb came from the living room. Ben took off his hat and coat and set his kit down so he didn't have to look at Herb.

"Well, you stayed long enough," Herb said. "What are we supposed to do, sit around waiting all night?"

"Donna forgot to tell me," Ben said. His voice shook. They didn't seem to notice. They were completely at ease.

"Sorry," Donna said. She locked her hands around Ben's arm. "You were rushed at dinner. I forgot to tell you before you made those calls…. By the way, you got two more. You want to take them? I told them I'd tell you when you came in." Ben nodded, pulled away from her. "I better go," he said. "It's some kind of epidemic. I'd say typhoid, but I swear I don't know where it's coming from."

"Too bad, darling," Donna said. She laughed. "Well, Herb, looks like the party is off."

Herb laughed. They waited for Ben to tell them to go ahead. The silence got awkward.

"I'm all dressed up, too," Donna said.

"Seems a shame. This is a new tie," Herb said.

Ben was at the front door, carrying his kit.

"You don't really want me to sit alone in this house all evening, do you, darling?" Donna said.

"Oh, no." He said it as if he'd just thought of it. "No sense in that. You and Herb go ahead." That was what they'd been waiting for.

It was typhoid all right. Where'd it come from? Why? His mind couldn't concentrate on such matters.

He didn't get home that night. They moved the known cases into the hospital, isolated them. They called a staff meeting for eight a.m. Ben shaved at the hospital, attended.

He sat in silence through two hours of talking and guessing. He didn't know what they discussed. The chief of staff stopped him afterwards in the corridor.

"You look bushed, Ben. You've been working too hard."

"Been up all night."

"Don't mean that. Twelve years of slavery is a long servitude, Ben. You need a rest. You need a change."

Ben laughed. "I'll buy a ticket to Europe."

He must have been more bushed than he knew. Because he did buy tickets to Europe. He had them in his pocket when he went home. He didn't mention them to Donna. She was asleep when he got there. He didn't wake her up.

The old man looked at Ben when he jabbed the vaccine needle in his arm. "You look out on your feet, Doc." He smiled and rubbed at his arm. "Don't let anything happen to you."

Ben glanced at the clock. Seven p.m. He called a nurse. "I'm calling a screaming halt," he said. "They've found the source—and I need some sleep."

Herb's car was parked out front. Donna met Ben at the door, smiling up at him, pushing up her lips to be kissed. He dropped his hat, had to retrieve it.

"Ben, you look like a ghost."

"I'm beat," he said. "Vaccinating the residents of Shanty Town. Preventive medicine. Seems the water supply down there is polluted." He looked over Donna's head at Herb Mason. "Also seems the people who own that property won't improve it."

Herb shrugged. "Why should they? Rents amount to nothing."

"The people amount to something."

"Transients? Bums? Dregs?" Herb looked along his nose. "Surely you're not telling me they wouldn't be better off dead."

"Look," Ben said. "I don't spend my time trying to save those people to listen to smart cracks about it."

"Ben," Donna said. "You're tired."

"Yes. I'm tired. Tired of smart lawyers and their clients who don't give a damn for human life."

"You need a soap box," Herb said, smiling.

"I just need clean air," Ben said. "I wish you'd get out, Herb. I tell you what, don't call me. I'll call you."

See how it is? He couldn't stand it any more, yet what could he do? How could he erase Herb's superior smile? How could he hope to keep Donna?

A doctor, his reputation, his practice, everything he'd worked for, one touch of scandal would ruin it. This way he could argue with Herb over something else that was vital to him, maybe end the affair.

Donna said, "Ben, I want you to apologize right now."

Ben shook his head. "I mean it, Herb. I don't want to see you for awhile… maybe when this business is cleared up."

"Ben, stop it," Donna said. "You can't talk to Herb like this. He has nothing to do with that epidemic."

"Except he represents the owners and I'm sick of the whole business."

Herb caught his arm. "Ben. Fella. Had no idea you felt so strongly. Why, I'm not going to lose you and Donna like this. I'll do something about it. I swear."

He winked at Donna, got his hat. "Sleep on it, Doc. You'll feel better." Ben saw the contempt in Herb's smile, saw what Herb really thought of Donna's husband.

He left the office at two the next afternoon. He drove to the nearest bar. He sat in the bar for two hours. He stared at the liquor in his glass. Two words kept swimming around in the alcohol in his brain. Preventive medicine.

"… tell you, I see her with him. Afternoons out driving. Looked right at her. I know her." The voice was low, six stools away. He'd have known whom he was talking about even if the bartender hadn't been trying to shut him up.

He got up, heart pounding. He bumped the six stools. This man was a son of a bitch. He'd tell him. He'd bust his mouth.

He stopped. The man's eyes widened, Ben saw the agony in them.

"God, Doc. I didn't know it was you." His voice broke. "God forgive me, Doc."

Ben stared at him. He wasn't a son of a bitch. He was just a guy. What would people say, Doc Taylor brawling in a bar? He bumped the rest of the stools on his way out.

A cop stopped him before he'd gone two blocks, siren wailing. When Ben pulled to the curb, he realized he was on the wrong side of the street.

The cop was snarling before he reached Ben's car. Then he recognized Ben. Ben had delivered all three of his kids. The last two weren't paid for. "Doc," he said. "Gee, Doc. You must have been working too hard."

"I'm drunk," Ben said. "I been drinking."

"Doc, you been working too hard. You're tired. Come on. Follow me home. Okay?"

Donna met him at the door. Always meeting him at the door. In his alcoholic clarity he saw it, you can't trust a wife who's always meeting you at the door.

"You've been drinking."

"Celebrating. We're going to Europe. Next week. You and I." When you love her, no matter what she's done, you don't want to let go. You'll do anything but let go.

"Are you joking?"

"Never more serious. You and I. How long? Don't know."

"Ben, we can't go to Europe. Why, everything is happening here. Ben, I don't want to go. Not now."

Ben looked at her, feeling the burn of tears behind the bridge of his nose. He tried to send Mason away; he wouldn't go. He offered her Europe, she didn't want to go, would hurry back.

He didn't sleep all night. He stared at the ceiling, watching it turn gray to black to gray again. He didn't make it to the office that morning. First time he'd missed in how many years?

Herb Mason dropped in at noon. Donna insisted he stay for lunch. Herb sipped black coffee, said, "Heard the damnedest thing, Ben. Heard people have been talking about Donna and me—even to your face."

Ben watched Donna go pale. "Whatever could they say about us?"

Herb said, "Damned little town. Little minds. Just want to say, fella, the three of us ought to stand together against this kind of talk. We've been friends too long to let something happen to spoil it."

"We certainly have," Donna said.

Ben didn't say anything. The silence stretched, got awkward.

When Herb was leaving, Ben said, "By the way, Herb, I've got to run up to Chicago for a couple days. Why don't you and Donna go along? We all need a few days in a big town."

Herb said, "I don't think I could."

"Sure you could. You've just about got to. What was it you said—stick together against those lies."

Herb glanced at Donna. Her nod was almost imperceptible. Herb said, "Okay, Ben. You're right, of course. Holiday together, the gossips will know what we think of their lies."

Herb and Donna wanted to go out that first night in Chicago. Ben told them no. They had a fourteenth floor suite overlooking Michigan Avenue, the outer drive, the lake. "I'm tired. Let me rest tonight. Why don't you and Donna go out?"

They tried not to appear too anxious. Ben called room service, ordered a fifth and mixers. "Have a couple drinks with me. Then you and Donna take in a club. Okay?"

"All right, sweets," Donna said. "If you insist."

Ben poured the drinks, mixing them one at a time. He dropped four tablets in Herb's glass. He wasn't worried about Herb's noticing the taste. Herb was so anxious to get out of here with Donna, he wasn't thinking about the whisky.

Herb managed to set his glass down before he toppled forward on his face. Ben heard Donna's sharp intake of breath.

Ben picked Herb up over his shoulder, carried him to the bed. Donna stared, rigid, holding her glass in her hand.

Ben stripped off Herb's clothes. Donna did not move. Ben got his surgical tools, prepared Herb for the operation.

Donna got to her feet. She tried to speak, but made no sound. Ben worked swiftly. It was a quick operation, quickly over.

Donna said, "God, Ben, why?"

Ben just looked at her. Finally her gaze lowered. She dropped her glass. It clattered dully on the rug.

Ben said, "I've tickets for Europe, Donna. The boat sails in the morning. I've made plane reservations for New York. I'm going. You can go with me." He jerked his head toward the man on the bed. "Or you can stay here with him. It's up to you."

Her teeth chattered. "I'll go with you, Ben." Her eyes were dead.

He nodded. "I thought you would."

They were packed. They checked out, caught a cab for Midway airport. Donna sat in the corner. She shook as if she were cold.

Ben looked at her. He felt nothing, no more than he had vaccinating the Shanty people, giving them their preventive medicine. He had done what he had to do, the only thing he could do. He still had Donna, Herb would never give him that superior smile again.

There was only one thing he regretted. He wouldn't be there when lover boy woke up in the morning.

Gil Brewer was about as prolific as anybody could be, cranking out novels and short stories galore. Stark House has already published four volumes of the short stuff and that is barely cracking the surface. When he was on, Brewer's books were as good as anything out there. Check out 13 French Street *or* The Red Scarf *to see what I mean. In 1970 he suffered a car crash and the effects of that, coupled with his alcoholism, took their toll. When he finally passed away in 1983, Harry Whittington had spent a lot of time at his bedside, comforting his old friend. This may not be the "best" Gil Brewer short story—I don't know what that would be—but it certainly has a little bit of everything Brewer did best....*

DIE, DARLING, DIE

Gil Brewer

1

As usual, he was waiting for her to go down to the beach. It would be easier to wait on the beach, but he was afraid if she saw him waiting, she wouldn't come. So he paced the warm room some more, watching the window. He went into the kitchenette, opened the refrigerator and drank some cold water from the water bottle. Then he rushed to the window again.

She was still up there. That was bad enough. It was the worst part of it, in fact.

He knew he would have to do something: change his room, leave the motel, get drunk, or ask her to marry him. The last idea was the one he desperately wanted, yet he feared it most. He knew he would accomplish none of the others.

It was pretty awful. Her name alone was enough to keep him awake all night. Miriam.

The Floridian Motel was two storied, built around a large court with fountains and palms and jungle landscape and mosaic paths. His room on the second floor faced West, directly opposite hers across the court.

The thing was, she went in for all-out sun bathing.

There was this over-large yellow screen. Each day, a little after noon, she carried the screen to the sundeck above her room. Exactly when the sun was right.

He would sit in a bath of perspiration and watch her shadow.

He knew he should tell her. He couldn't. Each day he waited for her to finish up there, and head for the Gulf beach across the stretch of lawn beyond the motel.

Suddenly he saw her up there, folding the screen.

He was wearing his khaki swimming shorts and leather moccasins. In his haste, he banged his foot against the bed. Dancing with pain, he grabbed a towel and walked as fast as he dared. Everybody in the motel knew what was going on, but he couldn't bring himself to run.

"Well, hello!" He surprised her at the corner of the motel, just as she stepped on the grass from the stairway to the second floor. She blushed under her darkening tan.

"Swimming?" he asked.

She almost nodded. They stood there staring at each other. She was wearing sandals, a two-piece white swim suit, and carrying an enormous red, white and blue beach towel.

"Gosh, Miriam." He moved a step toward her. She blushed still more and her lips parted as she pressed back against the stair railing, caught.

He knew she felt the same as himself. Neither would ever have to say anything.

"Are you going swimming too, Joe?"

They stood there. Her hair was absolutely black. Once he had touched it and it was like silk. Black silk. Her eyes were black, too—and wide and afraid. The fright in them scared him. He couldn't bring himself to pursue her as he might an ordinary girl. She was not ordinary.

"Are we just going to stand here, Joe?"

"I've been waiting for you."

"I know."

"You know?"

She turned quickly and started off across the grass.

He hurried after her. "What d'you mean?"

She paused. They were very close and he knew she wished she hadn't said that, for a strange look was in her eyes. She shook her head and turned toward the beach again.

"Miriam!"

He caught up with her just on the edge of the sea wall. He hardly dared look at her, the way it was with him. When she looked at him, he went right straight out of his head.

"What did you mean?"

They were close by a huge azalea bush in full bloom.

"Joe, please. I just knew you would be waiting—somewhere."

He took her hand. He suddenly moved without volition, compelled, grabbed her. She came against him and he held her brutally and tenderly and kissed her and she kissed back and he got his fingers twined in her hair and it was as if every muscle in his body tied knots and he couldn't speak or move.

"Joe," she said, pulling away. "The people."

He stood there shaking his head. "Miriam. Miriam."

"Goodness!" She turned, jumped from the sea wall onto the sand, and moved toward the blue-green waters of the Gulf.

Men and women from the motel lounged about on the white sands, swam, or sat humped over cool drinks in beach chairs under violently colored umbrellas provided by the establishment.

Miriam started unfurling the beach towel near the Lawtons, a middle-aged couple who were both slightly alcoholic. She saw Joe coming and hurried.

"Miriam, please."

"Joe!"

"Let's go down the beach."

She didn't want a scene. She let him take the towel, and went along with him, past the smiling eyes and whispered asides.

"What will they think, Joe?"

"I just want to talk with you."

"Please, Joe—this is far enough."

They were by a row of old pilings that stretched out into the water. A pelican billed its wing on one piling near shore.

Joe held her hands, tugged her down on the towel.

"I thought you were going swimming."

"I've got to talk with you. You know that."

"Please, Joe."

They were near the sea wall and couldn't be seen from behind. They were far enough from the other guests and he put his arms around her and held her down and kissed her again. He did it without thinking, compelled as before.

This time when she broke free, she leaped up and she was afraid. Not of him. Of something else. He didn't know what.

"If you don't go, I'll have to, Joe."

He stood up, took her hands and pulled her down again. She was breathing fast and so was he. Her smooth flesh was warm from the sun.

"Stop staring, Joe!"

He looked away. They sat there.

"I'm sorry," he said. "But what are we going to do?"

"I don't know what you mean," she spoke rapidly.

"Will you have dinner with me tonight?"

"No. I can't."

"Will you go out with me tonight? We could hit the night spots, dance a little?"

"No." She turned and looked at him. "Don't ask me again." Her leg touched his, but she didn't move it away. He knew it was doing the same thing to her as it was to him. Why did she act like this? Her fingers were clenched into the thick nap of the towel. She sat perfectly rigid. When she spoke, she didn't look at him and her voice shook. "You've never told me where you're from. Don't you work at all? What're you doing down here?"

"Vacation." He explained automatically, terribly conscious of her leg, her nearness. Knowing, she tried to change the subject. He wanted things to be in the open. He wanted to tell her how he watched her behind the screen. He wanted her to speak what he knew she felt. He was dizzy because none of this happened and he couldn't break through to her and he didn't know what was frightening her.

"Vacation from where?"

"Davenport. It's a vitamin plant. Make all sorts of junk. Pills, you know?" So he told her all the rest. Betty's father was president. They wanted Joe to marry Betty and be vice president. Only Joe had been working too hard, they said. So the vacation. Only because Betty's folks were the kind they were, it wasn't really because he worked too hard. It was so Betty could make sure by dating all the unobjectionable hopefuls in town while he was away. He had never told anybody that he wasn't sure himself, how he felt about Betty. He'd gone along with it. "One of those things. Glad it happened. Never liked chemistry, or vitamins. I'm not going back. You're my vitamin and I'm stuck with you."

He swallowed and looked at her and her eyes were misty.

He pretended not to notice. She looked small and luscious and helpless and scared and he wished he didn't hunger for her so. Somehow it wasn't right. He asked:

"How about you? What are you doing here?"

She turned, rising to her knees, and looked at him. She leaned toward him and placed both warm palms against his face. Her gaze was quick, up and down the beach, then at him. "I wish—" she said. Then she kissed him. They clung to each other, his hands tugging at her back, twisting in her hair. She tried to wriggle away, yet somehow not wanting to break the fierce demand of her lips. She sank her fingernails into his arms and stood up. "Stay away from me, Joe! Go back to her."

"Why are you like this? Miriam....Please—"

"We can't. I mean it—I mean it. Stay away!"

His mind was foggy with her.

She turned, ran up the length of the beach, and walked swiftly across the grass toward the motel.

He followed and knocked on the door of her apartment.

"Here," he said, when she opened the door. "You forgot your towel."

She snatched it from his hand and slammed the door. He tried to catch the door and open it again. She locked it.

"Joe, don't ever come here again!" She spoke through the louvered door window, then snapped the Venetian blinds shut.

"Miriam."

She didn't answer.

Finally he turned and started along the second floor outside landing, moving in a kind of dream toward his rooms.

"Mister Morley?"

He turned. It was the desk clerk, Kirkham, padding toward him from the nearest stairway; a short, stocky man wearing a yellow sports shirt sprouting green palms.

"Been looking all over for you, Mister Morley. There was a man in the office, asking for you."

"Who?"

"Some friend of yours from town."

He nodded at the clerk and turned away toward his room. Mistake. He didn't know anybody from town.

Miriam. He had to see her tonight. Whether she thought she didn't want it, or not. He knew what she did want.

He loved her.

The door was unlocked. He recalled that he hadn't locked it, but this didn't entitle strangers to free entrance.

"What's going on?"

"Hello," the man across the room said. "You Morley?"

He stepped on into the room. Somebody else closed the door.

"That's Morley," the one who closed the door said. "He was down on the beach with her. I saw them."

"All right, Stewart. You run along, now."

The door closed behind Stewart.

2

"My name's Thompson, Morley. We tried to get hold of you before entering. You weren't around. We had to come in."

"Now you can get out."

"Easy, now."

Thompson had been seated in the contour chair by the window. He stood up, reached into his jacket pocket, brought out a wallet. Joe saw the gun as the jacket flipped open.

"I'm with the police."

Joe read the ID card and Thompson put it away.

"Satisfactory?" Thompson said.

Joe looked at him. Thompson was tall and thin, his face untouched by any hint of humor, his pale blue eyes very calm. His gray gabardine suit was wrinkled and his dark hair quite neatly combed.

Joe looked beyond Thompson toward her room across the court. The sun slanted yellowly across the top of the motel, shining into the court. It left the far wall in shadow and he thought he saw her move past her window.

"We're going to have to use your room. You either cooperate, or you don't," Thompson said. "We've made provision for either way."

"What's all this about?" The sound of his voice was dim. There was a kind of dimness inside him just then.

Thompson returned to his chair, glanced out the window, then looked at Joe. "How is she?"

"What?"

"How's Miriam?"

A sudden urgency seemed to plane just beneath the surface of his skin. He stepped over to Thompson, standing close. "Tell me what this is about!"

Thompson sighed. "That's my job. That's what I planned. Now it's difficult, because you're all jammed up over her, aren't you?"

Joe breathed slowly, waiting.

"All right," Thompson said. "Got to tell you, anyway. You've hooked onto a wrong one. Not only that, but you're in the middle of something I don't figure you want to be in."

"What's it got to do with her?"

Thompson lifted a hand, dropped it on the arm of the chair. He drew a long breath, looked sourly at Joe. "She tell you about her husband?"

"What are you trying to say?"

"Husband. Her man. No, of course not—she didn't tell you." Thompson glanced out the window. Then he looked at his right foot, reached down and unlaced his shoe, eased his foot, then retied it. "How bad is it, Morley? How deep you got it for this one?"

"Watch what you say."

"Relax, friend."

"I mean it."

Thompson looked at him and cussed softly.

Joe stood there watching, listening. He believed what the man had said, but that was all he believed. Then suddenly he didn't even believe that. Husband? Miriam?

"She's a doll, isn't she?" Thompson said. "Well, son—she's a killer's doll. A moll. A babe. A broad."

Joe stood there listening and it was as if his dream were a moth brightly burning in a candle's flame.

Thompson was enjoying this. You could tell. There was a flicker of life in the stale blue eyes. Thompson was wrong. He had to be.

"Get out of here," Joe said.

"Not that easy, Morley. Cooperate or not—remember?" Thompson leaned back in the chair, stretched, glanced out the window, then at Joe. "Her husband's Frank Garrett. Basically, that is. He has a string of aliases. One week ago, he engineered a bank holdup near Coral Gables. There were two men with him. They got one hundred and seventy-three thousand dollars. A great deal of money. Garrett killed a cashier, shot him in the face. Coming through Miami, he murdered both men with him, left them in the stolen getaway car. Only we were tipped."

"Tipped."

"About his wife, his little doll, Morley. She's here, waiting for him."

He stood there staring at Thompson. He went into the kitchenette, opened the refrigerator and took out the water bottle.

"Say, I could go some of that," Thompson said.

Joe found two glasses, poured one full, overflowed the other. He left the water bottle on the sink, took the glasses into the living room and handed Thompson one. He set his own on the floor. Then he headed for a chair. He sat down. Thompson got up, took the glass of water from the floor and handed it to him.

"Drink up. You need it. This all you got—water?"

Joe drank it and set the glass on the windowsill.

Thompson said brusquely, "All right. She got under your skin. Now it's over. Now you know."

"You're here—waiting for him?"

"In a way, yes."

"But why here—why not over there?"

"If it was only that easy. It's not."

Thompson returned to the window and settled into the contour chair. The sun lingered on the maroon carpet. "We got this tip. Legitimate—very legitimate. You see, somewhere in this damned hotel, there's a hired gunman." Thompson shrugged. "We don't know where. He's here on account of a double-cross. Garrett wasn't working for himself. He's hid the money. Only he knows where. This gunman is only concerned with the double-cross. Has orders, what they call a contract. He has to fill it."

It seemed as though the room had become a dark hollow, containing only Thompson's self-satisfied voice.

"I still don't understand."

"Well, he's waiting to kill Garrett. We figure it'll be a rifle, straight into that apartment over there—see? Your room is best for keeping an eye on things, that's why we're here." Thompson lifted a pair of field glasses from beneath the chair, set them down again. "Is it clear now, Morley?"

Joe came fast across the room to Thompson. "What about her?"

"What about her."

"She's in danger. She could be killed."

Thompson shrugged. He shook his head. He looked out the window and picked at the arm of the chair.

"Didn't you hear me?"

"Little Miriam's got herself into a pickle."

"Listen," Joe said. "You listen to me. You've got her wrong. She's nothing like that."

"Are they, ever? You're not going to tell her any of this, are you?"

They watched each other.

Thompson said, "Who knows? Maybe you're the killer. Wouldn't that be nifty."

"Damn you!"

"Relax. Seriously, though—we've tried to screen everybody as best we can. Not very good, at that. It could be anybody." He scrubbed his chin, looked at his watch. He stood up, stripped his jacket off, dropped it over the back of the chair and sat down again. His revolver was holstered on the left side of his belt. It had shiny black grips. "It's no fooling, you know— Morley? There really is a killer and he's going to kill Garrett. Thing is, we've got to stop him—somehow. We've got to find where Garrett hid that money. Somehow. Clear, now?"

He looked at Thompson. Then he turned and ran for the door.

"I'd hate to shoot you," Thompson said quickly.

Joe paused.

"But I would. Thing is, Morley—we need you."

He stood with his back to Thompson, one hand on the doorknob.

"You going to help us, Morley?"

The doorknob twisted in his fingers. He let go, and the one called Stewart came into the room and closed the door.

"Not a sign, Lew," Stewart said.

"Who are the possibles?" Thompson said.

Stewart looked at Joe. "You going someplace?"

"Not yet, he isn't."

Stewart lounged against the door in white flannel slacks and a blue sports shirt. He needed a shave and his yellow hair was dank. Thompson glanced at Stewart and stood up. He pulled the tails of his shirt free, so his shirt covered his gun.

"That's better," Stewart said. "Be nice if whoever the guy is got a look at that."

"How about it?" Thompson said. "Any possibles?"

"All of them are possibles."

Somebody knocked on the door.

Thompson motioned to Stewart. Stewart pussyfooted across the room into the kitchenette, out of sight. Thompson grabbed his jacket and the field glasses and went after Stewart. Then he poked his head around the wall.

"Morley, we got to trust you. Get rid of whoever it is."

Joe opened the door.

"My name's Foster," the man at the door said. "You have any iodine?"

"Iodine?"

"Hate to bother you. I cut my hand on the ice tray. I'm going to run into town for some iodine, but I figured I'd better put something on it."

Foster showed Joe his arm. There was a scratch cut deeply across the back of his hand. It was bleeding, but not badly. Foster was wearing a blue-and-white checked bathrobe. He had red hair with touches of gray at the temples and he kept pursing his mouth as he looked at the cut on his hand.

"Damned ice trays," Foster said.

"I'm sorry. I haven't anything for that. Listen, why not try the office?"

"Yes. I guess you're right."

Stewart came out of the kitchenette, whistling. He brushed past Joe and Foster in the doorway. "See you tonight, O. K.?"

"Right," Joe said.

Foster kept looking at his hand. "Sorry to bother you. I'll try the office."

"That's it," Joe said. He watched Foster trot away toward the stairway from the second-floor landing.

"Close the door," Thompson said.

He closed the door and looked at Thompson. Thompson started to say something. The door opened and Stewart returned.

"Nuts," Stewart said. "He did cut his hand. Blood on the sink and the ice tray, too."

"You mean, you went into his apartment?" Joe said.

"Right. He's way off any line of fire, Lew. Down on the corner. Couldn't possibly use a rifle from there. I checked for one, quick as I could. No sign."

"There wouldn't be," Thompson said. He glanced at Joe and went over to the contour chair and slumped down, putting his feet up. He rubbed one foot with the other. "All right, Morley. How d'you stand now?"

"Why should he use a rifle?" Joe said.

Thompson looked at Stewart. "What you know?"

"He's coming around," Stewart said.

"I'm not anything," Joe told them. "I'm just asking you. How come you think he'll use a rifle?"

"You got inside information?"

Joe looked at both of them in turn. Then he moved across the room and sat down and looked at his hands and thought how warm and vigorous her body had been. It sent his blood awake and he could taste the smooth caress of her lips. He smacked his hands together.

"Stands to reason a rifle," Stewart said. "He wants to get away, whoever he is. He don't want to show himself, he can help it. So a rifle."

"Well, Morley?" Thompson said. "You still got that itch?"

Joe looked at him. There was a kind of helplessness inside him and he thought of Betty and Davenport, Iowa. Then Miriam, and the way her lips were again, and the hot touch of her soft bare leg.

"Shut up!" he said.

"There's the Lawtons," Stewart said. "Next door, here. But she don't look like she would stick it with a killer, and Lawton don't look the type."

"Do they, ever?"

"No. Then there's Holcomb, on the other side. He could be our boy. He's a nervous cat, Lew. All alone. He's down in the bar, last I knew. Keeps watching the clock."

"We can't do a thing," Thompson said. "That's the curse of it. We make one wrong move, we'll blow the whole thing up. They'll knock Garrett off someplace else. Maybe he'll get tipped."

"By her?"

"Who knows. Morley, you going to help us?"

"You have other men here?" Joe said. "How many?"

"Never mind. It's taken care of. You know too much already. We got to use you, Morley." Thompson sat up, put his feet on the floor. "How about it?"

"How?"

"We want you to go ahead with her, just like you have. Maybe she'll give it away, somehow. Maybe she'll tip you when Garrett's supposed to show."

"That's the hell of it," Stewart said. "He could come any time."

Joe looked at them, trying to think beyond the fog of her. He couldn't. They were giving him a chance. They were asking him.

"All right," he said.

"Maybe he's just hot for the babe," Stewart said.

"We'll take the chance," Thompson said.

"Another crack like that, I'll blow this whole thing," Joe said.

"He's got backbone," Stewart said. "We'd just run you in, son. Say—well, molesting women. See? But honest—we need your help. Why in hell you think we're here?"

"Stewart," Thompson said. "You take off. Don't come back unless you've got something good. It'll look fishy, the way you're running in and out."

"All right." Stewart frowned. He left the room.

"What do you want me to do?" Joe asked.

"Find her and stick with her. See what you can get." Thompson smiled. Just his lips, nothing in the eyes at all. "Concerning what we want. All right?"

"All right."

"You've committed yourself, Morley. To the law."

"Yes. All right."

"No errors. It could go bad for you now."

Joe got up and started for the door.

"Get dressed first," Thompson said. "She's not going swimming again. I can see her over there." He raised the field glasses to his eyes and his lips quirked. "Can't say as I blame you, either, Morley."

Joe went into the bedroom, stripped off the khaki shorts and took a cold shower. It didn't do any good.

3

On the way down to the bar, an hour later, he saw the man called Holcomb. Very smooth and efficient looking. He had met him the first day at the motel. Holcomb was seated on the stairs, nervously smoking a cigarette. He edged out of the way as Joe came down.

"Nice afternoon," Joe said.

"Is it? It stinks, for your information."

Joe kept on going. At the bottom of the stairs, he paused and glanced back. Holcomb was standing there, picking tobacco off his lip.

Thompson had told Joe that their tip had said the killer would use a rifle and that he was a dead shot. Holcomb seemed too nervous for that. But you couldn't tell. Maybe the nervousness was an act.

Suddenly everybody in the motel was suspect. He knew how Thompson and Stewart felt.

Miriam.

She wasn't in the bar. He ordered a beer, drank half of it and decided to try her room. The sky was flaming in the West, the sun a huge orange ball resting on purple clouds. There was a stiff, salty breeze.

Holcomb was lounging in a deck chair around the corner from the side of the motel where Miriam's room was.

"You got the inside track," Holcomb said. "Haven't you?"

"What?"

"Hell, you know what I mean."

Holcomb was a bit tight. You could see it around the eyes. He kept smoking his cigarette, lounging there, staring up at Joe.

"She didn't come out," Holcomb said. "I been waiting."

"Oh."

"Devil with it. There's others."

Holcomb stood up. He flicked his half-smoked cigarette over the railing, looked once at Joe, and sauntered off along the landing. His heels smacked loudly, echoing around the inside of the court.

Joe went on down to Miriam's door.

She didn't answer when he knocked.

"If you don't open up, I'll smash it in," he said. He did not speak loud, placing his lips close to the open louvered windows.

"All right."

The sound of her voice changed everything for him. It was gentle and afraid. She was not just a plain broad, and he didn't care anyway. Damn Thompson. Stewart, too.

The door opened. "I thought I told you, Joe."

He looked past her head. The apartments on this side ran straight through the motel wall. He could see beyond, through the living room window and across the court into his own rooms. He could not see Thompson. He knew Thompson had pulled the blinds and was watching with the damned field glasses plastered to his face.

"Miriam."

She brushed past him, her purse swinging on one arm and started to close the door. He thrust her back inside and went along with her. As the door closed, he held her arms and looked into her eyes.

"What's the matter, Joe?"

"Nothing. You know I want to see you. Why do you do this to me?"

"I've told you. You've got to leave me be."

He stepped close to her. She stepped back. He did it again, until they were shielded by the kitchen wall from Thompson and his glasses.

"Joe—stop!"

He got his hands on her and held her up against him, running his hands up and down her back. She was wearing a white linen dress and he felt it slide on silk with the warm soft flesh underneath. Her head came back. Her eyes were very black. It was as if she were trying to pull away and fighting to stay.

Suddenly she changed. She bent to him and their mouths came together. It was a bright pain, almost unbearable, then it was like drowning and wanting to drown. Her purse dropped. It struck with a thud. She arched back and he bent to retrieve it.

"Listen, Joe—all right—listen."

She held to him, looking at him, holding him with her eyes, too. He forgot the purse.

"All right," she said. "But I've got to tell you something. You've got to promise me."

"Miriam."

"Come." She pulled at his hand, smiling now, her eyes very black. "Sit down," she said. He could smell her perfume in the room and she stood against him, her knees touching his.

He tried to pull her down. She held herself stiff, smiling at him, then not smiling. He went crazy, his arms around her. She gripped her fingers in his hair.

"I'm a nurse, Joe. It's serious with me, if I lose this job. I'm waiting here, you see?"

"Miriam." He listened, remembering Thompson. Not caring about anything, unable to care.

"They're bringing this old woman here, see, Joe? I've got to be the kind— you know? Very exacting and with nothing in the way, especially not like you. See? She's coming here from the North, New York. To stay here. I'm her nurse."

"When's she coming?"

"Soon. I have to be just right."

"Come here."

"Yes. All right. Then you'll have to go—quickly. But afterwards, Joe. After she comes. Then we'll work something out. We could—something, yes—anything."

"Yes," he said huskily. "Yes."

"I'm human, Joe. I'm human."

"Now go," she said. They stood by the door. She kept pushing at him with her hand, smiling and not smiling, her eyes dull, but still very black.

"You're a nurse?"

She looked at him. "Yes. Now go. Don't come near me. Not until I say so. You think I'd let something like this get away from us? Never, Joe. It's too good."

"A nurse."

"Yes, I—what do you mean?"

"Nothing. Just that you'd be a fine nurse."

"You don't believe me, do you?"

"Sure. Sure I believe you."

"Wait. Wait, then you've got to go."

She started through the kitchen, then saw her purse there on the floor. She snatched it up. She opened her purse, brought out a card.

"Here, just read it."

He did. She was a registered nurse. Miriam Hall.

He looked at her. She dropped the card in her purse, snapped it shut. She turned, took the purse into the bedroom, came back pushing at her thick hair, loosening it.

She was a nurse.

"Miriam. Tonight. We could have dinner, then—"

"Then what? Sure." She pushed him toward the door, opened it and pushed him outside. "Sure. You want me to lose this job? Listen, we wait for something like this, Joe. It means a lot."

"You will let me know?"

She closed the door, only one eye and her red lips showing. "Now, just what do you think?"

He wanted to go back inside.

She closed the door, locked it, and he heard her say, "Go away, Joe."

"It's like I'm rooted."

"Joe, go away!"

It seemed as if there was panic in her voice. He realized suddenly that he might antagonize her. He didn't want that.

He turned and walked along the landing. By the time he reached the corner, he caught himself thinking of Betty, back in Davenport. Now that was an odd thing. My gosh, what was he going to tell Thompson....

"She's a nurse."

"Oh, great. I thought you were never getting out of there."

He walked past Thompson into the bedroom. Thompson was using the field glasses. "She's changing her clothes again." Thompson looked at him. "That's the second clean dress today. I can't see so well."

"The sun's going down."

"That's bad."

"She has lights."

"What did she say?" Thompson came into the bedroom and looked at him. Joe sat on the bed and stared at the floor.

"She's a nurse. I didn't tip her to anything."

"What are you thinking about?"

Joe looked at him. Then at the floor again.

Thompson went back into the living room. "It's getting dark fast now. Does she pull her blinds?"

"Not so far."

"This is the bad part. Night. The logical time. Did it seem like it might be tonight?"

"I think you're wrong about her."

"Sure. You going to be with her tonight?"

"No."

"Dinner?"

"No."

"Why not? Why didn't you fix it?"

"She said she's a nurse."

"Look, Morley. Come off it, please? For me. This is important." He came back into the bedroom. "Don't just sit there. You said you'd help us."

"I've done all I can do. All right." He looked at Thompson and told him everything she'd said. "And I believe her. She just isn't like what you said."

"You poor kid, you," Thompson said. "Well, all right. What can I do?" He went back into the other room. Joe heard him settle in the contour chair.

"I've done all I can," Joe said.

Thompson didn't answer.

"What do we do now?"

"Somehow, I detect a different tone to your voice, Morley. You've changed since you left this room."

Joe didn't answer him. He went into the bathroom and looked at his face. Then he went into the kitchen. The water bottle was still there on the sink, the water tepid. He filled it from the tap and returned it to the refrigerator. Then he drew himself a glass of water and slowly drank it.

"When you going home to Davenport?"

"How'd you know?"

"When you registered."

He set the glass down and stared at it.

A nurse, she said she was.

"Have some food sent up, Morley. A good lot, so we can both eat. I'm not leaving the room."

"So I have to stick around?"

"It looks that way. If you go out and eat, I don't eat. Be a little peculiar, having dinner sent up after you've eaten."

"We just going to sit here?"

"Get comfortable, pal." Thompson cleared his throat. "How old are you, Morley?"

"Twenty-two."

"I see. Got a girl back home?"

"What's it to you?"

Thompson didn't answer.

"Yeah, sort of," Joe said.

"Don't you wonder what she's doing?"

Joe didn't say anything.

4

The night slowly progressed into morning. Stewart came in about three and relieved Thompson at the window until five. Thompson slept in the contour chair. Joe did not sleep. None of the waiting did any good. Joe imagined they had men posted around to see if Garrett would come during the night, but when he asked Thompson, the detective didn't reply.

There were no lights after midnight in Miriam's apartment, and Thompson with the field glasses said she wore a long nightgown and was going to bed. Once, at about eleven thirty, they thought they had something. She came to the window overlooking the landing and the court and waved her arms. She was only taking some deep breathing.

They had breakfast sent up, and like dinner, they shared the one plate. It didn't even seem foolish to Joe anymore.

"Now what?" he said, after he wheeled the tray outside the door and locked the door.

"We wait some more."

"Did Stewart have anything new?"

"Nothing."

"How long will you wait?"

"Until something happens." Thompson looked like the very dickens.

"You can use my razor," Joe told him.

"I can't leave the window. I got a feeling." Thompson watched Miriam's place....

One o'clock in the afternoon, Miriam appeared on the sundeck above her apartment with the yellow screen. She was wearing her bathing suit. She set the screen up and stepped inside. Her shadow was very clear today, like a moving black paper cut-out silhouetted by the sun. Only you knew it wasn't paper. She lay down and they could only see the curved contour of her back just above the low parapet of the sundeck.

"Stewart thinks it's the desk clerk," Thompson said. He sighed and squeezed his eyes with thumb and forefinger. Then he rubbed both eyes with the heel of his hand. "He's a transient. They only hired him five days ago."

"That's right. There was a different man on the desk."

"Yeah."

Somebody whistled from beyond the court.

"Here it is," Thompson said.

"What?"

"We have to play it close," Thompson said. He came out of the chair, holding the field glasses. "We want Garrett alive. We could take him now, but we want the other one, too. He's got to give himself away. We've got every room spotted."

"You mean Garrett's coming?"

Thompson's hands shook a little holding the glasses to his eyes. "He's over there. He's reading something she wrote."

Joe stared toward her apartment, sick and a little lost. He saw a man's shadow in there. Thompson dropped the glasses, started for the door.

"You stay right here, Morley. Don't go outside. I've got to move." He went to the door. Joe wanted to say something. He didn't know what. "Lock the door," Thompson said. "And stay here." He was gone.

Joe looked over there, through the window. He saw the man come up onto the sundeck and move toward the screen. The man looked around, then stepped behind the screen, his shadow sharp. He was wearing a white Palm Beach suit.

Joe heard the door open and thought it was Thompson, remembering he hadn't locked it. He turned and looked at the shiny revolver in the man's hand.

"Get away from the window," Foster said. "In the kitchen."

Foster still wore the blue-and-white checked bathrobe. Joe thought crazily for a moment that he was here for more iodine, knowing all the time who he really was. He backed into the kitchen.

"Yeah," Foster said. His red hair was messed up, and his face sheened with perspiration. He held the revolver on Joe and reached behind the refrigerator. He brought out a rifle with a scope sight and Joe stared.

"Turn around," Foster said. "Fast, now."

Joe turned. He got halfway around when the gun smashed against his head. He sprawled out, the pain bright white deep into his shoulders.

He looked over there and came to his knees. Foster was at the window, holding the rifle. Joe went for him, his head one big ache. The rifle fired. Joe landed on Foster and the rifle fell outside the window, the stock snicking against the blinds.

He smashed at Foster's face. He tried to see over across there, on the sundeck.

"If you killed her!" He punched at Foster and they rolled out across the floor. "She was there too!" Joe said. He got his hands on Foster's throat, kneeling on his arms. Foster spat directly upward and Joe flinched.

"Jerk!" Foster said.

Joe fought to regain the hold. Foster wouldn't let him. The man was wiry and there was a crazed look in his eyes. He broke free, then came at Joe, coming to his feet, kicking.

Joe caught his foot and Foster sat down hard.

Somehow, he had to get to Thompson. That's all he could think now.

Then he heard her scream. He knew it was Miriam.

"Damn it!" Foster said.

The two of them stood close together, kneeling on the floor and Joe knew he had him. The man was no good with his fists. He got in a low solid punch and Foster bent over, and Joe brought his right up without even thinking. Foster fell back, groaning.

Joe went over to the window and jerked up the blinds.

She screamed again. He saw her running across the edge of the parapet. The sun slanted off her body, her hair fleeing black and high above her shoulders.

"Wait!"

It was Thompson who called. Joe saw him running across the roof toward the sundeck.

Then he saw Garrett, lying there by the yellow screen, holding the gun in his hand.

Joe knew what was going to happen. He didn't move, he wanted to do something, at least to speak. He just stood there.

Garrett fired the gun once. Joe heard Garrett's voice, "Die, darling, die...." Miriam went straight out into free air. She fell toward the court and struck and Joe saw that, too. He turned away.

"Watch it," Stewart said.

Foster was on his knees, looking at Stewart who'd just come through the door.

"You all right, Morley?"

Joe brushed past him. He heard Stewart tell him to wait, but he didn't wait. He went on through the door and toward the stairway to the roof. He climbed the stairs trying to shake the fog out of his mind.

She was a nurse, he thought. Lying down there.

Miriam....

He started along the roof. He didn't look down into the court. He couldn't make himself look down there.

"Morley."

Thompson was standing over there by the yellow screen.

"Yes."

He came across the sundeck. There were three other plainclothes men standing around, looking at the thing by the yellow screen.

"You all right, kid?"

Joe heard Stewart yell across the court.

"We got him, Lew. It was Foster, just like you said."

Thompson waved back. There was no expression on his face. He looked at Joe.

"How about it, Morley? You all right?"

"I'm all right. He shot her."

"That's right."

Joe moved over to the screen.

"We got it out of him before he died, though. Thank cripes for that, eh?"

"Sure."

Joe looked at Garrett. A young man, in a bloody Palm Beach suit, lying dead on the sundeck. Garrett's eyes were partially open and he was very pale.

"Hit him in the chest, too. Right in the chest," Thompson said. "Look here."

He took Joe's arm. He showed him the hole in the screen and they both heard Stewart calling. Stewart came up to them.

"She set him up for it," Stewart said. "She and Foster were working together."

"I'm darned," Thompson said.

Joe looked at the blood on the yellow screen.

"Foster said she nearly messed it up, the way she was with young Casanova, here."

"Easy," Thompson said.

"Foster says he didn't wise up we were here, even," Stewart said. "How about that? We're getting good."

"You mean," Joe said, "she brought him, her own husband up here—so Foster could get a good clean shot at him? At his shadow, standing up behind the screen?" He stared at Stewart. "Is that what you mean?"

Stewart nodded. "She left a note for him, in her room."

"Nifty," Thompson said.

"She said she was a nurse," Joe said. "She even had a card to prove it."

Thompson and Stewart looked at each other.

"Going back to Davenport, kid?" Thompson said.

Joe looked at Stewart, then Thompson, and remembered Betty. He wondered about her for a moment, then thought of Miriam again.

"You feel all right?" Thompson said.

"Yes. I feel all right." He paused. "It was the purse, that's what it was. I couldn't figure out why she did that, for a minute. She must have had a gun in her purse. It sounded like it, when it fell on the floor. She didn't want me to see it."

"What?" Thompson said.

Joe shook his head and turned away.

Day Keene (real name Gunard Hjerstedt) epitomized the writer flexible enough and talented enough to make the transition across multiple forms of media. After a career as an actor, he became the principal writer for the Little Orphan Annie radio show, then turned into a prolific pulp writer, moved on to paperback originals, and eventually ending up writing mainstream novels. A pro's pro, the story offered here is a carny story, oddly enough a sub-genre unto itself beneath the aegis of crime fiction. Fredric Brown's Madball *and William Lindsay Gresham's* Nightmare Alley *are classic examples in novel form. Here Keene shows he definitely knows the life....*

THE GEEK-GIRL

Day Keene

I drove into Langley at 10 o'clock on a hot Monday morning with the show strung out behind me like the tail on a red bone-dog. The town was typical of its type, small and Southern, built around an ancient brick courthouse rising out of a square of chinch bug-ravaged grass.

Bull Haney was riding with me. He looked at the name on the bank and remembered the name on the cotton gin we'd passed on the edge of town.

"This guy John R. Langley must be the local big shot."

I braked for the traffic light on the corner of 4th and Main. "Must be."

Haney spat over the side of the car. "Probably the town was named after him, huh?"

I said, "More likely his grandfather. Or even back before that. A man would have to be older than the original Siamese twins to have this burg named after him."

Stopped in the humid heat, you could smell decaying vegetation and dry rot. It was the first Monday in the month, and court day. There were quite a few people in the square, mostly small farmers and share croppers, but the only local I saw who showed any enthusiasm over the banner on the open, cream-colored Caddy I was driving was a freckle-faced 8-year-old girl with a cheerful gap where her two front teeth had been.

She stood on one foot on the curb, scratching a chubby leg with the dusty toes of her other foot, grinning, "Hit's the carnival come t' town."

I reached over the side of the car and gave her a handful of tickets to the various rides and shows. "On the house, sister. Come have a good time. And tell all your friends we're in town."

She showed me the gap in her teeth. "Gee. Thanks. Thanks a lot, Mister."

Bull grinned at me. "Some tough guy. I thought you never gave a sucker a break."

"Kids," I told him, "are different."

The young cop under the light waved me on. "Okay. Let's go, Carnie."

It was the way he said it. Like we were white trash. I started to open the door of the car and Bull laid his hand on my arm.

Bull put a fresh chew in his cheek. "Could be Langley doesn't care for carnivals. Could be it's a Sunday-School town."

I drove on slowly. "Could be."

Kenny, my advance man, had done a good job of papering. There were show cards in most of the store windows, and two– and three-sheets plastered on every available wall and billboard; but I didn't like the feel of the town. It was too quiet, almost as if it were peopled by zombies. Still, the people on the walks and in the stores looked normal, the same people you find in any town.

There was a prison gang cutting weeds a few blocks from the fairgrounds. As usual, they begged for cigarets. I slowed to throw out a couple of packs, and one of the pot-bellied guards waved me on with his shotgun.

"Get goin', Carnie. These boys are bad babies."

"What did they do?" Bull asked. "Spit on the sidewalk, or something?"

A few of the prisoners laughed. The other guard raised his rifle. He looked like he might shoot. I lifted my hand to him and drove on.

It wasn't much of a fairgrounds. There were two beat-up horse and cattle barns, a produce shed, a few smaller buildings and a weathered exhibition hall. A wooden grandstand was peeling white paint. The small oval pacing track was overgrown with Johnson grass and beggarweed.

The lot, however, wasn't bad. It was fairly level, on the edge of a muddy river fringed with Chinaberry trees. Bull got out and started to mark off the midway and spot his canvas trucks. Duke and Mabel drove up beside me.

"Geeze, is it hot!" Mabel said.

"Who booked this one?" Duke asked.

I said, "I did."

He pushed his straw sailor on the back of his head. "Okay. Okay. Don't get sore about it, Giff. It's your show. All I am is a talker."

The usual swarm of kids had followed the convoy of trucks through town. I watched the ride and canvas trucks wheel onto the lot and begin to unload and set up, then I walked back through the dust and the orderly confusion down to the row of house trailers lining up on the bank of the river.

There was a spring to the turf. The heat and dust felt familiar. As I passed Flo's trailer she opened the screen door and called, "Who picked this lemon out of a hat?"

I said, "I did."

Flo eased her 500 pounds to the ground. "Well, I always hope for the best. But if I was running the mitt camp I wouldn't have to look in my crystal ball to tell you you've picked a bloomer." She looked at the kids swarming over the lot, carrying tent stakes and chairs, earning a ride on the whip-the-whip or the Ferris wheel of the carousel. "The principal industry in and around Langley seems to be having children."

I said, "A man has to do something," and walked down to the river.

It hadn't changed. It was still shallow and red with mud, rising swift and clean and narrow back in the hills, then broadening out and slowing and filling with mud as it flowed down into the flatlands. Like a man's life.

I stood a long time looking upstream through the shimmering haze of heat, then walked back the way I'd come. Bull had most of his canvas laid out and was starting to raise his center poles. The grease monkeys were busy with the rides. Here and there a booth had been knocked together. Tent by tent, show by show, ride by ride, the midway was beginning to take form. I was watching the Ferris wheel go up when a police car trailing a plume of dust wailed down the highway and pulled into the lot.

Bull picked up a tent stake. "I knew it."

A tall, sallow-faced man in his middle 50s got out on the right-hand side of the car and pushed a battered white Stetson still farther back on his head.

"Who's in charge heah?" he asked.

I walked over to where he was standing. "I am. The name is Morgan. I own the show."

He didn't offer to shake hands. "I'm Sheriff Willis." He looked at my wide-brimmed panama and $200 silk suit. Neither of them impressed him. "Haven't I seen you before?"

I said, "That's possible. I was born in the part of the state."

"And how long have you been in the carnival business?"

I considered my answer. "For quite some time. In fact, since shortly after I got out of the Army. Yeah. For quite some years."

"And you've never heard of such a thing as buying a license to play a town?"

I stuck a cigaret in my mouth. "Of course. My advance man, Jack Kenny, always arranges for a reader at the same time he papers a town."

Willis shook his head at me. "Then this is one time he slipped up."

The uniformed deputy driving the car got out. Something was bothering him. I didn't like him on sight. "I never heard of no Morgans around here, except a passel of clay-eaters up in the hills. You carnies are all alike, a bunch of liars and clip artists."

I asked, "What's the matter with you, buster? You spend a dime on a corn game and fail to win a TV set?"

He came around the car fast. I let his punch slip past my ear and bounced his head off the dusty hood of the police car with a short left to his jaw.

Bull picked up the tent stake again. "And he tells me no rough stuff."

The deputy got to his feet, clawing at his holstered gun. Poker-faced,

Willis pushed him back against the car. "Stop it, you fool."

The punk looked at the gathering semi-circle of talkers, pitchmen, roustabouts and grease monkeys, each of them armed with the first thing he'd snatched up.

Willis turned back to me. "Now about that license?"

I lit the cigaret I'd stuck in my mouth. "Okay. Let's go down to the courthouse and find out."

Bull opened the off door of the Caddy. "I'll go with you. Just for luck."

Duke tested the edge of the switchblade he was holding by pointedly paring a thumb nail. "Have fun. But be back in half an hour."

The deputy gave him a dirty look, and he and Willis got back in the police car. I followed them into town. There were even more cars and people in the square than before. All of them looked hot. Even the leaves of the trees drooped limp and lifeless-looking in the sun.

A colored boy who looked like he might be a trusty was making vague motions with a broom on the worn stone steps of the courthouse. Willis asked him where Judge Langley was.

"He in his office, Sheriff," the boy told him. "He about t' hold cou't, I think."

The shaded interior of the courthouse held an illusion of coolness. Up on the second floor, Willis opened an unmarked door and motioned us in.

"This is Morgan, the owner of the carnival that's playin' the fair," Willis told a man back of a desk. "He *says* he thought his advance man made arrangements for a license."

"I see," Judge Langley said.

I liked him even less than I'd liked the deputy. He was a waxen-faced man in his middle 40s, with deep purple circles under his eyes.

"I see," he repeated. "What kind of a show do you run, Mr. Morgan?"

"A clean show. No grift."

"All you carnival men say that." He sunk the hook. "All right. A license will cost you $200 a day for seven days, payable in advance and non-refundable. And the first money-wheel you spin, or the first complaint we get, we'll close you down. And that goes for dirty shows, too. Now if that isn't satisfactory, you can load your show back on your trucks and pull on."

The usual reader cost from $20 to $50 a day for towns the size of Langley; he expected me to beef. I fooled him by counting out fourteen $100 bills. "Now if you'll write me a receipt."

He gave me a straight look but wrote out a receipt. "You must want to play Langley."

"I do."

He started to ask why. Before he could, the hall door opened again and two uniformed town policemen, one of them the lad who'd been directing traffic, came in with a struggling girl between them.

"For God's sake," His Honor exploded. "Court is supposed to be in session. I—"

He got a good look at the girl and forgot whatever he'd been about to say.

She was barefoot, blonde, not more than 19, and built like a combined Jane Russell and Marilyn Monroe. More, most of what she had showed. All she had on was a thin silk dress and, in struggling with the cops, the silk had split in the damndest places. If you disregarded the blank look in her eyes, her face was as pretty as her body.

Langley had trouble getting his lips wet enough to suit him. "What's she done?" he asked finally.

The young officer was embarrassed. "I don't rightly know how to charge her, Judge. I'm directing traffic on 4th and Main, see? And she comes walking across 4th dressed like she is now. And all the guys on the walk are hollerin' an whistlin' at her. And when I ask her what's the idea, she either can't or won't talk."

"What's your name, Miss?" Langley asked her.

Standing as she was, supported by the two cops, her blonde hair hanging over her face, the girl looked incredibly lovely and wanton. She brushed her hair back with one hand and tried to smile, at the same time making a mewing sound in her throat.

"See what I mean?" the cop said.

Langley asked Willis if she was local.

The poker-faced sheriff shook his head. "Not for 200 miles. We don't grow 'em that purty."

Langley looked back at the little blonde. "Has she any money or any identification on her?"

The young cop's face grew even redder. "Naw. She ain't got nawthin' on her but that dress."

His Honor used a clean pocket handkerchief to pat at the fine film of perspiration that was beading on his upper lip. "That makes it vagrancy and indecent exposure. Fifty dollars or 30 days, on each count."

He asked the girl if she had $100. A troubled look replaced her smile and she made the mewing sound again.

For some reason it seemed to amuse His Honor. "Well, don't worry, honey," he said. "Perhaps I can find some way for you to work out your fine."

The air in the office grew sticky. Sheriff Willis looked out the window. The cop who'd done the talking looked down at his polished shoes. The girl began to cry.

"Now, look here—" Bull began.

I laid another $100 bill on top of the 14 bills I'd placed on Langley's desk. "Perhaps that won't be necessary. There's her fine money on both charges. What's more, I'll give her a job on the show and that will take care of the vagrancy angle."

Langley scowled at me. "What can a mute girl do on a carnival?"

I took off my coat and wrapped it around her. "I'll think of something. I can probably make a geek of her."

The word puzzled His Honor. "What's a geek?"

I nodded for Bull to open the office door. "In this case, a wild girl. You know—" I went into a phony spiel—"—See Zaz Za, half animal, half woman, the beautiful little wild girl who spent her childhood with the wolves."

"That's a lot of baloney," Willis said.

"You yokels buy it," Bull told him.

I asked the girl, "Would you like to work for me, Miss?"

She made the same mewing sound again, but this time smiling an bobbing her head. I watched Langley's face as I closed the door behind us. I could expect trouble from him. He wasn't accustomed to being pushed around. His great-grandfather had founded Langley. He owned a bank and a cotton gin. He was a judge. In Langley, he was the law. He was used to getting what he wanted.

He wanted my little blonde geek....

The girl rode between us, seemingly content to be where she was. Neither Bull nor I spoke until we were almost back to the lot. Then, passing the prison gang Bull couldn't stand it any longer.

"This sudden insanity. How come?"

I glanced sideways at him. "What insanity?"

He told me. "First you lay out $200 a day to play a town that isn't worth a double-sawbuck." He looked at the girl between us. "Now her."

I said, "What I lay out for a license to play a town is my business. As for the little geek—what did you expect me to do, leave her there in the custody of His Honor? You know as well as I do what was in store for her."

"Yeah. Sure," Bull agreed with me. "But—"

Her big blue eyes round and frightened, the little golden geek scratched at my shirt sleeve and made the mewing sound again, as if she were agreeing with me. It was the damnedest thing I'd ever heard. I could feel my flesh crawl.

"Where'd you come from, Miss?" I asked her.

She continued to mew.

I tried again. "You live around here?"

She shook her head and mewed even more earnestly.

Bull used his handkerchief to mop at the back of his neck. "For God's sake, cut it out," he said. "Don't ask her no more questions. It makes cold chills run up and down my back just to listen to her."

I waved pleasantly at the pot-bellied Crackers guarding the lads cutting weeds and turned into the carnival lot. "Then, can be I'll get my money back. If she does that to you, think what she'll do to the yokels."

For just having set up the midway, there was a fair-sized crowd on the lot, as many adults now as there were children. Both the concessions and the rides were getting a good play, but neither the girl-show, the five-in-one nor the muscle-camp had made their first pitch.

When Duke saw the car he stopped cleaning his nails with the switchblade, snapped it shut and picked up his talker's cane. I let Bull out at the cook-house and drove on down to Flo's trailer.

Flo had hooked into the portable power plant. After the outside heat the air-conditioned trailer felt good. The little geek perched on the edge of Flo's bed, looking from Flo to me as I explained what I wanted.

"First put a pair of pants and a bra on her. Then fit her up with a short dress, you know, uneven and kind of jagged around the edges." I had an inspiration. "Like Moonbeam McSwine wears in the Li'l Abner cartoon. Let plenty of her show, but keep her decent."

"Yeah. Sure. I get you," Flo said.

"Then tell Duke to figure out some way to use her in the pit show. Maybe he can just ask her questions and she can act wild like and mew back at him. The yokels should go for that."

"They should," Flo agreed. She was practical. "But what are you going to use for a blow-off?"

I thought a moment. "We can stuff a boiled chicken with catchup and she can tear it apart with her teeth. The towners will think she's eating it raw." I looked at the little blonde. "You think you could do that, honey, for, say, $50 a week and your keep?"

Smiling, she mewed and bobbed her head at me. Then, when I stood up, she stood up to go with me.

"No. You stay here," I said. "For the time being at least. You're going to live with Flo."

She looked disappointed. I opened the screen door, turned back. I thought of something else. The girl's golden hair was too well combed. "And before Duke makes his first pitch, smear some dirt on her face and snarl her hair." I illustrated what I meant. "See? Like this."

Touching her was a mistake. It was like touching an open 220-volt circuit. She came alive under my hand and pressed her body against mine. Her lips were sweet and soft. I liked the smell of her hair.

I pried the girl loose with an effort.

"She seems to like you," Flo said.

I drove away from the trailer with Flo smiling, amused, and the little blonde geek standing in the open doorway, mewing after me, her blue eyes hurt and disappointed.

Back in the office-trailer I loosened the knot in my tie and picked a fifth of rum from the built-in liquor cabinet. Then, kicking off my shoes, I lay down on the leather lounge and drank warm rum from the bottle. Life was a complex affair. A man thought he knew what he wanted. He subjugated everything else to one aim. He sweat and lived toward one point. Then, with the score for which he was shooting almost within his grasp, he was ready to chump off like a yokel. I even considered kissing my money goodby and ordering Bull to reload the show and pull on. But I'd lived with my one big idea too long. I wasn't going to toss it away now. When the bottle was empty, I slept.

It was night when I awakened. Outside, the midway was alive with sound. I could hear the rhythmic creaking of the Ferris wheel, the tinkle of the carrousel organ, the tap of the talkers' canes as they made their pitches, and the shouts of the juice-joint and game men, the whole blended together by laughter and excited voices.

It was a good life. I liked it. I showered and put on clean clothes and walked down the crowded midway to the cookhouse for a cup of coffee.

Hugo was grinning from ear to ear, his white chef's cap cocked on one side of his head. "I guess you can pick 'em, Giff. It looks like the rest of us were wrong about this stand. The crowd ain't much for pretty, but there's sure a hell of a lot of them an' they ain't got no fishhooks in their pockets."

"Crackers are like that," I told him. "They'll spend their last dime to pleasure themselves and their families even if they have to live on sowbelly and grits for the next six months."

"You're a Cracker yourself, ain't you, Giff?"

"Let's say I used to be." I looked at the crowd milling up and down the midway. "Funny. They don't look it, but most of them are good family men. Another thing, you can push them just so far. Then they don't break, they fight back."

Hugo was puzzled. "What do you mean by that?"

I finished my coffee and stood up. "Nothing. It was just an observation."

The coffee washed the rum out of my mouth. I felt good. I felt fine. I walked back up the midway to the fairgrounds to look up the president of the fair association. According to my contract, the fair association had agreed to a guarantee of $900; but after the bobble about the reader I wanted to make certain.

I found him in a small office in the horse barn. He was nursing a Mason jar of corn whisky. He said that the guarantee was correct; that he'd held out for 30 per cent of the gross but it had been so long since Langley had had a carnival that rather than lose the booking, he had allowed Jack Kenny to talk him into the cash guarantee, with all admission money going to the fair association.

He was pretty deep into the jar. "I don't know, though, why we bother to hold a fair. It's the same thing every year. I don't know why we just don't mail him the ribbons."

"Mail who the ribbons?"

"John R. Every year it's the same. He gets the blue ribbon for the best bull, the best steer in its class, the best bale of cotton. If he baked a pie, I suppose we'd have to give him the blue ribbon for the best cook of the show."

I refused the drink he offered. "Who's John R.?"

He hiccupped. "His Honor, John R. Langley."

I sat on the edge of the desk. "It's that bad, huh?"

He took the drink I'd refused. "Worse. I hear how he treated you. Think what it means to live here, with him playing God 365 days a year! When the old man was alive, it wasn't so bad. But now with John R. in the saddle, there isn't a merchant or a farmer in the county who can call his soul his own." He twiddled an imaginary fife. "His Honor pipes the tune and we dance."

"How come?"

"He owns the bank. He owns the cotton gin. Every third farmer in the county is paying him interest and afraid to say 'spit' on Sunday for fear John R. will make him trouble of some kind. And we merchants make our living off the farmers and have to bank with him."

He got up and looked in his filing case and brightened as he found a full Mason jar. He unscrewed the cap and offered the jar to me. I needed a drink. I took one. I'd forgotten how good corn whisky can be. Time was when I'd drunk a lot of it.

The fair president's name was Meager. He continued, "I wouldn't mind it half so much if he wasn't so damned smug about everything. It's the women and the church people who really run every town or county. They could do something if they would. But John R. has them fooled. He doesn't drink or smoke or chew. Because he gives $5,000 a year to the church and spouts oily platitudes at every school-board and town meeting, the women and the preachers think he's one of the twelve disciples. I could tell you which one." He bought himself a drink. "Every woman in this town would buy herself a pair of iron britches before she'd let him get near her, if they knew the truth."

"He's that bad, huh?"

"He's worse. Believe me, Mr. Morgan, he's wrecked plenty of homes around here; then he's either bought off or scared off the husband, with the wife too ashamed to talk," he confided. "I even hear there's plenty of hell goes on nights in the courthouse basement, especially after His Honor has tucked away some teen-age or hill girl for 30 days for some minor breach of the peace. And afterward, like the wives, the girls are too ashamed or too scared to talk."

It was hot in the small office. I said, "That's hard to believe."

Meager hooted at me. "Ha. I remember one case during the war, right near the end, some girl from back in the hills. I don't remember the name of the family, but her husband had been ETO and they'd transferred him to the Pacific with a two-week States-side leave in between. Anyway, the girl was a little honey and her guy had been gone for about four months when it happened."

"When what happened?"

"When Langley got his hands on her. That was just about the same time the young billy she was married to was walking ashore on Iwo. She got into a little trouble over a bad check that turned out to be good, but before it did, His Honor had tucked her away for 30 days for his own convenience. She was only 17, and pretty, and they say it was pitiful what happened to the kid. She was young, emotional, see? And even if what happened wasn't her fault, she felt she'd let her man down. She was ashamed and she was desperate. So when Langley did let her go, she didn't go home."

"Where did she go?"

"Into the river. In the deep hole just this side of the bridge. That's how it come out she was four months pregnant. At the autopsy, see? Langley and his crowd claimed she was ashamed on account of the check business, but everyone in the know knew better."

"What did her husband do?"

"What could he do? He was in the South Pacific. Then when he did come home, I suppose he wasn't sure. A thing like that is hard to prove. Besides, even if he went to the chair for killing Langley it wouldn't bring her back."

I stood up. Meager's story had made me restless. I had to change the subject. "Well, I'd best get back to the lot. Anyway, I'm glad the guarantee is straight. With the excessive license fee I'll be lucky if I break even on the stand."

Meager stopped me at the door of the office. "Hey. What's this I hear about you snatching some fresh meat away from the tiger? I hear she's a little honey. I'll bet His Honor was furious."

"He wasn't pleased."

"Is she really crazy?"

I shook my head. "I doubt it."

I walked back to the midway. Business was holding up and getting better every minute. Duke had tipped his pitch for the girl-show and had moved over to the five-in-one, using Flo for his bally, and the lean-gutted Crackers and townsmen and their wives were roaring with laughter as Flo, quivering all over, sang *Why Not Take All of Me?* along with the simple dance step she was doing.

I waited for Duke to finish his ballyhoo and followed the crowd into the freak show. Even with the sidewalls raised and laced the big tent was almost unbearably hot. It smelled of freshly washed bodies and soft soap and gasoline.

The crowd gawked at the neon-tube swallower and the skeleton man and the usual run of attractions, but it could hardly wait until Duke came to the geek-girl.

Flo had done a good job on her. Her dress was an old burlap potato sack, tied around her slim middle with rope. Her hair was snarled and flecked with straw. There were smudges of dirt on her face. Somewhere, either Flo or Duke had dug up a rusty chain and fastened it to a peg, then around one of her ankles. As Duke moved the crowd over to her she squirmed about in the straw with which her pen was lined. She looked like a wild girl— the type of wild girl any man in his right mind would vote as the wild girl with whom he'd like to be lost in the jungle. Any jungle.

More, she was a clever little actress. As Duke began his spiel she stopped wriggling in the straw and stood up, and every woman in the tent gasped and every man sucked in his breath as she began to mew and preen herself in a piece of broken mirror, pausing from time to time to smile at the men in the crowd, like an amorous young tigress admiring her reflection in a river an wanting all male tigers to admire her.

The yarn Duke had thought up wasn't much. But it served. The crowd was too busy gawking at the little geek to listen to what he was saying. I wasn't surprised to see Judge Langley in the crowd. He stood cool and distinguished-looking in a crisp white linen suit, flanked on one side by Sheriff Willis and on the other by the young punk I'd slugged. His Honor couldn't keep his eyes off the girl.

For a geek, the kid was the best I'd ever seen. When Duke came to the part in his spiel about her eating nothing but raw meat, he picked a naked boiled chicken from a tray of raw chickens and tossed it to her. She caught it in mid air and bit the neck off with so much realism that the catchup with which it was filled squirted all over her, and two women in the front row fainted.

The deep circles under his eyes even more pronounced, Judge Langley said something to Willis. The sheriff nodded, took a step forward and stopped as the little geek licked thoughtfully at the simulated blood on one bare arm. Then, still holding the partly gnawed chicken in one hand, she untied the rope around her waist, casually pulled the sack dress over her head and returned to gnawing at the chicken as naked as she'd been born. What had looked like flesh-colored pants and bra was *flesh*!

The crowd in the tent went crazy. The men wanted to stay. Their wives tried to drag them away. I watched Langley. His face was as white as bond paper. It was a tremendous effort for him to breathe. Without looking away from the nude girl he said something to Willis and the punk. The three of them began to force their way through the milling crowd up to where Duke was trying frantically to get the dress back on the girl.

I got to the pen before Langley could. In the eight years Duke and I had worked together it was the first time I'd ever seen him flustered. He gasped:

"How was I to know she'd pull a trick like this? And when Flo and I rigged her up, she had both pants and a bra on. I saw 'em on her!"

"Disgusting," Langley said. "A venal and lewd exhibition. You're closed down as of now, Morgan. We won't tolerate such filth in Langley."

The little geek stopped mewing at me and hissed at him. Then snatching the burlap from Duke she threw the gnawed chicken in Langley's face and slipped the sack over her body.

His Honor wiped at the catchup on his lapel. "Load your trucks and get out of town, Morgan."

I protested, "But that's hardly fair to me. You can see for yourself that the girl is mentally unbalanced. I run a good clean show. How could I know this would happen?"

The young deputy was smug. "Don't try to give us that, Morgan."

Still white-faced, Langley wet his dry lips. "Well, what are you waiting for, Sheriff Willis? You know the statutes as well as I do. Arrest that girl!"

Duke asked, "For what?"

Langley said, "Indecent exposure and giving an indecent exhibition."

Some woman in the crowd backed him. "You tell them, Judge Langley. For shame."

Still other women backed her. There were cries of "Disgusting—shameful." Then somewhere in the back of the tent some babe called, "They ought to be tarred and feathered and run out of town on a rail, all of them."

Judge Langley continued, "I was afraid something like this might happen. That's why I set the license fee as high as I did, hoping that you'd move on."

I protested, "So she took off her clothes. You can't arrest the kid. She isn't in her right mind. She can't be. What she needs is medical treatment."

Langley patted the geek with his eyes so hard he had to wet his lips again before he could speak. "That will be attended to. I'll phone Atlanta in the morning and have a psychiatrist fly down to examine her. You can rest assured all her civil rights will be protected."

"And tonight?"

"We shall be forced to incarcerate her. For her own good." He raised a perspiring palm. "And before you ask, bail is refused. A girl like this could be a grave threat to the morals of our children."

Some of the women backed him again. I could see why Meager, the president of the fair committee, felt as he did. "She spends the night in a cell, huh?"

Langley's eyes tugged at the fringes of the burlap covering her thighs. "That is correct."

I leaned on the side of the pen and looked at the little geek. "He's the law, honey. He claims he has to arrest you. Do you want to go with him?"

She shook her head.

"What do you want to do?"

She smiled shyly, then put her arms around my neck and mewed earnestly in my face. She then cupped the back of my head in her hands and kissed me full on the lips, making hoarse animal sounds in her throat, leaving no doubt in the mind of anyone what she wanted to do.

Color flooded Langley's thin face.

The babe who'd said it before repeated her crack about how we should be tarred and feathered.

"I knew there was something between those two," the deputy said. "No wonder he paid her fine."

I said, "That's a lie."

Flo forced her way through the crowd to back me. "You men are making something out of nothing. The girl is sick in her mind. And Giff hasn't touched her. He brought her directly to my trailer and she hasn't been out of my sight since."

Willis smeared a little butter on his sheriff's badge. "Naturally you'd lie. You carnival people always stick together." He reached out a sunburned hand and caught the geek by one shoulder. "All right, sister. Let's go."

I slapped his hand away. "Uh uh."

"Meaning what?" Willis asked.

"Meaning no. The girl stays here."

I backed what I'd said by drawing the revolver I'd slipped into my belt before leaving the office trailer. Both Bull and Duke stepped up and stood beside me. In the sudden silence that followed, the babe in the back of the tent repeated, like some damn parrot:

"Tarred and feathered. That's what they ought to be."

His hand hovering over the butt of the gun strapped to his thigh, Sheriff Willis looked at Judge Langley for instructions.

His Honor shook his head. "No. Don't try to take her now. We don't want a riot. We have to think of the good of the whole," he added smugly. "Innocent women and children might be hurt. We'll go for now." He turned his wet eyes on me. "But we'll be back."

The little geek's arms felt soft and warm around my neck.

"We'll be here," I assured him.

Except for a work light here and there the midway had been dark for three hours. Now, one by one, as the patrons of the fair decided there wasn't going to be any excitement after all, the lights in the fairground proper winked out. The last of the cars drove out of the parking lot. All that was left was moon and starlight and a dim light in one window of the horse barn. I imagined Meager was either counting up the day's take or wrestling with another Mason jar.

Sitting on the stoop of the office trailer, Bull patted the turf with a tent stake. "If the sheriff and his boys are coming back, I wish they'd show."

"Have patience. They'll be back," I told him.

I walked down to the highway to see if the guards I'd posted were still in their proper places, and awake.

"Some fun, eh?" Hugo said.

I looked at the weapon with which he'd armed himself and took the meat cleaver away from him. "Uh uh. Get yourself a tent stake. You want to kill somebody?"

Hugo was disappointed. "Yeah. Sure. Why not?"

I dropped the cleaver in the cook-house as I continued my rounds. All the boys were in their places. Satisfied, I turned off the work lights and looked in through the screen door of Flo's trailer.

"How go things in here?" I asked Flo.

The fat woman put a finger to her lips. "Shh. The kid is asleep."

I looked past her at the bed. The little geek's golden hair was spread out on the pillow, like a halo. The shimmering nylon of one of Flo's nightgowns enveloped her body like a silk cocoon. Even asleep she was breathtakingly beautiful.

Flo pressed the back of a fat hand to her forehead. "I don't blame you for standing up for her, Giff. She's got us in a mess of trouble, but it was all you could do.

"Funny," Flo said. "I mean that she should drop into Langley the same day we pull into town. You think she's really a geek?"

I lit a cigaret. "Could be."

Flo looked up at the one remaining light, a yellow lantern in the cook-house. "Look, Giff—"

"What?"

Flo opened the door of the trailer and came outside with me. "You hurried me down here so fast after the trouble in the tent, I didn't have a chance to eat night lunch."

I laughed. "And your stomach's growling, huh?"

Flo looked wistfully at the lantern. "You said it. Do you think it would be all right if I leave her alone long enough to walk up and grab a quick mug of coffee and a few sandwiches?"

I said, "Of course. Hugo is down on the highway but there's a big pot of coffee on the stove and a pile of sandwiches on the table. Take your time. It could be they aren't coming back. If they do try to rush the lot I doubt if they'll get this far. Besides, I'll keep an eye on the trailer."

Flo looked in at the little geek, started to say something and changed her mind. "It's your show."

She waddled off up the midway. I stood a long time after she had gone, with my face pressed to the screen of the trailer door. As if she felt me watching her, the little geek opened her eyes, looked at me without expression, then closed her eyes again.

I wiped my face with my handkerchief and walked on down to the river. It looked different by moonlight, older. Like a boy might change into a man; sure, certain of himself. The river was like that. You couldn't see the hills. The slow-flowing water was black, sinister, relentless looking. Nothing could change its course, not even a pregnant 17-year-old girl.

"*Where did she go?*" I'd asked the man.

"*Into the river,*" he'd told me.

I sucked hard at my cigaret, then flipped it into the water as somewhere up near the highway, Bull or one of the other boys called, "Giff."

I walked back through the dark toward the voice. It wasn't Bull, it was Duke and he was holding a squirming something in his arms. When Duke saw me he set it on the ground and said, "Just wait till you hear this."

My freckle-faced little friend, to whom I had given the handful of free tickets when we hit town, smoothed her rumpled dress as I knelt in front of her. "That man grabbed me," she said, indignant. "After I runned out from town as fast as I could run."

Duke squatted down beside us. "I'm sorry, kid. It's just we're all a little nervous. And when you flashed on the lot I didn't quite know what you were. Now tell Giff what you told me."

She said, "Some of the men have got a big pot of tar, on wheels, right down in the courthouse square." Her words came out so fast I had trouble separating them. "An' feathers, too. An' my own pappy is there. Ma wanted him t' go home, but he wouldn't. He said we should sleep in the car acause he wouldn't miss the fun for a barrel of monkeys. An' Sheriff Willis an' Depity Ames are a givin' all the men whisky. An' as soon as the tar is real hot they are a comin' out heah an' put it on you an' the big ol' girl who took off her clothes. An' that's why I runned out t' tell you."

I hugged her a moment. "I'm glad you did."

The men in the circle around us started muttering.

I said, "Thanks. Thanks a lot for telling us, honey." I stood up and patted her lightly. "Now you scoot back for town. And you do just like your daddy told you. You crawl into your car and go to sleep."

When she had gone, Bull asked, "So what do we do now?"

I said, "We wait. And remember this, all of you. Don't hit anyone too hard. If we get hurt, it's too bad. If we kill one of them, it's murder."

The men faded back into the night. I looked over at the cook tent. Flo was sitting on a bench working on a pile of sandwiches. I doubted if she'd leave until the stack was gone. Since her glands had begun to kick up, all she had to live for was her stomach. And sliced-chicken sandwiches was one of her favorite foods.

Bull asked, "Where's the geek?"

I said, "In Flo's trailer. I look in on her from time to time."

He resumed patting at the turf with the tent stake he was holding. "You'd better. That no-good Langley was leaking at the mouth all the time he was looking at her."

"The guy can't be normal," Duke said. "God knows no one likes a good time any more than I do. But from the look on his face, he must be one of them satyrs."

The silence lengthened and deepened. Midnight crawled down the unlighted midway and met 1 o'clock. Then, out in the night, a mile or so away, a siren began to wail, softly at first, then with growing undulations that filled the dark countryside.

It was a development I hadn't expected.

Hugo hurried up from the highway. "Some of the guys in the road camp must have escaped. That's coming from their barracks. I seen it this afternoon when I was driving around trying to pick up a case of fresh eggs."

"They won't come here," Bull said.

I lit a cigaret, took two quick puffs and snuffed it out. "I'm not so sure about that. Langley's a heel, but he's smart. So is the sheriff. They may have figured they might need help to take us, and had that punk of a deputy tip the boys in the road camp that if they should happen to find the gates unlocked and sort of wander out and help clean up the carnival lot, every carnie head they cracked would lop so many months off their sentence. On the other hand, it could be a cover."

"Yeah. I see what you mean," Bull said. "For the benefit of the state police. 'So somebody wrecked the Giff Morgan show. Now ain't that too bad? It must have been some of the boys who escaped from the road gang.'"

Tiny, one of the wrestlers in the muscle-show, rubbed at the scar tissue over his right eye. "That still wouldn't explain away the tar and feathers."

I crumpled the duck I'd snuffed between my fingers and let the tobacco dribble to the ground. "His Honor doesn't have to explain anything. He *is* the law."

It was almost 2 o'clock when they came, crawling along the highway without lights on their cars, only the red glow from the fire box under the tar pot giving them away.

"Hey, Rube!" Duke called softly, and the answer rippled back from all four corners of the lot.

"Hey, Rube!"

There were four times as many of them as there were of us, most of them nasty drunk; for the most part, poolroom cowboys and hangers-on around the courthouse, with a leavening of small farmers and share croppers with more whisky than they could carry and honing for some excitement.

A big drunk rushed past me in the dark, shouting, "Git Morgan. The ones we want is Morgan an' the wild girl."

I hit him so hard he stopped as if he'd run into a brick wall. Then the fighting became general.

A few of the men were wearing handkerchief masks. Two of them backed me up against the canvas side wall, shouting, "We've got Morgan," and trying to make it stick. I recognized one of them as Willis's deputy.

"Come back for more, eh?" I asked him.

He wasn't feeling any pain. "Ya ya ya," he jeered. "When we get through with you this time, you're going to wish you'd kept right on going instead of being so damn smart."

I slugged his partner unconscious and swung at him and missed. He rushed me, swinging wild lefts and rights any doll in the girl-show could have parried. I mashed his nose flat with his face, then leaving him screaming on the ground I snatched up a piece of oily waste, touched my lighter to it, and tossed it up on top of the girl-show. Almost immediately flames leaped to the sky, just as if the canvas had been soaked in gasoline. The flames leaped to the freak-show tent next door. It burned as brightly as the girl-show, and a few seconds later the raucous clang of the fire bell in Langley joined the diminishing undulations of the prison-camp siren. From where the locals in Langley stood it must have looked as if the whole damn fairgrounds was on fire.

More, Hugo had been right about the road-camp boys. I could spot at least 15 shaved heads in the mob, and the boys didn't like the light. As the leaping flames soared even higher, they led the race back toward the highway, and as many carnies lying in reserve got up from behind packing cases and truck wheels and fought them back to the midway.

I heard the siren wail of a fire truck, traveling fast, and beat off two locals, who were beginning to lose their enthusiasm for the whole affair, long enough to glance toward town. There were two fire trucks on their way, and back of the revolving red lights there were 20 or more pairs of headlights, undoubtedly from the cars of awakened householders who thought the fairgrounds was on fire. Almost as many cars were coming from the other direction, as farmers with prize horses and cattle in the fairgrounds barns came in to rescue their stock.

Trapped between the two, the tar-and-feather mob stopped fighting and tried to take to the fields. The carnie, on top now, bowled them over like so many clay pigeons in the lead gallery. I kicked the punk deputy in the teeth to give him something to chew on and walked to the front of the midway.

Ignoring all of us, the firemen went to work on the tents and the dry grass around them, trying to prevent the flames from spreading to the horse and cattle barns. The people in the cars, all of them hastily dressed, a good sprinkling of women among them, crossed from the highway to the lot, picking their way among the courthouse hangers-on who were rocking on the turf, nursing cracked heads and split noses.

A fat man who looked like he might be a merchant, or maybe a prosperous farmer, tucked more of his night shirt into his pants as he looked from the bubbling tar pot to the wrecked midway.

"What the hell's going on here?" he asked.

I used the back of one hand to wipe a smear of blood from my lips. "It would seem some of your local boys don't like carnivals." I pointed to a few of the shave heads. "And someone let out some of your *real* bad boys to help burn us out and tar and feather me and the little girl I befriended today."

Still more cars and more men and women arrived—the solid, substantial element of Langley. Holding one hand over his mouth, the young punk of a deputy tried to sneak away and I caught him by the collar of his shirt and threw him up against one of the turnstiles.

One of the newcomers asked, "What are you doing here, Ames? Why are you out of uniform? And where is Sheriff Willis?"

The punk opened his mouth, then closed it. There was nothing he could say.

Meager, drunk as a coot, wove up to where I was standing. "Knew somethin' was goin' on," he said thickly. "Thash why I called the fire department as soon as I saw some of your tents were on fire. I said t' myself, I said, some of the boys are pickin' on that nice carnival man jush because he was good t' a poor li'l crazy girl."

I let out a shout, "The geek!" and ran down the torn-up midway with most of the crowd at my heels.

Flo was lying on the ground outside her trailer, moaning softly and holding one hand to her jaw. Both the screen and solid doors of the trailer were closed, but through the open windows the insistence of a man and the piteous mewing of the little geek were plainly audible.

It made my flesh crawl to hear her. From the collective gasp that went up from the crowd, most of them felt the same way.

There was the sound of a fist thudding on flesh. The girl's scream was a tortured moan in her throat. "Damn you," the man cursed her. "Stop fighting me, you crazy little fool."

The trailer door was bolted on the inside. I wrenched it open so hard both it and the screen door came off, the opening framing the wide trailer bed.

As nude as she'd been in the pit, her blue eyes wide with terror, the little blonde geek, almost at the end of her strength, was feebly struggling with Langley.

In the sudden silence that followed, I asked, "What's the idea, Your Honor? Couldn't you wait until you and your stooge sheriff got her down to the courthouse?"

Flo sat up, still holding her jaw. "He's the one who hit me. That rube sheriff, I mean. He wanted the guy inside to sneak the geek back into town while his gillies were beating on you boy. But His Honor was hell-determined. He said he had plenty of time and he'd waited as long as he intended to wait."

"Where's the sheriff now?" I asked her.

Flo said, "He banged on the door of the trailer when the fire siren began to wail, then took off down the river bank. At the rate he was running, he should be in Georgia by now."

It was almost the same scene I'd been through in the freak show, with a different target now. One of the housewives come out from town said, "Disgusting." Another one said, "For shame. And the poor girl couldn't even scream for help."

His face as white as the sheet on which he had been struggling, Judge Langley got to his feet and attempted to arrange his disordered clothes with hands that shook so badly he couldn't accomplish his purpose. He didn't look distinguished now. He looked like what he was.

One of the men who'd been in the first crowd, a lad in overalls and with a bridge of freckles across his nose, cried, "*Sold.* The carnival is a disgrace to Langley County, you told us. And the carrying on of Morgan and his wild girl a menace to the morals of our children."

Langley looked at him with wet eyes, then away.

Another, even longer, silence followed and I knew what the crowd was thinking, remembering whispered stories; how the man, crouching in shame and terror in the trailer doorway, had treated them like dub sheep because he owned the bank, because he owned the cotton gin, because he was a judge, because he was the law. And maybe some of the women had other, more personal thoughts.

One of them repeated, "And she couldn't even scream."

A gaunt-faced Bible-reading farmer added, grimly, "Just like it says in the good Book. And his *sin* shall cast him out."

Langley tried to speak and couldn't. His tongue was stuck to the roof of his mouth and there wasn't enough water inside him to moisten it. It had all leaked out through his pores.

Behind him, the little geek sat up on the bed and wrapped a sheet around her, modestly. Then, tears streaming down her cheeks, she pointed at Langley's back and mewed.

That tore it. The disgust and revulsion of the crowd turned to anger. The same girl who'd cried it before repeated:

"Tarred and feathered. That's what he ought to be."

Male voices took up the cry: some eager to cover up what they'd come to the lot to do; the newcomers righteously outraged, dumb, plodding sheep— who'd revolted.

The lad with the bridge of freckles across his nose reached through the trailer doorway and caught hold of Langley. "Come out of that. By God, no man sells *me.*"

Langley screamed and tried to pull away.

"Get the tar ready," a man shouted.

Still other eager hands helped pull Langley out of the trailer and worried his disordered clothes from his body.

The sheet wrapped around her like a sarong, the little geek padded barefoot to the door of the trailer to watch. I pushed her head down on my shoulder as two dozen shouting men hurried the screaming, terror-stricken thing that had once been a man up the midway.

"No. Don't look, honey," I told her.

But *I* did, enjoying every minute; thinking, every time Langley screamed, of the girl the president of the fair association had told me about—the little hill girl whom Langley had molested and driven to suicide while her husband was on Iwo.

Morning was hot and dry. What with one thing and another, I hadn't slept all night. My throat felt parched and there was an empty feeling in my head, as if I'd tied on a good one.

Duke came out of his trailer and straightened the knot in his tie as he looked at the loading trucks. He didn't seem too much surprised. "We're moving on, eh, Giff?"

I said, "I got on the phone this morning and picked up a still-date over in Shelby. Thursday, Friday, and Saturday. For the American Legion. After what happened here last night, I don't imagine that Langley is in much of a carnival mood."

Duke lit his first cigaret of the morning. "Probably not. But I bet the churches do a good business."

"Without doubt."

Mabel came out of the trailer, still working on her pin curlers and sporting a fresh black eye.

"Who hung one on you?" I asked her.

Duke answered before she could. "I did. Just before it's time to get up this morning, I'm lying there thinking about what happened last night and I suddenly realize the voice of the dame in the freak-show, the one who first started the tar-and-feather business, was sort of familiar. So I shake Mabel awake and ask her to say something. And what do you know? It was her!"

"So you hung one on her, huh?"

"Yeah."

Mabel's voice was shrill. "I tried to tell him you said I should yell it. But Duke wouldn't believe me."

"Naturally not," Duke said. "Yelling a dumb thing like that. You could have caused a lot of trouble. In fact, you did."

"How many times you yell it, Mabel?" I asked.

She counted on her fingers. "Four times. Three times in the freak show. An' once in front of the trailer." Her vacuous smile widened to show still more of her pink gums. "An' the fourth time, it took."

I counted four $50 bills into her hand. "Thanks. Thanks a lot, kid." I added a fifth $50. "And that's for the black eye."

She pulled up her skirt and stuffed the bills into the top of one of her nylons. "Gee. Thanks a lot, Giff. Any time you want I should yell anything else, you just say the word."

Duke took off his straw sailor and mopped at the leather sweatband. "Hey. What goes on? I don't get it."

I said, "There's a lot of things we don't understand."

He stood a moment trying to figure it out, then walked Mabel on down the dismantled midway toward the cook-house, where Hugo was beating the triangle for breakfast, and yelling, "Come and get it."

Bull opened the screen door behind me and stepped to the ground, swearing softly.

I asked, "What's eating you?"

He said, "I was just checking on the insurance. And what do you think I find?"

"What?"

He looked at me thoughtfully. "You canceled the fire insurance on the girl-show and freak-show tents two days before we pulled into Langley. No wonder the damn things burned like they'd been soaked in gasoline."

"So?"

He shook his head. "So nothing. It's your show. It's just I'm beginning to understand." He called to Mabel and Duke and walked on down to the cook-house for breakfast.

It was hot sitting in the sun. I got up and went inside the trailer. It was almost as hot inside. I poured a glass of cold water. It helped some but not much. There was a hard lump in my stomach. My throat still felt parched. I decided what I needed was a drink and I was opening a fresh bottle when the screen door of the trailer opened and the little geek came in.

She looked the same, still, somehow different. It was the bright look in her eyes,, for one thing. For two more: her artistically applied make-up and the smart pastel-colored suit she was wearing. Her lips moved and now, instead of the unnatural mewing sounds, she said in a sultry voice, "Make it two."

She smiled. "I'm still a little shaky. I thought I'd been around, but that thing last night was really close."

"Too close," I admitted as I made the drinks. "Still, all in all, it went well."

She sipped her drink. "Well? Hell, it was perfect. You could give Cecil B. DeMille lessons."

The drink didn't help the parched feeling in my throat. I still felt emotionally drained.

She sat on the leather lounge I used for a bed and crossed one knee over the other. "You thought a lot of her, didn't you, Giff?"

It was the first time she'd ever called me anything but Mr. Morgan, or honey. I liked the sound of my name in her mouth. "She was my wife." I opened the safe and took out an envelope and laid it on the lounge beside her. "And while we're on the subject, there's the two grand we agreed on."

"I was all right as a geek?"

"You were perfect."

She sat running the envelope through her fingers. "Two grand is a lot of money for a night club entertainer used to making $80 a week."

The parched feeling in my throat persisted. "It's yours. You earned it."

"Yes," she admitted. "I did. And now?"

I didn't know what to do with my drink. I drank it. "What do you mean by that?"

Her half-smile turned wry. "Just what I said. You got what you wanted. You're even. You broke the guy. Even if he lives he'll never dare show his face in Langley. So why should you go on with your guts all snarled up inside of you, in love with a tombstone, afraid to love again."

I chewed on a hunk of ice. "What's it to you?"

The smile left her lips. "Possibly plenty. Maybe I don't hate anyone. Then again, it could be I'm in love with a guy who had guts enough to do something about his hate outside of crying in his beer."

I didn't say anything.

She wet her lips with her tongue. "Well, if that's all there is to it, if you'll have one of your boys run me up town to where I parked my car before I went into my act—"

I asked it flatly. "You're in a hurry to go?"

She said as flatly, "No."

I reached out and touched her cheek. "Look, kid," I said, uncertain what to say. "I—"

She took my hand and pulled me down beside her, treating me like I'd treated her the night before. Only she was soft and sweet-smelling and I wanted to bury my face against her throat and never come up again.

"Don't look back. Please," she begged me. "It's all over and done with."

"Sure."

"Was she as pretty as I am?"

"No. She was just a Cracker kid."

"But she was carrying your child?"

"Yeah."

She pressed my face closer to the soft sweetness of her and there was a note almost of awe in her voice. "I'm a woman. I can have children. I'd make you a good wife, Giff."

The parched ache in the roof of my mouth went away and the hard lump in my stomach dissolved. I raised my face and looked at her. "How do you know I'd make a good husband?"

She smiled.

I kissed her, gently at first, then with a growing need—and I wasn't alone anymore. I'd never be alone again. She was everything I'd missed, everything I'd needed and wanted for years, a blonde kid that I'd met in a night club.

It was a long time later when Bull rapped on the screen door of the trailer. "We're ready to pull out, Giff," he called.

The little blonde lay back in my arms. "What's your name again, honey?" I asked her.

"Mrs. Morgan to you," she told me, as her lips found mine again.

Helen Nielsen wrote eighteen novels and nearly fifty short stories, many of them for Alfred Hitchcock's Mystery Magazine. *She also wrote television scripts for shows like* Perry Mason, Alcoa Theater, Alfred Hitchcock Presents, *and* 87th Precinct. *Her first novel,* Gold Cost Nocturne, *was turned into the 1954 Terence Clark film,* Blackout. *Known as a master of suspense, her stories were often set in the otherwise sunny southern California. She wrote in a variety of styles and seemed bent on not repeating herself. Regardless, her storytelling is superb throughout her catalog and this story is no different....*

WOMAN MISSING

Helen Nielsen

Einar Peterson's body was wearying of life. He slept at the touch of his silvered head on the pillow; but when his wife Amelia, fastened her hands on his shoulders and shook with all her housewife strength, he awakened, trying to remember where he was, and why he was no longer the boy he'd been dreaming of, sailing his small boat on a bright Sunday on Lake Vattern. Without his glasses, Amelia's face bobbed above him like a pale balloon.

"Einar—Einar. Something's wrong in back!"

"What? Where?" Einar mumbled.

"In the tenant's house in back. I think it's Mrs. Tracy sick again."

Einar Peterson pulled himself up in the bed and groped on the night table until his slightly arthritic fingers located his eye glasses. With them in place, the pale balloon now had gray hair and troubled eyes.

"Mrs. Tracy?" he repeated. "What is it, Mother? What's wrong?"

"I don't know. I woke up because of the lights in the driveway and the motor running."

"Maybe it's the Mister."

"In the driveway? You know the Mister always comes home up the alley. Anyway, it's only ten-thirty. I looked at the clock when the lights woke me up. Get up, Einar. Go see. That poor little Mrs. Tracy—"

Amelia liked to worry about people, and the night air was damp and chilly outside the blankets. Einar didn't want to get up; but now he could see that the light reflected on his wife's face wasn't from the ceiling fixture—it was from a glaring beam outside the bedroom window, and the noise he heard wasn't from the old refrigerator in the kitchen—it was the sound of an automobile motor. Reluctantly, he parted himself from snug comfort and padded to the window to which Amelia had preceded him.

"Somebody went back to the tenant house," she whispered. "It was a man."

"Did you see him?" Einar asked.

"Hush, not so loud. No, I didn't see; but I heard the footsteps. I think it must be a doctor."

"A doctor! Why would a doctor leave the motor running?"

"I think it's an ambulance. There's a funny light on top."

The window was open two inches. Einar lifted the sash quietly and poked out his head. Amelia was right. The automobile he saw certainly did have a light on top.

"It's a taxi," he said.

"A taxi? Here?"

"Quiet!" Einar drew back inside. "Somebody's coming."

Einar Peterson watched the brightness in front of the headlights; but the heavy, man-like footsteps skirted the light and passed by the window in shadows. They stopped at the taxi. A door opened; then silence behind the idling motor, and darkness behind the lights except for the small, round glow of a cigarette.

"Look," Amelia whispered. "She's coming."

Linda Tracy was such a very young woman, it was difficult to realize that she was married to Mr. Tracy and would have been the mother of his child if it had been God's will. She looked more like one of Einar Peterson's teen-age grand-daughters except for something…. Einar Peterson's mind always caught on that odd feeling when he thought of Mrs. Tracy. Something. She walked rapidly into the headlights, head down except for an instant when she turned and stared almost directly at the dark window behind which the two unseen watchers were hidden. She was wearing a light colored coat and very noisy heels, and, this they would remember to tell the police, a very fearful expression on her face. She passed the window and entered the cab. The glow of a burning cigarette spun into space and was lost in the darkness. The door of the taxi slammed shut. In a matter of seconds, the taxi was gone.

"Well," said Amelia. "What was that?"

Einar Peterson removed his glasses and padded back to the bed.

"Einar, I'm worried. Mrs. Tracy never goes out at night. Her lights always go off just after ten o'clock. Einar—"

Einar's answer was a snore. She lowered the window to within two inches of the sill and returned to bed; but she didn't sleep. There was something strange about Linda Tracy. Amelia had never mentioned her feelings to anyone, not even Einar; but there was something….

Chester Tracy was a slight, sandy-haired man with a peering face. That was how he impressed Sergeant Mike Shelly. He had probably started peering when he was a kid, his nose pressed against the store windows full of Christmas toys he would never receive. Children who had done that never lost the look; it grew older with them. There was fear in his face, too; fear muted by shock. Shelly had to pry words out of him.

"When did you get home, Mr. Tracy?" he asked. "At what time—exactly."

Tracy was possibly forty. He wore suntan cotton pants and a brown leather zipper jacket with an I.D. badge from Flight Research pinned to the breast pocket. The photo on the badge would have embarrassed the Passport Bureau.

"The usual time," he said. "I work the 5:45 p.m. to 2:45 a.m. shift."

"What time?" Shelly persisted.

"It takes me eighteen minutes to drive home. I've clocked it a hundred times—just to keep awake. It may take eighteen and a half if I miss the green light at Slauson."

"Then you were home at a few minutes past three."

"At three minutes past—exactly. I looked at the kitchen clock when I came in."

"The light was on?" Shelly asked.

"It's always on when I come home. Linda leaves it for me when she goes to bed."

"And so everything seemed normal."

"Until I started down the hall to the bathroom," Tracy said. "I saw that the bedroom door was open. It's usually closed because of that light in the kitchen. I looked in to see if Linda was all right, and that's when I discovered—" Tracy's eyes were less glazed now. Emotion was breaking through the numbness. "Why are you asking all these dumb questions?" he demanded. "My wife's gone—don't you understand? I called you because Linda's gone!"

A missing wife can mean many things—Mike Shelly had carried a police badge in his pocket long enough to know that. He'd talked to the old people up front, but he had to question Tracy alone. Outside, Shelly's partner, Sergeant Keonig, was searching the grounds. Inside, Shelly stood in a living room just large enough for one small divan and two slip-covered chairs, pried away at Chester Tracy, and puzzled over the photographs he'd found in a double frame on the side table. One side of the frame showed Linda Tracy close-up: blonde, smiling, lovely; the other held a full length Linda attired in an abbreviated bathing suit: blonde, smiling, lovely. She was nineteen years old. The forty-year-old man with the peering face had told him that.

"I know that your wife's gone," Shelly answered quietly. "I'm looking for her. I've been looking for her ever since I got here. A photograph isn't enough, Mr. Tracy. I need to know what kind of woman your wife is."

Reactions could be startling, particularly in the pre-dawn hours of a torturous night. Color flooded to Chester Tracy's face.

"What kind of woman?" he echoed. "Is that any way to talk to a man in my position?"

"Mr. Tracy—"

"She's my wife. That's the kind of woman she is! She's my wife!"

If someone had bought the finest toy in the shop for that kid with his faced pressed against the window, and then taken it away, the emotional response would have matched what was written on Chester Tracy's face.

"I was thinking more of her habits," Shelly explained. "Where she goes. Who she sees...."

"But she doesn't see anyone! She doesn't go anywhere—not without me! My wife lost a baby four months ago. Since that time, she hadn't been well. She never goes out unless I take her in the car."

"Where do you go?"

"To the market. Once in awhile to a drive-in movie."

"Never to friends?"

"With me working the hours I work? I went on swing shift for the extra money after Linda got pregnant. Since then, we have no friends. Ask the Petersons up front. Linda walks up to get the mail every morning—the box is on Peterson's house. That's as much as she goes out without me. Every night I call home during the ten o'clock coffee break—"

"Ten o'clock," Shelly echoed. "Did you talk to your wife at ten o'clock tonight?"

"I did."

"Did she seem nervous or upset?"

"No more than usual. Linda's been nervous and upset ever since she lost the baby. That's why I call her every night. I catch her just before she takes her sleeping pills—"

Tracy's voice ceased as the front door opened. It was Keonig. He glanced at Tracy; then turned to Sergeant Shelly.

"I didn't find a single footprint," he said. "This house is built on a cement slab. It extends along the right side for the width of about ten feet, all the way to the alley. There's an old station wagon parked on that extension."

"That's mine," Tracy volunteered.

"In front," Keonig added, "the cement narrows to a walk leading to Peterson's driveway—the way we came. I'd hoped our man might have stepped off the walk and left a print in the soft flower bed under the Petersons' windows, but all I found was this—"

Cupped in the palm of Keonig's hand was a cigarette butt—standard brand, filter tip.

"Peterson said the man who came for Mrs. Tracy tossed a cigarette into the flower bed," Shelly reflected. "Keep it."

"It was all I could find," Keonig repeated.

"Try the bathroom," Shelly said. "Or does your wife keep those sleeping pills in her bedroom, Mr. Tracy?" Shelly set the double-framed photograph back on the table and turned toward the hall. "You take the bathroom," he told Keonig, "and I'll take the bedroom. You come with me, Tracy. I'll need you."

In a square cell with one window, curtained, shade drawn, the bed was turned down and a soft, pink nightgown laid out for its missing occupant. Shelly studied the display while Chester Tracy, at his request, took stock of his wife's closet.

"I think there's a blue dress missing," he reported.

"A blue dress," Shelly repeated.

"Sort of a suit. You know, a dress with a jacket over it."

"What else?" Shelly prodded. "Shoes?"

The shoe rack held, at quick glance, a good dozen pairs of slippers and pumps.

"I think she usually wore black pumps with the blue dress," Chester said. "I don't see them here."

"Black shoes," Shelly echoed. "What coat?"

"The Petersons said a light coat. That would be the one she called a cashmere. It was new. I got it for her with my last big overtime check." Shelly picked up one of the pumps from the rack and examined it. Size 5A. It was clear plastic with a spike heel. He turned it over in his hands. The soles were badly worn, especially at the toe. The heels weren't.

"Are these new, too?" he asked.

"I got them for her for Christmas," Chester answered.

"Is anything else missing?"

The question kept Chester busy, while Shelly examined the rest of the rack. Most of the shoes were dress pumps or sandals, but there was one conspicuous pair of walking flats. When Keonig came in from the bathroom with the sleeping pills, Shelly still held one of the flats in his hand. A small crust of dried mud loosened at the prod of his fingernail and fell to the floor.

"I had to dig, but I found them in the medicine chest," Keonig said. "Now maybe you'll tell me why."

"Because Mrs. Tracy took sleeping pills every night after her husband's ten o'clock call."

"Not tonight," Keonig said.

"Obviously. That's interesting, isn't it? Let me see that bottle." It was nearly half full. Shelly read the prescription label and frowned. "Dr. Youngston," he read aloud. "Two pills before retiring. 10-7-59. Keonig, what's the date?"

"It was the twelfth of January at midnight," Keonig answered.

"Dr. Youngston," Shelly mused. "Your wife did see someone outside of this house, Tracy. Who else?"

The man still seemed to be in a state of shock. He groped for words. "I told you—no one."

"At any time—before your marriage."

"I didn't know Linda very long before our marriage. Leo talked me into going to this party—"

"Leo? Leo who?"

"Leo Manfred. We worked together at Flight Research. Look, why don't you stop asking these questions? Why don't you look for that cab?"

"Where can I find Leo Manfred?" Shelly persisted.

"I don't know! At home, I suppose. I lost track of Leo when I went on nights. I don't even know if he's with Flight Research now."

"But he did know your wife?"

"That was months ago—seven, eight months ago."

"Leo Manfred and Dr. Youngston." Shelly slipped the bottle of pills into his pocket. "Who else, Tracy? Who else knew that your wife would be here alone at ten-thirty? Who might she have gone with without fear?"

"But she was afraid," Keonig protested. "The Petersons said—"

"Who else, Tracy?"

Chester Tracy sank down on the edge of the bed. The kid with his face pressed against the window wanted to cry; but the kid was a man of forty, and so, instead, he took a pack of cigarettes from his pocket, standard brand, no filter tip, pulled out one cigarette and held it between thumb and forefinger, until the thumb clenched white and the cigarette snapped in two. He looked up.

"I can't think!" he protested. "You're the police. Find my wife! Please, find my wife!"

> Linda Tracy, white Caucasian, female. Age: 19. Height 5'3".
> Weight, 110. Blonde hair, Hazel eyes. Probably wearing a blue
> jacket dress, black pumps, and a light tan cashmere coat. Last
> seen entering a taxi at 1412 North....

A description of the missing woman was going out over the police radio before Shelly and Keonig left the Peterson property. Shelly took a turn about the premises, while Keonig used the telephone. It was still a good hour before dawn, and a light fog had wrapped the world in a close, damp blanket. At the side of the tenant house, Shelly found the station wagon, the windshield and windows curtained with moisture. Beyond it, the paved area terminated at an unpaved alleyway. He took a few steps into the alley and peered toward the street lamp at the nearest corner. It was at least four lots distant—darkness and fog prohibited a closer guess—and no back yard taxpayer units such as the Petersons had added were in evidence. This was the route by which Chester Tracy had arrived home—the only other access to the property except the front drive. Underfoot, the stubborn adobe had absorbed most of a none too recent gravel topping, and the pale light from the corner lamp caught in small, wet shallows of leftover rain. Shelly scraped his shoes clean on the parking slab and returned to the car and Keonig.

"It's a break—that cab business," Keonig said. "A cab can be traced."

"I know it can," Shelly mused. "That's what is bothering me."

A cab can be traced, but it takes time. Time to check each office of each company; run down each call sheet; pry out of bed a driver who had worked most of the night. Meanwhile, a sun rises, a city comes awake, the air begins to fill with the aromas of coffee, frying bacon, and, predominantly, carbon monoxide. Shelly couldn't wait. The Southern Area telephone directory listed a Dr. Carl Youngston on Manchester Boulevard; hours: nine to five.

At ten minutes before nine, Mike Shelly waited in the foyer of a handsome new medical building and watched a slender, blond young man in a gray topcoat unlock the slab door leading to Dr. Youngston's office. He stooped to retrieve an advertising folder that had been deposited in the mail slot, and arose pulling a pair of tortoise-rimmed glasses from an inner pocket. These he donned in time to bring the full width and height of Mike Shelly into focus.

Surprise didn't seem to unnerve the doctor.

"Do you have an appointment?" he asked.

Shelly's appointment was a badge that bridged all priorities. Inside the office, Dr. Youngston removed his topcoat, straightened a tie that caught the blue of his eyes behind the tortoise rims, and then scrutinized the bottle of sleeping pills Shelly now held in his hand.

"Linda Tracy," he read aloud. "Two every night before retiring. Yes, I remember Mrs. Tracy. Quite a young woman. Quite—" He hesitated. "—attractive," he added.

"You *remember* Mrs. Tracy." Shelly echoed. "Isn't she your patient now?"

"I suppose she is. Her record is in my files. It's just that I haven't seen her for some time."

"Since she lost her baby?"

"Oh, yes. Certainly. Before, at the time, and after."

"She took it hard, then?"

"Every woman takes it hard. Some may seem indifferent, but that's superficial."

"But doesn't a miscarriage affect different women in different ways?"

Dr. Youngston wasn't over thirty-five. His blond hair was clipped close; his clean-shaven face had a military alertness about it.

"What's your problem, Sergeant?" he queried. "Is Mrs. Tracy in trouble?"

"Why do you ask that question?"

"Why is a police officer at my door when I open the office in the morning?"

"It could be Mr. Tracy who's in trouble."

"Mr. Tracy was never my patient. Mrs. Tracy was."

"You're using the past tense again, Doctor."

"All right, Sergeant, I'll take your bait. Has Mrs. Tracy been murdered?"

It was early morning, but the fog had lifted and the sun was shining through the windows. The world was bright, and Dr. Youngston didn't seem a morbid-minded man.

"That's an interesting thought," Shelly mused, "but, so far as the police know, Mrs. Tracy is only the victim of abduction."

"Abduction? What do you mean?"

"I'm not sure. That's why I came to you. A doctor does more than treat the body, doesn't he? You have to understand something of the psychological make-up of the patient."

"I'm merely an obstetrician," Youngston protested.

"Merely? Wouldn't an obstetrician need to know quite a bit about feminine psychology—not to mention family relationships? Now, consider this situation, Doctor. Knowing Mrs. Tracy, and there you have me at an advantage, what would you make of it if I told you that some man, unidentified, had called for her in a taxi last night at ten-thirty while her husband was at work on the night shift. The landlord and his wife, awakened by the sound of the motor outside the window, got out of bed and watched through the window. They saw the taxi waiting. Moments later, they heard a man—careful, apparently, not to step into the beam of the headlights—come from the Tracy house at the rear of the lot."

"I'm familiar with the Tracy house at the rear of the lot," Dr. Youngston said. "I was called there when Mrs. Tracy lost her child."

"Good. You see the picture, then. Shortly after the man reached the cab, Mrs. Tracy came from the house. She didn't avoid the lights. The landlord and his wife both insist that she looked frightened. She went to the cab, entered it, and the cab drove off."

Youngston had followed the story carefully.

"And hasn't been heard of since, I presume."

"Exactly," Shelly said. "By the way, could I trouble you for a cigarette, Doctor?"

"Sorry," Youngston answered. "I never acquired the habit." He appeared thoughtful for a moment, then asked, "What does the cab driver have to say?"

"We're tracking him down now," Shelly replied. "What I'm interested in is your reaction. What do you think happened last night?"

It was a tough question to spring on a man so early in the morning. Youngston frowned, thoughtfully.

"While Mr. Tracy was at work, did you say?"

"Night shift—5:45 to 2:45. Calls his wife every night during the ten o'clock coffee break to make sure she's all right."

Dr. Youngston took the pill bottle from Shelly's hand and studied the label again.

"Being a physician," he said, slowly, "my mind may run in a rut; but isn't it possible that the man who came in the cab told Mrs. Tracy that her husband had been injured on the job?"

"Highly possible," Shelly agreed. "But why did he tell her that?"

"She was a very attractive woman," the doctor suggested.

"Is that what you see typed on the prescription label, Doctor?"

Youngston didn't answer with words. Instead, he went to his files. A few minutes later, he returned with the information that Linda Tracy had come to him on the seventh of October complaining of severe nervous tension and an inability to sleep. He had given her a prescription for sixty pills, together with the admonition not to use more than two at a time.

"How many pills would you guess are in that bottle, Doctor?" Shelly asked.

Youngston adjusted his glasses.

"I won't guess," he said. "I'll just ask. How many, Sergeant?"

"Twenty-eight," Shelly said. "That means only thirty-two pills used, or sixteen nights—"

"It's not unusual for a patient to fail to follow instructions," Youngston said.

"—out of better than three months," Shelly concluded. "Has Mrs. Tracy been back since you issued that prescription?"

"No," Youngston said. "If she had, it would have been entered in the files."

"When she came, did she come alone?"

Dr. Youngston hesitated. "No," he said, thoughtfully. "Mr. Tracy was with her. In fact, it was he who made her come. He was always very concerned about her."

"How did he take it when she lost the baby?"

"Hard. No, actually, not too hard. It was Mrs. Tracy's safety that concerned him. He had an almost paternal—" Youngston paused until the silence grew awkward. "—possessiveness," he added.

"Did Mrs. Tracy reciprocate?"

Youngston smiled wryly.

"With paternal possessiveness?"

"You know what I mean. Did she love him?"

"That's a peculiar question, Sergeant."

"But a necessary one, Doctor. For a few months you were close to this woman—closer than anyone. Closer even than her husband in many ways. Did she seem a happy woman?"

"Sergeant, a pregnant woman is every kind of woman. Happy, unhappy, fearful, miserable—"

"Dr. Youngston. I remind you, for sixteen nights, consecutively or otherwise, Linda Tracy took the sleeping pills you prescribed for her and, presumably, went to sleep. And yet, her husband told me that he called his wife every night at ten o'clock just before she took her sleeping pills and went to bed. Somebody lied, Doctor. Either Chester Tracy lied to me, or Linda Tracy lied to her husband. That's why I asked you if the woman who disappeared last night loved her husband."

Dr. Youngston wasn't naïve. People married for many reasons;

occasionally, love. He hesitated a long time before replying.

"I can't answer that," he said.

"Can't, or won't, Doctor?"

"Can't, Sergeant. You need facts, don't you? Ask me something I can answer factually, and I'll cooperate."

He was adamant. This was the time for diagnosis, analysis, conjecture, or just plain old-fashioned gossip; but Dr. Youngston had chosen none of these, and there was a hardness about his mouth that was impervious to change. Shelly recognized defeat when he met it.

"Just one more question," he said. "What was Mrs. Tracy's condition, aside from nervousness, when you last saw her?"

"Physically—excellent," Youngston said.

"Thank you, Doctor. If you think of anything else—factual, of course, that might help us, my name is Shelly. Mike Shelly. You can reach me at headquarters."

Twenty-eight pills in a bottle, and dried mud on her walking shoes. The words made a kind of jingle in Shelly's mind. He was still looking for Linda Tracy—not, of course, in that small room at headquarters where Chester Tracy was pleading for action:

"Haven't you found that cab driver yet? My God, my wife's been gone for nearly twelve hours!"

"We've located the cab company, Mr. Tracy. It's one of the big ones, and it took a while to trace the call sheet. The driver was a man named Berendo—Don Berendo."

"What does he say?"

"He's off duty. We've sent a couple of men to pick him up."

"All right, all right! But when are you going to find Linda? My God!"

No, Shelly couldn't take much of Chester Tracy. A man with more control was easier to interview. A man half a head taller than Tracy, wiry but strong. Black curly hair, teeth that gleamed white in an easy smile.

His name was Leo Manfred. He was thirty-ish. He lived in a small apartment over a garage that housed—visible through raised doors—half a section of discarded rental furnishings, a single horse trailer, and a two-year-old convertible with trailer hitch. The interior of the apartment, furnished chiefly by two large couches and a jazz-playing stereo set, was profusely decorated with mounted photos of horses, as well as a small collection of loving cups. Manfred himself was attired in fitted twill pants, a heavy-knit turtle neck sweater, and western boots. Between the white teeth was a rough brier pipe, which he removed at the sight of Shelly's badge. It was still early in the morning, and he hadn't expected a visitor.

"Just got back from the stable," he explained. "Showing a horse I've got to sell to a prospective buyer. A Palomino, good strain. I like to work him out early when he's frisky."

"I thought you were on the day shift," Shelly said.

"What? Where?"

"At Flight Research."

And so the call was official, with Leo Manfred involved enough to have given Sergeant Shelly reason to acquire some background. There was no evidence of Manfred's easy smile now.

"Not for a week," he said.

"What happened a week ago?"

"I quit. Life's too short to waste on a job you don't like."

Manfred stepped back to the stereo set and tuned down the volume. The jazz continued behind the conversation like a muted heartbeat.

"Low pay?" Shelly queried.

"Good pay," Manfred said. "I just wanted a change. Look, what is this? Did somebody make off with the payroll?"

"Somebody," Shelly answered, "made off with Chester Tracy's wife."

Mike Shelly appreciated good jazz, and what was coming from the stereo was very good jazz. It was smooth and cool and well organized, and so was Leo Manfred, who took this information with just a trace of muscular reaction in his face that only an expert could have noticed. And then he waited, because, if he waited, Mike Shelly would have to stop listening to the jazz and tell the story that had previously been told to the only other man known to have been acquainted with Linda Tracy.

"Why have you told me this?" he asked, when Shelly finished.

"Chester Tracy mentioned your name."

"Does he think I made off with Linda?"

Manfred's facial expression was controlled, but his voice wasn't. An unmistakable note of derision had crept into his tone.

"Is something wrong with Linda Tracy?" Shelly asked.

"No comment," Manfred answered.

"In that case, I'll have to ask where you were last night at ten-thirty."

Chester Tracy had named two men who knew his wife. One was a doctor who didn't smoke; the other was a man with a horse to sell who had one forefinger laced tightly around the stem of a brier pipe.

"Now I'm getting it," Manfred said. "I introduced Linda to Chester—he must have told you that."

"He did," Shelly answered.

"And now you want to know what I know about her. Well, I don't. Linda was half of a double date I once went on. I don't think I even knew her last name before she nailed Chester."

"Nailed?" Shelly echoed.

"She was one of those, that's why I gave her to Chester. She was hunting, and Chester had that certain look."

The face of a kid pressed against the window, Shelly thought.

"The potential husband look," Manfred explained. "I don't have it. Most women sense that right away; to some it has to come subtly—like a blow on the head."

"How did it come to Linda?" Shelly asked.

He was getting tired of jazz. The photos of horses mounted on the walls were more interesting. Some of them had Leo Manfred astride the horse, standing beside the horse; one was of Manfred introducing the horse to a beautiful blonde. Both Manfred and the blonde were wearing dark glasses, but both were recognizable. The blonde was Linda Tracy.

"Who was the other half of the blind date?" Shelly prodded. "A Palomino?"

Manfred said nothing for a few seconds. His face was still controlled, but his glands didn't know it. The frown lines on his forehead were getting moist.

"Look," he said, suddenly, "I wasn't even in the city last night. I drove down to San Diego yesterday to see about a job I'm angling for. I didn't get back until almost midnight."

"Did you drive alone?"

"Alone? Sure. Sergeant, I knew this girl a couple of weeks before I introduced her to Chester. We went dancing—things like that. Pairing her off with Chester was a joke. He was afraid of women. I had no idea he'd fall for her. My guess is that Linda was just too much woman for Chester. I think she rigged that whole deal last night in order to get away from him."

"Why?" Shelly demanded.

"Love in bloom. Linda was always the romantic type. She had a big imagination."

"She's not the only one," Shelly said dryly. "If Mrs. Tracy wanted to run off with another man, she could have staged a fight with Chester and then disappeared. We would have classed it as just another domestic quarrel and waited seventy-two hours before issuing a Missing Persons bulletin."

It was good jazz, but it ended. Leo Manfred walked to the stereo set and switched it off. For a moment, his back was to Shelly, and in that moment, it seemed to stiffen.

When he turned around, he said, "I was only trying to be helpful, Sergeant."

"Thanks," Shelly answered. "You can be a lot more helpful if you find someone in San Diego, or on the road back, who can verify the story that you were driving home alone at ten-thirty last night."

Don Berendo. He still looked sleepy. A pile of comb-resistant black hair crowded for space on the top of his head, spilling over to his forehead. He hadn't had time to shave before being taken in for questioning, and his beard came out black. He wore a brown leather jacket, and twisted his taxi driver's cap in his hands.

"I picked this guy up at the airport," he said. "He came out of the Inter-Continental waiting room and hailed me just as I was getting ready to pull away after unloading a gent and a lady who were flying to Paris. Must have been all of seventy—both of them, but cute as a couple of kids starting out on a honeymoon. Paris." Berendo's face broke in a sleepy smile. "I bet they have a devil of a time at the Folies Bergere."

"The man who came out of the waiting room," Keonig prodded. "What was he like?"

"Him? Let's see. He wore a raincoat—one of those Private Eye kind, and a brown felt hat with the brim snapped down, and dark glasses."

"Dark glasses *and* a raincoat?" Shelly echoed.

"You get all kinds at International, Sergeant."

"How tall was he?" Keonig asked. "How heavy? Fat or thin?"

Berendo scowled. He stared at Keonig; he stared at Shelly. Then he stared at Chester Tracy, who crouched at the edge of his chair listening with his whole body. Suddenly, Berendo brightened.

"He was about my size," he said "About medium. I didn't get a good look at his face—that hat brim and the glasses."

"Did he have luggage?" Shelly asked.

"No, he didn't. I asked about that. 'It's checked through,' he told me. 'I have to go home. I forgot something.' Then he gave me that address—the place you call Peterson's where this guy, Tracy, lives. He kept telling me to hurry."

"What time was it when you picked him up?"

"Ten after ten. I marked it on my sheet. I got him to the address he gave me before ten-thirty. He told me to wait in the drive with the motor running while he went to the place in the back. He was gone about two minutes. When he came back, I thought we'd go again; but he just opened the back door and stood there smoking a cigarette. A minute or so later, the woman came."

"You saw my wife?" Chester demanded. "How did she look?"

"Scared," Berendo said. "No, there's a better word—shocked."

"As if she'd received bad news?" Shelly suggested.

"Something like that. She got into the cab and the guy after her. I backed out of the drive and started back to the airport, thinking we had a plane to catch and wondering, I'll tell you, how a guy could go off and forget a woman like that at home."

"Did they talk?" Keonig asked. "Did you hear any conversation?"

Berendo hesitated. "I was pretty busy driving," he said at last. "Wait—there was something. The cigarette. The guy gave her a cigarette. She must have been nervous because she used three matches trying to get a light."

"She used the matches?" Shelly repeated. "The man didn't give her a light?"

"No. He didn't even sit near her. He sat on one side of the seat and she sat on the other—all tense. I thought maybe they'd had a fight and that was why he had to go back for her. You know where Airport Boulevard crosses Century—that intersection just before you pull into the airport? Well, I was barreling along, still thinking I had a plane to catch, and I started to speed up so's I'd make the green. This guy leans forward and says, 'Turn left here!' I slam on the brakes thinking he's kidding. 'Look, Mister,' I started to say; but he comes right back at me. 'I said, turn left here!' Okay, so he's the customer. I turned left."

"Where did you go then?" Shelly asked.

"Just about half a block—to this engineering place, Flight Research. 'Stop here,' he says, and I stopped. The woman got out and the man got out and paid me. 'Shall I wait' I ask him. 'Don't bother," he said. I couldn't figure it, but, like I said, you get all kinds."

"Did they go inside?" Keonig queried.

"That's the funny thing," Berendo answered. "I started to pull out into traffic again, but I smelled something burning. I stopped and looked in the back. This woman had dropped her cigarette and the floor mat was smoldering. I stopped and yanked open the back door, and I naturally looked back at where I'd let them out because I was thinking a few choice things I'd like to say, and they were gone."

"What do you mean—gone?"

"What I said—gone! I felt downright spooky."

"Do you mean that they had gone inside the building?" Shelly demanded.

"They couldn't have gone inside the building. It sets way back off the street—one of those real modern places with no windows, just a big glass entrance to a lobby with a reception desk and a row of doors behind it. A couple of months ago, they landscaped in front and put in a long, winding walk of some kind of flagstone, or maybe slate. They put in new grass, that kind you never have to cut, and trees and shrubs so it doesn't look like a factory at all. At night they've got ground lights on the walk, and the lights shining out from that lobby. There was nobody on the walk and nobody in the lobby."

"They might have gone through one of the inner doors," Keonig suggested.

And then Don Berendo smiled sleepily, but knowingly. "That walk goes back a good two hundred feet," he said, "and I hadn't even got pulled away from the curb. What did they use for transportation—rockets?"

There was only one way to check Berendo's story—a trip to Flight Research. It was a little past eleven when Shelly and Keonig arrived. Berendo was right. The walk, slate slabs set in white gravel, formed a huge S curving back to the plate glass entrance. The entire foyer was visible from the street.

"It was dark," Keonig reminded. "The shrubs might have thrown shadows."

"The shrubs might have given shelter," Shelly said.

Halfway to the doors, at the first reverse curve of the walk, a cluster of semi-tropical growth raised a barrier which fanned back to join the edge of the building. Shelly stepped off the walk onto the Dicondra. The growth was tight and cushiony, like a closely woven carpet. It absorbed footprints and sprang back into place. But the foliage, he discovered, was more than decorative. It hid from the street the less scenic tight wire fence which enclosed the loading and parking areas at the side and rear of the building. At first, there seemed to be no break in the fence; then Shelly noticed a small gate, probably for the gardener's use. He started toward it, then stopped. Behind the foliage, there was a break in the grass—a small, round hole about the size of a penny with one side slightly flattened. Nearby, a sprinkler embedded in the earth was leaking, releasing just enough moisture to soften the ground. Shelly's eyes scanned the area. There were no other holes. He continued to the gate, Keonig at his heels, and found it locked. Over a buzzer on the wall of the building was a small sign: "Ring For Admittance." Shelly rang. Moments later, a uniformed guard appeared, demanded I.D. cards and received instead, police badges. The gate opened. From the inside, Shelly turned and examined the lock.

"Can this be set to remain unlocked?" he asked.

"From the inside," the guard answered.

"That's good enough," Shelly said.

They continued past the guard, past the loading platform, and on to where the parking lot fanned out before them in six rows of double parked vehicles. By this time, a shirt-sleeved official, summoned by the guard, joined them to inquire the nature of their business. His badge announced that he was C. H. Dawson, Supervisor. Dep't. E.

"How many employees do you have here?" Shelly asked.

"Four hundred and fifty—approximately," Dawson replied. "Three hundred on the day shift and a hundred and fifty on swing and graveyard."

"Skeleton crews," Keonig suggested.

"Somewhat. You see, we produce high precision equipment for the Air Force. The day shift is largely production, but much of our experimental work demands around the clock schedules. We keep skeleton shop and shipping crew at night, but a fairly complete technical force."

Shelly was still staring at the parking lot.

"Precision equipment," he said. "That means I.D. cards and gate inspection for all employees of all shifts."

"Exactly."

"And no one could enter or leave these premises, by foot or by automobile, who wasn't known to either the guard or the receptionist on duty."

"Not without proper credentials," Dawson replied. "What is the difficulty, officers? We have an Air Force Intelligence officer inside."

"It's nothing like that," Shelly said. And then he paused, reflecting. "Around the clock," he said musingly. "Mr. Dawson, do you have anyone in the plant now who was here all last night?"

Dawson smiled wearily. "Several," he admitted, "including myself. We're running some tests—"

"Do you know an employee named Chester Tracy?"

For a moment it seemed that he'd hit a blank wall, and then Dawson brightened. Chester. Of course he knew Chester. He was in charge of the tool crib, night shift.

"Did you see him last night?"

Dawson was puzzled, but still cooperative. Chester'd spent most of the night in the lab, but had stepped out for a coffee—

"At what time?" Shelly asked.

"Time? We lose all sense of time when we're running tests. No, I do remember. It was eleven. Just eleven. I looked at the clock over the coffee machine, still thinking I might get home by midnight. Well, I'm still here."

"Where was Chester?"

"At the machine. The sugar pull jammed and he loosened it for me. 'It's a dull night,' he said. 'I need something to keep me awake.' I think he was making an excuse for being there when it wasn't time for the regular break. Some shop men never lose their awe of the white collar, even when it's open at the neck and frayed on both sides." And then Dawson paused and seemed to reflect on the total conversation. "I hope Chester isn't in some kind of trouble," he said, "—or his wife."

"Why do you mention his wife?" Keonig asked.

"Because she's not well. I know for a fact that Chester telephones her every night during the ten o'clock break. One night—oh, six weeks or so ago—I found him at the phones, frantic. We had a big wind that night and the telephone wires were down. He explained how nervous she had been since losing their child. He was so upset, I told him to goof off and go home to see how she was taking the storm."

"Goof off?" Shelly said.

"It was a simple matter for Chester. His work is chiefly at the beginning and the end of the shift. He could duck out the loading exit without being missed."

"Did he do it?"

"Yes, he did. About forty-five minutes later, I noticed he was back in the crib. I kidded him about not even turning off the motor, and he told me that his wife was asleep and he hadn't wanted to disturb her. Chester's a conscientious worker, Officer. I wouldn't have made such a suggestion to anyone else."

"He still had to drive past the gateman," Shelly observed.

"Yes, he did."

"Would there be any way of finding out if anyone drove out of your parking lot last night between shift changes?"

There was a way. It took a little time, and left everything as it had been in the first place. Two army officers had left the parking lot, and also the wife of one of the late working technicians who had brought him a dietetic supper. No one else. That left only one question to ask the cooperative Mr. Dawson.

"Did you know a former employee named Leo Manfred?" Shelly inquired.

This time Dawson smiled. "The 'Don Juan' of the drafting board," he said. "Leo was a good man, but he's a drifter. He's left us before. He'll be back when it blows over."

"When what blows over, Mr. Dawson?"

"Whatever made him decide it was time to move on—a woman, probably. Leo loves 'em, but leaves 'em." Then Dawson paused and examined the expressionless faces before him. "I don't suppose it would do any good if I asked what this inquiry is all about," he added.

Shelly gave him the only possible reply.

"As much good," he said, "as if we asked what you were testing last night."

Back on the sidewalk, Mike Shelly stood for awhile watching the traffic at the intersection in front of the airport entrance. Most of it bound for the airport consisted of taxi cabs. He counted six before Keonig called him back to the radio car. They were wanted at headquarters. Dr. Youngston had come in to make a statement.

Factual. That was the word Shelly had left with Dr. Youngston. He waited alone in a small room. His statement, he prefaced, was confidential.

"This is Sergeant Keonig," Shelly explained. "He's working on the case with me."

"Very well," Youngston said. "I suppose I should have told you this when you called at my office this morning, but I hadn't had the time to absorb the gravity of the situation. Besides, there are moments between a doctor and a patient that are as sacred as those between a confessor and a priest. I told you that I was called to the Tracy home when Mrs. Tracy lost her child. I was called by Mrs. Peterson. It was all over then, but Mrs. Tracy wasn't aware of what had happened. When I told her, she said something that might have a bearing on her disappearance."

"What did she say?" Shelly asked.

"She called out for someone."

"Her husband?"

"Her husband's name is Chester. The name she called was Leo."

Youngston might have said more, but he didn't have the opportunity. There was a sound from the doorway; Youngston, Shelly, Keonig, all turned at once. Chester Tracy stood staring at them with tragic eyes.

"Leo—" he echoed.

"I thought we were alone," Youngston protested.

"He took Linda. Leo. I'll kill him!"

Chester Tracy was in the doorway one instant; gone from it the next. A moment of shocked surprise, and then Shelly led the exodus to the door. The corridor was already empty; the elevator indicator was starting downward.

"Who is Leo?" Keonig demanded. "Where is he?"

Leo was a target on the other side of the city. Leo was in a garage apartment Shelly had visited once, and Chester Tracy probably a dozen times. Now the elevator indicator had reached street level, and Tracy would be racing for his station wagon. With a grim face, Shelly watched the indicator crawl upward again.

"Leo," he said, "is where we're going right now!"

On the far side of the garage apartment, the side not visible from the street, a sliding glass door opened onto a small sun deck. Shortly after noon, the sun leaned across the roof and bathed the deck in winter warmth. Leo Manfred sprawled in a low-slung deck chair. He still wore his boots and western pants, but had removed the sweater. He tossed his dark glasses on a nearby cocktail table and closed his eyes. He might have fallen asleep if it weren't for an annoying sound in the driveway below. Finally, it ceased and Leo relaxed. He remained relaxed until a shadow fell across his naked chest. Without benefit of the direct sun, the air was cold. Leo opened his eyes and looked up. Chester Tracy stood over him with a trench coat over his right arm and a brown felt hat in his left hand. He watched Leo's eyes open, and then tossed the hat on his chest in a gesture of contempt.

Leo slid one foot to the floor for leverage.

"Chester—" he said.

The coat slid off Chester's arm. In his hand, he held a gun. There was no time for conversation; only an instant for action. Tossing the hat in Chester's face, Leo lunged forward. Chester had time to fire one shot, wildly, and then Leo's arms were about his body, hurling him back into the room behind the glass doors. When Chester fell, Leo broke free and ran for the front stairway. He had scrambled down to the garage level when suddenly brought up short by the solid substance of Mike Shelly, pistol in hand.

"Drop that gun!" Shelly ordered.

Leo whirled. Chester stood above him at the top of the stairs. He'd retrieved the gun and was leveling it at Leo's head.

"I found the raincoat," he yelled, "and the brown hat—"

"Drop the gun!" Shelly repeated.

"I found 'em—in Leo's closet!"

"Drop it or I'll shoot it out of your hand!"

It wasn't just Mike Shelly facing Chester now; Keonig had come up behind him. Slowly, the gun lowered—then dropped.

"Come down," Shelly said.

Chester obeyed. He came down and stood within a few feet of Leo, while Keonig raced upstairs to find and bring back the hat and coat. At the sight of them, Chester found his voice.

"Make him tell what he's done with my Linda," he demanded. "Make Leo tell!"

"I haven't done anything with Linda," Leo protested. "I was in San Diego—"

"You took her away in a taxi! You always were crazy about Linda!"

Shelly took the hat and coat from Keonig's hands. Both showed signs of a lot of use.

"*I* was crazy about Linda?" Leo howled. "Let's get this straight. Linda was crazy about me! Why do you think she married you, Chester? I'll tell you why. Because she was crazy about me and I wouldn't have her. She married you out of spite—"

Chester no longer had a gun, but he had a body. Before anyone could stop him, he rushed at Leo and hurled him back against the chrome handle of a refrigerator stacked among the landlord's furnishings. Leo groaned and staggered forward, and then the door of the refrigerator slowly opened, bringing Mike Shelly's search to an end. All of the racks had been removed to make room for Linda Tracy's body.

"My God!" Leo gasped. "Oh, my God!"

It was Dr. Youngston who recovered first from the shock of discovery. He went to the body and made a quick examination. Linda Tracy had been struck a blow on the head "—with the usual blunt instrument," he said. "Dead for at least twelve hours."

"A little longer," Shelly said quietly. "Since about 10:55 last night."

His words sounded strange against the stunned silence which still pervaded the garage.

"How do you know that?" Keonig demanded.

"Because," Shelly answered, "if it takes eighteen minutes to drive from Flight Research to the Tracy house, it must take the same time to drive from the Tracy house to Flight Research. Think back, Keonig. The cab driver told us that he had picked up a man wearing a trench coat, a brown felt hat, and dark glasses at ten minutes past ten in front of the Inter-Continental waiting room at the airport. He drove to the Tracy address, reaching it shortly before 10:30, picked up Linda Tracy and drove to Flight Research where he discharged his passengers."

"Where they promptly disappeared," Keonig added. "Completely."

"But they didn't. They stepped behind the shrubbery and started to walk toward the gate in the wide fence, and then—" Shelly handed the coat and hat back to Keonig and went to the body. It was fully clothed—light tan coat, blue suit, black pumps. He wrenched loose the right pump and examined the heel. It was very high and narrow with a tip about the size of a penny with one side flattened. "Dr. Youngston, if a woman wearing a pump such as this were struck a heavy blow, hard enough to kill, from the back, left side, wouldn't the weight of her body fall on the right foot?"

"I suppose it would," Youngston said.

Shelly's thumb pricked at the residue of dried mud on the heel. "The grass on the grounds at Flight Research doesn't leave tracks," he mused, "but there was one small round hole near a leaky sprinkler valve that would just fit this heel. A woman's shoes are very interesting, particularly Mrs. Tracy's. She has a pair of plastic slippers in her closet less than a month old; but the soles are worn down as if she'd been doing a lot of dancing. And she has a pair of walking shoes in that same closet with mud on them. Now there's no mud on the way to the mail box, but there could be mud in the unpaved alley leading to the street."

Still holding the pump, Shelly made his way past a dazed Leo and a stunned Chester to the trunk of Leo's convertible. He opened it and peered inside. A jack, a tire iron, a spare tire and a folded saddle blanket. He shook out the blanket with one hand and then tossed it back inside the trunk.

"And then," he continued, "there's the matter of the sleeping pills Linda Tracy didn't take—but told her husband she did. What was to stop her, after that ten o'clock call, from slipping out the back way, walking down the alley, and meeting some Prince Charming to take her to the ball? But, like Cinderella, she had a witching hour—three a.m. Before three, when faithful husband returned, she had to be back in bed, asleep."

"Cinderella slipped up," Keonig observed.

"So did Linda Tracy. And so did her killer."

"I was in San Diego!" Leo protested. "I was on the road driving home at 10:55!"

"What about the night the wind blew down the telephone wires?" Shelly demanded. "Where were you then?"

Leo didn't answer. He was still struggling with shock.

"Weren't you waiting in your convertible at the end of the alley—"

"I didn't kill her," Leo protested.

"—wearing that trench coat and the brown hat—"

"I went out with her a few times, that's all. Just—just a few times—"

"—under the street lamp where you could be watched by anyone who had cause to be suspicious?"

"I didn't want to go out with her!" Leo cried. "I was sick of her. That's why I put in for this job in San Diego."

"He's lying—" Chester began.

"No," Shelly said, firmly, "I don't think he is. But rumors fly fast in a small plant, don't they? What did you think when you heard that Leo Manfred had quit and was moving south, Mr. Tracy? Were you afraid he was going to take your wife with him?"

The question caught Chester Tracy by surprise. He blinked stupidly, like a man blinded by sudden light.

"It's Leo's coat," he stammered. "It's Leo's hat—"

"Yes, and your wife had seen both of them often enough to have recognized Leo in an instant if he'd been the man who came for her in the cab. But she couldn't have recognized a new trench coat and a new hat—particularly not if she'd been called at ten o'clock and told that her husband had been injured on the job and the company was sending someone after her in a cab. The man who came for her was careful not to talk more than necessary. He sat on the opposite side of the seat. When he gave her a cigarette—not the brand he smoked, but a brand picked up in the airport waiting room where he must have kept the coat and hat in a locker—he let her get her own light. There could be only one reason for such caution."

Shelly stood with the black pump in his hands, and the tense faces of four men before him. But one face was more tense than the others.

"If Linda Tracy hadn't been upset," he added, "she would have recognized the man who came for her, in spite of his disguise. She knew him well enough. He was her husband."

"No!" Tracy protested. "It was Leo—"

"It was meant to sound like Leo when the cab driver told his story, as you knew he would do. That cab bothered me from the beginning. It was too easy to trace. Hadn't you been watching your wife since the night Dawson sent you home to inadvertently discover that she wasn't taking her pills at ten o'clock?"

"I work!" Tracy said. "I work nights!"

"But Dawson showed you a way to get in and out of the plant any time you wanted to without being missed. You knew she was going out with Manfred, and you knew Manfred was moving. You killed your wife, Mr. Tracy."

"No—"

"And made a clumsy attempt to frame Leo Manfred. The way you pushed him against that refrigerator just now was a little obvious. If Manfred had put your wife's body in there, he wouldn't have stood within twenty feet of it!"

Chester Tracy's station wagon was parked just outside the open garage. Shelly went to it and opened the tailgate. Early in the morning, the windows had been curtained with fog; nothing inside could be seen. But now he found a canvas tarpaulin, old and dirty but spotted with stains the police lab would find interesting.

"Time of death: approximately 10:55, Doctor," he said, "and then the body was carried to the parking lot until the usual time. After that, Chester Tracy went inside to have a cup of coffee before finishing his shift. But it wasn't a dull night, was it, Tracy?"

Shelly turned around and waited for a protest that didn't come. Chester Tracy had lowered his head and was crying, softly.

"Linda," he said. "My Linda—"

He had the face of a kid who had been given the loveliest toy in the shop window—and broken it.

Lorenz Heller wrote under a number of pseudonyms, including Larry Heller, Larry Holden, Laura Hale, Burt Sims, and his most well-known name, Frederick Lorenz. Heller was known for writing deeper characters than were often found in the fiction of the times. His background as a sailor allowed him to pen exciting seafaring adventures but he also became a Floridian— his evocative style blended perfectly with the hot, sultry weather and made for a perfect match of character and atmosphere. The story below is a prime example....

BACKBITE

Frederick Lorenz

Through the field glasses, Howard's red hunting coat was very clearly visible a half mile ahead through the light stand of Australian pine and palmetto. Satisfied, Geste slid the glasses back into the leather case that clipped to his belt. Now he knew exactly where Howard was going. He was heading almost due east toward the big marsh ten miles beyond the Placido River, a two-day trip on foot but there wasn't any other way to get there. There were no roads, and a plane couldn't land in the sump-ridden slough. A 'copter might get in, but the point was that it took a woodsman like Howard to find the spot in the first place. *And* get back out of it alive.

That was the whole thing, getting back alive. Anybody could have blundered into that marsh, but it took a real woodsman to get back out of it. A woodsman like Howard. Or like himself, Geste thought with satisfaction. He was as good, or better, a woodsman as Howard.

It was a real hunter's paradise, that swamp. The ducks swarmed there more thickly than mosquitoes, and it had never been shot over because it was too tricky to get in and out of. Men had gotten lost in there and turned up years later as skeletons.

Two of us are going in, Geste thought with grim satisfaction, *but I'm the only one coming out this time.*

He'd owed this to Howard for a long time, ever since Howard had married Mary Alice Freeman right, so to speak, from under Geste's nose, because Geste had been courting her at the time. Geste had taken an awful riding at the time, because it had always been his boast that once a woman went out with Clyde Geste, she was spoiled for any other man. And Mary Alice had been no ordinary woman. Her pappy owned the biggest citrus grove in middle Florida, and she was a woman for marrying, not just playing around.

Not, Geste thought sourly, like Beth Savage. He could spit when he thought of her. There wasn't any more to her than a handful of feathers, and it had been fun in the beginning. It had taken her quite awhile to come to his way of thinking, and when she did, it was all tears and sobs and clutching and "we belong to each other."

Beth's brothers had a ranch about two miles south where they were breeding Brahma cattle, but they were poorer than the poor cousins of church mice. Geste didn't want to marry into anything like that. But if he hung around, those three big, hard-fisted Savage brothers would make short work of him if he tried to back down—especially after telling Beth he would marry her.

Hell, he thought bitterly, you always told them you'd marry them. None of them took it serious. It was just something you said so their conscience didn't bother them afterwards.

That was why he had sold out his gas station and had five thousand dollars in his wallet. He didn't want to marry into any ragtag-bob-tail outfit like the Savage's.

But first he had this little score to settle with Howard for taking that Mary Alice Freeman deal right from under his nose. If it hadn't been for Howard, he'd of been in solid with the Freemans by this time and wouldn't have a thing to worry about for the rest of his life, instead of having to run from the Savages, the way he was.

Howard was heading straight for the Hatchet Marsh. Geste had no doubt of it now. He'd camp over-night, probably, just the other side of the Placido River, but it was in the marsh itself that he was going to give it to Howard. They'd never find him, once he sank into the mud of the swamp, and, even if they did, Geste would be long gone by that time.

And the beauty of it was, he didn't even have to kill him. He had that all planned. All it needed was a load of birdshot straight in the face, and Howard would take care of the rest of it. A blind man, when you right down to it, would actually kill himself in the swamp, blundering into the nearest sinkhole.

With five thousand dollars, Geste could start up again in, say, Tampa or maybe even Miami. He tracked Howard till sundown when, just as he expected, Howard made camp on the east bank of the Placido River. Geste crossed about a half mile to the south and made his own camp there, cradling his shotgun in a cabbage palm where the wet wouldn't get at it. He made a quick lean-to of palmetto fronds and stretched out under them in his sleeping bag. It would be about noon tomorrow when Howard would reach the edges of the marsh and begin hunting. The ducks were there by the million. Ducks, egrets, white and blue herons, and all kinds of wild life in spendthrift abundance. 'Gators, 'coons, 'possum, even black bear. Everything.

Geste awakened at sunrise the next morning and made a quick meal from the cold grits and sausage he had carried with him. He made his pack and trudged upriver to pick up Howard's track again. In about an hour or so he'd be able to pick up Howard through the glasses. At just about that time, Howard would be crossing the open savannah, which would take at least two hours. After that, it would be easy to follow him into the marsh. The sound of Howard's gun would be the guide from there on.

It was at eight-thirty that Geste came to the western edge of the savannah and took the glasses from the leather case at his belt and swept the wide, grassy space before him.

He frowned. There was no sign of Howard's red coat, which should have been very easy to pick up in the powerful glasses. He swept the space slowly again from south to north. Howard should have been half way across by now and clearly visible. Intently, he swept every inch of the grassy flatness before him. He swore and went over it twice again. He lowered the glasses and bit his lip. Howard was not out there, and he should have been.

Howard couldn't possibly have started before sunrise. Nobody but a fool would try to go through that country in the dark, and Howard wasn't a fool. In addition to the sink holes, there were snakes—copperheads, cottonmouths, rattlers, even the little deadly coral snakes.

Geste raised the glasses once again and went over the area, covering every speck of it. Howard was definitely not out there.

For the first time, Geste looked back over his shoulder. Howard, too, he suddenly remembered, carried field glasses. His heart began to beat a little faster. Suppose Howard had spotted him the day before? Howard was no fool. Howard knew that Geste had it in for him ever since he had married Mary Alice Freeman. Howard would know why he was being followed.

If he could kill Howard out here in the marsh country, it would be just as easy for Howard to kill him. Even a disabling wound would be mortal out here. A gunshot leg. It was practically a whole day's travel back to the highway, with nothing but the Savage brothers' ranch in between.

Geste wanted desperately to scan the savannah again with the glasses, but he knew it was futile. Howard was not out there on it, and from now on, every minute wasted was a minute lost. He had to travel fast and straight out of here. He was certain now that Howard had spotted him sometime during the day before, and was now coming up behind him, circling through the Australian pine and palmetto country.

His mind worked sharply. He threw off his sleeping bag, his knapsack, and everything, in fact, except his shotgun. His best plan would be to quarter north toward the highway, skirting the fringe of the Savage ranch, and come out the road about ten miles above Sanibar. He could always get a lift back, and, by cutting north like that, he would be working away from Howard.

Now that he had his plan, he was perfectly cool. Grimly, he thought, *the hunter hunted*. This had started out to be such an easy thing, but now it had turned out to be a life-or-death race for the highway. Once on the highway, he knew, Howard would never dare take a shot at him. He would be safe on the highway. And after that, he would pick up his car in Sanibar and light out for Tampa or Miami.

He set out northwest at a dogtrot. He was too good a woodsman to need a compass. One glance at the sun in the eastern sky was enough to set him on his way.

He ran for about a half hour and that was just about all he could take at that pace. The sweat poured off him and his leg muscles felt like constricting springs. He was dizzy and he cursed the quart of "shine" that he had drunk the night before in celebration of his selling the gas station so quickly. It was taking its toll now. He reeled under the shade of a water oak and lay prone on the ground, gasping for breath, but almost immediately he sat up and, with shaking hands, took out the glasses and looked back through the sparse growth of pine through which he had just come. He caught a movement and hurriedly focused on it, but it was only a family of 'coons grubbing over the cake of cold grits and sausage he had left behind.

Damn, had he come only such a short distance that he could still see the 'coons through his glasses!

He forced himself to his feet, but he did not run this time. Howard was in no better shape than he was. Nobody could really run through that palmetto. A steady pace was best. He settled down to a bent-kneed stride that really covered ground.

It was lonely country out here. An eagle wheeled in the sky, its small white head bent as it scanned the waters below for fish. An owl mourned in the swamp behind him. His heart leaped into his throat when, with a dry clatter, a small deer leaped up in the path and fled through the rustling fans of palmetto.

His throat was dry and his tongue was a rasp in his mouth, but he had left his water bottle behind with everything else when he started his flight toward the highway.

In the beginning he stopped only every quarter of an hour to take out the glasses and scan the trail behind him, but soon he had them to his eyes every few minutes. It was almost noon when he spotted Howard's red coat to the south of him. His heart stopped and he leaned forward, as if those few inches would bring him a closer view of Howard. He frantically spun the adjustment wheel and Howard came sharply into focus. Howard was standing beside a banyan tree, scanning the area with *his* field glasses.

Geste gasped. Before this, he thought Howard would be carrying a shotgun—but now he saw Howard's gun leaning against the tree. It was a rifle. A shotgun had a short range, but a rifle could carry accurately up to about a mile, mounted with a 'scope. He tried desperately to see if the gun had a 'scope, but it was leaning the wrong way against the tree.

With trembling hands, he shoved the glasses back into their case and picked up his shotgun. He suddenly noticed that it was getting darker, and he glanced up at the sky. Heavy clouds were coming in from the Gulf to the west. There was going to be rain, and this whole country would be a bog once the rains started.

There was no time to skirt the Savage ranch now. He would have to cut across it, but even so, he could still pass a good half mile to the south of the ranch house with practically no chance of running into any of Beth's big brothers.

He set out at a long, loping stride. In five minutes, he stopped and looked back again. Howard was coming definitely toward him now, the rifle cradled in his arm. Geste swore and pushed on faster.

His heart was in his mouth all the way across the Savage ranch. Finally, he was in the rough palmetto again, and he breathed easier. It was only seven miles to the highway now, but a very tough seven miles, waist-high palmetto all the way. His breath was harsh in his open mouth as he bulled through the slashing undergrowth of knife-edged leaves and prickly pear.

He should have known better. He was a good woodsman, and he knew that this was rattlesnake country. He should have heard that warning whirr, but he didn't. He was not aware of the snake until, as thick through the body as his upper arm, it struck him in the leg.

For a moment he stood frozen in horror. Then, in a frenzy, he leveled the shotgun and blew its head off. His hand flew to his belt for his hunting knife to gash the wound and suck out the poison, but the knife wasn't there. He hadn't brought it. He hadn't intended to go hunting, except for Howard, and he hadn't brought the knife.

He tried to keep calm. The thing to do when you're snake-bit, is to keep calm. Don't run. Running stimulates the heart action and the poison goes through you faster. He sat down on the ground, gripping his leg just above the bite, wondering frantically what to do.

The sweat poured off him. It poured into his eyes, down his ribs, and he could even feel it trickling in his hair. And then he felt what he knew was the first action of the venom—a sharp stab in his heart. His world exploded into a whiteness, and he screamed.

When he opened his eyes again, he was barely conscious. He knew he was being carried across someone's shoulder and he could see the matted redness of a hunting coat under him. He moaned feebly and tried to push himself away. A hand tightened around his wrist, and Howard's voice said reassuringly:

"Take it easy, Geste. You'll be okay. I think I got most of the poison out, but I'm getting you to a phone as fast as I can so we can get a doctor. The Savage boys' ranch house is just over the rise...."

In Ed Gorman's short fiction he usually finds a despicable act and turns it into a sort of uniquely human story, and "Angie" is no exception. Ed was Stark House's first Associate Editor and Stark House wouldn't be what it is today without the interest and passion Ed shared with Greg Shepard on "forgotten" paperback original books and writers. Ed was an award-winning author, writing in westerns, horror, science fiction and of course, mysteries and crime fiction. He was a prolific anthologist as well as a critical blogger whose entries across the years were a not to be missed treasure of the writers and fiction he loved.

ANGIE

Ed Gorman

Roy said, "He heard us last night."

Angie said, "Heard what?"

"Heard us talking about Gina."

"No, he didn't. He was asleep."

"That's what I thought. But I went back to the can one time and I saw his door was open and I looked in there and he was sittin' up in bed, wide awake. Listenin'."

"He probably'd just woken up."

"He heard us talkin'."

"How do you know?"

"I asked him," Roy said.

"Yeah? And what did he say?"

"He said he didn't."

"See, I told ya."

"Well, he was lyin'."

"How do you know?" she said.

"He's my son, ain't he? That's how I know. I could tell by his face."

"So what if he did hear?"

Roy looked at her, astonished. "So what if he did? He'll go to the cops."

"The cops? Roy, you're crazy. He's nine years old and he's your son."

"That little bastard don't give two turds about me, Angie. He was strictly a mama's boy. And now that he knows...."

He didn't need to say it. Angie had been waitressing at a truck stop when she'd met Roy. He was living in a trailer with his son, Jason, and his wife, Gina. He went for Angie immediately. On her nights off, he'd take her to Cedar Rapids, where they'd go to a couple of dance clubs. They always had a great time except when Roy got real drunk and started trouble with black guys who were dating white girls. Roy had some friends who were always talking about blowing up places with blacks and Jews and gays in them. Roy always gave them a certain percentage of his robbery money. That's what Roy did. He robbed banks, usually small-town ones that were located on the edge of town. Roy was a pro. He figured everything out carefully in advance. He knew the exit routes and where the banks kept the video surveillance cameras, and he checked out the teller windows in advance to see which clerk looked most vulnerable. He'd served six years in Fort Madison for sticking up a gas station when he was nineteen. He was thirty-six now and vowed never to be caught again. What she liked about him was that he had a goal in life. There was this one bank in Des Moines where he said he could get half a million on a payroll Friday. They'd go to Vegas and then they'd go see this whites-only compound up in the Utah mountains. That was the only part that Angie didn't like. She didn't understand politics and Roy and his buddies always carrying on about Jews and gays and colored people bored her. She had a way of looking awake when she was really not awake. She did that practically every time Roy and his buddies started talking about some militia deal they had heard about and intended to join. The wife got wind of the courtship between Roy and Angie, though, and raised hell. She wouldn't give him a divorce, and she threatened to tell the cops about all his robberies all over the Midwest. So one rainy night he killed her.

Shoved a knife into her right breast, which silenced her, and then cut her throat. He loaded her into a body bag and packed a hundred pounds of hand weights in there with her and then drove his two-year-old Ford out to the river that very moonglow night and threw her in just below the dam. The only trouble Roy had was his son, Jason. The kid just kept wailin' and carryin' on about where's my mom, where's my mom? He hadn't wanted the kid in the first place, had beat the shit out of her, but she still wouldn't get an abortion. Even back then he'd had the dream of this big Des Moines bank on payroll Friday, and who wanted a kid along when you had all the cash with you? But Gina had her way and Roy was stuck with the little prick. And now Jason had overheard him talkin' about killin' his mother. Roy knew that somehow, some way, the little prick would turn him in.

Roy said, "Don't worry, I'll handle it."

She watched him carefully. "Sometimes you scare the shit out of me, Roy. You really do. He's your own flesh and blood."

"I didn't want him. Gina wanted him."

"And you killed Gina."

"For you," he said. "I killed her for you." Then, "Shit, honey, here we go again. Arguin'. This ain't what I want and it ain't what you want, either. You c'mere now." Then, "A kid like that, he's a ball and chain."

He liked it when she sat in his lap. He liked to feel her up to the point that his erection got so big and bulgy it was downright painful. She'd wriggle on it and make him even crazier. Then, as now, they'd go in on their big mussed sleepwarm bed and do the trick.

Afterward, today, he said, "I better get into town. I want to be there at noontime. See what the place is like around then."

He was scoping out a bank. He was planning to rob it day after tomorrow. Their cash supply was way way down. The trailer park manager was on Roy's ass for back rent. Roy said, "Don't say nothin' to him when he gets home from school."

"All right."

"You just let me handle everything."

"All right."

"It'll be better for us," Roy said, trying to make her feel better. "Haulin' that kid everywhere we go, that isn't the kind of life we want. We want to be free, babe. That's just the kind of people we are. Free."

Roy had killed people before and it had never bothered her. But never a kid before, that she knew of. And his own kid to boot.

He kissed her breasts a final time and then said, "I'll figure out what to do about Jason and then you'n me'll go dancing' tonight. Okay?"

"Okay, Roy."

Roy was going to kill him for sure.

One day, when Angie was thirteen, her grandmother said, "That body of hers is going to get her in trouble someday." The irony being that Grandmother herself had a body just like it—killer breasts and hips that made young men weep in public—when she'd been young. And so had Angie's mother, the person Grandmother was talking to. The thing being that the worst trouble Grandmother had ever gotten in was getting knocked up by a soldier home on leave from WW2, a pregnancy that had brought Angie's mother into the world. The worst Suzie had ever gotten into, in turn, was getting knocked up by a Vietnam soldier home on leave, a pregnancy that had brought Angie into the world.

Angie, however, got into a lot more trouble than just spreading her sweet young thighs. She saw a TV show one night where this beautiful girl was referred to as a "kept woman," a woman who lounged about an expensive apartment all day, looking just great, while this older man paid her rent, gave her endless numbers of gifts, and practically groveled every time the kept woman was even faintly displeased. An Iowa girl with a wondrous body like Angie's, was it any wonder she'd want to be a kept woman, too?

When she was fifteen, she ran away from home in the company of a thirty-two-year-old woman from Omaha who took her to a hotel in Des Moines. Angie slept with ten men in three years and made just over a thousand dollars. One of the men had been black, and that gave her some pause. She could just hear her dad if he ever found out about her (A) screwing men for money or (B) screwing a black man for money.

She went back home. Her dad, who worked as an appliance service repair man for Al's American Appliances, didn't have the money for a private shrink so they sent her to the county Human Services Department, where she saw this counselor for free. She spent two hours filling out the Minnesota Multiphasic Personality Test, which just about bored her ass off. He kept peeking in the room and asking her if she was about done. That's what he pretended to do, anyway. What he was really doing was staring at her breasts. He'd fallen in love with them the moment they walked in the door. She ended up screwing him on the side. He had a wife who worked at Wal-Mart in Cedar Rapids and two little girls, one of whom was lame in some way and whom he got all sad about sometimes. He was thirty-eight and bald and felt guilty about screwing her and cheating on his wife and all but he said that her tits just made him dizzy when he touched them, just dizzy. He kept her in rap CDs. She loved rap. The way the gangsters in the rap videos took care of their girlfriends.

That's what she wanted. She wanted to meet some guy who'd give her a life of ease. A kept woman. No work. No hassle. No sweat. Just sit around some fancy apartment and read comic books and watch TV and porno movies. She loved porno movies. The thing was, she didn't like sex very much, except for masturbating, but if sex was the price she had to pay for a life of ease, so be it.

She dropped the counselor as soon as she managed to get through high school. She got a job in Cedar Rapids as a clerk in a Target store. She lasted three weeks. She took her paycheck and bought a very sexy dress and then she started hanging out in the lawyer bars downtown. Her first couple of months, things went pretty good. She hadn't found a guy who'd make her an official kept woman, but she'd found several guys who'd give her a little money now and then, enough money for a nice little apartment and a six-year-old Oldsmobile.

But things did not go well after a time. She caught the clap and profoundly displeased a couple of the men who gave her money. Then she ran into two men who were long of tongue but short of wallet, a car salesman who drove them around in sleek new Caddies, and a supper club owner who wore her like a pinkie ring. They were full of promises but had no real money. The Caddie man had two wives and two alimonies; and the supper club man owed the IRS boys so much in back taxes, he could barely afford a pack of gum. He'd had a supper club over in Rock Island several years back, and he'd been charged with tax evasion, later dropped to a simple (if overwhelming) tax debt.

Then, the worst thing of all happened. On the night of her twenty-sixth birthday, Angie got busted for prostitution. She was in a downtown bar sitting with a couple of hookers she knew getting birthday party drunk, when one of the lawyers suggested they all go out to his houseboat. Well, they did, and the cops followed them. Angie insisted that she accepted gifts but never cash for sex per se but it was a distinction apparently too subtle for the minds of the gendarmes. They hated these two particular lawyers and were gleeful about arresting them. Cedar Rapids had a new police station and Angie was impressed with it. She saw a couple of cute young cops, too, and thought she wouldn't mind dating a cop. It was probably fun. She was booked and fingerprinted and charged. It all, like much of Angie's life, had a dream-like quality. She was just walking through it—as if her life was a TV show and she was simply watching it—the reality of her trouble not hitting her until the next day when her name appeared in the paper. The Cedar Rapids paper was read by everybody in her hometown. Angie called home and tried to explain. Her mother was in tears, her father enraged. They told her not, definitely not, to attend the family reunion two weekends hence.

Now it was two years later and Angie was living with Roy, who robbed banks and killed people when he thought it was necessary. She saw plainly now that he was never going to have the kind of money it took to make her a kept woman. Hell, he'd even hinted a few times that she should get another waitress job to help out with the rent and the food. Plus, there were the people he'd killed, three that she knew of for sure. The only one that really bothered her was his wife. Killing his wife was a real personal thing, and it scared Angie. Killing his own son scared her even more.

She spent the afternoon getting depressed about her bikinis. School would be out in a week. Swimming pools would be opening up. Time to flaunt her body. But this year there was too much of her body to flaunt. She'd put on twenty pounds. Ripples of cellulite could be seen on the back of her thighs. She wished now Roy hadn't talked her into getting his name tattooed on both her boobs.

At three-thirty, Jason came home. He was a skinny, sandy-haired kid with a lot of freckles and eyeglasses so thick they made you feel sorry for him. Kids like Jason always got picked on by other kids.

Something was wrong. He usually went to the refrigerator and got himself some milk and a piece of the pie Angie always kept on hand for both of them. Roy had a whiskey tooth, not a sweet tooth. Then Jason usually sat at the dining room table and watched Batman. But not today. He just muttered a greeting and went back to his little room and closed the door.

Something really was wrong and she figured she knew what it was. She slipped a robe on over her bikini—you shouldn't be around him, your tits hangin' out that way, Roy said whenever she wore a bikini around the trailer—and went back to his room and knocked gently. She could never figure out what he thought of her. He was almost always polite but never more than that.

"I'm asleep," he said.

She giggled. "If you were asleep, you couldn't say 'I'm asleep.'"

"I just don't feel like talkin', Angie."

She decided to risk it. "You heard us talkin' last night, didn't you, Jason?"

There was a long silence. "No."

"About your mom."

"No."

"About what happened to her."

There was another long silence. "He killed her. I heard him say so."

So Roy was right. The kid had heard.

She opened the door and went in. He lay on the bed. He still had his sneakers on. A Spawn comic book lay across his chest. Sunlight angled in through the dirty window on the west wall and picked out the blond highlights in his hair.

She went over and sat down next to him. The springs made a noise. She tried not to think about her weight, or how her bikinis fit her. She was definitely going on a diet. She was going to be a kept woman, and one thing a kept woman had to do was keep her body good.

She said, "I just wanted you to know that I didn't have nothin' to do with it, what he did, I mean."

"Yeah," he said. "I know."

"And I also wanted you to know that your daddy isn't a bad man."

"Yes, he is."

"Sometimes he is. But not all the time."

"He broke your rib, didn't he?"

"He didn't mean to hit me that hard. He was just drunk was all. If he'd been sober, he wouldn't have hit me that hard."

"They say in school that a man shouldn't hit a woman at all."

"Well," she said, "you know what your daddy says about schools. That they're run by Jews and gays and colored people."

He stared at her. "I'm gonna turn him in."

She got scared. "Oh, honey, don't you ever say that to your daddy." She knew that Roy was looking for an excuse, any excuse, to kill Jason. "Promise me you won't. He'd get so mad he'd—"

She didn't need to finish her sentence. She sensed that the kid knew what she was talking about.

She said, "Is that a good comic book?"

"Not as good as Batman."

"Then how come you don't get Batman?"

"I already read it for this month."

"Oh."

She leaned forward and kissed him on the forehead. She'd never done that before. He was a nice kid. "You remember what I said now. You never say anything in front of your daddy about turnin' him in. You hear me?"

"Yeah, I guess so."

"You take a nap now."

She stood up.

Her mother had once said, "You give a man plenty of starch and a good piece of meat, he'll never complain about you or your cookin'." Angie had told this to Roy once and he'd grinned at her and pawed one of her breasts and said, "All depends on what kind of meat you're talkin' about." At the time, Angie had found his remark hilarious. There was nothing to smile about as she made the Kraft cheese and macaroni while the pork chops sizzled in the oven.

He was going to kill his own son. She couldn't get over it. His own son.

Forty-five minutes later, the three of them ate dinner. As always, Jason said grace to himself the way his mom had taught him. While he did this, Roy made a face and rolled his eyes. Little sissy son-of-a-bitch, he'd drunkenly said to Jason one night, sayin' grace like that.

Roy said, "Guess what I found today?"

Angie said, "What?"

"I was talkin' to the boy."

"Oh," Angie said, irritated with his tone of voice. "Pardon me for living." She got up from the table and carried her dishes to the sink.

"Guess what I found today?" Roy said to Jason.

"What?"

"A real great spot for fishin'."

"Oh."

"For you and me. I always wanted to teach you how to fish."

"I thought you hated to fish," Jason said.

"Not anymore. I love fishin', don't I, babe?"

"Yeah," Angie said from the sink, where she was cleaning off her plate. "He loves fishin'."

Angie knew immediately that Roy had figured out how to kill the kid. He hated fishing, and even more he hated to do anything with the kid.

After supper, Jason went into his room. Most kids would be out playing in the warm spring night. Not Jason. He had a little twelve-inch TV in there and he had a lot of X-Files novels, too. He was well set up.

While she was doing the dishes, and Roy was sitting at the table nursing a Hamms from the bottle and watching some skin on the Playboy Channel, she said, "You're gonna do it."

"Yes, I am."

"He's your own flesh and blood."

He came over and pressed against her. He had a hard-on. Seems he always had a hard-on. She didn't have no complaints in that department. He groped her and kissed her neck and said, "We're free kind of people, Angie. Free. And with the kid along, we'll never be free. Especially with what he knows about us. One phone call from him and we'll be in the slammer."

"But he's your own son."

Jason's door opened. He went to the john. Roy said, "You let me take care of it."

Twenty minutes later, Roy and Jason left. She couldn't think of any way to stop them without coming right out and warning Jason about what was going on.

She paced. She paced and gunned whiskey from a Smurfs glass. She was so agitated her heart felt like thunder in her chest and every few minutes her right arm jerked grotesquely.

And then she remembered the gun. She didn't even know what kind of gun it was. One of her lawyer friends had given it to her once when one of her old boyfriends was hassling her. She'd shot it a few times. She knew how to use it. She kept it in the bureau underneath the crotchless panties Roy had bought her, his joke always being that he'd personally eaten the crotch out of them.

She got the gun and she went after them. Her only thought was the river. About half a mile on the other side of some hardwoods was a cliff and below it fast water that ran to a dam near Cedar Rapids. One time they'd been walking and Roy said it was a perfect place to throw a body. His cellmate, a lifer Roy had a lot of respect for, had said that while bodies did occasionally wash up right away, there was a better chance they'd give you a five-, six-day head start from the law.

The dying day was indigo in the sky, indigo and salmon pink and mauve spreading like a stain beneath a few northeasterly thunderheads and a biting wind that tasted of rain. Rainstorms always scared her. When she was little, she'd always hidden in the closet, her two older sisters laughing at her, scaredy-pants, scaredy-pants. But she didn't care. She'd hidden anyway.

The way she found them, they were sitting on a picnic table near the cliff, father and son, just talking. Darkness was slowly making them grainy, and soon would make them invisible.

Roy said, "What the hell you doing here?"

"She can be here if she wants to," Jason said.

She smiled. The kid liked her and that made her feel good.

"I guess I need to go to the bathroom," Jason said.

He walked over to the hardwoods and disappeared.

"I was afraid you already did something to him," Angie said.

He looked at her. Shrugged. "It's harder than I thought it would be."

"He's your own flesh and blood."

"Yeah, yeah, I guess that's it. I started to do it a couple times but I couldn't go through with it. I mean, it's not like shootin' a stranger or anything."

"Let's go back."

He shook his head. "Oh, no. You go back alone."

"But if you can't do it, why you want to stay out here?"

"I didn't say I can't do it. I just said it's harder than I thought it was. It's just gonna take me a little time is all. Now, you get that sweet ass of yours back home and wait for me. We'll be pullin' out tonight."

"Pullin' out?"

They could see Jason coming back toward them.

"Yeah," Roy said in a whispering voice, "school'll be askin' questions, him not around anymore. Better off pullin' out tonight."

Jason walked up. "Dad tell you there's twenty-pound fish in that river?"

"Yeah," she said, "that's what he said."

"Angle's got to get back home. She's makin' us a surprise."

"A surprise?" Jason said, excited. "What kinda surprise?"

"Well, if she tells ya, it won't be much of a surprise, will it?"

Jason grinned. "No, I guess not."

"You head home, babe," Roy said. "We'll be up'n a while."

She wanted to argue but you didn't argue with Roy. You didn't argue and win, anyway. And you got bruises and bumps and breaks for not winning.

"Guess I better go," she said.

"I can't wait to see the surprise," Jason said.

She went back but she didn't go home. She stood inside the hardwoods, inside the shadows, inside the night, and watched them.

He couldn't do it. That's what she was hoping. That when it came right down to it, he just couldn't do it. She said a couple of prayers.

But he did it. Pulled the gun out, grabbed Jason by the shoulder and started dragging him across the grassy space between picnic table and cliff.

All this was instinct: her running, her screaming. Roy looked real pissed when he saw her. He got distracted from the kid and the kid tried wrestling himself away, swinging his arms wild, trying to kick, trying to bite.

Roy didn't have any warning about her gun. She got up close to him and jerked it out of the back pocket of her Levi's and killed him point-blank. Three bullets in the side of the head.

He went over on his side and shit his pants before he hit the ground. The smell was awful.

The weird thing was how the kid reacted. You'd think he'd be grateful that she'd killed the son-of-a-bitch. But he knelt next to Roy and wailed and rocked back and forth and held a dead cold white hand in his hand and then wailed some more.

Maybe, she thought, maybe it was because his mom was dead, too. Maybe losin' both your folks, maybe it was too much to handle, even if your own flesh-and-blood dad had tried to kill you.

She dragged Roy over and pushed him off the cliff into the river. The stars were on the water tonight and the choppy waves glistened.

She dragged the boy away. He fought at first, biting, kicking, wrestling, and all. She let him have a good hard slap, though, and that settled him down. He kept cryin' but he did what she told him. "How you doin'?"

"All right."

"You hungry?"

"Sort of, I guess."

"You'll like Colorado. Wait till you see the mountains."

"You didn't have to kill him."

"He was gonna kill you."

He didn't say anything for a long time. They were nearing the Nebraska border. The land was getting flatter. Cows, crying with prairie sorrow, tossed in their earthen beds, while night birds collected chorus-like in the trees, making the leafy branches thrum with their song. It was nice with the windows rolled down and all the summery Midwest roaring in your ears.

Sixty-three miles before they hit the border, just after ten o'clock, they found the Empire Motel, one of those 1950s jobs with the office in the middle and eight stucco-sided rooms fanned out on either side.

Angle rented a room and bought a bunch of candy and potato chips from the vending machine. She rented a sci-fi video from the manager for Jason.

She got him into the shower and then into bed and played the movie for him. He didn't last long. He was asleep in no time. She turned out the lights and got into bed herself. She was tired. Or thought she was, anyway. But she couldn't sleep. She lay there and thought about Roy and about when she was a little girl and about being a kept woman. It had to happen for her someday. It just had to. Then she remembered what she'd looked like in those bikinis. God, she really had to go on a diet.

She lay like this for an hour. Then she heard car doors opening and male laughter. She decided to go peek out the window. Two nice-looking, nicely dressed guys were carrying a suitcase each into a room two doors away. They were driving this just-huge new Lincoln. Sight of them made her agitated. She wanted a drink and to hear some music. Maybe dance a little. And laugh. She needed a good laugh.

Fifteen minutes later, she was fixed up pretty good, white tank top and red short-shorts, the ones where her cheeks were exposed to erotic perfection, her hair all done up nice, and enough perfume so that she smelled really good. The kid wouldn't miss her. He'd be fine. He'd be sleeping and the door would be locked and he'd be just fine.

Their names were Jim Durbin and Mike Brady. They were from Cedar Rapids and they owned a couple of computer stores and they were going to open a big new one in Denver. Ordinarily, Jim would fly but Mike was scared to fly. And ordinarily, they would stay in a nicer motel than this but they couldn't find anything else on the road. Her excuse for knocking on their door this late was the front office didn't have a cigarette machine and she was out and she heard them still up and she wondered if either of them had a few cigarettes they'd loan her. Jim said he didn't smoke but Mike did.

Jim said he'd been trying for years to get Mike to quit. How do you like that? Jim said. Guy doesn't mind risking lung cancer every day of his life but he won't get on an airplane?

They had a nice bottle of I. W. Harper and invited her in.

It was obvious Mike was interested in her. Jim was married. Mike was just going through a divorce he called "painful." He said his wife ended running off with this doctor she was on this charity committee with. Jim said Mike needed a good woman to rebuild Mike's self-esteem. That was a word Angie heard a lot. She liked the daytime talk shows and they talked a lot about self-esteem. There was a transvestite prostitute on just last week, as a matter of fact, and Angie felt sorry for the poor thing. He/she said that's all he/she was looking for, self-esteem.

Angie got sort of drunk and spent her time talking to Mike while Jim took a shower and got ready for bed. Angie could tell he was taking a real long time to give Mike and her a chance to be alone. And then they were making out and his hands were all over her and then she was down on her knees next to his bed and doing him and he was gasping and groaning and bucking and just going crazy and it made her feel powerful and wonderful to make a man this happy, especially a broken-hearted one.

When Jim came back, wearing a red terry-cloth robe and rubbing his crew cut with a white towel, Angie and Mike were sitting in chairs and having another drink.

"So, what's going on?" Jim said.

"Well," Mike said, and he looked like a teenager, excited and nervous at the same time, "I was going to ask Angie if she'd like to come to Denver with me. Spend a couple of weeks while we get the grand opening all set up and everything."

Jim said, still rubbing his crew cut with the white towel, "This is a guy who does everything first-class, Angie, let me tell you. You should see his condo. The view of the city. Unbelievable."

"You like Jet Skiing?" Mike said.

"Sure," Angie said, though she wasn't exactly sure what it was.

"Well, I've got two Jet Skis and they're a ball. Believe me, we could have a lot of fun. You could stay at my condo and do what you like during the day—shop or whatever—and then at night, we'll get together again."

Jim said, "God, Angie, you're a miracle worker. This sounds like my old buddy Mike Brady. I haven't heard him sound this happy in three or four years."

Mike grinned. "Maybe I'm in love." And he leaned over and slid his arm around Angie's neck and gave her a big whiskey kiss on the mouth.

All she could think of was how strange it was. Maybe she'd met the man who was going to make her into a kept woman. And this one wasn't married, either. He could marry her somewhere down the line.

She said, "Wait till I tell Jason."

Mike gave her a funny look. "Jason? Who's Jason?"

Jim came over, too. "Yeah, who's Jason?"

"Oh, sort of my stepson, I guess you'd say."

"You're traveling with a kid?" Mike said.

"Yeah."

Mike didn't have to say anything. It was all in his face.

He'd been outlining an orgy of activities and she went and ruined it all with reality. A kid. A fucking kid.

"Oh," Mike said, finally.

"He's a real nice kid," Angie said. "Real quiet and everything."

"I'm sure he's a nice kid, Angie," Jim said. "But I don't think that's what Mike had in mind. Nothing against kids, you understand. I've got two of my own and Mike's got three."

"I love kids," Mike said, as if somebody had accused him otherwise.

"He wouldn't be any trouble," Angie said. "He really wouldn't."

Mike and Jim looked at each other and Jim said, looking at Angie now, "You know what we should do? Why don't we take your phone number, you know where you're staying in Omaha and everything, and then Mike can give you a call when he gets settled into his condo?"

Mike didn't have nerve enough to say goodbye so Jim was doing it for him.

A ball and chain, she remembered Roy said about Jason. Mike wasn't going to call. Jim was just saying that. And she'd be somewhere in Omaha, maybe with a waitress job or something. And pretty soon school would roll around and she'd have to worry about school clothes and getting him enrolled in a new school and everything. While somebody else would be living with Mike in his Denver condo, and Jet Skiing, whatever that was, and using Mike's American Express to buy new clothes and stuff.

She said, "You know if there's a river around here somewhere?"

"A river?" Jim said.

"Yes," she said. "A river."

Next morning at seven a.m. she knocked on the door. A sleepy pajamaed Jim opened it. "Hey," he said. "How's it goin'?" He sounded a little leery of seeing her. He'd obviously hoped they'd put the Denver matter to rest last night.

"Guess what?" she said.

"What?"

"I said I was sort of Jason's stepmother? Well, actually, I'm his aunt. My sister lives about ten miles from here and has troubles with depression. She wanted me to take him for a while but she stopped by the room here real early this morning and picked him up. Said she was feeling a lot better."

Mike could be seen over Jim's shoulder now. He said, excited, "So you don't have the kid anymore?"

"Free, white and twenty-one," she said.

"You're going to Denver!" he said.

Jim said, "I'm going to get some breakfast down the road. I'll be back in an hour or so."

He got dressed quick and left.

They did it their first time right in Mike's mussed bed. Only once or twice did she think of the kid, and how she'd smothered him in the room. She hadn't had any trouble finding the river. She had to give it to Roy. The ball-and-chain business. She had liked the kid but he really was a ball and chain.

A few hours later, they left for Denver. That night, they had spare ribs for supper at a roadside place. They drank a lot of wine, or vino, as Jim kept calling it, and Mike as a joke licked some of the rib sauce off her fingers. She was scared about later, when she went to sleep. Maybe she'd have nightmares about the kid. But she snuggled up to Mike real good and after they made love, they lay in the darkness sharing his cigarette and talking about Denver and she ended up not having any dreams at all.

Stark House has published several titles by Bill Pronzini, one of the most decorated writers of the era. His awards include the first ever Shamus Award, an Edgar, and was named a Grandmaster by the Mystery Writers of America in 2008. His book 1001 Midnights: The Aficionado's Guide to Mystery and Detective Fiction—*co-authored with his wife, Marcia Muller (herself an MWA Grandmaster)—won a Macavity Award and has been one of the most quoted reference books in the genre for decades. Bill has written more than three dozen titles in his "Nameless Detective" series and is a prolific anthologist as well. He writes the stuff, writes about the stuff, and collects the stuff—and does it all quite well indeed.*

NIGHT GAMES

Bill Pronzini

When Brennan was within two hundred yards of the island's wooded leeward shore, he cut off the skiff's dashboard and running lights and throttled the 40-horsepower outboard down to crawling speed. There was no moon, but a broad canopy of coldly winking stars provided enough light so that he could make out the slender strip of pebble beach—the only spot other than the inlet on the north shore where a boat could be landed safely. He shut off the engine as he neared the beach; swung out as soon as the skiff scraped onto pebbles, then dragged it halfway out of the water.

He ungloved his right hand and drew the silenced Beretta from the pouch at his belt, listening for the dogs. Nothing to hear other than the thin late-summer wind rustling branches in the pines, but that didn't have to mean they weren't somewhere nearby. The dogs were Dobermans, a breed that if properly trained could attack silently and swiftly under the cover of darkness. These two weren't reputed to be vicious, but you could never be sure about watchdogs.

The layout of the island was fixed in his memory. A topographical map he'd bought in Seattle had provided the contours, and the answers to a few discreet questions of area locals in Doe Bay had told him the rest of what he needed to know.

A quarter-mile wide and half-mile long, it was one of the smallest in a series of islands between the coast of Washington state and the southern tip of Vancouver Island. Volcanic in origin, some were large—Orcas Island had seven small communities on it—while others were unnamed vacation spots only big enough for a handful of buildings, the exclusive retreats of the well-to-do of Seattle and Bellingham. The waters surrounding them, frigid and treacherous in bad weather, were reachable only by private boat or ferry.

This one had been bought by a wealthy Seattle businessman in the early seventies as a summer retreat. He was dead now, and his surviving relatives had no interest in the property except as a source of rental income. One of those relatives had been a college acquaintance of Lukash's. A perfect place for Lukash to arrange to hole up for a while, or so he'd stupidly believed.

Brennan set off on a well-worn path that led north along the shoreline, one of five footpaths crisscrossing the island. Dressed in black clothing and a black woolen cap, he was a moving shadow etched against the still waters of Rosario Strait. Now and then he had to use the shielded beam of his LED penlight to guide him, but it wasn't far around to the east shore inlet. Not much more than a ten-minute walk, even in the midnight dark and at a retarded pace.

Where the path emerged from the woods he paused to reconnoiter. A squat boathouse bulked on the cove's near side, sided by a short wooden float. On the high ground above, the rest of the buildings were visible— main house, caretaker's cottage, utility shed where the generator that was the island's only source of power was housed. Diffused light showed at the cottage, but from this vantage point Brennan couldn't tell if it came from inside or an outside fixture. The main house, set at an angle overlooking the inlet and the open water beyond, appeared dark. If Lukash was in bed asleep, taking him would be that much easier.

Brennan made his way to the boathouse. Inside, with the door shut, he felt along the inshore wall; the structure was solidly built, with no large chinks between the boards that would leak flashes of light. The penlight showed him the two small craft anchored there. One, a fourteen-foot skiff similar to the one he'd rented in Doe Bay, belonged to the caretaker, a man named Denbow. The other was Lukash's inboard.

Brennan disabled the inboard first by removing the engine's rotor and sinking it into the dark water. Then he unbolted the outboard from the skiff's transom and sank that, removed the oars and pushed them out through the open end into the strait, where the currents would carry them away.

He still had the night to himself when he stepped back outside. No movement, no sounds except for the wind-rustle, the cry of a nightbird, the faint lapping of water against the float. All right, but where were the dogs? Penned up for some reason? A break, if so. Then he wouldn't have to shoot them.

Another path, this one of crushed oyster shells and wooden steps in a couple of places where the ground humped, led from the boathouse upslope a hundred yards or so to a terrace fronting the main house. Good-size place, built of pine logs and redwood, with a porch that wrapped around on three sides. The smaller, plainer caretaker's cottage stood at a distance to the south, the utility shed at an oblique angle between them.

Bent low, Brennan started up the incline to one side of the path so as to avoid making noise on the shells. He'd covered a third of the distance when he heard the muffled report.

No mistaking what it was—the gutty eruption of a shotgun. He couldn't tell where it had come from, only that it had been somewhere above. Whatever the reason for the shot, it hadn't been directed at him or he'd have seen the muzzle flash.

There was no second report. And the first hadn't set the dogs to barking.

Brennan ran up the rest of the way to the terrace, dodged across it past the shapes of wrought iron outdoor furniture. He crouched in the cover of shrubbery growing alongside the porch, watching, listening. Nothing to see, nothing to hear. The night was cloaked in silence again.

He waited another minute before moving again. He climbed half a dozen steps onto the porch, padded to a sliding glass door. Locked, curtains drawn behind it inside. Same with an adjacent window. He followed the porch around to the front, found the door and windows there equally secure, and went on around to the far side.

Another sliding glass door, this one with a dim yellow glow showing through a narrow gap between the closed curtains. Brennan laid an eye close to the glass. The gap was wide enough to allow him a partial view of what looked to be a study—desk, leather chairs, Indian rugs, native stone fireplace. A gooseneck desk lamp was the source of the light.

The other thing he saw, extended outward on the floor behind the desk, was a man's bent leg.

This door was unlocked. He slid it open with his gloved free hand, eased himself inside with the Beretta upraised. The room was empty except for the man on the floor. The silence here and in the rest of the house was acute.

He crossed to the desk, leaned over to look down. Sightless eyes stared up at him out of a middle-aged, bearded face. Anthony Lukash had been clean-shaven in the photo Brennan had been given but there was no mistaking that mole on the left cheek. Lukash hadn't been dead very long; the blood was bright crimson around the hole between his eyes. Shot at close range with a small caliber handgun.

Nothing much surprised Brennan anymore, but this did. What the hell?

He straightened, scanned the room. A picture had been pulled away from the pine paneling next to the fireplace. The door to the wall safe behind it was wide open. Even at a distance he could tell that it was empty.

The desktop was bare except for the lamp; the drawers were full of nothing.

Nothing on the body, either.

Everything important gone, taken away. Laptop, cell phone; Lukash would have brought both, even though there was no internet service out here and cell service was sporadic. Flash disk. Hard copy of the design specs, if he'd printed one. And the $75,000 in cash.

The inner study door opened into a short hallway. With the aid of the penlight, Brennan looked into the rest of the rooms. Waste of a couple of minutes, but he had to be sure the house was empty.

He went out through the study door, down off the porch. From the south corner he had a clear look at the caretaker's cottage. The light still burned over there. An inside light, its glow brighter now because the front door stood half open.

The wind had picked up, its faint disturbance of the trees and shrubbery all there was to hear. Shapes and shadows all stationary within the range of vision. Brennan ran across to the near side of the cottage, away from the lighted doorway. Paused there long enough to listen to the silence, then climbed a side set of steps and edged along a narrow porch to the door.

He went in fast, fanning left and right with the Beretta. Small, cluttered living room, the odor of cheap whiskey strong in the air. And another dead man on the floor.

This one was tall, thin, sprawled belly-up in front of the hearth, his head and face a bloody red ruin. The fireplace stones and mantel behind him were peppered with buckshot, spattered with gore.

An open wallet lay beside the body. Brennan picked it up with his gloved hand, saw that it was empty of everything except for Arthur Denbow's Washington state driver's license, and dropped it. He didn't touch the body. He detoured around it, took a cursory look into the living room and the other three rooms. None of the missing items were here, either.

He quit the cottage through a door off the kitchen. At the rear was a wire-fenced kennel, and on a bed of pine needles and leaf mold near it he found the two Doberman watchdogs. A quick look with the penlight was all he needed to tell that each had been shot once in the head.

Lukash and the dogs killed with a handgun, the caretaker with a shotgun. Why the use of two different weapons? One thing seemed certain: the shooter had been known to the dogs; no stranger could get close enough to a pair of trained Dobermans to put bullets in their heads without being torn to pieces.

So who the hell was responsible for all this carnage? Somebody Lukash had contacted about disposal of the design specs? An acquaintance of Denbow's? It didn't figure to be anyone complicit in the original theft. All indications were that Lukash had acted alone. Used his position as a research engineer with the large industrial outfit known privately as the Company to embezzle the $75,000, then found a way to bypass security measures and steal the specs, and disappeared with both. Bright, crafty, gutsy, but with a couple of screws loose to have expected to get away clean.

As soon as the theft was discovered, the Company had called in the investigation firm Brennan worked for, specialists in cases of industrial espionage. He was their best field man, a loner whose methods were unorthodox and who now and then crossed the line. There were some who thought he had a screw loose himself, but he didn't care. Results, whatever it took to get them, was what he was paid for.

It had taken eight days to track Lukash and uncover the link to the old college acquaintance, the son of the island's deceased owner. The fact that he was still holed up here meant that he still had the goods in his possession. He hadn't tried to ransom them back to the Company so he must have intended on selling them to the highest bidder, domestic or foreign. Brennan didn't know what the specs were for, just that it was some sort of electronic device; he didn't want to know. All he needed to know was that the device was valuable and the Company wanted the specs and the money back—and Lukash taken out of commission, one way or another.

Well, that part of it had already been done by somebody else. The damn fool must have been careless in concealing his hideout, his hoard, or both. $75,000 in cash was more than enough to tempt the commission of a double murder; the specs even more so if the shooter had found out or guessed how much they were worth.

The crazy goddamn coincidence of Brennan's arrival and the slaughter was galling. His timing couldn't have been much worse. If he'd come out here this afternoon, or made the crossing just a couple of hours earlier tonight, he could have prevented all this from happening.

But it wasn't too late. The shooter and the plunder were still somewhere on the island. The boathouse had to be where he'd gone when he finished up here, and when he found both boats disabled he'd have known there was someone else on the island, someone alive and with a purpose.

What would he do then? Two options: stay put and try to repair one of the boats, or go hunting for the intruder or the craft he'd come in. He had to have a piece of luggage with him to hold the plunder, if nothing else; he wouldn't let go of it for long, or lug it on a hunt in the dark. And he had no way of knowing if the intruder was armed.

It hadn't been long since the shotgun blast. Chances were he was still in the boathouse.

From this vantage point Brennan could see only part of the structure. That portion was swathed in darkness, but that didn't have to mean anything. The shooter would have a flashlight and be careful how he used it.

Beyond the kennel was another stretch of pine woods. Brennan took a zigzag route to them, then headed downslope inside their outer edge. Thick-dark in there even so; he went slowly so as not to trip over something, stumble into one of the trees.

The stand of pines thinned as he neared the inlet. He halted at a point opposite the boathouse, separated from it by thirty yards of open ground coated with ferns. The only audible sounds were those made by the wind.

He stepped out of the tree cover and started over there, skirting a rotting moss-covered log—

Bright flash from the thick shadows at the inland corner, sudden explosive noise, stinging pain along his left side and enough impact to knock him off his feet.

He didn't stay where he fell; if he had, the second shotgun blast would have cut him in half. He rolled sideways, scrambled behind the rotting log in time to avoid being pinned by a flashlight beam.

Ambush. The son of a bitch had spotted him moving around up above.

Pain radiated along his right arm, his right side, but the charge of buckshot had been a glancing hit and missed a vital spot. He could still use his arm, but he'd lost the Beretta in the fall or the scramble.

For a few seconds the flash beam probed for him over and around the log, then winked out. Sharp clicking sound… a fresh shell being jacked into the chamber of a pump-action shotgun.

Brennan's hand was slick with blood from the arm wound. He sat up and wiped it off on his pant leg, sliding the hand downward to the cuff.

Slithery movement on the other side of the log.

Brennan yanked the cuff up, drew the backup .32 automatic holstered on his calf. At the same time he fumbled the penlight out with his left hand.

The dark shapes of man and upraised shotgun appeared not more than ten feet away, silhouetted against the starlit sky.

Brennan stabbed him with the penlight beam, freezing him just long enough to make him a clear target, and then fired five rounds as fast as he could squeeze the automatic's trigger. Killshots, one or more of them. The man grunted, jerked, went down fast and hard on top of the shotgun and stayed that way.

Brennan held the light on him while he sucked in air to get his breathing under control, then used the log as a fulcrum to shove onto his feet. He felt steady enough, the pain from the buckshot wounds ebbing now. When he turned the light on his arm and side he found the damage to be superficial, more blood than torn flesh and not too much of that. He wouldn't bleed to death before he got back to Doe Bay, and he could patch himself up in his motel room.

He found the Beretta easily enough, pocketed it. Then, with the toe of his shoe, he pushed the dead man over onto his back. Same age and size as the corpse in the caretaker's cottage: mid-forties, tall and gangly thin in a bullet-torn wool shirt and Levi's. The only items of interest in the pockets were a .32 caliber Ruger revolver and a California driver's license issued to a Thomas Kinsey. The face in the license photograph might have been the dead man's, but Brennan didn't think so.

No, Thomas Kinsey was the one in cottage with his head blown apart. This one was the caretaker, Denbow.

Substitution switch—that had been Denbow's game. He must have found out about Lukash's stash a few days ago, made contact with Kinsey—a man he knew, or a stranger he latched onto because of the resemblance—and lured him out to the island on some pretext or other. Maybe got him drunk enough to pass out, then went to shoot Lukash and claim the valuables. The dogs had been next, Kinsey the last to be disposed of with the shotgun.

Clever enough plan, a better one than Lukash's. Denbow would have left the island in Lukash's rented boat, abandoned the boat in Seattle or Bellingham, then gone anywhere he chose using Kinsey's ID. The bodies might not have been found for weeks. Two inhabitants of a lonely island murdered, with no apparent motive or suspects—a case to baffle the authorities for years.

Brennan, through blind luck, had spoiled the game and created an even more puzzling mystery—three human corpses, each shot with a different weapon. Not that it mattered to him. All that did matter was finishing what he'd been hired to do.

He found Lukash's computer and cell phone, the flash disk and bundles of cash, in a suitcase inside the boathouse where Denbow had stashed it before setting up his ambush. He carried the suitcase around to the gravel beach, taking his time, resting now and then to conserve his strength. Stowed it in the skiff's stern and wrestled the craft off the pebbles into the water.

The buckshot wounds were giving him hell again by the time he shoved off in the direction of Doe Bay. He ought to get a bonus from the Company, if not his employers, for what he'd been through tonight, but he probably wouldn't. They'd say it was all just part of the job.

Fletcher Flora was another writer whose name was never far from the pages of the digest magazines of the fifties and sixties. His work was seemingly everywhere and like Charles Runyon, he also wrote books under the "Ellery Queen" byline, three of them. Stark House has published four of his harder-edged novels, including Park Avenue Tramp in A Trio of Gold Medals, and a single volume containing three more of his books. Always entertaining, frequently sardonic, Flora is another author whose work is ripe for rediscovery. His body of work remains one of the great not-quite-forgotten "secrets" of the genre....

THE SILENT ONE

Fletcher Flora

That afternoon the old man put me after the bugs on the potato plants, and I was out there in the patch with the spray, cursing and grumbling some because I didn't want to do it, and about two o'clock along came Henry and Oliver carrying .22 rifles I don't mind saying it surprised me to see them together that way, because Henry never had anything to do with Oliver unless there was some reason he had to, and I stopped pumping the spray and looked at them, and Henry said, "You want to go after crows with us, Bruce?" and I said, "The old man says I got to spray the lousy potato plants, so I can't."

"That's tough," Henry said.

"It sure as hell is," I said.

"Well, we're going after crows," Henry said, and I said, "You told me that once," and he said, "I guess I did, at that."

"They're pretty hard to hit with a rifle," I said. "You got to get them sitting," he said.

"That's pretty hard, too," I said. "It's pretty hard to get close enough."

"Don't I know," he said, and I said, "Seems like they always hear you and fly away, no matter how quiet you are," and he said, "Seems like it, all right," and I said, "I bet you don't get a damn one."

He looked at me and said, "Put your money where your mouth is," and I said, "Oh, sure, sure," and then we both dropped it because neither one of us had a cent and couldn't have bet even if we'd wanted to, which we didn't, really.

Oliver didn't say anything at all, but just stood looking off across the potato patch and the pasture to the cornfield, and I saw that he had a fat lip, and said, "What happened to him?" and Henry said, "You mean old Oliver?" and I said, "Sure, I mean Oliver. Who else I mean?" and Henry said, "You mean his fat lip?" and I said, "Sure, I mean his fat lip."

Henry began to study Oliver's face without saying anything for a while, and as far as you could tell, Oliver didn't even know he was being studied, and as a matter of fact you'd have thought he hadn't even heard us talking about him. He just kept looking off the other way toward the cornfield, and there was this quiet kind of look on his face that was a kind of immune look, if you know what I mean, and it seemed to be out of reach of anything Henry and I could say or do. He was a damn queer kid when you came right down to it, and what Henry and I didn't like about him most was that he looked and acted more like a girl than a boy and was always very quiet and everything like that. When he was around, which wasn't any more often than we could help, we hardly ever said anything directly to him, but talked to each other *about* him, just like this time, like he was a stump or couldn't understand or speak up for itself if it wanted to.

Everyone called him Henry's brother, but he really wasn't. He was his step-brother, that's what he was, and Henry's father had got married to Oliver's mother about a year back, and there was old Henry stuck with Oliver and nothing he could do about it. He was a frail sort of kid, Oliver was, with thin arms and legs and a head too big for his body and eyes too big for his head, and he'd have looked very strange if he hadn't been so pretty, but as it was, he was so pretty in the face that you hardly noticed how queer he looked other places. Even now, with a fat lip, he was pretty.

After he'd studied Oliver a while, Henry said, "I hit him in the mouth," and held out his right hand in a fist to show how a knuckle was skinned, and I said, "What'd you hit him in the mouth for?"

"Well," Henry said, "he's always making me look bad, that's why," and I said, "About what?" and he said, "Oh, just about everything," and I said, "About what in particular that made you hit him in the mouth?" and he said, "Damn it, nothing in particular. You know how Oliver is. You keep wanting to hit him in the mouth, and sooner or later you do it."

"That's right," I said. "I'll admit I've wanted to hit him in the mouth a few times myself. What I can't figure out is, why the hell you taking him with you after crows?"

"Because I have to, that's why," Henry said.

I said, "Why do you have to?" and he said, "Because Oliver's old lady says we've got to be real brothers and do things together. I'll have to take him damn near every place I go, I guess. It's what I get for hitting him in the mouth. It sort of brought things to a head."

He always said Oliver's old lady, like she wasn't his own old lady at all, and I guess she wasn't really, just in a technical way because his old man had married her, and I started pumping the spray again, and said, "I don't mind telling you I'd hate to have Oliver tagging around after me all the time, and I'd probably wind up hitting him in the mouth again," and he said, "Well, I don't like it myself, and I may wind up the same way, but it'll be better all around if I can just hold out until it dies down sort of naturally.

To tell the truth, I don't think Oliver likes me any more than I like him, especially now, after what's happened."

"Well, I hope you get some crows," I said, "but I bet you don't."

"Thanks," he said. "You sure you can't come along? You could finish with the bugs after you get back."

"No. I couldn't do that. The old man said to spray the lousy potatoes, and when my old man says to do something he doesn't mean after I get through doing something else, he means first thing."

He said so-long then and said he'd come back by the potato patch and show me how many crows he got, and I said that was a laugh and he probably wouldn't have any and that I was ready to bet on it, though I wasn't, and he went down between two rows of potatoes and climbed through the barbed wire fence into the pasture. Oliver went after him and through the fence, too, and they went across the pasture and through the fence on the other side with Oliver tagging along about six steps behind all the way. After they got into the corn beyond the pasture, I couldn't see them any longer, and I finished pumping up the spray and went ahead with the bugs. It was getting pretty hot, and the spray didn't smell very good, stinking in fact, and I got to cursing and grumbling again, and the truth is, my old man would have taken the hide off me if he'd heard what I called him.

After a while I heard the little smack of a .22, and the crows began to raise hell all of a sudden, and I straightened up and looked and saw a black cloud of them rising from the tall hedgerow on the far side of the cornfield, and I said, "I bet he didn't get a damn one." I kept standing straight for a minute, watching the crows rise, but I was more listening than watching, because even when a crow is angry or excited or scared, his caw is still lazy-sounding and mournful, like he's grieving about something and isn't in any hurry because he knows he's going to have forever to grieve in, and it's about the saddest sound on earth. I don't know of any sadder ones, anyhow.

The black cloud stayed high against the blue sky above the hedge for a few minutes, and then the crows settled into the hedge again down a way from the place they'd risen from, and I turned and bent my back and started pumping the spray once more. After that for a while, I kept hearing the flat smack of the little .22's and the sad, raucous complaining of the crows, but I didn't stop again to look up, but kept right on after the bugs, cursing and grumbling and thinking that I'd never be a lousy farmer when I grew up, and it was a pretty long time later when I realized that the sounds of the .22's and the crows had stopped and hadn't started again. Old Henry's quit already, I thought, and I bet he didn't get a damn one. I happened to be at the end of a row at the lower end of the garden just then, and I stopped pumping and straightened up to look off toward the hedge beyond the cornfield, and I thought maybe Henry would be coming back, but I didn't see him, and then I thought that if he hadn't got any crows, he probably wouldn't come back by way of the garden at all, because he knew I'd ride him, and he wouldn't like it. My back was aching quite a bit, and I rubbed it and tried to stretch out the ache, and just then Oliver came out of the corn on the near side and started across the pasture, but Henry wasn't with him.

I wished old Oliver would stay away, because I didn't like him, and he always just stood around and made you uncomfortable by not saying anything, but he kept on coming, carrying the .22, and I waited for him. He came through the fence and up to me and stood looking at me, and he had this quiet expression on his face, his lips soft and still and his eyes like two big black pools in the shadows of his long lashes.

"Where's Henry?" I said.

"I think he's dead," he said.

From the way his voice sounded, he might have said, "I think he's gone home," or something like that, it was so undisturbed and natural, and I didn't get what he said at first, and after I got it, I thought he was joking, though it was a pretty poor kind of joke.

"Oh, sure," I said. "I know what happened, all right. He didn't get a damn crow just like I said, so he went home another way."

Oliver shook his head. "No. I shot him with my .22. It was an accident."

I began to get scared then, and I said, "What the hell you talking about?" and he said, "There's a hole right behind his ear. I'm pretty sure he's dead."

When he said that, I knew he meant it, and I'd never felt before like I felt at that moment, and I hope I never feel that way again, and the truth is, I acted crazy. I began running toward the fence, and then I stopped and ran back and said, "The old man's up in the barn. You go tell him to come down."

I didn't wait to see if he went, but tore out myself and lunged through the barbed wire fence into the pasture. One of the barbs hooked my jeans and ripped the flesh of one leg, and another barb on the upper strand almost took the shirt off my back, but I didn't even know this until later, and I went flying across to the fence on the other side and put a hand on the top of a post and vaulted over and bulled into the corn in a way that would have made the old man kick my backside around sixty acres if he'd seen me. On the opposite side of the cornfield, there wasn't any barbed wire fence, but the tall hedgerow instead that had thorns as bad as the barbs, and I pushed through it to the other side and stopped and looked around for Henry, but I didn't see him.

Then I did. Back from the hedge about thirty feet there was a grove of walnut trees, and Henry was lying among the trees on the ground, and I called his name, but he didn't move or answer. He was lying on his stomach with his head turned so that half of his face showed, and I went over and looked down at him. He looked queer, somehow not like Henry at all, and he was dead, all right, and the little hole was behind his ear. There was a dead crow on the ground beside him, so he'd got one after all, and I was glad he'd proved me wrong, and I only wished he could've come back by the potato patch and rubbed it into me a little.

I don't know how to say how I felt. However it was, it wasn't the way you'd expect a guy to feel. No way at all, mostly. Numb, I mean. I thought I ought to be doing something for old Henry, but of course there wasn't anything I could do that would make any difference, and I thought I ought to be showing how sorry I was, because I really liked him and was going to miss him and feel bad for a long time, maybe always, but nothing seemed to get into me or out of me through the numbness. Pretty soon the old man came up behind me with Oliver, and I looked at the old man, and his face was gray and craggy drawn tight over its bones.

Oliver stayed behind us a few steps, and finally the old man said to him over a shoulder, "How did it happen, Oliver?" and Oliver said, "Well, Henry was there, and I was in back of him, and all of a sudden the gun went off. I guess I didn't have the safety on." His voice was still the same as it had been in the potato patch, quiet and flat and undisturbed, and he stopped for a second or two and then said, "It was an accident."

The old man's voice sounded very angry. "Of course it was an accident," he said. "That's all these damn guns are good for. Accidents and tragedies. Now I don't know what to do." He paused and considered and then continued as if he were thinking aloud, "Seems to me when something like this happens you're supposed to leave things alone until someone comes to look them over. The sheriff or someone."

Behind him, Oliver said softly, "It was an accident," and the old man said in the angry voice, "I know it was an accident," and I turned and looked back at Oliver, and at first I was angry myself because it was all his fault that Henry was dead, and then in a flash I wasn't angry at all. I was afraid. Oliver was staring at the back of the old man's head, and his pretty face was very still, and his eyes were wide open and black and flat and intently calculating, and what I wanted to do was turn and run through the walnut grove and away from there as fast as I could. It's hard to explain or describe a fear like the fear I had.

The old man jerked into motion and went over and picked up Henry in his arms. "I don't care what the regular thing to do is," he said. "I'm going to take Henry across the fields to his own house. Come along, Oliver. Bruce, you go up to the yard. You can forget about the rest of the potatoes."

He walked away with Henry in his arms, and I watched him go along the hedgerow, and then I realized that Oliver hadn't made any move to follow yet. All at once he said, "Bruce," in his soft voice, and I forced myself to look at him, remembering how he'd come up to tell me that Henry was dead, how he'd walked in no hurry, as if he were just on his way home from somewhere or other with nothing much on his mind.

"What?" I said, and he said, "It's awful how accidents can happen, isn't it?" and then he just kept on standing there, not moving and not saying anything more, just staring at me with his wide black calculating eyes.

I turned and went back up to the house and sat in the yard in the sun, but I was cold and couldn't get warm, even though it was summer, and I wonder why it is they go to so much trouble in stories and movies describing or picturing things to scare you, because things like that are phony and easily forgotten, but the thing that really scares you and that you can't forget is maybe something that you've seen lots of times and don't even know what it's really like until you see it in a certain way at a certain time.

Like Oliver's face in the walnut grove, I mean.

In her essay collection "The Romantic Manifesto" Ayn Rand called Fredric Brown "an unusually ingenious writer" and I can't think of a more apt description. Brown wrote science fiction as well as crime fiction and could be wickedly funny in both the long and short form. I used to buy copies of his novel Martians, Go Home *and pass them out to friends who said they didn't like reading. He won an Edgar in 1947 for* The Fabulous Clipjoint *and no less a hardboiled maven than Mickey Spillane called Brown his favorite writer of all time. There are two books out there about Brown's life and work, a biography by Jack Seabrook, and the Chad Calkins published memoir by Brown's second wife. Both books shine a wonderful spotlight on Mr. Brown….*

BEWARE OF THE DOG

Fredric Brown

The seed of murder was planted in the mind of Wiley Hughes the first time he saw the old man open the safe.

There was money in the safe. Stacks of it.

The old man took three bills from one orderly pile and handed them to Wiley. They were twenties.

"Sixty dollars even, Mr. Hughes," he said. "And that's the ninth payment." He took the receipt Wiley gave him, closed the safe, and twisted the dial.

It was a small, antique-looking safe. A man could open it with a cold chisel and a good crowbar, if he didn't have to worry about how much noise he made.

The old man walked with Wiley out of the house and down to the iron fence. After he'd closed the gate behind Wiley, he went over to the tree and untied the dog again. Wiley looked back over his shoulder at the gate, and at the sign upon it: "Beware of the Dog."

There was a padlock on the gate too, and a bell button set in the gatepost. If you wanted to see old man Erskine you had to push that button and wait until he'd come out of the house and tied up the dog and then unlocked the gate to let you in.

Not that the padlocked gate meant anything. An ablebodied man could get over the fence easily enough. But once in the yard he'd be torn to pieces by that hound of hell Erskine kept for a watchdog.

A vicious brute, that dog.

A lean, underfed hound with slavering jaws and eyes that looked death at you as you walked by. He didn't run to the fence and bark. Nor even growl.

Just stood there, turning his head to follow you, with his yellowish teeth bared in a snarl that was the more sinister in that it was silent.

A black dog, with yellow hate-filled eyes, and a quiet viciousness beyond ordinary canine ferocity. A killer dog. Yes, it was a hound of hell, all right.

And a beast of nightmare, too. Wiley dreamed about it that night. And the next.

There was something he wanted very badly in those dreams. Or somewhere he wanted to go. And his way was barred by a monstrous black hound, with slavering jowls and eyes that looked death at you. Except for size, it was old man Erskine's watchdog.

The seed of murder grew.

Wiley Hughes lived, as it happened, only a block from the old man's house. Every time he went past it on his way to or from work he thought about it.

It would be so easy.

The dog? He could poison the dog. There were some things he wanted to find out, without asking about them. Patiently, at the office, he cultivated the acquaintance of the collector who had dealt with the old man before he had been transferred to another route.

He went out drinking with the man several times before the subject of the old man crept into the conversation—and then, after they'd discussed many other debtors.

"Old Erskine? The guy's a miser, that's all. He pays for that stock on time because he can't bear to part with a big chunk of money all at once. Ever see all the money he keeps in—?"

Wiley steered the conversation into safer channels. He didn't want to have discussed how much money the old man kept in the house. "Ever see a more vicious dog than that hound of his?"

The other collector shook his head. "And neither did anybody else. That mutt hates even the old man. Can't blame him for that, though; the old geezer half starves him to keep him fierce."

"The hell," said Wiley. "How come he doesn't jump Erskine then?"

"Trained not to, that's all. Nor Erskine's son—he visits there once in a while. Nor the man who delivers groceries. But anybody else he'd tear to pieces."

And then Wiley Hughes dropped the subject like a hot coal and began to talk about the widow who was always behind in her payments and who always cried if they threatened to foreclose.

The dog tolerated two people besides the old man. And that meant that if he could get past the dog without harming it, or it harming him, suspicion would be directed toward those two people.

It was a big if, but then the fact that the dog was underfed made it possible. If the way to a man's heart is through his stomach, why not the way to a dog's heart?

It was worth trying.

He went about it very carefully. He bought the meat at a butcher shop at the other side of town. He took every precaution that night, when he left his own house heading into the alley, that no one would see him.

Keeping to the middle of the alley, he walked past old man Erskine's fence, and kept walking. The dog was there, just inside the fence, and it kept pace with him, soundlessly.

He threw a piece of meat over the fence and kept walking.

To the corner and back again. He walked just a little closer to the fence and threw another piece of meat over. This time he saw the dog leave the fence and run for the meat.

He returned home, unseen, and feeling that things were working out his way. The dog was hungry; it would eat meat he threw to it. Pretty soon it would be taking food from his hand, through the fence.

He made his plans carefully, and omitted no factor.

The few tools he would need were purchased in such a way that they could not be traced to him. And wiped off fingerprints; they would be left at the scene of the burglary.

He studied the habits of the neighborhood and knew that everyone in the block was asleep by one o'clock, except for two night workers who didn't return from work until four-thirty.

There was the patrolman to consider. A few sleepless nights, at a darkened window gave him the information that the patrolman passed at one and again at four.

The hour between two and three, then, was the safest. And the dog. His progress in making friends with the dog had been easier and more rapid than he had anticipated. It took food from his hand, through the bars of the alley fence.

It let him reach through the bars and pet it. He'd been afraid of losing a finger or two the first time he'd tried that. But the fear had been baseless.

The dog had been as starved for affection as it had been starved for food.

Hound of hell, hell! He grinned to himself at the extravagance of the descriptive phrase he had once used.

Then came the night when he dared climb over the fence. The dog met him with little whimpers of delight. He'd been sure it would, but he'd taken every precaution two pairs of trousers, three shirts, and a scarf wrapped many times around his throat. And meat to offer, more tempting than his own. There was nothing to it, after that.

Friday, then, was to be that night. Everything was ready.

So ready that between eight o'clock in the evening and two in the morning, there was nothing for him to do. So ready he set and muffled his alarm, and slept.

Nothing to the burglary at all. Or the murder.

Down the alley, taking extra precautions this time that no one saw him. There was enough moonlight for him to read, and to grin at the "Beware of the Dog" sign on the back gate.

Beware of the dog! That was a laugh, now. He handed it a piece of meat through the fence, patted its head while it ate, and went up toward the house.

His crowbar opened a window, easily.

Silently he crept up the stairs to the bedroom of the old man, and there he did what it was necessary for him to do in order to be able to open the safe without danger of being heard.

The murder was really necessary, he told himself. Stunned—even tied up—the old man might possibly have managed to raise an alarm. Or might have recognized his assailant, even in the darkness.

The safe offered a bit more difficulty than he had anticipated, but not too much. Well before three o'clock—with an hour's factor of safety—he had it open and had the money.

It was only on his way out through the yard, after everything had gone perfectly, that Wiley Hughes began to worry and to wonder whether he had made any possible mistake. There was a brief instant of panic.

But then he was safely home, and he thought over every step he had taken, and there was no possible clue that would lead the police to suspect Wiley Hughes.

Inside the house, in sanctuary, he counted the money under a light that wouldn't show outside. Monday he would put it in a safe deposit box he had already rented under an assumed name.

Meanwhile, any hiding place would serve. But he was taking no chances; he had prepared a good one. That afternoon he had spaded the big flower bed in the back yard.

Now, keeping close under cover of the fence, so he could not be seen in the remotely possible case of a neighbor looking from a window, he scooped a hollow in the freshly spaded earth.

No need to bury it deep; a shallow hole, refilled, in the freshly turned soil would be best, and would never on earth be detected by human eyes. He wrapped the money in oiled paper, buried it, and covered the hole carefully, leaving no trace whatsoever.

By four o'clock he was in bed, and lay there thinking pleasantly of all the things that he could do with the money once it would be safe for him to begin spending it.

It was almost nine when he awakened the next morning. And again, for a moment, there was reaction and panic. For seconds that seemed hours as he lay rigidly, trying to recall everything he had done. Step by step he went over it and gradually confidence returned.

He had been seen by no one; he had left no possible clue.

His cleverness in getting past the dog without killing it would certainly throw suspicion elsewhere.

It had been easy, so easy for a clever man to commit a crime without leaving a single lead. Ridiculously easy. There was no possible—

Through the open window of his bedroom he heard voices that seemed excited about something. One of them sounded like the voice of the policeman on the day shift. Probably, then, the crime had been discovered. By why—?

He ran to the window and looked out.

A little knot of people were gathered in the alley behind his house, looking into the yard.

His gaze turned more directly downward and he knew then that he was lost. Across the freshly turned earth of the flower bed, strewn in wild profusion, was a disorderly array of banknotes, like flat green plants that had sprouted too soon.

And asleep on the grass, his nose beside the torn oiled paper in which Wiley had brought him the meat and which Wiley had used later to wrap the banknotes, was the black dog.

The dangerous, vicious, beware-of-the-dog, the hound of hell, whose friendship he had won so thoroughly that it had dug its way under the fence and followed him home.

When I've read books or watched movies or television shows about hit men, there's always been a nagging little voice in the back of my head. Assuming you can actually find someone to bump off your intended victim, can you really get away with it? If you've ever wondered about some of the same things I did, you might find the following story enjoyable....

HIT ME

Rick Ollerman

Every night it seemed Amanda was on me when I came home late, nagging from the jump about where I'd been, why I kept staying out so late, and on and on and on. *Jesus, woman*, I wanted to scream. *Why can't you just give it up already?*

It would be great if I could tell her that it takes time to set certain things up but that would be self-defeating. So I just kept making up stories: work kept me late, some of the guys and I went out for beers, Joe needed help with his car, Charlie was celebrating whatever. Don't worry, things would get back to normal soon. Anytime now. Really.

"Can't you at least call and tell me what's going on with you?" she'd ask. "I hate all this worrying."

"Sure," I said, apologizing. But I never did. I wasn't putting a lot of stock in her feelings just then. She could ask whatever questions she liked as far as I was concerned, as long as she stayed the hell out of my way. This would all end sometime in the near future, I knew. Just as soon as I could find someone I trusted enough to kill her.

I married my wife when she was still gorgeous. A figure you could die for, Mediterranean features that were just off enough—a small bump on her nose, a crooked chin, slightly bucked teeth—that gave her that exotic look while being just enough to keep her from the cover-girl good looking type. She was beautiful, though. Those flaws may not have been what a modeling agency looked for, but they made men turn their heads when she entered a crowd. And when she wore a bikini or something designed to show off her bust line or her waist....

But that was twenty six years ago. We'd raised two kids who were long out of the house and even further from our lives. What's the point in having kids that suck up all your time, most of your money, then end up hating you and taking off, never giving a damn about seeing you again?

Now the middle-aged spread had gotten hold of Amanda. Those hips aren't what they once were, the backs of those thighs were more cottage cheese than nylon ads. They still looked good in something loose or baggy but that wasn't what I wanted her wearing to bed.

The thing that really bothered me was that we weren't all that old. We were both in our early fifties, not too old to find love again. Yes, we were in love once, but time and the kids had worn all that away. Why not get a divorce, give us each a chance to start anew?

I asked her about it. It wasn't hard, but I realized later it was a mistake. At first Amanda didn't believe I was serious, but I didn't back down. Gradually she realized I meant what I was saying but she wouldn't budge from telling me she still loved me, we were soul mates and she wanted to be with me forever.

"What the hell for?" I yelled. "We barely sleep together anymore, we used to complete each other's sentences and now we talk over each other instead. The kids couldn't care less one way or the other. We don't kiss goodnight, we don't kiss each other good morning, and half the time I don't even know what you're doing."

"You're my soul mate," she'd say quietly, starting to accept my feelings. "I can't let you go."

"Maybe we were once, but things change. Life changes," I said. "Maybe we both did, too. The point is we're kidding ourselves now."

"I don't want a divorce."

And that became the mantra. I'd try again every few months. Amanda started seeing a therapist. Good, I thought. Tell it to someone else. She wanted me to go with her but I refused. I already knew what needed to happen. The question was how to do it.

One of the problems was that Amanda had more money than I did. When her parents had passed and she was left a good bit of inheritance, especially after we'd sold their house on Long Island. I wanted my half of that money. I was her husband. I was entitled to it. But I knew she wouldn't give up a cent if I walked out. The lawyers would probably get more than I did.

Months went by after I first suggested we split up. The therapist seemed to be helping Amanda but I was growing more and more miserable. Now that it was out in the open, I just wanted it done. I wanted things over. But I needed a settlement that gave me what I had coming. I just knew Amanda wouldn't give it to me.

I started spending more and more time away from home. That's how I met Rita, at one of the bars some of us went to after work. She was a waitress and she had no interest in what a bunch of salesmen from an industrial refrigeration equipment manufacturer did, but I'd stopped wearing my ring—something else that pissed off Amanda—and I made Rita laugh. At first I thought she must be that weird kind of chick that liked gallows humor but then I thought it was more than that. She actually thought I was joking about my life when I was actually complaining about it.

We started a little something on the side. It wasn't much but it was a good distraction from what was going on at home with my wife. Half the time when I went home I just fell asleep on the living room couch, not even bothering to go all the way up to bed. After a while I wasn't even sure Amanda noticed.

Things were going well with Rita and at some point I started to have thoughts of Amanda just not coming home one day. I wanted her to drive off to her little bookkeeping job at the country club across town and just… not come home. Oh, I wasn't picturing her in any flaming car wrecks or anything, it's not like I had a *lot* of hate or anger against her. I just wanted her gone. Just… gone.

But she'd leave in the morning, I'd leave in the morning, eventually I'd come home and there she'd be, always there, always waiting.

I grew angrier more of the time, became short-tempered. She'd say something to be nice and I'd bite her head off. A couple of times I must have had some sort of look in my eye because she'd sob and tell me to just go ahead and hit her. Like she thought it was something I wanted to do, something I needed to get out of my system. Strange stuff, I thought.

But it did get me thinking: what if I did hit her? Would that be enough to make her leave?

It wasn't something I could do anyway. She'd call the cops, I'd get arrested, maybe even lose my job, but I'd certainly risk any access I had to that dough sitting in her own checking account. We each had one and either of us could sign checks on the two accounts but that didn't do me a whole lot of good. If I wrote the one check, cleared her out, what would I do then? Run? She'd sure as hell want it back and I knew she'd involve the police.

Clearly we were in a rut the size of the Mariana Trench. I still wouldn't go to counseling because I thought it would resolve exactly nothing. She still wouldn't give up the divorce, lord knew why. What the hell did I have to do? She didn't seem keen on having an accident and I kept coming home, night after night, to her car parked on her side of the two-car garage, just like always.

Always.

It was too much. I wished she'd just die, but it wasn't like I could kill her, give her some untraceable drug that would give her a heart attack and then disappear from her system before the post-mortem. I couldn't do anything. When a spouse dies, the first person the cops look at is the other one. Everyone knows that. In the grand scheme of things, that probably cut down on a lot of murders, but it didn't help me any. I couldn't kill anyone anyway. I was a refrigeration salesman, for chrissake.

That shouldn't stop anyone else from taking a whack at it, though.

How do you go about hiring a hitman? As far as I could tell, you just sort of put it out there, let it be known that there was something you wanted done, that you'd pay for it, but it was a bad thing and it had to be a secret. I was intrigued. I didn't *have* to go through with anything, did I? So there was no real harm in asking around, trying to find the right someone. I could always back out. If I didn't actually pay anybody to do anything, or even negotiate hard terms, I might not even be guilty of conspiracy.

It was an interesting thought. To me, anyway. I put it to Rita the next night I saw her. I made a joke out of it, even though I was serious, because she still thought everything I said was half a joke anyway.

"There are some guys around here," she said. "You hear things, but I can't believe they're true."

"Why not?" I asked her, giving her a quick rub beneath her bar apron.

"Not here, silly," she said, stepping back with a twinkle in her eye.

"Why don't you believe those things?"

"Well, look at that guy over there." She gave a sideways indication with her pencil. "Like I said, you hear things, but if they were real, would he still be sitting there, coming in here two or three nights a week?" She shook her head, one of her large hoop earrings getting caught up in her curls. "He'd have to be in jail or something, wouldn't he?"

Not if he was any good, I thought.

"Well, okay," I told her, not wanting to seem too interested. "So am I seeing you tonight?"

She winked at me. "I'm off at twelve."

I knew Rita would ask about it later and I'd just tell her she made me curious. I'd make her think it was all her idea.

I took the stool next to the guy at the bar she'd pointed out and ordered a beer. The bartender set out a coaster, poured a draft and set it down in front of me. He didn't ask for money so I knew I could take care of it later. The guy I was interested in was to my left and I sat turned on my stool so that he was in front of me.

"Hey, there," I said, my hand shaking so much I had to put down my beer without taking a sip.

He turned his head slowly, gave me a quick glance, said, "Hey," and turned back to his own drink.

I forced a large gulp from my beer and set it back down, but too hard, and only halfway on the coaster. The guy in front of me turned around again. It seemed to be now or never.

"I heard you— do things," I said.

"Oh, yeah?" he said, raising an eyebrow. He turned around to face me. "What kind of things?"

"Oh, I don't know." Stupid answer! He was going to think I was an asshole. "Quiet ones." It was the best I could do.

Now he looked me over more carefully. "You want to talk quiet things?" he asked.

I was nervous but tried not to show it. I nodded once.

"Hmm," he said, reaching forward to my two-thirds full beer and picking it up. I thought he was about to drink it in front of me, maybe lift his leg on my trouser leg, but instead he flicked his wrist and dumped it down the front of my shirt.

"What the—" I jumped up, pulling the cold shirt away from my chest.

"Oh, I'm sorry." He nodded toward the back of the bar, where the rest rooms were. "Let me help you with that."

"No, it's okay," I said, thinking, what a wingnut, when he took me by the elbow and started to guide me.

"I need to know if you're wearing anything—electronic," he said quietly.

I understood now. This gave me an almost giddy sort of feeling as we went around to the men's room. Could I really have found someone, just like that?

He seemed to know what he was about once we were inside. There was only one stall and it was empty. He leaned his back against the door and told me to strip.

"Just the shirt, or...."

"Everything," he said.

I slid off my shoes and then dropped my pants, took off my jacket and handed that to him when he held out his hand. I pulled my tie over my head then unbuttoned my shirt.

"All the way off," he said.

It wanted to stick to me as I peeled it off, not caring about the smell, and now I was down to my underwear and dark brown socks.

"Drop the shorts."

I did, down to my ankles and he said, "That's enough." I pulled them up as he finished going through the pockets of my jacket. He handed it back but kept the wallet.

"Get dressed."

The wet shirt was harder going back on than it had been coming off, but I managed as he read out the information on my driver's license and credit cards.

"So, Mr. Paul Dutton," he said to me, tossing the billfold on the sink counter. "What is it you think I can do for you?"

"First," I said, working my tie back into place. "What do I call you?"

After a second, he said, "You can call me Dave."

"Dave," I said. "I have a hypothetical situation I'd like to talk to you about."

"Sure you do," he said.

Back at the bar, our heads close together and our voices kept low, I told him everything and I was surprised at how little there was to actually say. He didn't care about any of the history between me and Amanda, and why should he?

"So," I finally said. "If this is something that someone, you know, actually wanted to do, what would be the next step?"

Dave finished a fresh beer and singled the bartender over and asked for both of our checks. We waited while he ripped two tickets from a pad and slid them toward us. "Thank you," Dave told him.

"Here," he said, handing me the checks. "You take care of these. I'll handle the tip."

I took the papers but was impatient for my answer. Dave pulled a small group of bills from his pocket and held out a dollar. "I'd like to have about ten thousand of these," he said, and dropped it and a five on the beer-speckled bar top.

Ten grand, I thought. Ten grand and no more Amanda. A good divorce attorney would cost more than that.

This wasn't a done deal, though. I wasn't an idiot. All the while I spent with Rita that night at her place before I finally went home and collapsed on my living room couch, I was wondering how to protect myself. Getting the money shouldn't be a problem. I wasn't in a particular rush so I could withdraw some cash from the bank a couple of times a week, get the money together pretty quickly. Nothing suspicious by itself, and I wasn't planning on being much of a suspect.

That was the tricky part. There were two ways that I'd read people got busted for doing what I was trying to do. The first way was by asking around too much, getting yourself noticed. Someone would call the cops and the next thing you knew, the guy anxious to be the one to off your wife turned out to be an undercover cop. So far I'd minimized that by getting lucky with Rita, but I wasn't going to count on it.

The second problem was more complex. Suppose I did hire someone like Dave to kill my wife. I'd have an airtight alibi, be out of town, make all the right moves, and even if the cops suspected foul play, they wouldn't be able to prove a thing.

On the other hand, a hitman is already a criminal, or if not, a screw-up of the worst order. Who would agree to kill someone for money if they didn't already have the kind of past that made them cold enough to actually do it? Either way, the chances of them running afoul of the law at some point down the line was high, to say the least. And if they got jammed up? All they'd have to do is say the magic words: *give me something I can plea down to, and in return I'll give you a guy who paid to have his wife killed.*

I'd be the insurance policy of whoever I hired and that was not where I wanted to be. The first thought was having the hitman killed as soon as the job was done, but then the same problems still applied. Where would it end?

And I couldn't kill Dave. Jesus, what if I screwed up and he came back at me? No, I wasn't a murderer. A cheater, yes, a man wanting out of a marriage without giving up what he'd earned, sure, but if I was a killer myself this whole thing would probably be shaping up a completely different way.

So how did I make sure he wasn't a cop, and how did I make sure he couldn't come back on me later? It didn't take long for me to think of it— it was almost the same answer.

The next morning Amanda shook me awake from the couch. I stretched like a cat and asked if she'd made any coffee. She ignored me.

"You didn't come to bed last night. Again."

"Yeah, well, I got in late and I didn't want to wake you."

"God," she said, waving her hand in front of her face. "You smell like a bar the morning after."

I wanted to ask, "The morning after *what*?" but there was no point in engaging. "Yeah, the coolers went out at Jimmy's Pub yesterday afternoon. He asked us to help him out, you know."

"What do you guys know about service? You're salesmen."

I felt myself start to get angry, which was ridiculous because this was all a big lie anyway. "You think that means we don't know anything else? That we sell shit we don't know how it works? I tell you, I may not be so quick with those tools, but I can work my way around most things."

"Did you?"

"Did I what?"

"Did you fix Jimmy's problem?"

"Well of course we did," I said, running a hand through my hair. I smelled what was on it and I thought of my time with Rita last night. Soon that could be every night. Or no night. That I wouldn't have any more limits was the point. "Then Jimmy kept our mugs full the rest of the evening. It was only right."

Amanda started walking toward the kitchen. "Sure. It was only right."

I couldn't tell if she believed me and more importantly, I didn't care. I needed to shave and shower and get to work. I had some phone calls to make and I couldn't do them from home.

The first guy that sounded good on the phone happened to be an ex-cop. That could make him a good private investigator but it also made me think about what getting involved with someone with possible ties to the cops could mean. Then I thought it could be a strength. The more I thought about it, though, the more I liked it; the risks outweighed the rewards. So I hired him.

I gave him the whole story, about this scumbag named Dave who I thought was boning my wife. She had some money and damn it, that money was *ours*, not some boy-toy's she picked up at god knows where. The

PI's name was Cody, Ben Cody, and he wanted to know how long this had been going on. Hell, I didn't know. I was making it all up, wasn't I? The trick was to be vague enough to make him believe I was just the dumbass husband here.

The second you tell a PI you think your wife is fooling around, they've got the case halfway mapped out in their mind. The key for me was feeding him what he needed to keep going.

The first thing I asked for was information on this Dave character. I told Cody where he could find Dave—no, I didn't know his last name—but I did know he spent his time at the same place several nights a week. I told him I knew a waitress who could point the guy out to him, and that of course was Rita. I didn't tell her about it. I wanted her surprise to be genuine.

So that part was taken care of. Cody said he should have something in a day or two, depending on when he got eyes on Dave. These guys. They sure could talk tough when they wanted. But it gave me a little time to figure out what I needed to do for step two.

When I got home that night Amanda had made a special dinner for the two of us, something with fish. I hate fish. She had gone to a lot of trouble to match the wine to the rest of it, though, and I could tell she was making some sort of effort here. I wasn't sure just what until after we'd eaten and she came right out with it.

"We have walls," she said.

I looked around dining room with mock astonishment. "So that's what's keeping the ceiling up."

"No, stop it, Paul. I'm serious. I make the effort, I try to be a good wife to you, and it seems that whenever there's progress, whenever we take one step forward, another wall goes up. My therapist says we can't keep doing this."

"We've been married a long time, baby," I said, pouring the last of the wine into my glass. "People get used to each other, they accommodate."

"But they still *connect*, Paul. They still have sex or make love or screw or whatever you want to call it. They still hold each other and want to be held. We should be closer together after twenty years, Phil, not further apart."

And the Cubs should have won the series at least six time since I've been born. I'm over that, too. "Amanda, this is a very stressful time for me right now. I've got work—"

"You never used to have this much work."

"I'm making connections, baby. If I don't do it, it's going to be someone else. And when the new jobs open up, they'll be the ones filling them."

"But honey," she said, reaching out and covering one of my hands with hers. "We don't need the money anymore. Things don't have to change that much."

I pulled my hand away and used the napkin in my lap to dab away invisible crumbs. "But that's *your* money, Amanda. I'm trying to do something for me, something that makes *me* feel good on my own."

She pulled back then, sitting up straighter in her chair. "I can understand that, I think," she said. "But what about all this time with your friends? Where did all this come from?"

"Honey, the guys, they need help doing things. We're bonding. This goes back to the office, too. I want to be that guy, the one that helps everyone out. When they open that branch across the river, I want them to think there's only one guy they can give it to."

"Sure," she said. "The guy always willing to stay out late and help a friend out, no matter how long it takes or how late it is. That guy's you, isn't it?"

"Sure is, baby."

She tried one more time. "But don't you see the barriers it puts up between us? I haven't felt close to you for— I don't know how long."

"Menopause," I said, and I saw her blush. "Or what do they call it—pre-menopause? Maybe this shit isn't all me, you know. There's two sides to this street."

"But that's—"

"Honey, if we have a wall here, think of it like I'm taking one down somewhere else. I can't do it all at once. If we're building walls here, they don't have to be forever. I just have to work on one thing at a time. Right now it's all about that branch office."

She surrendered. I knew she would. "Would you like some dessert?" she asked. "I picked up some strawberries—"

Whoah, I had to cut this off in a hurry. The last thing I wanted was having to kill a couple of hours in the sack with Amanda when Rita was done at work at midnight and we had a dessert of our own we'd been planning for two days.

I told Amanda it would have to wait. Maybe tomorrow? My buddy Chuck is still moving out of his apartment and has to be out by Friday. There's no other time to get his crap out of there than at night.

Amanda hung her head in resignation.

"Look, it's almost over. If only that guy would learn to pack up before we got there, we'd have been done days ago. But he's going to owe me, Amanda. He'll be in my corner."

"Okay, Paul," she said, and began gathering dishes together.

"You want any help here?"

"No," she said, like I knew she would. "You get going. Maybe the sooner you go the earlier you'll come home."

Yeah, I thought, not fricking likely. Not with Rita waiting….

The first report from Ben Cody cleared the way for things to continue. I'd already gone to the bank once, withdrawing three grand in cash.

According to Cody, "Dave" was really a guy named Mitchell Johnson, an ex-Army grunt who'd served two terms in Iraq. He was discharged honorably but Cody couldn't find any sort of steady employment for Johnson since he'd been out of the service, but that he could keep digging.

"That's not what's important," I told him. "It's what he's doing with my wife."

And this is where part two began.

Through Rita I knew that Dave/Mitchell was likely to be at the bar tonight. I told Cody he should be there around nine-thirty, and to see what happened. I told him Amanda had made up some clumsy excuse to go out "with the girls" and that I suspected something was up.

Then I surprised Amanda that night saying I thought it would be nice if she came out with me to dinner, maybe catch up with some of the boys she hadn't seen in a while. There was a mix of happiness and confusion on her face.

"Why tonight?" she asked.

"Oh, I don't know," and I reached over and gave her a kiss on the cheek. "Walls, maybe."

She ran upstairs to change clothes.

"Dress sexy," I called up after her. "I don't want the boys thinking their next branch manager is married to some sort of scrub."

The next part was a little awkward. We ate at a small Italian joint, nothing fancy, a few miles from the bar. "Where are your friends?" Amanda asked.

I made a show of checking my phone. "Looks like they bagged it tonight. There's been a problem at Froelich's and some of them have been pulling rugged hours trying to nail it down." Froelich's was one of the larger grocery chains in town and we'd put in a refrigeration system in one of their new warehouses. As Amanda's face fell, I told her, "But they should be over at the bar in a little while."

We finished our food and I led her out. I'd encouraged her to drink a bit more than she usually would and as she stumbled slightly out to the car, she had that rosy glow to her cheeks that could mean just about anything.

Especially in a picture.

We got to the bar at about quarter to nine. I thought we might be cutting it a bit close and I tried not to let my nervousness show. As expected, Dave was sitting at his usual bar seat. Rita came up and pretended not to know me, just like we talked about the night before. I told her I didn't see any of my friends yet, so maybe my wife and I should just sit at the bar until they arrived.

Steam was almost visible coming from Rita's darkened complexion but I winked at her and mouthed the words, "Don't worry." I guided Amanda to the bar and the open stool next to Dave. I got to hand it to the man, he was cool about it. He looked at Amanda, then at me, and said, "Hello."

Amanda took it from there. "Oh, do you know my husband? I'm Amanda." She held out her hand for a quick shake.

"Call me Dave," he said. Standing behind Amanda I gave Dave a quick head shake that only he could see. "No, I haven't had the pleasure."

The two of us shook hands. I passed off two folded hundred dollar bills as I let go and he deftly made them disappear. The bartender came over and I ordered a Manhattan for Amanda, a beer for myself, and told him to bring Dave whatever it was he was having.

"Now," I said, kissing Amanda quickly on the cheek. "I have to make a quick stop in the restroom."

"Hurry back," she said.

I turned and Rita was staring daggers at me and I motioned for her to meet me around the corner.

"What the—"

"Calm down, sweetie," I said. "There's a reason for all this. I think she's close to agreeing to the divorce. I'm trying to sweeten the deal with some booze, get her out and a little high, nothing to it."

Rita poked me in the chest, harder than I expected. "There better not be."

"Trust me, honey," I said as she turned and went back to work.

I really did have to go to the bathroom and thirty seconds later Dave came in.

"The hell's going on, man?" He held up the two hundred dollar bills like they were an insult.

"Chill, dude," I said. "We were out for dinner and I thought we'd stop in, give you a chance to see her. The money's down payment on the rest. Or keep it for expenses. I don't really care as long as you do the job right."

He looked from side to side as if he didn't already know we were alone. "Fine. Might make it easier later when… you know."

"That's what I thought," I said, although I really hadn't. "One problem, though. I might have to run out, do a thing with a friend, and then come back."

"So?"

I couldn't tell if he was getting suspicious or not. "So buy her a few drinks. She's half in the bag already. I'll dash out of here, won't be gone an hour, tops."

Dave chewed on the corner of his mustache, said, "Okay. I'll give you an hour. But if I think she thinks something's up, I'm gone."

"That's fine," I said, almost shoving him out of the bathroom. "Just go make some small talk while I call my friends."

When I got out to the bar Amanda's Manhattan was half gone, her cheeks were shining, and she seemed to be laughing at every other word Dave was saying. When she reached out and touched his knee with her fingers,

I knew this could work if I could only get out of there quickly enough.

My phone was in my hand when I approached the pair and told Amanda there was a crisis at Froelich's and that it could only be handled at night when the warehouse could be shut down. I told her they needed me but I'd be gone sixty minutes at most. Would she mind....

Dave stepped right in with, "I can look after her for an hour—Paul, was it? If that's all right with the two of you."

"Can you stand it, darling?" I asked Amanda. I could see the happiness in her eyes dim just the slightest bit—oh, no, here we go again, she was probably thinking—but she told me it was okay.

"Don't have too much fun, you two," I said as I went back around the bar and out into the rear parking lot. It should work either way, but I thought it would be better if Ben Cody didn't see me there just then.

"Well, there definitely appears to be something going on, Mr. Dutton," Cody said as he slid a stack of color photos across his desk toward me. "It looks like you may have been right."

The pictures were of Amanda and her new friend Dave from the night before. I'd gotten her drunk enough to be inappropriately affectionate with a stranger, at least outwardly, but Cody didn't know that. To him it looked like something else entirely.

Things were starting well.

I put my fist up to my clenched lips, as though Cody had just confirmed my worst fears. My face said, I just can't believe this, and out loud I muttered, "What do we do next?"

"Well," said Cody. "I understand what you're going through. I'm sorry for all your pain. But you have to understand that we do see this every day in our line of work. You need to protect what's yours but I think we need to get more than this, and then you can consider your options."

Yes, yes, I nodded. I agreed completely. I told Cody I was supposed to drive out of town that night for work but how could I leave her now?

He let me sit on that for a while, until I asked, "You can follow this guy Mitchell, whatever his name, keep tabs on him?"

"Or we can follow your wife."

I waved my hand away, told him to do what he thought best. Cover them both for all I cared. My life was over.

I left his office, excited over what had been accomplished in such a short time. This was going to work. I could feel it.

From my cell phone I called Amanda and told her that I did indeed have to drive out of town for work. But I also told her I'd be back, possibly with good news.

"Is this about the new opening?" she asked.

I told her I didn't want to jinx it but that she should make reservations at her favorite restaurant and that I would meet her there, late. She genuinely sounded excited for me but all I cared about was that she went ahead and made the plans. She promised she would and we hung up.

What she didn't know was that I had taken her cell phone out of her purse that morning. Using that, my next call was to "Dave." I told her where Amanda would be tonight, and when.

"What do you want me to do about it?" he asked. "I'm not going to do the thing there, in the restaurant."

All I wanted him to do was bump into her again, just one more time. I told him not to worry, I'd be there a short time later, but I'd been thinking about it and he was right that the more familiar she was with him the easier it would be for him to get close. When he needed to.

"I'll be there," he said. "But this is it. When I do her I don't want her to be calling out my name because we've become such bosom buddies."

No, I told him, this would be it. After this, he'd be able to ring our doorbell, get himself invited in, and then do whatever needed to be done.

We hung up. I was very pleased, though I was shocked when Amanda's cell phone went off on the seat next to me. I looked at the incoming number: it was my own house. Amanda was looking for her phone.

"Sorry, honey," I said. "I must have picked it up by mistake." She'd just have to do without it this morning.

I never went out of town and I never went to the restaurant, either. Rita had the night off and we spent the evening doing all the things I'd wanted to do to her since we met, only this time without the late night time restrictions. When I finally dragged myself away, Rita clung to me, begging me to stay. Not yet, I told her. Not yet. But soon.

Since I had Amanda's phone, I had the convenient excuse of not being able to call her to tell her my trip was making me late. I skipped the restaurant and drove home, expecting her to already be there. And she was, taking a shower after arriving about half an hour before me.

"Where the hell were you?" she asked, crossly.

"I couldn't get back in time," I said. "I would have called you but by the time I knew, I realized I still had your cell phone."

"You could have called the restaurant."

I hadn't thought of that. "I didn't think of that, darling. I am so sorry. How long did you wait?"

"Long enough," she said coolly, turning the water off and pulling back the shower curtain. I turned my eyes away. After being with Rita all night I thought it was only appropriate.

"And the job?" she asked.

"Time will tell," I told her, but what I really wanted to know was how much time she'd spent with "Dave."

Ben Cody told me the next day, showing me yet another stack of photos, showing Amanda and Dave apparently sharing a bottle of wine.

"Did—did they go somewhere together?" I asked.

"No, not last night. Your wife seemed sort of antsy, as though she felt exposed. Was that a restaurant the two of you have been to before?"

I told him it was.

"Well, she had made reservations for herself and her husband. She probably thought someone might recognize this other character as not you."

"You're probably right," I told him. I wrote him a final check then and there, thanking him for everything and telling him I had to think.

"Strange," I said. "She's been saying some things lately about wanting to get back to being closer to me."

He shook his head and handed me a half-inch thick manila envelope, thanked me for hiring his agency, and told me he was sorry things had turned out this way.

Sure you are, I thought. But I sure wasn't.

Dave called me later that afternoon. He sounded spooked.

"I want to do it tonight," he said. "Last night was…."

I didn't care what last night was. I just didn't want him losing his nerve.

"You got it," I said. "I'll go home and pack and take off. You're sure you're good?"

"Oh, I've got this," he told me. "But I've got to do this now. I'm not sure this getting to know her—"

Oh for god's sake. "You don't have feelings for the bitch, do you?"

Amanda threw up a huge fuss when I told her about the last minute trip. But this was it, I told her. This was the big one. The announcement for the new branch would be made next week and I had been summoned to corporate for a special meeting.

"This has to stop," she said.

"Oh, it will," I said. "I promise. It all ends tonight."

And it did. When I drove in the next morning the police were everywhere. I'd stuffed my cell phone in the bottom of my suitcase where I'd be sure not to hear it and when I pulled up to the field of blue flashing lights up and down my street, saw the pylon blockades and the strings of police tape, I pulled my car over and went up to the nearest cop. The only thing he would say was to tell me to stand back. I told him I lived on that street.

"What's your name?" he asked.

I told him, and he asked me my address. He told me to wait and walked a few feet away, speaking into the radio clipped to his shoulder. A few minutes later, two men in suits walked out of the crowd and said, "Mr. Dutton?"

They told me the story, and I grew more and more frantic. When they told me about Amanda, her strangled body on the kitchen floor, I had to turn away to hide my triumph. I had it all now: the money, Rita. And I had Dave, but in an entirely different way.

Of course Ben Cody came forward and gave a statement about Dave's/Mitchell's seeming affair with Amanda. The police went looking but couldn't find him. Which was all the same to me. Easier, if anything.

Amanda and I had both had wills made and the disposition of the house and all the money was clear. It was mine. All of it. And no one would be able to take it away.

The hardest thing was keeping Rita at bay for a while. If my wife were dead, she'd say, why couldn't we be together? I kept telling her we needed to stay apart for a little while, make it look good. Part of me wondered if maybe I shouldn't dump Rita altogether and start over as a free agent. But that would take a bit of easing back. I didn't want to piss her off any more than I needed to.

I'd done it, the perfect crime. I'd murdered my wife and the hitman I'd hired couldn't come forth without getting clobbered himself. I had the photos of him with my wife. I was rich with no strings, and as a cherry on top of the cake, I actually got the branch manager job at the new facility. Everything was golden.

Until the police came back.

You remember all those trips I took? All that time I spent with Rita, the getting home late, the excuses I made to get out of being home on time? It turned out my bitch of a wife hadn't trusted me. She didn't know what was going, didn't think I'd possibly cheat on her, but she felt she had to know.

So she did what anyone with a little bit of money and half a brain would do: she hired a private detective.

And this guy was every bit as good as Ben Cody, let me tell you. The Scott Porter Agency out of Sarasota, the Cadillac to my four cylinder Ford. They had me coming and going with Rita so often that nothing I said was believable to anybody. Did I really work late on such and such a night? Did I really help Joe move some furniture on this date, or have business out of town this particular weekend?

Of course I hadn't. They arrested Rita and even charged her, but they let her bond out. Me? They locked me up and kept me there. The lawyer I had was the best I could get but without Amanda's money I could never have paid his retainer.

He thought I might have a chance if I could produce the mysterious Dave, who Ben Cody so helpfully identified as Mitchell Johnson, but he was nowhere to be found. The cops didn't seem to much care, either, they felt he'd turn up soon enough.

But they had the one they were after. I was the one that set it all up. My wife would still be alive if not for me. He was the hitter, but I was the killer.

See what I mean about hiring a hitman? You had to be careful. If you didn't do it just right it could really screw up your life.

As I mentioned in the introduction to this volume, Greg Shepard took over Stark House Press after the rest of the family members found reasons to leave the fledgling house behind. He has made it what it is today—as one reviewer has stated, Stark House is "doing God's work"—and continues to bring books and authors to the reading public's attention. Through additional imprints like Black Gat (mass market format titles) and Staccato Crime (crime fiction from the jazz age) he continues to increase the scope of that old good stuff that has been gone for too long. And oh, yeah, he writes a bit, too....

AXE

Gregory Shepard

He didn't know why they wouldn't believe him. He hadn't tried to kill that girl. It was the other way around. She'd tried to kill him. Why couldn't they see that? The evidence was right there. It was obvious.

What was he doing in jail anyway? She was the one who should be behind bars.

They were out to get him. Plain and simple. First her friends had lied to get him arrested, and then the officer had lied to keep him here. And what had he done?

Defended himself! The right of every law-abiding citizen within the sanctity of their own home. Wasn't it guaranteed by the Bill of Rights or the Declaration of Independence or something? He knew it was in there somewhere. A man's home is his castle.

And those damn lawyers. They actually wanted him to plead guilty. What the hell were they thinking? The first one to come along had actually wanted him to plead guilty by reason of insanity. That was just plain crazy. He'd had to fire him right away.

The next one had to bring up those previous arrests, as if he'd been guilty of those as well. He'd never been found guilty of hitting that guy. It was all hearsay. No one had proved anything. Why bring up the past? What did that have to do with anything?

So here he was, stuck in jail.

A year later.

Was this justice? Clearly, they'd already violated his rights to a quick and speedy trial.

It wasn't his fault that all the lawyers were crooks. It wasn't his fault he couldn't get a fair trial. He wanted his day in court. Oh yes, he wanted to tell them all just how it had happened. He'd show them what a conniving bitch that Rhonda woman is—her and all her friends. Dope fiends.

Alcoholics. Thieves. Liars, each and every one of them.

He remembered that night like it was yesterday.

He was sitting on his couch in the living room, having a smoke. It was just getting dark out. He'd lived in his place for only a few weeks and hadn't bothered to get the living room light fixed yet, so the only light in that room came from the bedroom behind him and the kitchen to his right. Too dark to read, maybe, but not so dark that he couldn't tell what was going on.

Oh yeah, he knew what was going on.

There'd been a pounding on his door.

"Open up, asshole, I know you're in there!" she'd screamed at him.

The landlady's daughter, Rhonda, had been kicked out of the place the month before and still had a bunch of her crap still lying around—tools, toys, stuff she'd stolen all over town.

He'd been afraid when he heard that pounding. He'd been dreading her return all day.

"I've come for my stuff, so open the goddamn door!"

He'd cringed inside, but decided to get it over with and had just got up from the couch when the door flew open and Rhonda stood framed in the doorway, the angel of death. Her nine-year-old son stood behind her, peering around her immense figure.

What had happened next? Oh yeah, after Rhonda broke down the door, she'd grabbed a baseball bat that was propped up against the living room wall. Grabbed it and started swinging.

He tried to back up but she was too fast for him. She'd swung the bat right at his face. Didn't he have all these missing teeth to prove it? Rhonda swung that bat and hit him in the mouth.

He'd staggered, his glasses flying. What could he see without his glasses? The rest was a blur. All he could figure was that she'd slipped and fallen on the axe. What else could have happened? He sure didn't hit her with it, and they didn't have any fingerprints to prove otherwise.

Rhonda had slipped and hit her head on the axe. She came up screaming, "He's trying to kill me, Jesse, run, run!" And there's the kid screaming, "He's trying to kill my mom!" And they both take off through the house, through the bedroom, through the bathroom, through the storage area and out the side door.

Hell, he didn't know why they choose to run that way. They just did. What could he see anyway? She'd knocked off his glasses. He was just afraid for his life.

He must have chased her out, though, because everyone had seen him outside the place. What had he done next?

There were a bunch of Rhonda's friends milling around, and people were spilling out of the bar that sat in front of his house. Bunch of lowlife scum, all rushing over to poor Rhonda who slipped on the wet lawn and lay dazed on the ground—like she hadn't deserved to fall on that axe.

One of them even had the nerve to take that rotten little kid of hers aside like she wanted to protect him, like he was going to do anything to him in front of all of these people. He wasn't that stupid.

The woman held tight to the boy. She looked him in the face and said, "You're going to prison for what you've done."

What the hell had he done? "She gets what she deserves," was all he said. Sure, and they'll probably bring that up in court, taking it all out of context. Well, it was her word against his. He'd show them. He'd prove his case. Even if he had to represent himself.

So here he sat in the courtroom, listening to all of the prosecution's rotten lies. All of the supposed witnesses—friends of Rhonda's! What did you expect them to do but lie? Even her rotten little kid Jesse got up on the stand and lied. Tried to get the jury to believe that he'd actually let Rhonda and Jesse into his place voluntarily. That they were just strolling through the house peacefully collecting their things when all of a sudden he'd gone berserk, picked up one of the axes she'd left lying around—probably stolen, too, if you wanted to know the truth—and swung it at her head. What a crock.

Why would he try to kill her? He hardly knew her. And where was the blood stains on the axe if he did? There weren't any—it was still sitting propped up against the wall. And who'd checked the blood to even make sure it was human? Nobody. And who had read him his Miranda Rights? No one. They didn't have a case and they knew it. All the prosecution had was lying witnesses, nothing more.

He'd beaten cases like this before, he'd do it again.

He sat there shaking his head. Incredible. He sure hoped the jury didn't actually believe this stuff. He hoped that they could see that the kid had obviously been coached in his lies. That Rhonda's friends were just trying to back her up.

Now it was his turn to ask some questions. Rhonda was on the stand. He fumbled through his papers. He wanted to get this right.

"Rhonda, isn't it true that are a known drug abuser?"

The prosecuting attorney, Miss Wilson, rose to her feet.

"Your honor, we're been over this before. I must protest this line of questioning."

The judge looked him directly in the eye. "Mr. Riesling, we've discussed this already. Objection sustained. The jury is asked to please disregard the question."

He decided to change his tact. He picked up his Bible and clutched it to his chest.

"Rhonda, on the night of the alleged offense, didn't you make accusations against me in front of a witness? Didn't you call me a Nazi, and threaten me?"

Rhonda looked a lot smaller in the witness stand than she did while she was ranting in his living room. She looked scared. She should be.

"I asked you not to threaten my son. That's all."

"I never threatened your son. Besides, he shouldn't have been messing around my car anyway. I think he broke into it. My radio was tampered with. The little thief needs some discipline anyway, what with a drug addict for a mother."

"Again I must object, your honor. Mr. Riesling is badgering the witness."

"Objection sustained. You may ask the witness questions, Mr. Riesling, questions that pertain to the night of the alleged incident. The jury is once again instructed to disregard the statements made by Mr. Riesling regarding Miss Caneda."

He couldn't believe it. What a kangaroo court! He permitted himself a lawyerly grimace.

"Rhonda, isn't it a known fact that most of the stuff you left in my house was stolen, and that you—"

"Objection, your honor. Same reason."

The judge's mouth looked tight. "The jury will be excused."

"Your honor, how can I state my case if you won't let me prove that Rhonda is a drug-taking, alcoholic, stealing liar? It's just her word against mine."

"Mr. Riesling, please be quiet. We have been over this before and you may not ask these questions. The jury is temporarily excused. Please wait outside. You will be called back very shortly."

"I object, your honor. This trial is a mockery of justice! I can't ask any of my questions. Obviously, there's a conspiracy against me!"

"Mr. Riesling, please be quiet. I won't ask you again."

He sat down and let the jury file out. He couldn't tell if he was reaching any of them, but he sure hoped so. Couldn't they see what a travesty of justice this really was? What could he do to get his story told?

He knew that the jury felt he was crazy for defending himself. Well, what could he do? The lawyers were out to get him. He couldn't even get his witnesses called. He was going to call Mrs. Beeson, his landlady and Rhonda's mother, but they probably wouldn't let him ask her any questions about Rhonda either.

He was just going to have to put himself on the stand. That's all there was to it. Then he could tell the whole story. He'd make them see.

"For the record, please state your full name."

"Clifford Maynard Riesling, your honor."

"You may begin your questioning, Miss Wilson."

The prosecuting attorney was practically rubbing her hands together in anticipation.

"Mr. Riesling, isn't it true that in 1992 you were arrested in Seattle for attempted murder?"

"I was never in Seattle that year. I was living in my van, traveling around. I think I was down south, or somewhere in Minnesota that year. But not in Seattle."

"Mr. Riesling, I have a copy of the arrest sheet right here. Would you like to review it to see if it jogs your memory?" She instructed the bailiff to deliver the arrest sheet to him.

He shrugged the paper aside. "More lies. You can write anything you want on those arrest sheets. Doesn't make them true. I wasn't in Seattle that year. I don't know where you got that sheet, but it wasn't me, and you can't prove that it was."

Miss Wilson's eyebrow rose. "Okay, Mr. Riesling, isn't it true that you were arrested more recently"—here she looked at her notes—"in August of 1999, in fact, in McKinleyville, for striking a man on the head with a lead pipe? I have that arrest sheet as well, and will present it as People's Exhibit No. 24."

He looked around the room. What is this? When was he going to get a chance to tell his side of the story? This wasn't what they were supposed to be asking him. He hadn't been able to ask any questions about Rhonda's past. What was going on here?

"They never proved a thing. Just hearsay. I object, your honor. I couldn't ask these kinds of questions. This isn't fair."

"Objection overruled, Mr. Riesling. You may continue, Miss Wilson."

"On the night in question, Mr. Riesling, when you claim to have been hit by a baseball bat, knocking out several of your teeth, why did you not mention this incident to the officer who arrived at the scene?"

"I don't know. I guess I was still confused."

"Mr. Riesling, I have a photo here taken of you the night of the arrest. It has already been entered in as evidence. Let me point out to you that you have no facial bruises nor marks of any kind on your face. But in your opening statement you indicate that Miss Caneda struck you forcibly with a baseball bat. How do you explain the lack of bruises, Mr. Riesling?"

"I don't know. Maybe she didn't hit me as hard as I thought."

"Hard enough to knock out most of your teeth, but not hard enough to cause a bruise?"

"It's possible."

"Mr. Riesling, didn't you in fact state to the arresting officer that Miss Caneda approached you first with a pair of scissors, and in a subsequent interview, with gardening shears?"

"I was confused that night. After she hit me, I didn't know what to think. I was dazed. She'd knocked off my glasses, as I told you. I couldn't really see what she had. But it must have been a bat. I mean, there was a bat in the room, right? It must have been a bat she hit me with."

"Okay." Miss Wilson looked through her notes again. "Mr. Riesling, isn't it true that in a letter you wrote to Mrs. Beeson while in jail, that you threatened your original lawyer, a Mr. Nate Weinstein? The phrase I am referring to is this: 'When I get out of here, I'm going to shoot that sonabitch in the ass with a twelve-gauge shotgun.' Were these your words?"

"I didn't write that letter."

"I have a copy of that letter here, which was confiscated at the time of its original posting. I would like to enter it as People's Exhibit No. 25, your honor."

The letter was brought forth by the bailiff.

"Mr. Riesling, would you take a look at this letter? Isn't this your handwriting?"

"Might be. Kinda hard to tell. Could be anyone's writing. They take your letters and make changes in them all the time."

"Did you or did you not threaten to shoot Mr. Weinstein with a 12-gauge shotgun?"

"Nope, never did. That's not my letter and you can't prove that it is. They fake stuff like this all the time when they really want to get you. They add things and change things."

"So, Mr. Riesling, you deny writing this letter, which clearly has your signature at the bottom of the page in your own handwriting?"

"Oh, I may have written part of the letter, but they changed things around. This letter isn't the same one I wrote. Nope, not the same at all."

This has taken the wind out of her sails. He can see that Miss Wilson is growing frustrated. No way is he going to admit to anything up here. They can ask anything they want.

"The letter is the same thing as all that other fake evidence you've brought in. Doesn't prove a thing. Fake evidence and lying witnesses don't prove a thing."

"Okay, let's go back to the evening in question. You maintain that Rhonda slipped and fell on the axe, which is shown in People's Exhibit No. 7 resting against the wall. Isn't it true that there was a second axe, Mr. Riesing, a small hand axe? The broken handle is shown on the floor in People's Exhibit No. 8."

"I don't know anything about any axes. I already told you that. She must have slipped and fallen on the axe leaning against the wall."

"If you look closely at the photo, Exhibit No. 7, Mr. Riesling"—and here Miss Wilson holds up a blown-up photo of the room taken the night of the incident and points to a large axe that rests against the living room wall—"do you see any blood around the axe? Or any sign of disturbance caused by the weight of Miss Caneda falling upon the axe?"

"Nope."

"And yet there is a large pool of blood in the bedroom doorway, where Miss Caneda says that you attacked her. How do you account for the blood in the doorway if Miss Caneda fell on the axe that is standing several yards away?"

"I don't know. I told you, my glasses were knocked off. I couldn't see a thing."

"Where do you suppose this blood came from, Mr. Riesling?"

"I don't know. Maybe she fell on the axe and staggered over to the door and lay there for a moment. It was too dark for me to tell where she was without my glasses."

"Mr. Riesling, we've all watched you during the trial taking your glasses off and on as you've read through your notes. You're not wearing your glasses now. Isn't it true that you are far-sighted, and can see better at a distance without your glasses than with them?"

"No, that's not true at all. I'm just not wearing them right now is all. Doesn't prove a thing."

Miss Wilson's eyebrow shot up again.

"Mr. Riesling, on the night of the alleged attack, several witnesses have stated that you were in your home for almost an hour before the investigating officer arrived. What were you doing during this period of time?"

"Nothing. There was a crowd outside. All of her friends, Rhonda's drinking buddies from the bar, fellow drug addicts. Known drug addicts, if I could bring my witnesses to prove it. They were milling around. I wasn't going to go out there and get jumped again. I was afraid for my life. Look, you don't know what it's like to be attacked in your own home by a crazy person with a baseball bat. I was just too scared to come out."

"Weren't you in fact disposing of evidence, Mr. Riesling? Hiding the head of the axe you used to strike Rhonda Caneda across the scalp? Hiding the head of the axe that broke off when you struck her with such force that it shattered the handle?"

"No, no, no, and you can't prove it. All's you got is a bunch of lying witnesses and a bunch of fake photos all blown up nice and large to impress the jury. And fake letters to make me out to be a murdering psychopath. And a judge that doesn't let me call my own witnesses. Well, I didn't try to kill her and I'm not crazy, and you can't get me to admit a thing. It's just their word against mine, and you know it."

The judge interrupted him. "Mr. Riesling, calm down. We're going to take a recess now. Remember, members of the jury, that you are not to discuss the details of this case with anyone outside the courtroom, nor between yourselves. The court is adjourned for fifteen minutes. We will re-adjourn at 10:30."

He'd done the best he could. He'd taken almost an hour when introducing his case before the jury, setting all his suspicions before the twelve men and women. He'd cast as many aspersions on Rhonda as he could get away with. He'd denied everything, and summed up by repeating everything he'd said when he introduced his case, spending at least ninety minutes this time. He'd been on a streak up there.

He'd talked about being a vet. He'd told them what a non-violent person he really was, what little reason he had to attack Rhonda in the first place. He'd held the Bible in front of him like a shield, hoping the jury could see what a God-fearing Christian he really was, deep down inside.

He was so glad he had an all-white jury. Boy, that had made him nervous when that black woman almost got on. He'd challenged her as quick as he could.

And that old Jew, all hooked nose and stringy beard. No way was he going to plead his case before a Jew. He'd already dealt with that problem with his ex-lawyer. Fortunately, the guy got himself excused before he had to challenge him.

Surely these twelve people could see that he was honest. He just wanted to live his life. He just wanted to be left alone. Besides, they'd never find that axe head, not now, and not as long as they looked.

Why couldn't they just leave him alone? If Rhonda had left him alone she wouldn't have needed five hours of stitches to put her scalp back together. She'd deserved everything she got, she and her meddling son.

They couldn't prove a thing.

Tim Lockhart is an up and coming novelist with clear and strong affinities to the classic noir writers of the past. He is a lawyer and former Navy office who has worked with the CIA, the DIA, and the Office of Naval Intelligence. He's written articles for a number of publications and—so far—five novels for Stark House. If they don't put you in the mood for the old, classic crime stories by Cain and Brewer, I don't know what will....

LAST NIGHT AT SKIPPER'S LOUNGE

Timothy J. Lockhart

When he pushed through the wooden door, its paint more peeled than he remembered and its glass porthole more smeared, the place looked almost the same, only smaller and shabbier. The bar still ran along the left wall, tables and chairs to the right, and the tiny bandstand was still at the back too close to the restrooms.

Standing behind the bar was the man everyone called "The Skipper," only older now and more grizzled than he'd been when Mackey had come here during Aviation Officer Candidate School. The Skipper was said to be a retired chief who acquired his nickname by commanding a tugboat in Norfolk. All that was really known about him was that he'd settled in Pensacola and opened the Lounge. Mackey had never heard the old man's real name, but both he and his bar had become legendary in the "Fly Navy" fraternity.

Although he couldn't see the Skipper's feet, Mackey knew the man was wearing mismatched socks, probably the red and green of navigation lights. The standing bet was that if anyone caught him wearing matching socks, the Skipper would buy a round for the house. In over thirty years of operating the Lounge, the Skipper had yet to pay up. After tonight—which was to be the last night, as Mackey had read in *Navy Times* two weeks ago—he never would.

Mackey stood just inside the door, looking at the array of flight suits and helmets, squadron stickers and plaques, and hundreds of framed photos of fliers. All those things and a wide variety of other items related to naval aviation—even a banged-up tail hook—covered the brick walls or hung from the ceiling. The Skipper and his patrons had obviously added to the display in the twenty-four years since Mackey had been in the bar.

Mackey surveyed the crowd, which was light at this early hour of 9:30 p.m. The place would be packed later on, both because it was a summer Saturday night at the beach and because the Skipper was finally closing the bar.

This last night at Skipper's Lounge was what had made Mackey return.

He'd stayed away before to avoid running into former squadron mates who knew why he'd had to retire from the Navy after only twenty years. People who, he knew, might feel obliged to be polite to his face—or maybe not— but could be counted on to do something entirely different when his back was turned.

Mackey's flying had always been good if not spectacular, and he'd done his collateral duties efficiently enough. But he'd never managed to keep away from his brother officers' wives and girlfriends or, toward the end when more women were in the military, his sister officers—and some of those Navy women were married too.

That unfortunate trait—earning Mackey the call sign "Tomcat" even though he'd never flown F-14s—finally caught up with him when his squadron executive officer found out about Mackey's affair with the XO's wife. He made sure Mackey was transferred to a desk in a dungeon somewhere with an equally dark detaching fitness report to drag along with him. After that Mackey knew he'd never see O-5. His briefer highlighted the negative FITREP, and the promotion board shot Mackey down with a unanimous vote of "drop from further consideration."

Mackey got a beer from the assistant bartender and drifted along the walls for several minutes, looking at various display items. He knew what he was searching for but couldn't remember its exact location.

Looking at the wall, Mackey didn't see the young woman until he bumped into her, making her spill some of her drink down the front of her low-cut sundress.

"Oh, sorry. I need to look where I'm going." Mackey passed her a paper napkin. "Here, maybe this will help."

"Thanks." Her tone was cool, not rude, and she seemed, surprisingly, to be by herself. Mackey reflexively wondered if he might have a chance with her even though she appeared to be in her mid-twenties, two decades younger than he was.

She began dabbing at her chest, and Mackey wanted to stare at her half-exposed breasts, their tan as never-ending as the Pacific. But he forced his eyes to stay on hers as he also forced a polite smile.

When her dress was as dry as she could get it, she glanced around for a place to drop the napkin, didn't see one, and reluctantly offered it to Mackey. She saw him looking into her eyes, and, as he'd figured, decorum compelled her to smile back.

"The least I can do is buy you another drink."

"No, thanks. I haven't finished this one."

"Please—it's only fair that I replace the one I spilled. What are you drinking?"

She hesitated slightly before saying, "Gin and tonic."

"Fine. I'll be right back."

He quickly found a place at the bar and came back in just a couple of minutes. He switched drinks with her, putting the almost finished one on a nearby table, and clinked the neck of his beer bottle against her glass. "Cheers."

"Cheers," she said, looking more closely at him. "Are you a Navy pilot?"

"Was. I got out because I could make more money on the outside." He actually made less money, and unless he started doing better as a sales rep for the pharmaceutical company, he might soon be looking for yet another job.

"Oh, I see. What did you fly?"

"Hornets—F-18s." He'd really been a helicopter pilot, but he knew women were more attracted to jet jocks.

"Interesting."

She moved closer to him. She was of medium height, slim but curved with blonde hair lighter than his own medium brown. She had a pretty face set off by bright hazel eyes that were close to the same shade as his. For a moment he wondered if he'd seen her somewhere before, but he didn't think so. She was attractive enough that he didn't think he'd have forgotten.

"Were any of these things yours?" She gestured toward the wall.

"Yes, somewhere. That's what I was looking for when I should have been looking out for you." He laughed enough to keep things light.

"Let's find them. I'd like to see."

It was like spinning the dial on a safe and hearing the first tumbler click into place. That "let's" told him that he might be able to get in as long as he didn't rush things. He knew how to wait—the good hunter learns how to wait.

"Okay. I'd like to see them myself." He led the way around the room, occasionally pointing out pictures of people he knew, or some unusual artifact. He tried to sound knowledgeable without seeming cocky or even worse, boring. She said the right things and nodded at the right places, so he thought he was making some headway.

After a short while, he came to the right spot. His yellow-and-blue ball cap and his running shirt in the same colors with the class number across the front. They all had nicknames on the other side—"Mac" on his because he didn't get the other one till later.

And the photo of his Navy classmates with their Marine Corps drill instructor standing to one side. They were all in their PT gear and he and the rest of the students were smiling, but their DI looked as pissed off as ever. After they hammed it up for the camera, he made them do fifty pushups to finish that session of physical training. Seeing the photo again made him happy and sad at the same time, a strange feeling he couldn't explain.

He pointed to the picture. "Those are the guys I went through basic training with here in Pensacola."

"You all look so young."

"We were—almost all of us right out of college. I was the second-youngest guy in the class."

She looked at him, smiling again, then turned back to the photo. "And which one is you? Let's see—here?"

He looked at the face she was touching through the glass. "Yep, that's me. Aviation Officer Candidate Will Mackey. Check out that buzz cut."

She laughed. "You look better with the haircut you have now."

The second tumbler clicked. "Thanks." He knew better than to say anything more in response to the compliment. "But now you know my name and I don't know yours."

"Lisa."

"That's a nice name."

"Oh, do you think all Lisas are nice?"

"I haven't known that many."

"I'll bet. I thought fighter jocks were supposed to get around."

He chuckled for an answer and said, "Say, are you hungry? We can get something to eat. The burgers here aren't bad." They weren't good either, but he thought it was too soon to suggest they go somewhere else.

"No, I'm fine. I had something before I came."

"So did I." He'd gone back to the Oyster Reef, a seafood place he and his classmates had haunted once they were granted liberty. The dinner had been all right, but neither the décor nor the food was as good as he remembered. As he got older he noticed that nothing seemed as good as it had been years earlier, not the places, not the food, not even the women. Booze was about the same—hell, booze had always been the same—but that was it.

"In that case you probably need another beer."

He knew a hint when he heard one. "Okay, grab that table, and I'll get us another round."

She sat close to him at the table and asked him questions about his days in the Navy. She seemed to be something of a fighter-jock groupie, so he told her a couple of sea stories. Then he began asking her about herself, not pressing for anything really personal but maintaining a lot of eye contact and really listening to her answers.

She was a native of Pensacola, an only child. After high school she'd gone to Florida State for a while, but it didn't take, so she'd returned home and gone to community college for an associate's degree. She'd become a dental hygienist and liked her job well enough to keep doing it. She also liked movies, the beach, and traveling—not that she had the time or money to travel much.

"Maybe you can travel more someday. Especially if you have a friend to go with you." He hoped that remark was as subtle as he'd tried to make it but at the same time knew it couldn't be.

Had he traveled much? Yeah, sure, for the Navy. All around the world. He'd seen some of the worst places of the prettiest places on Earth. Would he tell her about some of the places? Well, okay, if she really wanted him to.

He made it good, speaking to her of taking off from an aircraft carrier and then landing on it, the enormous ship looking like a postage stamp from a few thousand feet. He told her about watching the sun rise over Guantánamo Bay, Cuba, the lush, green smell of the island coming to him on the early morning breeze. He told her about watching the sun set off Fremantle, Australia, with the unfamiliar southern stars coming into view.

She listened closely, nodding, asking an occasional question, and not looking around at the other people in the increasingly crowded bar. By the time he thought he'd said enough, the place was packed and it was getting hard to talk over the noise of the crowd. When the band cranked up conversation became almost impossible.

They'd each had about four drinks, and although the alcohol hadn't affected him much, her eyes looked a bit out of focus, and she was slurring slightly. He knew she didn't need any more to drink now, and if she wanted something later, he had a bottle at his place.

Which is where he suggested they go now. Getting too hard to talk in here. Quiet at the Navy Inn on base. He had a suite—implying they wouldn't be in his bedroom—with a balcony that faced the bay. There was a moon out, and with the night wind it would feel good to sit there and watch the moonlight over the water.

She demurred a couple of times to let him know she wasn't easy, but when he didn't push too hard, didn't try to make the decision for her, she reconsidered. Oh, all right, maybe for an hour or so. The view did sound pretty.

Despite the noise all around him, he heard the third tumbler click into place. Now all he had to do was reach down and open the door.

As they left he took one last look around. He'd never see this place again. He was leaving it behind just as he'd left AOCS behind, the Navy behind. All those days when the promise of life was still before him, when he hadn't known what he'd since learned the hard way—how the blaze of youth inevitably burns down into the embers of middle age.

Then, even though he fought against it and willed the thought not to come, he realized that he had already left the best part of his life behind and that this night would simply mark that leaving. Something made him question—and this was a first—whether he still wanted this young woman. Maybe he'd be better off if he simply said goodnight and left. Maybe she would too.

But he told himself he'd gone to too much trouble to abandon the project now. And it had been a while since he'd slept with anyone this young. Someone who, if not inexperienced, was at least not as jaded as his usual hook-up.

To avoid the hassle of getting her car on base, they went in his car. He promised to bring her back, but he didn't say when, and she didn't ask.

They didn't talk much on the way there. He tried asking her a few more questions about herself, but she gave him only short, vague answers, and he sensed she needed to be quiet for a while. Maybe she was thinking about something deep. Or maybe, after the loud noise of the bar, she was just enjoying the silence.

He showed his ID to the bored gate guard, who didn't ask to see hers, and waved them through. He drove to the Navy Inn and parked as close as he could to the entrance. He thought he might have to help her out of the car, but she managed it all right, fumbling only a little.

He gave her that Tomcat smile that had always worked so well, and after a moment she smiled back. Then he led the way to the front door and inside to the elevators. The desk clerk, an older woman, looked at them and frowned, probably because of their age difference. Whatever.

When the elevator door opened, he helped her inside and then punched the button for the third floor. Thinking of the clerk's frown, he punched it harder than he'd intended. That startled Lisa, but she didn't say anything.

When they got to his suite, he opened the door and stood aside for her to enter. She went in, looked at the small living room, and excused herself to go to the bathroom, taking her purse with her. While she was gone, he mixed two drinks, Jim Beam and water over ice, keeping both of them light.

He went to the balcony and slid the glass door open. It was almost midnight, and the air had cooled from oppressively hot to merely warm but it was still heavy with humidity and acrid with the smell of salt. He sat and admired the view, which was almost as good as he'd described.

In a few minutes she joined him. When she came out on the balcony, he stood and offered her a glass. "Sorry—no gin and tonic. I'm more a bourbon drinker myself."

She nodded and had some of her drink. She didn't seemed to care that it was different. She took a seat and he did likewise.

"Mind if I smoke?"

"No, go ahead."

She pulled cigarettes and lighter from her purse. "Want one?"

He did, but it had been hard to quit, and he didn't want to resume the habit. "No, thanks."

When she had a cigarette going, she looked out over the bay and said, "You were right—this is a pretty view."

"I'm glad you like it."

She had some more of her drink. "I'm glad you weren't kidding about it."

"Did you think I was?"

She turned to look at him. "Well, a girl never knows. Men have lied to me before."

"And one or two women have lied to me. I guess that's just how the game is played."

"It is a game, isn't it? Until things turn serious, and then it isn't." She gave him a look he couldn't interpret.

"I know what you mean." But he really didn't. Despite having been married twice—why he didn't know—he'd never been serious about a woman. Well, never serious about anything but getting one into bed.

She tapped ash on the balcony rail. "Have you ever been in love?"

Her question caught him off guard, but after a moment he realized what answer she wanted. "Uh, sure, a time or two. Unfortunately, things just didn't work out. How about you?"

She looked down at her glass, tracing its rim with a forefinger. "No, not really. Infatuated a couple of times. But I haven't met a man I could really love. I'm beginning to wonder if I'll ever meet one."

"Sure you will. You're young—you've got plenty of time."

"I guess. But my mom had me when she was younger then I am now."

"Is she still with the man?"

"Oh, no, she passed away three years ago. Cancer." She waved her cigarette. "Not from this—breast cancer."

"I'm sorry." He knew the phrase was trite, but in this case he really meant it. He had a sense that she missed her mother.

"It was bad, especially toward the end. We got close—finally—and then, just like that, she was gone."

"I'm sorry," he repeated. "And your father…?"

"I never knew him." Her flat tone cut off any further questions. She finished her drink, dropped the cigarette butt into it, and stood.

From the abrupt way she moved, he thought perhaps he'd misjudged the signals earlier. Maybe she was going to ask him to take her back to her car. If that was it, he'd do it, he decided, instead of just calling a cab. He'd take her even though he would be disappointed not to spend the night with her.

But she surprised him. "It's late. Let's go to bed."

He paused so that he wouldn't seem too eager, but he was careful not to pause so long that she might reconsider. "All right."

They went into the bedroom, and he waited to see how she wanted to get undressed. Some women liked to undress in the bathroom, some liked to undress in front of him, and some liked to have him undress them.

This woman turned to face him and began removing her clothes. First her shoes, then the sundress, then the strapless, push-up bra. Finally she stepped out of her brief panties. She was tan all over, which he liked, and also shaved all over, which he always found a bit unsettling.

She gave him that uncertain smile a woman uses when she's naked in front of a man for the first time and needs reassurance. He smiled back and began getting undressed himself as she slid beneath the covers.

He'd left a light on in the living room, and that gave just enough illumination when he turned out the lights in the bedroom. He found her in the shadows and began kissing her. Her response was warm if not as eager as he'd hoped.

As a lover she was experienced enough to know what she liked and to be able to discover what he did. But she didn't make love in the absent, mechanical way he'd started noticing in women his own age.

No, this was more like when he was younger, say about this girl's age. He didn't say "girl" out loud anymore—you couldn't do that in the PC age—but he still thought of unmarried women in their twenties as "girls," and he still thought that word fit them better.

She satisfied him, and he did his best to satisfy her. Although he couldn't be sure, he didn't think she was faking when she gasped and tensed her muscles as though shot through with electricity. Certainly she seemed content afterward. He'd cranked up the AC, and now the room seemed almost chilly, so he kept the covers over them and she snuggled into his side.

He was sleepy but forced himself to stay awake in case she wanted to talk. Some women did, afterward, and Lisa turned out to be one of them.

"That was nice." Her breath tickled the hair on his chest.

"Yes, very nice. I'm glad you wanted to stay."

"It's been a while. I hope you don't think I jump into bed with every man I meet."

"Of course not. I think we just hit it off."

"Oh, that can happen." She chuckled. "Especially after a few drinks."

She paused before saying, "It happened to my mother. She met a guy, a Navy pilot in flight training here. In fact, she met him at that same bar—that's why I went there tonight, the bar's last night. That's what she said—they 'hit it off.'"

She sounded as though she wanted to tell the story, so he prompted her. "And…?"

"Well, they were together for a while. Just a few weeks, not even months. But she loved him."

"What happened? Did they break up?"

"She said he just quit calling, stopped coming around. She got him on the phone a time or two, but he said he was busy with flight training, didn't have time to see her. You know, that sort of crap."

Yes, he knew. He'd often used work as an excuse when he'd grown tired of a woman.

"But he left her a little something to remember him by. Two things, actually."

"What?"

"One was me."

He'd seen that coming. "I understand—that's why you never knew him."

"Right. Never even saw a picture of him. She said she didn't have one, and maybe she didn't. She told me nothing else about him—I don't think she knew much, actually."

"She never tried to find him, not even to get child support?"

"I don't think so. She was a proud, independent woman. I guess she figured that if he didn't want to commit, she wouldn't try to force him to. Even if he was the only man she ever really loved."

"So what was the other thing?"

"Oh, something silly. Kind of sweet too, I guess. After they first…became intimate, he gave her a miniature set of pilot's wings."

That didn't surprise Mackey either. He'd heard of guys doing that—in fact, after he'd heard about it, he'd done it himself a few times, mostly before he finished flight training and didn't even have the right to wear wings.

But it was a hassle to keep buying the wings—especially once you'd gotten what you were after—and he didn't want to end up giving a set to some girl who'd already received one from somebody else. So he'd quit doing it.

"They were kind of like jewelry only she never wore them. She just kept them in her purse to remember him by."

She stroked his arm, her fingertips brushing across his skin. "I still have them—the only thing of his that I have."

He didn't know what to say to that, so he kissed her forehead and then lay back as though he wanted to sleep. She must have said all she wanted to say, because she soon went to sleep herself, snoring lightly. Eventually he drifted off himself.

He woke up early—all those zero-dark-thirty Navy mornings had left him unable to sleep late. Lisa was still fast asleep, maybe from all she'd had to drink, so he was able to ease out of bed without waking her. He pulled on gym shorts and a T-shirt and padded out to the bar, where he readied the coffee pot and switched it on.

He went to the balcony and quietly slid the door open. The sun felt warm even though it was still low in the east, and he knew it was going to be another sultry day in Pensacola.

Well, AOCS was a long time ago, so at least he wouldn't have to go for a two-mile run in the heat, maybe getting stuck with carrying the battalion flag the whole way. Or sweat through close-order rifle drill on the grinder, the DI yelling obscenities in his ear.

No, all that was past. Gone like many other things he'd done in his life—some of which he regretted. He'd never been one to regret much, but it seemed to him now, with two ex-wives, an only child who was practically a stranger, and his dead-end job simply a way to pay bills, that maybe a little regret was in order.

Thinking that way, and frowning despite the bay view tourists paid to see, he suddenly wanted a cigarette. For a moment he thought again about how hard it had been to quit, but the urge was strong, and he muttered,

"Fuck it."

He went inside and found her purse on the coffee table. The purse was invitingly open, with the cigarettes on top of everything else, but he had to dig for the lighter. As he searched, something pricked his finger, and he snatched his hand back. Sucking the coppery pearl of blood on his finger, he opened the purse wider with his other hand and looked inside.

There was the lighter and something golden flashed next to it. He took out the lighter and then, with more care, took out the shiny thing.

It was a miniature set of pilot's wings. For a moment he was confused—if they were her mother's wings, they should have been tarnished, but these were shiny bright. The girl must polish them, he thought, probably while thinking of the father she'd never known. Resting the wings in his palm, he could feel that one of the two butterfly clasps was missing, and his finger had found the exposed pin.

The coffee wasn't quite ready, so he took the cigarettes, lighter, and miniature wings out on the balcony and closed the door behind him to keep the Florida climate out of the suite. He put the wings on a little table and lit a cigarette. The taste wasn't as good as he remembered, but after two or three drags he felt the familiar relaxation and hoped he hadn't just become a smoker again. Well, he told himself, one butt wouldn't hurt.

He took a few more puffs, savoring each, and then went inside to get a cup of the coffee. He checked on the girl, and she was still sound asleep. He went back on the balcony to enjoy his coffee and finish the cigarette.

He crushed the spent filter in the dirt of a wilting potted plant on the concrete balcony. He sipped some more coffee, picked up the wings, and cradled them in his palm.

He looked at the familiar device of a downward-pointing shield on a ship's twin-fluked anchor, thick, heavy rope looping around its top and bottom, and the strong feathered wings spreading out to either side. He remembered how proud he'd been when he'd first worn his wings, how proud his parents had been of him. Both were dead now, their best reasons for anyone's pride buried with them.

My God, he thought. This trip was supposed to be an attempt at fun, and here I am feeling lousy. I should be happy—I had a good time last night, and I proved I can still give a twenty-something girl a good time. Well, enough of being blue. We only live once, and I'm going to enjoy myself while I'm doing it.

Thinking that way lifted his spirits a little, and he toyed with the wings in his hand, watching the sun, higher now, glint off them.

Then he dropped the wings and had to scramble to stop them from bouncing on the concrete and going over the edge. He was able to cover them with his bare foot, the uncovered pin feeling sharp but not pricking the calloused skin as it had his finger.

As he carefully picked up the wings, he noticed something on the back.

Tiny scratches.

The sea breeze found him, and despite the coffee and the warmth of the sun, he felt a chill. He didn't have his reading glasses—glasses he hated, having had until recently the excellent vision required in pilots—so he had to squint and hold the wings out from his face to examine the markings.

When he'd heard about giving a set of wings to a conquest, he'd also heard about marking the wings in some way. After all, some of these girls slept around, and you'd at least want her to know which set you'd given her.

Some guys scratched their initials on the backs of wings, but Mackey didn't like the idea of using something that could point so clearly back to him.

He peered at the wings, trying to read the marks that looked as though they'd been made with another pin, or maybe the tip of a sharp knife. They were tiny, but Mackey could just make them out. And that made him colder.

He tried to tell himself that the three letters could have been the initials of someone whose first name began with an M. Maybe Mike somebody. He'd known a lot of Mikes in the Navy. But he knew that the other two letters—the a and the c—were lower case. So they weren't initials.

Her hair, her eyes…Suddenly he knew why she had seemed so familiar.

Mackey stumbled to his feet, knocking over the little table and spilling his coffee. He started to go inside, then bent and heaved the coffee and everything else in his stomach onto the withered plant. When he didn't think any more would come up, he stood and leaned against the wall, the rough concrete rubbing his face like sandpaper.

He didn't move for a couple of minutes. When he thought he could walk normally, he went inside and put the cigarettes and lighter back in her purse. Then he dropped in the wings, carefully keeping their back turned away so he wouldn't have to look at those initials again.

He went into the bedroom and began picking up the clothes he'd worn the night before. Although he moved quietly, the girl stirred into wakefulness.

She opened her eyes—those bright hazel eyes—and looked at him. "Hi." She ventured a smile, which he did his best to return, but he knew it was a feeble effort. "I really slept, didn't I? I don't usually sleep this late."

"It's not too late. I mean, it's not that late. You sleep some more. I, uh, I'm going to pick up the Sunday paper."

"Okay." She yawned, stretched, and burrowed deeper under the covers. "Maybe just a few more minutes."

All he could see of her was her hair and the side of her face. He studied her profile, trying to remember.

Maybe it had been that girl who'd come to the Lounge with a couple of her friends. With the help of his buddies, Mackey had peeled her away from the others, bought her a few drinks, even danced with her some. They'd gone out a few times. Her name had been…what? He tried but couldn't remember. The names and even the faces were indistinct now, all lost to time.

All lost.

He dressed quickly in the living room. He found his wallet, phone, and car keys and eased out the door, leaving only his shaving gear and a couple of changes of clothing behind. There was nothing in the suite with his name on it, and the room was paid for through this morning.

She'd probably wait a couple of hours before deciding he wasn't coming back. She'd be angry, really pissed, maybe even mad enough to try to find him.

But she probably couldn't. Mackey was a common surname, and he'd kept a low profile on the internet, not using social media for the same reason he'd always had an unlisted landline, and, after mobiles came in, used burners to juggle his various women.

No, as far as he and the girl were concerned, this was the end of the line. Now she would have to take a cab back to her car. For a moment he wished he'd left her some money for that, but he wasn't going back. Not for that. Not for anything.

As he went down in the elevator, stomach acid burned hot in his throat, and he wondered if there really was a hell.

He pulled out of the parking lot, drove off the base, and headed west. He could be in New Orleans in less than three hours.

Back in the Navy Inn, the girl rolled over after the door shut as quietly as Mackey could manage it. She smiled as she got out of bed, still naked, went to the window, and watched a disheveled Navy pilot with a rancid soul finish pulling on his shoes as he crawled into the car that had brought them here the night before.

Then she laughed out loud. The noise sounded strange in the empty room, but she couldn't help herself. She laughed again, louder. This was for you, Barbara, she thought. All for you.

She knew she was free now, free of the promise she had made to her best friend. Her "twin," as people had referred to them since they'd been little girls.

I got him for you, Barb.

I found him. It wasn't easy, but I did it.

And I got him. Lisa only wished Barbara could know what she'd done to the son of a bitch.

Mackey had tried his old, tired routine but this time there'd been no magic to it. He'd lost his own game and damned himself forever.

She went to the bathroom and started a long, hot shower.

Robert W. Chambers was a master of the weird supernatural tale, stories that appeared supernatural in nature but usually had more human-related solutions. He is perhaps best known for his story collection The King in Yellow, *about an imaginary play of the same name that drives its readers mad. Stark House has published a four-volume collection of his weird literature, plus two more volumes of his fiction. Here is a story that brings Chambers' strong atmospheric style to a group of men compelled to stay in one place a bit too long....*

BARBARIANS

Robert W. Chambers

CHAPTER I
FED UP

So this is what happened to the dozen-odd malcontents who could no longer stand the dirty business in Europe and the dirtier politicians at home.

There was treachery in the Senate, treason in the House. A plague of liars infested the Republic; the land was rotting with plots.

But if the authorities at Washington remained incredulous, stunned into impotency, while the din of murder filled the world, a few mere men, fed up on the mess, sickened while awaiting executive galvanization, and started east to purge their souls.

They came from the four quarters of the continent, drawn to the decks of the mule transport by a common sickness and a common necessity. Only two among them had ever before met. They represented all sorts, classes, degrees of education and of ignorance, drawn to a common rendezvous by coincidental nausea incident to the temporary stupidity and poltroonery of those supposed to represent them in the Congress of the Great Republic.

The rendezvous was a mule transport reeking with its cargo, still tied up to the sun-scorched wharf where scores of loungers loafed and gazed up at the rail and exchanged badinage with the supercargo.

The supercargo consisted of this dozen-odd fed-up ones—eight Americans, three Frenchmen and one Belgian.

There was a young soldier of fortune named Carfax, recently discharged from the Pennsylvania State Constabulary, who seemed to feel rather sure of a commission in the British service.

Beside him, leaning on the blistering rail, stood a self-possessed young man named Harry Stent. He had been educated abroad; his means were ample; his time his own. He had shot all kinds of big game except a Hun, he told another young fellow—a civil engineer—who stood at his left and whose name was Jim Brown.

A youth on crutches, passing along the deck behind them, lingered, listening to the conversation, slightly amused at Stent's game list and his further ambition to bag a Boche.

The young man's lameness resulted from a trench acquaintance with the game which Stent desired to hunt. His regiment had been, and still was, the 2nd Foreign Legion. He was on his way back, now, to finish his convalescence in his old home in Finistère. He had been a writer of stories for children. His name was Jacques Wayland.

As he turned away from the group at the rail, still amused, a man advancing aft spoke to him by name, and he recognized an American painter whom he had met in Brittany.

"You, Neeland?"

"Oh, yes. I'm fed up with watchful waiting."

"Where are you bound, ultimately?"

"I've a hint that an Overseas unit can use me. And you, Wayland?"

"Going to my old home in Finestère where I'll get well, I hope."

"And then?"

"Second Foreign."

"Oh. Get that leg in the trenches?" inquired Neeland.

"Yes. Came over to recuperate. But Finestère calls me. I've *got* to smell the sea off Eryx before I can get well."

A pleasant-faced, middle-aged man, who stood near, turned his head and cast a professionally appraising glance at the young fellow on crutches.

His name was Vail; he was a physician. It did not seem to him that there was much chance for the lame man's very rapid recovery.

Three muleteers came on deck from below—all young men, all talking in loud, careless voices. They wore uniforms of khaki resembling the regular service uniform. They had no right to these uniforms.

One of these young men had invented the costume. His name was Jack Burley. His two comrades were, respectively, "Sticky" Smith and "Kid" Glenn. Both had figured in the squared circle. All three were fed up. They desired to wallop something, even if it were only a leather-rumped mule.

Four other men completed the supercargo—three French youths who were returning for military duty and one Belgian. They had been waiters in New York. They also were fed up with the administration. They kept by themselves during the voyage. Nobody ever learned their names. They left the transport at Calais, reported, and were lost to sight in the flood of young men flowing toward the trenches.

They completed the odd dozen of fed-up ones who sailed that day on the suffocating mule transport in quest of something they needed but could not find in America—something that lay somewhere amid flaming obscurity in that hell of murder beyond the Somme—their souls' salvation perhaps.

Twelve fed-up men went. And what happened to all except the four French youths is known. Fate laid a guiding hand on the shoulder of Carfax and gave him a gentle shove toward the Vosges. Destiny linked arms with Stent and Brown and led them toward Italy. Wayland's rendezvous with Old Man Death was in Finestère. Neeland sailed with an army corps, but Chance met him at Lorient and led him into the strangest paths a young man ever travelled.

As for Sticky Smith, Kid Glenn and Jack Burley, they were muleteers. Or thought they were. A muleteer has to do with mules. Nothing else is supposed to concern him.

But into the lives of these three muleteers came things never dreamed of in their philosophy—never imagined by them even in their cups.

As for the others, Carfax, Brown, Stent, Wayland, Neeland, this is what happened to each one of them. But the episode of Carfax comes first. It happened somewhere north of the neutral Alpine region where the Vosges shoulder their way between France and Germany.

After he had exchanged a dozen words with a staff officer, he began to realize, vaguely, that he was done in.

CHAPTER II
MAROONED

"Will they do anything for us?" repeated Carfax.

The staff officer thought it very doubtful. He stood in the snow switching his wet puttees and looking out across a world of tumbled mountains. Over on his right lay Germany; on his left, France; Switzerland towered in ice behind him against an arctic blue sky.

It grew warm on the Falcon Peak, almost hot in the sun. Snow was melting on black heaps of rocks; a black salamander, swollen, horrible, stirred from its stiff lethargy and crawled away blindly across the snow.

"Our case is this," continued Carfax; "somebody's made a mistake. We've been forgotten. And if they don't relieve us rather soon some of us will go off our bally nuts. Do you get me, Major?"

"I beg your pardon—"

"Do you understand what I've been saying?"

"Oh, yes; quite so."

"Then ask yourself, Major, how long can four men stand it, cooped up here on this peak? A month, two months, three, five? But it's going on ten months—ten months of solitude—silence—not a sound, except when the snowslides go bellowing off into Alsace down there below our feet." His bronzed lip quivered. "I'll get aboard one if this keeps on."

He kicked a lump of ice off into space; the staff officer glanced at him and looked away hurriedly.

"Listen," said Carfax with an effort; "we're not regulars—not like the others. The Canadian division is different. Its discipline is different—in spite of Salisbury Plain and K. of K. In my regiment there are half-breeds, pelt-hunters, Nome miners, Yankees of all degrees, British, Canadians, gentlemen adventurers from Cosmopolis. They're good soldiers, but do you think they'd stay here? It is so in the Athabasca Battalion; it is the same in every battalion. They wouldn't stay here ten months. They couldn't. We are free people; we can't stand indefinite caging; we've got to have walking room once every few months."

The staff officer murmured something.

"I know; but good God, man! Four of us have been on this peak for nearly ten months. We've never seen a Boche, never heard a shot. Seasons come and go, rain falls, snow falls, the winds blow from the Alps, but nothing else comes to us except a half-frozen bird or two."

The staff officer looked about him with an involuntary shiver. There was nothing to see except the sun on the wet, black rocks and the whitewashed observation station of solid stone from which wires sagged into the valley on the French side.

"Well—good luck," he said hastily, looking as embarrassed as he felt. "I'll be toddling along."

"Will you say a word to the General, like a good chap? Tell him how it is with us—four of us all alone up here since the beginning. There's Gary, Captain in the Athabasca Battalion, a Yankee if the truth were known; there's Flint, a cockney lieutenant in a Calgary battery; there's young Gray, a lieutenant and a Prince Edward Islander; and here's me, a major in the Yukon Battalion—four of us on the top of a cursed French mountain—ten months of each other, of solitude, silence—and the whole world rocking with battles—and not a sound up here—not a whisper! I tell you we're four sick men! We've got a grip on ourselves yet, but it's slipping. We're still fairly civil to each other, but the strain is killing. Sullen silences smother irritability, but—" he added in a peculiarly pleasant voice, "I expect we are likely to start killing each other if somebody doesn't get us out of here very damn quick."

The staff captain's lips formed the words, "Awfully sorry! Good luck!" but his articulation was indistinct, and he went off hurriedly, still murmuring.

Carfax stood in the snow, watching him clamber down among the rocks, where an alpinist orderly joined them.

Gary presently appeared at the door of the observation station. "Has he gone?" he inquired, without interest.

"Yes," said Carfax.

"Is he going to do anything for us?"

"I don't know.... *No!*"

Gary lingered, kicked at a salamander, then turned and went indoors.

Carfax sat down on a rock and sucked at his empty pipe.

Later the three officers in the observation station came out to the door again and looked at him, but turned back into the doorway without saying anything. And after a while Carfax, feeling slightly feverish, went indoors, too.

In the square, whitewashed room Gray and Flint were playing cut-throat poker; Gary was at the telephone, but the messages received or transmitted appeared to be of no importance. There had never been any message of importance from the Falcon Peak or to it. There was likely to be none.

Ennui, inertia, dry rot—and four men, sometimes silently, sometimes violently cursing their isolation, but always cursing it—afraid in their souls lest they fall to cursing one another aloud as they had begun to curse in their hearts.

Months ago rain had fallen; now snow fell, and vast winds roared around them from the Alps. But nothing else ever came to the Falcon Peak, except a fierce, red-eyed *Lämmergeyer* sheering above the peak on enormous pinions, or a few little migrating birds fluttering down, half frozen, from the high air lanes. Now and then, also, came to them a staff officer from below, British sometimes, sometimes French, who lingered no longer than necessary and then went back again, down into friendly deeps where were trees and fields and familiar things and human companionship, leaving them to their hell of silence, of solitude, and of each other.

The tide of war had never washed the base of their granite cliffs; the highest battle wave had thundered against the Vosges beyond earshot; not even a deadened echo of war penetrated those silent heights; not a Taube floated in the zenith.

In the squatty, whitewashed ruin which once had been the eyrie of some petty predatory despot, and which now served as an observatory for two idle divisions below in the valley, stood three telescopes. Otherwise the furniture consisted of valises, trunks, a table and chairs, a few books, several newspapers, and some tennis balls lying on the floor,

Carfax seated himself at one of the telescopes, not looking through it, his heavy eyes partly closed, his burnt-out pipe between his teeth.

Gary rose from the telephone and joined the card players. They shuffled and dealt listlessly, seldom speaking save in monosyllables.

After a while Carfax went over to the card table and the young lieutenant cashed in and took his place at the telescope.

Below in the Alsatian valley spring had already started the fruit buds, and a delicate green edged the lower snow line.

The lieutenant spoke of it wistfully; nobody paid any attention; he rose presently and went outdoors to the edge of the precipice—not too near, for fear he might be tempted to jump out through the sunshine, down into that inviting world of promise below.

Far underneath him—very far down in the valley—a cuckoo called. Out of the depths floated the elfin halloo, the gaily malicious challenge of spring herself, shouted up melodiously from the plains of Alsace—*Cuckoo! Cuckoo! Cuckoo!*—You poor, sullen, frozen foreigner up there on the snowy rocks!—*Cuckoo! Cuckoo! Cuckoo!*

The lieutenant of Yukon infantry, whose name was Gray, came back into the room.

"There's a bird of sorts yelling like hell below," he said to the card players.

Carfax ran over his cards, rejected three, and nodded. "Well, let him yell," he said.

"What is it, a Boche dicky-bird insulting you?" asked Gary, in his Yankee drawl.

Flint, declining to draw cards, got up and went out into the sunshine. When he returned to the table, he said: "It's a cuckoo.... I wish to God I were out of this," he added.

They continued to play for a while without apparent interest. Each man had won his comrades' money too many times to care when Carfax added up debit and credit and wrote down each man's score. In nine months, alternately beggaring one another, they had now, it appeared, broken about even.

Gary, an American in British uniform, twitched a newspaper toward himself, slouched in his chair, and continued to read for a while. The paper was French and two weeks old; he jerked it about irritably.

Gray, resting his elbows on his knees, sat gazing vacantly out of the narrow window. For a smart officer he had grown slovenly.

"If there was any trout fishing to be had," he began; but Flint laughed scornfully.

"What are you laughing at? There must be trout in the valley down there where that bird is," insisted Gray, reddening.

"Yes, and there are cows and chickens and houses and women. What of it?"

Gary, in his faded service uniform of a captain, scowled over his newspaper. "It's bad enough to be here," he said heavily; "so don't let's talk about it. Quit disputing."

Flint ignored the order.

"If there was anything sportin' to do—"

"Oh, shut up," muttered Carfax. "Do you expect sport on a hog-back?"

Gray picked up a tennis ball and began to play it against the whitewashed stone wall, using the palm of his hand. Flint joined him presently; Gary went over to the telephone, set the receiver to his ear and spoke to some officer in the distant valley on the French side, continuing a spiritless conversation while watching the handball play. After a while he rose, shambled out and down among the rocks to the spring where snow lay, trodden and filthy, and the big, black salamanders crawled half stupefied in the sun. All his loathing and fear of them kindled again as it always did at sight of them. "Dirty beasts," he muttered, stumping and stumbling among the stunted fir trees; "some day they'll bite some of these damn fools who say they can't bite. And that'll end 'em."

Flint and Gray continued to play handball in a perfunctory way while Carfax looked on from the telephone without interest. Gary came back, his shoes and puttees all over wet snow.

"Unless," he said in a monotonous voice, "something happens within the next few days I'll begin to feel queer in my head; and if I feel it coming on, I'll blow my bally nut off. Or somebody's." And he touched his service automatic in its holster and yawned.

After a dead silence:

"Buck up," remarked Carfax; "think how our men must feel in Belfort, never letting off their guns. Ross rifles, too—not a shot at a Boche since the damn war began!"

"God!" said Flint, smiting the ball with the palm of his hand, "to think of those Ross rifles rusting down there and to think of the pink-skinned pigs they could paunch so cleanly. Did you ever paunch a deer? What a mess of intestines all over the shop!"

Gary, still standing, began to kick the snow from his shoes. Gray said to him: "For a dollar of your Yankee money I'd give you a shot at me with your automatic—you're that slack at practice."

"If it goes on much longer like this I'll not have to pay for a shot at anybody," returned Gary, with a short laugh.

Gray laughed too, disagreeably, stretching his facial muscles, but no sound issued.

"We're all going crazy together up here; that's my idea," he said. "I don't know which I can stand most comfortably, your voices or your silence. Both make me sick."

"Some day a salamander will nip you; then you'll go loco," observed Gary, balancing another tennis ball in his right hand. "Give me a shot at you?" he added. "I feel as though I could throw it clean through you. You look soft as a pudding to me."

Far, clear, from infinite depths, the elf-like hail of the cuckoo came floating up to the window.

To Flint, English born, the call meant more than it did to Canadian or Yankee.

"In Devon," he said in an altered voice, "they'll be calling just now. There's a world of primroses in Devon.... And the thorn is as white as the damned snow is up here."

Gary growled his impatience and his profile of a Greek fighter showed in clean silhouette against the window.

"Aw, hell," he said, "did I come out here for this?—nine months of it?" He hurled the tennis ball at the wall. "Can the home talk, if you don't mind."

The cuckoo was still calling.

"Did you ever play cuckoo," asked Carfax, "at ten shillings a throw? It's not a bad game—if you're put to it for amusement."

Nobody replied; Gray's sunken, boyish face betrayed no interest; he continued to toss a tennis ball against the wall and catch it on the rebound.

Toward sundown the usual Alpine chill set in; a mist hung over the snow-edged cliffs; the rocks breathed steam under a foggy and battered moon.

CHAPTER III
CUCKOO!

Carfax, on duty, sat hunched up over the telephone, reporting to the fortress.

Gray came in, closed the wooden shutters, hung blankets over them, lighted an oil stove and then a candle. Flint took up the cards, looked at Gary, then flung them aside, muttering.

Nobody attempted to read; nobody touched the cards again. An orderly came in with soup. The meal was brief and perfectly silent.

Flint said casually, after the table had been cleared: "I haven't slept for a month. If I don't get some sleep I'll go queer. I warn you; that's all. I'm sorry to say it, but it's so."

"They're dirty beasts to keep us here like this," muttered Gary—"nine months of it, and not a shot."

"There'll be a few shots if things don't change," remarked Flint in a colourless voice. "I'm getting wrong in my head. I can feel it."

Carfax turned from the switchboard with a forced laugh: "Thinking of shooting up the camp?"

"That or myself," replied Flint in a quiet voice; "ever since that cuckoo called I've felt queer."

Gary, brooding in his soiled tunic collar, began to mutter presently: "I once knew a man in a lighthouse down in Florida who couldn't stand it after a bit and jumped off."

"Oh, we've heard that twenty times," interrupted Carfax wearily.

Gray said: "*What* a jump!—I mean down into Alsace below—"

"You're all going dotty!" snapped Carfax. "Shut up or you'll be doing it—some of you."

"I can't sleep. That's where I'm getting queer," insisted Flint. "If I could get a few hours' sleep now—"

"I wish to God the Boches could reach you with a big gun. That would put you to sleep, all right!" said Gray.

"This war is likely to end before any of us see a Fritz," said Carfax. "I could stand it, too, except being up here with such"—his voice dwindled to a mutter, but it sounded to Gary as though he had used the word "rotters."

Flint's face had a white, strained expression; he began to walk about, saying aloud to himself: "If I could only sleep. That's the idea—sleep it off, and wake up somewhere else. It's the silence, or the voices—I don't know which. You dollar-crazy Yankees and ignorant Provincials don't realize what a cuckoo is. You've no traditions, anyway—no past, nothing to care for—"

"Listen to 'Arry!" retorted Gary—" 'Arry and his cuckoo!"

Carfax stirred heavily. "Shut up!" he said, with an effort. "The thing is to keep doing something—something—anything—except quarrelling."

He picked up a tennis ball. "Come on, you funking brutes! I'll teach you how to play cuckoo. Every man takes three tennis balls and stands in a corner of the room. I stand in the middle. Then you blow out the candle. Then I call 'cuckoo!' in the dark and you try to hit me, aiming by the sound of my voice. Every time I'm hit I pay ten shillings to the pool, take my place in a corner, and have a shot at the next man, chosen by lot. And if you throw three balls apiece and nobody hits me, then you each pay ten shillings to me and I'm cuckoo for another round."

"We aim at random?" inquired Gray, mildly interested.

"Certainly. It must be played in pitch darkness. When I call out cuckoo, you take a shot at where you think I am. If you all miss, you all pay. If I'm hit, I pay."

Gary chose three tennis balls and retired to a corner of the room; Gray and Flint, urged into action, took three each, unwillingly.

"Blow out the candle," said Carfax, who had walked into the middle of the room. Gary blew it out and the place was in darkness.

They thought they heard Carfax moving cautiously, and presently he called, "Cuckoo!" A storm of tennis balls rebounded from the walls; "Cuckoo!" shouted Carfax, and the tennis balls rained all around him.

Once more he called; not a ball hit him; and he struck a match where he was seated upon the floor.

There was some perfunctory laughter of a feverish sort; the candle was relighted, tennis balls redistributed, and Carfax wrote down his winnings.

The next time, however, Gray, throwing low, caught him. Again the candle was lighted, scores jotted down, a coin tossed, and Flint went in as cuckoo.

It seemed almost impossible to miss a man so near, even in total darkness, but Flint lasted three rounds and was hit, finally, a stinging smack on the ear. And then Gary went in.

It was hot work, but they kept at it feverishly, grimly, as though their very sanity depended upon the violence of their diversion. They threw the balls hard, viciously hard. A sort of silent ferocity seemed to seize them. A chance hit cut the skin over Flint's cheekbone, and when the candle was lighted, one side of his face was bright with blood.

Early in the proceedings somebody had disinterred brandy and Schnapps from under a bunk. The room had become close; they all were sweating.

Carfax emptied his iced glass, still breathing hard, tossed a shilling and sent in Gary as cuckoo.

Flint, who never could stand spirits, started unsteadily for the candle, but could not seem to blow it out. He stood swaying and balancing on his heels, puffing out his smooth, boyish cheeks and blowing at hazard.

"You're drunk," said Gray, thickly; but he was as flushed as the boy he addressed, only steadier of leg.

"What's that?" retorted Flint, jerking his shoulders around and gazing at Gray out of glassy eyes.

"Blow out that candle," said Gary heavily, "or I'll shoot it out! Do you get that?"

"Shoot!" repeated Flint, staring vaguely into Gary's bloodshot eyes; "you shoot, you old slacker—"

"Shut up and play the game!" cut in Carfax, a menacing roar rising in his voice. "You're all slackers—and rotters, too. Play the game! Keep playing—hard!—or you'll go clean off your fool nuts!"

Gary walked heavily over and knocked the tennis balls out of Flint's hands.

"There's a better game than that," he said, his articulation very thick; "but it takes nerve—if you've got it, you spindle-legged little cockney!"

Flint struck at him aimlessly. "I've got nerve," he muttered, "plenty of nerve, old top! What d'you want? I'm your man; I'll go you—eh, what?"

"Go on with the game, I tell you!" bawled Carfax.

Gary swung around: "Wait till I explain—"

"No, don't wait! Keep going! Keep playing! Keep doing something, for God's sake!"

"Will you wait!" shouted Gary. "I want to tell you—"

Carfax made a hopeless gesture: "It's talk that will do the trick for us all—"

"I want to tell you—"

Carfax shrugged, emptied his full glass with a gesture of finality.

"Then talk, damn you! And we'll all be at each other's throats before morning."

Gary got Gray by the elbow: "Reggie, it's this way. We flip up for cuckoo. Whoever gets stuck takes a shot apiece from our automatics in the legs—eh, what?"

"It's perfectly agreeable to me," assented Gray, in the mincing, elaborate voice characteristic of him when drunk.

Flint wagged his head. "It's a sportin' game. I'm in," he said.

Gary looked at Carfax. "A shot in the dark at a man's legs. And if he gets his—it will be Blighty in exchange for hell."

Carfax, sullen with liquor, shoved his big hand into his pocket, produced a shilling, and tossed it.

A brighter flush stained the faces which ringed him; the risky hazard of the affair cleared their sick minds to comprehension.

Tails turned uppermost; Flint and Gary were eliminated. It lay between Carfax and Gray, and the older man won.

"Mind you fire low," said the young fellow, with an excited laugh, and walked into the middle of the room.

Gary blew out the candle. Presently from somewhere in the intense darkness Gray called "Cuckoo!" and instantly a slanting red flash lashed out through the gloom. And, when the deafening echo had nearly ceased: "Cuckoo!"

Another pistol crashed. And after a swimming interval they heard him moving. "Cuckoo!" he called; a level flame stabbed the dark; something fell, thudding through the staccato uproar of the explosion. At the same moment the outer door opened on the crack and Carfax's orderly peeped in.

Carfax struck a match with shaky fingers; the candle guttered, sank, flared on Flint, who was laughing without a sound. "Got the beggar, by God!" he whispered—"through the head! Look at him. Look at Reggie Gray! Tried for his head and got him—"

He reeled back, chuckling foolishly, and levelled at Carfax. "Now I'll get you!" he simpered, and shot him through the face.

As Carfax pitched forward, Gary fired.

"Missed me, by God!" laughed Flint. "Shoot? Hell, yes. I'll show you how to shoot—"

He struck the lighted candle with his left hand and laughed again in the thick darkness.

"Shoot? I'll show you how to shoot, you old slacker—"

Gary fired.

After a silence Flint giggled in the choking darkness as the door opened cautiously again, and shot at the terrified orderly.

"I'm a cockney, am I? And you don't think much of the Devon cuckoos, do you? Now I'll show you that I understand all kinds of cuckoos—"

Both flashes split the obscurity at the same moment. Flint fell back against the wall and slid down to the floor. The outer door began to open again cautiously.

But the orderly, half dressed, remained knee-deep in the snow by the doorway.

After a long interval Gary struck a match, then went over and lit the candle. And, as he turned, Flint fired from where he lay on the floor and Gary swung heavily on one heel, took two uncertain steps. Then his pistol fell clattering; he sank to his knees and collapsed face downward on the stones.

Flint, still lying where he had fallen, partly upright, against the wall, began to laugh, and died a few moments later, the wind from the slowly opening door stirring his fair hair and extinguishing the candle.

And at last, through the opened door crept Carfax's orderly; peered into the darkness within, shivering in his unbuttoned tunic, his boots wet with snow.

Dawn already whitened the east; and up out of the ghastly fog edging the German Empire, silhouetted, monstrous, against the daybreak, soared a *Lämmergeyer*, beating the livid void with enormous, unclean wings.

The orderly heard its scream, shrank, cowering, against the door frame as the huge bird's ferocious red and yellow eyes blazed level with his.

Suddenly, above the clamor of the *Lämmergeyer*, the shrill bell of the telephone began to ring.

The terrible racket of the *Lämmergeyer* filled the sky; the orderly stumbled into the room, slipped in a puddle of something wet, sent an empty bottle rolling and clinking away into the darkness; stumbled twice over prostrate bodies; reached the telephone, half fainting; whispered for help.

After a long, long while, the horror still thickly clogging vein and brain, he scratched a match, hesitated, then holding it high, reeled toward the door with face averted.

Outside the sun was already above the horizon, flashing over Haut Alsace at his feet.

The *Lämmergeyer* was a speck in the sky, poised over France.

Up out of the infinite and sunlit chasm came a mocking, joyous hail—up through the sheer, misty gulf out of vernal depths: *Cuck*-oo! *Cuck*-oo! *Cuck*-oo!

Edward Phillips Oppenheim was known as "The Prince of Storytellers," writing over a hundred novels and more than three dozen short story collections. His writing was smooth and filled with rascals and society members aplenty, blazing with puzzles and intrigue. The Great Impersonation, published between the wars in 1920, is widely considered one of the best spy novels of all time. At his best he is as compulsively readable as anyone. He was so popular he graced the cover of Time *magazine's September 12th, 1927 issue. Stark House has reprinted a pair of his novels, including one that was extremely rare (previously only six extant copies) as well as two collections of previously unpublished short stories.*

POLITICS PAYS BEST

E. Phillips Oppenheim

Radford's old friends at K Department of the Foreign Office were delighted to see him. Everyone pushed his surreptitious newspaper into the waste-paper basket and looked up from his property pile of accumulated papers with a sigh of relief. There were six of them in the room, and all were well known to their visitor.

"Radford, my son," Bonham Lewis, the senior, declared, "you were a wise man when you left us. Things are getting worse and worse—more work, less pay, slower promotion. The modern government office is nothing more nor less than a sweating den. Have a cigarette?"

Radford accepted the cigarette but shook his head at the proffered chair.

"I am waiting to see the chief," he explained. "That's why I looked in upon this hive of industry."

"Some dark work on hand," Dick Graham, generally called "the office boy," remarked. "If there's ever anything doing at all in the blood-and-thunder business, it's given to the outsiders. Why doesn't one of us get a chance sometimes to swagger round the picturesque capitals of Europe in disguise, with a revolver in his hip pocket?"

"Nothing of the sort left nowadays," Radford sighed. "What you call the picturesque capitals of Europe are sordid dumping grounds off broken energies and chilled ambitions. All this peace talk seems to have sapped the life out of everything."

"Crime," one of the others declared, looking up from his task, "the criminal world—that's where the only fun is to be found. You knew something when you chucked us, Radford. I wonder why the boss has sent for you this time. Things are as flat as ditch water everywhere."

"Except at Geneva," Bonham Lewis put in cryptically. "One hears queer things from Geneva."

"And you'll go on hearing them," a man from the other side of the room observed, "so long as we keep about thirty K7 men haunting the place. They must earn their money somehow."

A commissionaire entered the room. He beckoned mysteriously to Radford. Names were seldom mentioned in the department.

"This way, sir, if you please."

Radford threw away his cigarette.

"Well, so long, you fellows!" he said. "If any of you have need of a rest cure at any time, you know my telephone number."

"Take us on as sleuths the next juicy murder case you get," Dick Graham begged.

"The police keep those to themselves," Radford replied. "Bye-bye!"

His guide led him down the familiar corridor, into the dignified-looking apartment at the end—the "apex of the triangle," someone had once said, between the Home Office, the Foreign Office and Scotland Yard. Radford had seldom crossed the threshold without a thrill, and even now he could scarcely fail to remember that he had left it often enough on missions which had involved the covering up of his tracks, and the making of his will. His chief, older and more worn in features, but otherwise unchanged, welcomed him with a grasp of the hand, and pointed to the visitor's armchair.

"Sit down, Radford," he invited. "Nothing very exciting for you this time, I'm afraid. Glad you happen to be free, all the same."

"One advantage of my humble efforts," Radford remarked, "is that I can choose my clients."

"Of course you can," the other agreed, "with a banking account like yours. Be thankful always for your millionaire uncle. You'd have rusted to death if you'd stayed here."

The Minister leaned back, and looked up at the ceiling with half-closed eyes. For several moments he did not speak. At length—

"I wonder, Radford," he asked, "if you happened to remember, during the time you were established in Switzerland, coming across a man named Cantanerri? He's by way of being a prince or something, I believe, but of course you wouldn't hear of anything of that sort during the war."

"Cantanerri?" Radford repeated thoughtfully. "I remember the fellow. We were doing very much the same type of job—dashes across the frontier just as far as a certain railway station, for information. Naturally, he wasn't quite so active as I was, because he wasn't in the war at that time."

"Just so," the other murmured. "See much of him?"

"Very little. It was rather a delicate question whom he was working for in those days. I gave him rather a clear berth, and he treated me the same way. I did do him a good turn once, though," Radford went on reflectively. "It was the last day I ever saw him. I always thought he was working on his own passport, but apparently he wasn't, although his country hadn't come into the war them. For some reason or other, there was an extra watch kept one night when we landed at Geneva. He was just in front of me at the passport station, and they kept us waiting nearly ten minutes whilst they looked at his passport, inside and out and upside down. I could see the name on it—'Humbert, Jeweler, Place de Valenciennes, Geneva.' The man kept on looking at his photograph and then at him.

"'No one on board you happen to know, I suppose?' he asked Cantanerri.

"I pushed in at once, pretending to be impatient. It was a cold night anyway.

"'I can tell you who he is,' I volunteered. 'I bought my last watch at his shop—Humbert, Place de Valenciennes.'

"They let him through all right after that. He slipped away on the quay, without stopping to thank me, and I've never seen him since."

"A stroke of luck, perhaps," the Minister observed. "Cantanerri is over here in London now. Nothing against that, of course. He belongs to a friendly nation—an ally, in fact, if alliances which existed in those days count any longer—and we've nothing against his presence here at all, but there's a feeling that we should rather like to know why he's deserted his beloved capital for London just at this time of year. His, of course, is a very aristocratic family, but he has very few connections here. Do you still belong to the St. Luke's Club?"

"At the present moment I do," Radford replied, a little ruefully. "If I go on getting any more dud players for partners and millionaire experts for opponents I shall have to chuck it though."

"Well, don't chuck it just yet," the Minister begged. "We'll see you through a trifle of gambling if it's necessary. Cantanerri spends most of his afternoons, and a portion of his evenings there, I believe. Seems the only thing he cares to do. I wonder if you'd mind dropping in now and then. We'd like a report—just the ordinary X. D. sort of thing. Can you manage it, do you think?"

"I daresay I could," Radford acknowledged, a little surprised, "But what's the matter with the Department?"

"A whim of B. J.'s," the Minister explained. "He argues that Cantanerri belongs to a friendly nation, that he would recognize any of our staff, or would be very likely to, at any rate, and would resent inquiries being made as to his business here. There's a certain amount of reason in that, you know. We've asked you to help us before, under the same conditions, and I think it would be as well not to run any risk of trouble just now. This peace talk seems to have set everyone on edge. Drop in and see us whenever you've anything to report, however trifling it is. If you want any help, of course you can have it from MI6, but I'd rather we weren't officially connected with even the vaguest sort of inquiries."

"That's quite all right, sir," Radford promised, as he rose to his feet. "I haven't a large staff, but they're quite enough to deal with any ordinary matters, and I keep them well out of sight."

The Minister made a note in his diary.

"You shan't be kept waiting," he assured him. "I'll see that you have the entrée."

Radford entered the card room of his club about five o'clock that afternoon, to find himself plunged into an alien atmosphere. There were four or five ordinary rubbers going on, to which no one was paying the slightest attention. Around one table, situated in an alcove and reserved for the high game, however, at least a dozen spectators were standing. Radford made his way toward it and touched a friend on the arm. "What's the excitement, Jim?" he inquired.

Jim Holderness, a rising young diplomatist, turned and nodded.

"Some very high play," he confided. "They're playing at sovereign points, and a monkey on the rubber."

"Who the mischief's 'they'?"

"Harvey Wren, Burridge, a man who is a stranger to me, and a Prince something or other—Cantanerri, I think his name is. I don't know whether he's Spanish, Italian or Rumanian, but he's a magnificent player, although he has rotten luck."

Radford changed his position a little and studied the man opposite him. Prince Cantanerri was a person of very dignified presence. His face was pale, his hair faintly streaked with gray—otherwise jet black. His forehead was broad and massive, his eyes tired, his mouth finely cut but supercilious. He played his cards, gathered or waved away the tricks with an air of complete indifference. There was neither a smile upon his face, nor any sign of discontent with the scores at the end of the game were added up. He helped himself occasionally to a cigarette from a quaintly chased silver box which stood by his side.

"Collyer ought to paint him as The Silent Gambler," Radford's friend whispered. "He's been playing these stakes here now for three afternoons, nearly always with rotten cards and a dud partner. No one has ever heard him make a complaint, or even a comment. Yesterday, for once in a while, he cut with Wren, and, would you believe it, Wren, who never does that sort of thing, revoked when they had the rubber sitting. He never said a word."

Radford nodded.

"The Silent Gambler," he murmured. "Yes, I should think that would be a good name for him."

"Ever met him?"

"Once. He was playing for even higher stakes then."

"Winning or losing?"

"He won that time."

Cantanerri was dummy and leaned back in his chair with a faint yawn.

He looked incuriously beyond the table, and his eyes met Radford's. There was not a flicker of recognition in them, yet they lingered. Radford knew perfectly well, although neither made any sign, that he was recognized. Old habits prevail—especially habits of discipline. Radford wandered away. In the morning he called at Downing Street.

"Nothing much to report, sir," he said to his chief. "You're quite right about Cantanerri being at the St. Luke's Club. He's there nearly every afternoon and most evenings, and he's playing such stakes as they've never attempted there before for contract bridge. I saw him lose two thousand yesterday afternoon, and they say that his week's account is over eleven thousand."

"An expensive amusement," the Minister meditated. "Don't lose sight of him, Radford. We're very much interested in Price Cantanerri—more so every day, as a matter of fact. Has he recognized you?"

"I think so," Radford answered. "He hasn't spoken though. As a matter of fact, he seldom speaks to anyone—sits there like a waxen figure of silent elegance."

"Don't lose sight of him," the Minister insisted. "He may speak to you any day."

"No particular line of action?" Radford inquired.

His chief shook his head.

"Everything obvious is dealt with," he confided. "We know that he has the royal suite at the Greek Park Hotel, that he lunches or dines usually in his room, and that he only this afternoon left a card at his Embassy."

"Is he still in the Service?"

"Who knows? See you tomorrow, perhaps, Radford, or the next day. Don't neglect us—or the club. Very good thing for a busy man, a club. Keeps him in touch with his friends, and—er—all sorts of interesting things. Take my advice, Radford, don't miss a day."

Radford took his chief's advice, or rather carried out his instructions, and became an habitué instead of a casual visitor to his club, at times playing a little dilettante bridge, at times joining the group of watchers around the big table. Rumors of the high play had spread through the West End, and the star performers from other clubs who had the entrée to the St. Luke's joined the limited company of gamblers, so that sometimes there were two tables playing for results which were almost reminiscent of the old Crockford and Almack days. Steadily, throughout it all, the Prince played his cards faultlessly, but with the same lack of enthusiasm. He held Yarboroughs without complaint, repeatedly drew the weakest partners without a flicker of an eyelid, until his ill fortune became the talk of the club....

Radford, who had made no effort to claim his acquaintance, came face to face with him one day upon the stairs. Prince Cantanerri paused with his hand upon the banister.

"We are old acquaintances, I think, Major Radford," he said.

"You have an excellent memory, Prince," Radford replied.

The Prince led the way into the smoking room on the first floor, and pointed to an easy-chair next the one which he had himself selected.

"Yes," he acknowledged, "I have a good memory. It was part of the equipment of our profession in those days. How do you pass your time now, Major—now that the drums have ceased to roll?"

"Ignominiously, I'm afraid you'll think," Radford confessed. "I have devoted the few gifts I possess to private practice."

The Prince raised his eyebrows.

"I do not understand," he admitted.

"The problems I used to tackle for the Government," Radford explained, "I tackle now—or rather their equivalent—for whoever chooses to hire me. In other words, I am a private inquiry agent—detective, if you have no objection to the term."

The Prince gave no outward sign of disapproval, but Radford was well aware that nothing but his perfect manners and unusual gifts of restraint had checked his exclamation of surprise at the announcement.

"It is a profession no doubt in your country admirably conducted," he remarked. "In mine we know little of it. Our police rather resent interference."

"So they do here sometimes," Radford agreed. "At the same time there is considerable latitude about my enterprises. Any honorable adventure which, for various reasons, is best undertaken by a third party, I attempt to deal with if commissioned by an acceptable client.... And you—you preserve your old interests?"

"Politics exist no longer for me, nor patriotism as it is generally understood," the Prince confided. "I am not persona grata with the powers which rule my country. One must find one's thrills, if ever, in the turning of a card on a green baize table. The clank of a saber or the gleam of suspicion in a gray eye, which might mean a bullet in ten seconds—those things have passed. I still feel sometimes, though," he added under his breath, "that there was more excitement in presenting for his inspection a forged passport to a curious official, than there is in picking up those thirteen cards of fate. What do you think, Major?"

Radford threw away his cigarette and lit another.

"I have my work," he pointed out, "and Nature never made a gambler of me."

The Prince rose slowly to his feet. A respectful message had been brought to him from the bridge room.

"Nature made a gambler of me for all time," he acknowledged. "Au revoir, my friend."

The meeting had been after lunch, and later in the afternoon Radford paid his customary visit to the Foreign Office. His chief was interested.

"So the Prince is no longer connected with the politics of his country," he mused. "Well, that is news. There are three great figureheads, each one of whom has something to say about his government, church, state and people, and Cantanerri has been supposed to be the only man in touch with all three."

"He gave me to understand," Radford reported, "that his political interests were dead."

"He still loses?"

"Enormously. And in a sense unjustly. I should call him the finest player of the lot of them, but he always seems handicapped by bad cards or indifferent partners. He must be enormously rich."

"He is supposed to be. You spoke of your profession to him?"

"I did."

"Did he make any comment?'

"No spoken one," Radford acknowledged. "I should imagine, however, that I do not exist for him any longer. It is worth while my keeping on?"

The Minister seemed shocked.

"You're doing marvelously, Radford," he pronounced, "a good deal more marvelously than you realize perhaps. Don't be late tomorrow afternoon. I may have to go down to Windsor at six o'clock."

"I'm to come, even if there is nothing to report?"

"You're to come even if there is nothing that you think worthwhile reporting," was the firm reply.

About a week later Radford was opening his letters in his office library when he received what was perhaps the greatest surprise of his life. There was a knock at the door—his secretary had not yet arrived—and in response to Radford's nonchalant "Come in" the Prince di Cantanerri made deliberate entrance. He closed the door behind him, removed his hat and touched the cigarette in its long amber holder which he was smoking.

"You permit, Major?" he asked.

"Certainly," Radford assented. "Take a chair, won't you? Forgive my seeming astonished. I don't often get such early morning visitors."

The Prince sank gracefully into the proffered chair. He seemed to bring with him into the little apartment a mingled odor of fine Egyptian tobacco, and an elusive but virile perfume as of a man fresh from his toilet. Less definitely, too, he brought an atmosphere of elegance and perfect poise. Radford pushed the rest of his letters away and seated himself at his desk.

"It seems ridiculous to imagine, Prince," he said, "that you have come here to consult me professionally."

"It is, nevertheless, a fact," Cantanerri acknowledged. "I have been thinking over some of those words of yours in connection with your profession—'any honorable adventure which, for various reasons, is best undertaken by a third party.' Those were very nearly your exact words, I think, Major?"

"Quite likely," Radford agreed.

"On those lines," the Prince went on, leaning forward to knock the ash from his cigarette into a tray upon the corner of the table," I wish you to act for me. Before I explain the exact nature of the commission, will you allow my servant, who waits outside, to bring in a small parcel?"

"Certainly."

The Prince raised his voice slightly, and, leaning forward, struck the panel of the door with the end of his Malacca cane.

"Antonio," he directed, "you can enter."

A typical Italian butler, dressed in complete black, made his appearance. He carried a package of considerable size under his arm and held his bowler hat in the other hand. His anxious eyes were fixed upon his master, who spoke to him in rapid Italian. The package was deposited carefully upon Cantanerri's knee. With a reverential salute to the latter, and a polite one to Radford, the man took his leave.

"The service which I shall require of you, Major Radford," the Prince began, his fingers playing tenderly, almost reverentially, with the fastenings of the box upon his knee, "is a simple one, but it involves a certain amount of explanation. I take it for granted that secrecy is amongst the guarantees of your service."

"Naturally," Radford acquiesced, "if a client intrusts me with his confidence, even if I am unable to serve him, my discretion may be taken as a matter of course."

"It is perhaps no secret to you," the Prince continued calmly, "to learn that I have lost a considerable sum of money since my arrival in this country."

"No secret at all," Radford admitted. "Pretty hard luck you've had too. I never saw anyone hold worse cards."

The Prince shrugged his shoulders.

"The fortune will change," he said. "Meanwhile, it is a regrettable fact that I am short of money. Tomorrow, at the St. Luke's Club, I shall be asked for a cheque for nineteen thousand pounds. I also owe a considerable sum which I lost at *chemin de fer* a few nights ago. It is not my custom to be one hour late in the payment of a debt of honor."

Radford moved uneasily in his place. The Prince produced a gold knife from his pocket and proceeded to cut the strings of the packet. The paper fell away, disclosing a black oak box, flat and oblong, with worn, brass clasps, and two locks, one at each end. With a key from his chain the Prince turned both and swung open the lid. Inside, the box was lined with purple velvet, and the whole of the interior was taken up by an oil painting in a worn, gilt frame of beautiful design. For nearly a minute the Prince, with his monocle thrust firmly into his eye, held the picture upon his knees and studied it. For the first time, it seemed to Radford, there was a slight change in his expression. His eyes had lost their cold, indifferent gleam. He turned the picture toward Radford almost reluctantly.

"I am not aware whether you are a student of medieval art, Major Radford," he said. "If so, you will know at once the divine fingers which produced this work."

Radford adjusted his spectacle and leaned forward. For some considerable time he said nothing. A sense of perplexity oppressed him. The picture was of a Madonna, kneeling, with the Child by her side.

"The picture naturally suggests Fra Lippo Lippi," Radford remarked thoughtfully—"the grouping and background, and even the profile of the Madonna—the clarity of the flesh tints too. Yes, it is very reminiscent of Fra Lippo Lippi."

"It should be," the Prince observed, "for it is his work. It is The Kneeling Madonna, which very few, even of the great picture lovers, have seen. It has hung for many generations in the gallery of a castle of mine in the Apennines, which few tourists have ever heard of, much less visited."

Radford said nothing. He was still studying the picture.

"You find it beautiful?" the Prince asked gently.

"I find it beautiful but perplexing," was the hesitating reply.

The Prince's eyebrows were languidly raised. It was almost the only gesture which he ever permitted himself.

"Perplexing?"

"I do not pretend to be an expert," Radford continued. "My judgment as against the judgment of an expert is not worth a snap of the fingers, but I should have imagined that to have been the work of one of Lippo Lippi's disciples, or hangers-on in the studio, rather than his own."

The Prince smiled tolerantly.

"You must remember," he explained, as he carefully closed the box, "that The Kneeling Madonna was probably amongst the earliest of Fra Lippo Lippi's greater productions. He painted it in those hectic days when he was first tasting the sweet agony of liberty. However, let that pass. Shall I continue?"

"If you please," Radford begged.

"You are doubtless aware of a certain law of my country," the Prince went on, "which forbids the exportation of its art treasures, even when privately owned."

"I have heard of it."

"It is doubtful whether the law could ever be upheld against me, as I have the King's signed permission to deal with my own property in such ways as I think fit, but the law is a lengthy process, and I need the money."

"There is, I believe," Radford reflected, "a very heavy penalty—"

The Prince's beautifully shaped hand, gently uplifted, checked further speech from Radford.

"A Cantanerri is subject to no laws. Steps might be taken to prevent the picture leaving the country, if it were not too late, but a penalty cannot be inflicted. I shall proceed?"

"I shall be very glad to hear anything you have to say, Prince," Radford replied. "You will understand, however, I am sure, that the disposal of *objets d'art* such as this scarcely comes within the scheme of my activities."

The Prince smiled once more—indulgently this time.

"I should scarcely have sought out anyone of your profession, Major Radford," he confided, "for an ordinary transaction of this nature. In this case, however, what you have to do, if you consent to act as my agent, is a very easy task indeed. I wish to leave the picture in your keeping on the sole condition that you do not handle it or remove it from its box. In say an hour's time I should like you to ring up the firm of Levine. You will ask to speak to Jacob Levine. You will tell him that a certain picture has been deposited in your charge which is subject to his inspection this afternoon not later than three o'clock. If he is satisfied he may take it away with him on leaving behind with you an open cheque for eighty thousand pounds. That money you will draw from the bank and bring to me at the St. Luke's Club this afternoon."

Radford was for the moment speechless.

"I'm not to mention the name of the picture or discuss it in any way with Levine?" he asked.

"Certainly not. There is, in fact, no necessity. He knows all about the picture. All that you have to do is to unlock the box—see, I give you here the key—and to allow Jacob Levine to take the picture away with him if he hands you the cheque for eighty thousand pounds. The only other condition I make is that you do not leave this place until the transaction is concluded. So far as regards your fee, I suggest the sum of a thousand pounds, which you may deduct from the amount you bring me."

"The fee is wonderful," Radford murmured, "but supposing Levine, on examining the picture, is not prepared to buy it?"

The Prince had the patient air of one dealing with a troublesome child.

"If there should be any question of that sort," he said, "telephone to me at the St. Luke's Club…. Everything, I think, is understood?"

"Everything."

The Prince placed his precious parcel upon Radford's desk and picked up his hat. He was evidently one of the old-fashioned school to whom handshaking is not an acceptable form of greeting or farewell. With a slight but gracious inclination of the head, he turned toward the door.

"We shall meet later in the day, Major Radford," he remarked.

"I hope so," was the somewhat dazed response.

The great man from the Foreign Office showed not the slightest hesitation in acceding to Radford's somewhat diffidently proffered request. Within twenty minutes of his brief telephone conversation, he was seated in Radford's easy-chair.

"It's very kind indeed of you to come, sir," Radford declared warmly. "I would not have ventured to suggest such a thing, but you will understand, I am sure, the curious position I am placed in. You wish to know every slight happening in connection with the Prince. Very good! As I told you over the phone, he arrived here before ten o'clock this morning. He brought with him this picture"—Radford, producing the key from his pocket, commenced to unlock the box—"and my instructions are that Mr. Jacob Levine, who is, I suppose, the great picture dealer, will call here upon receiving a message from me, and will leave me an open cheque for eighty thousand pounds, which money I am to take to the Prince at the St. Luke's Club, and a portion of which he needs, I believe, to defray his accounts there. I am to deduct a fee of a thousand pounds."

"A pleasant little sum," the Minister murmured. "It all seems very simple, Radford. You were quite right to keep me posted at once, but what's your trouble?"

"Just this," Radford pointed out, opening the box, and displaying its contents. "I wonder whether you know anything about pictures, sir? I happen to know just a little."

"Nothing at all," the Minister confessed frankly. "What's wrong with it?"

"Well, the Prince declares that it is a genuine Fra Lippo Lippi picture, entitled The Kneeling Madonna. I never heard of such a picture, and, to tell you the truth, sir, although it's a very interesting painting, from my poor judgment I should never have believed it to have been a Fra Lippo Lippi at all."

The Minister whistled.

"So that's your trouble, is it, Radford?" he remarked.

"That's it, sir. I don't believe for a single moment that Levine will accept the picture as genuine, and I should say that the odds against my handling that cheque are about a hundred to one. If I don't handle it, what's going to happen to the Prince tonight when the clerk sends him up his account at the St. Luke's Club?"

The Minister examined the picture and stroked his chin. Then he looked at Radford, and there was a twinkle in his eyes.

"Let us hope, Radford," he said, "that you're not such a great art expert as you think."

"I am to carry on then, sir?"

The Minister took the picture from its case and handled it for a moment with curious, inquisitive fingers. Then he replaced it.

"Carry on, by all means, my dear Radford," he enjoined, "and let me know how the affair ends. It seems to me incredible that the Prince should be deceived in such a manner, or attempt to deceive anyone else."

"I think I can let you know now, sir, how it is likely to end," Radford replied, "but I'll ring you up, or come round."

Whereupon Radford's second distinguished visitor of the morning took his leave. The third arrived punctually at two o'clock. Radford recognized him at once—a short, squat man, with eyeglasses which hung always over the bridge of his nose, a gray, trimly kept mustache, thick lips but piercing eyes.

"What about the picture, Major?" he said briskly.

Radford unfastened the locks, and stood it upon his desk. The famous art critic peered at it, took it out of its case, carried it to the light and fondled it with his thick, pudgy fingers. Presently he brought it back to the box.

"Wonderful!" he murmured, with a farewell glance. "Lock it up, young man."

He drew his chair to the desk, produced a fountain pen and began to write. Radford watched him in amazement. He wrote swiftly and without hesitation:

Pay to Major Radford, or order, the sum of eighty thousand pounds.

"You're satisfied with the picture?" Radford ventured to inquire.

Jacob Levine shot a swift look at him.

"If the prince had asked a hundred thousand he could have had it," he replied, tucking the parcel under his arm, and taking his leave.

Radford, a little dazed, called for his car and drove to his bank. He passed a credit slip across the counter with Mr. Levine's cheque.

"I want to draw out the whole of that amount," he told the clerk. "I'm in no hurry for a few minutes if you like to telephone over to Mr. Levine's place."

"Quite unnecessary, sir," the clerk assured him. "Mr. Levine sent word in this afternoon that a cheque for eighty thousand pounds would be presented, and that it was O. K."

"Very thoughtful of him," Radford observed. "Thousand-pound notes, please."

At twelve o'clock on the following morning Radford was once more ushered into the familiar room where his chief sat waiting for him. As he took the chair to which the latter good-humoredly pointed, a little gasp of surprise escaped him. On the farther end of the long table was a familiar package.

"Well, finish your story, Radford," the Minister invited.

"I'm beginning to think you know about as much of it as I do, sir," was the wondering rejoinder. "Levine came, gave me a cheque for the picture, the bank cashed the cheque, I handed over the money to the Prince, who pushed it into his pocket as though it were a packet of treasury notes. I hung about the Club most of the evening. The Prince paid his account, and for once had a streak of luck. He must have won eleven or twelve thousand pounds."

The other nodded.

"I can see where your eyes are wandering, Radford," he remarked. "You've been very useful in this matter, and although I can rely upon your discretion I shall have to apologize for leaving you still a little in the dark. This much, however, you shall know. Cantanerri was ruined by the war, treated badly by his government and is practically penniless. He reverted to his old profession—this time rather more on his own account. He discovered what we have all known for many months—that there is a new political plot brewing which started at Geneva last year, which involves at some time or other, I fear, another European war, a regrouping of the Balkan states, and I think I may as well add of Poland and of Hungary. The prime mover in this you can guess to be Germany, and the country which she is anxious to secure as her ally is Cantanerri's native land. That much we knew, but what we were at our wits' end to discover was the bribe Germany was prepared to offer. Cantanerri discovered that for us in his own capital. Damned clever fellow, that! He knew that nothing would satisfy us but the original documents, and you know now the way he solved the problem of getting them out of his country.

"He got permission to sell one of his so-called works of art, which, although, mind you many people think a very beautiful picture, is, as you surmised, the work of one of Fra Lippo Lippi's disciples; and the original documents were packed in the back of it, the government stamp giving it a free exit. Levine was willing to oblige, and there we are! We have what we want, the Prince has eighty thousand pounds, you have what I hope you will consider an adequate fee, and two of our ambassadors in foreign countries are under notice of recall to be replaced by stronger men. No one can every associate Cantanerri with the business, as he has never been near any of us—and you have been a very useful agent."

Radford picked up his hat.

"After all, sir," he said, as he took his leave, "crime is all very well, but I think that politics pay best."

Sid Fleischman was an entertainer at heart. When he was fifteen he traveled in vaudeville as a magician. He tried his hand at writing and became known for writing humorous fiction as well as children's books. He wrote for Hollywood, including the John Wayne/Lauren Bacall movie Blood Alley. *Fleischman was not only recognized with a Newbery Medal winner but he was also a National Book Awards finalist. Vastly overlooked—though not by Stark House—are his exotic adventure mysteries, which set a standard few writers can match. They are true seat-of-your pants thrillers in the best paperback original tradition.*

SECRETARIES MAKE SUCH NICE WIVES

A. S. Fleischman

To begin with, it was a rotten day. The Mexican sun was in hiding and the track at Agua Caliente was muddy from last night's rain. Paul Stevens, the film star, hadn't picked a winner in any of the first five races. "Let's go, baby," he said, turning to Kathryne. "They cleaned me—but good."

His wife—who had been Mrs. Stevens only two weeks—smiled with a proud twinkle in her eyes. She had picked two winners. "Any time you care to borrow my crystal ball," she said, "just let me know."

"Okay, Mrs. Moneybags," he grinned. "You'll pay the dinner check."

Paul's sedan was at a far end of the parking lot. They began to walk. "Paul—you're not sorry you married me," Kathryne muttered, suddenly serious. "I mean—you could have married a name. Secretaries come a dime a dozen."

The actor wrapped his arm around her waist and gripped her reassuringly. "I'm not complaining," he said. They reached the car and Paul unlocked the door.

"Mind if we join you, Stevens?" It was a voice from behind. Paul had been inattentive to the sound of footsteps that had followed him out the gate. He turned sharply. A man and woman, in casual sports clothes, faced him. The man seemed about 40, he thought. The woman, younger and very thin, appeared cat-like nervous and wore dark sun glasses. Her cheeks were drawn.

"Sorry, chum," the actor replied. "We're not going your way." Autograph hunters could often be a nuisance.

"Let's not waste each other's time," the man said with a fixed smile. "Unfortunately, ol' man, I'm armed. You're taking us across the border. Please—get in."

Paul looked at Kathryne and she returned his own astonishment. They got in, and the strangers took the back seat. The actor backed the sedan out and turned on to the highway.

"What's going to prevent me," Paul asked, "from turning you in at the border while the car is being searched?"

The man threw his head back and laughed briefly. "You do have a sense of humor, ol' man. I'll be perfectly frank with you. I can't afford to be caught." He leaned forward and placed his arm over the front seat. A small pistol lay in his oversize palm. "Do we understand each other, my friend?"

"Perfectly," the actor murmured.

"At no time," the stranger went on in an even voice, "will you or your companion leave your seats during the border inspection. We're simply your Hollywood friends down for the races."

Tijuana lay behind them. The sedan crossed the narrow bridge only a few blocks from the border gates where a short double line of cars waited. Paul took the outside line, stopping behind a station wagon.

The station wagon in front of him cleared customs and Paul pulled forward. He killed the engine, and the inspector, a red-faced giant in baggy uniform, bent down to the window.

"Nationality?" he inquired of the back seat.

"American," the man answered politely.

"American."

"Where were you born?"

"Kansas City."

"New York."

There were no accents to arouse his suspicions and the inspector turned to Paul and Kathryne. Before he put his routine questions to them, he recognized Paul and his face because a bustling smile.

"You're Paul Sevens, the movie star!"

Paul confessed and wondered if there wasn't some way to convey to the lunkhead that there was dynamite in the back seat.

"Say—I hate to trouble you," the officer said, pulling a small notebook from his breast pocket. "My kid collects autographs. You wouldn't mind putting down your John Henry, would you?"

What a break! "Not a bit," Paul replied anxiously. He could write a quick note for help and the two uninvited travelers would be helpless to stop him.

Paul hardly had the book in hand when the man in the back seat leaned forward. "Perhaps the inspector would like our autographs too," he smiled.

"Sure would," the customs man said enthusiastically. "All of you sign."

That was that, Paul thought. He finished his signature and handed the book to Kathryne. She signed and passed the page into the back seat.

"Thanks a million," the inspector grinned, when the book was returned. "Now I'll have to make a routine check of your car."

While he was searching the luggage compartment three high school girls piled out of a red convertible alongside and shoved paper and pencil at the actor and his group. While they giggled and gawked, the back seat kept a sharp eye on Paul and Kathryne. In each case they made sure their own signatures were written last.

"Okay," the inspector smiled, waving Paul off and turning his attention to the red convertible.

Paul started the engine and pulled on to the highway leading into San Diego. "Now what?" he asked irritably. "Can we drop you off at the city jail?"

The passengers were obviously relieved at having safely crossed the border. "That address won't do," he laughed. "We'll leave you at 12th and Market. And we do want to thank you for the lift, ol' man."

It wasn't until the siren shrilled up from behind that Paul noticed a police car racing up from behind. Reflexively, he yanked his foot of the accelerator.

"Step on it, you idiot!"

The stranger had lost his poise. His head and shoulders appeared between Paul and Kathryne. The gun was in his hand. He braced the muzzle against her temple. "Give it the gas or I'll blow the lady's head to bits."

It was no time for argument. Paul jammed the accelerator to the floor. He caught a glance at Katheryne—she looked frightened but composed.

The siren wailed nearer. Two sirens. A distant shot exploded—the police were trying for his tires!

Paul's speedometer climbed dangerously. A blowout now and they'd all be killed! It was time to take a chance—

Without warning he jammed the brake pedal to the floor. The sedan careened sidewise, whined off the road and stopped short of a eucalyptus sapling. The man pitched forward, his body sailing into the front seat except for his legs. Paul reached for the gun. He caught the man's wrist and twisted until the gun dropped. Kathryne had shielded her face with her hands and had struck the dashboard. She was dazed, but okay.

The police closed in. A service revolver was thrust upon them. An officer gestured for all to get out of the car.

Paul explained what had taken place. The pair of strangers were given a hasty search. On the man were found a number of small containers of heroin—taped to his waist.

There was murder in the smuggler's eyes. "You tipped 'em off. I'll get you!" He was handcuffed to the woman and both were led to the police car.

"We've your wife to thank," the officer explained, who was treating Kathryne's bruises. "She wrote the words 'help' 'follow' in shorthand as the middle initial in her signature. One of the girls in the red convertible alongside you could read the stuff. She tipped us off."

Paul bent down and kissed Kathryne on her turned up nose. "Officer," he smiled, "take it from me. Secretaries make nice wives."

Many of the writers in this collection have been praised for the number of stories they've published in multiple genres, but Robert Silverberg undoubtedly leads the way. He is a legend chiefly in the realm of science fiction but he has written at least a little bit of everything else, including non-fiction. I remember well teaching myself to juggle in front of the bathroom mirror as I read the serialization of Lord Valentine's Castle; *the first edition release may have been the first hardcover I ever purchased. Collections of his work are a joy to read, accompanied as many of them are by Silverberg's own reminiscences and stories-behind-the-story recountings.*

THE DEAD MAN'S EYES

Robert Silverberg

On a crisp afternoon of high winds late in the summer of 2017 Frazier murdered his wife's lover, a foolish deed that he immediately regretted. To murder anyone was stupid, when there were so many more effective alternatives available; but even so, if murder was what he had to do, why murder the *lover*? Two levels of guilt attached there: not only the taking of a life, but the taking of an irrelevant life. If you had to kill someone, he told himself immediately afterward, then you should have killed *her*. She was the one who had committed the crime against the marriage, after all. Poor Hurwitt had been only a means, a tool, virtually an innocent bystander. Yes, kill *her*, not him. Kill yourself, even. But Hurwitt was the one he had killed, a dumb thing to do and done in a dumb manner besides.

It had all happened very quickly, without premeditation. Frazier was attending a meeting of the Museum trustees, to discuss expanding the Hall of Mammals. There was a recess; and because the day was so cool, the air so crystalline and bracing, he stepped out on the balcony that connected the old building with the Pilgersen Extension for a quick breather. Then the sleek bronze door of the Pilgersen opened far down the way and a dark-haired man in a grubby blue-gray lab coat appeared. Frazier saw at once, by the rigid set of his high shoulders and the way his long hair fluttered in the wind, that it was Hurwitt.

He wants to see me, Frazier thought. He knows I'm attending the meeting today and he's come out here to stage the confrontation at last, to tell me that he loves my famous and beautiful wife, to ask me bluntly to clear off and let him have her all to himself.

Frazier's pulse began to rise, his face grew hot. Even while he was thinking that it was oddly old-fashioned to talk of *letting* Hurwitt have Marianne, that in fact Hurwitt had probably already had Marianne in every conceivable way and vice versa but that if now he had some idea of setting up housekeeping with her—unbelievable, unthinkable!—this was hardly the appropriate place to discuss it with him, another and more primordial area of his brain was calling forth torrents of adrenaline and preparing him for mortal combat.

But no: Hurwitt didn't seem to have ventured onto the balcony for any man-to-man conference with his lover's husband. Evidently he was simply taking the shortcut from his lab in the Pilgersen to the fourth-floor cafeteria in the old building. He walked with his head down, his brows knitted, as though pondering some abstruse detail of trilobite anatomy, and he took no notice of Frazier at all.

"Hurwitt?" Frazier said finally, when the other man was virtually abreast of him.

Caught by surprise, Hurwitt looked up, blinking. He appeared not to recognize Frazier for a moment. For that moment he was frozen in mid-blink, his unkempt hair a dark halo about him, his awkward rangy body off balance between strides, his peculiar glinting eyes flashing like yellow beacons. In fury Frazier imagined this man's bony nakedness, pale and gaunt, probably with sparse ropy strands of black hair sprouting on a white chest, imagined those long arms wrapped around Marianne, imagined those huge knobby fingers cupping her breasts, imagined that thin-lipped wide mouth covering hers. Imagined the grubby lab coat lying crumpled at the foot of the bed, and her silken orange wrap beside it. That was what sent Frazier over the brink, not the infidelities themselves, not the thought of the sweaty embraces—there was plenty of that in each of her films, and it had never meant a thing to him, for he knew it was only well-paid make-believe—and not the rawboned look of the man or his uncouth stride or even the manic glint of those strange off-color eyes, those eerie topaz eyes, but the lab coat, stained and worn with a button missing and a pocket-flap dangling, lying beside Marianne's discarded silk. For her to take such a lover, a pathetic dreary poker of fossils, a hollow-chested laboratory drudge—no, no, no—

"Hello, Loren," Hurwitt said. He smiled amiably, he offered his hand. His eyes, though, narrowed and seemed almost to glow. It must be those weird eyes, Frazier thought, that Marianne has fallen in love with. "What a surprise, running into you out here."

And stood there smiling, and stood there holding out his hand, and stood there with his frayed lab coat flapping in the breeze.

Suddenly Frazier was unable to bear the thought of sharing the world with this man an instant longer. He watched himself as though from a point just behind his own right ear as he went rushing forward, seized not Hurwitt's hand but his wrist, and pushed rather than pulled, guiding him swiftly backward toward the parapet and tipping him up and over. It took perhaps a quarter of a second. Hurwitt, gaping, astonished, rose as though floating, hovered for an instant, began to descend. Frazier had one last look at Hurwitt's eyes, bright as glass, staring straight into his own, photographing his assailant's face; and then Hurwitt went plummeting downward.

My God, Frazier thought, peering over the edge. Hurwitt lay face down in the courtyard five stories below, arms and legs splayed, lab coat billowing about him.

He was at the airport an hour later, with a light suitcase that carried no more than a day's change of clothing and a few cosmetic items. He flew first to Dallas, endured a 90-minute layover, went on to San Francisco, doubled back to Calgary as darkness descended, and caught a midnight special to Mexico City, where he checked into a hotel using the legal commercial alias that he employed when doing business in Macao, Singapore, and Hong Kong. Standing on the terrace of a tower thirty stories above the Zona Rosa, he inhaled musky smog, listened to the squeals of traffic and the faint sounds of far-off drums, watched flares of green lightning in the choking sky above Popocatepetl, and wondered whether he should jump. Ultimately he decided against it. He wanted to share nothing whatever with Hurwitt, not even the manner of his death. And suicide would be an overreaction anyway. First he had to find out how much trouble he was really in.

The hotel had InfoLog. He dialed in and was told that queries were billed at five million pesos an hour, pro rated. Vaguely he wondered whether that was as expensive as it sounded. The peso was practically worthless, wasn't it? What could that be in dollars, a hundred bucks, five hundred, maybe? Nothing.

"I want Harvard Legal," he told the screen. "Criminology. Forensics. Technical. Evidence technology." Grimly he menued down and down until he was near what he wanted. "Eyeflash," he said. "Theory, techniques. Methods of detail recovery. Acceptance as evidence. Reliability of record. Frequency of reversal on appeal. Supreme Court rulings, if any."

Back to him, in surreal fragments which, at an extra charge of three million pesos per hour, pro rated, he had printed out for him, came blurts of information:

Perceptual pathways in outer brain layers....broad-scale optical architecture....images imprinted on striate cortex, or primary visual cortex....inferior temporal neurons....cf. McDermott and Brunetti, 2007, utilization of lateral geniculate body as storage for visual data....inferior temporal cortex....uptake of radioactive glucose....downloading....degrading of signal....degeneration period....Pilsudski signal-enhancement filter....Nevada vs. Bensen, 2011....hippocampus simulation....amygdala....acetylcholine....U.S. Supreme Court, 23 March 2012....cf Gross and Bernstein, 13 Aug 2003....Mishkin....Appenzeller....

Enough. He shuffled the printouts in a kind of hard-edged stupor until dawn; and then, after a hazy calculation of time-zone differentials, he called his lawyer in New York. It took four bounces, but the telephone tracked him down in the commute, driving in from Connecticut.

Frazier keyed in the privacy filter. All the lawyer would know was that some client was calling; the screen image would be a blur, the voice would be rendered universal, generalized, unidentifiable. It was more for the lawyer's protection than Frazier's: there had been nasty twists in jurisprudence lately, and lawyers were less and less willing to run the risk of being named accomplices after the fact. Immediately came a query about the billing. Bill to my hotel room, Frazier replied, and the screen gave him a go-ahead.

"Let's say I'm responsible for causing a fatal injury and the victim had a good opportunity to see me as the act was occurring. What are the chances that they can recover eyeflash pictures?"

"Depends on how much damage was received in the process of the death. How did it happen?"

"Privileged communication?"

"Sorry. No."

"Even under filter?"

"Even. If the mode of death was unique or even highly distinctive and unusual, how can I help but draw the right conclusion? And then I'll know more than I want to know."

"It wasn't unique," Frazier said. "Or distinctive, or unusual. But I still won't go into details. I can tell you that the injury wasn't the sort that would cause specific brain trauma. I mean, nothing like a bullet between the eyes, or falling into a vat of acid, or—"

"All right. I follow. This take place in a major city?"

"Major, yes."

"In Missouri, Alabama, or Kentucky?"

"None of those," said Frazier. "It took place in a state where eyeflash recovery is legal. No question of that."

"And the body? How long after death do you estimate it would have been found?"

"Within minutes, I'd say."

"And when was that?"

Frazier hesitated. "Within the past twenty-four hours."

"Then there's almost total likelihood that there's a readily recoverable photograph in your victim's brain of whatever he saw at the moment of death. Beyond much doubt it's already been recovered. Are you sure he was looking at you as he died?"

"Straight at me."

"My guess is there's probably a warrant out for you already. If you want me to represent you, kill the privacy filter so I can confirm who you are, and we'll discuss our options."

"Later," Frazier said. "I think I'd rather try to make a run for it."

"But the chances of your getting away with—"

"This is something I need to do," said Frazier. "I'll talk to you some other time."

He was almost certainly cooked. He knew that. He had wasted critical time running frantically back and forth across the continent yesterday, when he should have been transferring funds, setting up secure refuges, and such. The only question now was whether they were already looking for him, in which case there'd be blocks on his accounts everywhere, a passport screen at every airport, worldwide interdicts of all sorts. But if that was so they'd already have traced him to this hotel. Evidently they hadn't, which meant that they hadn't yet uncovered the Southeast Asian trading alias and put interdicts on that. Well, it was just a lousy manslaughter case, or maybe second-degree at worst: they had more serious things to worry about, he supposed.

Checking out of the hotel without bothering about breakfast, he headed for the airport and used his corporate credit card to buy himself a flight to Belize. There he bought a ticket to Surinam, and just before his plane was due to leave he tried his personal card in the cash disburser and was pleasantly surprised to find that it hadn't yet been yanked. He withdrew the maximum. Of course now there was evidence that Loren Frazier had been in Belize this day, but he wasn't traveling as Frazier, and he'd be in Surinam before long, and by the time they traced him there, assuming that they could, he'd be somewhere else, under some other name entirely. Maybe if he kept dodging for six or eight months he'd scramble his trail so thoroughly that they'd never be able to find him. Did they pursue you forever, he wondered? A time must come when they file and forget. Of course, he might not want to keep running forever, either. Already he missed Marianne. Despite what she had done.

He spent three days in Surinam at a little pastel-green Dutch hotel at the edge of Paramaribo, eating spicy noodle dishes and waiting to be arrested. Nobody bothered him. He used a cash machine again, keying up one of his corporate accounts and transferring a bundle of money into the account of Andreas Schmidt of Zurich, which was a name he had used seven years ago for some export-import maneuvers involving Zimbabwe and somehow, he knew not why, had kept alive for eventualities unknown. This was an eventuality, now. When he checked the Schmidt account he found that there was money in it already, significant money, and that his Swiss passport had not yet expired. The Swiss charge-d'affaires in Guyana was requested to prepare a duplicate for him. A quick boat trip up the Marowijne River took him to St. Laurent on the French Guiana side of the river, where he was able to hire a driver to take him to Cayenne, and from there he flew to Georgetown in Guyana. A smiling proxy lawyer named

Chatterji obligingly picked up his passport for him from the Swiss, and under the name of Schmidt he went on to Buenos Aires. There he destroyed all his Frazier documentation. He resisted the temptation to find out whether there was a Frazier interdict out yet. No sense handing them a trail extending down to Buenos Aires just to gratify his curiosity. If they weren't yet looking for him because he had murdered Hurwitt, they'd be looking for him on a simple missing-persons hook by this time. One way or another, it was best to forget about his previous identity and operate as Schmidt from here on.

This is almost fun, he thought.

But he missed his wife terribly.

While sitting in sidewalk cafes on the broad Avenida de 9 Julio, feasting on huge parrilladas sluiced down by carafe after carafe of red wine, he brooded obsessively on Marianne's affair. It made no sense. The world-famous actress and the awkward rawboned paleontologist: why? How was it possible? She had been making a commercial at the museum—Frazier, in fact, had helped to set the business up in his capacity as a member of the board of trustees—and Hurwitt, who was the head of the department of invertebrate paleontology, or some such thing, had volunteered to serve as the technical consultant. Very kind of him, everyone said. Taking time away from his scientific work. He seemed so bland, so juiceless: who could suspect him of harboring lust for the glamorous film personality? Nobody would have imagined it. But things must have started almost at once. Some chemistry between them, beyond all understanding. People began to notice, and then to give Frazier strange little knowing looks. Eventually even he caught on. A truly loving husband is generally just about the last one to know, because he will always put the best possible interpretation on the data. But after a time the accumulation of data becomes impossible to overlook or deny or reason away. There are always small changes when something like that has begun: they start to read books of a kind they've never read before, they talk of different things, they may even show some new moves in bed. Then comes the real carelessness, the seemingly unconscious slips that scream the actual nature of the situation. Frazier was forced finally to an acceptance of the truth. It tore at his heart. There was no room in their marriage for such stuff. Despite his money, despite his power, he had never gone in for the casual morality of the intercontinental set, and neither, so he thought, had Marianne. This was the second marriage for each: the one that was supposed to carry them happily on to the finish. And now look.

"Se or? Another carafe?"

"No," he said. "Yes. Yes." He stared at his plate. It was full of sausages, sweetbreads, grilled steak. Where had all that come from? He was sure he had eaten everything. It must have grown back. Moodily he stabbed a plump blood sausage and ate without noticing. Took a drink. They mixed the wine with seltzer water here, half and half. Maybe it helped you put away those tons of meat more easily.

Afterward, strolling along the narrow, glittering Calle Florida with the stylish evening promenade flowing past him on both sides, he caught sight of Marianne coming out of a jeweler's shop. She wore gaucho leathers, emerald earrings, skin-tight trousers of gold brocade. He grunted as though he had been struck and pressed his elbows against his sides as one might do if expecting a second blow. Then an elegant young Argentinian uncoiled himself from a curbside table and trotted quickly toward her, and they laughed and embraced and ran off arm in arm, sweeping right past him without even a glance. He remembered, now: women all over the world were wearing Marianne's face this season. This one, in fact, was too tall by half a head. But he would have to be prepared for such incidents wherever he went. Mariannes everywhere, bludgeoning him with their beauty and never even knowing what they had done. He found himself wishing that the one who had been sleeping with that museum man was just another Marianne clone, that the real one was at home alone now, waiting for him, wondering, wondering.

In Montreal six weeks later, using a privacy filter and one of his corporate cards, he risked putting through a call to his apartment and discovered that there was an interdict on his line. When he tried the office number an android mask appeared on the screen and he was blandly told that Mr. Frazier was unavailable. The android didn't know when Mr. Frazier would be available. Frazier asked for Markman, his executive assistant, and a moment later a bleak, harried, barely recognizable face looked out at him. Frazier explained that he was a representative of the Bucharest account, calling about a highly sensitive matter. "Don't you know?" Markman said. "Mr. Frazier's disappeared. The police are looking for him." Frazier asked why, and Markman's face dissolved in an agony of shame, bewilderment, protective zeal. "There's a criminal charge against him," Markman whispered, nearly in tears.

He called his lawyer next and said, "I'm calling about the Frazier case. I don't want to kill the filter but I imagine you won't have much trouble figuring out who I am."

"I imagine I won't. Just don't tell me where you are, okay?"

The situation was about as he expected. They had recovered the murder prints from the dead man's eyes: a nice shot, embedded deep in the cortical tissue, Frazier looming up against Hurwitt, nose to nose, a quick cut to the hand reaching for Hurwitt' arm, a wild free-form pan to the sky as Frazier lifted Hurwitt up and over the parapet. "Pardon me for saying this, but you looked absolutely deranged," the lawyer told him. "The prints were on all the networks the next day. Your eyes—it was really scary. I'm absolutely sure we could get impairment of faculties, maybe even crime of passion. Suspended sentence, but of course there'd be rehabilitation. I don't see any way around that, and it could last a year or two, and you might not be as effective in your profession afterward, but considering the circumstances—"

"How's my wife?" Frazier said. "Do you know anything about what she's been doing?"

"Well, of course I don't represent her, you realize. But she does get in the news. She's said to be traveling."

"Where?"

"I couldn't say. Look, I can try to find out, if you'd like to call back this time tomorrow. Only I suggest that for your own good you call me at a different number, which is—"

"For my good or for yours?" Frazier said.

"I'm trying to help," said the lawyer, sounding annoyed.

He took refresher courses in French, Italian, and German to give himself a little extra plausibility in the Andreas Schmidt identity, and cultivated a mild Teutonic accent. So long as he didn't run up against any real Swiss who wanted to gabble with him in Romansch or Schwyzerdeutsch he suspected he'd make out all right. He kept on moving, Strasbourg, Athens, Haifa, Tunis. Even though he knew that no further fund transfers were possible, there was enough money stashed under the Schmidt accounts to keep him going nicely for ten or fifteen years, and by then he hoped to have this thing figured out.

He saw Mariannes in Tel Aviv, in Heraklion on Crete, and in Sidi bou Said, just outside Tunis. They were all clones, of course. He recognized that after just a quick queasy instant. Still, seeing that delicate high-bridged nose once again, those splendid amethyst eyes, those tight auburn ringlets, it was all he could do to keep himself from going up to them and throwing his arms around them, and he had to force himself each time to turn away, biting down hard on his lip.

In London, outside the Connaught, he saw the real thing. The Connaught was where they had spent their wedding trip back in '07, and he winced at the sight of its familiar grand façade, and winced even more when Marianne came out, young and radiant, wearing a shimmering silver cloud. Dazzling light streamed from her. He had no doubt that this was no trendy clone but the true Marianne: she moved in that easy confident way, with that regal joy in her own beauty, that no cosmetic surgeon could ever impart even to the most intent imitator. The pavement itself seemed to do her homage. But then Frazier saw that the man on whose arm she walked was himself, young and radiant too, the Loren Frazier of that honeymoon journey of seven years back, his hair dark and thick, his love of life and success and his magnificent new wife cloaking him like an imperial mantle; and Frazier realized that he must merely be hallucinating, that the breakdown had moved on to a new and more serious stage. He stood gaping while Mr. and Mrs. Frazier swept through him like the phantoms they were and away in the direction of Grosvenor Square, and then he staggered and nearly fell. To the Connaught doorman he admitted that he was unwell, and because he was well dressed and spoke with the hint of an accent and was able to find a twenty-sovereign piece in the nick of time the doorman helped him into a cab and expressed his deepest concern. Back at his own hotel, ten minutes over on the other side of Mayfair, he had three quick gins in a row and sat shivering for an hour before the image faded from his mind.

"I advise you to give yourself up," the lawyer said, when Frazier called him from Nairobi. "Of course you can keep on running as long as you like. But you're wearing yourself out, and sooner or later someone will spot you, so why keep on delaying the inevitable?"

"Have you spoken to Marianne lately?"

"She wishes you'd come back. She wants to write to you, or call you, or even come and see you, wherever you are. But I've told her you refuse to provide me with any information about your location. Is that still your position?"

"I don't want to see her or hear from her."

"She loves you."

"I'm a homicidal maniac. I might do the same thing to her that I did to Hurwitt."

"Surely you don't really believe—"

"No," Frazier said. "Not really."

"Then let me give her an address for you, at least, and she can write to you."

"It could be a trap, couldn't it?"

"Surely you can't possibly believe—"

"Who knows? Anything's possible."

"A postal box in Caracas, say," the lawyer suggested, "and let's say that you're in Rio, for the sake of the discussion, and I arrange an intermediary to pick up the letter and forward it care of American Express in Lima, and then on some day of your own choosing, known to nobody else, you make a quick trip in and out of Peru and—"

"And they grab me the moment I collect the letter," Frazier said. "How stupid do you think I am? You could set up forty intermediaries and I'd still have to create a trail leading to myself if I want to get the letter. Besides, I'm not in South America any more. That was months ago."

"It was only for the sake of the dis—" the lawyer said, but Frazier was gone already.

He decided to change his face and settle down somewhere. The lawyer was right: all this compulsive traveling was wearing him down. But by staying in one place longer than a week or two he was multiplying the chances of being detected, so long as he went on looking like himself. He had always wanted a longer nose anyway, and not quite so obtrusive a chin, and thicker eyebrows. He fancied that he looked too Slavic, though he had no Eastern European ancestry at all. All one long rainy evening at the mellow old Addis Ababa Hilton he sketched a face for himself that he thought looked properly Swiss: rugged, passionate, with the right mix of French elegance, German stolidity, Italian passion. Then he went downstairs and showed the printout to the bartender, a supple little Portuguese.

"Where would you say this man comes from?" Frazier asked.

"Lisbon," the bartender replied at once. "That long jaw, those lips— unmistakably Lisbon, though perhaps his grandmother on his mother's side is of the Algarve. A man of considerable distinction, I would say. But I do not know him, Senhor Schmidt. He is no one I know. You would like your dry martini, as usual?"

"Make it a double," Frazier said.

He had the work done in Vienna. Everyone agreed that the best people for that sort of surgery were in Geneva, but Switzerland was the one country in the world he dared not enter, so he used his Zurich banking connections to get him the name of the second-best people, who were said to be almost as good, remarkably good, he was told. That seemed high praise indeed, Frazier thought, considering it was a Swiss talking about Austrians. The head surgeon at the Vienna clinic, though, turned out to be Swiss himself, which provided Frazier with a moment of complete terror, pretending as he was to be a native of Zurich. But the surgeon had been at his trade long enough to know that a man who wants his perfectly good face transformed into something entirely different does not wish to talk about his personal affairs. He was a big, cheerful extravert named Randegger with a distinct limp. Skiing accident, the surgeon explained. Surely getting your leg fixed must be easier than getting your face changed, Frazier thought, but he decided that Randegger was simply waiting for the off season to undergo repair. "This will be no problem at all," Randegger told him, studying Frazier's printout. "I have just a few small suggestions." He went deftly to work with a light-pen, broadening the cheekbones, moving the ears downward and forward. Frazier shrugged. Whatever you want, Dr. Randegger, he thought. Whatever you want. I'm putty in your hands.

It took six weeks from first cut to final healing. The results seemed fine to him—suave, convincing, an authoritative face—though at the beginning he was afraid it would all come apart if he smiled, and it was hard to get used to looking in a mirror and seeing someone else. He stayed at the clinic the whole six weeks. One of the nurses wore the Marianne face, but the body was all wrong, wide hips, startling steatopygous rump, short muscular legs. Near the end of his stay she lured him into bed. He was sure he'd be impotent with her, but he was wrong. There was only one really bad moment, when she reared above him and he couldn't see her body at all, only her beautiful, passionate, familiar face.

Even now, he couldn't stop running. Belgrade, Sydney, Rabat, Barcelona, Milan: they went by in a blur of identical airports, interchangeable hotels, baffling shifts of climate. Almost everywhere he went he saw Mariannes, and sometimes was puzzled that they never recognized him, until he remembered that he had altered his face: why should they know him now, even after the seven years of their marriage? As she traveled he began to see another ubiquitous face, dark and Latin and pixyish, and realized that Marianne's vogue must be beginning to wane. He hoped that some of the Mariannes would soon be converting themselves to this newer look. He had never really felt at ease with all these simulacra of his wife, whom he still loved beyond all measure.

That love, though, had become inextricably mixed with anger. He could not even now stop thinking about her incomprehensible, infuriating violation of the sanctity of their covenant. It had been the best of marriages, amiable, passionate, close, a true union on every level. He had never even thought of wanting another woman. She was everything he wanted; and he had every reason to think that his feelings were reciprocated. That was the worst of it, not the furtive little couplings she and Hurwitt must have enjoyed, but the deeper treason, the betrayal of their seeming harmony, her seemingly whimsical destruction of the hermetic seal that enclosed their perfect world.

He had overreacted, he knew. He wished he could call back the one absurd impulsive act that had thrust him from his smooth and agreeable existence into this frantic wearisome fugitive life. And he felt sorry for Hurwitt, who probably had been caught up in emotions beyond his depth, swept away by the astonishment of finding himself in Marianne's arms. How could he have stopped to worry, at such a time, about what he might be doing to someone else's marriage? How ridiculous it had been to kill him! And to stare right into Hurwitt's eyes, incontrovertibly incriminating himself, while he did! If he needed any proof of his temporary insanity, the utter foolishness of the murder would supply it.

But there was no calling any of it back. Hurwitt was dead; he had lived on the run for—what, two years, three?—and Marianne was altogether lost to him. So much destruction achieved in a single crazy moment. He wondered what he would do if he ever saw Marianne again. Nothing violent, no, certainly not. He had a sudden image of himself in tears, hugging her knees, begging her forgiveness. For what? For killing her lover?

For bringing all sorts of nasty mess and the wrong kind of publicity into her life? For disrupting the easy rhythms of their happy marriage? No, he thought, astonished, aghast. What do I have to be forgiven for? From her, nothing. She's the one who should go down on her knees before me. I wasn't the one who was fooling around. And then he thought, No, no, we must forgive each other. And after that he thought, Best of all, I must take care never to have anything to do with her for the rest of my life. And that thought cut through him like a blade, like Dr. Randegger's fiery scalpel.

Six months later he was walking through the cavernous, ornate lobby of the Hotel de Paris in Monte Carlo when he saw a Marianne standing in front of a huge stack of suitcases against a marble pillar no more than twenty feet from him. He was inured to Mariannes by this time and at first the sight of her had no impact; but then he noticed the familiar monogram on the luggage, and recognized the intricate little bows of red plush cord with which the baggage tags were tied on, and he realized that this was the true Marianne at last. Nor was this any hallucination like the Connaught one. She was visibly older, with a vertical line in her left cheek that he had never seen before. Her hair was a darker shade and somehow more ordinary in its cut, and she was dressed simply, no radiance at all. Even so, people were staring at her and whispering. Frazier swayed, gripped a nearby pillar with his suddenly clammy hand, fought back the impulse to run. He took a deep breath and went toward her, walking slowly, impressively, his carefully cultivated distinguished-looking-Swiss-businessman walk.

"Marianne?" he said.

She turned her head slightly and stared at him without any show of recognition.

"I do look different, yes," he said, smiling.

"I'm sorry, but I don't—"

A slender, agile-looking man five or six years younger than she, wearing sunglasses, appeared from somewhere as though conjured out of the floor. Smoothly he interpolated himself between Frazier and Marianne. A lover? A bodyguard? Simply part of her entourage? Pleasantly but forcefully he presented himself to Frazier as though saying, Let's not have any trouble now, shall we?

"Listen to my voice," Frazier said. "You haven't forgotten my voice. Only the face is different."

Sunglasses came a little closer. Looked a little less pleasant.

Marianne stared.

"You haven't forgotten, have you, Marianne?" Frazier said.

Sunglasses began to look definitely menacing.

"Wait a minute," Marianne said, as he glided into a nose-to-nose with Frazier. "Step back, Aurelio." She peered through the shadows. "Loren?"

she said.

Frazier nodded. He went toward her. At a gesture from Marianne, Sunglasses faded away like a genie going back into the bottle. Frazier felt strangely calm now. He could see Marianne's upper lip trembling, her nostrils flickering a little. "I thought I never wanted to see you again," he said. "But I was wrong about that. The moment I saw you and knew it was really you, I realized that I had never stopped thinking about you, never stopped wanting you. Wanting to put it all back together."

Her eyes widened. "And you think you can?"

"Maybe."

"What a damned fool you are," she said, gently, almost lovingly, after a long moment.

"I know. I really messed myself up, doing what I did."

"I don't mean that," she said. "You messed us both up with that. Not to mention him, the poor bastard. But that can't be undone, can it? If you only knew how often I prayed to have it not have happened." She shook her head. "It was nothing, what he and I were doing. Nothing. Just a silly fling, for Christ's sake. How could you possibly have cared so much?"

"What?"

"To *kill* a man, for something like that? To wreck three lives in half a second? For *that*?"

"What?" he said again. "What are you telling me?"

Sunglasses suddenly was in the picture again. "We're going to miss the car to the airport, Marianne."

"Yes. Yes. All right, let's go."

Frazier watched, numb, immobile. Sunglasses beckoned and a swarm of porters materialized to carry the luggage outside. As she reached the vast doorway Marianne turned abruptly and looked back, and in the dimness of the great lobby her eyes suddenly seemed to shift in color, to take on the same strange topaz glint that he had imagined he had seen in Hurwitt's. Then she swung around and was gone.

An hour later he went down to the Consulate to turn himself in. They had a little trouble locating him in the list of wanted fugitives, but he told them to keep looking, going back a few years, and finally they came upon his entry. He was allowed half a day to clear up his business affairs, but he said he had none to clear up, so they set about the procedure of arranging his passage to the States, while he watched like a tourist who is trying to replace a lost passport.

Coming home was like returning to a foreign country that he had visited a long time before. Everything was familiar, but in an unfamiliar way. There were endless hearings, conferences, psychological examinations. His lawyers were excessively polite, as if they feared that one wrong word would cause him to detonate, but behind their silkiness he saw the contempt that the orderly have for the self-destructive. Still, they did their job well. Eventually he drew a suspended sentence and two years of rehabilitation, after which, they told him, he'd need to move to some other city, find some appropriate line of work, and establish a stable new existence for himself. The rehabilitation people would help him. There would be a probation period of five years when he'd have to report for progress conferences every week.

At the very end one of the rehab officers came to him and told him that his lawyers had filed a petition asking the court to let him have his original face back. That startled him. For a moment Frazier felt like a fugitive again, wearily stumbling from airport to airport, from hotel to hotel.

"No," he said. "I don't think that's a good idea at all. The man who had that face, he's somebody else. I think I'm better off keeping this one. What do you say?"

"I think so too," said the rehab man.

Barry N. Malzberg is perhaps best known for his work in science fiction but he has written crime fiction and men's action under a variety of pseudonyms, as well. His work as an essayist on the field of science fiction is ignored at the reader's peril; see Breakfast in the Ruins *and* The Bend at the End of the Road. *He is a stylist who is at times comic, subversive, and never shy. Stark House has published novels, multiple volumes of short stories, and the complete Lone Wolf series, most with new introductions or afterwords written by the author. If you haven't encountered Malzberg before, here is a short-short that gives you a quick taste....*

DISORDERLY

Barry N. Malzberg

Henry Wilson came home at six to find his wife Flora lying quite dead on the sofa, an open bottle of barbiturates clenched in her left hand, a suicide note draped across her chest.

Carefully putting down his briefcase and washing his hands from knuckle to elbow, Henry straightened out the house, closed the window shades and then picked up the note and read it.

> *Dear Henry: I am sorry to do this but it is the only way for both of us. You have made your life intolerable and now you have done the same to me. I can no longer live in a house like a glass cage and I cannot leave because—and this is the truth—there is no other way of life for me. So I leave you and I hope that things will be better for you and for me. I hope too that you learn something. Your wife, Flora*

The note was typed and she had not signed it.

Henry looked at it and his wife's body for a very long time; then he straightened out the house a bit, getting the furniture back in place and raising Flora's corpse so that he could take some of the minute dust off the couch. He flicked the shades a few times, put the desk in order—Flora had left the typewriter uncovered—and then, when he was sure that everything was in place, he picked up the phone and called the police.

"My wife has killed herself," he said. "I came home to find her on the couch. It was an overdose of sleeping pills. No, she's dead; I checked her breathing. I live at sixteen West Street on the ground floor. My apartment has a white door. I just painted it last week."

"Hold on," said a competent voice, "and we'll be right out."

"She's dead," Henry repeated and hung up.

In the few minutes before the police came there were still things which Henry saw he had to do, now that he had a chance to look the apartment over carefully. He closed the cabinet of the television set. He took a broom and flicked some grains of bread off the kitchen floor. He checked the bedroom to make sure that the bed he had made that morning was not rumpled. He changed the pillow case—there were a few tear drops on it and they had stained. He made up the garbage and disposed of it.

When he was certain that he had done everything to the best of his ability, Henry sat by the body of his dead wife and waited for the police. He waited for what seemed a long time, but, eventually they came. He heard the siren outside. He got up and opened the door for them.

Two policemen came up the walk, a short one and a tall one.

"My name is Rogers," the short one said, "and this is O'Toole. You called the station house a few minutes ago?"

"That's right," Henry said. "My name is Henry Wilson and my wife has killed herself."

"Killed herself, huh?" O'Toole said. "Well, let's just check this out."

"Before you go in," Henry said, "would you do me a favor and wipe your shoes off on the rug outside? We have a new carpet and—"

O'Toole gave Henry a strange look.

"Your wife killed herself?" he said.

"Yes. If you'd just do me the favor—"

Rogers and O'Toole shrugged, looking at Henry carefully, and obediently scuffed their shoes in the hall, then followed Henry inside.

"That her?" Rogers said, pointing to the couch.

"That's her. I came home and found her dead."

The two policemen went to the couch, leaned over.

"She's dead all right," O'Toole said. "When did you discover this?"

"When I came home from work about half an hour ago. I work in a bank. I'm a teller."

"Looks like suicide, all right," Rogers said, picking up the empty bottle which Henry had centered on the coffee table. "She must of took forty of these things."

"It was a terrible shock," Henry said.

"Let's check out the place," said O'Toole. "Mind if we look around in here?"

"Not at all. You'll find that our home—*my* home—is quite neat."

The two officers disappeared into the bedroom and began to move things around; Henry shuddered as he heard the room being disarranged. Then one of them went into the bathroom and began to flush the toilet repeatedly. Henry twitched.

O'Toole came back in by himself. "You had any indications that your wife might commit suicide?"

"No," said Henry, taking a chair and putting it neatly against one of the walls, sitting down on it. "None at all."

"Any trouble between you two?"

"None at all," said Henry. "Oh, we had our disagreements. She wasn't a very good housekeeper and I've always felt strongly about those things. But we've been married for two years and I thought we were very happy."

"Then why did she kill herself?"

Henry rubbed an infinitesimal scratch on his left shoetip. "I haven't the faintest idea, officer."

"Well," Rogers said, coming back into the room and taking off his hat. "I guess we better call down the precinct and get them over here. It looks like suicide. I'm sorry, Mr.—uh."

"Wilson," Henry said.

"Just wait a minute," said O'Toole, taking another chair from under the table and sitting down in it so heavily that it groaned and made Henry jump. "I just want to ask Mr. Wilson one or two questions. You said you came home to find her dead on the couch. Any suicide note?"

"Suicide note? Well, yes."

"What did it say?"

"Well, it didn't make much sense. Something about being unhappy, I think; about being sorry to leave me. She typed it and she made a lot of errors."

"I see," said O'Toole. "Where is it?"

"What?"

"The note. Where is it? It's evidence, you know. Where did you put it?"

"Put it?" said Henry. "Well, I don't know. I mean I'm not sure where it is now."

O'Toole gave Rogers a long, meaningful look and Rogers swung his head, peered at Henry. "You don't know?" Rogers said. "You don't now where your wife's suicide note is? Maybe you don't know because there wasn't a suicide note? Is that it?"

"Oh yes, there was. I read it. It was just that I—well, I incinerated it. I cleaned up the apartment a little and I put it in a bag and took everything downstairs to the incinerator."

"Well, now, is that so?" said O'Toole.

"I had to get rid of it, you see. I can't stand sloppiness. That was Flora's problem. She didn't know how to keep house and I had to do everything myself. I can't stand things lying around."

"So, you incinerated your wife's suicide note," said Rogers, "and then you cleaned up the place a little. So in other words, it's just your word that she left a note. It's just your word that she killed herself, right? You could have poisoned her and left her with that empty bottle on the couch and for all we know it would be suicide, right? It could be that way, huh, my friend?"

"But it didn't happen that way," Henry said, "and I wish you wouldn't raise your voice. I told you, I can't stand disorder. I cleaned up everything."

"I'm going to call the precinct," O'Toole said heavily. "You're in custody

Mr.—uh."

"Wilson," Rogers said.

"Wilson," said O'Toole.

"But I told you," Henry said, straining in his chair. "I told—"

But it was never revealed exactly what Henry had told them for at the first clinging, cold touch of the handcuffs on his wrist, the dirty brass touching his own skin, Henry gasped and sprawled over his rug in a perfect faint, knocking over his chair and disarranging his room. It was fortunate that he was not conscious to see the disarray because it would have upset him even more.

The autopsy showed that it was barbiturates, of course. But that did Henry very little good at all. The shocking disorder of the cell in which he had been confined for two weeks completely undermined his sanity and although the judge was very sympathetic, there was nothing to do but to remand him to a mental institution for an indeterminate time. Henry is still there and although the outlook is uncertain he has brought a better appearance to the day rooms.

Flora might have been pleased.

We close this collection with a story from the great Bruno Fischer. While it was written in the early 1940s it wasn't published until Gary Lovisi finally unearthed it for a collection for his own Gryphon Books imprint. It's so well done the story could almost have been written today. Fischer started out writing for the "weird menace" pulps but transitioned to the world of paperback originals after that market collapsed. His novels were published by Lion and Dell and of course, Gold Medal, and sold millions of copies. If you haven't read him before....

INSTRUCTION FOR MURDER

Bruno Fischer

Behind me I heard Paul McGee's voice suddenly demand: "What's wrong with a man marrying a girl fifteen years his junior?"

That came apropos of nothing. We had not been discussing marriage or even women. Our talk had begun with my year abroad and had reached the usual topic of writers when they are together: publishers, royalties, movie sales, work in progress. Then, as McGee had started to mix another batch of cocktails, I had moved over to a window to watch the rain slanting down toward the street five stories below.

I said without turning from the window: "So that's it. One of Broadway's most famous bachelors is at last succumbing. She's an actress, of course."

"No," he said. Then he laughed weakly. "I'm working on a play with that theme. I want to hear your opinion on the subject so that I can put your words in the mouth of one of my characters. We plagiarize our friends' thoughts, we writers."

A sedan pulled up in front of the apartment house. A girl got out—a small, slim thing in a bright yellow slicker. She was followed by a man with a slouch hat pulled down over his forehead and the collar of his topcoat up about his neck. For perhaps a minute they stood in the rain, apparently arguing. She was tugging at his sleeve, and he was shaking his head. Suddenly she rose to her toes and moved against him. Their lips met and held. His arms went around her slicker. It made a charming picture: two young people kissing in the rain.

"Well?" McGee asked impatiently. "Haven't you any opinion on the subject?"

I turned from the window. "None. If they love each other, let them marry. It depends on the individuals."

McGee nodded as he poured the cocktails. "Precisely."

"You liar," I said. "That's no play. Who's the girl, Paul?"

Grinning broadly, he handed me one of the cocktails. He was a tall man, rather wide at the shoulders, with hardly any hair and a deeply lined face. He looked older than his forty years, yet I could see how a much younger woman could fall for him. He had not only fame and money, which is always an inducement, he was, in addition, a swell guy.

"Always the detective writer," he commented. "No chance of hiding anything from you, Walt."

The doorbell rang. McGee put down his glass and strode across the room. I heard the door swing open and then voices in the foyer.

A girl said: "Congratulate us, Paul. We were married today. This is my brand-new husband, Chester Patterson."

There were the vague mutters of men acknowledging introductions, then McGee's voice rose: "Come in and celebrate."

The girl in the yellow slicker I had seen in the street entered first. The man with the turned-up topcoat collar followed. Immediately behind was McGee. He was smiling, but it was a smile wholly confined to his lips.

"Leona, I want you to meet my friend, Walt Bligh," McGee said. "Walt, my secretary, Leona Diamond—or, rather, Patterson."

She extended a hand to me and her grip was surprisingly hearty for so small a girl. She was rather nice-looking—merry blue eyes, a pert little nose, and a perpetual smile.

At once I knew. It was as simple as that—a middle-aged man and his pretty stenographer. Sometimes it turned out all right and sometimes it turned out like this. Poor Paul!

I turned to the man in the topcoat. "And this is Chester Patterson," McGee was saying.

Patterson would be young and handsome. That completed the pattern.

Our palms brushed momentarily. He was a big man, showing signs of fleshiness, which in a few years would grow into fatty bulges. His eyes were too light and too small, and his lips too thin. But probably I was over critical. I was trying to dislike him because of what he had done, through no fault of his own, to Paul McGee.

McGee was mixing more cocktails. That smile was still clamped on his face like a mask, and it had about as much life in it as a mask. The girl was at his side, gushing: "We were married at about four. The first one I wanted to tell the good news to was you. Chester wasn't so keen on coming, but he's never met you, and he doesn't know what a sweet old thing you are."

I winced for McGee. Sweet old thing! Why, I was only a couple of years younger than McGee, and I'm practically a young man. How cruel young girls can be in their thoughtlessness.

McGee managed to retain the smile. "You minx!" he said. "So that's why you wanted the day off!"

The drinks were poured, and we drank to the happiness of the bride and groom. Then we sat down. It was pretty uncomfortable. Three of us had nothing to say. Leona sat next to her husband on the couch and toyed delightedly with his fingers and chattered about how they would live in a two-room Village apartment, and of how Chester expected a raise from his firm.

After awhile she, too, stopped talking. She shifted closer to Patterson and rested her cheek against his arm. McGee went to the cocktail shaker and mixed drinks with his back turned toward them.

I thought: Why don't they go and leave poor Paul alone?

"Say, are you Walt Bligh, the detective story writer?" Patterson asked suddenly.

I nodded. If he asks me how I manage to think up my plots, I told myself, there'll be violence.

Instead he delivered himself of the second of the two statements people invariably make when they are introduced to detective fiction writers. "I bet you guys couldn't solve a real murder," he asserted smugly.

"We're writers," I retorted, "not detectives."

"Still, you pretend to know a lot about it."

I wasn't sure what he was trying to get at. His tone indicated that he was trying to pick an argument, but why with me? Probably he was a bit overawed at being in the presence of two rather well–known writers and was trying to impress Leona that he was as good as they were any day.

"All right," I said, "I'd make a marvelous detective, only there's more money in writing. So what?"

He shifted one knee over the other. "You know, the trouble with you detective writers is you make the murders too complicated," he advised me in a patronizing manner. "A pal of mine—a real detective—he told me if you want to kill somebody, make it simple. The more complicated a murder, the easier it is to find who did it. He told me this: do like the racketeers— shoot a man in the street and run like hell and nobody would ever get you."

"Or be a good-looking woman," I said. I figured that any talk would be better than the uncomfortable silence. "In that case, simply murder the man you want to and say that he tried to attack you. The reason will hold even if he happens to be your husband. It's been done in this state. Only be careful to maintain a tearful, martyred, soul-crushed attitude in order to get the public on your side. I'd give odds of a thousand to one that no jury would convict you."

"But suppose you're a man?" Patterson asked.

"Then don't get caught," I said. "There are various ways in which—"

"What's this, instructions on how to commit murder?" McGee interrupted. "How about another drink?"

Three of us accepted cocktails. Leona let hers remain untouched on the coffee table. When Patterson put his glass down, she stood up.

"I think we'll be going, Paul. Thanks for the party."

Patterson looked up at her without moving. "Tell him, Lee," he said.

"We'll have to talk it over more fully, Chester."

"Then I'll tell him," Patterson declared.

McGee stood in the middle of the room rolling the thin stem of the cocktail glass between his long fingers. The smile was on his lips, always on his lips, but I looked at his eyes and turned away quickly.

"Have you anything to tell me, Leona?" he asked quietly.

"Sure," Patterson said. "Lee's quitting her job as your secretary. I won't have my wife all alone with a man all day in a bachelor apartment."

I could have smacked him for the way he put it. Leona cried: "Please, Chester! I said we'd talk it over between ourselves." Two dots of embarrassment showed on her cheeks.

"A writer's office is his home," McGee said.

"That's why I don't want her to work for you." Patterson stood up. "There's nothing to talk over, Lee. Let's get going."

McGee said: "Just a minute, Leona."

There was an incisive quality in his voice. I saw Patterson bunch his shoulders as if he expected trouble. Languidly, I rose and moved behind Patterson. I confess that I was hoping that McGee would start something.

But McGee's manner turned gentle as he looked at Leona. They were facing each other, he and Leona, standing only a foot or two apart, and I saw a bond of sympathy and understanding leap between their eyes.

"Do you want to quit your job, Leona?" McGee asked gently.

"I—" Leona began. Her eyes shifted to her husband. There was sympathy and understanding between herself and Paul McGee, but she loved Chester Patterson. So she said to McGee: "Yes, Paul. I'm sorry."

They left. For a little while McGee stood looking at the empty doorway which led to the foyer. Then he went to the coffee table and poured a stiff hooker of rye, straight.

"I'm not fifteen years older," he said wryly. "It's closer to eighteen years."

I went for my coat and shook his hand warmly. He'll get over it, I thought. There are other women. But at that moment, I knew, he wanted to be alone.

I suppose I should have made it my business to see a great deal of Paul McGee, take him out to parties and introduce new women to him, but during the next few weeks I was busy making corrections and reading proofs of my latest novel, and I hadn't much time for anybody. Once in those two weeks I met him in the lobby of a theater during intermission. He was alone, standing against a wall and smoking. My companion and I joined him for a few minutes. His manner was as charming as ever, but I noticed tired lines under his eyes and a slackness about the mouth. After the show my companion and I looked for him, thinking to make a night of it with him. We couldn't find him.

Then, fifteen days after I had met Leona and Chester Patterson in McGee's apartment, I saw the newspaper headline.

I was having a late breakfast at the hotel where I was staying. A man facing me at a nearby table hunched over a tabloid as he drank his coffee. I couldn't help seeing the headline: BRIDE SLAYS HUSBAND. Nothing unusual in that for a tabloid story.

Then I was craning forward, trying to get a good look at the full-page photograph of a woman. I think I must have appeared a little ridiculous as I brought my chin almost level with the table top. But the owner of the tabloid merely considered me impudent. He scowled at me across the top of the paper and spread it out flat on his table.

Flushing, I returned to the business of breaking eggs into an egg cup. Of course that couldn't have been a photograph of Leona Patterson. All the same, as soon as I finished my eggs I went out to the newsstand in the hotel lobby.

A pert little face leaped up at me from the top tabloid of a huge pile. I stood staring at it until the man behind the stand demanded: "Paper, mister?" Selecting one copy of every morning paper, I returned to the dining room.

The story was played up more sensationally in the tabloids, but the essential facts were the same in all the papers.

Beautiful Leona Patterson, a private secretary, had murdered Chester Patterson, her husband of two weeks, at eleven p.m. last night. When police arrived at the tiny Greenwich Village apartment in response to her telephone call, they found the body of Chester Patterson sprawled on the living room rug. Death had been caused by a carving knife, which still protruded from his heart. The same knife had also inflicted several minor wounds on his body.

Leona Patterson sat huddled in an armchair. She was dry-eyed, staring at nothing at all. Her dress was torn and she wore only one shoe. A deep gash on which the blood had already clotted ran down her cheek.

"He tried to attack me," Leona Patterson told the police. "He was a beast. I found that out shortly after we were married. He came home very drunk and—and we struggled. I didn't know what I was doing. Everything went black. The carving knife was on the table in the kitchenette. Somehow it was in my hands—and then...."

I couldn't finish my breakfast. I sat over the papers, not reading them any more, just sitting there and burning cigarets. There wasn't any blood in my fingertips.

Presently I arose and took a cab to Paul McGee's apartment. He wasn't in; I hadn't really expected him to be. I returned to my hotel loaded with afternoon papers. There wasn't much additional news about the murder, except that Paul McGee, the famous playwright, who had been her employer until her marriage, had offered to foot the expenses of her defense. There was a one-column photograph of McGee in most of the papers.

As I rode up the elevator, two men were discussing the murder. One commented with a wise clucking of his tongue: "Wise guy, this McGee. He chisels into the murder and gets a million dollars worth of free publicity. I hear his 'The Last Madman' wasn't doing so well. I bet by tomorrow it's sold out for the next three months."

Both men laughed. In that laughter there was sincere admiration for a man who had put over a clever business deal. I would have enjoyed taking a couple of swings at them. Instead I looked at my toes until I reached my floor.

I phoned McGee's apartment every thirty minutes. No answer. At about four o'clock my own phone rang. Somehow I knew before I lifted the receiver that it was McGee.

"Walt? You heard the dreadful news, of course?" McGee sounded very tired.

"Yes," I said. "I'm sorry, Paul."

"Walt, we've got to get the poor girl off. She has very little money. I'm going to hire the best legal talent there is. You know a great deal about these things, Walt. What do you think of Monty Silverberg?"

"He'll get her off."

There was a pause. Then McGee asked: "You don't think there's any danger that she'll be found guilty?"

"She'll be freed," I said. "She followed my instructions very carefully."

I could hear McGee breathing heavily at the other end of the wire. "Walt, for God's sake, be reasonable. It simply happened that way."

"Is that why you phoned me, to ask me not to go to the district attorney and tell him that she followed my instructions for murdering and getting away with it?"

There was bitterness in my voice. For I felt that some of Chester Patterson's blood was on my hands.

"He was a beast. The way he treated the poor girl!"

"I can think of better ways of divorce," I said, "than murder."

"You don't understand, Walt. It happened the way she said. I spoke to her a little while ago. She went temporarily insane."

I said quietly, "Don't worry, Paul. I won't tell about that conversation. It won't do any good. The formula is fool-proof. Tell her to be sure to weep a great deal and show her legs when she's on the witness stand."

He hung up on me.

I didn't see Paul McGee until the trial, and he made no attempt to get in touch with me. But I attended the trial. It was more than curiosity that drew me to it. I could not rid myself of the notion that I was involved, that, if I hadn't tried to make conversation that evening in McGee's apartment, Chester Patterson would now be alive.

The trial was front-page news. The state tried to show that the murder was willful and premeditated, and I must say that the assistant district attorney made out something of a case.

The medical examiner testified that Chester Patterson had been stabbed in the right shoulder, the abdomen, and the right hip before the final thrust into his heart had finished him, and that he believed that Patterson had been either unconscious or so incapacitated by the three wounds as to have been unable to offer further resistance when the knife was jabbed into his heart. He further stated that Patterson had been dead for at least forty minutes before Leona telephoned the police.

It looked bad, but not too bad. And when Montgomery Silverberg got into action, it was a field day for the defense. Two men testified that they had been drinking with Patterson the evening of the murder, that he had been very drunk when he had left them to go home. Others stated that Patterson always turned nasty when drunk and had engaged in frequent brawls. A young woman artist who lived in the apartment next to the Pattersons told of how she had often heard them quarrel, that on several nights she had heard Leona shriek and weep as if she were being beaten.

Then Leona took the stand. I had convinced myself that she was a cold-blooded, calculating murderer who had faithfully followed my suggestion. But when she told her story my heart went out to her in spite of myself. Because, after all, much of what she told must have been the truth. There was no doubt that Chester Patterson had been an extremely unpleasant person with whom to live.

Dressed in a simple green frock, she looked utterly helpless. And very attractive. She had aged since the last time I had seen her: her shoulders drooped and there were lines of weariness under her eyes. She did not show much of her legs; she did not have to. There wasn't a man in the courtroom who didn't automatically clench his hands at the thought of the brute she had been foolish enough to marry.

Paul McGee sat in the first row, his half-bald head thrust forward. I had an impulse to go over to him, to place my arm comfortingly about his shoulders. When we had met in the aisle or in the hall, we had nodded curtly to each other. Now I felt sorry for him. He wasn't to blame; any man in love would have acted the same way.

Leona, in a tight voice which occasionally cracked, told how she had met Chester Patterson at a party three weeks before she had married him and had been completely swept off her feet by his virile handsomeness. Then one day they had gone to the Municipal Building to get their marriage license, and forty-eight hours later they had been married. She wasn't quite sure how it had happened; she had been in a daze of love and happiness.

A couple of days after they had started living together, she had snapped out of the daze. It was as if she had seen him for the first time. Making her quit her job with McGee had been the beginning. He had been absolutely domineering, brutally so when drunk, and he had drunk a great deal. And he had been insanely jealous. Before they had been married a week, he had accused her of having affairs with every male she greeted in the hall or in the street, including the grocery man on the corner. They had had several bitter quarrels.

On the night of the murder he had returned home very drunk and had immediately begun to berate her. The quarrel had started about nothing; he was simply in an ugly mood. She had informed him, then, that she was going to leave him, and had started for the bedroom to pack. He had grabbed her, slapped her face, scratched her cheek. She had flailed out against him. He had backed her up against the kitchenette table and her hand had closed on the handle of the carving knife. She had been crazy with fear and rage. The knife hadn't been so much a deadly weapon as something with which to defend herself. She had struck out at him....

There was an audible relaxation of tension when she finished her story. People coughed, moved in their seats, whispered to each other. But I continued to sit rigid. I couldn't breathe, something was choking me.

For I knew that part of Leona Patterson's story was a lie. Perhaps Chester Patterson had deserved to die, but that wasn't it. She hadn't told the truth about the murder.

She bore up splendidly under the cross-examination. As for the wounds on Patterson's body before the final thrust was made, she didn't know about them. She couldn't remember clearly just what had happened. She had struck out at him, had kept striking until he was on the floor; and then, with a feeling of horror which almost caused her to faint, she had realized that he was dead.

Why had she waited forty minutes before she had called the police? She had an answer for that, too. She had pulled herself up on a chair, had sat there, numb, horrified, thinking of taking her own life. Time hadn't meant anything. Four minutes or four hours might have passed for all she knew. Finally she had dragged herself to the telephone, asked for the police, said: "I have just killed my husband."

Perfectly understandable. She had brushed aside the prosecutor's two most telling points. As a matter of fact, the prosecution had never had much of a case. Because she admitted freely that she had killed Chester Patterson.

The assistant district attorney did his best in the summation, but he hadn't a chance. He appealed to reason. He pointed out that if Leona Patterson were freed, any woman who wanted to slay her husband could do so with impunity. She had only to say that he abused her.

Montgomery Silverberg's address to the jury was, as always, a masterpiece of pathos. I left in the middle of it.

There was a bar a block from the courthouse. I drank an endless number of rye highballs. Phrases ran through my head: moral duty as a citizen, farcical trial, tragedy of two wrecked lives and one dead body, murder is never justifiable.

A couple of hours later a newsboy came in with the late afternoon papers, which announced that Leona Patterson had been found not guilty. Of course. That was simple justice. But the jury didn't know it. I believed that they had freed a murderer. I ordered another drink.

I was still sleeping off my drunk the following morning when the telephone awoke me. Mr. Paul McGee was in the lobby and wished to see me.

"No!" I snapped and slammed the phone on its cradle.

I did not go back to sleep and I did not get up. I lay wide-eyed looking up at the ceiling. McGee and I had been friends for about twelve years. I had been very fond of him. I still was. Perhaps that's why it hurt so much.

After a while somebody knocked at my door. All right, I thought. Let it come now. I slipped out of bed and let Paul McGee in.

We looked at each other for several seconds. Then McGee stuck out his hand. "I'm going away from some time, Walt. My ship leaves at midnight."

I took his hand, of course, but there was nothing to the handshake. I asked: "With Leona?"

He dropped his eyes to his feet like an abashed schoolboy. "She'll be on the ship. Ostensibly we're not traveling together. We don't want the papers to find out so soon after the trial. We'll be married quietly in Paris."

It was my cue to wish him luck. I didn't, couldn't. I tightened the cord of my pajamas and walked to a table and picked up a pack of cigarets and said: "Have one, Paul."

He didn't reach for the cigaret. The lines of his face had grown deeper. He coughed to clear his throat before he started to speak.

"I know what's eating you, Walt. You think Leona has played you for a sucker. You think you gave her the idea of how to murder Patterson and get away with it. You can't forgive her, and because of the way I feel about her you're taking it out on me, too. But I swear to heaven it wasn't like that. She's not a cold-blooded murderer. Patterson was a—"

"You can drop the act with me," I broke in wearily. "I know that Leona didn't murder her husband."

Slowly I extracted a cigaret from the pack and lit it. Then I looked up at McGee. His lips were parted and there was no color in his face.

I thought: Let's have it out. Maybe that will take it off my mind.

So I said: "You killed Chester Patterson."

Sometimes people cry when they should laugh and laugh when they should cry. Paul McGee smiled. But it was utterly phoney. I had seen him smile like that when Leona had told him she had married Chester Patterson.

"Are you trying to play at being the mastermind of one of your novels?" he commented dryly.

"It didn't require masterminding," I said. "I'm the only one who knew all the factors involved. I'm sure others were puzzled about how Leona could possibly have killed Patterson in the way she described. Patterson was twice her size and five times as strong. She might have taken him by surprise and stabbed him once. But three times before the mortal thrust? What was he doing during that time? Cheering her on? No, it didn't make sense. I'm sure it puzzled the assistant district attorney, but naturally he didn't bring it up because it would have weakened his case against Leona. He was sure she was guilty. Her confession put everybody off the track. It was meant to."

McGee had dropped into a chair. I had never before seen a more beaten, hopeless expression on a man's face.

"If Leona didn't kill him, who did?" I went on. "There was only one answer. As the trial developed, the picture straightened out. It must have been something like this: The night of the murder you were in the Pattersons' apartment. Maybe Leona, realizing that she had made a tragic mistake and feeling utterly miserable, had turned to you for comfort. She phoned you to come over, or else you had simply dropped in to see her. While you were there, Patterson returned home. He was drunk and vicious and jealous. He lunged for you, tried to beat you up. You grabbed the knife and killed him. Then you and Leona talked over what to do. That accounts for the lapse between the murder and the time the police were called."

"All right," McGee said. "But it was self-defense."

"Was it? He was down on the floor, either helpless or unconscious, when you thrust the knife into his heart. That was deliberate, the act of a killer. That was murder. And then, letting Leona take the rap!"

"Please, Walt!" McGee was on his feet, trembling. His voice wasn't steady, either. "Please try to understand. She didn't call me. She was suffering in silence, alone. I decided to call on the Pattersons. He was out. She blurted out everything and you can imagine how I felt. Then he came in and, as you said, we fought. I'm no weakling, but he was younger and stronger and would probably have beaten me to a pulp. I got the knife in my hand and simply let him have it. I didn't know how many times I had stabbed him until I heard the medical report. I was overwhelmed by rage, by hatred. You can understand that, Walt."

"Sure. And I understand why you let Leona take the rap for you."

"I didn't want to, Walt," he cried. "Even though it looked bad for me. I was in the man's apartment alone with his wife. She'd been my secretary. It would be brought out that she had been unhappy with her husband. What chance would I have? We talked it over, Leona and I, with the body lying only a few feet away. We had become suddenly very calm, as if we were already in our graves. And she told me that she loved me. She had known it for several days now. Perhaps it was a rebound from having lived with Patterson, I don't know. But it should have been the happiest moment of my life. Instead it made everything worse.

"Then she suggested that she confess to the murder. She recalled what you told us. She could get away with it; I probably wouldn't. Of course I wouldn't hear of it at first. But she brought me around. Heroics are all right in my plays, but this was real life. We were dealing with our future happiness. We had a chance, but only through a certain amount of sacrifice on her part. So in the end I gave in. She tore her dress, scratched herself. I slipped out of the apartment; nobody had seen me come or go."

There was a silence which was stifling.

Presently Paul McGee said: "Aren't you going to call the police?"

I shrugged. "Fortunately, I haven't that ethical problem to struggle with. There is not a scrap of evidence against you. You have simply to say I'm crazy and the police will believe you. As far as the police and the public are concerned, Leona Patterson murdered her husband."

The last sentence hurt him. He cringed back in his chair. That must have been on his mind, that now Leona would be forever branded a murderer.

I said: "If I had called the police before I had just spoken, you would have blurted out the same confession to them. I forced the confession from you, then once again instructed you on how to get away with murder. Was I justified? I don't know. What's right and wrong? Perhaps the only guilty party was Chester Patterson. If he had deserved to live he would be alive today. And you and Leona— you're not vicious, you're not murderers. You're merely two people who have gotten into a terrible mess. Some people would say you don't deserve happiness for what you did. Maybe now you'll never find it."

I don't think he was listening to me. Not that I was really talking to him. The words were for myself.

I went over to him and placed my hand on his shoulder. "So long, Paul," I said. "Give my best to Leona."

He stood up and nodded and left.

He had forgotten to shake hands, to say good-bye. No matter. I stepped out of my pajamas and took an ice-cold shower.

THE END

Acknowledgements

"Hangover" by Charles Runyon, MANHUNT, *December 1960*

"A Matter of Balance" by Peter Rabe, *previously unpublished © copyright 2024*

"Invitation to an Accident" by Wade Miller, ELLERY QUEEN'S MYSTERY MAGAZINE, *July 1955*

"The Tormented" by James McKimmey, THE MAN FROM U.N.C.L.E. MAGAZINE, *August 1967*

"Murderer #2" by Jean Potts, ALFRED HITCHCOCK'S MYSTERY MAGAZINE, *January 1961*

"To Kill a Wife" by Lionel White, MURDER!, *September 1956*

"So Curse the Day" by Jada M. Davis, *previously unpublished © copyright 2024*

"Art for Money's Sake" by Dan J. Marlowe, THE ELKS MAGAZINE, *February 1970*

"Chester Drum Takes Over" by Stephen Marlowe, ELLERY QUEEN'S ANTHOLOGY #25, *Spring-Summer 1973*

"Sleep Without Dreams" by Frank Kane, MANHUNT, *February 1956*

"The Memory Guy" by Henry Kane, EDGAR WALLACE MYSTERY MAGAZINE, *March 1966*

"Nothing in My Way" by Orrie Hitt, SMASHING DETECTIVE STORIES, *July 1955*

"Preventive Medicine" by Harry Whittington, TRAPPED, *August 1956*

"Die, Darling, Die" by Gil Brewer, JUSTICE, *January 1956*

"The Geek-Girl" by Day Keene, ADAM, *October 1953*

"Woman Missing" by Helen Nielsen, ALFRED HITCHCOCK'S MYSTERY MAGAZINE, *May 1960*

"Backbite" by Frederick Lorenz, JUSTICE, *January* 1956

"Angie" by Ed Gorman, 999: NEW TALES OF HORROR AND SUSPENSE, Avon Books, *1999*

"Night Games" by Bill Pronzini, BULLETS AND OTHER HURTING THINGS: A TRIBUTE TO BILL CRIDER, *Down & Out Books 2021*

"The Silent One" by Fletcher Flora, HUNTED, *December 1955*

"Beware of the Dog" by Fredric Brown, EDGAR WALLACE MYSTERY MAGAZINE, *March 1966*

"Hit Me" by Rick Ollerman, DOWN & OUT: THE MAGAZINE, *Volume 1, Number 1 2017*

"Axe" by Gregory Shepard, *previously unpublished © copyright 2024*

"Last Night at Skipper's Lounge" by Timothy J. Lockhart, DOWN & OUT: THE MAGAZINE, *Volume 1, Issue 2 2017*

"Barbarians" by Robert W. Chambers, D. Appleton and Company, *1917*

"Politics Pays Best" by E. Phillips Oppenheim, THE COUNTRY GENTLEMAN, *February 1930*

"Secretaries Make Such Nice Wives" by A. S. Fleischman, TORONTO STAR WEEKLY, *1946*

"The Dead Man's Eyes" by Robert Silverberg, PLAYBOY, *August 1988*

"Disorderly" by Barry N. Malzberg, THE MAN FROM U.N.C.L.E. MAGAZINE, *January 1968*

"Instruction for Murder" by Bruno Fischer, A MATE FOR MURDER: AND OTHER TALES FROM THE PULPS, Gryphon Books 1992

BLACK GAT BOOKS offers the best in reprint crime fiction from the 1950s-1970s. New titles appear every month, and each book is sized to 4.25" x 7", just like they used to be. Collect them all.

Harry Whittington · A Haven for the Damned #1 ·
Charlie Stella · Eddie's World #2
Leigh Brackett · Stranger at Home #3
John Flagg · The Persian Cat #4
Malcolm Braly · Felony Tank #6
Vin Packer · The Girl on the Best Seller List #7
Orrie Hitt · She Got What She Wanted #8
Helen Nielsen · The Woman on the Roof #9
Lou Cameron · Angel's Flight #10
Gary Lovisi · The Affair of Lady Westcott's Lost Ruby / The Case of the Unseen Assassin #11
Arnold Hano · The Last Notch #12
Clifton Adams · Never Say No to a Killer #13
Ed Lacy · The Men From the Boys #14
Henry Kane · Frenzy of Evil #15
William Ard · You'll Get Yours #16
Bert & Dolores Hitchens · End of the Line #17
Noël Calef · Frantic #18
Ovid Demaris · The Hoods Take Over #19
Fredric Brown · Madball #20
Louis Malley · Stool Pigeon #21
Frank Kane · The Living End #22
Ferguson Findley · My Old Man's Badge #23
Paul Connolly · Tears are for Angels #24
E. P. Fenwick · Two Names for Death #25
Lorenz Heller · Dead Wrong #26
Robert Martin · Little Sister #27
Calvin Clements · Satan Takes the Helm #28

Jack Karney · Cut Me In #29
George Benet · The Hoodlums #30
Jonathan Craig · So Young, So Wicked #31
Edna Sherry · Tears for Jessie Hewitt #32
William O'Farrell · Repeat Performance #33
Marvin Albert · The Girl With No Place to Hide #34
Edward S. Aarons · Gang Rumble #35
William Fuller · Back Country #36
Robert Silverberg · The Killer #37
William R. Cox · Make My Coffin Strong #38
A. S. Fleischman · Blood Alley #39
Harold R. Daniels · The Girl in 304 #40
William H. Duhart · The Deadly Pay-Off #41
Robert Ames · Awake and Die #42
Charles Runyon · Object of Lust #43
Paul Conant - Dr. Gatskill's Blue Shoes #44
Asa Bordages - Murders in Silk #45
Darwin Teilhet - Take Me As I Am #46
Stephen Marlowe - Blonde Bait #47
Jonathan Latimer - The Fifth Grave #48
Andrew Coburn - Off Duty #49
Basil Heatter - Any Man's Girl #50
Day Keene - Acapulco G.P.O. #51
John P. Browner - Death of a Punk #52
Glenn Canary - The Trailer Park Girls #53
Jacquin Sanders - Freakshow #54
John & Ward Hawkins - The Floods of Fear #55
Richard Jessup - Night Boat to Paris #56
Arnold Drake - The Steel Noose #57
William Vance - Bait #58

Stark House Press
1315 H Street, Eureka, CA 95501 (707) 498-3135
griffinskye3@sbcglobal.net   www.StarkHousePress.com
Available from your local bookstore or direct from the publisher